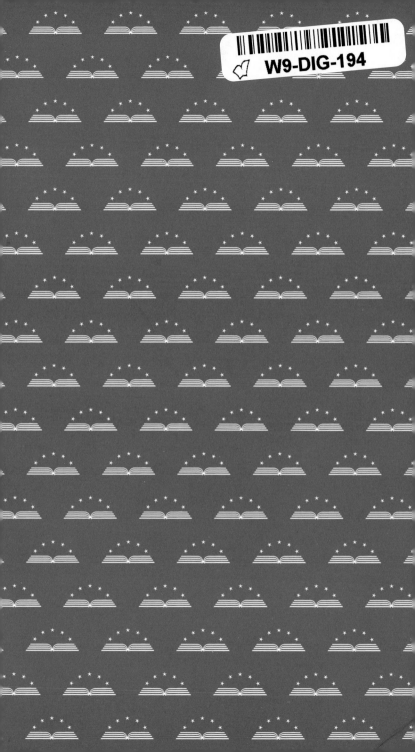

SHIRLEY JACKSON

Shirley Jackson

NOVELS AND STORIES
The Lottery
The Haunting of Hill House
We Have Always Lived in the Castle
Other Stories and Sketches

THE LIBRARY OF AMERICA

JOYCE CAROL OATES
SELECTED THE CONTENTS FOR THIS VOLUME

Contents

THE LOTTERY

OR, THE ADVENTURES OF JAMES HARRIS

For my mother and father

I

She saith, That after their Meetings, they all make very low Obey-
sances to the Devil, who appears in black Cloaths, and a little Band.
He bids them Welcome at their coming, and brings Wine or Beer,
Cakes, Meat, or the like. He sits at the higher end. . . . They Eat,
Drink, Dance and have Musick. At their parting they use to say,
Merry meet, merry part.

Joseph Glanvil: *Sadducismus Triumphatus*

The Intoxicated

H E WAS just tight enough and just familiar enough with the house to be able to go out into the kitchen alone, apparently to get ice, but actually to sober up a little; he was not quite enough a friend of the family to pass out on the living-room couch. He left the party behind without reluctance, the group by the piano singing "Stardust," his hostess talking earnestly to a young man with thin clean glasses and a sullen mouth; he walked guardedly through the dining-room where a little group of four or five people sat on the stiff chairs reasoning something out carefully among themselves; the kitchen doors swung abruptly to his touch, and he sat down beside a white enamel table, clean and cold under his hand. He put his glass on a good spot in the green pattern and looked up to find that a young girl was regarding him speculatively from across the table.

"Hello," he said. "You the daughter?"

"I'm Eileen," she said. "Yes."

She seemed to him baggy and ill-formed; it's the clothes they wear now, young girls, he thought foggily; her hair was braided down either side of her face, and she looked young and fresh and not dressed-up; her sweater was purplish and her hair was dark. "You sound nice and sober," he said, realizing that it was the wrong thing to say to young girls.

"I was just having a cup of coffee," she said. "May I get you one?"

He almost laughed, thinking that she expected she was dealing knowingly and competently with a rude drunk. "Thank you," he said, "I believe I will." He made an effort to focus his eyes; the coffee was hot, and when she put a cup in front of him, saying, "I suppose you'd like it black," he put his face into the steam and let it go into his eyes, hoping to clear his head.

"It sounds like a lovely party," she said without longing, "everyone must be having a fine time."

"It is a lovely party." He began to drink the coffee, scalding hot, wanting her to know she had helped him. His head

5

steadied, and he smiled at her. "I feel better," he said, "thanks to you."

"It must be very warm in the other room," she said soothingly.

Then he did laugh out loud and she frowned, but he could see her excusing him as she went on, "It was so hot upstairs I thought I'd like to come down for a while and sit out here."

"Were you asleep?" he asked. "Did we wake you?"

"I was doing my homework," she said.

He looked at her again, seeing her against a background of careful penmanship and themes, worn textbooks and laughter between desks. "You're in high school?"

"I'm a Senior." She seemed to wait for him to say something, and then she said, "I was out a year when I had pneumonia."

He found it difficult to think of something to say (ask her about boys? basketball?), and so he pretended he was listening to the distant noises from the front of the house. "It's a fine party," he said again, vaguely.

"I suppose you like parties," she said.

Dumbfounded, he sat staring into his empty coffee cup. He supposed he did like parties; her tone had been faintly surprised, as though next he were to declare for an arena with gladiators fighting wild beasts, or the solitary circular waltzing of a madman in a garden. I'm almost twice your age, my girl, he thought, but it's not so long since I did homework too. "Play basketball?" he asked.

"No," she said.

He felt with irritation that she had been in the kitchen first, that she lived in the house, that he must keep on talking to her. "What's your homework about?" he asked.

"I'm writing a paper on the future of the world," she said, and smiled. "It sounds silly, doesn't it? I think it's silly."

"Your party out front is talking about it. That's one reason I came out here." He could see her thinking that that was not at all the reason he came out here, and he said quickly, "What are you saying about the future of the world?"

"I don't really think it's got much future," she said, "at least the way we've got it now."

"It's an interesting time to be alive," he said, as though he were still at the party.

"Well, after all," she said, "it isn't as though we didn't *know* about it in advance."

He looked at her for a minute; she was staring absently at the toe of her saddle shoe, moving her foot softly back and forth, following it with her eyes. "It's really a frightening time when a girl sixteen has to think of things like that." In my day, he thought of saying mockingly, girls thought of nothing but cocktails and necking.

"I'm seventeen." She looked up and smiled at him again. "There's a terrible difference," she said.

"In my day," he said, overemphasizing, "girls thought of nothing but cocktails and necking."

"That's partly the trouble," she answered him seriously. "If people had been really, honestly scared when you were young we wouldn't be so badly off today."

His voice had more of an edge than he intended ("When *I* was young!"), and he turned partly away from her as though to indicate the half-interest of an older person being gracious to a child: "I imagine we thought we were scared. I imagine all kids sixteen—seventeen—think they're scared. It's part of a stage you go through, like being boy-crazy."

"I keep figuring how it will be." She spoke very softly, very clearly, to a point just past him on the wall. "Somehow I think of the churches as going first, before even the Empire State building. And then all the big apartment houses by the river, slipping down slowly into the water with the people inside. And the schools, in the middle of Latin class maybe, while we're reading Cæsar." She brought her eyes to his face, looking at him in numb excitement. "Each time we begin a chapter in Cæsar, I wonder if this won't be the one we never finish. Maybe we in our Latin class will be the last people who ever read Cæsar."

"That would be good news," he said lightly. "I used to hate Cæsar."

"I suppose when you were young everyone hated Cæsar," she said coolly.

He waited for a minute before he said, "I think it's a little silly for you to fill your mind with all this morbid trash. Buy yourself a movie magazine and settle down."

"I'll be able to get all the movie magazines I want," she said insistently. "The subways will crash through, you know, and the little magazine stands will all be squashed. You'll be able to pick up all the candy bars you want, and magazines, and lipsticks and artificial flowers from the five-and-ten, and dresses lying in the street from all the big stores. And fur coats."

"I hope the liquor stores will break wide open," he said, beginning to feel impatient with her, "I'd walk in and help myself to a case of brandy and never worry about anything again."

"The office buildings will be just piles of broken stones," she said, her wide emphatic eyes still looking at him. "If only you could know exactly what *minute* it will come."

"I see," he said. "I go with the rest. I see."

"Things will be different afterward," she said. "Everything that makes the world like it is now will be gone. We'll have new rules and new ways of living. Maybe there'll be a law not to live in houses, so then no one can hide from anyone else, you see."

"Maybe there'll be a law to keep all seventeen-year-old girls in school learning sense," he said, standing up.

"There won't be any schools," she said flatly. "No one will learn anything. To keep from getting back where we are now."

"Well," he said, with a little laugh. "You make it sound very interesting. Sorry I won't be there to see it." He stopped, his shoulder against the swinging door into the dining-room. He wanted badly to say something adult and scathing, and yet he was afraid of showing her that he had listened to her, that when he was young people had not talked like that. "If you have any trouble with your Latin," he said finally, "I'll be glad to give you a hand."

She giggled, shocking him. "I still do my homework every night," she said.

Back in the living-room, with people moving cheerfully around him, the group by the piano now singing "Home on the Range," his hostess deep in earnest conversation with a tall, graceful man in a blue suit, he found the girl's father and said, "I've just been having a very interesting conversation with your daughter."

His host's eye moved quickly around the room. "Eileen? Where is she?"

"In the kitchen. She's doing her Latin."

"'*Gallia est omnia divisa in partes tres,*'" his host said without expression. "I know."

"A really extraordinary girl."

His host shook his head ruefully. "Kids nowadays," he said.

The Daemon Lover

S HE had not slept well; from one-thirty, when Jamie left and she went lingeringly to bed, until seven, when she at last allowed herself to get up and make coffee, she had slept fitfully, stirring awake to open her eyes and look into the half-darkness, remembering over and over, slipping again into a feverish dream. She spent almost an hour over her coffee—they were to have a real breakfast on the way—and then, unless she wanted to dress early, had nothing to do. She washed her coffee cup and made the bed, looking carefully over the clothes she planned to wear, worried unnecessarily, at the window, over whether it would be a fine day. She sat down to read, thought that she might write a letter to her sister instead, and began, in her finest handwriting, "Dearest Anne, by the time you get this I will be married. Doesn't it sound funny? I can hardly believe it myself, but when I tell you how it happened, you'll see it's even stranger than that. . . ."

Sitting, pen in hand, she hesitated over what to say next, read the lines already written, and tore up the letter. She went to the window and saw that it was undeniably a fine day. It occurred to her that perhaps she ought not to wear the blue silk dress; it was too plain, almost severe, and she wanted to be soft, feminine. Anxiously she pulled through the dresses in the closet, and hesitated over a print she had worn the summer before; it was too young for her, and it had a ruffled neck, and it was very early in the year for a print dress, but still. . . .

She hung the two dresses side by side on the outside of the closet door and opened the glass doors carefully closed upon the small closet that was her kitchenette. She turned on the burner under the coffeepot, and went to the window; it was sunny. When the coffeepot began to crackle she came back and poured herself coffee, into a clean cup. I'll have a headache if I don't get some solid food soon, she thought, all this coffee, smoking too much, no real breakfast. A headache on her wedding day; she went and got the tin box of aspirin from the bathroom closet and slipped it into her blue pocketbook. She'd have to change to a brown pocketbook if she wore the print dress, and the only brown pocketbook she had was shabby. Helplessly, she stood looking from the blue pocketbook to the print dress, and then put the pocketbook down and went and got her coffee and sat down near the window, drinking her coffee, and looking carefully around the one-room apartment. They planned to come back here tonight and everything must be correct. With sudden horror she realized that she had forgotten to put clean sheets on the bed; the laundry was freshly back and she took clean sheets and pillow cases from the top shelf of the closet and stripped the bed, working quickly to avoid thinking consciously of why she was changing the sheets. The bed was a studio bed, with a cover to make it look like a couch, and when it was finished no one would have known she had just put clean sheets on it. She took the old sheets and pillow cases into the bathroom and stuffed them down into the hamper, and put the bathroom towels in the hamper too, and clean towels on the bathroom racks. Her coffee was cold when she came back to it, but she drank it anyway.

When she looked at the clock, finally, and saw that it was after nine, she began at last to hurry. She took a bath, and used one of the clean towels, which she put into the hamper and replaced with a clean one. She dressed carefully, all her underwear fresh and most of it new; she put everything she had worn the day before, including her nightgown, into the hamper. When she was ready for her dress, she hesitated before the closet door. The blue dress was certainly decent, and clean, and fairly becoming, but she had worn it several times with Jamie, and there was nothing about it which made it special for a wedding day. The print dress was overly pretty, and new to Jamie, and yet wearing such a print this early in the year was certainly rushing the season. Finally she thought, This is my wedding day, I can dress as I please, and she took the print dress down from the hanger. When she slipped it on over her head it felt fresh and light, but when she looked at herself in the mirror she remembered that the ruffles around the neck did not show her throat to any great advantage, and the wide swinging skirt looked irresistibly made for a girl, for someone who would run freely, dance, swing it with her hips when she walked. Looking at herself in the mirror she thought with revulsion, It's as though I was trying to make myself look prettier than I am, just for him; he'll think I want to look younger because he's marrying me; and she tore the print dress off so quickly that a seam under the arm ripped. In the old blue dress she felt comfortable and familiar, but unexciting. It isn't what you're wearing that matters, she told herself firmly, and turned in dismay to the closet to see if there might be anything else. There was nothing even remotely suitable for her marrying Jamie, and for a minute she thought of going out quickly to some little shop nearby, to get a dress. Then she saw that it was close on ten, and she had no time for more than her hair and her make-up. Her hair was easy, pulled back into a knot at the nape of her neck, but her make-up was another delicate balance between looking as well as possible, and deceiving as little. She could not try to disguise the sallowness of her skin, or the lines around her eyes, today, when it might look as though she were only doing it for her wedding, and yet she could not bear the thought of Jamie's bringing to marriage anyone who looked haggard and lined. You're thirty-four years old after *all*, she told herself cruelly in the bathroom mirror. Thirty, it said on the license.

It was two minutes after ten; she was not satisfied with her clothes, her face, her apartment. She heated the coffee again and sat down in the chair by the window. Can't do anything more now, she thought, no sense trying to improve anything the last minute.

Reconciled, settled, she tried to think of Jamie and could not see his face clearly, or hear his voice. It's always that way with someone you love, she thought, and let her mind slip past today and tomorrow, into the farther future, when Jamie was established with his writing and she had given up her job, the golden house-in-the-country future they had been preparing for the last week. "I used to be a wonderful cook," she had promised Jamie, "with a little time and practice I could remember how to make angel-food cake. And fried chicken," she said, knowing how the words would stay in Jamie's mind, half-tenderly. "And Hollandaise sauce."

Ten-thirty. She stood up and went purposefully to the phone. She dialed, and waited, and the girl's metallic voice said, ". . . the time will be exactly ten-twenty-nine." Half-consciously she set her clock back a minute; she was remembering her own voice saying last night, in the doorway: "Ten o'clock then. I'll be ready. Is it really *true*?"

And Jamie laughing down the hallway.

By eleven o'clock she had sewed up the ripped seam in the print dress and put her sewing-box away carefully in the closet. With the print dress on, she was sitting by the window drinking another cup of coffee. I could have taken more time over my dressing after all, she thought; but by now it was so late he might come any minute, and she did not dare try to repair anything without starting all over. There was nothing to eat in the apartment except the food she had carefully stocked up for their life beginning together: the unopened package of bacon, the dozen eggs in their box, the unopened bread and the unopened butter; they were for breakfast tomorrow. She thought of running downstairs to the drugstore for something to eat, leaving a note on the door. Then she decided to wait a little longer.

By eleven-thirty she was so dizzy and weak that she had to go downstairs. If Jamie had had a phone she would have called him then. Instead, she opened her desk and wrote a note: "Jamie, have gone downstairs to the drugstore. Back in five minutes." Her pen leaked onto her fingers and she went into the bathroom and washed, using a clean towel which she replaced. She tacked the note on the door, surveyed the apartment once more to make sure that everything was perfect, and closed the door without locking it, in case he should come.

In the drugstore she found that there was nothing she wanted to eat except more coffee, and she left it half-finished because she suddenly realized that Jamie was probably upstairs waiting and impatient, anxious to get started.

But upstairs everything was prepared and quiet, as she had left it, her note unread on the door, the air in the apartment a little stale from too many cigarettes. She opened the window and sat down next to it until she realized that she had been asleep and it was twenty minutes to one.

Now, suddenly, she was frightened. Waking without preparation into the room of waiting and readiness, everything clean and untouched since ten o'clock, she was frightened, and felt an urgent need to hurry. She got up from the chair and almost ran across the room to the bathroom, dashed cold water on her face, and used a clean towel; this time she put the towel carelessly back on the rack without changing it; time enough for that later. Hatless, still in the print dress with a coat thrown on over it, the wrong blue pocketbook with the aspirin inside in her hand, she locked the apartment door behind her, no note this time, and ran down the stairs. She caught a taxi on the corner and gave the driver Jamie's address.

It was no distance at all; she could have walked it if she had not been so weak, but in the taxi she suddenly realized how imprudent it would be to drive brazenly up to Jamie's door, demanding him. She asked the driver, therefore, to let her off at a corner near Jamie's address and, after paying him, waited till he drove away before she started to walk down the block. She had never been here before; the building was pleasant and old, and Jamie's name was not on any of the mailboxes in the vestibule, nor on the doorbells. She checked the address; it was right, and finally she rang the bell marked "Superintendent." After a minute or two the door buzzer rang and she opened the door and went into the dark hall where she hesitated until a door at the end opened and someone said, "Yes?"

She knew at the same moment that she had no idea what to ask, so she moved forward toward the figure waiting against the light of the open doorway. When she was very near, the figure said, "Yes?" again and she saw that it was a man in his shirtsleeves, unable to see her any more clearly than she could see him.

With sudden courage she said, "I'm trying to get in touch with someone who lives in this building and I can't find the name outside."

"What's the name you wanted?" the man asked, and she realized that she would have to answer.

"James Harris," she said. "Harris."

The man was silent for a minute and then he said, "Harris." He turned around to the room inside the lighted doorway and said, "Margie, come here a minute."

"What now?" a voice said from inside, and after a wait long enough for someone to get out of a comfortable chair a woman joined him in the doorway, regarding the dark hall.

"Lady here," the man said. "Lady looking for a guy name of Harris, lives here. Anyone in the building?"

"No," the woman said. Her voice sounded amused. "No men named Harris here."

"Sorry," the man said. He started to close the door. "You got the wrong house, lady," he said, and added in a lower voice, "or the wrong guy," and he and the woman laughed.

When the door was almost shut and she was alone in the dark hall she said to the thin lighted crack still showing, "But he *does* live here; I know it."

"Look," the woman said, opening the door again a little, "it happens all the time."

"Please don't make any mistake," she said, and her voice was very dignified, with thirty-four years of accumulated pride. "I'm afraid you don't understand."

"What did he look like?" the woman said wearily, the door still only part open.

"He's rather tall, and fair. He wears a blue suit very often. He's a writer."

"No," the woman said, and then, "Could he have lived on the third floor?"

"I'm not sure."

"There was a fellow," the woman said reflectively. "He wore a blue suit a lot, lived on the third floor for a while. The Roysters lent him their apartment while they were visiting her folks upstate."

"That might be it; I thought, though. . . ."

"This one wore a blue suit mostly, but I don't know how tall he was," the woman said. "He stayed there about a month."

"A month ago is when—"

"You ask the Roysters," the woman said. "They come back this morning. Apartment 3B."

The door closed, definitely. The hall was very dark and the stairs looked darker.

On the second floor there was a little light from a skylight far above. The apartment doors lined up, four on the floor, uncommunicative and silent. There was a bottle of milk outside 2C.

On the third floor, she waited for a minute. There was the

sound of music beyond the door of 3B, and she could hear voices. Finally she knocked, and knocked again. The door was opened and the music swept out at her, an early afternoon symphony broadcast. "How do you do," she said politely to this woman in the doorway. "Mrs. Royster?"

"That's right." The woman was wearing a housecoat and last night's make-up.

"I wonder if I might talk to you for a minute?"

"Sure," Mrs. Royster said, not moving.

"About Mr. Harris."

"*What* Mr. Harris?" Mrs. Royster said flatly.

"Mr. James Harris. The gentleman who borrowed your apartment."

"O Lord," Mrs. Royster said. She seemed to open her eyes for the first time. "What'd he do?"

"Nothing. I'm just trying to get in touch with him."

"O Lord," Mrs. Royster said again. Then she opened the door wider and said, "Come in," and then, "Ralph!"

Inside, the apartment was still full of music, and there were suitcases half-unpacked on the couch, on the chairs, on the floor. A table in the corner was spread with the remains of a meal, and the young man sitting there, for a minute resembling Jamie, got up and came across the room.

"What about it?" he said.

"Mr. Royster," she said. It was difficult to talk against the music. "The superintendent downstairs told me that this was where Mr. James Harris has been living."

"Sure," he said. "If that was his name."

"I thought you lent him the apartment," she said, surprised.

"*I* don't know anything about him," Mr. Royster said. "He's one of Dottie's friends."

"Not *my* friends," Mrs. Royster said. "No friend of mine." She had gone over to the table and was spreading peanut butter on a piece of bread. She took a bite and said thickly, waving the bread and peanut butter at her husband. "Not *my* friend."

"You picked him up at one of those damn meetings," Mr. Royster said. He shoved a suitcase off the chair next to the radio and sat down, picking up a magazine from the floor next to him. "I never said more'n ten words to him."

"You said it was okay to lend him the place," Mrs. Royster

said before she took another bite. "You never said a word against him, after *all*."

"*I* don't say anything about *your* friends," Mr. Royster said.

"If he'd of been a friend of mine you would have said *plenty*, believe me," Mrs. Royster said darkly. She took another bite and said, "Believe me, he would have said *plenty*."

"That's all I want to hear," Mr. Royster said, over the top of the magazine. "No more, now."

"You see." Mrs. Royster pointed the bread and peanut butter at her husband. "That's the way it is, day and night."

There was silence except for the music bellowing out of the radio next to Mr. Royster, and then she said, in a voice she hardly trusted to be heard over the radio noise, "Has he gone, then?"

"Who?" Mrs. Royster demanded, looking up from the peanut butter jar.

"Mr. James Harris."

"Him? He must've left this morning, before we got back. No sign of him anywhere."

"Gone?"

"Everything was fine, though, perfectly fine. I told you," she said to Mr. Royster, "I told you he'd take care of everything fine. I can always tell."

"You were lucky," Mr. Royster said.

"Not a thing out of place," Mrs. Royster said. She waved her bread and peanut butter inclusively. "Everything just the way we left it," she said.

"Do you know where he is now?"

"Not the slightest idea," Mrs. Royster said cheerfully. "But, like I said, he left everything fine. Why?" she asked suddenly. "You looking for *him*?"

"It's very important."

"I'm sorry he's not here," Mrs. Royster said. She stepped forward politely when she saw her visitor turn toward the door.

"Maybe the super saw him," Mr. Royster said into the magazine.

When the door was closed behind her the hall was dark again, but the sound of the radio was deadened. She was half-way down the first flight of stairs when the door was opened and Mrs. Royster shouted down the stairwell, "If I see him I'll tell him you were looking for him."

What can I do? she thought, out on the street again. It was impossible to go home, not with Jamie somewhere between here and there. She stood on the sidewalk so long that a woman, leaning out of a window across the way, turned and called to someone inside to come and see. Finally, on an impulse, she went into the small delicatessen next door to the apartment house, on the side that led to her own apartment. There was a small man reading a newspaper, leaning against the counter; when she came in he looked up and came down inside the counter to meet her.

Over the glass case of cold meats and cheese she said, timidly, "I'm trying to get in touch with a man who lived in the apartment house next door, and I just wondered if you know him."

"Whyn't you ask the people there?" the man said, his eyes narrow, inspecting her.

It's because I'm not buying anything, she thought, and she said, "I'm sorry. I asked them, but they don't know anything about him. They think he left this morning."

"I don't know what you want *me* to do," he said, moving a little back toward his newspaper. "I'm not here to keep track of guys going in and out next door."

She said quickly, "I thought you might have noticed, that's all. He would have been coming past here, a little before ten o'clock. He was rather tall, and he usually wore a blue suit."

"Now how many men in blue suits go past here every day, lady?" the man demanded. "You think I got nothing to do but—"

"I'm sorry," she said. She heard him say, "For God's sake," as she went out the door.

As she walked toward the corner, she thought, he must have come this way, it's the way he'd go to get to my house, it's the only way for him to walk. She tried to think of Jamie: where would he have crossed the street? What sort of person was he actually—would he cross in front of his own apartment house, at random in the middle of the block, at the corner?

On the corner was a newsstand; they might have seen him

there. She hurried on and waited while a man bought a paper and a woman asked directions. When the newsstand man looked at her she said, "Can you possibly tell me if a rather tall young man in a blue suit went past here this morning around ten o'clock?" When the man only looked at her, his eyes wide and his mouth a little open, she thought, he thinks it's a joke, or a trick, and she said urgently, "It's very important, please believe me. I'm not teasing you."

"*Look*, lady," the man began, and she said eagerly, "He's a writer. He might have bought magazines here."

"What you want him for?" the man asked. He looked at her, smiling, and she realized that there was another man waiting in back of her and the newsdealer's smile included him. "Never mind," she said, but the newsdealer said, "Listen, maybe he did come by here." His smile was knowing and his eyes shifted over her shoulder to the man in back of her. She was suddenly horribly aware of her over-young print dress, and pulled her coat around her quickly. The newsdealer said, with vast thoughtfulness, "Now I don't know for sure, mind you, but there might have been someone like your gentleman friend coming by this morning."

"About ten?"

"About ten," the newsdealer agreed. "Tall fellow, blue suit. I wouldn't be at all surprised."

"Which way did he go?" she said eagerly. "Uptown?"

"Uptown," the newsdealer said, nodding. "He went uptown. That's just exactly it. What can I do for you, sir?"

She stepped back, holding her coat around her. The man who had been standing behind her looked at her over his shoulder and then he and the newsdealer looked at one another. She wondered for a minute whether or not to tip the newsdealer but when both men began to laugh she moved hurriedly on across the street.

Uptown, she thought, that's right, and she started up the avenue, thinking: He wouldn't have to cross the avenue, just go up six blocks and turn down my street, so long as he started uptown. About a block farther on she passed a florist's shop; there was a wedding display in the window and she thought, This is my wedding day after all, he might have gotten flowers to bring me, and she went inside. The florist came out of the back of the shop, smiling and sleek, and she said, before he could speak, so that he wouldn't have a chance to think she was buying anything: "It's *terribly* important that I get in touch with a gentleman who may have stopped in here to buy flowers this morning. *Terribly* important."

She stopped for breath, and the florist said, "Yes, what sort of flowers were they?"

"I don't know," she said, surprised. "He never—" She stopped and said, "He was a rather tall young man, in a blue suit. It was about ten o'clock."

"I see," the florist said. "Well, *really*, I'm afraid. . . ."

"But it's *so* important," she said. "He may have been in a hurry," she added helpfully.

"Well," the florist said. He smiled genially, showing all his small teeth. "For a *lady*," he said. He went to a stand and opened a large book. "Where were they to be sent?" he asked.

"Why," she said, "I don't think he'd have sent them. You see, he was coming—that is, he'd *bring* them."

"Madam," the florist said; he was offended. His smile became deprecatory, and he went on, "Really, you must realize that unless I have *something* to go on. . . ."

"*Please* try to remember," she begged. "He was tall, and had a blue suit, and it was about ten this morning."

The florist closed his eyes, one finger to his mouth, and thought deeply. Then he shook his head. "I simply *can't*," he said.

"Thank you," she said despondently, and started for the door, when the florist said, in a shrill, excited voice, "Wait! Wait just a moment, madam." She turned and the florist, thinking again, said finally, "Chrysanthemums?" He looked at her inquiringly.

"Oh, *no*," she said; her voice shook a little for a minute before she went on. "Not for an occasion like this, I'm sure."

The florist tightened his lips and looked away coldly. "Well, of *course* I don't know the *occasion*," he said, "but I'm almost certain that the gentleman you were inquiring for came in this morning and purchased one dozen chrysanthemums. No delivery."

"You're *sure?*" she asked.

"Positive," the florist said emphatically. "That was absolutely the man." He smiled brilliantly, and she smiled back and said, "Well, thank you very much."

He escorted her to the door. "Nice corsage?" he said, as they went through the shop. "Red roses? Gardenias?"

"It was very kind of you to help me," she said at the door.

"Ladies always look their best in flowers," he said, bending his head toward her. "Orchids, perhaps?"

"No, thank you," she said, and he said, "I hope you find your young man," and gave it a nasty sound.

Going on up the street she thought, Everyone thinks it's so *funny:* and she pulled her coat tighter around her, so that only the ruffle around the bottom of the print dress was showing.

There was a policeman on the corner, and she thought, Why don't I go to the police—you go to the police for a missing person. And then thought, What a fool I'd look like. She had a quick picture of herself standing in a police station, saying, "Yes, we were going to be married today, but he didn't come," and the policemen, three or four of them standing around listening, looking at her, at the print dress, at her too-bright make-up, smiling at one another. She couldn't tell them any more than that, could not say, "Yes, it looks silly, doesn't it, me all dressed up and trying to find the young man who promised to marry me, but what about all of it you don't know? I have more than this, more than you can see: talent, perhaps, and humor of a sort, and I'm a lady and I have pride and affection and delicacy and a certain clear view of life that might make a man satisfied and productive and happy; there's more than you think when you look at me."

The police were obviously impossible, leaving out Jamie and what he might think when he heard she'd set the police after him. "No, no," she said aloud, hurrying her steps, and someone passing stopped and looked after her.

On the coming corner—she was three blocks from her own street—was a shoeshine stand, an old man sitting almost asleep in one of the chairs. She stopped in front of him and waited, and after a minute he opened his eyes and smiled at her.

"Look," she said, the words coming before she thought of them, "I'm sorry to bother you, but I'm looking for a young man who came up this way about ten this morning, did you see him?" And she began her description, "Tall, blue suit, carrying a bunch of flowers?"

The old man began to nod before she was finished. "I saw him," he said. "Friend of yours?"

"Yes," she said, and smiled back involuntarily.

The old man blinked his eyes and said, "I remember I thought, You're going to see your girl, young fellow. They all go to see their girls," he said, and shook his head tolerantly.

"Which way did he go? Straight on up the avenue?"

"That's right," the old man said. "Got a shine, had his flowers, all dressed up, in an awful hurry. You got a girl, I thought."

"Thank you," she said, fumbling in her pocket for her loose change.

"She sure must of been glad to see him, the way he looked," the old man said.

"Thank you," she said again, and brought her hand empty from her pocket.

For the first time she was really sure he would be waiting for her, and she hurried up the three blocks, the skirt of the print dress swinging under her coat, and turned into her own block. From the corner she could not see her own windows, could not see Jamie looking out, waiting for her, and going down the block she was almost running to get to him. Her key trembled in her fingers at the downstairs door, and as she glanced into the drugstore she thought of her panic, drinking coffee there this morning, and almost laughed. At her own door she could wait no longer, but began to say, "Jamie, I'm here, I was so worried," even before the door was open.

Her own apartment was waiting for her, silent, barren, afternoon shadows lengthening from the window. For a minute she saw only the empty coffee cup, thought, He has been here waiting, before she recognized it as her own, left from the morning. She looked all over the room, into the closet, into the bathroom.

"I never saw him," the clerk in the drugstore said. "I know because I would of noticed the flowers. No one like that's been in."

The old man at the shoeshine stand woke up again to see her standing in front of him. "Hello again," he said, and smiled.

"Are you *sure?*" she demanded. "Did he go on up the avenue?"

"I watched him," the old man said, dignified against her tone. "I thought, There's a young man's got a girl, and I watched him right into the house."

"What house?" she said remotely.

"Right there," the old man said. He leaned forward to point. "The next block. With his flowers and his shine and going to see his girl. Right into her house."

"Which one?" she said.

"About the middle of the block," the old man said. He looked at her with suspicion, and said, "What you trying to do, anyway?"

She almost ran, without stopping to say "Thank you." Up on the next block she walked quickly, searching the houses from the outside to see if Jamie looked from a window, listening to hear his laughter somewhere inside.

A woman was sitting in front of one of the houses, pushing a baby carriage monotonously back and forth the length of her arm. The baby inside slept, moving back and forth.

The question was fluent, by now. "I'm sorry, but did you see a young man go into one of these houses about ten this morning? He was tall, wearing a blue suit, carrying a bunch of flowers."

A boy about twelve stopped to listen, turning intently from one to the other, occasionally glancing at the baby.

"Listen," the woman said tiredly, "the kid has his bath at ten. Would I see strange men walking around? I ask you."

"Big bunch of flowers?" the boy asked, pulling at her coat. "Big bunch of flowers? I seen him, missus."

She looked down and the boy grinned insolently at her. "Which house did he go in?" she asked wearily.

"You gonna divorce him?" the boy asked insistently.

"That's not nice to ask the lady," the woman rocking the carriage said.

"Listen," the boy said, "I seen him. He went in there." He

pointed to the house next door. "I followed him," the boy said. "He give me a quarter." The boy dropped his voice to a growl, and said, " 'This is a big day for me, kid,' he says. Give me a quarter."

She gave him a dollar bill. "Where?" she said.

"Top floor," the boy said. "I followed him till he give me the quarter. Way to the top." He backed up the sidewalk, out of reach, with the dollar bill. "You gonna divorce him?" he asked again.

"Was he carrying flowers?"

"Yeah," the boy said. He began to screech. "You gonna divorce him, missus? You got something on him?" He went careening down the street, howling, "She's got something on the poor guy," and the woman rocking the baby laughed.

The street door of the apartment house was unlocked; there were no bells in the outer vestibule, and no lists of names. The stairs were narrow and dirty; there were two doors on the top floor. The front one was the right one; there was a crumpled florist's paper on the floor outside the door, and a knotted paper ribbon, like a clue, like the final clue in the paper-chase.

She knocked, and thought she heard voices inside, and she thought, suddenly, with terror, What shall I say if Jamie is there, if he comes to the door? The voices seemed suddenly still. She knocked again and there was silence, except for something that might have been laughter far away. He could have seen me from the window, she thought, it's the front apartment and that little boy made a dreadful noise. She waited, and knocked again, but there was silence.

Finally she went to the other door on the floor, and knocked. The door swung open beneath her hand and she saw the empty attic room, bare lath on the walls, floorboards unpainted. She stepped just inside, looking around; the room was filled with bags of plaster, piles of old newspapers, a broken trunk. There was a noise which she suddenly realized as a rat, and then she saw it, sitting very close to her, near the wall, its evil face alert, bright eyes watching her. She stumbled in her haste to be out with the door closed, and the skirt of the print dress caught and tore.

She knew there was someone inside the other apartment,

because she was sure she could hear low voices and sometimes laughter. She came back many times, every day for the first week. She came on her way to work, in the mornings; in the evenings, on her way to dinner alone, but no matter how often or how firmly she knocked, no one ever came to the door.

Like Mother Used to Make

D AVID TURNER, who did everything in small quick movements, hurried from the bus stop down the avenue toward his street. He reached the grocery on the corner and hesitated; there had been something. Butter, he remembered with relief; this morning, all the way up the avenue to his bus stop, he had been telling himself butter, don't forget butter coming home tonight, when you pass the grocery remember butter. He went into the grocery and waited his turn, examining the cans on the shelves. Canned pork sausage was back, and corned-beef hash. A tray full of rolls caught his eye, and then the woman ahead of him went out and the clerk turned to him.

"How much is butter?" David asked cautiously.

"Eighty-nine," the clerk said easily.

"Eighty-nine?" David frowned.

"That's what it is," the clerk said. He looked past David at the next customer.

"Quarter of a pound, please," David said. "And a half-dozen rolls."

Carrying his package home he thought, I really ought not to trade there any more; you'd think they'd know me well enough to be more courteous.

There was a letter from his mother in the mailbox. He stuck it into the top of the bag of rolls and went upstairs to the third floor. No light in Marcia's apartment, the only other apartment on the floor. David turned to his own door and unlocked it, snapping on the light as he came in the door. Tonight, as every night when he came home, the apartment looked warm and friendly and good; the little foyer, with the neat small table and four careful chairs, and the bowl of little marigolds against the pale green walls David had painted himself; beyond, the kitchenette, and beyond that, the big room where David read and slept and the ceiling of which was a perpetual trouble to him; the plaster was falling in one corner and no power on earth could make it less noticeable. David consoled himself for the plaster constantly with the thought that perhaps if he had not taken an apartment in an old brownstone the plaster would not be falling, but then, too, for the money he paid he could not have a foyer and a big room and a kitchenette, anywhere else.

He put his bag down on the table and put the butter away in the refrigerator and the rolls in the breadbox. He folded the empty bag and put it in a drawer in the kitchenette. Then he hung his coat in the hall closet and went into the big room, which he called his living-room, and lighted the desk light. His word for the room, in his own mind, was "charming." He had always been partial to yellows and browns, and he had painted the desk and the bookcases and the end tables himself, had even painted the walls, and had hunted around the city for the exact tweedish tan drapes he had in mind. The room satisfied him: the rug was a rich dark brown that picked up the darkest thread in the drapes, the furniture was almost yellow, the cover on the studio couch and the lampshades were orange. The rows of plants on the window sills gave the touch of green the room needed; right now David was looking for an ornament to set on the end table, but he had his heart set on a low translucent green bowl for more marigolds, and such things cost more than he could afford, after the silverware.

He could not come into this room without feeling that it was the most comfortable home he had ever had; tonight, as always, he let his eyes move slowly around the room, from couch to drapes to bookcase, imagined the green bowl on the end table, and sighed as he turned to the desk. He took his pen from the holder, and a sheet of the neat notepaper sitting in one of the desk cubbyholes, and wrote carefully: "Dear Marcia, don't forget you're coming for dinner tonight. I'll expect you about six." He signed the note with a "D" and picked up the key to Marcia's apartment which lay in the flat pencil tray on his desk. He had a key to Marcia's apartment because she was never home when her laundryman came, or when the man came to fix the refrigerator or the telephone or the windows, and someone had to let them in because the landlord was reluctant to climb three flights of stairs with the pass key. Marcia had never suggested having a key to David's apartment, and he had never offered her one; it pleased him to have only one key to his home, and that safely in his own pocket; it had a pleasant feeling to him, solid and small, the only way into his warm fine home.

He left his front door open and went down the dark hall to the other apartment. He opened the door with his key and turned on the light. This apartment was not agreeable for him to come into; it was exactly the same as his: foyer, kitchenette, living-room, and it reminded him constantly of his first day in his own apartment, when the thought of the careful home-making to be done had left him very close to despair. Marcia's home was bare and at random; an upright piano a friend had given her recently stood crookedly, half in the foyer, because the little room was too narrow and the big room was too cluttered for it to sit comfortably anywhere; Marcia's bed was unmade and a pile of dirty laundry lay on the floor. The window had been open all day and papers had blown wildly around the floor. David closed the window, hesitated over the papers, and then moved away quickly. He put the note on the piano keys and locked the door behind him.

In his own apartment he settled down happily to making dinner. He had made a little pot roast for dinner the night before; most of it was still in the refrigerator and he sliced it in fine thin slices and arranged it on a plate with parsley. His plates were orange, almost the same color as the couch cover, and it was pleasant to him to arrange a salad, with the lettuce on the orange plate, and the thin slices of cucumber. He put coffee on to cook, and sliced potatoes to fry, and then, with his dinner cooking agreeably and the window open to lose the odor of the frying potatoes, he set lovingly to arranging his table. First, the tablecloth, pale green, of course. And the two fresh green napkins. The orange plates and the precise cup and saucer at each place. The plate of rolls in the center, and the odd salt and pepper shakers, like two green frogs. Two glasses —they came from the five-and-ten, but they had thin green bands around them—and finally, with great care, the silverware. Gradually, tenderly, David was buying himself a complete set of silverware; starting out modestly with a service for two, he had added to it until now he had well over a service for four, although not quite a service for six, lacking salad forks and soup spoons. He had chosen a sedate, pretty pattern, one that would be fine with any sort of table setting, and each morning he gloried in a breakfast that started with a shining silver spoon for his grapefruit, and had a compact butter knife for his toast and a solid heavy knife to break his eggshell, and a fresh silver spoon for his coffee, which he sugared with a particular spoon meant only for sugar. The silverware lay in a tarnish-proof box on a high shelf all to itself, and David lifted it down carefully to take out a service for two. It made a lavish display set out on the table—knives, forks, salad forks, more forks for the pie, a spoon to each place, and the special serving pieces—the sugar spoon, the large serving spoons for the potatoes and the salad, the fork for the meat, and the pie fork. When the table held as much silverware as two people could possibly use he put the box back on the shelf and stood back, checking everything and admiring the table, shining and clean. Then he went into his living-room to read his mother's letter and wait for Marcia.

The potatoes were done before Marcia came, and then suddenly the door burst open and Marcia arrived with a shout and fresh air and disorder. She was a tall handsome girl with a loud voice, wearing a dirty raincoat, and she said, "I didn't forget, Davie, I'm just late as usual. What's for dinner? You're not mad, are you?"

David got up and came over to take her coat. "I left a note for you," he said.

"Didn't see it," Marcia said. "Haven't been home. Something smells good."

"Fried potatoes," David said. "Everything's ready."

"Golly." Marcia fell into a chair to sit with her legs stretched out in front of her and her arms hanging. "I'm tired," she said. "It's cold out."

"It was getting colder when I came home," David said. He was putting dinner on the table, the platter of meat, the salad, the bowl of fried potatoes. He walked quietly back and forth from the kitchenette to the table, avoiding Marcia's feet. "I don't believe you've been here since I got my silverware," he said.

Marcia swung around to the table and picked up a spoon. "It's beautiful," she said, running her finger along the pattern. "Pleasure to eat with it."

"Dinner's ready," David said. He pulled her chair out for her and waited for her to sit down.

Marcia was always hungry; she put meat and potatoes and salad on her plate without admiring the serving silver, and started to eat enthusiastically. "Everything's beautiful," she said once. "Food is wonderful, Davie."

"I'm glad you like it," David said. He liked the feel of the fork in his hand, even the sight of the fork moving up to Marcia's mouth.

Marcia waved her hand largely. "I mean everything," she said, "furniture, and nice place you have here, and dinner, and everything."

"I *like* things this way," David said.

"I know you do." Marcia's voice was mournful. "Someone should teach me, I guess."

"You *ought* to keep your home neater," David said. "You ought to get curtains at least, and keep your windows shut."

"I never remember," she said. "Davie, you are the most *wonderful* cook." She pushed her plate away, and sighed.

David blushed happily. "I'm glad you like it," he said again, and then he laughed. "I made a pie last night."

"A pie." Marcia looked at him for a minute and then she said, "Apple?"

David shook his head, and she said, "Pineapple?" and he shook his head again, and, because he could not wait to tell her, said, "Cherry."

"My *God*!" Marcia got up and followed him into the kitchen and looked over his shoulder while he took the pie carefully out of the breadbox. "Is this the first pie you ever made?"

"I've made two before," David admitted, "but this one turned out better than the others."

She watched happily while he cut large pieces of pie and put them on other orange plates, and then she carried her own plate back to the table, tasted the pie, and made wordless gestures of appreciation. David tasted his pie and said critically, "I think it's a little sour. I ran out of sugar."

"It's perfect," Marcia said. "I always loved a cherry pie really *sour*. This isn't sour enough, even."

David cleared the table and poured the coffee, and as he was setting the coffeepot back on the stove Marcia said, "My doorbell's ringing." She opened the apartment door and listened, and they could both hear the ringing in her apartment. She pressed the buzzer in David's apartment that opened the downstairs door, and far away they could hear heavy footsteps starting up the stairs. Marcia left the apartment door open and came back to her coffee. "Landlord, most likely," she said. "I didn't pay my rent again." When the footsteps reached the top of the last staircase Marcia yelled, "Hello?" leaning back in her chair to see out the door into the hall. Then she said, "Why, Mr. Harris." She got up and went to the door and held out her hand. "Come in," she said.

"I just thought I'd stop by," Mr. Harris said. He was a very large man and his eyes rested curiously on the coffee cups and empty plates on the table. "I don't want to interrupt your dinner."

"*That's* all right," Marcia said, pulling him into the room. "It's just Davie. Davie, this is Mr. Harris, he works in my office. This is Mr. Turner."

"How do you do," David said politely, and the man looked at him carefully and said, "How do you do?"

"Sit down, sit down," Marcia was saying, pushing a chair forward. "Davie, how about another cup for Mr. Harris?"

"Please don't bother," Mr. Harris said quickly, "I just thought I'd stop by."

While David was taking out another cup and saucer and getting a spoon down from the tarnish-proof silverbox, Marcia said, "You like homemade pie?"

"Say," Mr. Harris said admiringly, "I've forgotten what homemade pie *looks* like."

"Davie," Marcia called cheerfully, "how about cutting Mr. Harris a piece of that pie?"

Without answering, David took a fork out of the silverbox and got down an orange plate and put a piece of pie on it. His plans for the evening had been vague; they had involved perhaps a movie if it were not too cold out, and at least a short talk with Marcia about the state of her home; Mr. Harris was settling down in his chair and when David put the pie down silently in front of him he stared at it admiringly for a minute before he tasted it.

"Say," he said finally, "this is certainly some pie." He looked at Marcia. "This is really *good* pie," he said.

"You like it?" Marcia asked modestly. She looked up at David and smiled at him over Mr. Harris' head. "I haven't made but two, three pies before," she said.

David raised a hand to protest, but Mr. Harris turned to him and demanded, "Did you ever eat any better pie in your life?"

"I don't think Davie liked it much," Marcia said wickedly, "I think it was too sour for him."

"I *like* a sour pie," Mr. Harris said. He looked suspiciously at David. "A cherry pie's *got* to be sour."

"I'm glad you like it, anyway," Marcia said. Mr. Harris ate the last mouthful of pie, finished his coffee, and sat back. "I'm sure glad I dropped in," he said to Marcia.

David's desire to be rid of Mr. Harris had slid impercepti-bly into an urgency to be rid of them both; his clean house, his nice silver, were not meant as vehicles for the kind of fatuous banter Marcia and Mr. Harris were playing at together; almost roughly he took the coffee cup away from the arm Marcia had stretched across the table, took it out to the kitchenette and came back and put his hand on Mr. Harris' cup.

"Don't bother, Davie, honestly," Marcia said. She looked up, smiling again, as though she and David were conspirators against Mr. Harris. "I'll do them all tomorrow, honey," she said.

"Sure," Mr. Harris said. He stood up. "Let them wait. Let's go in and sit down where we can be comfortable."

Marcia got up and led him into the living-room and they sat down on the studio couch. "Come on in, Davie," Marcia called.

The sight of his pretty table covered with dirty dishes and cigarette ashes held David. He carried the plates and cups and silverware into the kitchenette and stacked them in the sink and then, because he could not endure the thought of their sitting there any longer, with the dirt gradually hardening on them, he tied an apron on and began to wash them carefully. Now and then, while he was washing them and drying them and putting them away, Marcia would call to him, sometimes,

"Davie, what *are* you doing?" or, "Davie, won't you stop all that and come sit down?" Once she said, "Davie, I don't want you to wash all those dishes," and Mr. Harris said, "Let him work, he's happy."

David put the clean yellow cups and saucers back on the shelves—by now, Mr. Harris' cup was unrecognizable; you could not tell, from the clean rows of cups, which one he had used or which one had been stained with Marcia's lipstick or which one had held David's coffee which he had finished in the kitchenette—and finally, taking the tarnish-proof box down, he put the silverware away. First the forks all went together into the little grooves which held two forks each—later, when the set was complete, each groove would hold four forks—and then the spoons, stacked up neatly one on top of another in their own grooves, and the knives in even order, all facing the same way, in the special tapes in the lid of the box. Butter knives and serving spoons and the pie knife all went into their own places, and then David put the lid down on the lovely shining set and put the box back on the shelf. After wringing out the dishcloth and hanging up the dish towel and taking off his apron he was through, and he went slowly into the living-room. Marcia and Mr. Harris were sitting close together on the studio couch, talking earnestly.

"My *father's* name was James," Marcia was saying as David came in, as though she were clinching an argument. She turned around when David came in and said, "Davie, you were so nice to do all those dishes yourself."

"That's all right," David said awkwardly. Mr. Harris was looking at him impatiently.

"I should have helped you," Marcia said. There was a silence, and then Marcia said, "Sit down, Davie, won't you?"

David recognized her tone; it was the one hostesses used when they didn't know what else to say to you, or when you had come too early or stayed too late. It was the tone he had expected to use on Mr. Harris.

"James and I were just talking about. . . ." Marcia began and then stopped and laughed. "What *were* we talking about?" she asked, turning to Mr. Harris.

"Nothing much," Mr. Harris said. He was still watching David.

"Well," Marcia said, letting her voice trail off. She turned to David and smiled brightly and then said, "Well," again.

Mr. Harris picked up the ashtray from the end table and set it on the couch between himself and Marcia. He took a cigar out of his pocket and said to Marcia, "Do you mind cigars?" and when Marcia shook her head he unwrapped the cigar tenderly and bit off the end. "Cigar smoke's good for plants," he said thickly, around the cigar, as he lighted it, and Marcia laughed.

David stood up. For a minute he thought he was going to say something that might start, "Mr. Harris, I'll thank you to. . . ." but what he actually said, finally, with both Marcia and Mr. Harris looking at him, was, "Guess I better be getting along, Marcia."

Mr. Harris stood up and said heartily, "Certainly have enjoyed meeting you." He held out his hand and David shook hands limply.

"Guess I better be getting along," he said again to Marcia, and she stood up and said, "I'm sorry you have to leave so soon."

"Lots of work to do," David said, much more genially than he intended, and Marcia smiled at him again as though they were conspirators and went over to the desk and said, "Don't forget your key."

Surprised, David took the key of her apartment from her, said good night to Mr. Harris, and went to the outside door.

"Good night, Davie honey," Marcia called out, and David said "Thanks for a simply *wonderful* dinner, Marcia," and closed the door behind him.

He went down the hall and let himself into Marcia's apartment; the piano was still awry, the papers were still on the floor, the laundry scattered, the bed unmade. David sat down on the bed and looked around. It was cold, it was dirty, and as he thought miserably of his own warm home he heard faintly down the hall the sound of laughter and the scrape of a chair being moved. Then, still faintly, the sound of his radio. Wearily, David leaned over and picked up a paper from the floor, and then he began to gather them up one by one.

Trial by Combat

WHEN Emily Johnson came home one evening to her furnished room and found three of her best handkerchiefs missing from the dresser drawer, she was sure who had taken them and what to do. She had lived in the furnished room for about six weeks and for the past two weeks she had been missing small things occasionally. There had been several handkerchiefs gone, and an initial pin which Emily rarely wore and which had come from the five-and-ten. And once she had missed a small bottle of perfume and one of a set of china dogs. Emily had known for some time who was taking the things, but it was only tonight that she had decided what to do. She had hesitated about complaining to the landlady because her losses were trivial and because she had felt certain that sooner or later she would know how to deal with the situation herself. It had seemed logical to her from the beginning that the one person in the rooming-house who was home all day was the most likely suspect, and then, one Sunday morning, coming downstairs from the roof, where she had been sitting in the sun, Emily had seen someone come out of her room and go down the stairs, and had recognized the visitor. Tonight, she felt, she knew just what to do. She took off her coat and hat, put her packages down, and, while a can of tamales was heating on her electric plate, she went over what she intended to say.

After her dinner, she closed and locked her door and went downstairs. She tapped softly on the door of the room directly below her own, and when she thought she heard someone say, "Come in," she said, "Mrs. Allen?," then opened the door carefully and stepped inside.

The room, Emily noticed immediately, was almost like her own—the same narrow bed with the tan cover, the same maple dresser and armchair; the closet was on the opposite side of the room, but the window was in the same relative position. Mrs. Allen was sitting in the armchair. She was about sixty. More than twice as old as I am, Emily thought, while she stood in the doorway, and a lady still. She hesitated for a few seconds, looking at Mrs. Allen's clean white hair and her neat, dark-blue house coat, before speaking. "Mrs. Allen," she said, "I'm Emily Johnson."

Mrs. Allen put down the *Woman's Home Companion* she had been reading and stood up slowly. "I'm very happy to meet you," she said graciously. "I've seen you, of course, several times, and thought how pleasant you looked. It's so seldom one meets anyone really"—Mrs. Allen hesitated—"really nice," she went on, "in a place like this."

"I've wanted to meet you, too," Emily said.

Mrs. Allen indicated the chair she had been sitting in. "Won't you sit down?"

"Thank you," Emily said. "You stay there. I'll sit on the bed." She smiled. "I feel as if I know the furniture so well. Mine's just the same."

"It's a shame," Mrs. Allen said, sitting down in her chair again. "I've told the landlady over and over, you can't make people feel at home if you put all the same furniture in the rooms. But she maintains that this maple furniture is clean-looking and cheap."

"It's better than most," Emily said. "You've made yours look much nicer than mine."

"I've been here for three years," Mrs. Allen said. "You've only been here a month or so, haven't you?"

"Six weeks," Emily said.

"The landlady's told me about you. Your husband's in the Army."

"Yes. I have a job here in New York."

"My husband was in the Army," Mrs. Allen said. She gestured at a group of pictures on her maple dresser. "That was a long time ago, of course. He's been dead for nearly five years." Emily got up and went over to the pictures. One of them was of a tall, dignified-looking man in Army uniform. Several were of children.

"He was a very distinguished-looking man," Emily said. "Are those your children?"

"I had no children, to my sorrow," the old lady said. "Those are nephews and nieces of my husband's."

Emily stood in front of the dresser, looking around the room. "I see you have flowers, too," she said. She walked to the window and looked at the row of potted plants. "I love flowers," she said. "I bought myself a big bunch of asters tonight to brighten up my room. But they fade so quickly."

"I prefer plants just for that reason," Mrs. Allen said. "But why don't you put an aspirin in the water with your flowers? They'll last much longer."

"I'm afraid I don't know much about flowers," Emily said. "I didn't know about putting an aspirin in the water, for instance."

"I always do, with cut flowers," Mrs. Allen said. "I think flowers make a room look so friendly."

Emily stood by the window for a minute, looking out on Mrs. Allen's daily view: the fire escape opposite, an oblique slice of the street below. Then she took a deep breath and turned around. "Actually, Mrs. Allen," she said, "I had a reason for dropping in."

"Other than to make my acquaintance?" Mrs. Allen said, smiling.

"I don't know quite what to do," Emily said. "I don't like to say anything to the landlady."

"The landlady isn't much help in an emergency," Mrs. Allen said.

Emily came back and sat on the bed, looking earnestly at Mrs. Allen, seeing a nice old lady. "It's so slight," she said, "but someone has been coming into my room."

Mrs. Allen looked up.

"I've been missing things," Emily went on, "like handkerchiefs and little inexpensive jewelry. Nothing important. But someone's been coming into my room and helping themselves."

"I'm sorry to hear it," Mrs. Allen said.

"You see, I don't like to make trouble," Emily said. "It's just that someone's coming into my room. I haven't missed anything of value."

"I see," Mrs. Allen said.

"I just noticed it a few days ago. And then last Sunday I was coming down from the roof and I saw someone coming out of my room."

"Do you have any idea who it was?" Mrs. Allen asked.

"I believe I do," Emily said.

Mrs. Allen was quiet for a minute. "I can see where you wouldn't like to speak to the landlady," she said finally.

"Of course not," Emily said. "I just want it to stop."

"I don't blame you," Mrs. Allen said.

"You see, it means someone has a key to my door," Emily said pleadingly.

"All the keys in this house open all the doors," Mrs. Allen said. "They're all old-fashioned locks."

"It *has* to stop," Emily said. "If it doesn't, I'll have to do something about it."

"I can see that," Mrs. Allen said. "The whole thing is very unfortunate." She rose. "You'll have to excuse me," she went on. "I tire very easily and I must be in bed early. I'm so happy you came down to see me."

"I'm so glad to have met you at last," Emily said. She went to the door. "I hope I won't be bothered again," she said. "Good night."

"Good night," Mrs. Allen said.

The following evening, when Emily came home from work, a pair of cheap earrings was gone, along with two packages of cigarettes which had been in her dresser drawer. That evening she sat alone in her room for a long time, thinking. Then she wrote a letter to her husband and went to bed. The next morning she got up and dressed and went to the corner drugstore, where she called her office from a phone booth and said that she was sick and would not be in that day. Then she went back to her room. She sat for almost an hour with the door slightly ajar before she heard Mrs. Allen's door open and Mrs. Allen come out and go slowly down the stairs. When Mrs. Allen had had time to get out onto the street, Emily locked her door and, carrying her key in her hand, went down to Mrs. Allen's room.

She was thinking, I just want to pretend it's my own room, so that if anyone comes I can say I was mistaken about the floor. For a minute, after she had opened the door, it seemed as though she *were* in her own room. The bed was neatly made and the shade drawn down over the window. Emily left the door unlocked and went over and pulled up the shade. Now that the room was light, she looked around. She had a sudden sense of unbearable intimacy with Mrs. Allen, and thought,

This is the way she must feel in my room. Everything was neat and plain. She looked in the closet first, but there was nothing in there but Mrs. Allen's blue house coat and one or two plain dresses. Emily went to the dresser. She looked for a moment at the picture of Mrs. Allen's husband, and then opened the top drawer and looked in. Her handkerchiefs were there, in a neat, small pile, and next to them the cigarettes and the earrings. In one corner the little china dog was sitting. Everything is here, Emily thought, all put away and very orderly. She closed the drawer and opened the next two. Both were empty. She opened the top one again. Besides her things, the drawer held a pair of black cotton gloves, and under the little pile of her handkerchiefs were two plain white ones. There was a box of Kleenex and a small tin of aspirin. For her plants, Emily thought.

Emily was counting the handkerchiefs when a noise behind her made her turn around. Mrs. Allen was standing in the doorway watching her quietly. Emily dropped the handkerchiefs she was holding and stepped back. She felt herself blushing and knew her hands were trembling. Now, she was thinking, now turn around and tell her. "Listen, Mrs. Allen," she began, and stopped.

"Yes?" Mrs. Allen said gently.

Emily found that she was staring at the picture of Mrs. Allen's husband; such a thoughtful-looking man, she was thinking. They must have had such a pleasant life together, and now she has a room like mine, with only two handkerchiefs of her own in the drawer.

"Yes?" Mrs. Allen said again.

What does she want me to say, Emily thought. What could she be waiting for with such a ladylike manner? "I came down," Emily said, and hesitated. My voice is almost ladylike, too, she thought. "I had a terrible headache and I came down to borrow some aspirin," she said quickly. "I had this awful headache and when I found you were out I thought surely you wouldn't mind if I just borrowed some aspirin."

"I'm so sorry," Mrs. Allen said. "But I'm glad you felt you knew me well enough."

"I never would have dreamed of coming in," Emily said, "except for such a bad headache."

"Of course," Mrs. Allen said. "Let's not say any more about it." She went over to the dresser and opened the drawer. Emily, standing next to her, watched her hand pass over the handkerchiefs and pick up the aspirin. "You just take two of these and go to bed for an hour," Mrs. Allen said.

"Thank you." Emily began to move toward the door. "You've been very kind."

"Let me know if there's anything more I can do."

"Thank you," Emily said again, opening the door. She waited for a minute and then turned toward the stairs to her room.

"I'll run up later today," Mrs. Allen said, "just to see how you feel."

The Villager

Miss Clarence stopped on the corner of Sixth Avenue and Eighth Street and looked at her watch. Two-fifteen; she was earlier than she thought. She went into Whelan's and sat at the counter, putting her copy of the *Villager* down on the counter next to her pocketbook and *The Charterhouse of Parma*, which she had read enthusiastically up to page fifty and only carried now for effect. She ordered a chocolate-frosted and while the clerk was making it she went over to the cigarette counter and bought a pack of Kools. Sitting again at the soda counter, she opened the pack and lit a cigarette.

Miss Clarence was about thirty-five, and had lived in Greenwich Village for twelve years. When she was twenty-three she had come to New York from a small town upstate because she wanted to be a dancer, and because everyone who wanted to study dancing or sculpture or book-binding had come to Greenwich Village then, usually with allowances from their families to live on and plans to work in Macy's or in a bookshop until they had enough money to pursue their art. Miss Clarence, fortunate in having taken a course in shorthand and typing, had gone to work as a stenographer in a coal and coke concern. Now, after twelve years, she was a private secretary in the same concern, and was making enough money to live in a good Village apartment by the park and buy herself smart clothes. She still went to an occasional dance recital with another girl from her office, and sometimes when she wrote to her old friends at home she referred to herself as a "Village die-hard." When Miss Clarence gave the matter any thought at all, she was apt to congratulate herself on her common sense in handling a good job competently and supporting herself better than she would have in her home town.

Confident that she looked very well in her gray tweed suit and the hammered copper lapel ornament from a Village jewelry store, Miss Clarence finished her frosted and looked at her watch again. She paid the cashier and went out into Sixth Avenue, and began to walk briskly uptown. She had estimated correctly; the house she was looking for was just west of Sixth Avenue, and she stopped in front of it for a minute, pleased with herself, and comparing the building with her own presentable apartment house. Miss Clarence lived in a picturesque brick and stucco modern; this house was wooden and old, with the very new front door that is deceptive until you look at the building above and see the turn-of-the-century architecture. Miss Clarence compared the address again with the ad in the *Villager*, and then opened the front door and went into the dingy hallway. She found the name Roberts and the apartment number, 4B. Miss Clarence sighed and started up the stairs.

She stopped and rested on the third landing, and lit another one of her cigarettes so as to enter the apartment effectively. At the head of the stairs on the fourth floor she found 4B, with a typed note pinned on the door. Miss Clarence pulled the note loose from the thumbtack that held it, and took it over into the light. "Miss Clarence—" she read, "I had to run out for a few minutes, but will be back about three-thirty. Please come on in and look around till I get back—all the furniture is marked with prices. Terribly sorry. Nancy Roberts."

Miss Clarence tried the door and it was unlocked. Still holding the note, she went in and closed the door behind her. The room was in confusion: half-empty boxes of papers and books were on the floor, the curtains were down, and the furniture piled with half-packed suitcases and clothes. The first thing Miss Clarence did was go to the window; on the fourth floor, she thought, maybe they would have a view. But she could see only dirty roofs and, far off to the left, a high building crowned with flower gardens. Someday I'll live *there*, she thought, and turned back to the room.

She went into the kitchen, a tiny alcove with a two-burner stove and a refrigerator built underneath, with a small sink on one side. Don't do much cooking, Miss Clarence thought, stove's never been cleaned. In the refrigerator were a bottle of milk and three bottles of Coca-Cola and a half-empty jar of peanut butter. Eat all their meals out, Miss Clarence thought. She opened the cupboard: a glass and a bottle opener. The other glass would be in the bathroom, Miss Clarence thought; no cups: she doesn't even make coffee in the morning. There was a roach inside the cupboard door; Miss Clarence closed it hurriedly and went back into the big room. She opened the bathroom door and glanced in: an old-fashioned tub with feet, no shower. The bathroom was dirty, and Miss Clarence was sure there would be roaches in there too.

Finally Miss Clarence turned to the crowded room. She lifted a suitcase and a typewriter off one of the chairs, took off her hat and coat, and sat down, lighting another one of her cigarettes. She had already decided that she could not use any of the furniture—the two chairs and the studio bed were maple; what Miss Clarence thought of as Village Modern. The small end-table bookcase was a nice piece of furniture, but there was a long scratch running across the top, and several glass stains. It was marked ten dollars, and Miss Clarence told herself she could get a dozen new ones if she wanted to pay that price. Miss Clarence, in a mild resentment of the coal and coke company, had done her quiet apartment in shades of beige and off-white, and the thought of introducing any of this shiny maple frightened her. She had a quick picture of young Village characters, frequenters of bookshops, lounging on the maple furniture and drinking rum and Coke, putting their glasses down anywhere.

For a minute Miss Clarence thought of offering to buy some books, but the ones packed on top of the boxes were mostly art books and portfolios. Some of the books had "Arthur Roberts" written inside; Arthur and Nancy Roberts, Miss Clarence thought, a nice young couple. Arthur was the artist, then, and Nancy . . . Miss Clarence turned over a few of the books and came across a book of modern dance photographs; could Nancy, she wondered affectionately, be a dancer?

The phone rang and Miss Clarence, on the other side of the room, hesitated for a minute before walking over and answering it. When she said hello a man's voice said, "Nancy?"

"No, I'm sorry, she's not home," Miss Clarence said.

"Who's this?" the voice asked.

"I'm waiting to see Mrs. Roberts," Miss Clarence said.

"Well," the voice said, "this is Artie Roberts, her husband. When she comes back ask her to call me, will you?"

"Mr. Roberts," Miss Clarence said. "Maybe you can help me, then. I came to look at the furniture."

"Who are you?"

"My name is Clarence, Hilda Clarence. I was interested in buying the furniture."

"Well, Hilda," Artie Roberts said, "what do you think? Everything's in good condition."

"I can't quite make up my mind," Miss Clarence said.

"The studio bed's as good as new," Artie Roberts went on, "I've got this chance to go to Paris, you know. That's why we're selling the stuff."

"That's wonderful," Miss Clarence said.

"Nancy's going on back to her family in Chicago. We've got to sell the stuff and get everything fixed up in such a short time."

"I know," Miss Clarence said. "It's too bad."

"Well, Hilda," Artie Roberts said, "you talk to Nancy when she gets back and she'll be glad to tell you all about it. You won't go wrong on any of it. I can guarantee that it's comfortable."

"I'm sure," Miss Clarence said.

"Tell her to call me, will you?"

"I certainly will," Miss Clarence said.

She said good-bye and hung up.

She went back to her chair and looked at her watch. Three-ten. I'll wait till just three-thirty, Miss Clarence thought, and then I'll leave. She picked up the book of dance photographs, slipping the pages through her fingers until a picture caught her eye and she turned back to it. I haven't seen this in years, Miss Clarence thought—Martha Graham. A sudden picture of herself at twenty came to Miss Clarence, before she ever came to New York, practicing the dancer's pose. Miss Clarence put the book down on the floor and stood up, raising her arms. Not as easy as it used to be, she thought, it catches you in the shoulders. She was looking down at the book over her shoulder, trying to get her arms right, when there was a knock and the door was opened. A young man—about Arthur's age, Miss Clarence thought—came in and stood just inside the door, apologetically.

"It was partly open," he said, "so I came on in."

"Yes?" Miss Clarence said, dropping her arms.

"You're Mrs. Roberts?" the young man asked.

Miss Clarence, trying to walk naturally over to her chair, said nothing.

"I came about the furniture," the man said. "I thought I might look at the chairs."

"Of course," Miss Clarence said. "The price is marked on everything."

"My name's Harris. I've just moved to the city and I'm trying to furnish my place."

"It's very difficult to find things these days."

"This must be the tenth place I've been. I want a filing cabinet and a big leather chair."

"I'm afraid . . ." Miss Clarence said, gesturing at the room.

"I know," Harris said. "Anybody who has that sort of thing these days is hanging on to it. I write," he added.

"Really?"

"Or, rather, I *hope* to write," Harris said. He had a round agreeable face and when he said this he smiled very pleasantly. "Going to get a job and write nights," he said.

"I'm sure you won't have much trouble," Miss Clarence said.

"Some one here an artist?"

"Mr. Roberts," Miss Clarence said.

"Lucky guy," Harris said. He walked over to the window. "Easier to draw pictures than write any time. This place is certainly nicer than mine," he added suddenly, looking out the window. "Mine's a hole in the wall."

Miss Clarence could not think of anything to say, and he turned again to look at her curiously. "You an artist, too?"

"No," Miss Clarence said. She took a deep breath. "Dancer," she said.

He smiled again, pleasantly. "I might have known," he said. "When I came in."

Miss Clarence laughed modestly.

"It must be wonderful," he said.

"It's hard," Miss Clarence said.

"It must be. You had much luck so far?"

"Not much," Miss Clarence said.

"I guess that's the way everything is," he said. He wandered over and opened the bathroom door; when he glanced in Miss

Clarence winced. He closed the door again without saying anything and opened the kitchen door.

Miss Clarence got up and walked over to stand next to him and look into the kitchen with him. "I don't cook a lot," she said.

"Don't blame you, so many restaurants." He closed the door again and Miss Clarence went back to her chair. "I can't eat breakfasts out, though. That's one thing I can't do," he said.

"Do you make your own?"

"I try to," he said. "I'm the worst cook in the world. But it's better than going out. What I need is a wife." He smiled again and started for the door. "I'm sorry about the furniture," he said. "Wish I could have found something."

"That's all right."

"You people giving up housekeeping?"

"We have to get rid of everything," Miss Clarence said. She hesitated. "Artie's going to Paris," she said finally.

"Wish I was." He sighed. "Well, good luck to both of you."

"You, too," Miss Clarence said, and closed the door behind him slowly. She listened for the sound of his steps going down the stairs and then looked at her watch. Three-twenty-five.

Suddenly in a hurry, she found the note Nancy Roberts had left for her and wrote on the back with a pencil taken from one of the boxes: "My dear Mrs. Roberts—I waited until three-thirty. I'm afraid the furniture is out of the question for me. Hilda Clarence." Pencil in hand, she thought for a minute. Then she added: "P.S. Your husband called, and wants you to call him back."

She collected her pocketbook, *The Charterhouse of Parma*, and the *Villager*, and closed the door. The thumbtack was still there, and she pried it loose and tacked her note up with it. Then she turned and went back down the stairs, home to her own apartment. Her shoulders ached.

My Life with R. H. Macy

AND the first thing they did was segregate me. They segre-gated me from the only person in the place I had even a speaking acquaintance with; that was a girl I had met going down the hall who said to me: "Are you as scared as I am?" And when I said, "Yes," she said, "I'm in lingerie, what are you in?" and I thought for a while and then said, "Spun glass," which was as good an answer as I could think of, and she said, "Oh. Well, I'll meet you here in a sec." And she went away and was segregated and I never saw her again.

Then they kept calling my name and I kept trotting over to wherever they called it and they would say ("They" all this time being startlingly beautiful young women in tailored suits and with short-clipped hair), "Go with Miss Cooper, here. She'll tell you what to do." All the women I met my first day were named Miss Cooper. And Miss Cooper would say to me: "What are you in?" and I had learned by that time to say, "Books," and she would say, "Oh, well, then, you belong with Miss Cooper here," and then she would call "Miss Cooper?" and another young woman would come and the first one would say, "13-3138 here belongs with you," and Miss Cooper would say, "What is she in?" and Miss Cooper would answer, "Books," and I would go away and be segregated again.

Then they taught me. They finally got me segregated into a classroom and I sat there for a while all by myself (that's how far segregated I was) and then a few other girls came in, all wearing tailored suits (I was wearing a red velvet afternoon frock) and we sat down and they taught us. They gave us each a big book with R. H. Macy written on it, and inside this book were pads of little sheets saying (from left to right): "Comp. keep for ref. cust. d.a. no. or c.t. no. salesbook no. salescheck no. clerk no. dept. date M." After M there was a long line for Mr. or Mrs. and the name, and then it began again with "No. item. class. at price. total." And down at the bottom was writ-ten ORIGINAL and then again, "Comp. keep for ref.," and "Paste yellow gift stamp here." I read all this very carefully. Pretty soon a Miss Cooper came, who talked for a little while on the advantages we had in working at Macy's, and she talked about the salesbooks, which it seems came apart into a sort of road map and carbons and things. I listened for a while, and when Miss Cooper wanted us to write on the little pieces of paper, I copied from the girl next to me. That was training.

Finally someone said we were going on the floor, and we descended from the sixteenth floor to the first. We were in groups of six by then, all following Miss Cooper doggedly and wearing little tags saying BOOK INFORMATION. I never did find out what that meant. Miss Cooper said I had to work on the special sale counter, and showed me a little book called *The Stage-Struck Seal*, which it seemed I would be selling. I had gotten about halfway through it before she came back to tell me I had to stay with my unit.

I enjoyed meeting the time clock, and spent a pleasant half-hour punching various cards standing around, and then someone came in and said I couldn't punch the clock with my hat on. So I had to leave, bowing timidly at the time clock and its prophet, and I went and found out my locker number, which was 1773, and my time-clock number, which was 712, and my cash-box number, which was 1336, and my cash-register number, which was 253, and my cash-register-drawer number, which was K, and my cash-register-drawer-key number, which was 872, and my department number, which was 13. I wrote all these numbers down. And that was my first day.

My second day was better. I was officially on the floor. I stood in a corner of a counter, with one hand possessively on *The Stage-Struck Seal*, waiting for customers. The counter head was named 13-2246, and she was very kind to me. She sent me to lunch three times, because she got me confused with 13-6454 and 13-3141. It was after lunch that a customer came. She came over and took one of my stage-struck seals, and said "How much is this?" I opened my mouth and the customer said "I have a D. A. and I will have this sent to my aunt in Ohio. Part of that D. A. I will pay for with a book dividend of 32 cents, and the rest of course will be on my account. Is this book price-fixed?" That's as near as I can remember what she said. I smiled confidently, and said "Certainly; will you wait just one moment?" I found a little piece of paper in a drawer under the counter: it had "Duplicate Triplicate" printed across the front in big letters. I took down the customer's name and address, her aunt's name and address, and wrote carefully across the front of the duplicate triplicate "1 Stg. Strk. Sl." Then I smiled at the customer again and said carelessly: "That will be seventy-five cents." She said "But I have a D. A." I told her that all D. A.'s were suspended for the Christmas rush, and she gave me seventy-five cents, which I kept. Then I rang up a "No Sale" on the cash register and I tore up the duplicate triplicate because I didn't know what else to do with it.

Later on another customer came and said "Where would I find a copy of Ann Rutherford Gwynn's *He Came Like Thunder*?" and I said "In medical books, right across the way," but 13-2246 came and said "That's philosophy, isn't it?" and the customer said it was, and 13-2246 said "Right down this aisle, in dictionaries." The customer went away, and I said to 13-2246 that her guess was as good as mine, anyway, and she stared at me and explained that philosophy, social sciences and Bertrand Russell were all kept in dictionaries.

So far I haven't been back to Macy's for my third day, because that night when I started to leave the store, I fell down the stairs and tore my stockings and the doorman said that if I went to my department head Macy's would give me a new pair of stockings and I went back and I found Miss Cooper and she said, "Go to the adjuster on the seventh floor and give him this," and she handed me a little slip of pink paper and on the bottom of it was printed "Comp. keep for ref. cust. d.a. no. or c.t. no. salesbook no. salescheck no. clerk no. dept. date M." And after M, instead of a name, she had written 13-3138. I took the little pink slip and threw it away and went up to the fourth floor and bought myself a pair of stockings for $.69 and then I came down and went out the customers' entrance.

I wrote Macy's a long letter, and I signed it with all my numbers added together and divided by 11,700, which is the number of employees in Macy's. I wonder if they miss me.

II

The ignorant *Looker-on* can't imagine what the *Limner* means by those seemingly *rude Lines* and *Scrawls*, which he intends for the *Rudiments* of a *Picture*, and the *Figures of Mathematick Operation* are *Nonsense*, and *Dashes* at a *Venture*, to one uninstructed in *Mechanicks*. We are in the Dark to *one another's* Purposes and Intendments; and there are a thousand Intrigues in our little Matters, which will not presently confess their Design, even to *sagacious Inquisitors*.

Joseph Glanvil: *Sadducismus Triumphatus*

The Witch

T HE coach was so nearly empty that the little boy had a seat all to himself, and his mother sat across the aisle on the seat next to the little boy's sister, a baby with a piece of toast in one hand and a rattle in the other. She was strapped securely to the seat so she could sit up and look around, and whenever she began to slip slowly sideways the strap caught her and held her halfway until her mother turned around and straightened her again. The little boy was looking out the window and eating a cookie, and the mother was reading quietly, answering the little boy's questions without looking up.

"We're on a river," the little boy said. "This is a river and we're on it."

"Fine," his mother said.

"We're on a bridge over a river," the little boy said to himself.

The few other people in the coach were sitting at the other end of the car; if any of them had occasion to come down the aisle the little boy would look around and say, "Hi," and the stranger would usually say, "Hi," back and sometimes ask the little boy if he were enjoying the train ride, or even tell him he was a fine big fellow. These comments annoyed the little boy and he would turn irritably back to the window.

"There's a cow," he would say, or, sighing, "How far do we have to go?"

"Not much longer now," his mother said, each time.

Once the baby, who was very quiet and busy with her rattle and her toast, which the mother would renew constantly, fell over too far sideways and banged her head. She began to cry, and for a minute there was noise and movement around the mother's seat. The little boy slid down from his own seat and ran across the aisle to pet his sister's feet and beg her not to cry, and finally the baby laughed and went back to her toast, and the little boy received a lollipop from his mother and went back to the window.

"I saw a witch," he said to his mother after a minute. "There was a big old ugly old bad old witch outside."

"Fine," his mother said.

"A big old ugly witch and I told her to go away and she went away," the little boy went on, in a quiet narrative to himself, "she came and said, 'I'm going to eat you up,' and I said, 'no, you're not,' and I chased her away, the bad old mean witch."

He stopped talking and looked up as the outside door of the coach opened and a man came in. He was an elderly man, with a pleasant face under white hair; his blue suit was only faintly touched by the disarray that comes from a long train trip. He was carrying a cigar, and when the little boy said, "Hi," the man gestured at him with the cigar and said, "Hello yourself, son." He stopped just beside the little boy's seat, and leaned against the back, looking down at the little boy, who craned his neck to look upward. "What you looking for out that window?" the man asked.

"Witches," the little boy said promptly. "Bad old mean witches."

"I see," the man said. "Find many?"

"My father smokes cigars," the little boy said.

"All men smoke cigars," the man said. "Someday you'll smoke a cigar, too."

"I'm a man already," the little boy said.

"How old are you?" the man asked.

The little boy, at the eternal question, looked at the man suspiciously for a minute and then said, "Twenty-six. Eight hunnerd and forty eighty."

His mother lifted her head from the book. "Four," she said, smiling fondly at the little boy.

"Is that so?" the man said politely to the little boy. "Twenty-six." He nodded his head at the mother across the aisle. "Is that your mother?"

The little boy leaned forward to look and then said, "Yes, that's her."

"What's your name?" the man asked.

The little boy looked suspicious again. "Mr. Jesus," he said.

"*Johnny*," the little boy's mother said. She caught the little boy's eye and frowned deeply.

"That's my sister over there," the little boy said to the man. "She's twelve-and-a-half."

"Do you love your sister?" the man asked. The little boy stared, and the man came around the side of the seat and sat down next to the little boy. "Listen," the man said, "shall I tell you about my little sister?"

The mother, who had looked up anxiously when the man sat down next to her little boy, went peacefully back to her book.

"Tell me about your sister," the little boy said. "Was she a witch?"

"Maybe," the man said.

The little boy laughed excitedly, and the man leaned back and puffed at his cigar. "Once upon a time," he began, "I had a little sister, just like yours." The little boy looked up at the man, nodding at every word. "My little sister," the man went on, "was so pretty and so nice that I loved her more than anything else in the world. So shall I tell you what I did?"

The little boy nodded more vehemently, and the mother lifted her eyes from her book and smiled, listening.

"I bought her a rocking-horse and a doll and a million lollipops," the man said, "and then I took her and I put my hands around her neck and I pinched her and I pinched her until she was dead."

The little boy gasped and the mother turned around, her smile fading. She opened her mouth, and then closed it again as the man went on, "And then I took and I cut her head off and I took her head—"

"Did you cut her all in pieces?" the little boy asked breathlessly.

"I cut off her head and her hands and her feet and her hair and her nose," the man said, "and I hit her with a stick and I killed her."

"Wait a minute," the mother said, but the baby fell over sideways just at that minute and by the time the mother had set her up again the man was going on.

"And I took her head and I pulled out all her hair and—"

"Your little *sister*?" the little boy prompted eagerly.

"My little sister," the man said firmly. "And I put her head in a cage with a bear and the bear ate it all up."

"Ate her *head* all up?" the little boy asked.

The mother put her book down and came across the aisle.

She stood next to the man and said, "Just what do you think you're doing?" The man looked up courteously and she said, "Get out of here."

"Did I frighten you?" the man said. He looked down at the little boy and nudged him with an elbow and he and the little boy laughed.

"This man cut up his little sister," the little boy said to his mother.

"I can very easily call the conductor," the mother said to the man.

"The conductor will *eat* my mommy," the little boy said. "We'll chop her head off."

"And little sister's head, too," the man said. He stood up, and the mother stood back to let him get out of the seat. "Don't ever come back in this car," she said.

"My mommy will eat *you*," the little boy said to the man.

The man laughed, and the little boy laughed, and then the man said, "Excuse me," to the mother and went past her out of the car. When the door had closed behind him the little boy said, "How much longer do we have to stay on this old train?"

"Not much longer," the mother said. She stood looking at the little boy, wanting to say something, and finally she said, "You sit still and be a good boy. You may have another lollipop."

The little boy climbed down eagerly and followed his mother back to her seat. She took a lollipop from a bag in her pocketbook and gave it to him. "What do you say?" she asked.

"Thank you," the little boy said. "Did that man really cut his little sister up in pieces?"

"He was just teasing," the mother said, and added urgently, "Just *teasing*."

"Prob'ly," the little boy said. With his lollipop he went back to his own seat, and settled himself to look out the window again. "Prob'ly he was a witch."

The Renegade

I T WAS eight-twenty in the morning. The twins were loiter-
ing over their cereal, and Mrs. Walpole, with one eye on
the clock and the other on the kitchen window past which the
school bus would come in a matter of minutes, felt the unreasonable irritation that comes with being late on a school
morning, the wading-through-molasses feeling of trying to
hurry children.

"You'll have to walk," she said ominously, for perhaps the
third time. "The bus won't wait."

"I'm hurrying," Judy said. She regarded her full glass of
milk smugly. "I'm closer to through than Jack."

Jack pushed his glass across the table and they measured
meticulously, precisely. "No," he said. "Look how much more
you have than me."

"It doesn't *matter*," Mrs. Walpole said, "it doesn't *matter*.
Jack, *eat* your cereal."

"She didn't have any more than me to start with," Jack said.
"Did she have any more than me, Mom?"

The alarm clock had not gone off at seven as it should. Mrs.
Walpole heard the sound of the shower upstairs and calculated
rapidly; the coffee was slower than usual this morning, the
boiled eggs a shade too soft. She had only had time to pour
herself a glass of fruit juice and no time to drink it. *Someone*—
Judy or Jack or Mr. Walpole—was going to be late.

"*Judy*," Mrs. Walpole said mechanically, "*Jack*."

Judy's hair was not accurately braided. Jack would get off
without his handkerchief. Mr. Walpole would certainly be irritable.

The yellow-and-red bulk of the school bus filled the road
outside the kitchen window, and Judy and Jack streaked for
the door, cereal uneaten, books most likely forgotten. Mrs. Walpole followed them to the kitchen door, calling, "Jack, your
milk money; come straight home at noon." She watched them
climb into the school bus and then went briskly to work
clearing their dishes from the table and setting a place for Mr.

Walpole. She would have to have breakfast herself later, in the breathing-spell that came after nine o'clock. That meant her wash would be late getting on the line, and if it rained that afternoon, as it certainly might, nothing would be dry. Mrs. Walpole made an effort, and said, "Good morning, dear," as her husband came into the kitchen. He said, "Morning," without glancing up and Mrs. Walpole, her mind full of unfinished sentences that began, "Don't you think other people ever have any feelings or—" started patiently to set his breakfast before him. The soft-boiled eggs in their dish, the toast, the coffee. Mr. Walpole devoted himself to his paper, and Mrs. Walpole, who wanted desperately also to say, "I don't suppose you notice that I haven't had a chance to eat—" set the dishes down as softly as she could.

Everything was going smoothly, although half-an-hour late, when the telephone rang. The Walpoles were on a party line, and Mrs. Walpole usually let the phone ring her number twice before concluding that it was really their number; this morning, before nine o'clock, with Mr. Walpole not half-through his breakfast, it was an unbearable intrusion, and Mrs. Walpole went reluctantly to answer it. "Hello," she said forbiddingly.

"Mrs. Walpole," the voice said, and Mrs. Walpole said, "Yes?" The voice—it was a woman—said, "I'm sorry to bother you, but this is—" and gave an unrecognizable name. Mrs. Walpole said, "Yes?" again. She could hear Mr. Walpole taking the coffeepot off the stove to pour himself a second cup.

"Do you have a dog? Brown-and-black hound?" the voice continued. With the word *dog* Mrs. Walpole, in the second before she answered, "Yes," comprehended the innumerable aspects of owning a dog in the country (six dollars for spaying, the rude barking late at night, the watchful security of the dark shape sleeping on the rug beside the double-decker beds in the twins' room, the inevitability of a dog in the house, as important as a stove, or a front porch, or a subscription to the local paper; more, and above any of these things, the dog herself, known among the neighbors as Lady Walpole, on an exact par with Jack Walpole or Judy Walpole; quiet, competent, exceedingly tolerant), and found in none of them a reason for such an early morning call from a voice which she realized now was as irritable as her own.

"Yes," Mrs. Walpole said shortly, "I own a dog. Why?"

"Big brown-and-black hound?"

Lady's pretty markings, her odd face. "Yes," Mrs. Walpole said, her voice a little more impatient, "yes, that is certainly my dog. Why?"

"He's been killing my chickens." The voice sounded satisfied now; Mrs. Walpole had been cornered.

For several seconds Mrs. Walpole was quiet, so that the voice said, "Hello?"

"That's perfectly ridiculous," Mrs. Walpole said.

"This morning," the voice said with relish, "your dog was chasing our chickens. We heard the chickens at about eight o'clock, and my husband went out to see what was the matter and found two chickens dead and he saw a big brown-and-black hound down with the chickens and he took a stick and chased the dog away and then he found two more dead ones. He says," the voice went on flatly, "that it's lucky he didn't think to take his shotgun out with him because you wouldn't have any more dog. Most awful mess you ever saw," the voice said, "blood and feathers everywhere."

"What makes you think it's *my* dog?" Mrs. Walpole said weakly.

"Joe White—he's a neighbor of yours—was passing at the time and saw my husband chasing the dog. Said it was your dog."

Old man White lived in the next house but one to the Walpoles. Mrs. Walpole had always made a point of being courteous to him, inquired amiably about his health when she saw him on the porch as she passed, had regarded respectfully the pictures of his grandchildren in Albany.

"I see," Mrs. Walpole said, suddenly shifting her ground. "Well, if you're absolutely *sure*. I just can't believe it of Lady. She's so gentle."

The other voice softened, in response to Mrs. Walpole's concern. "It *is* a shame," the other woman said. "I can't tell you how sorry I am that it happened. But . . ." her voice trailed off significantly.

"Of course we'll take care of the damage," Mrs. Walpole said quickly.

"No, no," the woman said, almost apologetically. "Don't even *think* about it."

"But of *course*—" Mrs. Walpole began, bewildered.

"The dog," the voice said. "You'll have to do something about the dog."

A sudden unalterable terror took hold of Mrs. Walpole. Her morning had gone badly, she had not yet had her coffee, she was faced with an evil situation she had never known before, and now the voice, its tone, its inflection, had managed to frighten Mrs. Walpole with a word like "something."

"How?" Mrs. Walpole said finally. "I mean, what do you want me to do?"

There was a brief silence on the other end of the wire, and then the voice said briskly, "I'm sure I don't know, missus. I've always heard that there's no way to stop a chicken-killing dog. As I say, there was no damage to speak of. As a matter of fact, the chickens the dog killed are plucked and in the oven now."

Mrs. Walpole's throat tightened and she closed her eyes for a minute, but the voice went inflexibly on. "We wouldn't ask you to do anything except take care of the dog. Naturally, you understand that we can't have a dog killing our chickens?"

Realizing that she was expected to answer, Mrs. Walpole said, "Certainly."

"So . . ." the voice said.

Mrs. Walpole saw over the top of the phone that Mr. Walpole was passing her on his way to the door. He waved briefly to her and she nodded at him. He was late; she had intended to ask him to stop at the library in the city. Now she would have to call him later. Mrs. Walpole said sharply into the phone, "First of all, of course, I'll have to make sure it's my dog. If it *is* my dog I can promise you you'll have no more trouble."

"It's your dog all right." The voice had assumed the country flatness; if Mrs. Walpole wanted to fight, the voice implied, she had picked just the right people.

"Good-bye," Mrs. Walpole said, knowing that she was making a mistake in parting from this woman angrily; knowing that she should stay on the phone for an interminable apologetic conversation, try to beg her dog's life back from this stupid inflexible woman who cared so much for *her* stupid chickens.

Mrs. Walpole put the phone down and went out into the kitchen. She poured herself a cup of coffee and made herself some toast.

I am not going to let this bother me until after I have had my coffee, Mrs. Walpole told herself firmly. She put extra butter on her toast and tried to relax, moving her back against the chair, letting her shoulders sag. Feeling like this at nine-thirty in the morning, she thought, it's a feeling that belongs with eleven o'clock at night. The bright sun outside was not as cheerful as it might be; Mrs. Walpole decided suddenly to put her wash off until tomorrow. They had not lived in the country town long enough for Mrs. Walpole to feel the disgrace of washing on Tuesday as mortal; they were still city folk and would probably always be city folk, people who owned a chicken-killing dog, people who washed on Tuesday, people who were not able to fend for themselves against the limited world of earth and food and weather that the country folk took so much for granted. In this situation as in all such others —the disposal of rubbish, the weather stripping, the baking of angel-food cake—Mrs. Walpole was forced to look for advice. In the country it is extremely difficult to "get a man" to do things for you, and Mr. and Mrs. Walpole had early fallen into the habit of consulting their neighbors for information which in the city would have belonged properly to the superintendent, or the janitor, or the man from the gas company. When Mrs. Walpole's glance fell on Lady's water dish under the sink, and she realized that she was indescribably depressed, she got up and put on her jacket and a scarf over her head and went next door.

Mrs. Nash, her next-door neighbor, was frying doughnuts, and she waved a fork at Mrs. Walpole at the open door and called, "Come in, can't leave the stove." Mrs. Walpole, stepping into Mrs. Nash's kitchen, was painfully aware of her own kitchen with the dirty dishes in the sink. Mrs. Nash was wearing a shockingly clean house dress and her kitchen was freshly washed; Mrs. Nash was able to fry doughnuts without making any sort of a mess.

"The men do like fresh doughnuts with their lunch," Mrs. Nash remarked without any more preamble than her nod and invitation to Mrs. Walpole. "I always try to get enough made ahead, but I never do."

"I wish I could make doughnuts," Mrs. Walpole said. Mrs. Nash waved the fork hospitably at the stack of still-warm doughnuts on the table and Mrs. Walpole helped herself to one, thinking: This will give me indigestion.

"Seems like they all get eaten by the time I finish making them," Mrs. Nash said. She surveyed the cooking doughnuts and then, satisfied that she could look away for a minute, took one herself and began to eat it standing by the stove. "What's wrong with you?" she asked. "You look sort of peaked this morning."

"To tell you the truth," Mrs. Walpole said, "it's our dog. Someone called me this morning that she's been killing chickens."

Mrs. Nash nodded. "Up to Harris'," she said. "I know."

Of course she'd know by now, Mrs. Walpole thought.

"You know," Mrs. Nash said turning again to the dough-nuts, "they do say there's nothing to do with a dog kills chick-ens. My brother had a dog once killed sheep, and I don't know *what* they didn't do to break that dog, but of course nothing would do it. Once they get the taste of blood." Mrs. Nash lifted a golden doughnut delicately out of the frying kettle, and set it down on a piece of brown paper to drain. "They get so's they'd rather kill than eat, hardly."

"But what can I *do*?" Mrs. Walpole asked. "Isn't there *anything*?"

"You can try, of course," Mrs. Nash said. "Best thing to do first is tie her up. Keep her tied, with a good stout chain. Then at least she won't go chasing no more chickens for a while, save you getting her killed *for* you."

Mrs. Walpole got up reluctantly and began to put her scarf on again. "I guess I'd better get a chain down at the store," she said.

"You going downstreet?"

"I want to do my shopping before the kids come home for lunch."

"Don't buy any store doughnuts," Mrs. Nash said. "I'll run

up later with a dishful for you. You get a good stout chain for that dog."

"Thank you," Mrs. Walpole said. The bright sunlight across Mrs. Nash's kitchen doorway, the solid table bearing its plates of doughnuts, the pleasant smell of the frying, were all symbols somehow of Mrs. Nash's safety, her confidence in a way of life and a security that had no traffic with chicken-killing, no city fears, an assurance and cleanliness so great that she was willing to bestow its overflow on the Walpoles, bring them doughnuts and overlook Mrs. Walpole's dirty kitchen. "Thank you," Mrs. Walpole said again, inadequately.

"You tell Tom Kittredge I'll be down for a pork roast later this morning," Mrs. Nash said. "Tell him to save it for me."

"I shall." Mrs. Walpole hesitated in the doorway and Mrs. Nash waved the fork at her.

"See you later," Mrs. Nash said.

Old man White was sitting on his front porch in the sun. When he saw Mrs. Walpole he grinned broadly and shouted to her, "Guess you're not going to have any more dog."

I've got to be nice to him, Mrs. Walpole thought, he's not a traitor or a bad man by country standards; anyone would tell on a chicken-killing dog; but he doesn't have to be so pleased about it, she thought, and tried to make her voice pleasant when she said, "Good morning, Mr. White."

"Gonna have her shot?" Mr. White asked. "Your man got a gun?"

"I'm so worried about it," Mrs. Walpole said. She stood on the walk below the front porch and tried not to let her hatred show in her face as she looked up at Mr. White.

"It's too bad about a dog like that," Mr. White said.

At least he doesn't blame *me*, Mrs. Walpole thought. "Is there anything I can do?" she said.

Mr. White thought. "Believe you might be able to cure a chicken-killer," he said. "You get a dead chicken and tie it around the dog's neck, so he can't shake it loose, see?"

"Around her neck?" Mrs. Walpole asked, and Mr. White nodded, grinning toothlessly.

"See, when he can't shake it loose at first he tries to play with it and then it starts to bother him, see, and then he tries to roll it off and it won't come and then he tries to bite it off and it won't come and then when he sees it won't come he thinks he's never gonna get rid of it, see, and he gets scared. And then you'll have him coming around with his tail between his legs and this thing hanging around his neck and it gets worse and worse."

Mrs. Walpole put one hand on the porch railing to steady herself. "What do you do then?" she asked.

"Well," Mr. White said, "the way I heard it, see, the chicken gets riper and riper and the more the dog sees it and feels it and smells it, see, the more he gets to hate chicken. And he can't ever get rid of it, see?"

"But the dog," Mrs. Walpole said. "Lady, I mean. How long do we have to leave it around her neck?"

"Well," Mr. White said with enthusiasm, "I guess you leave it on until it gets ripe enough to fall off by itself. See, the head. . . ."

"I see," Mrs. Walpole said. "Would it work?"

"Can't say," Mr. White said. "Never tried it myself." His voice said that *he* had never had a chicken-killing dog.

Mrs. Walpole left him abruptly; she could not shake the feeling that if it were not for Mr. White, Lady would not have been identified as the dog killing the chickens; she wondered briefly if Mr. White had maliciously blamed Lady because they were city folk, and then thought, No, no man around here would bear false witness against a dog.

When she entered the grocery it was almost empty; there was a man at the hardware counter and another man leaning against the meat counter talking to Mr. Kittredge, the grocer. When Mr. Kittredge saw Mrs. Walpole come in he called across the store, "Morning, Mrs. Walpole. Fine day."

"Lovely," Mrs. Walpole said, and the grocer said, "Bad luck about the dog."

"I don't know what to do about it," Mrs. Walpole said, and the man talking to the grocer looked at her reflectively, and then back at the grocer.

"Killed three chickens up to Harris's this morning," the grocer said to the man and the man nodded solemnly and said, "Heard about that."

Mrs. Walpole came across to the meat counter and said,

"Mrs. Nash said would you save her a roast of pork. She'll be down later to get it."

"Going up that way," the man standing with the grocer said. "Drop it off."

"Right," the grocer said.

The man looked at Mrs. Walpole and said, "Gonna have to shoot him, I guess?"

"I hope not," Mrs. Walpole said earnestly. "We're all so fond of the dog."

The man and the grocer looked at one another for a minute, and then the grocer said reasonably, "Won't do to have a dog going around killing chickens, Mrs. Walpole."

"First thing you know," the man said, "someone'll put a load of buckshot into him, he won't come home no more." He and the grocer both laughed.

"Isn't there any way to cure the dog?" Mrs. Walpole asked.

"Sure," the man said. "Shoot him."

"Tie a dead chicken around his neck," the grocer suggested. "That might do it."

"Heard of a man did that," the other man said.

"Did it help?" Mrs. Walpole asked eagerly.

The man shook his head slowly and with determination.

"You know," the grocer said. He leaned his elbow on the meat counter; he was a great talker. "You know," he said again, "my father had a dog once used to eat eggs. Got into the chicken-house and used to break the eggs open and lick them up. Used to eat maybe half the eggs we got."

"That's a bad business," the other man said. "Dog eating eggs."

"Bad business," the grocer said in confirmation. Mrs. Walpole found herself nodding. "Last, my father couldn't stand it no more. Here half his eggs were getting eaten," the grocer said. "So he took an egg once, set it on the back of the stove for two, three days, till the egg got good and ripe, good and hot through, and that egg smelled pretty bad. Then—I was there, boy twelve, thirteen years old—he called the dog one day, and the dog come running. So I held the dog, and my daddy opened the dog's mouth and put in the egg, red-hot and smelling to heaven, and then he held the dog's mouth closed so's the dog couldn't get rid of the egg anyway except swallow it." The grocer laughed and shook his head reminiscently.

"Bet that dog never ate another egg," the man said.

"Never touched another egg," the grocer said firmly. "You put an egg down in front of that dog, he'd run's though the devil was after him."

"But how did he feel about you?" Mrs. Walpole asked. "Did he ever come near *you* again?"

The grocer and the other man both looked at her. "How do you mean?" the grocer said.

"Did he ever *like* you again?"

"Well," the grocer said, and thought. "No," he said finally, "I don't believe you could say's he ever did. Not much of a dog, though."

"There's one thing you ought to try," the other man said suddenly to Mrs. Walpole, "you really want to cure that dog, there's one thing you ought to try."

"What's that?" Mrs. Walpole said.

"You want to take that dog," the man said, leaning forward and gesturing with one hand, "take him and put him in a pen with a mother hen's got chicks to protect. Time she's through with him he won't never chase another chicken."

The grocer began to laugh and Mrs. Walpole looked, bewildered, from the grocer to the other man, who was looking at her without a smile, his eyes wide and yellow, like a cat's.

"What would happen?" she asked uncertainly.

"Scratch his eyes out," the grocer said succinctly. "He wouldn't ever be able to *see* another chicken."

Mrs. Walpole realized that she felt faint. Smiling over her shoulder, in order not to seem discourteous, she moved quickly away from the meat counter and down to the other end of the store. The grocer continued talking to the man behind the meat counter and after a minute Mrs. Walpole went outside, into the air. She decided that she would go home and lie down until nearly lunchtime, and do her shopping later in the day.

At home she found that she could not lie down until the breakfast table was cleared and the dishes washed, and by the time she had done that it was almost time to start lunch. She was standing by the pantry shelves, debating, when a dark shape crossed the sunlight in the doorway and she realized that Lady was home. For a minute she stood still, watching Lady. The dog came in quietly, harmlessly, as though she had spent the morning frolicking on the grass with her friends, but there were spots of blood on her legs and she drank her water eagerly. Mrs. Walpole's first impulse was to scold her, to hold her down and beat her for the deliberate, malicious pain she had inflicted, the murderous brutality a pretty dog like Lady could keep so well hidden in their home; then Mrs. Walpole, watching Lady go quietly and settle down in her usual spot by the stove, turned helplessly and took the first cans she found from the pantry shelves and brought them to the kitchen table.

Lady sat quietly by the stove until the children came in noisily for lunch, and then she leaped up and jumped on them, welcoming them as though they were the aliens and she the native to the house. Judy, pulling Lady's ears, said, "Hello, Mom, do you know what Lady did? You're a bad bad dog," she said to Lady, "you're going to get shot."

Mrs. Walpole felt faint again and set a dish down hastily on the table. "Judy Walpole," she said.

"She *is* Mom," Judy said. "She's going to get shot."

Children don't realize, Mrs. Walpole told herself, death is never real to them. Try to be sensible, she told herself. "Sit down to lunch, children," she said quietly.

"But, *Mother*," Judy said, and Jack said, "She *is*, Mom."

They sat down noisily, unfolding their napkins and attacking their food without looking at it, eager to talk.

"You *know* what Mr. Shepherd said, Mom?" Jack demanded, his mouth full.

"Listen," Judy said, "we'll tell you what he said."

Mr. Shepherd was a genial man who lived near the Walpoles and gave the children nickels and took the boys fishing. "He says Lady's going to get shot," Jack said.

"But the spikes," Judy said. "Tell about the spikes."

"The *spikes*," Jack said. "Listen, Mommy. He says you got to get a collar for Lady. . . ."

"A strong collar," Judy said.

"And you get big thick nails, like spikes, and you hammer them into the collar."

"All around," Judy said. "Let *me* tell it, Jack. You hammer these nails all around so's they make spikes inside the collar."

"But it's loose," Jack said. "Let *me* tell this part. It's loose and you put it around Lady's neck. . . ."

"And—" Judy put her hand on her throat and made a strangling noise.

"Not *yet*," Jack said. "Not *yet*, dopey. First you get a long long long long rope."

"A *real* long rope," Judy amplified.

"And you fasten it to the collar and then we put the collar on Lady," Jack said. Lady was sitting next to him and he leaned over and said, "Then we put this real sharp spiky collar around your neck," and kissed the top of her head while Lady regarded him affectionately.

"And then we take her where there are chickens," Judy said, "and we show her the chickens, and we turn her loose."

"And make her chase the chickens," Jack said. "And *then*, and then, when she gets right up close to the chickens, we puuuuuuull on the rope—"

"And—" Judy made her strangling noise again.

"The spikes cut her head off," Jack finished dramatically.

They both began to laugh and Lady, looking from one to the other, panted as though she were laughing too.

Mrs. Walpole looked at them, at her two children with their hard hands and their sunburned faces laughing together, their dog with blood still on her legs laughing with them. She went to the kitchen doorway to look outside at the cool green hills, the motion of the apple tree in the soft afternoon breeze.

"Cut your head right off," Jack was saying.

Everything was quiet and lovely in the sunlight, the peaceful sky, the gentle line of the hills. Mrs. Walpole closed her eyes, suddenly feeling the harsh hands pulling her down, the sharp points closing in on her throat.

After You, My Dear Alphonse

Mrs. Wilson was just taking the gingerbread out of the oven when she heard Johnny outside talking to someone.

"Johnny," she called, "you're late. Come in and get your lunch."

"Just a minute, Mother," Johnny said. "After you, my dear Alphonse."

"After *you*, my dear Alphonse," another voice said.

"No, after *you*, my dear Alphonse," Johnny said.

Mrs. Wilson opened the door. "Johnny," she said, "you come in this minute and get your lunch. You can play after you've eaten."

Johnny came in after her, slowly. "Mother," he said, "I brought Boyd home for lunch with me."

"Boyd?" Mrs. Wilson thought for a moment. "I don't believe I've met Boyd. Bring him in, dear, since you've invited him. Lunch is ready."

"Boyd!" Johnny yelled. "Hey, Boyd, come on in!"

"I'm coming. Just got to unload this stuff."

"Well, hurry, or my mother'll be sore."

"Johnny, that's not very polite to either your friend or your mother," Mrs. Wilson said. "Come sit down, Boyd."

As she turned to show Boyd where to sit, she saw he was a Negro boy, smaller than Johnny but about the same age. His arms were loaded with split kindling wood. "Where'll I put this stuff, Johnny?" he asked.

Mrs. Wilson turned to Johnny. "Johnny," she said, "what did you make Boyd do? What is that wood?"

"Dead Japanese," Johnny said mildly. "We stand them in the ground and run over them with tanks."

"How do you do, Mrs. Wilson?" Boyd said.

"How do you do, Boyd? You shouldn't let Johnny make you carry all that wood. Sit down now and eat lunch, both of you."

"Why shouldn't he carry the wood, Mother? It's his wood. We got it at his place."

69

"Johnny," Mrs. Wilson said, "go on and eat your lunch."

"Sure," Johnny said. He held out the dish of scrambled eggs to Boyd. "After you, my dear Alphonse."

"After *you*, my dear Alphonse," Boyd said.

"After *you*, my dear Alphonse," Johnny said. They began to giggle.

"Are you hungry, Boyd?" Mrs. Wilson asked.

"Yes, Mrs. Wilson."

"Well, don't you let Johnny stop you. He always fusses about eating, so you just see that you get a good lunch. There's plenty of food here for you to have all you want."

"Thank you, Mrs. Wilson."

"Come on, Alphonse," Johnny said. He pushed half the scrambled eggs on to Boyd's plate. Boyd watched while Mrs. Wilson put a dish of stewed tomatoes beside his plate.

"Boyd don't eat tomatoes, do you, Boyd?" Johnny said.

"*Doesn't* eat tomatoes, Johnny. And just because you don't like them, don't say that about Boyd. Boyd will eat *anything*."

"Bet he won't," Johnny said, attacking his scrambled eggs.

"Boyd wants to grow up and be a big strong man so he can work hard," Mrs. Wilson said. "I'll bet Boyd's father eats stewed tomatoes."

"My father eats anything he wants to," Boyd said.

"So does mine," Johnny said. "Sometimes he doesn't eat hardly anything. He's a little guy, though. Wouldn't hurt a flea."

"Mine's a little guy, too," Boyd said.

"I'll bet he's strong, though," Mrs. Wilson said. She hesitated. "Does he . . . work?"

"Sure," Johnny said. "Boyd's father works in a factory."

"There, you see?" Mrs. Wilson said. "And he certainly has to be strong to do that—all that lifting and carrying at a factory."

"Boyd's father doesn't have to," Johnny said. "He's a foreman."

Mrs. Wilson felt defeated. "What does your mother do, Boyd?"

"My mother?" Boyd was surprised. "She takes care of us kids."

"Oh. She doesn't work, then?"

"Why should she?" Johnny said through a mouthful of eggs. "You don't work."

"You really don't want any stewed tomatoes, Boyd?"

"No, thank you, Mrs. Wilson," Boyd said.

"No, thank you, Mrs. Wilson, no, thank you, Mrs. Wilson, no, thank you, Mrs. Wilson," Johnny said. "Boyd's sister's going to work, though. She's going to be a teacher."

"That's a very fine attitude for her to have, Boyd." Mrs. Wilson restrained an impulse to pat Boyd on the head. "I imagine you're all very proud of her?"

"I guess so," Boyd said.

"What about all your other brothers and sisters? I guess all of you want to make just as much of yourselves as you can."

"There's only me and Jean," Boyd said. "I don't know yet what I want to be when I grow up."

"We're going to be tank drivers, Boyd and me," Johnny said. "Zoom." Mrs. Wilson caught Boyd's glass of milk as Johnny's napkin ring, suddenly transformed into a tank, plowed heavily across the table.

"Look, Johnny," Boyd said. "Here's a foxhole. I'm shooting at you."

Mrs. Wilson, with the speed born of long experience, took the gingerbread off the shelf and placed it carefully between the tank and the foxhole.

"Now eat as much as you want to, Boyd," she said. "I want to see you get filled up."

"Boyd eats a lot, but not as much as I do," Johnny said. "I'm bigger than he is."

"You're not much bigger," Boyd said. "I can beat you running."

Mrs. Wilson took a deep breath. "Boyd," she said. Both boys turned to her. "Boyd, Johnny has some suits that are a little too small for him, and a winter coat. It's not new, of course, but there's lots of wear in it still. And I have a few dresses that your mother or sister could probably use. Your mother can make them over into lots of things for all of you, and I'd be very happy to give them to you. Suppose before you leave I make up a big bundle and then you and Johnny can take it over to your mother right away . . ." Her voice trailed off as she saw Boyd's puzzled expression.

"But I have plenty of clothes, thank you," he said. "And I don't think my mother knows how to sew very well, and anyway I guess we buy about everything we need. Thank you very much, though."

"We don't have time to carry that old stuff around, Mother," Johnny said. "We got to play tanks with the kids today."

Mrs. Wilson lifted the plate of gingerbread off the table as Boyd was about to take another piece. "There are many little boys like you, Boyd, who would be very grateful for the clothes someone was kind enough to give them."

"Boyd will take them if you want him to, Mother," Johnny said.

"I didn't mean to make you mad, Mrs. Wilson," Boyd said.

"Don't think I'm angry, Boyd. I'm just disappointed in you, that's all. Now let's not say anything more about it."

She began clearing the plates off the table, and Johnny took Boyd's hand and pulled him to the door. "'Bye, Mother," Johnny said. Boyd stood for a minute, staring at Mrs. Wilson's back.

"After you, my dear Alphonse," Johnny said, holding the door open.

"Is your mother still mad?" Mrs. Wilson heard Boyd ask in a low voice.

"I don't know," Johnny said. "She's screwy sometimes."

"So's mine," Boyd said. He hesitated. "After *you*, my dear Alphonse."

Charles

T HE day my son Laurie started kindergarten he renounced corduroy overalls with bibs and began wearing blue jeans with a belt; I watched him go off the first morning with the older girl next door, seeing clearly that an era of my life was ended, my sweet-voiced nursery-school tot replaced by a long-trousered, swaggering character who forgot to stop at the corner and wave good-bye to me.

He came home the same way, the front door slamming open, his cap on the floor, and the voice suddenly become raucous shouting, "Isn't anybody *here*?"

At lunch he spoke insolently to his father, spilled his baby sister's milk, and remarked that his teacher said we were not to take the name of the Lord in vain.

"How *was* school today?" I asked, elaborately casual.

"All right," he said.

"Did you learn anything?" his father asked.

Laurie regarded his father coldly. "I didn't learn nothing," he said.

"Anything," I said. "Didn't learn anything"

"The teacher spanked a boy, though," Laurie said, addressing his bread and butter. "For being fresh," he added, with his mouth full.

"What did he do?" I asked. "Who was it?"

Laurie thought. "It was Charles," he said. "He was fresh. The teacher spanked him and made him stand in a corner. He was awfully fresh."

"What did he do?" I asked again, but Laurie slid off his chair, took a cookie, and left, while his father was still saying, "See here, young man."

The next day Laurie remarked at lunch, as soon as he sat down, "Well, Charles was bad again today." He grinned enormously and said, "Today Charles hit the teacher."

"Good heavens," I said, mindful of the Lord's name, "I suppose he got spanked again?"

"He sure did," Laurie said. "Look up," he said to his father.

"What?" his father said, looking up.

"Look down," Laurie said. "Look at my thumb. Gee, you're dumb." He began to laugh insanely.

"Why did Charles hit the teacher?" I asked quickly.

"Because she tried to make him color with red crayons," Laurie said. "Charles wanted to color with green crayons so he hit the teacher and she spanked him and said nobody play with Charles but everybody did."

The third day—it was Wednesday of the first week—Charles bounced a see-saw on to the head of a little girl and made her bleed, and the teacher made him stay inside all during recess. Thursday Charles had to stand in a corner during story-time because he kept pounding his feet on the floor. Friday Charles was deprived of blackboard privileges because he threw chalk.

On Saturday I remarked to my husband, "Do you think kindergarten is too unsettling for Laurie? All this toughness, and bad grammar, and this Charles boy sounds like such a bad influence."

"It'll be all right," my husband said reassuringly. "Bound to be people like Charles in the world. Might as well meet them now as later."

On Monday Laurie came home late, full of news. "Charles," he shouted as he came up the hill; I was waiting anxiously on the front steps. "Charles," Laurie yelled all the way up the hill, "Charles was bad again."

"Come right in," I said, as soon as he came close enough. "Lunch is waiting."

"You know what Charles did?" he demanded, following me through the door. "Charles yelled so in school they sent a boy in from first grade to tell the teacher she had to make Charles keep quiet, and so Charles had to stay after school. And so all the children stayed to watch him."

"What did he do?" I asked.

"He just sat there," Laurie said, climbing into his chair at the table. "Hi, Pop, y'old dust mop."

"Charles had to stay after school today," I told my husband. "Everyone stayed with him."

"What does this Charles look like?" my husband asked Laurie. "What's his other name?"

"He's bigger than me," Laurie said. "And he doesn't have any rubbers and he doesn't ever wear a jacket."

Monday night was the first Parent-Teachers meeting, and only the fact that the baby had a cold kept me from going; I wanted passionately to meet Charles's mother. On Tuesday Laurie remarked suddenly, "Our teacher had a friend come to see her in school today."

"Charles's mother?" my husband and I asked simultaneously.

"Naaah," Laurie said scornfully. "It was a man who came and made us do exercises, we had to touch our toes. Look." He climbed down from his chair and squatted down and touched his toes. "Like this," he said. He got solemnly back into his chair and said, picking up his fork, "Charles didn't even *do* exercises."

"That's fine," I said heartily. "Didn't Charles want to do exercises?"

"Naaah," Laurie said. "Charles was so fresh to the teacher's friend he wasn't *let* do exercises."

"Fresh again?" I said.

"He kicked the teacher's friend," Laurie said. "The teacher's friend told Charles to touch his toes like I just did and Charles kicked him."

"What are they going to do about Charles, do you suppose?" Laurie's father asked him.

Laurie shrugged elaborately. "Throw him out of school, I guess," he said.

Wednesday and Thursday were routine; Charles yelled during story hour and hit a boy in the stomach and made him cry. On Friday Charles stayed after school again and so did all the other children.

With the third week of kindergarten Charles was an institution in our family; the baby was being a Charles when she cried all afternoon; Laurie did a Charles when he filled his wagon full of mud and pulled it through the kitchen; even my husband, when he caught his elbow in the telephone cord and pulled telephone, ashtray, and a bowl of flowers off the table, said, after the first minute, "Looks like Charles."

During the third and fourth weeks it looked like a reformation in Charles; Laurie reported grimly at lunch on Thursday of the third week, "Charles was so good today the teacher gave him an apple."

"What?" I said, and my husband added warily, "You mean Charles?"

"Charles," Laurie said. "He gave the crayons around and he picked up the books afterward and the teacher said he was her helper."

"What happened?" I asked incredulously.

"He was her helper, that's all," Laurie said, and shrugged.

"Can this be true, about Charles?" I asked my husband that night. "Can something like this happen?"

"Wait and see," my husband said cynically. "When you've got a Charles to deal with, this may mean he's only plotting."

He seemed to be wrong. For over a week Charles was the teacher's helper; each day he handed things out and he picked things up; no one had to stay after school.

"The P.T.A. meeting's next week again," I told my husband one evening. "I'm going to find Charles's mother there."

"Ask her what happened to Charles," my husband said. "I'd like to know."

"I'd like to know myself," I said.

On Friday of that week things were back to normal. "You know what Charles did today?" Laurie demanded at the lunch table, in a voice slightly awed. "He told a little girl to say a word and she said it and the teacher washed her mouth out with soap and Charles laughed."

"What word?" his father asked unwisely, and Laurie said, "I'll have to whisper it to you, it's so bad." He got down off his chair and went around to his father. His father bent his head down and Laurie whispered joyfully. His father's eyes widened.

"Did Charles tell the little girl to say *that*?" he asked respectfully.

"She said it *twice*," Laurie said. "Charles told her to say it *twice*."

"What happened to Charles?" my husband asked.

"Nothing," Laurie said. "He was passing out the crayons."

Monday morning Charles abandoned the little girl and said the evil word himself three or four times, getting his mouth washed out with soap each time. He also threw chalk.

My husband came to the door with me that evening as I set out for the P.T.A. meeting. "Invite her over for a cup of tea after the meeting," he said. "I want to get a look at her."

"If only she's there," I said prayerfully.

"She'll be there," my husband said. "I don't see how they could hold a P.T.A. meeting without Charles's mother."

At the meeting I sat restlessly, scanning each comfortable matronly face, trying to determine which one hid the secret of Charles. None of them looked to me haggard enough. No one stood up in the meeting and apologized for the way her son had been acting. No one mentioned Charles.

After the meeting I identified and sought out Laurie's kindergarten teacher. She had a plate with a cup of tea and a piece of chocolate cake; I had a plate with a cup of tea and a piece of marshmallow cake. We maneuvered up to one another cautiously, and smiled.

"I've been so anxious to meet you," I said. "I'm Laurie's mother."

"We're all so interested in Laurie," she said.

"Well, he certainly likes kindergarten," I said. "He talks about it all the time."

"We had a little trouble adjusting, the first week or so," she said primly, "but now he's a fine little helper. With occasional lapses, of course."

"Laurie usually adjusts very quickly," I said. "I suppose this time it's Charles's influence."

"Charles?"

"Yes," I said, laughing, "you must have your hands full in that kindergarten, with Charles."

"Charles?" she said. "We don't have any Charles in the kindergarten."

Afternoon in Linen

I T WAS a long, cool room, comfortably furnished and happily placed, with hydrangea bushes outside the large windows and their pleasant shadows on the floor. Everyone in it was wearing linen—the little girl in the pink linen dress with a wide blue belt, Mrs. Kator in a brown linen suit and a big, yellow linen hat, Mrs. Lennon, who was the little girl's grandmother, in a white linen dress, and Mrs. Kator's little boy, Howard, in a blue linen shirt and shorts. Like in *Alice Through the Looking-Glass*, the little girl thought, looking at her grandmother; like the gentleman all dressed in white paper. I'm a gentleman all dressed in pink paper, she thought. Although Mrs. Lennon and Mrs. Kator lived on the same block and saw each other every day, this was a formal call, and so they were drinking tea.

Howard was sitting at the piano at one end of the long room, in front of the biggest window. He was playing "Humoresque" in careful, unhurried tempo. I played that last year, the little girl thought; it's in G. Mrs. Lennon and Mrs. Kator were still holding their teacups, listening to Howard and looking at him, and now and then looking at each other and smiling. I could still play that if I wanted to, the little girl thought.

When Howard had finished playing "Humoresque," he slid off the piano bench and came over and gravely sat down beside the little girl, waiting for his mother to tell him whether to play again or not. He's bigger than I am, she thought, but I'm older. I'm ten. If they ask me to play the piano for them now, I'll say no.

"I think you play very nicely, Howard," the little girl's grandmother said. There were a few moments of leaden silence. Then Mrs. Kator said, "Howard, Mrs. Lennon spoke to you." Howard murmured and looked at his hands on his knees.

"I think he's coming along very well," Mrs. Kator said to Mrs. Lennon. "He doesn't like to practise, but I think he's coming along well."

"Harriet loves to practise," the little girl's grandmother said.

78

"She sits at the piano for hours, making up little tunes and singing."

"She probably has a real talent for music," Mrs. Kator said. "I often wonder whether Howard is getting as much out of his music as he should."

"Harriet," Mrs. Lennon said to the little girl, "won't you play for Mrs. Kator? Play one of your own little tunes."

"I don't know any," the little girl said.

"Of course you do, dear," her grandmother said.

"I'd like very much to hear a little tune you made up yourself, Harriet," Mrs. Kator said.

"I don't know any," the little girl said.

Mrs. Lennon looked at Mrs. Kator and shrugged. Mrs. Kator nodded, mouthing "Shy," and turned to look proudly at Howard.

The little girl's grandmother set her lips firmly in a tight, sweet smile. "Harriet dear," she said, "even if we don't want to play our little tunes, I think we ought to tell Mrs. Kator that music is not our forte. I think we ought to show her our really fine achievements in another line. Harriet," she continued, turning to Mrs. Kator, "has written some poems. I'm going to ask her to recite them to you, because I feel, even though I may be prejudiced"—she laughed modestly—"even though I probably *am* prejudiced, that they show real merit."

"Well, for heaven's sake!" Mrs. Kator said. She looked at Harriet, pleased. "Why, dear, I didn't know you could do anything like that! I'd really *love* to hear them."

"Recite one of your poems for Mrs. Kator, Harriet."

The little girl looked at her grandmother, at the sweet smile, and at Mrs. Kator, leaning forward, and at Howard, sitting with his mouth open and a great delight growing in his eyes. "Don't know any," she said.

"Harriet," her grandmother said, "even if you don't remember any of your poems, you have some written down. I'm sure Mrs. Kator won't mind if you read them to her."

The huge merriment that had been gradually taking hold of Howard suddenly overwhelmed him. "Poems," he said, doubling up with laughter on the couch. "Harriet writes poems." He'll tell all the kids on the block, the little girl thought.

"I do believe Howard's jealous," Mrs. Kator said.

"Aw," Howard said. "I wouldn't write a poem. Bet you couldn't make *me* write a poem if you *tried*."

"You couldn't make me, either," the little girl said. "That's all a lie about the poems."

There was a long silence. Then "Why, Harriet!" the little girl's grandmother said in a sad voice. "What a thing to say about your grandmother!" Mrs. Kator said. "I think you'd better apologize, Harriet," the little girl's grandmother said. Mrs. Kator said, "Why, you certainly *had* better."

"I didn't do anything," the little girl muttered. "I'm sorry."

The grandmother's voice was stern. "Now bring your poems out and read them to Mrs. Kator."

"I don't have any, honestly, Grandma," the little girl said desperately. "Honestly, I don't have any of those poems."

"Well, *I* have," the grandmother said. "Bring them to me from the top desk drawer."

The little girl hesitated for a minute, watching her grandmother's straight mouth and frowning eyes.

"Howard will get them for you, Mrs. Lennon," Mrs. Kator said.

"Sure," Howard said. He jumped up and ran over to the desk, pulling open the drawer. "What do they look like?" he shouted.

"In an envelope," the grandmother said tightly. "In a brown envelope with 'Harriet's poetry' written on the front."

"Here it is," Howard said. He pulled some papers out of the envelope and studied them a moment. "Look," he said. "Harriet's poems—about stars." He ran to his mother, giggling and holding out the papers. "Look, Mother, Harriet's poetry's about stars!"

"Give them to Mrs. Lennon, dear," Howard's mother said. "It was very rude to open the envelope first."

Mrs. Lennon took the envelope and the papers and held them out to Harriet. "Will you read them or shall I?" she asked kindly. Harriet shook her head. The grandmother sighed at Mrs. Kator and took up the first sheet of paper. Mrs. Kator leaned forward eagerly and Howard settled down at her feet, hugging his knees and putting his face against his leg to keep from laughing. The grandmother cleared her throat, smiled at Harriet, and began to read.

"'The Evening Star,'" she announced.

"When evening shadows are falling,
  And dark gathers closely around,
  And all the night creatures are calling,
  And the wind makes a lonesome sound,

"I wait for the first star to come out,
  And look for its silvery beams,
  When the blue and green twilight is all about,
  And grandly a lone star gleams."

Howard could contain himself no longer. "Harriet writes poems about stars!"

"Why, it's lovely, Harriet dear!" Mrs. Kator said. "I think it's really lovely, honestly. I don't see what you're so shy about it for."

"There, you see, Harriet?" Mrs. Lennon said. "Mrs. Kator thinks your poetry is very nice. Now aren't you sorry you made such a fuss about such a little thing?"

He'll tell all the kids on the block, Harriet thought. "I didn't write it," she said.

"Why, Harriet!" Her grandmother laughed. "You don't need to be so modest, child. You write very nice poems."

"I copied it out of a book," Harriet said. "I found it in a book and I copied it and gave it to my old grandmother and said I wrote it."

"I don't believe you'd do anything like that, Harriet," Mrs. Kator said, puzzled.

"I did *so*," Harriet maintained stubbornly. "I copied it right out of a book."

"Harriet, I don't believe you," her grandmother said.

Harriet looked at Howard, who was staring at her in admiration. "I copied it out of a book," she said to him. "I found the book in the library one day."

"I can't imagine her saying she did such a thing," Mrs. Lennon said to Mrs. Kator. Mrs. Kator shook her head.

"It was a book called"—Harriet thought a moment—"called *The Home Book of Verse*," she said. "That's what it was. And I copied every single word. I didn't make up *one*."

"Harriet, is this true?" her grandmother said. She turned to Mrs. Kator. "I'm afraid I must apologize for Harriet and for reading you the poem under false pretenses. I never dreamed she'd deceive me."

"Oh, they do," Mrs. Kator said deprecatingly. "They want attention and praise and sometimes they'll do almost anything. I'm sure Harriet didn't mean to be—well, dishonest."

"I did *so*," Harriet said. "I wanted everyone to think I wrote it. I said I wrote it on purpose." She went over and took the papers out of her grandmother's unresisting hand. "And you can't look at them any more, either," she said, and held them in back of her, away from everyone.

Flower Garden

AFTER living in an old Vermont manor house together for almost eleven years, the two Mrs. Winnings, mother and daughter-in-law, had grown to look a good deal alike, as women will who live intimately together, and work in the same kitchen and get things done around the house in the same manner. Although young Mrs. Winning had been a Talbot, and had dark hair which she wore cut short, she was now officially a Winning, a member of the oldest family in town and her hair was beginning to grey where her mother-in-law's hair had greyed first, at the temples; they both had thin sharp-featured faces and eloquent hands, and sometimes when they were washing dishes or shelling peas or polishing silverware together, their hands, moving so quickly and similarly, communicated more easily and sympathetically than their minds ever could. Young Mrs. Winning thought sometimes, when she sat at the breakfast table next to her mother-in-law, with her baby girl in the high-chair close by, that they must resemble some stylized block print for a New England wallpaper; mother, daughter, and granddaughter, with perhaps Plymouth Rock or Concord Bridge in the background.

On this, as on other cold mornings, they lingered over their coffee, unwilling to leave the big kitchen with the coal stove and the pleasant atmosphere of food and cleanliness, and they sat together silently sometimes until the baby had long finished her breakfast and was playing quietly in the special baby corner, where uncounted Winning children had played with almost identical toys from the same heavy wooden box.

"It seems as though spring would never come," young Mrs. Winning said. "I get so tired of the cold."

"Got to be cold some of the time," her mother-in-law said. She began to move suddenly and quickly, stacking plates, indicating that the time for sitting was over and the time for working had begun. Young Mrs. Winning, rising immediately to help, thought for the thousandth time that her mother-in-law would never relinquish the position of authority in her own house until she was too old to move before anyone else.

"And I wish someone would move into the old cottage," young Mrs. Winning added. She stopped halfway to the pantry with the table napkins and said longingly, "If only *someone* would move in before spring." Young Mrs. Winning had wanted, long ago, to buy the cottage herself, for her husband to make with his own hands into a home where they could live with their children, but now, accustomed as she was to the big old house at the top of the hill where her husband's family had lived for generations, she had only a great kindness left toward the little cottage, and a wistful anxiety to see some happy young people living there. When she heard it was sold, as all the old houses were being sold in these days when no one could seem to find a newer place to live, she had allowed herself to watch daily for a sign that someone new was coming; every morning she glanced down from the back porch to see if there was smoke coming out of the cottage chimney, and every day going down the hill on her way to the store she hesitated past the cottage, watching carefully for the least movement within. The cottage had been sold in January and now, nearly two months later, even though it seemed prettier and less worn with the snow gently covering the overgrown garden and icicles in front of the blank windows, it was still forlorn and empty, despised since the day long ago when Mrs. Winning had given up all hope of ever living there.

Mrs. Winning deposited the napkins in the pantry and turned to tear the leaf off the kitchen calendar before selecting a dish towel and joining her mother-in-law at the sink. "March already," she said despondently.

"They *did* tell me down at the store yesterday," her mother-in-law said, "that they were going to start painting the cottage this week."

"Then that *must* mean someone's coming!"

"Can't take more than a couple of weeks to paint inside that little house," old Mrs. Winning said.

It was almost April, however, before the new people moved in. The snow had almost melted and was running down the street in icy, half-solid rivers. The ground was slushy and miserable to walk on, the skies grey and dull. In another month the first amazing green would start in the trees and on the ground, but for the better part of April there would be cold rain and perhaps more snow. The cottage had been painted inside, and new paper put on the walls. The front steps had been repaired and new glass put into the broken windows. In spite of the grey sky and the patches of dirty snow the cottage looked neater and firmer, and the painters were coming back to do the outside when the weather cleared. Mrs. Winning, standing at the foot of the cottage walk, tried to picture the cottage as it stood now, against the picture of the cottage she had made years ago, when she had hoped to live there herself. She had wanted roses by the porch; that could be done, and the neat colorful garden she had planned. She would have painted the outside white, and that too might still be done. Since the cottage had been sold she had not gone inside, but she remembered the little rooms, with the windows over the garden that could be so bright with gay curtains and window boxes, the small kitchen she would have painted yellow, the two bedrooms upstairs with slanting ceilings under the eaves. Mrs. Winning looked at the cottage for a long time, standing on the wet walk, and then went slowly on down to the store.

The first news she had of the new people came, at last, from the grocer a few days later. As he was tying the string around the three pounds of hamburger the large Winning family would consume in one meal, he asked cheerfully, "Seen your new neighbors yet?"

"Have they moved in?" Mrs. Winning asked. "The people in the cottage?"

"Lady in here this morning," the grocer said. "Lady and a little boy, seem like nice people. They say her husband's dead. Nice-looking lady."

Mrs. Winning had been born in the town and the grocer's father had given her jawbreakers and licorice in the grocery store while the present grocer was still in high school. For a while, when she was twelve and the grocer's son was twenty, Mrs. Winning had hoped secretly that he would want to marry her. He was fleshy now, and middle-aged, and although he still called her Helen and she still called him Tom, she belonged now to the Winning family and had to speak critically to him, no matter how unwillingly, if the meat were tough or the butter price too high. She knew that when he spoke of the new neighbor as a "lady" he meant something different than if he had spoken of her as a "woman" or a "person." Mrs. Winning knew that he spoke of the two Mrs. Winnings to his other customers as "ladies." She hesitated and then asked, "Have they really moved in to stay?"

"She'll have to stay for a while," the grocer said drily. "Bought a week's worth of groceries."

Going back up the hill with her package Mrs. Winning watched all the way to detect some sign of the new people in the cottage. When she reached the cottage walk she slowed down and tried to watch not too obviously. There was no smoke coming from the chimney, and no sign of furniture near the house, as there might have been if people were still moving in, but there was a middle-aged car parked in the street before the cottage and Mrs. Winning thought she could see figures moving past the windows. On a sudden irresistible impulse she turned and went up the walk to the front porch, and then, after debating for a moment, on up the steps to the door. She knocked, holding her bag of groceries in one arm, and then the door opened and she looked down on a little boy, about the same age, she thought happily, as her own son.

"Hello," Mrs. Winning said.

"Hello," the boy said. He regarded her soberly.

"Is your mother here?" Mrs. Winning asked. "I came to see if I could help her move in."

"We're all moved in," the boy said. He was about to close the door, but a woman's voice said from somewhere in the house, "Davey? Are you talking to someone?"

"That's my mommy," the little boy said. The woman came up behind him and opened the door a little wider. "Yes?" she said.

Mrs. Winning said, "I'm Helen Winning. I live about three houses up the street, and I thought perhaps I might be able to help you."

"Thank you," the woman said doubtfully. She's younger than I am, Mrs. Winning thought, she's about thirty. And pretty. For a clear minute Mrs. Winning saw why the grocer had called her a lady.

"It's so nice to have someone living in this house," Mrs. Winning said shyly. Past the other woman's head she could see the small hallway, with the larger living-room beyond and the door on the left going into the kitchen, the stairs on the right, with the delicate stair-rail newly painted; they had done the hall in light green, and Mrs. Winning smiled with friendship at the woman in the doorway, thinking, She *has* done it right; this is the way it should look after all, she knows about pretty houses.

After a minute the other woman smiled back, and said, "Will you come in?"

As she stepped back to let Mrs. Winning in, Mrs. Winning wondered with a suddenly stricken conscience if perhaps she had not been too forward, almost pushing herself in. . . . "I hope I'm not making a nuisance of myself," she said unexpectedly, turning to the other woman. "It's just that I've been wanting to live here myself for so long." Why did I say that, she wondered; it had been a very long time since young Mrs. Winning had said the first thing that came into her head.

"Come see *my* room," the little boy said urgently, and Mrs. Winning smiled down at him.

"I have a little boy just about your age," she said. "What's your name?"

"Davey," the little boy said, moving closer to his mother. "Davey William MacLane."

"My little boy," Mrs. Winning said soberly, "is named Howard Talbot Winning."

The little boy looked up at his mother uncertainly, and Mrs. Winning, who felt ill at ease and awkward in this little house she so longed for, said, "How old are you? My little boy is five."

"I'm five," the little boy said, as though realizing it for the first time. He looked again at his mother and she said graciously, "Will you come in and see what we've done to the house?"

Mrs. Winning put her bag of groceries down on the slim-legged table in the green hall, and followed Mrs. MacLane into the living-room, which was L-shaped and had the windows Mrs. Winning would have fitted with gay curtains and flower-boxes. As she stepped into the room Mrs. Winning realized, with a quick wonderful relief, that it was really going to be all right, after all. Everything, from the andirons in the fireplace to the books on the table, was exactly as Mrs. Winning might have done if she were eleven years younger; a little more informal, perhaps, nothing of quite such good quality as young Mrs. Winning might have chosen, but still richly, undeniably right. There was a picture of Davey on the mantel, flanked by a picture which Mrs. Winning supposed was Davey's father; there was a glorious blue bowl on the low coffee table, and around the corner of the L stood a row of orange plates on a shelf, and a polished maple table and chairs.

"It's lovely," Mrs. Winning said. This could have been mine, she was thinking, and she stood in the doorway and said again, "It's perfectly lovely."

Mrs. MacLane crossed over to the low armchair by the fireplace and picked up the soft blue material that lay across the arm. "I'm making curtains," she said, and touched the blue bowl with the tip of one finger. "Somehow I always make my blue bowl the center of the room," she said. "I'm having the curtains the same blue, and my rug—when it comes!—will have the same blue in the design."

"It matches Davey's eyes," Mrs. Winning said, and when Mrs. MacLane smiled again she saw that it matched Mrs. MacLane's eyes too. Helpless before so much that was magic to her, Mrs. Winning said "*Have* you painted the kitchen yellow?"

"Yes," Mrs. MacLane said, surprised. "Come and see." She led the way through the L, around past the orange plates to the kitchen, which caught the late morning sun and shone with clean paint and bright aluminum; Mrs. Winning noticed the electric coffeepot, the waffle iron, the toaster, and thought, *she* couldn't have much trouble cooking, not with just the two of them.

"When I have a garden," Mrs. MacLane said, "we'll be able to see it from almost all the windows." She gestured to the broad kitchen windows, and added, "I love gardens. I imagine I'll spend most of my time working in this one, as soon as the weather is nice."

"It's a good house for a garden," Mrs. Winning said. "I've heard that it used to be one of the prettiest gardens on the block."

"I thought so too," Mrs. MacLane said. "I'm going to have flowers on all four sides of the house. With a cottage like this you can, you know."

Oh, I know, I know, Mrs. Winning thought wistfully, remembering the neat charming garden she could have had, instead of the row of nasturtiums along the side of the Winning house, which she tended so carefully; no flowers would grow well around the Winning house, because of the heavy old maple trees which shaded all the yard and which had been tall when the house was built.

Mrs. MacLane had had the bathroom upstairs done in yellow, too, and the two small bedrooms with overhanging eaves were painted green and rose. "All garden colors," she told Mrs. Winning gaily, and Mrs. Winning, thinking of the oddly-matched, austere bedrooms in the big Winning house, sighed and admitted that it would be wonderful to have window seats under the eaved windows. Davey's bedroom was the green one, and his small bed was close to the window. "This morning," he told Mrs. Winning solemnly, "I looked out and there were four icicles hanging by my bed."

Mrs. Winning stayed in the cottage longer than she should have; she felt certain, although Mrs. MacLane was pleasant and cordial, that her visit was extended past courtesy and into curiosity. Even so, it was only her sudden guilt about the three pounds of hamburger and dinner for the Winning men that drove her away. When she left, waving good-bye to Mrs. MacLane and Davey as they stood in the cottage doorway, she had invited Davey up to play with Howard, Mrs. MacLane up for tea, both of them to come for lunch some day, and all without the permission of her mother-in-law.

Reluctantly she came to the big house and turned past the bolted front door to go up the walk to the back door, which all the family used in the winter. Her mother-in-law looked up as she came into the kitchen and said irritably, "I called the store and Tom said you left an hour ago."

"I stopped off at the old cottage," Mrs. Winning said. She put the package of groceries down on the table and began to take things out quickly, to get the doughnuts on to a plate and the hamburger into the pan before too much time was lost.

With her coat still on and her scarf over her head she moved as fast as she could while her mother-in-law, slicing bread at the kitchen table, watched her silently.

"Take your coat off," her mother-in-law said finally. "Your husband will be home in a minute."

By twelve o'clock the house was noisy and full of mud tracked across the kitchen floor. The oldest Howard, Mrs. Winning's father-in-law, came in from the farm and went silently to hang his hat and coat in the dark hall before speaking to his wife and daughter-in-law; the younger Howard, Mrs. Winning's husband, came in from the barn after putting the truck away and nodded to his wife and kissed his mother; and the youngest Howard, Mrs. Winning's son, crashed into the kitchen, home from kindergarten, shouting, "Where's dinner?"

The baby, anticipating food, banged on her high-chair with the silver cup which had first been used by the oldest Howard Winning's mother. Mrs. Winning and her mother-in-law put plates down on the table swiftly, knowing after many years the exact pause between the latest arrival and the serving of food, and with a minimum of time three generations of the Winning family were eating silently and efficiently, all anxious to be back about their work: the farm, the mill, the electric train; the dishes, the sewing, the nap. Mrs. Winning, feeding the baby, trying to anticipate her mother-in-law's gestures of serving, thought, today more poignantly than ever before, that she had at least given them another Howard, with the Winning eyes and mouth, in exchange for her food and her bed.

After dinner, after the men had gone back to work and the children were in bed, the baby for her nap and Howard resting with crayons and coloring book, Mrs. Winning sat down with her mother-in-law over their sewing and tried to describe the cottage.

"It's just perfect," she said helplessly. "Everything is so pretty. She invited us to come down some day and see it when it's all finished, the curtains and everything."

"I was talking to Mrs. Blake," the elder Mrs. Winning said, as though in agreement. "She says the husband was killed in an automobile accident. *She* had some money in her own name and I guess she decided to settle down in the country for the boy's health. Mrs. Blake said he looked peakish."

"She loves gardens," Mrs. Winning said, her needle still in her hand for a moment. "She's going to have a big garden all around the house."

"She'll need help," the elder woman said humorlessly, "that's a mighty big garden she'll have."

"She has the *most* beautiful blue bowl, Mother Winning. You'd love it, it's almost like silver."

"Probably," the elder Mrs. Winning said after a pause, "probably her people came from around here a ways back, and *that's* why she's settled in these parts."

The next day Mrs. Winning walked slowly past the cottage, and slowly the next, and the day after, and the day after that. On the second day she saw Mrs. MacLane at the window, and waved, and on the third day she met Davey on the sidewalk. "When are you coming to visit my little boy?" she asked him, and he stared at her solemnly and said, "Tomorrow."

Mrs. Burton, next-door to the MacLanes, ran over on the third day they were there with a fresh apple pie, and then told all the neighbors about the yellow kitchen and the bright electric utensils. Another neighbor, whose husband had helped Mrs. MacLane start her furnace, explained that Mrs. MacLane was only very recently widowed. One or another of the townspeople called on the MacLanes almost daily, and frequently, as young Mrs. Winning passed, she saw familiar faces at the windows, measuring the blue curtains with Mrs. MacLane, or she waved to acquaintances who stood chatting with Mrs. MacLane on the now firm front steps. After the MacLanes had been in the cottage for about a week Mrs. Winning met them one day in the grocery and they walked up the hill together, and talked about putting Davey into the kindergarten. Mrs. MacLane wanted to keep him home as long as possible, and Mrs. Winning asked her, "Don't you feel terribly tied down, having him with you all the time?"

"I like it," Mrs. MacLane said cheerfully, "we keep each other company," and Mrs. Winning felt clumsy and ill-mannered, remembering Mrs. MacLane's widowhood.

As the weather grew warmer and the first signs of green showed on the trees and on the wet ground, Mrs. Winning and Mrs. MacLane became better friends. They met almost daily at the grocery and walked up the hill together, and twice Davey came up to play with Howard's electric train, and once Mrs. MacLane came up to get him and stayed for a cup of coffee in the great kitchen while the boys raced round and round the table and Mrs. Winning's mother-in-law was visiting a neighbor.

"It's such an old house," Mrs. MacLane said, looking up at the dark ceiling. "I love old houses; they feel so secure and warm, as though lots of people had been perfectly satisfied with them and they *knew* how useful they were. You don't get that feeling with a new house."

"This dreary old place," Mrs. Winning said. Mrs. MacLane, with a rose-colored sweater and her bright soft hair, was a spot of color in the kitchen that Mrs. Winning knew she could never duplicate. "I'd give anything in the world to live in your house," Mrs. Winning said.

"*I* love it," Mrs. MacLane said. "I don't think I've ever been so happy. Everyone around here is so nice, and the house is so pretty, and I planted a lot of bulbs yesterday." She laughed. "I used to sit in that apartment in New York and dream about planting bulbs again."

Mrs. Winning looked at the boys, thinking how Howard was half-a-head taller, and stronger, and how Davey was small and weak and loved his mother adoringly. "It's been good for Davey already," she said. "There's color in his cheeks."

"Davey loves it," Mrs. MacLane agreed. Hearing his name Davey came over and put his head in her lap and she touched his hair, bright like her own. "We'd better be getting on home, Davey boy," she said.

"Maybe our flowers have grown some since yesterday," said Davey.

Gradually the days became miraculously long and warm, and Mrs. MacLane's garden began to show colors and became an ordered thing, still very young and unsure, but promising rich brilliance for the end of the summer, and the next summer, and summers ten years from now.

"It's even better than I hoped," Mrs. MacLane said to Mrs. Winning, standing at the garden gate. "Things grow so much better here than almost anywhere else."

Davey and Howard played daily after the school was out for the summer, and Howard was free all day. Sometimes Howard stayed at Davey's house for lunch, and they planted a vegetable patch together in the MacLane back yard. Mrs. Winning stopped for Mrs. MacLane on her way to the store in the mornings and Davey and Howard frolicked ahead of them down the street. They picked up their mail together and read it walking back up the hill, and Mrs. Winning went more cheerfully back to the big Winning house after walking most of the way home with Mrs. MacLane.

One afternoon Mrs. Winning put the baby in Howard's wagon and with the two boys they went for a long walk in the country. Mrs. MacLane picked Queen Anne's lace and put it into the wagon with the baby, and the boys found a garter snake and tried to bring it home. On the way up the hill Mrs. MacLane helped pull the wagon with the baby and the Queen Anne's lace, and they stopped halfway to rest and Mrs. MacLane said, "Look, I believe you can see my garden all the way from here."

It was a spot of color almost at the top of the hill and they stood looking at it while the baby threw the Queen Anne's lace out of the wagon. Mrs. MacLane said, "I always want to stop here to look at it," and then, "Who is that *beautiful* child?"

Mrs. Winning looked, and then laughed. "He is attractive, isn't he," she said. "It's Billy Jones." She looked at him herself, carefully, trying to see him as Mrs. MacLane would. He was a boy about twelve, sitting quietly on a wall across the street, with his chin in his hands, silently watching Davey and Howard.

"He's like a young statue," Mrs. MacLane said. "So brown, and, will you look at that face?" She started to walk again to see him more clearly, and Mrs. Winning followed her. "Do I know his mother and fath—?"

"The Jones children are half-Negro," Mrs. Winning said hastily. "But they're all beautiful children; you should see the girl. They live just outside town."

Howard's voice reached them clearly across the summer air. "Nigger," he was saying, "nigger, nigger boy."

"Nigger," Davey repeated, giggling.

Mrs. MacLane gasped, and then said, "*Davey*," in a voice that made Davey turn his head apprehensively; Mrs. Winning had never heard her friend use such a voice, and she too watched Mrs. MacLane.

"Davey," Mrs. MacLane said again, and Davey approached slowly. "What did I hear you say?"

"Howard," Mrs. Winning said, "leave Billy alone."

"Go tell that boy you're sorry," Mrs. MacLane said. "Go at once and tell him you're sorry."

Davey blinked tearfully at his mother and then went to the curb and called across the street, "I'm sorry."

Howard and Mrs. Winning waited uneasily, and Billy Jones across the street raised his head from his hands and looked at Davey and then, for a long time, at Mrs. MacLane. Then he put his chin on his hands again.

Suddenly Mrs. MacLane called, "Young man— Will you come here a minute, please?"

Mrs. Winning was surprised, and stared at Mrs. MacLane, but when the boy across the street did not move Mrs. Winning said sharply, "Billy! Billy Jones! Come here at once!"

The boy raised his head and looked at them, and then slid slowly down from the wall and started across the street. When he was across the street and about five feet from them he stopped, waiting.

"Hello," Mrs. MacLane said gently, "what's your name?"

The boy looked at her for a minute and then at Mrs. Winning, and Mrs. Winning said, "He's Billy Jones. Answer when you're spoken to, Billy."

"Billy," Mrs. MacLane said, "I'm sorry my little boy called you a name, but he's very little and he doesn't always know what he's saying. But he's sorry, too."

"Okay," Billy said, still watching Mrs. Winning. He was wearing an old pair of blue jeans and a torn white shirt, and he was barefoot. His skin and hair were the same color, the golden shade of a very heavy tan, and his hair curled lightly; he had the look of a garden statue.

"Billy," Mrs. MacLane said, "how would you like to come and work for me? Earn some money?"

"Sure," Billy said.

"Do you like gardening?" Mrs. MacLane asked. Billy nodded soberly. "Because," Mrs. MacLane went on enthusiastically, "I've been needing someone to help me with my garden, and it would be just the thing for you to do." She waited a minute and then said, "Do you know where I live?"

"Sure," Billy said. He turned his eyes away from Mrs. Winning and for a minute looked at Mrs. MacLane, his brown eyes expressionless. Then he looked back at Mrs. Winning, who was watching Howard up the street.

"Fine," Mrs. MacLane said. "Will you come tomorrow?"

"Sure," Billy said. He waited for a minute, looking from Mrs. MacLane to Mrs. Winning, and then ran back across the street and vaulted over the wall where he had been sitting. Mrs. MacLane watched him admiringly. Then she smiled at Mrs. Winning and gave the wagon a tug to start it up the hill again. They were nearly at the MacLane cottage before Mrs. MacLane finally spoke. "I just can't stand that," she said, "to hear children attacking people for things they can't help."

"They're strange people, the Joneses," Mrs. Winning said readily. "The father works around as a handyman; maybe you've seen him. You see—" she dropped her voice—"the mother was white, a girl from around here. A local girl," she said again, to make it more clear to a foreigner. "She left the whole litter of them when Billy was about two, and went off with a white man."

"Poor children," Mrs. MacLane said.

"*They're* all right," Mrs. Winning said. "The church takes care of them, of course, and people are always giving them things. The girl's old enough to work now, too. She's sixteen, but. . . ."

"But what?" Mrs. MacLane said, when Mrs. Winning hesitated.

"Well, people talk about her a lot, you know," Mrs. Winning said. "Think of her mother, after all. And there's another boy, couple of years older than Billy."

They stopped in front of the MacLane cottage and Mrs.

MacLane touched Davey's hair. "Poor unfortunate child," she said.

"Children *will* call names," Mrs. Winning said. "There's not much you can do."

"Well . . ." Mrs. MacLane said. "Poor child."

The next day, after the dinner dishes were washed, and while Mrs. Winning and her mother-in-law were putting them away, the elder Mrs. Winning said casually, "Mrs. Blake tells me your friend Mrs. MacLane was asking around the neighbors how to get hold of the Jones boy."

"She wants someone to help in the garden, I think," Mrs. Winning said weakly. "She needs help in that big garden."

"Not *that* kind of help," the elder Mrs. Winning said. "You tell her about them?"

"She seemed to feel sorry for them," Mrs. Winning said, from the depths of the pantry. She took a long time settling the plates in even stacks in order to neaten her mind. She *shouldn't* have done it, she was thinking, but her mind refused to tell her why. She should have asked me first, though, she thought finally.

The next day Mrs. Winning stopped off at the cottage with Mrs. MacLane after coming up the hill from the store. They sat in the yellow kitchen and drank coffee, while the boys played in the back yard. While they were discussing the possibilities of hammocks between the apple trees there was a knock at the kitchen door and when Mrs. MacLane opened it she found a man standing there, so that she said, "Yes?" politely and waited.

"Good morning," the man said. He took off his hat and nodded his head at Mrs. MacLane. "Billy told me you was looking for someone to work your garden," he said.

"Why . . ." Mrs. MacLane began, glancing sideways uneasily at Mrs. Winning.

"I'm Billy's father," the man said. He nodded his head toward the back yard and Mrs. MacLane saw Billy Jones sitting under one of the apple trees, his arms folded in front of him, his eyes on the grass at his feet.

"How do you do," Mrs. MacLane said inadequately.

"Billy told me you said for him to come work your garden,"

the man said. "Well, now, I think maybe a summer job's too much for a boy his age, he ought to be out playing in the good weather. And that's the kind of work I do anyway, so's I thought I'd just come over and see if you found anyone yet."

He was a big man, very much like Billy, except that where Billy's hair curled only a little, his father's hair curled tightly, with a line around his head where his hat stayed constantly and where Billy's skin was a golden tan, his father's skin was darker, almost bronze. When he moved, it was gracefully, like Billy, and his eyes were the same fathomless brown. "Like to work this garden," Mr. Jones said, looking around. "Could be a mighty nice place."

"You were very nice to come," Mrs. MacLane said. "I certainly do need help."

Mrs. Winning sat silently, not wanting to speak in front of Mr. Jones. She was thinking, I wish she'd ask me first, this is impossible . . . and Mr. Jones stood silently, listening courteously, with his dark eyes on Mrs. MacLane while she spoke. "I guess a lot of the work would be too much for a boy like Billy," she said. "There are a lot of things I can't even do myself, and I was sort of hoping I could get someone to give me a hand."

"That's fine, then," Mr. Jones said. "Guess I can manage most of it," he said, and smiled.

"Well," Mrs. MacLane said, "I guess that's all settled, then. When do you want to start?"

"How about right now?" he said.

"Grand," Mrs. MacLane said enthusiastically, and then, "Excuse me for a minute," to Mrs. Winning over her shoulder. She took down her gardening gloves and wide straw hat from the shelf by the door. "Isn't it a lovely day?" she asked Mr. Jones as she stepped out into the garden while he stood back to let her pass.

"You go along home now, Bill," Mr. Jones called as they went toward the side of the house.

"Oh, why not let him stay?" Mrs. MacLane said. Mrs. Winning heard her voice going on as they went out of sight. "He can play around the garden, and he'd probably enjoy . . ."

For a minute Mrs. Winning sat looking at the garden, at the corner around which Mr. Jones had followed Mrs. MacLane, and then Howard's face appeared around the side of the door and he said, "Hi, is it nearly time to eat?"

"Howard," Mrs. Winning said quietly, and he came in through the door and came over to her. "It's time for you to run along home," Mrs. Winning said. "I'll be along in a minute."

Howard started to protest, but she added, "I want you to go right away. Take my bag of groceries if you think you can carry it."

Howard was impressed by her conception of his strength, and he lifted down the bag of groceries; his shoulders, already broad out of proportion, like his father's and his grandfather's, strained under the weight, and then he steadied on his feet. "Aren't I strong?" he asked exultantly.

"*Very* strong," Mrs. Winning said. "Tell Grandma I'll be right up. I'll just say good-bye to Mrs. MacLane."

Howard disappeared through the house; Mrs. Winning heard him walking heavily under the groceries, out through the open front door and down the steps. Mrs. Winning rose and was standing by the kitchen door when Mrs. MacLane came back.

"You're not ready to go?" Mrs. MacLane exclaimed when she saw Mrs. Winning with her jacket on. "Without finishing your coffee?"

"I'd better catch Howard," Mrs. Winning said. "He ran along ahead."

"I'm sorry I left you like that," Mrs. MacLane said. She stood in the doorway beside Mrs. Winning, looking out into the garden. "How *wonderful* it all is," she said, and laughed happily.

They walked together through the house; the blue curtains were up by now, and the rug with the touch of blue in the design was on the floor.

"Good-bye," Mrs. Winning said on the front steps.

Mrs. MacLane was smiling, and following her look Mrs. Winning turned and saw Mr. Jones, his shirt off and his strong back shining in the sun as he bent with a scythe over the long grass at the side of the house. Billy lay nearby, under the shade of the bushes; he was playing with a grey kitten. "I'm going to have the finest garden in town," Mrs. MacLane said proudly.

"You won't have him working here past today, will you?" Mrs. Winning asked. "Of course you won't have him any longer than just today?"

"But surely—" Mrs. MacLane began, with a tolerant smile, and Mrs. Winning, after looking at her for an incredulous minute, turned and started, indignant and embarrassed, up the hill.

Howard had brought the groceries safely home and her mother-in-law was already setting the table.

"Howard says you sent him home from MacLane's," her mother-in-law said, and Mrs. Winning answered briefly, "I thought it was getting late."

The next morning when Mrs. Winning reached the cottage on her way down to the store she saw Mr. Jones swinging the scythe expertly against the side of the house, and Billy Jones and Davey sitting on the front steps watching him. "Good morning, Davey." Mrs. Winning called, "is your mother ready to go downstreet?"

"Where's Howard?" Davey asked, not moving.

"He stayed home with his grandma today," Mrs. Winning said brightly. "Is your mother ready?"

"She's making lemonade for Billy and me," Davey said. "We're going to have it in the garden."

"Then tell her," Mrs. Winning said quickly, "tell her that I said I was in a hurry and that I had to go on ahead. I'll see her later." She hurried on down the hill.

In the store she met Mrs. Harris, a lady whose mother had worked for the elder Mrs. Winning nearly forty years before. "Helen," Mrs. Harris said, "you get greyer every year. You ought to stop all this running around."

Mrs. Winning, in the store without Mrs. MacLane for the first time in weeks, smiled shyly and said that she guessed she needed a vacation.

"Vacation!" Mrs. Harris said. "Let that husband of yours do the housework for a change. He doesn't have nuthin' else to do."

She laughed richly, and shook her head. "Nuthin' else to do," she said. "The Winnings!"

Before Mrs. Winning could step away Mrs. Harris added, her laughter penetrated by a sudden sharp curiosity: "Where's

that dressed-up friend of yours get to? Usually downstreet together, ain't you?"

Mrs. Winning smiled courteously, and Mrs. Harris said,
laughing again, "Just couldn't believe those shoes of hers, first
time I seen them. Them shoes!"

While she was laughing again Mrs. Winning escaped to the
meat counter and began to discuss the potentialities of pork
shoulder earnestly with the grocer. Mrs. Harris only says what
everyone else says, she was thinking, are they talking like that
about Mrs. MacLane? Are they laughing at her? When she
thought of Mrs. MacLane she thought of the quiet house, the
soft colors, the mother and son in the garden; Mrs. MacLane's
shoes were green and yellow platform sandals, odd-looking
certainly next to Mrs. Winning's solid white oxfords, but so inevitably right for Mrs. MacLane's house, and her garden.
. . . Mrs. Harris came up behind her and said, laughing
again, "What's she got, that Jones fellow working for her
now?"

When Mrs. Winning reached home, after hurrying up the
hill past the cottage, where she saw no one, her mother-in-law
was waiting for her in front of the house, watching her come
the last few yards. "Early enough today," her mother-in-law
said. "MacLane out of town?"

Resentful, Mrs. Winning said only, "Mrs. Harris nearly drove
me out of the store, with her jokes."

"Nothing wrong with Lucy Harris getting away from that
man of hers wouldn't cure," the elder Mrs. Winning said. Together, they began to walk around the house to the back door.
Mrs. Winning, as they walked, noticed that the grass under the
trees had greened up nicely, and that the nasturtiums beside
the house were bright.

"I've got something to say to you, Helen," the elder Mrs.
Winning said finally.

"Yes?" her daughter-in-law said.

"It's the MacLane girl, about her, I mean. You know her so
well, you ought to talk to her about that colored man working
there."

"I suppose so," Mrs. Winning said.

"You *sure* you told her? You told her about those people?"

"I told her," Mrs. Winning said.

"He's there every blessed day," her mother-in-law said. "And working out there without his shirt on. He goes in the house."

And that evening Mr. Burton, next-door neighbor to Mrs. MacLane, dropped in to see the Howard Winnings about getting a new lot of shingles at the mill; he turned, suddenly, to Mrs. Winning, who was sitting sewing next to her mother-in-law at the table in the front room, and raised his voice a little when he said, "Helen, I wish you'd tell your friend Mrs. MacLane to keep that kid of hers out of my vegetables."

"Davey?" Mrs. Winning said involuntarily.

"No," Mr. Burton said, while all the Winnings looked at the younger Mrs. Winning, "no, the other one, the colored boy. He's been running loose through our back yard. Makes me sort of mad, that kid coming in spoiling other people's property. You know," he added, turning to the Howard Winnings, "you know, that does make a person mad." There was a silence, and then Mr. Burton added, rising heavily, "Guess I'll say good-night to you people."

They all attended him to the door and came back to their work in silence. I've got to do something, Mrs. Winning was thinking, pretty soon they'll stop coming to me first, they'll tell someone else to speak to *me*. She looked up, found her mother-in-law looking at her, and they both looked down quickly.

Consequently Mrs. Winning went to the store the next morning earlier than usual, and she and Howard crossed the street just above the MacLane house, and went down the hill on the other side.

"Aren't we going to see Davey?" Howard asked once, and Mrs. Winning said carelessly, "Not today, Howard. Maybe your father will take you out to the mill this afternoon."

She avoided looking across the street at the MacLane house, and hurried to keep up with Howard.

Mrs. Winning met Mrs. MacLane occasionally after that at the store or the post office, and they spoke pleasantly. When Mrs. Winning passed the cottage after the first week or so, she was no longer embarrassed about going by, and even looked at it frankly once or twice. The garden was going beautifully; Mr.

Jones's broad back was usually visible through the bushes, and Billy Jones sat on the steps or lay on the grass with Davey.

One morning on her way down the hill Mrs. Winning heard a conversation between Davey MacLane and Billy Jones; they were in the bushes together and she heard Davey's high familiar voice saying, "Billy, you want to build a house with me today?"

"Okay," Billy said. Mrs. Winning slowed her steps a little to hear.

"We'll build a big house out of branches," Davey said excitedly, "and when it's finished we'll ask my mommy if we can have lunch out there."

"You can't build a house just out of branches," Billy said. "You ought to have wood, and boards."

"And chairs and tables and dishes," Davey agreed. "And walls."

"Ask your mommy can we have two chairs out here," Billy said. "Then we can pretend the whole garden is our house."

"And I'll get us some cookies, too," Davey said. "And we'll ask my mommy and your daddy to come in our house." Mrs. Winning heard them shouting as she went down along the sidewalk.

You have to admit, she told herself as though she were being strictly just, you have to admit that he's doing a lot with that garden; it's the prettiest garden on the street. And Billy acts as though he had as much right there as Davey.

As the summer wore on into long hot days undistinguishable one from another, so that it was impossible to tell with any real accuracy whether the light shower had been yesterday or the day before, the Winnings moved out into their yard to sit after supper, and in the warm darkness Mrs. Winning sometimes found an opportunity of sitting next to her husband so that she could touch his arm; she was never able to teach Howard to run to her and put his head in her lap, or inspire him with other than the perfunctory Winning affection, but she consoled herself with the thought that at least they were a family, a solid respectable thing.

The hot weather kept up, and Mrs. Winning began to spend more time in the store, postponing the long aching walk up the hill in the sun. She stopped and chatted with the grocer, with other young mothers in the town, with older friends of her mother-in-law's, talking about the weather, the reluctance of the town to put in a decent swimming pool, the work that had to be done before school started in the fall, chickenpox, the P.T.A. One morning she met Mrs. Burton in the store, and they spoke of their husbands, the heat, and the hot-weather occupations of their children before Mrs. Burton said: "By the way, Johnny will be six on Saturday and he's having a birthday party; can Howard come?"

"Wonderful," Mrs. Winning said, thinking, His good white shorts, the dark blue shirt, a carefully-wrapped present.

"Just about eight children," Mrs. Burton said, with the loving carelessness mothers use in planning the birthday parties of their children. "They'll stay for supper, of course—send Howard down about three-thirty."

"That sounds so nice," Mrs. Winning said. "He'll be delighted when I tell him."

"I thought I'd have them all play outdoors most of the time," Mrs. Burton said. "In this weather. And then perhaps a few games indoors, and supper. Keep it simple—*you* know." She hesitated, running her finger around and around the top rim of a can of coffee. "Look," she said, "I hope you won't mind me asking, but would it be all right with you if I didn't invite the MacLane boy?"

Mrs. Winning felt sick for a minute, and had to wait for her voice to even out before she said lightly, "It's all right with me if it's all right with *you*; why do you have to ask *me?*"

Mrs. Burton laughed. "I just thought you might mind if he didn't come."

Mrs. Winning was thinking. Something bad has happened, somehow people think they know something about me that they won't say, they all pretend it's nothing, but this never happened to me before; I live with the Winnings, don't I? "Really," she said, putting the weight of the old Winning house into her voice, "why in the *world* would it bother me?" Did I take it too seriously, she was wondering, did I seem too anxious, should I have let it go?

Mrs. Burton was embarrassed, and she set the can of coffee down on the shelf and began to examine the other shelves studiously. "I'm sorry I mentioned it at all," she said.

Mrs. Winning felt that she had to say something further, something to state her position with finality, so that no longer would Mrs. Burton, at least, dare to use such a tone to a Winning, presume to preface a question with "I hope you don't mind me asking." "After all," Mrs. Winning said carefully, weighing the words, "she's like a second mother to Billy."

Mrs. Burton, turning to look at Mrs. Winning for confirmation, grimaced and said, "Good Lord, Helen!"

Mrs. Winning shrugged and then smiled and Mrs. Burton smiled and then Mrs. Winning said, "I do feel so sorry for the little boy, though."

Mrs. Burton said, "Such a sweet little thing, too."

Mrs. Winning had just said, "He and Billy are together *all* the time now," when she looked up and saw Mrs. MacLane regarding her from the end of the aisle of shelves; it was impossible to tell whether she had heard them or not. For a minute Mrs. Winning looked steadily back at Mrs. MacLane, and then she said, with just the right note of cordiality, "Good morning, Mrs. MacLane. Where is your little boy this morning?"

"Good morning, Mrs. Winning," Mrs. MacLane said, and moved on past the aisle of shelves, and Mrs. Burton caught Mrs. Winning's arm and made a desperate gesture of hiding her face and, unable to help themselves, both she and Mrs. Winning began to laugh.

Soon after that, although the grass in the Winning yard under the maple trees stayed smooth and green, Mrs. Winning began to notice in her daily trips past the cottage that Mrs. MacLane's garden was suffering from the heat. The flowers wilted under the morning sun, and no longer stood up fresh and bright; the grass was browning slightly and the rose bushes Mrs. MacLane had put in so optimistically were noticeably dying. Mr. Jones seemed always cool, working steadily; sometimes bent down with his hands in the earth, sometimes tall against the side of the house, setting up a trellis or pruning a tree, but the blue curtains hung lifelessly at the windows. Mrs. MacLane still smiled at Mrs. Winning in the store, and then one day they met at the gate of Mrs. MacLane's garden and, after hesitating for a minute, Mrs. MacLane said, "Can you come in for a few minutes? I'd like to have a talk, if you have time."

"Surely," Mrs. Winning said courteously, and followed Mrs. MacLane up the walk, still luxuriously bordered with flowering bushes, but somehow disenchanted, as though the summer heat had baked away the vivacity from the ground. In the familiar living-room Mrs. Winning sat down on a straight chair, holding herself politely stiff, while Mrs. MacLane sat as usual in her armchair.

"How is Davey?" Mrs. Winning asked finally, since Mrs. MacLane did not seem disposed to start any conversation.

"He's very well," Mrs. MacLane said, and smiled as she always did when speaking of Davey. "He's out back with Billy."

There was a quiet minute, and then Mrs. MacLane said, staring at the blue bowl on the coffee table, "What I wanted to ask you is, what on earth is gone wrong?"

Mrs. Winning had been holding herself stiff in readiness for some such question, and when she said, "I don't know what you mean," she thought, I sound exactly like Mother Winning, and realized, I'm enjoying this, just as *she* would; and no matter what she thought of herself she was unable to keep from adding, "*Is* something wrong?"

"Of course," Mrs. MacLane said. She stared at the blue bowl, and said slowly, "When I first came, everyone was so nice, and they seemed to like Davey and me and want to help us."

That's wrong, Mrs. Winning was thinking, you mustn't ever talk about whether people like you, that's bad taste.

"And the garden was going so well," Mrs. MacLane said helplessly. "And now, no one ever does more than just speak to us—I used to say 'Good morning' over the fence to Mrs. Burton and she'd come to the fence and we'd talk about the garden, and now she just says 'Morning' and goes in the house—and no one ever smiles, or anything."

This is dreadful, Mrs. Winning thought, this is childish, this is complaining. People treat you as you treat them, she thought; she wanted desperately to go over and take Mrs. MacLane's hand and ask her to come back and be one of the nice people again; but she only sat straighter in the chair and said, "I'm sure you must be mistaken. I've never heard anyone speak of it."

"*Are* you sure?" Mrs. MacLane turned and looked at her. "Are you sure it isn't because of Mr. Jones working here?"

Mrs. Winning lifted her chin a little higher and said, "Why on earth would anyone around here be rude to you because of Jones?"

Mrs. MacLane came with her to the door, both of them planning vigorously for the days some time next week, when they would all go swimming, when they would have a picnic, and Mrs. Winning went down the hill thinking, The nerve of her, trying to blame the colored folks.

Toward the end of the summer there was a bad thunderstorm, breaking up the prolonged hot spell. It raged with heavy wind and rain over the town all night, sweeping without pity through the trees, pulling up young bushes and flowers ruthlessly; a barn was struck on one side of town, the wires pulled down on another. In the morning Mrs. Winning opened the back door to find the Winning yard littered with small branches from the maples, the grass bent almost flat to the ground.

Her mother-in-law came to the door behind her. "Quite a storm," she said, "did it wake you?"

"I woke up once and went to look at the children," Mrs. Winning said. "It must have been about three o'clock."

"I was up later," her mother-in-law said. "I looked at the children too; they were both asleep."

They turned together and went in to start breakfast.

Later in the day Mrs. Winning started down to the store; she had almost reached the MacLane cottage when she saw Mrs. MacLane standing in the front garden with Mr. Jones standing beside her and Billy Jones with Davey in the shadows of the front porch. They were all looking silently at a great branch from one of the Burtons' trees that lay across the center of the garden, crushing most of the flowering bushes and pinning down what was to have been a glorious tulip bed. As Mrs. Winning stopped, watching, Mrs. Burton came out on to her front porch to survey the storm-damage, and Mrs.

MacLane called to her, "Good morning, Mrs. Burton, it looks like we have part of your tree over here."

"Looks so," Mrs. Burton said, and she went back into her house and closed the door flatly.

Mrs. Winning watched while Mrs. MacLane stood quietly for a minute. Then she looked up at Mr. Jones almost hopefully and she and Mr. Jones looked at one another for a long time. Then Mrs. MacLane said, her clear voice carrying lightly across the air washed clean by the storm: "Do you think I ought to give it up, Mr. Jones? Go back to the city where I'll never have to see another garden?"

Mr. Jones shook his head despondently, and Mrs. MacLane, her shoulders tired, went slowly over and sat on her front steps and Davey came and sat next to her. Mr. Jones took hold of the great branch angrily and tried to move it, shaking it and pulling until his shoulders tensed with the strength he was bringing to bear, but the branch only gave slightly and stayed, clinging to the garden.

"Leave it alone, Mr. Jones," Mrs. MacLane said finally. "Leave it for the next people to move!"

But still Mr. Jones pulled against the branch, and then suddenly Davey stood up and cried out, "There's Mrs. Winning! Hi, Mrs. Winning!"

Mrs. MacLane and Mr. Jones both turned, and Mrs. MacLane waved and called out, "Hello!"

Mrs. Winning swung around without speaking and started, with great dignity, back up the hill toward the old Winning house.

Dorothy and My Grandmother and the Sailors

THERE used to be a time of year in San Francisco—in late March, I believe—when there was fine long windy weather, and the air all over the city had a touch of salt and the freshness of the sea. And then, some time after the wind first started, you could look around Market Street and Van Ness and Kearney, and the fleet was in. That, of course, was some time ago, but you could look out around the Golden Gate, unbridged at that time, and there would be the battleships. There may have been aircraft carriers and destroyers, and I believe I recall one submarine, but to Dot and me then they were battleships, all of them. They would be riding out there on the water, quiet and competently grey, and the streets would be full of sailors, walking with the roll of the sea and looking in shop windows.

I never knew what the fleet came in for; my grandmother said positively that it was for refueling; but from the time the wind first started, Dot and I would become more aware, walking closer together, and dropping our voices when we talked. Although we were all of thirty miles from where the fleet lay, when we walked with our backs to the ocean we could feel the battleships riding somewhere behind and beyond us, and when we looked toward the ocean we narrowed our eyes, almost able to see across thirty miles and into a sailor's face.

It *was* the sailors, of course. My mother told us about the kind of girls who followed sailors, and my grandmother told us about the kind of sailors who followed girls. When we told Dot's mother the fleet was in, she would say earnestly, "Don't go near any sailors, you two." Once, when Dot and I were about twelve, and the fleet was in, my mother stood us up and looked at us intensely for a minute, and then she turned around to my grandmother and said, "I don't approve of young girls going to the movies alone at night," and my grandmother said, "Nonsense, they won't come this far down the peninsula; I *know* sailors."

Dot and I were permitted only one movie at night a week, anyway, and even then they sent my ten-year-old brother along with us. The first time the three of us started off to the movies together my mother looked at Dot and me again and then speculatively at my brother, who had red curly hair, and started to say something, and then looked at my grandmother and changed her mind.

We lived in Burlingame, which is far enough away from San Francisco to have palm trees in the gardens, but near enough so that Dot and I were taken into San Francisco, to the Emporium, to get our spring coats each year. Dot's mother usually gave Dot her coat money, which Dot handed over to my mother, and then Dot and I got identical coats, with my mother officiating. This was because Dot's mother was never well enough to go into San Francisco shopping, and particularly not with Dot and me. Consequently every year, some time after the wind started and the fleet came in, Dot and I, in service-weight silk stockings which we kept for that occasion, and each with a cardboard pocketbook containing a mirror, a dime for luck, and a chiffon handkerchief caught at one side and hanging down, got into the back seat of my mother's car with my mother and grandmother in the front, and headed for San Francisco and the fleet.

We always got our coats in the morning, went to the Pig'n'-Whistle for lunch, and then, while Dot and I were finishing our chocolate ice cream with chocolate sauce and walnuts, my grandmother phoned my Uncle Oliver and arranged to meet him at the launch which took us out to the fleet.

My Uncle Oliver was taken along partly because he was a man and partly because in the previous war he had been a radio operator on a battleship and partly because another uncle of mine, an Uncle Paul, was still with the Navy (my grandmother thought he had something to do with a battleship named the *Santa Volita*, or *Bonita*, or possibly *Carmelita*) and my Uncle Oliver was handy for asking people who looked like they might know my Uncle Paul if they did know him. As soon as we got on a boat my grandmother would say, as though she had never thought of it before, "Look, that one over there seems to be an officer; Ollie, just go over casually and ask him if he knows old Paul."

Oliver, having been one himself, didn't think that sailors were particularly dangerous to Dot and me if we had my mother and my grandmother with us, but he loved ships, and so he went with us and left us the minute we were on board; while we stepped cautiously over the clean decks eyeing the lifeboats apprehensively, my Uncle Oliver would touch the grey paint affectionately and go off in search of the radio apparatus.

When we met my Uncle Oliver at the launch he would usually buy Dot and me an ice-cream cone each and on the launch he would point out various boats around and name them for us. He usually got into a conversation with the sailor running the launch, and sooner or later he managed to say modestly, "I was to sea, back in '17," and the sailor would nod respectfully. When it came time for us to leave the launch and go up a stairway on to the battleship, my mother whispered to Dot and me, "Keep your skirts down," and Dot and I climbed the ladder, holding on with one hand and with the other wrapping our skirts tight around us into a bunch in front which we held on to. My grandmother always preceded us onto the battleship and my mother and Uncle Oliver followed us. When we got on board my mother took one of us by the arm and my grandmother took the other and we walked slowly around all of the ship they allowed us to see, excepting only the lowest levels, which alarmed my grandmother. We looked solemnly at cabins, decks which my grandmother said were aft, and lights which she said were port (both sides were port to my grandmother; she believed that starboard was up, in the sense that the highest mast always pointed at the north star). Usually we saw cannon—all guns were cannon—which my Uncle Oliver, in what must have been harmless teasing, assured my grandmother were kept loaded all the time. "In case of mutiny," he told my grandmother.

There were always a great many sight-seers on the battleships, and my Uncle Oliver was fond of gathering a little group of boys and young men around him to explain how the radio system worked. When he said he had been a radio operator back in '17 someone was sure to ask him, "Did you ever send out an S.O.S.?" and my Uncle Oliver would nod heavily, and say, "But I'm still here to tell about it."

Once, while my Uncle Oliver was telling about '17 and my

mother and my grandmother and Dot were looking over the rail at the ocean, I saw a dress that looked like my mother's and followed it for quite a way down the battleship before the lady turned around and I realized that it was not my mother and I was lost. Remembering what my grandmother had told me, that I was always safe if I didn't lose my head, I stood still and looked around until I isolated a tall man in a uniform with lots of braid. That will be a captain, I thought, and he will certainly take care of me. He was very polite. I told him I was lost and thought my mother and my grandmother and my friend Dot and my Uncle Oliver were down the boat a ways but I was afraid to go back alone. He said he would help me find them, and he took my arm and led me down the boat. Before very long we met my mother and my grandmother hurrying along looking for me with Dot coming along behind them as fast as she could. When my grandmother saw me she ran forward and seized my arm, pulling me away from the captain and shaking me. "You gave us the scare of our lives," she said.

"She was just lost, that's all," the captain said.

"I'm glad we found her in time," my grandmother said, walking backward with me to my mother.

The captain bowed and went away, and my mother took my other arm and shook me. "Aren't you ashamed?" she said. Dot stared at me solemnly.

"But he was a captain—" I began.

"He might have *said* he was a captain," my grandmother said, "but he was a marine."

"A marine!" my mother said, looking over the side to see if the launch was there to take us back. "Get Oliver and tell him we've seen enough," she said to my grandmother.

Because of what happened that evening, that was the last year we were allowed to see the fleet. We dropped Uncle Oliver off at home, as usual, and my mother and my grandmother took Dot and me to the Merry-Go-Round for dinner. We always had dinner in San Francisco after the fleet, and went to a movie and got home to Burlingame late in the evening. We always had dinner in the Merry-Go-Round, where the food came along on a moving platform and you grabbed it as it went by. We went there because Dot and I loved it, and next to the battleships it was the most dangerous place in San

Francisco, because you had to pay fifteen cents for every dish you took and didn't finish, and Dot and I were expected to pay for these mistakes out of our allowances. This last evening Dot and I lost forty-five cents, mainly because of a mocha cream dessert that Dot hadn't known was full of coconut. The movie Dot and I chose was full, although the usher outside told my grandmother there were plenty of seats. My mother refused to wait in line to get our money back, so my grandmother said we had to go on in and take our chances on seats. As soon as two seats were vacant my grandmother shoved Dot and me toward them, and we sat down. The picture was well under way when the two seats next to Dot emptied, and we were looking for my grandmother and my mother when Dot looked around suddenly and then grabbed my arm. "Look," she said in a sort of groan, and there were two sailors coming along the row of seats toward the empty ones. They reached the seats just as my mother and grandmother got down to the other end of the row, and my grandmother had just time to say loudly, "You leave those girls alone," when two seats a few aisles away were vacated and they had to go sit down.

Dot moved far over in her seat next to me and clung to my arm.

"What are they doing?" I whispered.

"They're just sitting there," Dot said. "What do you think I ought to do?"

I leaned cautiously around Dot and looked. "Don't pay any attention," I said. "Maybe they'll go away."

"*You* can talk," Dot said tragically, "they're not next to *you*."

"I'm next to *you*," I said reasonably, "that's pretty close."

"What are they doing now?" Dot asked.

I leaned forward again. "They're looking at the picture," I said.

"I can't stand it," Dot said. "I want to go home."

Panic overwhelmed both of us at once, and fortunately my mother and my grandmother saw us running up the aisle and caught us outside.

"What did they say?" my grandmother demanded. "I'll tell the usher."

My mother said if Dot would calm down enough to talk she would take us into the tea room next door and get us each a hot chocolate. When we got inside and were sitting down we told my mother and my grandmother we were fine now and instead of a hot chocolate we would have a chocolate sundae apiece. Dot had even started to cheer up a little when the door of the tea room opened and two sailors walked in. With one wild bound Dot was in back of my grandmother's chair, cowering and clutching my grandmother's arm. "Don't let them get me," she wailed.

"They followed us," my mother said tautly.

My grandmother put her arms around Dot. "Poor child," she said, "you're safe with us."

Dot had to stay at my house that night. We sent my brother over to Dot's mother to tell her that Dot was staying with me and that Dot had bought a grey tweed coat with princess lines, very practical and warmly interlined. She wore it all that year.

III

The Confession of *Margaret Jackson*, relict of *Tho. Stuart* in *Shaws*, who being examined by the Justices anent her being guilty of Witchcraft, declares . . . That forty years ago, or thereabout, she was at *Pollockshaw-croft*, with some few sticks on her back, and that the black Man came to her, and that she did give up herself unto the black Man, from the top of her head to the sole of her foot; and that this was after the Declarant's renouncing of her Baptism; and that the Spirit's name, which he designed her, was *Locas*. And that about the third or fourth of *January*, instant, or thereby, in the night-time, when she awaked, she found a Man to be in bed with her, whom she supposed to be her Husband; though her Husband had been dead twenty years, or thereby, and that the Man immediately disappeared: And declares, That this Man who disappeared was the Devil.

Joseph Glanvil: Sadducismus Triumphatus

Colloquy

THE doctor was competent-looking and respectable. Mrs. Arnold felt vaguely comforted by his appearance, and her agitation lessened a little. She knew that he noticed her hand shaking when she leaned forward for him to light her cigarette, and she smiled apologetically, but he looked back at her seriously.

"You seem to be upset," he said gravely.

"I'm very much upset," Mrs. Arnold said. She tried to talk slowly and intelligently. "That's one reason I came to you instead of going to Doctor Murphy—our regular doctor, that is."

The doctor frowned slightly. "My husband," Mrs. Arnold went on. "I don't want him to know that I'm worried, and Doctor Murphy would probably feel it was necessary to tell him." The doctor nodded, not committing himself, Mrs. Arnold noted.

"What seems to be the trouble?"

Mrs. Arnold took a deep breath. "Doctor," she said, "how do people tell if they're going crazy?"

The doctor looked up.

"Isn't that silly," Mrs. Arnold said. "I hadn't meant to say it like that. It's hard enough to explain anyway, without making it so dramatic."

"Insanity is more complicated than you think," the doctor said.

"I *know* it's complicated," Mrs. Arnold said. "That's the only thing I'm really *sure* of. Insanity is one of the things I mean."

"I beg your pardon?"

"That's my trouble, Doctor." Mrs. Arnold sat back and took her gloves out from under her pocketbook and put them carefully on top. Then she took them and put them underneath the pocketbook again.

"Suppose you just tell me all about it," the doctor said.

Mrs. Arnold sighed. "Everyone else seems to understand," she said, "and I don't. Look." She leaned forward and gestured with one hand while she spoke. "I don't understand the way people live. It all used to be so simple. When I was a little girl I used to live in a world where a lot of other people lived too and they all lived together and things went along like that with no fuss." She looked at the doctor. He was frowning again, and Mrs. Arnold went on, her voice rising slightly. "Look. Yesterday morning my husband stopped on his way to his office to buy a paper. He always buys the *Times* and he always buys it from the same dealer, and yesterday the dealer didn't have a *Times* for my husband and last night when he came home for dinner he said the fish was burned and the dessert was too sweet and he sat around all evening talking to himself."

"He could have tried to get it at another dealer," the doctor said. "Very often dealers downtown have papers later than local dealers."

"No," Mrs. Arnold said, slowly and distinctly, "I guess I'd better start over. When I was a little girl—" she said. Then she stopped. "Look," she said, "did there use to be words like psychosomatic medicine? Or international cartels? Or bureaucratic centralization?"

"Well," the doctor began.

"What do they *mean*?" Mrs. Arnold insisted.

"In a period of international crisis," the doctor said gently, "when you find, for instance, cultural patterns rapidly disintegrating . . ."

"International crisis," Mrs. Arnold said. "Patterns." She began to cry quietly. "He said the man had no *right* not to save him a *Times*," she said hysterically, fumbling in her pocket for a handkerchief, "and he started talking about social planning on the local level and surtax net income and geopolitical concepts and deflationary inflation." Mrs. Arnold's voice rose to a wail. "He really said deflationary inflation."

"Mrs. Arnold," the doctor said, coming around the desk, "we're not going to help things any this way."

"What is going to help?" Mrs. Arnold said. "Is everyone really crazy but me?"

"Mrs. Arnold," the doctor said severely, "I want you to get hold of yourself. In a disoriented world like ours today, alienation from reality frequently—"

"Disoriented," Mrs. Arnold said. She stood up. "Alienation," she said. "Reality." Before the doctor could stop her she walked to the door and opened it. "Reality," she said, and went out.

Elizabeth

JUST before the alarm went off she was lying in a hot sunny garden, with green lawns around her and stretching as far as she could see. The bell of the clock was an annoyance, a warning which had to be reckoned with; she moved uneasily in the hot sun and knew she was awake. When she opened her eyes and it was raining and she saw the white outline of the window against the grey sky, she tried to turn over and bury her face in the green grass, but it was morning and habit was lifting her up and dragging her away into the rainy dull day.

It was definitely past eight o'clock. The clock said so, the radiator was beginning to crackle, and on the street two stories below she could hear the ugly morning noises of people stirring, getting out to work. She put her feet reluctantly out from under the blankets and on to the floor, and swung herself up to sit on the edge of the bed. By the time she was standing up and in her bathrobe the day had fallen into its routine; after the first involuntary rebellion against every day's alarm she subsided regularly into the shower, make-up, dress, breakfast schedule which would take her through the beginning of the day and out into the morning where she could forget the green grass and the hot sun and begin to look forward to dinner and the evening.

Because it was raining and the day seemed unimportant she put on the first things she came to; a grey tweed suit that she knew was shapeless and heavy on her now that she was so thin, a blue blouse that never felt comfortable. She knew her own face too well to enjoy the long careful scrutiny that went with putting on make-up; toward four o'clock in the afternoon her pale narrow cheeks would warm up and fill out, and the lipstick that looked too purple with her dark hair and eyes would take on a rosier touch in spite of the blue blouse, but this morning she thought, as she had thought nearly every morning standing in front of her mirror, I wish I'd been a blonde; never realizing quite that it was because there were thin hints of grey in her hair.

She walked quickly around her one-room apartment, with a

sureness that came of habit rather than conviction; after more than four years in this one home she knew all its possibilities, how it could put on a sham appearance of warmth and welcome when she needed a place to hide in, how it stood over her in the night when she woke suddenly, how it could relax itself into a disagreeable unmade, badly-put-together state, mornings like this, anxious to drive her out and go back to sleep. The book she had read the night before lay face down on the end table, the ashtray next to it dirtied: the clothes she had taken off lay over the back of a chair, to be taken to the cleaner this morning.

With her coat and hat on, she made the bed quickly, pulling it straight on top over the wrinkles beneath, stuffed the clothes to go to the cleaner into the back of the closet, and thought, I'll dust and straighten and maybe wash the bathroom tonight, come home and take a hot bath and wash my hair and do my nails; by the time she had locked the apartment door behind her and started down the stairs, she was thinking, Maybe today I'll stop in and get some bright material for slip-covers and drapes. I could make them evenings and the place wouldn't look so dreary when I wake up mornings; yellow, I could get some yellow dishes and put them along the wall in a row. Like in *Mademoiselle* or something, she told herself ironically as she stopped at the front door, the brisk young businesswoman and her one-room home. Suitable for entertaining brisk young businessmen. I wish I had something that folded up into a bookcase on one side and a Sheraton desk on the other and opened out into a dining-room table big enough to seat twelve.

While she was standing just inside the door, pulling on her gloves and hoping the rain might stop in these few seconds, the door next to the stairway opened and a woman said, "Who's that?"

"It's Miss Style," she said, "Mrs. Anderson?"

The door opened wide and an old woman put her head out. "I thought it was that fellow has the apartment right over you," she said. "I been meaning to catch him about leaving them skis outside his door. Nearly broke my leg."

"I've been wishing I didn't have to go out. It's such a bad day."

The old woman came out of her room and went to the front door. She pulled aside the door curtain and looked out, wrapping her arms around herself. She was wearing a dirty house dress and the sight of her made Miss Style's grey tweed suit suddenly seem clean and warm.

"I been trying to catch that fellow for two days now," the old woman said. "He goes in and out so quiet." She giggled, looking sideways at Miss Style. "I nearly caught that man of yours night before last," she said. "He comes down the stairs quiet, too. I saw who it was in time," and she giggled again. "I guess all the men come downstairs quiet. All afraid of something."

"Well, if I'm going to go out I might as well do it," Miss Style said. She still stood in the doorway for a minute, hesitating before walking out into the day and the rain and the people. She lived on a fairly quiet street, where later there would be children shouting at each other and on a nice day an organ-grinder, but today in the rain everything looked dirty. She hated to wear rubbers because she had graceful slim feet; on a day like this she went slowly, stepping carefully between puddles.

It was very late; there were only a few people still sitting at the counter in the corner drugstore. She sat on a stool, reconciled to the time, and waited patiently until the clerk came down the counter with her orange juice. "Hello, Tommy," she said dismally.

"Morning, Miss Style," he said, "lousy day."

"Isn't it," she said. "A fine day not to go out."

"I came in this morning," Tommy said. "I would have given my right arm to stay home in bed. There ought to be a law against rain."

Tommy was little and ugly and alert; looking at him, Miss Style thought, He has to get up and come to work in the mornings just like I do and just like everyone else in the world; the rain is just another break in the millions of lousy things, in getting up and going to work.

"I don't mind snow," Tommy was saying, "and I don't mind the hot weather, but I sure do hate rain."

He turned suddenly when someone called him, and went dancing down to the other end of the counter, bringing up with a flourish before his customer. "Lousy day, isn't it?" he said. "Sure do wish I was in Florida."

Miss Style drank her orange juice, remembering her dream. A sharp recollection of flowers and warmth came into her mind, and then was lost before the cold driving rain outside.

Tommy came back with her coffee and a plate of toast. "Nothing like coffee to cheer you up in the morning," he said.

"Thanks, Tommy," she said, unenthusiastic. "How's your play coming, by the way?"

Tommy looked up eagerly. "Hey," he said, "I finished it, I meant to tell you. Finished the whole thing and sent it away day before yesterday."

Funny thing, she thought, a clerk in a drugstore, he gets up in the morning and eats and walks around and writes a play just like it was real, just like the rest of us, like me. "Fine," she said.

"I sent it to an agent a guy told me about, he said it was the best agent he knew."

"Tommy," she said, "why didn't you give it right to me?"

He laughed, looking down at the sugar bowl he was holding for her. "Listen," he said, "my friend said you didn't want stuff like mine, you want people, like, from out of town or something, they don't know if they're any good or not. Hell," he went on anxiously, "I'm not one of these guys fall for ads in the magazines."

"I see," she said.

Tommy leaned over the counter. "Don't get sore," he said, "You know what I mean, you know your business better than I do."

"I'm not sore," she said. She watched Tommy hurry away again, and she thought— Wait till I tell Robbie. Wait till I tell him the soda jerk thinks he's a bum.

"Listen," Tommy said to her, from halfway down the counter, "how long, do you think I ought to wait? How long will they take to read it, these agents?"

"Couple of weeks, maybe," she said. "Maybe longer."

"I figured it might be," he said. "You want more coffee today?"

"No, thanks," she said. She slid down from the stool and walked across the store to pay her check. They're probably going to buy that play, she was thinking, and I'm going to start eating in the hamburg joint across the street.

She went out into the rain again to see her bus just pulling up across the street. She ran for it, against the light, and pushed into the crowd of people getting on. With a kind of fury left over from Tommy and his play she thrust her way against the people, and a woman turned to her and said, "Who do you think you're pushing?" Vengefully she put her elbow into the woman's ribs and got on the bus first. She dropped her nickel in and got to the last available seat, and heard the woman behind her. "These people who think they can shove anybody around, they think they're important." She looked around to see if anyone knew who the woman was talking about; the man beside her on the seat next to the window was staring straight ahead with the infinitely tired expression of the early-morning bus passenger; two girls in the seat in front were looking out the window after a man passing, and in the aisle next to her the woman was standing, still talking about her. "People who think their business is the only important thing in the world. Think they can just push anyone around." No one in the bus was listening: everyone was wet and uncomfortable and crowded, but the woman went on monotonously— "Think no one else has a right to ride on buses."

She stared past the man out the window until the crowds coming into the bus pushed the woman past her down the aisle. When she came to her stop she was timid for a minute about pushing her way out, and when she reached the door the woman was near it, staring at her as though wanting to remember her face. "Dried-up old maid," the woman said loudly, and the people around her in the bus laughed.

Miss Style put on an expression of contempt, stepping carefully down to the curb, looking up just as the bus pulled away to see the woman's face still watching her from the window. She walked through the rain to the old building where her office was, thinking, That woman was just waiting for anyone to cross her path this morning, I wish I'd said something back to her.

"Morning, Miss Style," the elevator operator said.

"Morning," she said. She walked into the open-work iron elevator and leaned against the back wall.

"Bad day," the operator said. He waited for a minute and then closed the door. "Fine day not to go out," he said.

"Sure is," she said. I wish I'd said something to that woman in the bus, she was thinking. I shouldn't have let her get away with it, let the day start off like that, with a nasty incident, I should have answered her back and got to feeling good and pleased with myself. Start the day off right.

"Here you are," the operator said. "You don't have to go out again for quite a while."

"Glad of that," she said. She got out of the elevator and walked down the hall to her office. There was a light on inside, making the *ROBERT SHAX, Literary Agents,* stand out against the door. Looks almost cheerful, she thought, Robbie must be in early.

She had worked for Robert Shax for nearly eleven years. When she came to New York the Christmas she was twenty, a thin dark girl with neat clothes and hair and moderate ambition, holding on to her pocketbook with both hands, afraid of subways, she answered an ad, and met Robert Shax before she had even found a room to live in. It had been one of those windfall ads, an assistant wanted in a literary agency, and there was no one around to tell Elizabeth Style, asking people timidly how to find the address, that if she got the job it wasn't worth getting. The literary agency was Robert Shax and a thin clever man who had disliked Elizabeth so violently that after two years she had taken Robert Shax away to start his own agency. Robert Shax was on the door and on all the checks, and Elizabeth Style hid away in her office, wrote the letters, kept the records, and came out occasionally to consult the files she allowed Robert Shax to keep on display.

They had spent much time in the eight years trying to make this office look like a severe environment for a flourishing business: a miserable place that its owners were too busy to pretty up more than enough to meet the purposes of its clients. The door opened into a tight little reception room, painted tan the year before, with two cheap chrome and brown chairs, a brown linoleum floor, and a framed picture of a vase of flowers over the small desk which was occupied five afternoons a week by a Miss Wilson, a colorless girl who answered the phone sniffling. Beyond Miss Wilson's desk were two doors, which did not give the effect of limitless offices, stretching on down the building, that Robert Shax had hoped they might; the one on the left had, on the door, "Robert Shax," and the one on the right had, on the door, "Elizabeth Style," and through the pebbled glass doors you could see, dimly, the shape of the narrow window each office owned, crowding close enough to the door and walls to admit that the two offices together were no wider than the reception room, and to hint darkly that all that protected the privacy of Mr. Shax and Miss Style was a beaverboard partition painted to look like the walls.

Every morning Elizabeth Style came into the office with the idea that something might be done for it still, that somehow there might be a way to make it look respectable, with Venetian blinds or paneling or an efficient-looking bookcase with sets of classics and the newest books that Robert Shax had presumably sold to their publishers. Or even an end table with expensive magazines. Miss Wilson thought it would be nice to have a radio, but Robert Shax wanted an expensive office with heavy carpeting and desks sitting solidly on the floor and a battery of secretaries.

This morning the office looked more cheerful than usual, probably because it was still raining outside, or else because the lights were already on and the radiators were going. Elizabeth Style went over to the door of her office and opened it, saying, "Morning, Robbie," because, since there was no one in the office, there was no need to pretend that the beaverboard partitions were walls.

"Morning, Liz," Robbie said, and then, "Come on in, will you?"

"I'll take my coat off," she said. There was a tiny closet in the corner of her office where she hung up her coat, squeezing in back of the desk to do it. She noticed that there was mail on her desk, four or five letters and a bulky envelope that would be a manuscript. She spread the letters out to make sure there was nothing of any particular interest, and then went out of her office and opened the door of Robbie's.

He was leaning down over his desk, in an attitude meant to show extreme concentration; the faintly bald top of his head was toward her and his heavy round shoulders cut off the lower half of the window. His office was almost exactly like hers; it had a small filing cabinet and an autographed photograph of one of the few reasonably successful writers the firm had handled. The photograph was signed "To Bob, with deepest gratitude, Jim," and Robert Shax was fond of using it as a happy example in his office conversations with eager authors. When she had closed the door Elizabeth was only a step away from the straight visitor's chair slanting at the desk; she sat down and stretched her feet out in front of her.

"I got soaked coming in this morning," she said.

"It's an awful day," Robbie said, without looking up. When he was alone with her he relaxed the heartiness that he usually stocked in his voice: he let his face look tired and worried. He was wearing his good grey suit that day, and later, with other people around, he would look like a golfer, a man who ate good rare roast beef and liked pretty girls. "It's one hell of a day," he repeated. He looked up at her. "Liz," he said, "that goddamned minister is in town again."

"No wonder you look so worried," she said. She had been ready to complain at him, to tell him about the woman on the bus, to ask him to sit up straight and behave, but there was nothing to say. "Poor old Robbie," she said.

"There's a note from him," Robbie said. "I've got to go up there this morning. He's in that goddamned rooming-house again."

"What are you planning to tell him?"

Robbie got up and turned around to the window. When he got out of his chair he had just room to turn around to get to the window of the closet or the filing cabinet; on a pleasanter day she might have an amiable remark about his weight. "I don't know what in hell I'm planning to tell him," Robbie said. "I'll promise him something."

I know you will, she thought. She had the familiar picture of Robbie's maneuvers to escape an awkward situation in the back of her mind: she could see Robbie shaking the old man's hand briskly, calling him "sir" and keeping his shoulders back, saying that the old man's poems were "fine, sir, really magnificent," promising anything, wildly, just to get away. "You'll come back in some kind of trouble," she said mildly.

Robbie laughed suddenly, happily. "But he won't bother us for a while."

"You ought to call him up or something. Write him a letter," she said.

"Why?" She could see that he was pleased with the idea of coming back in trouble, of being irresponsible and what he would call carefree; he would make the long trip uptown to the minister's rooming-house by subway and take a taxi for the last two blocks to arrive in style, and sit for a tiresome hour talking to the old man, just to be carefree and what he might call gallant.

Make him feel good, she thought. He has to go, not me. "You shouldn't be trusted to run a business by yourself," she said. "You're too silly."

He laughed again and walked around the desk to pat her head. "We get along pretty well, don't we, Liz?"

"Fine," she said.

He was beginning to think about it now; he was holding his head up and his voice was filling out. "I'll tell him someone wants one of his poems for an anthology," he said.

"Just don't give him any money," she said. "He has more than we have now."

He went back to his closet and took out his coat, his good coat today, and threw it carelessly over his arm. He put his hat on the back of his head and picked up his brief case from the desk. "Got all the old guy's poems in here," he said. "I figured I could kill some time reading them aloud to him."

"Have a nice trip," she said.

He patted her on the head again, and then reached out for the door. "You'll take care of everything here?"

"I'll try to cope with it," she said.

She followed him out the door and started into her own office. Halfway across the outer office he stopped, not turning. "Liz?" he said.

"Well?"

He thought for a minute. "Seems like there was something I wanted to tell you," he said. "It doesn't matter."

"See you for lunch?" she asked.

"I'll be back about twelve-thirty," he said.

He closed the door and she heard his footsteps going

emphatically down the hall to the elevator; busy footsteps, she thought, in case anyone was listening in this fearful old building.

She sat for a minute at her desk, smoking and wishing she could paint her office walls a light green. If she wanted to stay late at night she could do it herself. It would only take one can of paint, she told herself bitterly, to do an office like this, with enough left over to do the front of the building. Then she put out her cigarette and thought, I've worked in it this long, maybe some day we'll get a million-dollar client and can move into a real office building where they have soundproof walls.

The mail on her desk was bad. A bill from her dentist, a letter from a client in Oregon, a couple of ads, a letter from her father, and the bulky envelope that was certainly a manuscript. She threw out the ads and the dentist's bill, which was marked "Please remit," set the manuscript and the other letter aside, and opened the letter from her father.

It was in his own peculiar style, beginning, "Dearest Daughter," and ending, "Yr. Afft. Father," and told her that the feed store was doing badly, that her sister in California was pregnant again, that old Mrs. Gill had asked after her the other day, and that he found himself very much alone since her mother's death. And he hoped she was well. She threw the letter into the wastebasket on top of the dentist's bill.

The letter from the client in Oregon wanted to know what had happened to a manuscript sent in three months before; the large bulky envelope contained a manuscript written in long-hand, from a young man in Allentown who wanted it sold immediately and their fee taken out of the editor's check. She glanced through the manuscript carelessly, turning over the pages and reading a few words on each; halfway through she stopped and read a whole page, and then turned back a little and read more. With her eyes still on the manuscript, she leaned over and reached into the bottom drawer of her desk, stirring papers around until she found a small, ten-cent notebook, partly filled with notes. She opened the notebook to a blank page, copied out a paragraph from the manuscript, thinking, I can switch that around and make it a woman instead of a man; and she made another note, "make W., use any name but Helen," which was the name of the woman in the story. Then she put the notebook away and set the manuscript to one side of her desk in order to swing up the panel of the desk that brought the typewriter upright. She took out a sheet of notepaper labeled "ROBERT SHAX, Literary Agents, Elizabeth Style, Fiction Department," and put it into the typewriter; she was just typing the young man's name and the address: General Delivery, Allentown, when she heard the outer door open and close.

"Hello," she called, without looking up.

"Good morning."

She looked up then; it was such a high, girlish voice. The girl who had come in was big and blonde, and walked across the little reception room as though she were prepared to be impressed no matter what happened to her there.

"Did you want to see me?" Elizabeth asked, her hands still resting on the typewriter keys. If God should have sent me a client, she thought, it won't hurt to look literary.

"I wanted Mr. Shax," the girl said. She waited in the doorway of Elizabeth's office.

"He was called out on very pressing business," Elizabeth said. "Did you have an appointment?"

The girl hesitated, as though doubting Elizabeth's authority.

"Not exactly," she said finally. "I'm supposed to be working here, I guess."

Seemed like there was something he wanted to tell me, Elizabeth thought, that coward. "I see," she said. "Come in and sit down."

The girl came in shyly, although with no apparent timidity. She figured it was his business to tell me, not hers, Elizabeth thought. "Did Mr. Shax tell you to come to work here?"

"Well," the girl said, deciding it was all right to trust Elizabeth, "on Monday about five o'clock I was asking for a job in all the offices in this building and I came here and Mr. Shax showed me around the office and he said he thought I could do the work all right." She thought back over what she had said. "You weren't here," she added.

"I couldn't have been," Elizabeth agreed. He's known since Monday and I find out, she thought, what is this, Wednesday? I find out on Wednesday when she shows up for work. "I didn't ask your name."

"Daphne Hill," the girl said meekly.

Elizabeth wrote "Daphne Hill" down on her memorandum and looked at it, partly to seem as if she was coming to an important decision and partly to see what "Daphne Hill" looked like written down.

"Mr. Shax said," the girl began, and stopped. Her voice was high and when she was anxious she opened her small brown eyes wide and blinked. Except for her hair, which was a pale blonde and curled all over the top of her head, she was clumsy and awkward, all dressed up for her first day at work.

"What did Mr. Shax say?" Elizabeth asked when the girl seemed to have subsided permanently.

"He said he wasn't satisfied with the girl he had now and I was to learn her job and get to do it and I was to come today because he was going to tell her yesterday that I was coming."

"Fine," Elizabeth said. "Can you type, do you suppose?"

"I guess so," the girl said.

Elizabeth looked at the letter in the typewriter on her desk and then said, "Well, you go on outside and sit at the desk out there and if the phone rings you answer it. Read or something."

"Yes, Miss Style," the girl said.

"And please close my office door," Elizabeth said. She watched the girl go out and close the door carefully. The things she had wanted to say to the girl were waiting to be said: maybe she could rephrase some of them for Robbie at lunch.

What does this mean, she thought suddenly in panic, Miss Wilson has been here almost as long as I have. Is he trying in his own heavy-handed fashion to beautify the office? He might better buy a bookcase; who is going to teach this incredible girl to answer the phone and write letters, even as well as Miss Wilson? Me, she thought at last. I'm going to have to drag Robbie out of this last beautiful impulsive gesture like always; the things I do for a miserable little office and a chance to make money. Anyway, maybe Daphne will help me paint the walls after five some day; maybe the one thing Daphne knows how to do is paint.

She turned back to the letter in the typewriter. An encouraging letter to a new client; it fell into a simple formula in her mind and she wrote it without hesitating, typing clumsily and amateurishly, but quickly. "Dear Mr. Burton," she wrote. "We have read your story with a good deal of interest. Your plot is well thought out, and we believe that the character of—" She stopped for a minute and turned back to the manuscript, opening it at random—"Lady Montague, in particular, is of more than usual merit. Naturally, in order to appeal to the better-paying markets, the story needs touching up by a skilled professional editor, a decisive selling service we are able to offer our clients. Our rates—"

"Miss Style?"

In spite of the beaverboard partitions, Elizabeth said, "If you want to talk to me, Miss Hill, come in."

After a minute Miss Hill opened the door and came in. Elizabeth could see her pocketbook on the desk outside, the lipstick and compact sitting next to it. "When does Mr. Shax get back?"

"Probably not till this afternoon. He went out on important business with a client," Elizabeth said. "Why, did anyone call?"

"No, I just wondered," Miss Hill said. She closed the door and went heavily back to her desk. Elizabeth looked again at the letter in the typewriter and then turned her chair around to put her still-wet feet on the radiator under the window. After a minute she opened the bottom drawer of her desk again and this time took out a pocket reprint of a mystery story. With her feet on the radiator she settled down to read.

Because it was raining, and because she was depressed and out of sorts, and because Robbie had not come by quarter to one, Elizabeth treated herself to a Martini while she was waiting, sitting uncomfortably on a narrow chair in the restaurant, watching other unimpressive people go in and out. The restaurant was crowded, the floors wet from the feet coming in from the rain, and it was dark and dismal. Elizabeth and Robbie had come here for lunch two or three times a week, ever since they had opened the office in the building near-by. The first day they had come had been in summer, and Elizabeth, in a sheer black dress—she remembered it still; she would be too thin for it now—and a small white hat and white gloves, had been excited and happy over the great new career opening out for her. She and Robbie had held hands across the table and talked enthusiastically: they were only going to stay in the old building for a year, or two at the most, and then they would have enough money to move uptown; the good clients who would come to the new Robert Shax Agency would be honest reputable writers, with large best-selling manuscripts; editors would go to lunch with them at sleek uptown restaurants, a drink before lunch would not be an extraordinary thing. The first order of stationery saying "ROBERT SHAX, Literary Agents, Elizabeth Style, Fiction Department," had not been delivered; they planned the letterhead at lunch that day.

Elizabeth thought about ordering another Martini and then she saw Robbie coming impatiently through the people in the aisles. He saw her across the room and waved at her, aware of people watching him, an executive late for a luncheon appointment, even in a dingy restaurant.

When he got to the table, his back to the room, his face was tired and his voice was quiet. "Finally made it," he said. He looked surprised at the empty Martini glass. "I haven't even had breakfast yet," he said.

"Did you have a bad time with the minister?"

"Terrible," he said. "He wants a book of his poems published this year."

"What did you tell him?" Elizabeth tried not to let her voice sound strained. Time enough for that later, she thought, when he feels like answering me.

"I don't know," Robbie said. "How the hell do I know what I told the old fool?" He sat down heavily. "Something about we'd do our best."

That means he's really made a mess of it, Elizabeth thought. If he did well he'd tell me in detail. She was suddenly so tired that she let her shoulders droop and sat stupidly staring off at the people coming in and out of the door. What am I going to say to him, she thought, what words will Robbie understand best?

"What are you looking so glum about?" Robbie asked suddenly. "No one made you go way the hell uptown without breakfast."

"I had a tough morning anyway," Elizabeth said. Robbie looked up, waiting. "I had a new employee to break in."

Robbie still waited, his face a little flushed, squinting at her; he was waiting to see what she was going to say before he apologized, or lost his temper, or tried to pass the whole thing off as a fine joke.

Elizabeth watched him: this is Robbie, she was thinking, I know what he's going to do and what he's going to say and what tie he's going to wear every day in the week, and for eleven years I have known these things and for eleven years I have been wondering how to say things to make him understand; and eleven years ago we sat here and held hands and he said we were going to be successful. "I was thinking of the day we had lunch here when we first started out together," she said quietly, and Robbie looked mystified. "The day we started out together," she repeated more distinctly. "Do you remember Jim Harris?" Robbie nodded, his mouth a little open. "We were going to make a lot of money because Jim was going to bring all his friends to us and then you had a fight with Jim and we haven't seen him since and none of his friends came to us and now we've got your friend the minister for a client and a beautiful picture of Jim on your office wall. Signed," she said. "Signed, with 'gratitude,' and if he was making enough money we'd be around trying to borrow from him even now."

"Elizabeth," Robbie said. He was confused between trying to look hurt and trying to see if anyone heard what she was saying.

"Even the boy in my corner drugstore." Elizabeth looked at him for a minute. "Daphne Hill," she said. "My God."

"I see," Robbie said, with a significant smile. "Daphne Hill." He turned when he saw the waitress coming. "Miss," he said loudly, and to Elizabeth, "I think you ought to have another drink. Cheer you up a little." When the waitress looked at him he said "Two Martinis," and turned back to Elizabeth, putting on the smile again. "I'm going to drink my breakfast," he said, and then he reached over and touched Elizabeth's hand. "Listen," he said, "Liz, if that's all that's bothering you. I was a dope, I thought you'd figured I'd done something wrong about the minister. Listen, Daphne's all right. I just thought we needed someone around who'd brighten the place up a little."

"You could have painted the wall," Elizabeth said tonelessly. When Robbie stared she said, "Nothing," and he went on, leaning forward seriously.

"Look," he said, "if you don't like this Daphne out she goes. There's no question about it, after all. We're in business together." He looked off into space and smiled reminiscently. "I remember those days, all right. We were going to do wonders." He lowered his voice and looked lovingly at Elizabeth. "I think we still can," he said.

Elizabeth laughed in spite of herself. "You'll have to go down the stairs more quietly," she said. "My janitor's wife thought you were the man who leaves skis out in the hall. She nearly broke a leg."

"Don't make fun of me," Robbie said. "Elizabeth, it really hurts me to see you let someone like Daphne Hill upset you."

"Of course it does," Elizabeth said. Robbie suddenly impressed her as funny. If only I could keep on feeling like this, she thought, even while she was laughing at him. "Here comes your breakfast for you to drink," she said.

"Miss," Robbie said to the waitress. "We'd like to order our lunch, please."

He handed the menu ceremoniously to Elizabeth and said to the waitress, "Chicken croquettes and French fried potatoes." Elizabeth said, "The same, please," and handed the menu back. When the waitress had gone Robbie picked up one of the Martinis and handed it to Elizabeth. "You need this, old girl," he said. He picked up the other and looked at her; then he lowered his voice to the same low affectionate tone, and said, "Here's to you, and our future success."

Elizabeth smiled at him sweetly and tasted her drink. She could see Robbie debating whether to toss his off all at once or to sip it slowly as though he didn't need it.

"If you drink it too fast you'll be sick, dear," she said. "Without your breakfast."

He tasted it delicately and then set it down. "Now let's talk seriously about Daphne," he said.

"I thought she was leaving," Elizabeth said.

He looked frightened. "Naturally, if you want it that way," he said stiffly. "Seems sort of rotten to hire a girl and fire her the same day because you're jealous."

"I'm not jealous," Elizabeth said. "I never said I was."

"If I can't have a good-looking girl in the office," Robbie said.

"You can," Elizabeth said. "I'd just like one who could type."

"Daphne can take care of the work all right."

"Robbie," Elizabeth said, and then stopped. Already, she thought, I don't want to laugh at him any more; I wish I could feel all the time like I did a minute ago, not like this. She looked at him carefully, his red face and the thin greying hair, and the heavy shoulders above the table; he was holding his head back and his chin firm because he knew she was looking at him. He thinks I'm awed, she thought, he's a man and he's cowed me. "Let her stay," Elizabeth said.

"After all," Robbie leaned back to let the waitress put his plate in front of him, "after all," he went on when the waitress had gone, "it isn't as though I didn't have the authority to hire someone for my own office."

"I know," Elizabeth said wearily.

"If you want to start a fuss about some small thing," Robbie said. The corners of his mouth were turned down and he refused to meet her eyes. "I can run my own office," he repeated.

"You're scared to death I might leave you some day," Elizabeth said. "Eat your lunch."

Robbie picked up his fork. "Naturally," he said, "I feel that it would be a shame to break up a pleasant partnership just because you were jealous."

"Never mind," Elizabeth said, "I won't go away anywhere."

"I hope not," Robbie said. He ate industriously for a minute. "I tell you what," he said suddenly, putting his fork down, "we'll try her out for a week and then if you don't think she's better than Miss Wilson she'll go."

"But I don't—" Elizabeth began. Then she said. "Fine. That way we can find out exactly how she'll suit us."

"Splendid idea," Robbie said. "Now I feel better." He reached across the table and this time patted her hand. "Good old Liz," he said.

"You know," Elizabeth said, "I feel so funny right now." She was looking at the doorway. "I thought I saw someone I knew."

Robbie turned around and looked at the doorway. "Who?"

"No one you know," Elizabeth said. "A boy from my home town. It wasn't the same person, though."

"Always think you see people you know in New York," Robbie said, turning back to his fork.

Elizabeth was thinking, it must have been talking about old times with Robbie and the two drinks I had, I haven't thought of Frank for years. She laughed out loud, and Robbie stopped eating to say, "What's the matter with you, anyway? People will think something's wrong."

"I was just thinking," Elizabeth said. Suddenly she felt that she must talk to Robbie, treat him as she would anyone else she knew well, like a husband almost. "I haven't thought about this fellow for years," she said. "It just brought a thousand things back to my mind."

"An old boy friend?" Robbie said without interest.

Elizabeth felt the same twinge of horror she might have felt fifteen years ago at the suggestion. "Oh, *no*," she said. "He took me to a dance once. My mother called up his mother and asked to have him take me."

"Chocolate ice cream with chocolate sauce," Robbie said to the waitress.

"Just coffee," Elizabeth said. "He was a wonderful boy," she said to Robbie. Why can't I stop myself? she was thinking, I haven't thought about this for years.

"Listen," Robbie said, "did you tell Daphne she could go out for lunch?"

"I didn't tell her anything," Elizabeth said.

"We better hurry then," Robbie said. "The poor kid must be starving."

Frank, Elizabeth thought. "Seriously," she said, "what did you and the minister decide?"

"I'll tell you later," Robbie said, "when I get my ideas straight. Right now I'm not so sure what we did decide."

And he'll spring it on me suddenly, Elizabeth thought, so I won't have time to think; he's just promised to publish the minister's poems at his own expense; or he's gone out of town, will I deal with it; or someone's going to sue us. Frank wouldn't have been in a place like this, anyway, if he's eating at all, it's some place where everything is quiet and they call him "sir" and the women are all beautiful. "It doesn't matter anyway," she said.

"Of course it doesn't," Robbie said. He evidently felt it was necessary to add one final clinching touch before they went back to Daphne Hill. "As long as we can fight it together, we'll come through everything fine," he said. "We work well together, Liz." He stood up and turned to get his coat and hat. His suit was wrinkled and he felt uncomfortable in it, from the way he moved his shoulders uneasily.

Elizabeth finished the last of her coffee. "You get fatter every day," she said.

He looked around at her, his eyes frightened. "You think I ought to start dieting again?" he asked.

They came up in the elevator together, standing in opposite corners, each looking off into space, through the iron grill-work of the elevator, into something private and secret. They had gone up and down in this elevator four or six or eight or ten times a day since they moved into the building, sometimes happily, sometimes coldly angry with one another, sometimes laughing or quarreling furiously with quick violent phrases; the elevator operator probably knew more about them than Elizabeth's landlady or the young couple who had the apartment across the hall from Robbie, and yet they got into the elevator daily and the elevator operator spoke to them civilly and stood with his back to them, riding up and down, entering briefly into their quarrels, possibly smiling with his back turned.

Today he said, "Weather still bad?" and Robbie said, "Worse than ever," and the operator said, "There ought to be a law against it," and let them off at their floor.

"I wonder what he thinks of us, the elevator man," Elizabeth said, following Robbie down the hall.

"Probably wishes he could get off that elevator for a while and sit down in an office," Robbie said. He opened the door of the office and said, "Miss Hill?"

Daphne Hill was sitting at the reception desk, reading the mystery Elizabeth had left to go out to lunch. "Hello, Mr. Shax," she said.

"Did you take that off my desk?" Elizabeth said, surprised for a minute into speaking at once without thinking.

"Wasn't it all right?" Daphne asked. "I didn't have anything to do."

"We'll find you plenty to do, young lady," Robbie said heartily, the brisk businessman again. "Sorry to keep you waiting for lunch."

"I went out and got something to eat," Daphne said.

"Good," Robbie said, looking sideways at Elizabeth. "We'll have to make some arrangement for the future."

"Hereafter," Elizabeth said sharply, "don't go into my office without permission."

"Sure," Daphne said, startled. "You want your book back?"

"Keep it," Elizabeth said. She went into her office and closed the door. She heard Robbie saying, "Miss Style doesn't like to have her things disturbed, Miss Hill," and then, "Come into my office, please." As though there were real partitions, Elizabeth thought. She heard Robbie go quickly into his office and Daphne pound her deliberate way after him, and the door close.

She sighed, and thought, I'll pretend they're real partitions; Robbie will. She noticed a note standing against her typewriter where she had left it with the letter to Mr. Burton still half-finished. She picked up the note and read it with heavy concentration to drown out Robbie's employer voice on the other side of the partition. The note was from Miss Wilson, and said:

"Miss Style, no one told me there was a new girl coming and since I've been working here so long I think you should have told me. I guess she can learn the work as well by herself. Please tell Mr. Shax to send me my money at home, the address is in the file as he knows. There was a call from a Mr. Robert Hunt for you, will you call him back at his hotel, the Addison House. Please tell Mr. Shax to send the money, it comes now to two weeks and an extra week for notice. Alice Wilson."

She must have been mad, Elizabeth thought, not to wait around for her money, she must have been furious, I guess Daphne was the first to tell her and she felt like I did; he'll never send her any money. She could hear Robbie's voice saying, "It's a terrible business, the most heart-breaking I know." He's talking about free-lance writing, she thought, Daphne probably wants to sell her life history.

She went out of the door of her office and around to Robbie's and knocked. If Robbie says, "Who is it?" she thought, I'll say "The elevator man, come up to sit down for a while." Then Robbie said, "Come on in, Liz, don't be silly."

"Robbie," she said, opening the door, "Miss Wilson was here and left a note."

"I forgot to tell you," Daphne said, "and I didn't get a chance yet anyway. She said to tell Mr. Shax to send her money."

"I'm sorry about this," Robbie said. "She should have been told yesterday. It's a damned shame for her to find out like this." Daphne was sitting in the one other chair in his office and he hesitated and then said, "Sit here, Elizabeth."

Elizabeth waited until he started to hoist himself up and then said, "That's all right, Robbie, I'm going back to work."

Robbie read Miss Wilson's letter carefully. "Miss Hill," he said, "make a note to send Miss Wilson her back pay and the extra week she asks for."

"I don't have anything to make a note on," Daphne said. Elizabeth took a pad and pencil off Robbie's desk and handed it to her, and Daphne made a solemn sentence on the first page of the pad.

"Who is this Hunt?" Robbie asked Elizabeth. "Your old boy friend?"

I know I shouldn't have told him, Elizabeth thought. "I think it's an old friend of my father's from home," she said.

"Better call him back," Robbie said, handing her the note.

"I shall," Elizabeth said. "Don't you think you'd better write Miss Wilson and explain what happened?"

Robbie looked dismayed, and then he said, "Miss Hill can do that this afternoon."

Elizabeth, carefully not looking at Daphne, said, "Fine idea. That will give her something to do."

She closed the door quietly when she went out and closed the door of her own office after herself to give the illusion of privacy. She knew that Robbie would listen to her talking on the phone; she had an odd picture of Robbie and Daphne, sitting silently one on either side of Robbie's desk, two heavy serious faces turned slightly to the partition, listening soberly to Elizabeth talking to her father's old friend.

She looked up the hotel number in the book, hearing

Robbie say, "Tell her we're all sincerely sorry, but that circumstances beyond my control, and so on. Make it as pleasant as possible. Remember to tell her we'll consider her for the first new job we have here."

Elizabeth dialed the number, waiting for the sudden silence in Robbie's office. She asked the hotel clerk for Mr. Robert Hunt, and when he answered she made her voice low, and said, "Uncle Robert? This is Beth."

He answered enthusiastically, "Beth! It's fine hearing your voice. Mom thought you'd be too busy to call back."

"Is she with you? How nice," Elizabeth said. "How are you both? How is Dad?"

"All fine," he said. "How are you, Beth?"

She kept her voice low. "Just grand, Uncle Robert, getting along so well. How long have you been here? And how long are you staying? And when can I see you?"

He laughed. "Mom is talking at me from this end and you're talking at me from that end," he said. "And I can't hear a word either of you is saying. How are you, anyway?"

"I'm grand," she said again.

"Beth," he said, "we're very anxious to see you. Got a lot of messages from home and all."

"I'm pretty busy," she said, "but I'd love to see you. How long are you staying?"

"Tomorrow," he said. "Just came in for a couple of days."

She was figuring quickly, even while her voice was saying, "Oh, no," with heavy dismay. "*Why* didn't you let me know?" she said.

"Mom wants me to tell you everyone sends their love," he said.

"I'm just sick," she said. Guilt drove her into accenting her words violently. "I don't know *how* I'm going to get to see you. Maybe tomorrow morning somehow?"

"Well," he said slowly, "Mom sort of had her heart set on going to Long Island tomorrow to see her sister, and they'll take us right to the train. We thought maybe you'd come along with us tonight."

"Oh, Lord," Elizabeth said, "I've got a dinner appointment I can't break. A client," she said, "you know."

"Isn't that a shame," he said. "We're going to a show;

thought you might come along. Mom," he called, "what's that show we're going to?" He waited for a minute and then said, "She doesn't remember either. The hotel got tickets for us."

"I wish I could," she said, "I just wish I could." She thought in spite of herself of the extra ticket they had been careful to buy, the two old people alone for dinner pretending they were celebrating in a strange city. They saved tonight for me, she thought. "If it had been any other person in the world, I could have broken it, but this is one of our best clients and I just don't dare."

"Of course not." There was so long a silence that Elizabeth said hastily, "How is Dad, anyway?"

"Fine," he said. "Everyone's fine. I guess he sort of wishes you were home now."

"I imagine he's lonesome," Elizabeth said, careful not to let her voice commit her to anything. She was anxious to end the phone call, dissociate herself from the Hunts and her father and the nagging hints that she should go home. I live in New York now, she told herself while the old man's voice continued with a monotonous series of anecdotes about her father and people she had known long ago; I live in New York by myself and I don't have to remember any of these people; Uncle Robert should be glad I talk to him at all.

"I'm so glad you called," she said suddenly, through his voice. "I've got to get back to work."

"Of course," he said apologetically. "Well, Beth, write to all of us, won't you? Mom is telling me to give you her love."

They hang on to me, she thought; they're holding me back, with their letters and their "Yrs. afftly.," and their sending love back and forth. "Good-bye," she said.

"Come back soon for a visit," he went on.

"I will when I can. Good-bye," Elizabeth said. She hung up on his "Good-bye," and then, "Oh, wait, Beth," when something more occurred to him. I couldn't listen any longer without being rude, she thought.

She heard Robbie's voice starting then in the next office, "And I guess you understand about things like answering the phone, and so on."

"I guess so," Daphne said.

*

Elizabeth went back to her letter to Mr. Burton, permanently curled from staying in the typewriter, and she heard Robbie and Daphne Hill talking for a while, about names of clients, and the two-button phone extension at the reception desk, and then she heard both of them go out to the reception desk and try the extension, two children, she thought, playing office. Occasionally she would hear Robbie's heavy laugh, and then, after a minute, Daphne laughing too, slow and surprised. In spite of all her attempts to concentrate on their rates for Mr. Burton she found herself listening, following Robbie and Daphne where they moved around the office. Once, louder than the slight murmur which had been going on between them, she heard Robbie's man-of-the-world voice saying, "Some quiet little restaurant," and then when the voice dropped back to its cautious tone she said to herself, Where they can talk. She waited, not to sound like an intruder, until she heard Daphne settle down solidly at the reception desk and Robbie start back for his own office. Then she said, "Robbie?"

There was a silence and then he came around and opened her office door. "You know I don't like you to yell in the office," he said.

She paused for a minute because she wanted to speak cordially. "We're going to have dinner together tonight?" she asked. They had dinner together four or five times a week, usually in the restaurant where they had had lunch, or in some small place near either Robbie's apartment or Elizabeth's. When she saw the corners of Robbie's mouth turn down and the faint turn of his head toward the outer office she raised her voice slightly. "I got out of seeing these fool people tonight," she said. "There's a lot I want to talk to you about."

"As a matter of fact, Liz," Robbie said, talking very quickly and in a low voice, "I'm afraid I'm going to be stuck for dinner." Not realizing that he was repeating what he had heard her say on the phone a few minutes before, he went on, putting on a look of annoyance, "I've got a dinner appointment I can't break, with a client." When Elizabeth looked surprised, he said, "The minister, I promised him this morning we'd get together again tonight. I haven't had a chance to tell you."

"Of course you can't break it," Elizabeth said easily. She waited, watching Robbie. He was sitting uneasily on the corner of her desk, playing absently with a pencil, wanting to leave and afraid to go too abruptly. What am I doing, Elizabeth thought suddenly, playing hide-and-seek? "Why don't you go to a movie or something?" she said.

Robbie laughed mournfully. "I wish I could," he said.

Elizabeth reached over and took the pencil away from him. "Poor old Robbie," she said. "You're all upset. You ought to get off somewhere and relax."

Robbie frowned anxiously. "Why should I?" he said. "Isn't this my office?"

Elizabeth made her voice tender. "You ought to get out of here for a few hours, Robbie, I'm serious. You won't be able to work this afternoon." She decided to allow herself one small spiteful dig. "Particularly if you have to see that old horror tonight," she said.

Robbie's mouth opened and closed, and then he said, "I can't think when it's such lousy weather. Rain drives me crazy."

"I know it does," Elizabeth said. She stood up. "You get your hat and coat on, and leave your brief case and everything here," she said, pushing him toward the door, "and then come back after sitting in a movie for a couple of hours and you'll feel like a million dollars to go out and out-talk the minister."

"I don't want to go out again in this weather," Robbie said.

"Stop and get a shave," Elizabeth said. She opened the door of her office and saw Daphne Hill staring at her. "Get a haircut," she said, touching the back of his head. "Miss Hill and I will get along fine without you. Won't we, Miss Hill?"

"Sure," Daphne said.

Robbie went uneasily into his office and came out a minute later carrying his wet coat and hat. "I don't know what you want me to go out for," he said.

"I don't know what you want to stay here for," Elizabeth said, escorting him to the outer door. "You're not good for anything when you feel like this." She opened the front door and he walked out. "See you later."

"See you later," Robbie said, starting down the hall.

Elizabeth watched him until he had gone into the elevator and then she closed the door behind her and turned to

Daphne Hill. "Is that letter to Miss Wilson anywhere near written?" she asked.

"I was just doing it," Daphne said.

"Bring it to me when you finish." Elizabeth went into her office and closed the door and sat down at the desk. Frank, she was thinking, it couldn't have been Frank. He would have said "Hello" or something, I haven't changed that much. If it was Frank, what was he doing around here? It won't do any good, she thought, there's no way of finding him anyway.

She took the telephone book from the corner of her desk and looked for Frank's name; it wasn't there, and she turned further until she came to the H's, running her finger down the page till she found Harris, James. Pulling the phone over she dialed the number and waited. When a man answered she said, "Is this Jim Harris?"

"That's right," he said.

"This is Elizabeth Style."

"Hello," he said. "How are you?"

"I've been waiting for you to get in touch with me," she said. "It's been a long time."

"I know it has," he said. "Somehow I never seem to get around—"

"I'll tell you what I called you about," she said. "Do you remember Frank Davis?"

"I remember him," he said. "What's he doing now?"

"That's what I wanted to ask you," she said.

"Oh. Well. . . ."

She waited a minute, and then went on, "One of these days I'm going to take you up on that standing dinner date."

"I hope you do," he said. "I'll call you."

Oh, no, she thought. "It seems like such a long time since we got together. Listen." She made her voice sound like this was a sudden idea, one of those unexpectedly brilliant things, "Why don't we make it tonight?"' He started to say something and she went on, "I've been dying to see you."

"You see, my kid sister's in town," he said.

"Can't she come along?" Elizabeth asked.

"Well," he said, "I guess so."

"Fine," Elizabeth said. "You come on down to my place for

a drink first, and bring the kid along, and we can have a grand talk about old times."

"Suppose I call you back?" he asked.

"I'm leaving the office now," Elizabeth said flatly. "I'll be running around all afternoon. So let's make it around seven?"

"All right," he said.

"I'm so pleased we made it tonight," Elizabeth said. "I'll see you later."

After she had hung up she sat for a minute with her hand on the phone, thinking, good old Harris, he never has a chance if you talk fast; he must get stuck for every dirty job around town. She laughed, pleased, and then stopped abruptly when Daphne knocked on the door; when Elizabeth said, "Come in," Daphne opened the door cautiously and put her head in.

"I finished the letter, Miss Style," she said.

"Bring it here," Elizabeth said, and then added, "please."

Daphne came in and held the letter out at arm's length. "It isn't very good," she said. "But it's my first letter by myself."

Elizabeth glanced at the letter. "It doesn't matter," she said. "Sit down, Daphne."

Daphne sat down gingerly on the edge of the chair. "Sit back," Elizabeth said. "That's the only chair I've got and I don't want you breaking it."

Daphne sat back and opened her eyes wide.

Elizabeth carefully opened her pocketbook and took out a pack of cigarettes and hunted for a match. "Just a minute," Daphne said eagerly, "I've got some." She hurried out to the outer office and came back with a package of matches. "Keep them," she said, "I've got plenty more."

Elizabeth lit her cigarette and put the matches down on the edge of the desk. "Now," she said, and Daphne leaned forward. "Where did you work before you started here?"

"This is my first job," Daphne said. "I just came to New York."

"Where did you come from?"

"Buffalo," Daphne said.

"So you came to New York to make your fortune?" Elizabeth asked. This is where I have dear Daphne, she was thinking, I've already made my fortune.

"I don't know," Daphne said. "My father brought us down here because his brother needed him in the business. We just moved here a couple of months ago."

If I had a family to take care of me, Elizabeth thought, I wouldn't have a job with Robert Shax. "What sort of an education have you had?"

"I went to high school in Buffalo," Daphne said. "I was in business school for a while."

"You want to be a writer?"

"No," Daphne said, "I want to be an agent, like Mr. Shax. And you," she added.

"It's a fine business," Elizabeth said. "You can make a lot of money at it."

"That's what Mr. Shax said. He was very nice about it."

Daphne was getting braver. She was eyeing Elizabeth's cigarette and had settled down comfortably in her chair.

Elizabeth was suddenly very tired; there was no sport in Daphne. "Mr. Shax and I were talking about you at lunch," she said deliberately.

Daphne smiled. When she smiled, and when she was sitting down, without the appearance of that big body resting precariously on small feet, Daphne was an attractive girl. In spite of the small brown eyes, with that incredible mop of hair, Daphne was very attractive. I'm so thin, Elizabeth thought, and she said with pleasure, "I think you'd better rewrite that letter to Miss Wilson, Daphne."

"Sure," Daphne said.

"Telling her," Elizabeth went on, "to come back to work as soon as she can."

"Back here?" Daphne asked, with the smallest beginning of alarm.

"Back here," Elizabeth said. She smiled. "I'm afraid Mr. Shax didn't have courage enough to tell you," she said. "Mr. Shax and I are, besides business partners," she said, "very good friends. Frequently Mr. Shax takes advantage of our friendship and leaves the disagreeable tasks for me to do."

"Mr. Shax didn't tell me anything," Daphne said.

"I didn't think he had," Elizabeth said, "when I saw how you went right ahead as though you were staying here."

Daphne was frightened. She's too stupid to cry, Elizabeth

thought, but she's going to have to have everything explained to her in detail. "Naturally," Elizabeth went on, "I don't like having to do this. Possibly I can make it easier for you by trying to help you get another job."

Daphne nodded.

"This may help you," Elizabeth said, "because Mr. Shax commented on it earlier, and it's the sort of thing men are particular about. Your appearance."

Daphne looked down at the ample front of her dress.

"Probably," Elizabeth said, "you already know this, and I'm very rude to comment on it, but I think you'd make a better impression and if you ever get a job you'd be able to work more comfortably if you wore something to the office instead of a silk dress. It makes you seem, somehow, as though you were just in from Buffalo."

"You want me to wear a suit or something?" Daphne asked. She spoke slowly and without malice.

"Something quieter, anyway," Elizabeth said.

Daphne looked Elizabeth up and down. "A suit like yours?" she asked.

"A suit would be fine," Elizabeth said. "And try to comb your hair down."

Daphne touched the top of her head tenderly.

"Try to be more orderly, in general," Elizabeth said. "You have beautiful hair, Daphne, but it would look more suitable to an office if you were to wear it more severely."

"Like yours?" Daphne asked, looking at the grey in Elizabeth's hair.

"Any way you please," Elizabeth said, "just so it doesn't look like a floor mop." She turned pointedly back to her desk, and after a minute Daphne rose. "Take this back," Elizabeth said, holding out the letter to Miss Wilson, "and rewrite it the way I told you to."

"Yes, Miss Style," Daphne said.

"You can go home as soon as you're through with the letter," Elizabeth said. "Leave it on your desk, along with your name and address and Mr. Shax will send you your day's pay."

"I don't care whether he does or not," Daphne said abruptly.

Elizabeth looked up for a minute and regarded Daphne

steadily. "Do you think you have any right to criticize Mr. Shax's decisions?" she asked.

For a few minutes Elizabeth sat at her desk waiting to see what Daphne would do; after the door had closed quietly behind Daphne and she had walked to her desk there had been a heavy silence; she's sitting at her desk there, Elizabeth thought, thinking it over. Then, finally, there was the small sound of Daphne's pocketbook, the snap of the catch opening, the movement of a hand searching against keys, papers; she's taking her compact out, Elizabeth thought, she's looking to see if what I said about her appearance is true; she's wondering if Robbie said anything, how he said it, whether I made it worse or smoothed it over for her. I should have told her he said she was a fat pig, or the ugliest thing he had ever seen; she might not even have seen through that. What's she doing now? Daphne had said "Damn" very distinctly; Elizabeth sat forward in her chair, not wanting to let any trace of action escape. Then there was the quiet sound of the typewriter; Daphne was typing the letter to Miss Wilson. Elizabeth shook her head slowly and laughed. She lighted a cigarette with one of Daphne's matches, still on the edge of the desk, and looked blankly at the letter to Mr. Burton, still in the typewriter. Sitting with one arm hooked over the back of the chair and the cigarette in her mouth, she typed slowly, with one finger, "The hell with you, Burton," and then tore the page out of the typewriter and threw it in the wastebasket. That's every single bit of work I've done today, she told herself, and it doesn't matter after looking at Daphne's face when I told her. She looked at her desk, the letters waiting to be answered, the criticisms by a professional editor waiting to be written, the complaints to be satisfied, and thought, I'll go on home. I can take a bath and clean the place and get some stuff for Jim and the kid sister; I'll only wait till Daphne leaves.

"Daphne?" she called.

After a hesitation: "Yes, Miss Style?"

"Aren't you through yet?" Elizabeth said; she could afford to let herself speak gently now. "That letter to Miss Wilson should only take a minute."

"Just getting ready to leave," Daphne said.

"Don't forget to leave your name and address."

There was a silence from the other room, and Elizabeth said to her closed door, raising her voice again, "Did you hear me?"

"Mr. Shax knows my name and address," Daphne said. The outer door opened, and Daphne said, "Good-bye."

"Good-bye," Elizabeth said.

She got out of the taxi at her corner, and after paying the man, she had a ten-dollar bill and some change in her pocketbook; this, with twenty dollars more in her apartment, was all the money she had until she could ask Robbie for more. Figuring quickly, she decided to take ten dollars of her money at home to get her through the evening; Jim Harris would have to pay for her dinner; ten dollars, then, for taxis and emergencies; she would ask Robbie for more tomorrow. The money in her pocketbook would go for liquor and cocktail things; she stopped in the liquor store on the corner and bought a bottle of rye, a fifth, so that she would have some to offer Robbie the next time he came down. With her bottle under her arm she went into the delicatessen and bought ginger ale; hesitantly she selected a bag of potato chips and then a box of crackers and a liverwurst spread to put on them.

She was unused to entertaining; she and Robbie spent evenings quietly together, seldom seeing any people except an occasional client and, sometimes, an old friend who invited them out. Because they were not married, Robbie was reluctant to take her anywhere where he might be embarrassed by her presence. They ate their meals in small restaurants, did their rare drinking at home or in a corner bar, saw neighborhood movies. When it was necessary for Elizabeth to invite people to visit her Robbie was not there; they had once given a party in Robbie's larger apartment to celebrate some great occasion, probably a client of some sort, and the party had been so miserable and the guest so uncomfortable that they had never given another and had been invited to only one or two.

Consequently Elizabeth, although she spoke so blithely of "coming down for a drink," was almost completely at a loss when people actually came. As she climbed the stairs to her apartment, her packages braced between her arm and her chin, she was worrying over and over the progress of having a drink, the passing of crackers, the taking of coats.

The appearance of her room shocked her; she had forgotten her hurried departure this morning and the way she had left things around; also, the apartment was created and planned for Elizabeth; that is, the hurried departure every morning of a rather unhappy and desperate young woman with little or no ability to make things gracious, the lonely ugly evenings in one chair with one book and one ashtray, the nights spent dreaming of hot grass and heavy sunlight. There was no possible arrangement of these things that would permit of a casual grouping of three or four people, sitting easily around a room holding glasses, talking lightly. In the early evening, with one lamp on and the shadows in the corners, it looked warm and soft, but you had only to sit down in the one armchair, or touch a hand to the grey wood end table that looked polished, to see that the armchair was hard and cheap, the grey paint chipping.

For a minute Elizabeth stood in the doorway holding her packages, trying clearly to visualize her room as it might be smoothed out by an affectionate hand, but the noise of footsteps above coming down the stairs drove her inside with the door shut and, once in, there was no clear vision; she had her feet on the unpolished floor; there was a dirty fingerprint on the inside doorknob. Robbie's, Elizabeth thought.

She opened the glass French doors that screened the kitchenette and put her packages down; the kitchenette was part of one wall, with a tiny stove built in under a cabinet, a sink installed over a refrigerator, and, over the sink, two shelves on which stood her collection of china: two plates, two cups and saucers, four glasses. She also owned a small saucepan, a frying-pan, and a coffeepot. She had bought all her small house furnishings in a five-and-ten a few years before, planning a tiny complete kitchen, where she could make miniature roasts for herself and Robbie, even bake a small pie or cookies, wearing a yellow apron and making funny mistakes at first. Although she had been a fairly competent cook when she first came to New York, capable of frying chops and potatoes, in the many years since she had been near a real stove she had lost all her knowledge except the fudge-making play in which she indulged herself occasionally. Cooking was, like everything else she had known, a decent honest knowledge meant to make her a capable happy woman ("the way to a man's heart," her mother used to say soberly), which, with the rest of her daily life, had sunk to a miniature useful only as a novelty on rare occasions.

She had to take down the four glasses and wash them; they were dusty from standing so long unused on the open shelf. She checked the refrigerator. For a while she had kept butter and eggs in the refrigerator, and bread and coffee in the cabinet, but they had grown mouldy and rancid before she had been able to make more than one breakfast from them; she was so often late and so seldom inclined to take time over her own breakfast.

It was only four-thirty; she had time to straighten things up and bathe and dress. Her first care was for the easy things in the apartment; she dusted the tables and emptied the ashtray, stopping to put her dustcloth down and pull the bedcovers even, smoothing the spread down to a regular roundness. She was tempted to take up the three small scatter rugs and shake them, and then wash the floor, but a glance at the bathroom discouraged her; they would certainly be in and out of the bathroom, and the floor and tub and even the walls badly needed washing. She used her dust cloth soaked in hot water from the tap, getting the floor clean at last; she put out clean towels from her small stock and started her bath water while she went back to finish the big room.

After all her haphazard work the room looked the same; still grey and inhospitable in the rainy afternoon light. She debated for a minute running downstairs for some bright flowers, and then decided that her money wouldn't last that far; they would only be in the room for a short while anyway, and with something to drink and something to eat any room should look friendly.

When she finished her bath it was nearly six, and dark enough to light the lamp on the end table. She walked barefoot across the room, feeling clean and freshened, conscious of the cologne she had put on, with her hair curling a little from the hot water. With the feeling of cleanness came an excitement; she would be happy tonight, she would be successful, something wonderful would happen to change her whole life.

Following out this feeling she chose a dark red silk dress from the closet; it was youthfully styled and without the grey in her hair it made her look nearer twenty than over thirty. She selected a heavy gold chain to wear with it, and thought, I can wear my good black coat, even if it's raining I'll wear it to feel nice.

While she dressed she thought about her home. Considered honestly, there was no way to do anything with this apartment, no yellow drapes or pictures would help. She needed a new apartment, a pleasant open place with big windows and pale furniture, with the sun coming in all day. To get a new apartment she needed more money, she needed a new job, and Jim Harris would have to help her; tonight would be only the first of many exciting dinners together, building into a lovely friendship that would get her a job and a sunny apartment; while she was planning her new life she forgot Jim Harris, his heavy face, his thin voice; he was a stranger, a gallant dark man with knowing eyes who watched her across a room, he was someone who loved her, he was a quiet troubled man who needed sunlight, a warm garden, green lawns. . . .

A Fine Old Firm

Mrs. Concord and her older daughter, Helen, were sitting in their living-room, sewing and talking and trying to keep warm. Helen had just put down the stockings she had been mending and walked over to the French doors that opened out on to the garden. "I wish spring would hurry up and get here," she was saying when the doorbell rang.

"Good Lord," Mrs. Concord said, "if that's company! The rug's all covered with loose threads." She leaned over in her chair and began to gather up the odds and ends of material around her as Helen went to answer the door. She opened it and stood smiling while the woman outside held out a hand and began to talk rapidly. "You're Helen? I'm Mrs. Friedman," she said. "I hope you won't think I'm just breaking in on you, but I have been so anxious to meet you and your mother."

"How do you do?" Helen said. "Won't you come in?" She opened the door wider and Mrs. Friedman stepped in. She was small and dark and wearing a very smart leopard coat. "Is your mother home?" she asked Helen just as Mrs. Concord came out of the living room.

"I'm Mrs. Concord," Helen's mother said.

"I'm Mrs. Friedman," Mrs. Friedman said. "Bob Friedman's mother."

"Bob Friedman," Mrs. Concord repeated.

Mrs. Friedman smiled apologetically. "I thought surely your boy would have mentioned Bobby," she said.

"Of course he has," Helen said suddenly. "He's the one Charlie's *always* writing about, Mother. It's so hard to make a connection," she said to Mrs. Friedman, "because Charlie seems so far away."

Mrs. Concord was nodding. "Of course," she said. "Won't you come in and sit down?"

Mrs. Friedman followed the Concords into the living-room and sat in one of the chairs not filled with sewing. Mrs. Concord waved her hand at the room. "It makes such a mess," she said, "but every now and then Helen and I just get to work and make things. These are kitchen curtains," she added, picking up the material she had been working on.

"They're very nice," Mrs. Friedman said politely.

"Well, tell us about your son," Mrs. Concord went on. "I'm amazed that I didn't recognize the name right away, but somehow I associate Bob Friedman with Charles and the Army, and it seemed strange to have his mother here in town."

Mrs. Friedman laughed. "That's just about the way I felt," she said. "Bobby wrote me that his friend's mother lived here only a few blocks from us, and said why didn't I drop in and say Hello."

"I'm so glad you did," Mrs. Concord said.

"I guess we know about as much about Bob as you do by now," Helen said. "Charlie's always writing about him."

Mrs. Friedman opened her purse, "I even have a letter from Charlie," she said. "I thought you'd like to take a look at it."

"Charles wrote you?" Mrs. Concord asked.

"Just a note. He likes the pipe tobacco I send Bobby," Mrs. Friedman explained, "and I put a tin of it in for him the last time I sent Bobby a package." She handed the letter to Mrs. Concord and said to Helen, "I imagine I could tell you all about yourselves, Bobby's said so much about all of you."

"Well," Helen said, "I know that Bob got you a Japanese sword for Christmas. *That* must have looked lovely under the tree. Charlie helped him buy it from the boy that had it—did you hear about that, and how they almost had a fight with the boy?"

"*Bobby* almost had a fight," Mrs. Friedman said. "Charlie was smart and stayed out of it."

"No, we heard it that *Charlie* was the one who got in trouble," Helen said. She and Mrs. Friedman laughed.

"Maybe we shouldn't compare notes," Mrs. Friedman said. "They don't seem to stick together on their stories." She turned to Mrs. Concord, who had finished the letter and handed it to Helen. "I was just telling your daughter how many complimentary things I've heard about you."

"We've heard a lot about you, too," Mrs. Concord said.

"Charlie showed Bob a picture of you and your two daughters. The younger one's Nancy, isn't it?"

"Nancy, yes," Mrs. Concord said.

"Well, Charlie certainly thinks a lot of his family," Mrs. Friedman said. "Wasn't he nice to write me?" she asked Helen.

"That tobacco must be good," Helen said. She hesitated for a minute and handed the letter back to Mrs. Friedman, who put it in her purse.

"I'd love to meet Charlie sometime," Mrs. Friedman said. "It seems as though I know him so well."

"I'm sure he'll want to meet you when he comes back," Mrs. Concord said.

"I hope it won't be long now," Mrs. Friedman said. All three were silent for a minute, and then Mrs. Friedman went on with animation, "It seems so strange that we've been living in the same town and it took our boys so far away to introduce us."

"This is a very hard town to get acquainted in," Mrs. Concord said.

"Have you lived here long?" Mrs. Friedman smiled apologetically. "Of course I know of your husband," she added. "My sister's children are in your husband's high school and they speak so highly of him."

"Really?" Mrs. Concord said. "My husband has lived here all his life. I came here from the West when I was married."

"Then it hasn't been hard for you to get settled and make friends," Mrs. Friedman said.

"No, I never had much trouble," Mrs. Concord said. "Of course most of our friends are people who went to school with my husband."

"I'm sorry Bobby never got a chance to study under Mr. Concord," Mrs. Friedman said. "Well. . . ." She rose. "I have certainly enjoyed meeting you at last."

"I'm so glad you came over," Mrs. Concord said. "It's like having a letter from Charles."

"And I know how welcome a letter can be, the way I wait for Bobby's," Mrs. Friedman said. She and Mrs. Concord started for the door and Helen got up and followed them. "My husband is very much interested in Charlie, you know. Ever since he found out that Charlie was studying law when he went into the Army."

"Your husband is a lawyer?" Mrs. Concord asked.

"He's the Friedman of Grunewald, Friedman & White,"

Mrs. Friedman said. "When Charlie is ready to start out for himself, perhaps my husband could find a place for him."

"That's awfully kind of you," Mrs. Concord said. "Charles will be so sorry when I tell him. You see, it's always been sort of arranged that he'd go in with Charles Satterthwaite, my husband's oldest friend. Satterthwaite & Harris."

"I believe Mr. Friedman knows the firm," Mrs. Friedman said.

"A fine old firm," Mrs. Concord said. "Mr. Concord's grandfather used to be a partner."

"Give Bob our best regards when you write him," Helen said.

"I will," Mrs. Friedman said. "I'll tell him all about meeting you. It's been very nice," she said, holding out her hand to Mrs. Concord.

"I've enjoyed it," Mrs. Concord said.

"Tell Charlie I'll send him some more tobacco," Mrs. Friedman said to Helen.

"I certainly will," Helen said.

"Well, good-bye then," Mrs. Friedman said.

"Good-bye," Mrs. Concord said.

The Dummy

IT WAS a respectable, well-padded restaurant with a good chef and a group of entertainers who called themselves a floor show; the people who came there laughed quietly and dined thoroughly, appreciating the principle that the check was always a little more than the restaurant and the entertainment and the company warranted; it was a respectable, likable restaurant, and two women could go into it alone with perfect decorum and have a faintly exciting dinner. When Mrs. Wilkins and Mrs. Straw came noiselessly down the carpeted staircase into the restaurant none of the waiters looked up more than once, quickly, few of the guests turned, and the head-waiter came quietly and bowed agreeably before he turned to the room and the few vacant tables far in the back.

"Do you *mind* being so far away from everything, Alice?" Mrs. Wilkins, who was hostess, said to Mrs. Straw. "We can wait for a table, if you like. Or go somewhere else?"

"Of course not." Mrs. Straw was a rather large woman in a heavy flowered hat, and she looked affectionately at the substantial dinners set on near-by tables. "I don't mind where we sit; this is really lovely."

"Anywhere will do," Mrs. Wilkins said to the headwaiter. "Not *too* far back if you can help it."

The headwaiter listened carefully and nodded, stepping delicately off between the tables to one very far back, near the doorway where the entertainers came in and out, near the table where the lady who owned the restaurant was sitting drinking beer, near the kitchen doors. "Nothing nearer?" Mrs. Wilkins said, frowning at the headwaiter.

The headwaiter shrugged, gesturing at the other vacant tables. One was behind a post, another was set for a large party, a third was somehow behind the small orchestra.

"This will do beautifully, Jen," Mrs. Straw said. "We'll sit right down."

Mrs. Wilkins hesitated still, but Mrs. Straw pulled out the chair on one side of the table and sat down with a sigh, setting her gloves and pocketbook on the extra chair beside her, and reaching to unfasten the collar of her coat.

"I can't say I *like* this," Mrs. Wilkins said, sliding into the chair opposite. "I'm not sure we can see anything."

"Of course we can," Mrs. Straw said. "We can see all that's going on, and of course we'll be able to hear everything. Would you like to sit here instead?" she finished reluctantly.

"Of course not, Alice," Mrs. Wilkins said. She accepted the menu the waiter was offering her and set it down on the table, scanning it rapidly. "The food is quite good here," she said.

"Shrimp casserole," Mrs. Straw said. "Fried chicken." She sighed. "I certainly am hungry."

Mrs. Wilkins ordered quickly, with no debate, and then helped Mrs. Straw choose. When the waiter had gone Mrs. Straw leaned back comfortably and turned in her chair to see all of the restaurant. "This is a lovely place," she said.

"The people seem to be very nice," Mrs. Wilkins said. "The woman who owns it is sitting over there, in back of you. I've always thought she looked very clean and decent."

"She probably makes sure the glasses are washed," Mrs. Straw said. She turned back to the table and picked up her pocketbook, diving deep into it after a pack of cigarettes and a box of wooden safety matches, which she set on the table. "I like to see a place that serves food kept nice and clean," she said.

"They make a lot of money from this place," Mrs. Wilkins said. "Tom and I used to come here years ago before they enlarged it. It was very nice then, but it attracts a better class of people now."

Mrs. Straw regarded the crabmeat cocktail now in front of her with deep satisfaction. "Yes, indeed," she said.

Mrs. Wilkins picked up her fork indifferently, watching Mrs. Straw. "I had a letter from Walter yesterday," she said.

"What'd he have to say?" Mrs. Straw asked.

"He seems fine," Mrs. Wilkins said. "Seems like there's a lot he doesn't tell us."

"Walter's a good boy," Mrs. Straw said. "You worry too much."

The orchestra began to play suddenly and violently and the lights darkened to a spotlight on the stage.

"I hate to eat in the dark," Mrs. Wilkins said.

"We'll get plenty of light back here from those doors," Mrs. Straw said. She put down her fork and turned to watch the orchestra.

"They've made Walter a proctor," Mrs. Wilkins said.

"He'll be first in his class," Mrs. Straw said. "Look at the dress on that girl."

Mrs. Wilkins turned covertly, looking at the girl Mrs. Straw had indicated with her head. The girl had come out of the doorway that led to the entertainers' rooms; she was tall and very dark, with heavy black hair and thick eyebrows, and the dress was electric green satin, cut very low, with a flaming orange flower on one shoulder. "I never did see a dress like that," Mrs. Wilkins said. "She must be going to dance or something."

"She's not a very pretty girl," Mrs. Straw said. "And look at the fellow with her!"

Mrs. Wilkins turned again, and moved her head back quickly to smile at Mrs. Straw. "He looks like a monkey," she said.

"So little," Mrs. Straw said. "I hate those flabby little blond men."

"They used to have such a nice floor show here," Mrs. Wilkins said. "Music, and dancers, and sometimes a nice young man who would sing requests from the audience. Once they had an organist, I think."

"This is our dinner coming along now," Mrs. Straw said. The music had faded down, and the leader of the orchestra, who acted as master of ceremonies, introduced the first number, a pair of ballroom dancers. When the applause started, a tall young man and a tall young woman came out of the entertainers' door and made their way through the tables to the dance floor; on their way they both gave a nod of recognition to the girl in electric green and the man with her.

"Aren't they graceful?" Mrs. Wilkins said when the dance started. "They always look so pretty, that kind of dancers."

"They have to watch their weight," Mrs. Straw said critically. "Look at the figure on the girl in green."

Mrs. Wilkins turned again. "I hope they're not comedians."

"They don't look very funny right now," Mrs. Straw said.

She estimated the butter left on her plate. "Every time I eat a good dinner," she said, "I think of Walter and the food we used to get in school."

"Walter writes that the food is quite good," Mrs. Wilkins said. "He's gained something like three pounds."

Mrs. Straw raised her eyes. "For heaven's sake!"

"What is it?"

"I think he's a ventriloquist," Mrs. Straw said. "I do believe he is."

"They're very popular right now," Mrs. Wilkins said.

"I haven't seen one since I was a kid," Mrs. Straw said. "He's got a little man—what do you call them?—in that box there." She continued to watch, her mouth a little open. "Look at it, Jen."

The girl in green and the man had sat down at a table near the entertainers' door. She was leaning forward, watching the dummy, which was sitting on the man's lap. It was a grotesque wooden copy of the man—where he was blond, the dummy was extravagantly yellow-haired, with sleek wooden curls and sideburns; where the man was small and ugly, the dummy was smaller and uglier, with the same wide mouth, the same staring eyes, the horrible parody of evening clothes, complete to tiny black shoes.

"I wonder how they happen to have a ventriloquist *here*," Mrs. Wilkins said.

The girl in green was leaning across the table to the dummy, straightening his tie, fastening one shoe, smoothing the shoulders of his coat. As she leaned back again the man spoke to her and she shrugged indifferently.

"I can't take my eyes off that green dress," Mrs. Straw said. She started as the waiter came softly up to her with the menu, waiting uneasily for their dessert orders, his eye on the stage where the orchestra was finishing a between-acts number. By the time Mrs. Straw had decided on apple pie with chocolate ice cream the master of ceremonies was introducing the ventriloquist ". . . and Marmaduke, a chip off the old block!"

"I hope it's not very long," Mrs. Wilkins said. "We can't hear from here anyway."

The ventriloquist and the dummy were sitting in the spotlight, both grinning widely, talking fast; the man's weak blond face was close to the dummy's staring grin, their black shoulders against one another. Their conversation was rapid; the audience was laughing affectionately, knowing most of the jokes before the dummy finished speaking, silent with interest for a minute and then laughing again before the words were out.

"I think he's terrible," Mrs. Wilkins said to Mrs. Straw during one roar of laughter. "They're always so coarse."

"Look at our friend in the green dress," Mrs. Straw said. The girl was leaning forward, following every word, tense and excited. For a minute the heavy sullenness of her face had vanished; she was laughing with everyone else, her eyes light. "*She* thinks it's funny," Mrs. Straw said.

Mrs. Wilkins drew her shoulders closer together and shivered. She attacked her dish of ice cream primly.

"I always wonder," she began after a minute, "why places like this, you know, with really good food, never seem to think about desserts. It's always ice cream or something."

"Nothing better than ice cream," Mrs. Straw said.

"You'd think they'd have pastries, or some nice pudding," Mrs. Wilkins said. "They never seem to give any *thought* to it."

"I've never seen anything like that fig-and-date pudding you make, Jen," Mrs. Straw said.

"Walter always used to say that was the best—" Mrs. Wilkins began, and was cut short by a blare from the orchestra. The ventriloquist and the dummy were bowing, the man bowing deeply from the waist and the dummy bobbing his head courteously; the orchestra began quickly with a dance tune, and the man and the dummy turned and trotted off the stage.

"Thank heavens," Mrs. Wilkins said.

"I haven't seen one of those for years," Mrs. Straw said.

The girl in green had risen, waiting for the man and the dummy to come back to the table. The man sat down heavily, the dummy still on his knee, and the girl sat down again, on the edge of her chair, asking him something urgently.

"What do *you* think?" he said loudly, without looking at her. He waved to a waiter, who hesitated, looking in back of him at the table where the woman who owned the restaurant was sitting alone. After a minute the waiter approached the man, and the girl said, her voice clear over the soft waltz the orchestra was playing, "Don't drink anything more, Joey, we'll go somewhere and eat."

The man spoke to the waiter, ignoring the girl's hand on his arm. He turned to the dummy, speaking softly, and the dummy's face and broad grin looked at the girl and then back at the man. The girl sat back, looking out of the corners of her eyes at the owner of the restaurant.

"I'd hate to be married to a man like that," Mrs. Straw said.

"He's certainly not a very good comedian," Mrs. Wilkins said.

The girl was leaning forward again, arguing, and the man was talking to the dummy, making the dummy nod in agreement. When the girl put a hand on his shoulder the man shrugged it away without turning around. The girl's voice rose again. "Listen, Joey," she was saying.

"In a minute," the man said. "I just want to have this one drink."

"Yeah, leave him alone, can't you?" the dummy said.

"You don't need another drink now, Joey," the girl said. "You can get another drink later."

The man said, "Look, honey, I've got a drink ordered. I can't leave before it comes."

"Why don't you make old deadhead shut up?" the dummy said to the man, "always making a fuss when she sees someone having a good time. Why don't you tell her to shut up?"

"You shouldn't talk like that," the man said to the dummy. "It's not nice."

"*I* can talk if I want to," the dummy said. "She can't make *me* stop."

"Joey," the girl said, "I want to talk to you. Listen, let's go somewhere and talk."

"Shut up for a minute," the dummy said to the girl. "For God's sake will you shut up for a minute?"

People at nearby tables were beginning to turn, interested in the dummy's loud voice, and laughing already, hearing him talk. "*Please* be quiet," the girl said.

"Yeah, don't make such a fuss," the man said to the dummy. "I'm just going to have this one drink. She doesn't mind."

"He's not going to bring you any drink," the girl said impatiently. "They told him not to. They wouldn't give you a drink here, the way you're acting."

"I'm acting fine," the man said.

"*I'm* the one making the fuss," the dummy said. "It's time someone told you, sweetheart, you're going to get into trouble acting like a wet blanket all the time. A man won't stand for it forever."

"Be quiet," the girl said, looking around her anxiously. "Everyone can hear you."

"Let them hear me," the dummy said. He turned his grinning head around at his audience and raised his voice. "Just because a man wants to have a good time she has to freeze up like an icebag."

"Now, Marmaduke," the man said to the dummy, "you'd better talk nicer to your old mother."

"Why, I wouldn't tell that old bag the right time," the dummy said. "If she doesn't like it here, let her get back on the streets."

Mrs. Wilkins' mouth opened, and shut again; she put her napkin down on the table and stood up. While Mrs. Straw watched blankly she walked over to the other table and slapped the dummy sharply across the face.

By the time she had turned and come back to her own table Mrs. Straw had her coat on and was standing.

"We'll pay on the way out," Mrs. Wilkins said curtly.

She picked up her coat and the two of them walked with dignity to the door. For a moment the man and girl sat looking at the dummy slumped over sideways, its head awry. Then the girl reached over and straightened the wooden head.

Seven Types of Ambiguity

THE basement room of the bookstore seemed to be enormous; it stretched in long rows of books off into dimness at either end, with books lined in tall bookcases along the walls, and books standing in piles on the floor. At the foot of the spiral staircase winding down from the neat small store upstairs, Mr. Harris, owner and sales-clerk of the bookstore, had a small desk, cluttered with catalogues, lighted by one dirty overhead lamp. The same lamp served to light the shelves which crowded heavily around Mr. Harris' desk; farther away, along the lines of book tables, there were other dirty overhead lamps, to be lighted by pulling a string and turned off by the customer when he was ready to grope his way back to Mr. Harris' desk, pay for his purchases and have them wrapped. Mr. Harris, who knew the position of any author or any title in all the heavy shelves, had one customer at the moment, a boy of about eighteen, who was standing far down the long room directly under one of the lamps, leafing through a book he had selected from the shelves. It was cold in the big basement room; both Mr. Harris and the boy had their coats on. Occasionally Mr. Harris got up from his desk to put a meagre shovelful of coal on a small iron stove which stood in the curve of the staircase. Except when Mr. Harris got up, or the boy turned to put a book back into the shelves and take out another, the room was quiet, the books standing silent in the dim light.

Then the silence was broken by the sound of the door opening in the little upstairs bookshop where Mr. Harris kept his best-sellers and art books on display. There was the sound of voices, while both Mr. Harris and the boy listened, and then the girl who took care of the upstairs bookshop said, "Right on down the stairs. Mr. Harris will help you."

Mr. Harris got up and walked around to the foot of the stairs, turning on another of the overhead lamps so that his new customer would be able to see his way down. The boy put his book back in the shelves and stood with his hand on the back of it, still listening.

When Mr. Harris saw that it was a woman coming down the

stairs he stood back politely and said, "Watch the bottom step. There's one more than people think." The woman stepped carefully down and stood looking around. While she stood there a man came carefully around the turn in the staircase, ducking his head so his hat would clear the low ceiling. "Watch the bottom step," the woman said in a soft clear voice. The man came down beside her and raised his head to look around as she had.

"Quite a lot of books you have here," he said.

Mr. Harris smiled his professional smile. "Can I help you?"

The woman looked at the man, and he hesitated a minute and then said, "We want to get some books. Quite a few of them." He waved his hand inclusively. "Sets of books."

"Well, if it's books you want," Mr. Harris said, and smiled again. "Maybe the lady would like to come over and sit down?" He led the way around to his desk, the woman following him and the man walking uneasily between the tables of books, his hands close to his sides as though he were afraid of breaking something. Mr. Harris gave the lady his desk chair and then sat down on the edge of his desk, shoving aside a pile of catalogues.

"This is a very interesting place," the lady said, in the same soft voice she had used when she spoke before. She was middle-aged and nicely dressed; all her clothes were fairly new, but quiet and well planned for her age and air of shyness. The man was big and hearty-looking, his face reddened by the cold air and his big hands holding a pair of wool gloves uneasily.

"We'd like to buy some of your books," the man said. "Some good books."

"Anything in particular?" Mr. Harris asked.

The man laughed loudly, but with embarrassment. "Tell the truth," he said, "I sound sort of foolish, now. But I don't know much about these things, like books." In the large quiet store his voice seemed to echo, after his wife's soft voice and Mr. Harris'. "We were sort of hoping you'd be able to tell us," he said. "None of this trash they turn out nowadays." He cleared his throat. "Something like Dickens," he said.

"Dickens," Mr. Harris said.

"I used to read Dickens when I was a kid," the man said. "Books like that, now, good books." He looked up as the boy who had been standing off among the books came over to them. "I'd like to read Dickens again," the big man said.

"Mr. Harris," the boy asked quietly.

Mr. Harris looked up. "Yes, Mr. Clark?" he said.

The boy came closer to the desk, as though unwilling to interrupt Mr. Harris with his customers. "I'd like to take another look at the Empson," he said.

Mr. Harris turned to the glass-doored bookcase immediately behind his desk and selected a book. "Here it is," he said, "you'll have it read through before you buy it at this rate." He smiled at the big man and his wife. "Some day he's going to come in and buy that book," he said, "and I'm going to go out of business from shock."

The boy turned away, holding the book, and the big man leaned forward to Mr. Harris. "I figure I'd like two good sets, big, like Dickens," he said, "and then a couple of smaller sets."

"And a copy of *Jane Eyre*," his wife said, in her soft voice. "I used to love that book," she said to Mr. Harris.

"I can let you have a very nice set of the Brontës," Mr. Harris said. "Beautiful binding."

"I want them to look nice," the man said, "but solid, for reading. I'm going to read through all of Dickens again."

The boy came back to the desk, holding the book out to Mr. Harris. "It still looks good," he said.

"It's right here when you want it," Mr. Harris said, turning back to the bookcase with the book. "It's pretty scarce, that book."

"I guess it'll be here a while longer," the boy said.

"What's the name of this book?" the big man asked curiously.

"*Seven Types of Ambiguity*," the boy said. "It's quite a good book."

"There's a fine name for a book," the big man said to Mr. Harris. "Pretty smart young fellow, reading books with names like that."

"It's a good book," the boy repeated.

"I'm trying to buy some books myself," the big man said to the boy. "I want to catch up on a few I've missed. Dickens, I've always liked his books."

"Meredith is good," the boy said. "You ever try reading Meredith?"

"Meredith," the big man said. "Let's see a few of your books," he said to Mr. Harris. "I'd sort of like to pick out a few I want."

"Can I take the gentleman down there?" the boy said to Mr. Harris. "I've got to go back anyway to get my hat."

"I'll go with the young man and look at the books, Mother," the big man said to his wife. "You stay here and keep warm."

"Fine," Mr. Harris said. "He knows where the books are as well as I do," he said to the big man.

The boy started off down the aisle between the book tables, and the big man followed, still walking carefully, trying not to touch anything. They went down past the lamp still burning where the boy had left his hat and gloves, and the boy turned on another lamp further down. "Mr. Harris keeps most of his sets around here," the boy said. "Let's see what we can find." He squatted down in front of the bookcases, touching the backs of the rows of books lightly with his fingers. "How do you feel about the prices?" he asked.

"I'm willing to pay a reasonable amount for the books I have in mind," the big man said. He touched the book in front of him experimentally, with one finger. "A hundred and fifty, two hundred dollars altogether."

The boy looked up at him and laughed. "That ought to get you some nice books," he said.

"Never saw so many books in my life," the big man said. "I never thought I'd see the day when I'd just walk into a bookstore and buy up all the books I always wanted to read."

"It's a good feeling."

"I never got a chance to read much," the man said. "Went right into the machine-shop where my father worked when I was much younger than you, and worked ever since. Now all of a sudden I find I have a little more money than I used to, and Mother and I decided we'd like to get ourselves a few things we always wanted."

"Your wife was interested in the Brontës," the boy said. "Here's a very good set."

The man leaned down to look at the books the boy pointed out. "I don't know much about these things," he said. "They look nice, all alike. What's the next set?"

"Carlyle," the boy said. "You can skip him. He's not quite what you're looking for. Meredith is good. And Thackeray. I think you'd want Thackeray; he's a great writer."

The man took one of the books the boy handed him and opened it carefully, using only two fingers from each of his big hands. "This looks fine," he said.

"I'll write them down," the boy said. He took a pencil and a pocket memorandum from his coat pocket. "Brontës," he said, "Dickens, Meredith, Thackeray." He ran his hand along each of the sets as he read them off.

The big man narrowed his eyes. "I ought to take one more," he said. "These won't quite fill up the bookcase I got for them."

"Jane Austen," the boy said. "Your wife would be pleased with that."

"You read all these books?" the man asked.

"Most of them," the boy said.

The man was quiet for a minute and then he went on, "I never got much of a chance to read anything, going to work so early. I've got a lot to catch up on."

"You're going to have a fine time," the boy said.

"That book you had a while back," the man said. "What was that book?"

"It's aesthetics," the boy said. "About literature. It's very scarce. I've been trying to buy it for quite a while and haven't had the money."

"You go to college?" the man asked.

"Yes."

"Here's one I ought to read again," the man said. "Mark Twain. I read a couple of his books when I was a kid. But I guess I have enough to start on." He stood up.

The boy rose too, smiling. "You're going to have to do a lot of reading."

"I like to read," the man said. "I really like to read."

He started back down the aisles, going straight for Mr. Harris' desk. The boy turned off the lamps and followed, stopping to get his hat and gloves. When the big man reached Mr.

Harris' desk he said to his wife, "That's sure a smart kid. He knows those books right and left."

"Did you pick out what you want?" his wife asked.

"The kid has a fine list for me." He turned to Mr. Harris and went on, "It's quite an experience seeing a kid like that liking books the way he does. When I was his age I was working for four or five years."

The boy came up with the slip of paper in his hand. "These ought to hold him for a while," he said to Mr. Harris.

Mr. Harris glanced at the list and nodded. "That Thackeray's a nice set of books," he said.

The boy had put his hat on and was standing at the foot of the stairs. "Hope you enjoy them," he said. "I'll be back for another look at that Empson, Mr. Harris."

"I'll try to keep it around for you," Mr. Harris said. "I can't promise to hold it, you know."

"I'll just count on it's being here," the boy said.

"Thanks, son," the big man called out as the boy started up the stairs. "Appreciate your helping me."

"That's all right," the boy said.

"He's sure a smart kid," the man said to Mr. Harris. "He's got a great chance, with an education like that."

"He's a nice young fellow," Mr. Harris said, "and he sure wants that book."

"You think he'll ever buy it?" the big man asked.

"I doubt it," Mr. Harris said. "If you'll just write down your name and address, I'll add these prices."

Mr. Harris began to note down the prices of the books, copying from the boy's neat list. After the big man had written his name and address, he stood for a minute drumming his fingers on the desk, and then he said, "Can I have another look at that book?"

"The Empson?" Mr. Harris said, looking up.

"The one the boy was so interested in." Mr. Harris reached around to the bookcase in back of him and took out the book. The big man held it delicately, as he had held the others, and he frowned as he turned the pages. Then he put the book down on Mr. Harris' desk.

"If he isn't going to buy it, will it be all right if I put this in with the rest?" he asked.

Mr. Harris looked up from his figures for a minute, and then he made the entry on his list. He added quickly, wrote down the total, and then pushed the paper across the desk to the big man. While the man checked over the figures Mr. Harris turned to the woman and said, "Your husband has bought a lot of very pleasant reading."

"I'm glad to hear it," she said. "We've been looking forward to it for a long time."

The big man counted out the money carefully, handing the bills to Mr. Harris. Mr. Harris put the money in the top drawer of his desk and said, "We can have these delivered to you by the end of the week, if that will be all right?"

"Fine," the big man said. "Ready, Mother?"

The woman rose, and the big man stood back to let her go ahead of him. Mr. Harris followed, stopping near the stairs to say to the woman, "Watch the bottom step."

They started up the stairs and Mr. Harris stood watching them until they got to the turn. Then he switched off the dirty overhead lamp and went back to his desk.

Come Dance with Me in Ireland

YOUNG Mrs. Archer was sitting on the bed with Kathy Valentine and Mrs. Corn, playing with the baby and gossiping, when the doorbell rang. Mrs. Archer, saying, "Oh, dear!," went to push the buzzer that released the outside door of the apartment building. "We *had* to live on the ground floor," she called to Kathy and Mrs. Corn. "Everybody rings our bell for everything."

When the inner doorbell rang she opened the door of the apartment and saw an old man standing in the outer hall. He was wearing a long, shabby black overcoat and had a square white beard. He held out a handful of shoelaces.

"Oh," Mrs. Archer said. "Oh, I'm terribly sorry, but—"

"Madam," the old man said, "if you would be so kind. A nickel apiece."

Mrs. Archer shook her head and backed away. "I'm afraid not," she said.

"Thank you anyway, Madam," he said, "for speaking courteously. The first person on this block who has been decently polite to a poor old man."

Mrs. Archer turned the doorknob back and forth nervously. "I'm awfully sorry," she said. Then, as he turned to go, she said, "Wait a minute," and hurried into the bedroom. "Old man selling shoelaces," she whispered. She pulled open the top dresser drawer, took out her pocketbook, and fumbled in the change purse. "Quarter," she said. "Think it's all right?"

"Sure," Kathy said. "Probably more than he's gotten all day." She was Mrs. Archer's age, and unmarried. Mrs. Corn was a stout woman in her middle fifties. They both lived in the building and spent a good deal of time at Mrs. Archer's, on account of the baby.

Mrs. Archer returned to the front door. "Here," she said, holding out the quarter. "I think it's a shame everyone was so rude."

The old man started to offer her some shoelaces, but his hand shook and the shoelaces dropped to the floor. He leaned heavily against the wall. Mrs. Archer watched, horrified,

"Good Lord," she said, and put out her hand. As her fingers touched the dirty old overcoat she hesitated and then, tightening her lips, she put her arm firmly through his and tried to help him through the doorway. "Girls," she called, "come help me, quick!"

Kathy came running out of the bedroom, saying, "Did you call, Jean?" and then stopped dead, staring.

"What'll I do?" Mrs. Archer said, standing with her arm through the old man's. His eyes were closed and he seemed barely able, with her help, to stand on his feet. "For heaven's sake, grab him on the other side."

"Get him to a chair or something," Kathy said. The hall was too narrow for all three of them to go down side by side, so Kathy took the old man's other arm and half-led Mrs. Archer and him into the living-room. "Not in the good chair," Mrs. Archer exclaimed. "In the old leather one." They dropped the old man into the leather chair and stood back. "What on earth do we do now?" Mrs. Archer said.

"Do you have any whiskey?" Kathy asked.

Mrs. Archer shook her head. "A little wine," she said doubtfully.

Mrs. Corn came into the living-room, holding the baby. "Gracious!" she said. "He's drunk!"

"Nonsense," Kathy said. "I wouldn't have let Jean bring him in if he were."

"Watch out for the baby, Blanche," Mrs. Archer said.

"Naturally," Mrs. Corn said. "We're going back into the bedroom, honey," she said to the baby, "and then we're going to get into our lovely crib and go beddy-bye."

The old man stirred and opened his eyes. He tried to get up.

"Now you stay right where you are," Kathy ordered, "and Mrs. Archer here is going to bring you a little bit of wine. You'd like that, wouldn't you?"

The old man raised his eyes to Kathy. "Thank you," he said.

Mrs. Archer went into the kitchen. After a moment's thought she took the glass from over the sink, rinsed it out, and poured some sherry into it. She took the glass of sherry back into the living-room and handed it to Kathy.

"Shall I hold it for you or can you drink by yourself?" Kathy asked the old man.

"You are much too kind," he said, and reached for the glass. Kathy steadied it for him as he sipped from it, and then he pushed it away.

"That's enough, thank you," he said. "Enough to revive me." He tried to rise. "Thank you," he said to Mrs. Archer, "and thank *you*," to Kathy. "I had better be going along."

"Not until you're quite firm on your feet," Kathy said. "Can't afford to take chances, you know."

The old man smiled. "*I* can afford to take chances," he said.

Mrs. Corn came back into the living-room. "Baby's in his crib," she said, "and just about asleep already. Does *he* feel better now? I'll bet he was just drunk or hungry or something."

"Of course he was," Kathy said, fired by the idea. "He was hungry. That's what was wrong all the time, Jean. How silly we were. Poor old gentleman!" she said to the old man. "Mrs. Archer is certainly not going to let you leave here without a full meal inside of you."

Mrs. Archer looked doubtful. "I have some eggs," she said.

"Fine!" Kathy said. "Just the thing. They're easily digested," she said to the old man, "and especially good if you haven't eaten for"—she hesitated—"for a while."

"Black coffee," Mrs. Corn said, "if you ask me. Look at his hands shake."

"Nervous exhaustion," Kathy said firmly. "A nice hot cup of bouillon is all he needs to be good as ever, and he has to drink it very slowly until his stomach gets used to food again. The stomach," she told Mrs. Archer and Mrs. Corn, "shrinks when it remains empty for any great period of time."

"I would rather not trouble you," the old man said to Mrs. Archer.

"Nonsense," Kathy said. "We've got to see that you get a good hot meal to go on with." She took Mrs. Archer's arm and began to walk her out to the kitchen. "Just some eggs," she said. "Fry four or five. I'll get you half a dozen later. I don't suppose you have any bacon. I'll tell you, fry up a few potatoes too. He won't care if they're half-raw. These people eat things like heaps of fried potatoes and eggs and—"

"There's some canned figs left over from lunch," Mrs. Archer said. "I was wondering what to do with them."

"I've got to run back and keep an eye on him," Kathy said.

"He might faint again or something. You just fry up those eggs and potatoes. I'll send Blanche out if she'll come."

Mrs. Archer measured out enough coffee for two cups and set the pot on the stove. Then she took out her frying pan. "Kathy," she said, "I'm just a little worried. If he really is drunk, I mean, and if Jim should hear about it, with the baby here and everything. . . ."

"Why, Jean!" Kathy said. "You should live in the country for a while, I guess. Women always give out meals to starving men. And you don't need to *tell* Jim. Blanche and I certainly won't say anything."

"Well," said Mrs. Archer, "you're sure he isn't drunk?"

"I know a starving man when I see one," Kathy said. "When an old man like that can't stand up and his hands shake and he looks so funny, that means he's starving to death. Literally starving."

"Oh, my!" said Mrs. Archer. She hurried to the cupboard under the sink and took out two potatoes. "Two enough, do you think? I guess we're really doing a good deed."

Kathy giggled. "Just a bunch of Girl Scouts," she said. She started out of the kitchen, and then she stopped and turned around. "You have any pie? They always eat pie."

"It was for dinner, though," Mrs. Archer said.

"Oh, give it to him," Kathy said. "We can run out and get some more after he goes."

While the potatoes were frying, Mrs. Archer put a plate, a cup and saucer, and a knife and fork and spoon on the dinette table. Then, as an afterthought, she picked up the dishes and, taking a paper bag out of a cupboard, tore it in half and spread it smoothly on the table and put the dishes back. She got a glass and filled it with water from the bottle in the refrigerator, cut three slices of bread and put them on a plate, and then cut a small square of butter and put it on the plate with the bread. Then she got a paper napkin from the box in the cupboard and put it beside the plate, took it up after a minute to fold it into a triangular shape, and put it back. Finally she put the pepper and salt shakers on the table and got out a box of eggs. She went to the door and called, "Kathy! Ask him how does he want his eggs fried?"

There was a murmur of conversation in the living-room and Kathy called back, "Sunny side up!"

Mrs. Archer took out four eggs and then another and broke them one by one into the frying-pan. When they were done she called out, "All right, girls! Bring him in!"

Mrs. Corn came into the kitchen, inspected the plate of potatoes and eggs, and looked at Mrs. Archer without speaking. Then Kathy came, leading the old man by the arm. She escorted him to the table and sat him down in a chair. "There," she said. "Now, Mrs. Archer's fixed you a lovely hot meal."

The old man looked at Mrs. Archer. "I'm very grateful," he said.

"Isn't that nice!" Kathy said. She nodded approvingly at Mrs. Archer. The old man regarded the plate of eggs and potatoes. "Now pitch right in," Kathy said. "Sit down, girls. I'll get a chair from the bedroom."

The old man picked up the salt and shook it gently over the eggs. "This looks delicious," he said finally.

"You just go right ahead and eat," Kathy said, reappearing with a chair. "We want to see you get filled up. Pour him some coffee, Jean."

Mrs. Archer went to the stove and took up the coffeepot.

"Please don't bother," he said.

"That's all right," Mrs. Archer said, filling the old man's cup. She sat down at the table. The old man picked up the fork and then put it down again to take up the paper napkin and spread it carefully over his knees.

"What's your name?" Kathy asked.

"O'Flaherty, Madam. John O'Flaherty."

"Well, John," Kathy said, "I am Miss Valentine and this lady is Mrs. Archer and the other one is Mrs. Corn."

"How do you do?" the old man said.

"I gather you're from the old country," Kathy said.

"I beg your pardon?"

"Irish, aren't you?" Kathy said.

"I am, Madam." The old man plunged the fork into one of the eggs and watched the yolk run out onto the plate. "I knew Yeats," he said suddenly.

"Really?" Kathy said, leaning forward. "Let me see—he was the writer, wasn't he?"

" 'Come out of charity, come dance with me in Ireland,' " the old man said. He rose and, holding on to the chair back, bowed solemnly to Mrs. Archer, "Thank you again, Madam, for your generosity." He turned and started for the front door. The three women got up and followed him.

"But you didn't finish," Mrs. Corn said.

"The stomach," the old man said, "as this lady has pointed out, shrinks. Yes, indeed," he went on reminiscently, "I knew Yeats."

At the front door he turned and said to Mrs. Archer, "Your kindness should not go unrewarded." He gestured to the shoelaces lying on the floor. "These," he said, "are for you. For your kindness. Divide them with the other ladies."

"But I wouldn't dream—" Mrs. Archer began.

"I insist," the old man said, opening the door. "A small return, but all that I have to offer. Pick them up yourself," he added abruptly. Then he turned and thumbed his nose at Mrs. Corn. "I hate old women," he said.

"Well!" said Mrs. Corn faintly.

"I may have imbibed somewhat freely," the old man said to Mrs. Archer, "but I never served bad sherry to my guests. We are of two different worlds, Madam."

"Didn't I tell you?" Mrs. Corn was saying. "Haven't I kept telling you all along?"

Mrs. Archer, her eyes on Kathy, made a tentative motion of pushing the old man through the door, but he forestalled her.

" 'Come dance with me in Ireland,' " he said. Supporting himself against the wall, he reached the outer door and opened it. "And time runs on," he said.

IV

We are never liable to be so betray'd and abused, till, by our vile *Dispositions* and *Tendencies*, we have forfeited the *tutelary* Care, and *Oversight* of the better Spirits; who, tho' generally they are our Guard and Defence against the Malice and Violence of evil *Angels*, yet it may well enough be thought, that some Time they may take their Leave of such as are swallow'd up by *Malice*, *Envy*, and *Desire* of *Revenge*, Qualities most contrary to their *Life* and *Nature*; leave them exposed to the *Invasion* and *Solicitations* of those *wicked Spirits*, to whom such hateful *Attributes* make them very suitable.

Joseph Glanvil: *Sadducismus Triumphatus*

Of Course

Mrs. Tylor, in the middle of a busy morning, was far too polite to go out on the front porch and stare, but she saw no reason for avoiding the windows; when her vacuuming or her dishwashing, or even the upstairs bedmaking, took her near a window on the south side of the house she would lift the curtain slightly, or edge to one side and stir the shade. All she could see, actually, was the moving van in front of the house, and various small activities going on between the movers; the furniture, what she could see of it, looked fine.

Mrs. Tylor finished the beds and came downstairs to start lunch, and in the short space of time it took her to get from the front bedroom window to the kitchen window a taxi had stopped in front of the house next door and a small boy was dancing up and down on the sidewalk. Mrs. Taylor estimated him; about four, probably, unless he was small for his age; about right for her youngest girl. She turned her attention to the woman who was getting out of the taxi, and was further reassured. A nice-looking tan suit, a little worn and perhaps a *little* too light in color for moving day, but nicely cut, and Mrs. Tylor nodded appreciatively over the carrots she was scraping. *Nice* people, obviously.

Carol, Mrs. Tylor's youngest, was leaning on the fence in front of the Tylor house, watching the little boy next door. When the little boy stopped dancing up and down Carol said, "Hi." The little boy looked up, took a step backward, and said, "Hi." His mother looked at Carol, at the Tylor house, and down at her son. Then she said, "Hello there" to Carol. Mrs. Tylor smiled in the kitchen. Then, on a sudden impulse she dried her hands on a paper towel, took off her apron, and went to the front door. "Carol," she called lightly, "Carol, dear." Carol turned around, still leaning on the fence. "What?" she said uncoöperatively.

"Oh, hello," Mrs. Tylor said to the lady still standing on the sidewalk next to the little boy. "I heard Carol talking to someone. . . ."

"The children were making friends," the lady said shyly.

Mrs. Tylor came down the steps to stand near Carol at the fence. "Are you our new neighbor?"

"If we ever get moved in," the lady said. She laughed. "Moving day," she said expressively.

"I know. Our name's Tylor," Mrs. Tylor said. "This is Carol."

"*Our* name is Harris," the lady said. "This is James Junior."

"Say hello to James," Mrs. Tylor said.

"And *you* say hello to Carol," Mrs. Harris said.

Carol shut her mouth obstinately and the little boy edged behind his mother. Both ladies laughed. "Children!" one of them said, and the other said, "Isn't it the way!"

Then Mrs. Tylor said, gesturing at the moving van and the two men moving in and out with chairs and tables and beds and lamps, "Heavens, isn't it terrible?"

Mrs. Harris sighed. "I think I'll just go crazy."

"Is there anything we can do to help?" Mrs. Tylor asked. She smiled down at James. "Perhaps James would like to spend the afternoon with us?"

"That *would* be a relief," Mrs. Harris agreed. She twisted around to look at James behind her. "Would you like to play with Carol this afternoon, honey?" James shook his head mutely and Mrs. Tylor said to him brightly, "Carol's two older sisters might, just *might* take her to the movies, James. You'd like *that* wouldn't you?"

"I'm afraid not," Mrs. Harris said flatly. "James does not go to movies."

"Oh, well, of course," Mrs. Tylor said, "lots of mothers *don't*, of course, but when a child has two older. . . ."

"It isn't that," Mrs. Harris said. "We do not go to movies, any of us."

Mrs. Tylor quickly registered the "any" as meaning there was probably a Mr. Harris somewhere around, and then her mind snapped back and she said blankly, "Don't go to movies?"

"Mr. Harris," Mrs. Harris said carefully, "feels that movies are intellectually retarding. We do not go to movies."

"Naturally," Mrs. Tylor said. "Well, I'm sure Carol wouldn't mind staying home this afternoon. She'd love to play with James. Mr. Harris," she added cautiously, "wouldn't object to a sandbox?"

"I want to go to the movies," Carol said.

Mrs. Tylor spoke quickly. "Why don't you and James come over and rest at our house for a while? You've probably been running around all morning."

Mrs. Harris hesitated, watching the movers. "Thank you," she said finally. With James following along behind her, she came through the Tylors' gate, and Mrs. Tylor said, "If we sit in the garden out back we can still keep an eye on your movers." She gave Carol a small push. "Show James the sand-box, dear," she said firmly.

Carol took James sullenly by the hand and led him over to the sandbox. "See?" she said, and went back to kick the fence pickets deliberately. Mrs. Tylor sat Mrs. Harris in one of the garden chairs and went over and found a shovel for James to dig with.

"It certainly feels good to sit down," Mrs. Harris said. She sighed. "Sometimes I feel that moving is the most terrible thing I have to do."

"You were lucky to get that house," Mrs. Tylor said, and Mrs. Harris nodded. "We'll be glad to get nice neighbors," Mrs. Tylor went on. "There's something so nice about con-genial people right next door. I'll be running over to borrow cups of sugar," she finished roguishly.

"I certainly hope you will," Mrs. Harris said. "We had such disagreeable people next door to us in our old house. Small things, you know, and they do irritate you so." Mrs. Tylor sighed sympathetically. "The radio, for instance," Mrs. Harris continued, "all day long, and so *loud*."

Mrs. Tylor caught her breath for a minute. "You must be sure and tell us if ours is ever too loud."

"Mr. Harris cannot bear the radio," Mrs. Harris said. "We do not own one, of course."

"Of course," Mrs. Tylor said. "No radio."

Mrs. Harris looked at her and laughed uncomfortably. "You'll be thinking my husband is crazy."

"Of course not," Mrs. Tylor said. "After all, lots of people don't like radios; my oldest nephew, now, he's just the *other* way—"

"Well," Mrs. Harris said, "newspapers, too."

Mrs. Tylor recognized finally the faint nervous feeling that

was tagging her; it was the way she felt when she was irrevoca-
bly connected with something dangerously out of control: her
car, for instance, on an icy street, or the time on Virginia's
roller skates. . . . Mrs. Harris was staring absent-mindedly at
the movers going in and out, and she was saying, "It isn't as
though we hadn't ever *seen* a newspaper, not like the movies at
all; Mr. Harris just feels that the newspapers are a mass degra-
dation of taste. You really never *need* to read a newspaper, you
know," she said, looking around anxiously at Mrs. Tylor.

"I never read anything but the—"

"And we took *The New Republic* for a *number* of years," Mrs.
Harris said. "When we were first married, of course. Before
James was born."

"What is your husband's business?" Mrs. Tylor asked
timidly.

Mrs. Harris lifted her head proudly. "He's a scholar," she
said. "He writes monographs."

Mrs. Tylor opened her mouth to speak, but Mrs. Harris
leaned over and put her hand out and said, "It's *terribly* hard
for people to understand the desire for a really peaceful life."

"What," Mrs. Tylor said, "what does your husband do for
relaxation?"

"He reads plays," Mrs. Harris said. She looked doubtfully
over at James. "Pre-Elizabethan, of course."

"Of course," Mrs. Tylor said, and looked nervously at
James, who was shoveling sand into a pail.

"People are really very unkind," Mrs. Harris said. "Those
people I was telling you about, next door. It wasn't only the
radio, you see. Three times they *deliberately* left their *New
York Times* on our doorstep. Once James nearly got it."

"Good Lord," Mrs. Tylor said. She stood up. "Carol," she
called emphatically, "don't go away. It's nearly time for lunch,
dear."

"Well," Mrs. Harris said. "I must go and see if the movers
have done anything right."

Feeling as though she had been rude, Mrs. Tylor said,
"Where is Mr. Harris now?"

"At his mother's," Mrs. Harris said. "He always stays there
when we move."

"Of course," Mrs. Tylor said, feeling as though she had been saying nothing else all morning.

"They don't turn the radio on while he's there," Mrs. Harris explained.

"Of course," Mrs. Tylor said.

Mrs. Harris held out her hand and Mrs. Tylor took it. "I do so hope we'll be friends," Mrs. Harris said. "As you said, it means such a lot to have really thoughtful neighbors. And we've been so unlucky."

"Of course," Mrs. Tylor said, and then came back to herself abruptly. "Perhaps one evening soon we can get together for a game of bridge?" She saw Mrs. Harris's face and said, "No. Well, anyway, we must all get together some evening soon." They both laughed.

"It does sound silly, doesn't it," Mrs. Harris said. "Thanks so much for all your kindness this morning."

"Anything we can do," Mrs. Tylor said. "If you want to send James over this afternoon."

"Perhaps I shall," Mrs. Harris said. "If you really don't mind."

"Of course," Mrs. Tylor said. "Carol, dear."

With her arm around Carol she walked out to the front of the house and stood watching Mrs. Harris and James go into their house. They both stopped in the doorway and waved, and Mrs. Tylor and Carol waved back.

"Can't I go to the movies," Carol said, "*please*, Mother?"

"I'll go with you, dear," Mrs. Tylor said.

Pillar of Salt

F OR some reason a tune was running through her head when she and her husband got on the train in New Hampshire for their trip to New York; they had not been to New York for nearly a year, but the tune was from farther back than that. It was from the days when she was fifteen or sixteen; and had never seen New York except in movies, when the city was made up, to her, of penthouses filled with Noel Coward people; when the height and speed and luxury and gaiety that made up a city like New York were confused inextricably with the dullness of being fifteen, and beauty unreachable and far in the movies.

"What *is* that tune?" she said to her husband, and hummed it. "It's from some old movie, I think."

"I know it," he said, and hummed it himself. "Can't remember the words."

He sat back comfortably. He had hung up their coats, put the suitcases on the rack, and had taken his magazine out. "I'll think of it sooner or later," he said.

She looked out the window first, tasting it almost secretly, savoring the extreme pleasure of being on a moving train with nothing to do for six hours but read and nap and go into the dining-car, going farther and farther every minute from the children, from the kitchen floor, with even the hills being incredibly left behind, changing into fields and trees too far away from home to be daily. "I love trains," she said, and her husband nodded sympathetically into his magazine.

Two weeks ahead, two unbelievable weeks, with all arrangements made, no further planning to do, except perhaps what theatres or what restaurants. A friend with an apartment went on a convenient vacation, there was enough money in the bank to make a trip to New York compatible with new snow suits for the children; there was the smoothness of unopposed arrangements, once the initial obstacles had been overcome, as though when they had really made up their minds, nothing dared stop them. The baby's sore throat cleared up. The plumber came, finished his work in two days, and left. The dresses had been altered in time; the hardware store could be left safely, once they had found the excuse of looking over new city products. New York had not burned down, had not been quarantined, their friend had gone away according to schedule, and Brad had the keys to the apartment in his pocket. Everyone knew where to reach everyone else; there was a list of plays not to miss and a list of items to look out for in the stores—diapers, dress materials, fancy canned goods, tarnishproof silverware boxes. And, finally, the train was there, performing its function, pacing through the afternoon, carrying them legally and with determination to New York.

Margaret looked curiously at her husband, inactive in the middle of the afternoon on a train, at the other fortunate people traveling, at the sunny country outside, looked again to make sure, and then opened her book. The tune was still in her head, she hummed it and heard her husband take it up softly as he turned a page in his magazine.

In the dining-car she ate roast beef, as she would have done in a restaurant at home, reluctant to change over too quickly to the new, tantalizing food of a vacation. She had ice cream for dessert but became uneasy over her coffee because they were due in New York in an hour and she still had to put on her coat and hat, relishing every gesture, and Brad must take the suitcases down and put away the magazines. They stood at the end of the car for the interminable underground run, picking up their suitcases and putting them down again, moving restlessly inch by inch.

The station was a momentary shelter, moving visitors gradually into a world of people and sound and light to prepare them for the blasting reality of the street outside. She saw it for a minute from the sidewalk before she was in a taxi moving into the middle of it, and then they were bewilderingly caught and carried on uptown and whirled out on to another sidewalk and Brad paid the taxi driver and put his head back to look up at the apartment house. "This is it, all right," he said, as though he had doubted the driver's ability to find a number so simply given. Upstairs in the elevator, and the key fit the door. They had never seen their friend's apartment before, but it was reasonably familiar—a friend moving from New Hampshire to New York carries private pictures of a home not erasable in a

few years, and the apartment had enough of home in it to settle Brad immediately in the right chair and comfort her with
instinctive trust of the linen and blankets.

"This is home for two weeks," Brad said, and stretched.
After the first few minutes they both went to the windows automatically; New York was below, as arranged, and the houses
across the street were apartment houses filled with unknown
people.

"It's wonderful," she said. There were cars down there, and
people, and the noise was there. "I'm so happy," she said, and
kissed her husband.

They went sight-seeing the first day; they had breakfast in an
Automat and went to the top of the Empire State building.
"Got it all fixed up now," Brad said, at the top. "Wonder just
where that plane hit."

They tried to peer down on all four sides, but were embarrassed about asking. "After all," she said reasonably, giggling
in a corner, "if something of mine got broken I wouldn't want
people poking around asking to see the pieces."

"If you owned the Empire State building you wouldn't
care," Brad said.

They traveled only in taxis the first few days, and one taxi
had a door held on with a piece of string; they pointed to it
and laughed silently at each other, and on about the third day,
the taxi they were riding in got a flat tire on Broadway and
they had to get out and find another.

"We've only got eleven days left," she said one day, and
then, seemingly minutes later, "we've already been here six
days."

They had got in touch with the friends they had expected to
get in touch with, they were going to a Long Island summer
home for a week end. "It looks pretty dreadful right now,"
their hostess said cheerfully over the phone, "and we're leaving
in a week ourselves, but I'd never *forgive* you if you didn't see
it *once* while you were here." The weather had been fair but
cool, with a definite autumn awareness, and the clothes in the
store windows were dark and already hinting at furs and vel-
vets. She wore her coat every day, and suits most of the time.
The light dresses she had brought were hanging in the closet
in the apartment, and she was thinking now of getting a

sweater in one of the big stores, something impractical for New Hampshire, but probably good for Long Island.

"I have to do some shopping, at least one day," she said to Brad, and he groaned.

"Don't ask me to carry packages," he said.

"You aren't up to a good day's shopping," she told him, "not after all this walking around you've been doing. Why don't you go to a movie or something?"

"I want to do some shopping myself," he said mysteriously. Perhaps he was talking about her Christmas present; she had thought vaguely of getting such things done in New York; the children would be pleased with novelties from the city, toys not seen in their home stores. At any rate she said, "You'll probably be able to get to your wholesalers at last."

They were on their way to visit another friend, who had found a place to live by a miracle and warned them consequently not to quarrel with the appearance of the building, or the stairs, or the neighborhood. All three were bad, and the stairs were three flights, narrow and dark, but there was a place to live at the top. Their friend had not been in New York long, but he lived by himself in two rooms, and had easily caught the mania for slim tables and low bookcases which made his rooms look too large for the furniture in some places, too cramped and uncomfortable in others.

"What a lovely place," she said when she came in, and then was sorry when her host said, "Some day this damn situation will let up and I'll be able to settle down in a really decent place."

There were other people there; they sat and talked companionably about the same subjects then current in New Hampshire, but they drank more than they would have at home and it left them strangely unaffected; their voices were louder and their words more extravagant; their gestures, on the other hand, were smaller, and they moved a finger where in New Hampshire they would have waved an arm. Margaret said frequently, "We're just staying here for a couple of weeks, on a vacation," and she said, "It's wonderful, so *exciting*," and she said, "We were *terribly* lucky; this friend went out of town just at the right. . . ."

Finally the room was very full and noisy, and she went into a corner near a window to catch her breath. The window had been opened and shut all evening, depending on whether the person standing next to it had both hands free; and now it was shut, with the clear sky outside. Someone came and stood next to her, and she said, "Listen to the noise outside. It's as bad as it is inside."

He said, "In a neighborhood like this someone's always getting killed."

She frowned. "It sounds different than before. I mean, there's a different sound to it."

"Alcoholics," he said. "Drunks in the streets. Fighting going on across the way." He wandered away, carrying his drink.

She opened the window and leaned out, and there were people hanging out of the windows across the way shouting, and people standing in the street looking up and shouting, and from across the way she heard clearly, "Lady, lady." They must mean me, she thought, they're all looking this way. She leaned out farther and the voices shouted incoherently but somehow making an audible whole, "Lady, your house is on fire, lady, lady."

She closed the window firmly and turned around to the other people in the room, raising her voice a little. "Listen," she said, "they're saying the house is on fire." She was desperately afraid of their laughing at her, of looking like a fool while Brad across the room looked at her blushing. She said again, "The *house* is on *fire*," and added, "They say," for fear of sounding too vehement. The people nearest to her turned and someone said, "She says the house is on fire."

She wanted to get to Brad and couldn't see him; her host was not in sight either, and the people all around were strangers. They don't listen to me, she thought, I might as well not be here, and she went to the outside door and opened it. There was no smoke, no flame, but she was telling herself, I might as well not be here, so she abandoned Brad in panic and ran without her hat and coat down the stairs, carrying a glass in one hand and a package of matches in the other. The stairs were insanely long, but they were clear and safe, and she opened the street door and ran out. A man caught her arm and said, "Everyone out of the house?" and she said, "No, Brad's still there." The fire engines swept around the corner, with people leaning out of the windows watching them, and the man holding her arm said, "It's down here," and left her. The fire was two houses away; they could see flames behind the top windows, and smoke against the night sky, but in ten minutes it was finished and the fire engines pulled away with an air of martyrdom for hauling out all their equipment to put out a ten-minute fire.

She went back upstairs slowly and with embarrassment, and found Brad and took him home.

"I was so frightened," she said to him when they were safely in bed, "I lost my head completely."

"You should have tried to find someone," he said.

"They wouldn't listen," she insisted. "I kept telling them and they wouldn't listen and then I thought I must have been mistaken. I had some idea of going down to see what was going on."

"Lucky it was no worse," Brad said sleepily.

"I felt trapped," she said. "High up in that old building with a fire; it's like a nightmare. And in a strange city."

"Well, it's all over now," Brad said.

The same faint feeling of insecurity tagged her the next day; she went shopping alone and Brad went off to see hardware, after all. She got on a bus to go downtown and the bus was too full to move when it came time for her to get out. Wedged standing in the aisle she said, "Out, please," and, "Excuse me," and by the time she was loose and near the door the bus had started again and she got off a stop beyond. "No one *listens* to me," she said to herself. "Maybe it's because I'm too polite." In the stores the prices were all too high and the sweaters looked disarmingly like New Hampshire ones. The toys for the children filled her with dismay; they were so obviously for New York children: hideous little parodies of adult life, cash registers, tiny pushcarts with imitation fruit, telephones that really worked (as if there weren't enough phones in New York that really worked), miniature milk bottles in a carrying case. "We get our milk from cows," Margaret told the salesgirl. "My children wouldn't know what these were." She was exaggerating, and felt guilty for a minute, but no one was around to catch her.

She had a picture of small children in the city dressed like their parents, following along with a miniature mechanical civilization, toy cash registers in larger and larger sizes that eased them into the real thing, millions of clattering jerking small imitations that prepared them nicely for taking over the large useless toys their parents lived by. She bought a pair of skis for her son, which she knew would be inadequate for the New Hampshire snow, and a wagon for her daughter inferior to the one Brad could make at home in an hour. Ignoring the toy mailboxes, the small phonographs with special small records, the kiddie cosmetics, she left the store and started home.

She was frankly afraid by now to take a bus; she stood on the corner and waited for a taxi. Glancing down at her feet, she saw a dime on the sidewalk and tried to pick it up, but there were too many people for her to bend down, and she was afraid to shove to make room for fear of being stared at. She put her foot on the dime and then saw a quarter near it, and a nickel. Someone dropped a pocketbook, she thought, and put her other foot on the quarter, stepping quickly to make it look natural; then she saw another dime and another nickel, and a third dime in the gutter. People were passing her, back and forth, all the time, rushing, pushing against her, not looking at her, and she was afraid to get down and start gathering up the money. Other people saw it and went past, and she realized that no one was going to pick it up. They were all embarrassed, or in too much of a hurry, or too crowded. A taxi stopped to let someone off, and she hailed it. She lifted her feet off the dime and the quarter, and left them there when she got into the taxi. This taxi went slowly and bumped as it went; she had begun to notice that the gradual decay was not peculiar to the taxis. The buses were cracking open in unimportant seams, the leather seats broken and stained. The buildings were going, too—in one of the nicest stores there had been a great gaping hole in the tiled foyer, and you walked around it. Corners of the buildings seemed to be crumbling away into fine dust that drifted downward, the granite was eroding unnoticed. Every window she saw on her way uptown seemed to be broken; perhaps every street corner was peppered with small change. The people were moving faster than ever before; a girl in a red hat appeared at the upper side of the taxi window and was gone beyond the lower side before you could see the hat; store windows were so terribly bright because you only caught them for a fraction of a second. The people seemed hurled on in a frantic action that made every hour forty-five minutes long, every day nine hours, every year fourteen days. Food was so elusively fast, eaten in such a hurry, that you were always hungry, always speeding to a new meal with new people. Everything was imperceptibly quicker every minute. She stepped into the taxi on one side and stepped out the other side at her home; she pressed the fifth-floor button on the elevator and was coming down again, bathed and dressed and ready for dinner with Brad. They went out for dinner and were coming in again, hungry and hurrying to bed in order to get to breakfast with lunch beyond. They had been in New York nine days; tomorrow was Saturday and they were going to Long Island, coming home Sunday, and then Wednesday they were going home, really home. By the time she had thought of it they were on the train to Long Island; the train was broken, the seats torn and the floor dirty; one of the doors wouldn't open and the windows wouldn't shut. Passing through the outskirts of the city, she thought, It's as though everything were traveling so fast that the solid stuff couldn't stand it and were going to pieces under the strain, cornices blowing off and windows caving in. She knew she was afraid to say it truly, afraid to face the knowledge that it was a voluntary neck-breaking speed, a deliberate whirling faster and faster to end in destruction.

On Long Island, their hostess led them into a new piece of New York, a house filled with New York furniture as though on rubber bands, pulled this far, stretched taut, and ready to snap back to the city, to an apartment, as soon as the door was opened and the lease, fully paid, had expired. "We've had this place every year for simply ages," their hostess said. "Otherwise we couldn't have gotten it *possibly* this year."

"It's an awfully nice place," Brad said. "I'm surprised you don't live here all year round."

"Got to get back to the city *some* time," their hostess said, and laughed.

"Not much like New Hampshire," Brad said. He was beginning to be a little homesick, Margaret thought; he wants to yell, just once. Since the fire scare she was apprehensive about large groups of people gathering together; when friends began to drop in after dinner she waited for a while, telling herself they were on the ground floor, she could run right outside, all the windows were open; then she excused herself and went to bed. When Brad came to bed much later she woke up and he said irritably, "We've been playing anagrams. Such crazy people." She said sleepily, "Did you win?" and fell asleep before he told her.

The next morning she and Brad went for a walk while their host and hostess read the Sunday papers. "If you turn to the right outside the door," their hostess said encouragingly, "and walk about three blocks down, you'll come to our beach."

"What do they want with our beach?" their host said. "It's too damn cold to do anything down there."

"They can look at the *water*," their hostess said.

They walked down to the beach; at this time of year it was bare and windswept, yet still nodding hideously under traces of its summer plumage, as though it thought itself warmly inviting. There were occupied houses on the way there, for instance, and a lonely lunchstand was open, bravely advertising hot dogs and root beer. The man in the lunchstand watched them go by, his face cold and unsympathetic. They walked far past him, out of sight of houses, on to a stretch of grey pebbled sand that lay between the grey water on one side and the grey pebbled sand dunes on the other.

"Imagine going swimming here," she said with a shiver. The beach pleased her; it was oddly familiar and reassuring and at the same time that she realized this, the little tune came back to her, bringing a double recollection. The beach was the one where she had lived in imagination, writing for herself dreary love-broken stories where the heroine walked beside the wild waves; the little tune was the symbol of the golden world she escaped into to avoid the everyday dreariness that drove her into writing depressing stories about the beach. She laughed out loud and Brad said, "What on earth's so funny about his Godforsaken landscape?"

"I was just thinking how far away from the city it seems," she said falsely.

The sky and the water and the sand were grey enough to

make it feel like late afternoon instead of midmorning; she was tired and wanted to go back, but Brad said suddenly, "Look at that," and she turned and saw a girl running down over the dunes, carrying her hat, and her hair flying behind her.

"Only way to get warm on a day like this," Brad remarked, but Margaret said, "She looks frightened."

The girl saw them and came toward them, slowing down as she approached them. She was eager to reach them but when she came within speaking distance the familiar embarrassment, the not wanting to look like a fool, made her hesitate and look from one to the other of them uncomfortably.

"Do you know where I can find a policeman?" she asked finally.

Brad looked up and down the bare rocky beach and said solemnly, "There don't seem to be any around. Is there something we can do?"

"I don't think so," the girl said. "I really need a policeman."

They go to the police for everything, Margaret thought, these people, these New York people, it's as though they had selected a section of the population to act as problem-solvers, and so no matter what they want they look for a policeman.

"Be glad to help you if we can," Brad said.

The girl hesitated again. "Well, if you *must* know," she said crossly, "there's a leg up there."

They waited politely for the girl to explain, but she only said, "Come *on*, then," and waved to them to follow her. She led them over the dunes to a spot near a small inlet, where the dunes gave way abruptly to an intruding head of water. A leg was lying on the sand near the water, and the girl gestured at it and said, "There," as though it were her own property and they had insisted on having a share.

They walked over to it and Brad bent down gingerly. "It's a leg all right," he said. It looked like part of a wax dummy, a death-white wax leg neatly cut off at top-thigh and again just above the ankle, bent comfortably at the knee and resting on the sand. "It's real," Brad said, his voice slightly different. "You're right about that policeman."

They walked together to the lunchstand and the man listened unenthusiastically while Brad called the police. When the police came they all walked out again to where the leg was lying and Brad gave the police their names and addresses, and then said, "Is it all right to go on home?"

"What the hell you want to hang around for?" the policeman inquired with heavy humor. "You waiting for the rest of him?"

They went back to their host and hostess, talking about the leg, and their host apologized, as though he had been guilty of a breach of taste in allowing his guests to come on a human leg; their hostess said with interest, "There was an arm washed up in Bensonhurst, I've been reading about it."

"One of these killings," the host said.

Upstairs Margaret said abruptly, "I suppose it starts to happen first in the suburbs," and when Brad said, "What starts to happen?" she said hysterically, "People starting to come apart."

In order to reassure their host and hostess about their minding the leg, they stayed until the last afternoon train to New York. Back in their apartment again it seemed to Margaret that the marble in the house lobby had begun to age a little; even in two days there were new perceptible cracks. The elevator seemed a little rusty, and there was a fine film of dust over everything in the apartment. They went to bed feeling uncomfortable, and the next morning Margaret said immediately, "I'm going to stay in today."

"You're not upset about yesterday, are you?"

"Not a bit," Margaret said. "I just want to stay in and rest."

After some discussion Brad decided to go off again by himself; he still had people it was important to see and places he must go in the few days they had left. After breakfast in the Automat Margaret came back alone to the apartment, carrying the mystery story she had bought on the way. She hung up her coat and hat and sat down by the window with the noise and the people far below, looking out at the sky where it was grey beyond the houses across the street.

I'm not going to worry about it, she said to herself, no sense thinking all the time about things like that, spoil your vacation and Brad's too. No sense worrying, people get ideas like that and then worry about them.

The nasty little tune was running through her head again, with its burden of suavity and expensive perfume. The houses across the street were silent and perhaps unoccupied at this time of day; she let her eyes move with the rhythm of the tune, from window to window along one floor. By gliding quickly across two windows, she could make one line of the tune fit one floor of windows, and then a quick breath and a drop down to the next floor; it had the same number of windows and the tune had the same number of beats, and then the next floor and the next. She stopped suddenly when it seemed to her that the windowsill she had just passed had soundlessly crumpled and fallen into fine sand; when she looked back it was there as before but then it seemed to be the windowsill above and to the right, and finally a corner of the roof.

No sense worrying, she told herself, forcing her eyes down to the street, stop thinking about things all the time. Looking down at the street for long made her dizzy and she stood up and went into the small bedroom of the apartment. She had made the bed before going out to breakfast, like any good housewife, but now she deliberately took it apart, stripping the blankets and sheets off one by one, and then she made it again, taking a long time over the corners and smoothing out every wrinkle. "*That*'s done," she said when she was through, and went back to the window. When she looked across the street the tune started again, window to window, sills dissolving and falling downward. She leaned forward and looked down at her own window, something she had never thought of before, down to the sill. It was partly eaten away; when she touched the stone a few crumbs rolled off and fell.

It was eleven o'clock; Brad was looking at blowtorches by now and would not be back before one, if even then. She thought of writing a letter home, but the impulse left her before she found paper and pen. Then it occurred to her that she might take a nap, a thing she had never done in the morning in her life, and she went in and lay down on the bed. Lying down, she felt the building shaking.

No sense worrying, she told herself again, as though it were a charm against witches, and got up and found her coat and hat and put them on. I'll just get some cigarettes and some letter paper, she thought, just run down to the corner. Panic caught her going down in the elevator; it went too fast, and when she stepped out in the lobby it was only the people standing around who kept her from running. As it was, she went quickly out of the building and into the street. For a minute she hesitated, wanting to go back. The cars were going past so rapidly, the people hurrying as always, but the panic of the elevator drove her on finally. She went to the corner, and, following the people flying along ahead, ran out into the street, to hear a horn almost overhead and a shout from behind her, and the noise of brakes. She ran blindly on and reached the other side where she stopped and looked around. The truck was going on its appointed way around the corner, the people going past on either side of her, parting to go around her where she stood.

No one even noticed me, she thought with reassurance, everyone who saw me has gone by long ago. She went into the drugstore ahead of her and asked the man for cigarettes; the apartment now seemed safer to her than the street—she could walk up the stairs. Coming out of the store and walking to the corner, she kept as close to the buildings as possible, refusing to give way to the rightful traffic coming out of the doorways. On the corner she looked carefully at the light; it was green, but it looked as though it were going to change. Always safer to wait, she thought, don't want to walk into another truck.

People pushed past her and some were caught in the middle of the street when the light changed. One woman, more cowardly than the rest, turned and ran back to the curb, but the others stood in the middle of the street, leaning forward and then backward according to the traffic moving past them on both sides. One got to the farther curb in a brief break in the line of cars, the others were a fraction of a second too late and waited. Then the light changed again and as the cars slowed down Margaret put a foot on the street to go, but a taxi swinging wildly around her corner frightened her back and she stood on the curb again. By the time the taxi had gone the light was due to change again and she thought, I can wait once more, no sense getting caught out in the middle. A man beside her tapped his foot impatiently for the light to change back; two girls came past her and walked out into the street a few steps to wait, moving back a little when cars came too close, talking busily all the time. I ought to stay right with them, Margaret thought, but then they moved back against her and the light changed and the man next to her charged into the street and the two girls in front waited a minute and then moved slowly on, still talking, and Margaret started to follow and then decided to wait. A crowd of people formed around her suddenly; they had come off a bus and were crossing here, and she had a sudden feeling of being jammed in the center and forced out into the street when all of them moved as one with the light changing, and she elbowed her way desperately out of the crowd and went off to lean against a building and wait. It seemed to her that people passing were beginning to look at her. What do they think of me, she wondered, and stood up straight as though she were waiting for someone. She looked at her watch and frowned, and then thought, What a fool I must look like, no one here ever saw me before, they all go by too fast. She went back to the curb again but the green light was just changing to red and she thought, I'll go back to the drugstore and have a coke, no sense going back to that apartment.

The man looked at her unsurprised in the drugstore and she sat and ordered a coke but suddenly as she was drinking it the panic caught her again and she thought of the people who had been with her when she first started to cross the street, blocks away by now, having tried and made perhaps a dozen lights while she had hesitated at the first; people by now a mile or so downtown, because they had been going steadily while she had been trying to gather her courage. She paid the man quickly, restrained an impulse to say that there was nothing wrong with the coke, she just had to get back, that was all, and she hurried down to the corner again.

The minute the light changes, she told herself firmly; there's no sense. The light changed before she was ready and in the minute before she collected herself traffic turning the corner overwhelmed her and she shrank back against the curb. She looked longingly at the cigar store on the opposite corner, with her apartment house beyond; she wondered, How do people ever manage to get there, and knew that by wondering, by admitting a doubt, she was lost. The light changed and she looked at it with hatred, a dumb thing, turning back and forth, back and forth, with no purpose and no meaning. Looking to either side of her slyly, to see if anyone were watching, she stepped quietly backward, one step, two, until she was well away from the curb. Back in the drugstore again she waited for some sign of recognition from the clerk and saw none; he regarded her with the same apathy as he had the first time. He gestured without interest at the telephone; he doesn't care, she thought, it doesn't matter to him who I call.

She had no time to feel like a fool, because they answered the phone immediately and agreeably and found him right away. When he answered the phone, his voice sounding surprised and matter-of-fact, she could only say miserably, "I'm in the drugstore on the corner. Come and get me."

"What's the matter?" He was not anxious to come.

"Please come and get me," she said into the black mouthpiece that might or might not tell him, "please come and get me, Brad. *Please*."

Men with Their Big Shoes

I T WAS young Mrs. Hart's first summer living in the country, and her first year being married and the mistress of a house; she was going to have her first baby soon, and it was the first time she had ever had anyone, or thought of having anyone, who could remotely be described as a maid. Young Mrs. Hart spent almost hours every day, while she was resting as the doctor told her to, in peacefully congratulating herself. When she was sitting in the rocking chair on the front porch she could look down the quiet street with the trees and gardens and kind people who smiled at her as they passed; or she could turn her head and look through the wide windows in her own house, into the pretty living-room with the chintz curtains and matching slip-covers and maple furniture; she could raise her eyes a little and look at the ruffled white curtains on the bedroom windows. It was a real house: the milkman left milk there every morning, the brightly painted pots in a row along the porch railing held real plants which grew and needed regular watering; you could cook on the real stove in the kitchen, and Mrs. Anderson was always complaining about the shoe marks on the clean floors, just like a real maid.

"It's the men who make dirt on the floor," Mrs. Anderson would say, regarding the print of a heel. "A woman, you watch them, she always puts her feet down quiet. Men with their big shoes." And she would flick carelessly at the mark with the dustcloth.

Although Mrs. Hart was unreasonably afraid of Mrs. Anderson, she had heard and read so much about how all housewives these days were intimidated by their domestic help that she was never surprised at first by her own timid uneasiness; Mrs. Anderson's belligerent authority, moreover, seemed to follow naturally from a knowledge of canning and burnt-sugar gravy and setting yeast rolls out to rise. When Mrs. Anderson, all elbows and red face, her hair pulled disagreeably tight, had presented herself first at the back door with an offer to help, Mrs. Hart had accepted blindly, caught between unwashed windows in a litter of unpacking and dust; Mrs. Anderson had started correctly with the kitchen, and made Mrs. Hart a hot cup of tea first thing; "You can't afford to get too tired," she said, eyeing Mrs. Hart's waist, "you got to be careful right along."

By the time Mrs. Hart discovered that Mrs. Anderson never got anything quite clean, never completely managed to get anything back where it belonged, it was incredible to think of doing anything about it. Mrs. Anderson's thumbprints were on all the windows and Mrs. Hart's morning cup of tea was a regular institution; Mrs. Hart put the water on to boil directly after breakfast and Mrs. Anderson made them each a cup of tea when she came at nine. "You need a hot cup of tea to start your day off right," she said amiably every morning, "it settles your stomach for the day."

Mrs. Hart never allowed herself to think further about Mrs. Anderson than to feel comfortably proud of having all the housework done for her ("a regular *treasure*," she wrote to her girl friends in New York, "and she fusses over me like I was actually *her* baby!"); it was not until Mrs. Anderson had been coming dutifully every morning for over a month that Mrs. Hart recognized with sickening conviction that the faint small uneasiness was justified.

It was a warm sunny morning, the first after a week of rain, and Mrs. Hart put on an especially pretty house dress— washed and ironed by Mrs. Anderson—and made her husband a soft-boiled egg for his breakfast, and went down the front walk with him to wave good-bye till he got to the corner and the bus which took him to his job at the bank in the neighboring town. Coming back up the walk to her house, Mrs. Hart admired the sunlight on the green shutters, and spoke affectionately to her next-door neighbor, who was out already sweeping her porch. Pretty soon I'll have my baby out in the garden in his play pen, Mrs. Hart thought, and left the front door open behind her for the sun to come in and soak into the floor. When she came into the kitchen, Mrs. Anderson was sitting at the table and the tea was poured.

"Good morning," Mrs. Hart said. "Isn't it a beautiful day?"

"Morning," Mrs. Anderson said. She waved at the tea. "I knew you was just out front so I got everything all ready. Can't start the day off without your cup of tea."

"I was beginning to think the sun would never come out again," Mrs. Hart said. She sat down and pulled her cup toward her. "It's so lovely to be dry and warm again."

"It settles your stomach, tea does," Mrs. Anderson said. "I already put the sugar in. You'll be having trouble with your stomach right along now."

"You know," Mrs. Hart said happily, "last summer about this time I was still working in New York and I didn't think Bill and I were *ever* going to get married. And now look at me," she added, and laughed.

"You never know what's going to happen to you," Mrs. Anderson said. "When things look worst, you'll either die or get better. I used to have a neighbor was always saying that." She sighed and rose, taking her cup with her to the sink. "Of course some of us never get much good coming along," she said.

"And then everything happened in about two weeks," Mrs. Hart said. "Bill got this job up here and the girls at the office gave us a waffle iron."

"It's up on the shelf," Mrs. Anderson said. She reached out for Mrs. Hart's cup. "You sit still," she said. "You'll never have another chance to take it easy like this."

"I can't remember to sit still all the time," Mrs. Hart said. "Everything's too exciting."

"It's for your own good," Mrs. Anderson said. "I'm only thinking of you."

"You've been very nice already," Mrs. Hart said dutifully, "coming to help every morning like this. And taking such good care of me."

"I don't want thanks," Mrs. Anderson said. "You just come through all right, that's all I want to see."

"But I really don't know what to do without you," Mrs. Hart said. That ought to be enough for today, she thought suddenly, and laughed aloud at the idea of a portion of gratitude doled out every morning to Mrs. Anderson, like a bonus on her hourly wage. It's true, though, she thought; I have to say it every day, sooner or later.

"You laughing about something?" Mrs. Anderson said, half-turning with her hard red wrists braced against the sink. "I say something funny?"

"I was just thinking," Mrs. Hart said quickly, "thinking about the girls I used to be in the office with. They'd be so jealous if they could see me now."

"Never know when they're well off," Mrs. Anderson said.

Mrs. Hart reached out and touched the yellow curtain at the window beside her, thinking of the one-room apartments in New York and the dark office. "I wish *I* could be cheerful these days," Mrs. Anderson went on.

Mrs. Hart dropped her hand quickly from the curtain and turned to smile sympathetically at Mrs. Anderson. "I know," she murmured.

"You never know how bad it can be," Mrs. Anderson said. She jerked her head toward the back door. "*He* was at it again. All night long." By now Mrs. Hart knew how to tell whether "*he*" meant Mr. Anderson or Mr. Hart; a gesture of Mrs. Anderson's head toward the back door and the path she took home every day meant Mr. Anderson; the same gesture toward the front door where every night Mrs. Hart met her husband meant Mr. Hart. "Not a minute's sleep for *me*," Mrs. Anderson was saying.

"Isn't that a shame," Mrs. Hart said. She stood up quickly and started for the back door. "Dish towels on the line," she explained.

"I'll do it, later," Mrs. Anderson said. "Cursing and yelling," she went on, "I thought I was going crazy. 'Why don't you go on and get out?' he says to me. Went over and opened the door wide as it would go and yelled so's all the neighbors could hear him. 'Why don't you get out?' he says."

"Terrible," Mrs. Hart said, her hand on the back door knob.

"Thirty-seven years," Mrs. Anderson said. She shook her head. "And he wants me to get out." She watched Mrs. Hart light a cigarette and said, "You shouldn't smoke. You'll likely be sorry if you go on smoking like that. That's why I never had any children," she went on. "What would I do, him acting like that with children around listening?"

Mrs. Hart walked across to the stove and looked into the teapot. "Believe I'll have another cup," she said. "Will you have another, Mrs. Anderson?"

"Gives me heartburn," Mrs. Anderson said. She put the freshly washed cup back on the table. "I just washed this," she said, "but it's your cup. And your house. I guess you can do what you want to."

Mrs. Hart laughed and brought the teapot over to the table. Mrs. Anderson watched her pour the tea and then took the teapot away. "I'll just wash this," she said, "before you decide to drink any more." She dropped her voice. "Too much liquid spoils the kidneys."

"I always drink a lot of tea and coffee," Mrs. Hart said.

Mrs. Anderson looked at the dried dishes standing on the drain of the sink, and then picked up three glasses in each great hand. "You sure had a lot of dirty glasses around this morning."

"I was just too tired last night to clean up," Mrs. Hart said. Besides, she thought, cleaning up is what I pay *her* for; and she added, making her voice light, "So I just left everything for you."

"It's my job to clean up after people," Mrs. Anderson said. "Someone always has to do the dirty work for the rest. You have a lot of company?"

"Some people my husband knows in town," Mrs. Hart said. "About six altogether."

"He shouldn't bring his friends home with you like *that*," Mrs. Anderson said.

Mrs. Hart thought of the pleasant chatter about the New York theatre and the local roadhouse where they all might go dancing soon, and the pretty compliments on her house, and showing the baby things to the two other young wives, and sighed. She had lost track of what Mrs. Anderson was saying.

"—Right in front of his own wife," Mrs. Anderson finished, and moved her head significantly toward the front door. "*He* do much drinking?"

"No, not much," Mrs. Hart said.

Mrs. Anderson nodded. "I know what you mean," she said. "You watch them taking one drink after another and you can't think of any way to tell them to stop. And then something makes them mad and first thing you know they're telling you to go on and get out." She nodded again. "There's nothing any woman can do but make sure when she does have to get out she sure has some place to go."

Mrs. Hart said carefully, "Now, Mrs. Anderson, I don't really think that all husbands—"

"You only been married a year," Mrs. Anderson said dismally, "and no one that's older around to tell you."

Mrs. Hart lit a second cigarette from the end of the first. "I'm really not at all worried about my husband's drinking," she said formally.

Mrs. Anderson stopped, holding a pile of clean plates. "Other women?" she asked. "Is *that* what it is?"

"What on *earth* makes you say that?" Mrs. Hart demanded. "Bill would no more *look*—"

"You need someone to be looking after you, times like this," Mrs. Anderson said. "Don't think I don't know; you just want to tell someone about it all. I guess all men treat their wives the same, only some of them are drinkers and some of them throw their money away on gambling and some of them chase every young girl they see." She laughed her abrupt laugh. "And some not so young, if you ask the wives," she said. "If most women knew how their husbands were going to turn out, there'd be less marrying going on."

"I think a successful marriage is the woman's responsibility," Mrs. Hart said.

"Mrs. Martin now, down at the grocery, she was telling me, the other day, some of the things *her* husband used to do before he died," Mrs. Anderson said. "You'd never suspect what some men do." She looked thoughtfully at the back door. "Some's worse than others, though. She thinks you're real sweet, Mrs. Martin does."

"That's nice of her," Mrs. Hart said.

"I didn't say nothing about *him*," Mrs. Anderson said, her head moving toward the front door. "I don't mention any names, not where anybody'd think I know the people."

Mrs. Hart thought of Mrs. Martin, keen-eyed and shrill, watching other people's groceries ("Two loaves of whole wheat today, Mrs. Hart? Company tonight, maybe?"). "I think she's such a nice person," Mrs. Hart said, wanting to add, You tell her I said so.

"I'm not saying she isn't," Mrs. Anderson said grimly. "You just don't want to let her figure out anything's wrong."

"I'm sure—" Mrs. Hart began.

"I *told* her," Mrs. Anderson said, "I said I was sure Mr. Hart never did any running around's far as I knew. Nor drinking like some. I said I felt like you might be my own daughter sometimes and no man was going to mistreat you while I was around."

"I wish," Mrs. Hart began again, a quick fear touching her; her kind neighbors watching her beneath their friendliness, looking out quietly from behind curtains, watching Bill, perhaps? "I don't think people ought to talk about other people," she said desperately, "I mean, I don't think it's fair to say things when you can't *know* for sure."

Mrs. Anderson laughed again suddenly and went over to open the mop closet. "You don't want to let anything scare you," she said, "not right now. Will I do the living-room this morning? I could get the little rugs out to air in the sun. It's just that *he*—" the back door "—got me all upset. You know."

"I'm sorry," Mrs. Hart said. "Isn't that a shame."

"Mrs. Martin said why didn't I come live with you folks," Mrs. Anderson said, searching violently in the mop closet, her voice sounding muffled and dusty. "Mrs. Martin was saying a young woman like you, just starting out, always needs a friend around."

Mrs. Hart looked down at her fingers twisting the handle of the cup; she had only drunk half her tea. It's too late now for me to walk into another room, she thought; I can always say Bill would never allow it. "I met Mrs. Martin in town a few days ago," she said. "She was wearing an awfully good-looking blue coat." She smoothed her house dress with her hand, and added irritably, "I wish I could get into a decent dress again."

" 'Why don't you get out?' he says to me." Mrs. Anderson backed out of the mop closet with a dustpan in one hand and a cleaning cloth in the other. "Drunk and cursing so's all the neighbors could hear. 'Why don't you get out?' I thought sure you'd hear him even up here."

"I'm sure he couldn't mean it," Mrs. Hart said, trying to make her voice sound final.

"*You* wouldn't stand for it," Mrs. Anderson said. She put the dustpan and cloth down and came over and sat down at the table opposite Mrs. Hart. "Mrs. Martin was thinking if you wanted me to I could come right into your spare room. Do all the cooking."

"You could," Mrs. Hart said amiably, "except that I'm going to put the baby in there."

"We'd put the baby in your room," Mrs. Anderson said. She laughed and gave Mrs. Hart's hand a push. "Don't worry," she said, "I'd keep out of your way. Well, and if you wanted to put the baby in with me then I could get up at night to feed it for you. Guess I could take care of a baby all right."

Mrs. Hart smiled cheerfully back at Mrs. Anderson. "I'd love to, of course," she said. "Some day. Right now of *course* Bill would never let me do it."

"Of course not," Mrs. Anderson said. "The men never do, do they? I told Mrs. Martin down at the grocery, she's the nicest little thing in the world, I said, but her husband wouldn't let the scrubwoman come live with them."

"Why, Mrs. Anderson," Mrs. Hart said, looking horrified, "saying things like that about yourself!"

"And another woman, one who's older and knows a little more," Mrs. Anderson said. "She might see a little more, too, maybe."

Mrs. Hart, her fingers tight on the teacup, caught a quick picture of Mrs. Martin, leaning comfortably across the counter ("I see you've got a new star boarder, Mrs. Hart. Mrs. Anderson'll see that you're taken good care of!"). And her neighbors, their frozen faces regarding her as she walked down to meet Bill at the bus; the girls in New York, reading her letters together and envying her ("Such a perfect *jewel*—she's going to live with us and do *all* the work!"). Looking up at Mrs. Anderson's knowing smile across the table, Mrs. Hart realized with a sudden unalterable conviction that she was lost.

The Tooth

THE bus was waiting, panting heavily at the curb in front of the small bus station, its great blue-and-silver bulk glittering in the moonlight. There were only a few people interested in the bus, and at that time of night no one passing on the sidewalk: the one movie theatre in town had finished its show and closed its doors an hour before, and all the movie patrons had been to the drugstore for ice cream and gone on home; now the drugstore was closed and dark, another silent doorway in the long midnight street. The only town lights were the street lights, the lights in the all-night lunchstand across the street, and the one remaining counter lamp in the bus station where the girl sat in the ticket office with her hat and coat on, only waiting for the New York bus to leave before she went home to bed.

Standing on the sidewalk next to the open door of the bus, Clara Spencer held her husband's arm nervously. "I feel so funny," she said.

"Are you all right?" he asked. "Do you think I ought to go with you?"

"No, of course not," she said. "I'll be all right." It was hard for her to talk because of her swollen jaw; she kept a handkerchief pressed to her face and held hard to her husband. "Are you sure *you'll* be all right?" she asked. "I'll be back tomorrow night at the latest. Or else I'll call."

"Everything will be fine," he said heartily. "By tomorrow noon it'll all be gone. Tell the dentist if there's anything wrong I can come right down."

"I feel so funny," she said. "Light-headed, and sort of dizzy."

"That's because of the dope," he said. "All that codeine, and the whisky, and nothing to eat all day."

She giggled nervously. "I couldn't comb my hair, my hand shook so. I'm glad it's dark."

"Try to sleep in the bus," he said. "Did you take a sleeping pill?"

"Yes," she said. They were waiting for the bus driver to

finish his cup of coffee in the lunchstand; they could see him through the glass window, sitting at the counter, taking his time. "I feel so *funny*," she said.

"You know, Clara," he made his voice very weighty, as though if he spoke more seriously his words would carry more conviction and be therefore more comforting, "you know, I'm glad you're going down to New York to have Zimmerman take care of this. I'd never forgive myself if it turned out to be something serious and I let you go to this butcher up here."

"It's just a *toothache*," Clara said uneasily, "nothing very serious about a *toothache*."

"You can't tell," he said. "It might be abscessed or something; I'm sure he'll have to pull it."

"Don't even talk like that," she said, and shivered.

"Well, it looks pretty bad," he said soberly, as before. "Your face so swollen, and all. Don't you worry."

"I'm not worrying," she said. "I just feel as if I were all tooth. Nothing else."

The bus driver got up from the stool and walked over to pay his check. Clara moved toward the bus, and her husband said, "Take your time, you've got plenty of time."

"I just feel funny," Clara said.

"Listen," her husband said, "that tooth's been bothering you off and on for years; at least six or seven times since I've known you you've had trouble with that tooth. It's about time something was done. You had a toothache on our honeymoon," he finished accusingly.

"Did I?" Clara said. "You know," she went on, and laughed, "I was in such a hurry I didn't dress properly. I have on old stockings and I just dumped everything into my good pocketbook."

"Are you sure you have enough money?" he said.

"Almost twenty-five dollars," Clara said. "I'll be home tomorrow."

"Wire if you need more," he said. The bus driver appeared in the doorway of the lunchroom. "Don't worry," he said.

"Listen," Clara said suddenly, "are you *sure* you'll be all right? Mrs. Lang will be over in the morning in time to make breakfast, and Johnny doesn't need to go to school if things are too mixed up."

"I know," he said.

"Mrs. Lang," she said, checking on her fingers. "I called Mrs. Lang, I left the grocery order on the kitchen table, you can have the cold tongue for lunch and in case I don't get back Mrs. Lang will give you dinner. The cleaner ought to come about four o'clock, I won't be back so give him your brown suit and it doesn't matter if you forget but be sure to empty the pockets."

"Wire if you need more money," he said. "Or call. I'll stay home tomorrow so you can call at home."

"Mrs. Lang will take care of the baby," she said.

"Or you can wire," he said.

The bus driver came across the street and stood by the entrance to the bus.

"Okay?" the bus driver said.

"Good-bye," Clara said to her husband.

"You'll feel all right tomorrow," her husband said. "It's only a toothache."

"I'm fine," Clara said. "Don't you worry." She got on the bus and then stopped, with the bus driver waiting behind her. "Milkman," she said to her husband. "Leave a note telling him we want eggs."

"I will," her husband said. "Good-bye."

"Good-bye," Clara said. She moved on into the bus and behind her the driver swung into his seat. The bus was nearly empty and she went far back and sat down at the window outside which her husband waited. "Good-bye," she said to him through the glass, "take care of yourself."

"Good-bye," he said, waving violently.

The bus stirred, groaned, and pulled itself forward. Clara turned her head to wave good-bye once more and then lay back against the heavy soft seat. Good Lord, she thought, what a thing to do! Outside, the familiar street slipped past, strange and dark and seen, unexpectedly, from the unique station of a person leaving town, going away on a bus. It isn't as though it's the first time I've ever been to New York, Clara thought indignantly, it's the whisky and the codeine and the sleeping pill and the toothache. She checked hastily to see if her codeine tablets were in her pocketbook; they had been standing, along with the aspirin and a glass of water, on the dining-room sideboard, but somewhere in the lunatic flight from her home she must have picked them up, because they were in her pocketbook now, along with the twenty-odd dollars and her compact and comb and lipstick. She could tell from the feel of the lipstick that she had brought the old, nearly finished one, not the new one that was a darker shade and had cost two-fifty. There was a run in her stocking and a hole in the toe that she never noticed at home wearing her old comfortable shoes, but which was now suddenly and disagreeably apparent inside her best walking shoes. Well, she thought, I can buy new stockings in New York tomorrow, after the tooth is fixed, after everything's all right. She put her tongue cautiously on the tooth and was rewarded with a split-second crash of pain.

The bus stopped at a red light and the driver got out of his seat and came back toward her. "Forgot to get your ticket before," he said.

"I guess I was a little rushed at the last minute," she said. She found the ticket in her coat pocket and gave it to him. "When do we get to New York?" she asked.

"Five-fifteen," he said. "Plenty of time for breakfast. One-way ticket?"

"I'm coming back by train," she said, without seeing why she had to tell him, except that it was late at night and people isolated together in some strange prison like a bus had to be more friendly and communicative than at other times.

"Me, I'm coming back by bus," he said, and they both laughed, she painfully because of her swollen face. When he went back to his seat far away at the front of the bus she lay back peacefully against the seat. She could feel the sleeping pill pulling at her; the throb of the toothache was distant now, and mingled with the movement of the bus, a steady beat like her heartbeat which she could hear louder and louder, going on through the night. She put her head back and her feet up, discreetly covered with her skirt, and fell asleep without saying good-bye to the town.

She opened her eyes once and they were moving almost silently through the darkness. Her tooth was pulsing steadily and she turned her cheek against the cool back of the seat in weary resignation. There was a thin line of lights along the ceiling of the bus and no other light. Far ahead of her in the bus she could see the other people sitting; the driver, so far away as to be only a tiny figure at the end of a telescope, was straight at the wheel, seemingly awake. She fell back into her fantastic sleep.

She woke up later because the bus had stopped, the end of that silent motion through the darkness so positive a shock that it woke her stunned, and it was a minute before the ache began again. People were moving along the aisle of the bus and the driver, turning around, said, "Fifteen minutes." She got up and followed everyone else out, all but her eyes still asleep, her feet moving without awareness. They were stopped beside an all-night restaurant, lonely and lighted on the vacant road. Inside, it was warm and busy and full of people. She saw a seat at the end of the counter and sat down, not aware that she had fallen asleep again when someone sat down next to her and touched her arm. When she looked around foggily he said, "Traveling far?"

"Yes," she said.

He was wearing a blue suit and he looked tall; she could not focus her eyes to see any more.

"You want coffee?" he asked.

She nodded and he pointed to the counter in front of her where a cup of coffee sat steaming.

"Drink it quickly," he said.

She sipped at it delicately; she may have put her face down and tasted it without lifting the cup. The strange man was talking.

"Even farther than Samarkand," he was saying, "and the waves ringing on the shore like bells."

"Okay, folks," the bus driver said, and she gulped quickly at the coffee, drank enough to get her back into the bus.

When she sat down in her seat again the strange man sat down beside her. It was so dark in the bus that the lights from the restaurant were unbearably glaring and she closed her eyes. When her eyes were shut, before she fell asleep, she was closed in alone with the toothache.

"The flutes play all night," the strange man said, "and the stars are as big as the moon and the moon is as big as a lake."

As the bus started up again they slipped back into the

darkness and only the thin thread of lights along the ceiling of the bus held them together, brought the back of the bus where she sat along with the front of the bus where the driver sat and the people sitting there so far away from her. The lights tied them together and the strange man next to her was saying, "Nothing to do all day but lie under the trees."

Inside the bus, traveling on, she was nothing; she was passing the trees and the occasional sleeping houses, and she was in the bus but she was between here and there, joined tenuously to the bus driver by a thread of lights, being carried along without effort of her own.

"My name is Jim," the strange man said.

She was so deeply asleep that she stirred uneasily without knowledge, her forehead against the window, the darkness moving along beside her.

Then again that numbing shock, and, driven awake, she said, frightened, "What's happened?"

"It's all right," the strange man—Jim—said immediately. "Come along."

She followed him out of the bus, into the same restaurant, seemingly, but when she started to sit down at the same seat at the end of the counter he took her hand and led her to a table. "Go and wash your face," he said. "Come back here afterward."

She went into the ladies' room and there was a girl standing there powdering her nose. Without turning around the girl said, "Cost's a nickel. Leave the door fixed so's the next one won't have to pay."

The door was wedged so it would not close, with half a match folder in the lock. She left it the same way and went back to the table where Jim was sitting.

"What do you want?" she said, and he pointed to another cup of coffee and a sandwich. "Go ahead," he said.

While she was eating her sandwich she heard his voice, musical and soft, "And while we were sailing past the island we heard a voice calling us. . . ."

Back in the bus Jim said, "Put your head on my shoulder now, and go to sleep."

"I'm all right," she said.

"No," Jim said. "Before, your head was rattling against the window."

Once more she slept, and once more the bus stopped and she woke frightened, and Jim brought her again to a restaurant and more coffee. Her tooth came alive then, and with one hand pressing her cheek she searched through the pockets of her coat and then through her pocketbook until she found the little bottle of codeine pills and she took two while Jim watched her.

She was finishing her coffee when she heard the sound of the bus motor and she started up suddenly, hurrying, and with Jim holding her arm she fled back into the dark shelter of her seat. The bus was moving forward when she realized that she had left her bottle of codeine pills sitting on the table in the restaurant and now she was at the mercy of her tooth. For a minute she stared back at the lights of the restaurant through the bus window and then she put her head on Jim's shoulder and he was saying as she fell asleep, "The sand is so white it looks like snow, but it's hot, even at night it's hot under your feet."

Then they stopped for the last time, and Jim brought her out of the bus and they stood for a minute in New York together. A woman passing them in the station said to the man following her with suitcases, "We're just on time, it's five-fifteen."

"I'm going to the dentist," she said to Jim.

"I know," he said. "I'll watch out for you."

He went away, although she did not see him go. She thought to watch for his blue suit going through the door, but there was nothing.

I ought to have thanked him, she thought stupidly, and went slowly into the station restaurant, where she ordered coffee again. The counter man looked at her with the worn sympathy of one who has spent a long night watching people get off and on buses. "Sleepy?" he asked.

"Yes," she said.

She discovered after a while that the bus station joined Pennsylvania Terminal and she was able to get into the main waiting-room and find a seat on one of the benches by the time she fell asleep again.

Then someone shook her rudely by the shoulder and said, "What train you taking, lady, it's nearly seven." She sat up and saw her pocketbook on her lap, her feet neatly crossed, a clock glaring into her face. She said, "Thank you," and got up and walked blindly past the benches and got on to the escalator. Someone got on immediately behind her and touched her arm; she turned and it was Jim. "The grass is so green and so soft," he said, smiling, "and the water of the river is so cool."

She stared at him tiredly. When the escalator reached the top she stepped off and started to walk to the street she saw ahead. Jim came along beside her and his voice went on, "The sky is bluer than anything you've ever seen, and the songs. . . ."

She stepped quickly away from him and thought that people were looking at her as they passed. She stood on the corner waiting for the light to change and Jim came swiftly up to her and then away. "Look," he said as he passed, and he held out a handful of pearls.

Across the street there was a restaurant, just opening. She went in and sat down at a table, and a waitress was standing beside her frowning. "You was asleep," the waitress said accusingly.

"I'm very sorry," she said. It was morning. "Poached eggs and coffee, please."

It was a quarter to eight when she left the restaurant, and she thought, if I take a bus, and go straight downtown now, I can sit in the drugstore across the street from the dentist's office and have more coffee until about eight-thirty and then go into the dentist's when it opens and he can take me first.

The buses were beginning to fill up; she got into the first bus that came along and could not find a seat. She wanted to go to Twenty-third Street, and got a seat just as they were passing Twenty-sixth Street; when she woke she was so far downtown that it took her nearly half-an-hour to find a bus and get back to Twenty-third.

At the corner of Twenty-third Street, while she was waiting for the light to change, she was caught up in a crowd of people, and when they crossed the street and separated to go different directions someone fell into step beside her. For a minute she walked on without looking up, staring resentfully at the sidewalk, her tooth burning her, and then she looked up, but there was no blue suit among the people pressing by on either side.

When she turned into the office building where her dentist was, it was still very early morning. The doorman in the office building was freshly shaven and his hair was combed; he held the door open briskly, as at five o'clock he would be sluggish, his hair faintly out of place. She went in through the door with a feeling of achievement; she had come successfully from one place to another, and this was the end of her journey and her objective.

The clean white nurse sat at the desk in the office; her eyes took in the swollen cheek, the tired shoulders, and she said, "You poor thing, you look worn out."

"I have a toothache." The nurse half-smiled, as though she were still waiting for the day when someone would come in and say, "My feet hurt." She stood up into the professional sunlight. "Come right in," she said. "We won't make you wait."

There was sunlight on the headrest of the dentist's chair, on the round white table, on the drill bending its smooth chromium head. The dentist smiled with the same tolerance as the nurse; perhaps all human ailments were contained in the teeth, and he could fix them if people would only come to him in time. The nurse said smoothly, "I'll get her file, doctor. We thought we'd better bring her right in."

She felt, while they were taking an X-ray, that there was nothing in her head to stop the malicious eye of the camera, as though the camera would look through her and photograph the nails in the wall next to her, or the dentist's cuff buttons, or the small thin bones of the dentist's instruments; the dentist said, "Extraction," regretfully to the nurse, and the nurse said, "Yes, doctor, I'll call them right away."

Her tooth, which had brought her here unerringly, seemed now the only part of her to have any identity. It seemed to have had its picture taken without her; it was the important creature which must be recorded and examined and gratified; she was only its unwilling vehicle, and only as such was she of interest to the dentist and the nurse, only as the bearer of her tooth was she worth their immediate and practised attention.

The dentist handed her a slip of paper with the picture of a full set of teeth drawn on it; her living tooth was checked with a black mark, and across the top of the paper was written "Lower molar; extraction."

"Take this slip," the dentist said, "and go right up to the address on this card; it's a surgeon dentist. They'll take care of you there."

"What will they do?" she said. Not the question she wanted to ask, not: What about me? or, How far down do the roots go?

"They'll take that tooth out," the dentist said testily, turning away. "Should have been done years ago."

I've stayed too long, she thought, he's tired of my tooth. She got up out of the dentist chair and said, "Thank you. Good-bye."

"Good-bye," the dentist said. At the last minute he smiled at her, showing her his full white teeth, all in perfect control.

"Are you all right? Does it bother you too much?" the nurse asked.

"I'm all right."

"I can give you some codeine tablets," the nurse said. "We'd rather you didn't take anything right now, of course, but I think I could let you have them if the tooth is really bad."

"No," she said, remembering her little bottle of codeine pills on the table of a restaurant between here and there. "No, it doesn't bother me too much."

"Well," the nurse said, "good luck."

She went down the stairs and out past the doorman; in the fifteen minutes she had been upstairs he had lost a little of his pristine morningness, and his bow was just a fraction smaller than before.

"Taxi?" he asked, and, remembering the bus down to Twenty-third Street, she said, "Yes."

Just as the doorman came back from the curb, bowing to the taxi he seemed to believe he had invented, she thought a hand waved to her from the crowd across the street.

She read the address on the card the dentist had given her and repeated it carefully to the taxi driver. With the card and the little slip of paper with "Lower molar" written on it and her tooth identified so clearly, she sat without moving, her hands still around the papers, her eyes almost closed. She thought

she must have been asleep again when the taxi stopped suddenly, and the driver, reaching around to open the door, said,
"Here we are, lady." He looked at her curiously.

"I'm going to have a tooth pulled," she said.

"Jesus," the taxi driver said. She paid him and he said,
"Good luck," as he slammed the door.

This was a strange building, the entrance flanked by medical
signs carved in stone; the doorman here was faintly professional, as though he were competent to prescribe if she did not
care to go any farther. She went past him, going straight ahead
until an elevator opened its door to her. In the elevator she
showed the elevator man the card and he said, "Seventh
floor."

She had to back up in the elevator for a nurse to wheel in an
old lady in a wheel chair. The old lady was calm and restful, sitting there in the elevator with a rug over her knees; she said,
"Nice day" to the elevator operator and he said, "Good to see
the sun," and then the old lady lay back in her chair and the
nurse straightened the rug around her knees and said, "Now
we're not going to worry," and the old lady said irritably,
"Who's worrying?"

They got out at the fourth floor. The elevator went on
up and then the operator said, "Seven," and the elevator
stopped and the door opened.

"Straight down the hall and to your left," the operator said.

There were closed doors on either side of the hall. Some of
them said "DDS," some of them said "Clinic," some of them
said "X-Ray." One of them, looking wholesome and friendly
and somehow most comprehensible, said "Ladies." Then she
turned to the left and found a door with the name on the card
and she opened it and went in. There was a nurse sitting
behind a glass window, almost as in a bank, and potted palms
in tubs in the corners of the waiting room, and new magazines
and comfortable chairs. The nurse behind the glass window
said, "Yes?" as though you had overdrawn your account with
the dentist and were two teeth in arrears.

She handed her slip of paper through the glass window and
the nurse looked at it and said, "Lower molar, yes. They called
about you. Will you come right in, please? Through the door
to your left."

Into the vault? she almost said, and then silently opened the door and went in. Another nurse was waiting, and she smiled and turned, expecting to be followed, with no visible doubt about her right to lead.

There was another X-ray, and the nurse told another nurse; "Lower molar," and the other nurse said, "Come this way, please."

There were labyrinths and passages, seeming to lead into the heart of the office building, and she was put, finally, in a cubicle where there was a couch with a pillow and a wash basin and a chair.

"Wait here," the nurse said. "Relax if you can."

"I'll probably go to sleep," she said.

"Fine," the nurse said. "You won't have to wait long."

She waited probably for over an hour, although she spent the time half-sleeping, waking only when someone passed the door; occasionally the nurse looked in and smiled, once she said, "Won't have to wait much longer." Then, suddenly, the nurse was back, no longer smiling, no longer the good hostess, but efficient and hurried. "Come along," she said, and moved purposefully out of the little room into the hallways again.

Then, quickly, more quickly than she was able to see, she was sitting in the chair and there was a towel around her head and a towel under her chin and the nurse was leaning a hand on her shoulder.

"Will it hurt?" she asked.

"No," the nurse said, smiling. "You know it won't hurt, don't you?"

"Yes," she said.

The dentist came in and smiled down on her from over her head. "Well," he said.

"Will it hurt?" she said.

"Now," he said cheerfully, "we couldn't stay in business if we hurt people." All the time he talked he was busying himself with metal hidden under a towel, and great machinery being wheeled in almost silently behind her. "We couldn't stay in business at all," he said. "All you've got to worry about is telling us all your secrets while you're asleep. Want to watch out for that, you know. Lower molar?" he said to the nurse.

"Lower molar, doctor," she said.

Then they put the metal-tasting rubber mask over her face and the dentist said, "You know," two or three times absent-mindedly while she could still see him over the mask. The nurse said "Relax your hands, dear," and after a long time she felt her fingers relaxing.

First of all things get so far away, she thought, remember this. And remember the metallic sound and taste of all of it. And the outrage.

And then the whirling music, the ringing confusedly loud music that went on and on, around and around, and she was running as fast as she could down a long horribly clear hallway with doors on both sides and at the end of the hallway was Jim, holding out his hands and laughing, and calling something she could never hear because of the loud music, and she was running and then she said, "I'm not afraid," and someone from the door next to her took her arm and pulled her through and the world widened alarmingly until it would never stop and then it stopped with the head of the dentist looking down at her and the window dropped into place in front of her and the nurse was holding her arm.

"Why did you pull me back?" she said, and her mouth was full of blood. "I wanted to go on."

"I didn't pull you," the nurse said, but the dentist said, "She's not out of it yet."

She began to cry without moving and felt the tears rolling down her face and the nurse wiped them off with a towel. There was no blood anywhere around except in her mouth; everything was as clean as before. The dentist was gone, suddenly, and the nurse put out her arm and helped her out of the chair. "Did I talk?" she asked suddenly, anxiously. "Did I say anything?"

"You said, 'I'm not afraid,'" the nurse said soothingly. "Just as you were coming out of it."

"No," she said, stopping to pull at the arm around her. "Did I *say* anything? Did I say where he is?"

"You didn't say *anything*," the nurse said. "The doctor was only teasing you."

"Where's my tooth?" she asked suddenly, and the nurse laughed and said, "All gone. Never bother you again."

She was back in the cubicle, and she lay down on the couch and cried, and the nurse brought her whisky in a paper cup and set it on the edge of the wash-basin.

"God has given me blood to drink," she said to the nurse, and the nurse said, "Don't rinse your mouth or it won't clot."

After a long time the nurse came back and said to her from the doorway, smiling, "I see you're awake again."

"Why?" she said.

"You've been asleep," the nurse said. "I didn't want to wake you."

She sat up; she was dizzy and it seemed that she had been in the cubicle all her life.

"Do you want to come along now?" the nurse said, all kindness again. She held out the same arm, strong enough to guide any wavering footstep; this time they went back through the long corridor to where the nurse sat behind the bank window.

"All through?" this nurse said brightly. "Sit down a minute, then." She indicated a chair next to the glass window, and turned away to write busily. "Do not rinse your mouth for two hours," she said, without turning around. "Take a laxative tonight, take two aspirin if there is any pain. If there is much pain or excessive bleeding, notify this office at once. All right?" she said, and smiled brightly again.

There was a new little slip of paper; this one said, "Extraction," and underneath, "Do not rinse mouth. Take mild laxative. Two aspirin for pain. If pain is excessive or any hemorrhage occurs, notify office."

"Good-bye," the nurse said pleasantly.

"Good-bye," she said.

With the little slip of paper in her hand, she went out through the glass door and, still almost asleep, turned the corner and started down the hall. When she opened her eyes a little and saw that it was a long hall with doorways on either side, she stopped and then saw the door marked "Ladies" and went in. Inside there was a vast room with windows and wicker chairs and glaring white tiles and glittering silver faucets; there were four or five women around the wash-basins, combing their hair, putting on lipstick. She went directly to the nearest of the three wash-basins, took a paper towel, dropped her pocketbook and the little slip of paper on the floor next to her, and fumbled with the faucets, soaking the towel until it was dripping. Then she slapped it against her face violently. Her eyes cleared and she felt fresher, so she soaked the paper again and rubbed her face with it. She felt out blindly for another paper towel, and the woman next to her handed her one, with a laugh she could hear, although she could not see for the water in her eyes. She heard one of the women say, "Where we going for lunch?" and another one say, "Just downstairs, prob'ly. Old fool says I gotta be back in half-an-hour."

Then she realized that at the wash-basin she was in the way of the women in a hurry so she dried her face quickly. It was when she stepped a little aside to let someone else get to the basin and stood up and glanced into the mirror that she realized with a slight stinging shock that she had no idea which face was hers.

She looked into the mirror as though into a group of strangers, all staring at her or around her; no one was familiar in the group, no one smiled at her or looked at her with recognition; you'd think my own face would know me, she thought, with a queer numbness in her throat. There was a creamy chinless face with bright blond hair, and a sharp-looking face under a red veiled hat, and a colorless anxious face with brown hair pulled straight back, and a square rosy face under a square haircut, and two or three more faces pushing close to the mirror, moving, regarding themselves. Perhaps it's not a mirror, she thought, maybe it's a window and I'm looking straight through at women washing on the other side. But there were women combing their hair and consulting the mirror; the group was on her side, and she thought, I hope I'm not the blonde, and lifted her hand and put it on her cheek.

She was the pale anxious one with the hair pulled back and when she realized it she was indignant and moved hurriedly back through the crowd of women, thinking, It isn't fair, why don't I have any color in my face? There were some pretty faces there, why didn't I take one of those? I didn't have time, she told herself sullenly, they didn't give me time to think, I could have had one of the nice faces, even the blonde would be better.

She backed up and sat down in one of the wicker chairs. It's mean, she was thinking. She put her hand up and felt her hair; it was loosened after her sleep but that was definitely the way she wore it, pulled straight back all around and fastened at the back of her neck with a wide tight barrette. Like a schoolgirl, she thought, only—remembering the pale face in the mirror—only I'm older than that. She unfastened the barrette with difficulty and brought it around where she could look at it. Her hair fell softly around her face; it was warm and reached to her shoulders. The barrette was silver; engraved on it was the name, "Clara."

"Clara," she said aloud. "*Clara?*" Two of the women leaving the room smiled back at her over their shoulders; almost all the women were leaving now, correctly combed and lipsticked, hurrying out talking together. In the space of a second, like birds leaving a tree, they all were gone and she sat alone in the room. She dropped the barrette into the ashstand next to her chair; the ashstand was deep and metal, and the barrette made a satisfactory clang falling down. Her hair down on her shoulders, she opened her pocketbook, and began to take things out, setting them on her lap as she did so. Handkerchief, plain, white, uninitialled. Compact, square and brown tortoise-shell plastic, with a powder compartment and a rouge compartment; the rouge compartment had obviously never been used, although the powder cake was half-gone. That's why I'm so pale, she thought, and set the compact down. Lipstick, a rose shade, almost finished. A comb, an opened package of cigarettes and a package of matches, a change purse, and a wallet. The change purse was red imitation leather with a zipper across the top; she opened it and dumped the money out into her hand. Nickels, dimes, pennies, a quarter. Ninety-seven cents. Can't go far on that, she thought, and opened the brown leather wallet; there was money in it but she looked first for papers and found nothing. The only thing in the wallet was money. She counted it; there were nineteen dollars. I can go a little farther on *that*, she thought.

There was nothing else in the pocketbook. No keys—shouldn't I have keys? she wondered—no papers, no address book, no identification. The pocketbook itself was imitation leather, light grey, and she looked down and discovered that she was wearing a dark grey flannel suit and a salmon pink blouse with a ruffle around the neck. Her shoes were black and stout with moderate heels and they had laces, one of which was untied. She was wearing beige stockings and there was a ragged tear in the right knee and a great ragged run going down her leg and ending in a hole in the toe which she could feel inside her shoe. She was wearing a pin on the lapel of her suit which, when she turned it around to look at it, was a blue plastic letter C. She took the pin off and dropped it into the ashstand, and it made a sort of clatter at the bottom, with a metallic clang when it landed on the barrette. Her hands were small, with stubby fingers and no nail polish; she wore a thin gold wedding ring on her left hand and no other jewelry.

Sitting alone in the ladies' room in the wicker chair, she thought, The least I can do is get rid of these stockings. Since no one was around she took off her shoes and stripped away the stockings with a feeling of relief when her toe was released from the hole. Hide them, she thought: the paper towel wastebasket. When she stood up she got a better sight of herself in the mirror; it was worse than she had thought: the grey suit bagged in the seat, her legs were bony, and her shoulders sagged. I look fifty, she thought; and then, consulting the face, but I can't be more than thirty. Her hair hung down untidily around the pale face and with sudden anger she fumbled in the pocketbook and found the lipstick; she drew an emphatic rosy mouth on the pale face, realizing as she did so that she was not very expert at it, and with the red mouth the face looking at her seemed somehow better to her, so she opened the compact and put on pink cheeks with the rouge. The cheeks were uneven and patent, and the red mouth glaring, but at least the face was no longer pale and anxious.

She put the stockings into the wastebasket and went barelegged out into the hall again, and purposefully to the elevator. The elevator operator said, "Down?" when he saw her and she stepped in and the elevator carried her silently downstairs. She went back past the grave professional doorman and out into the street where people were passing, and she stood in front of the building and waited. After a few minutes Jim came out of a crowd of people passing and came over to her and took her hand.

Somewhere between here and there was her bottle of

codeine pills, upstairs on the floor of the ladies' room she had left a little slip of paper headed "Extraction"; seven floors below, oblivious of the people who stepped sharply along the sidewalk, not noticing their occasional curious glances, her hand in Jim's and her hair down on her shoulders, she ran barefoot through hot sand.

Got a Letter from Jimmy

SOMETIMES, she thought, stacking the dishes in the kitchen, sometimes I wonder if men are quite sane, any of them. Maybe they're all just crazy and every other woman knows it but me, and my mother never told me and my roommate just didn't mention it and all the other wives think I know. . . .

"Got a letter from Jimmy today," he said, when he was unfolding his napkin.

So you got it at last, she thought, so he finally broke down and wrote you, maybe now it will be all right, everything settled and friendly again. . . . "What did he have to say?" she asked casually.

"Don't know," he said, "didn't open it."

My God, she thought, seeing it clearly all the way through right then. She waited.

"Going to send it back to him tomorrow unopened."

I could have figured that one out by myself, she thought. I couldn't have kept that letter closed for five minutes. I would have figured out something nasty like tearing it up and sending it back in little pieces, or getting someone to write a sharp answer for me, but I couldn't have kept it around for five minutes.

"Had lunch with Tom today," he said, as though the subject were closed, just exactly as though the subject were closed, she thought, just exactly as though he never expected to think about it again. Maybe he doesn't, she thought, my God.

"I think you ought to open Jimmy's letter," she said. Maybe it will all be just as easy as that, she thought, maybe he'll say all right and go open it, maybe he'll go home and live with his mother for a while.

"Why?" he said.

Start easy, she thought. You'll kill yourself if you don't. "Oh, I guess because I'm curious and I'll just die if I don't see what's in it," she said.

"Open it," he said.

Just watch me make a move for it, she thought. "Seriously," she said, "it's so silly to hold a grudge against a letter. Against

Jimmy, all right. But not to read a letter out of spite is silly." Oh God, she thought, I said silly. I said silly twice. That finishes it. If he hears me say he's silly I'm through, I can talk all night.

"Why should I read it?" he said, "I wouldn't be interested in anything he had to say."

"I would."

"Open it," he said.

Oh God, she thought, oh God oh God, I'll steal it out of his brief case, I'll scramble it up with his eggs tomorrow, but I won't take a dare like that, he'd break my arm.

"Okay," she said, "so I'm not interested." Make him think you're through, let him get nicely settled in his chair, let him get to the lemon pie, get him off on some other subject.

"Had lunch with Tom today," he said.

Stacking the dishes in the kitchen, she thought, Maybe he means it, maybe he could kill himself first, maybe he really wasn't curious and even if he were he'd drive himself into a hysterical state trying to read through the envelope, locked in the bathroom. Or maybe he just got it and said, Oh, from Jimmy, and threw it in his brief case and forgot it. I'll murder him if he did, she thought, I'll bury him in the cellar.

Later, when he was drinking his coffee, she said, "Going to show it to John?" John will die too, she thought, John will edge around it just like I'm doing.

"Show what to John?" he said.

"Jimmy's letter."

"Oh," he said. "Sure."

A tremendous triumph captured her. So he really wants to show it to John, she thought, so he just wants to see for himself that he's still mad, he wants John to say, Really, are you still mad at Jimmy? And he wants to be able to say yes. Out of her great triumph she thought, He really has been thinking about it all this time, too; and she said, before she could stop herself:

"Thought you were going to send it back unopened?"

He looked up. "I forgot," he said. "Guess I will."

I had to open my mouth, she thought. He forgot. The trouble is, she thought, he really did forget. It slipped his mind completely, he never gave it a second thought, if it was a snake it would have bit him. Under the cellar steps, she thought, with his head bashed in and his goddam letter under his folded hands, and it's worth it, she thought, oh it's worth it.

The Lottery

THE morning of June 27th was clear and sunny, with the fresh warmth of a full-summer day; the flowers were blossoming profusely and the grass was richly green. The people of the village began to gather in the square, between the post office and the bank, around ten o'clock; in some towns there were so many people that the lottery took two days and had to be started on June 26th, but in this village, where there were only about three hundred people, the whole lottery took less than two hours, so it could begin at ten o'clock in the morning and still be through in time to allow the villagers to get home for noon dinner.

The children assembled first, of course. School was recently over for the summer, and the feeling of liberty sat uneasily on most of them; they tended to gather together quietly for a while before they broke into boisterous play, and their talk was still of the classroom and the teacher, of books and reprimands. Bobby Martin had already stuffed his pockets full of stones, and the other boys soon followed his example, selecting the smoothest and roundest stones; Bobby and Harry Jones and Dickie Delacroix—the villagers pronounced this name "Dellacroy"—eventually made a great pile of stones in one corner of the square and guarded it against the raids of the other boys. The girls stood aside, talking among themselves, looking over their shoulders at the boys, and the very small children rolled in the dust or clung to the hands of their older brothers or sisters.

Soon the men began to gather, surveying their own children, speaking of planting and rain, tractors and taxes. They stood together, away from the pile of stones in the corner, and their jokes were quiet and they smiled rather than laughed. The women, wearing faded house dresses and sweaters, came shortly after their menfolk. They greeted one another and exchanged bits of gossip as they went to join their husbands. Soon the women, standing by their husbands, began to call to their children, and the children came reluctantly, having to be called four or five times. Bobby Martin ducked under his mother's grasping hand and ran, laughing, back to the pile of stones. His father spoke up sharply, and Bobby came quickly and took his place between his father and his oldest brother.

The lottery was conducted—as were the square dances, the teen-age club, the Halloween program—by Mr. Summers, who had time and energy to devote to civic activities. He was a round-faced, jovial man and he ran the coal business, and people were sorry for him, because he had no children and his wife was a scold. When he arrived in the square, carrying the black wooden box, there was a murmur of conversation among the villagers, and he waved and called, "Little late today, folks." The postmaster, Mr. Graves, followed him, carrying a three-legged stool, and the stool was put in the center of the square and Mr. Summers set the black box down on it. The villagers kept their distance, leaving a space between themselves and the stool, and when Mr. Summers said, "Some of you fellows want to give me a hand?" there was a hesitation before two men, Mr. Martin and his oldest son, Baxter, came forward to hold the box steady on the stool while Mr. Summers stirred up the papers inside it.

The original paraphernalia for the lottery had been lost long ago, and the black box now resting on the stool had been put into use even before Old Man Warner, the oldest man in town, was born. Mr. Summers spoke frequently to the villagers about making a new box, but no one liked to upset even as much tradition as was represented by the black box. There was a story that the present box had been made with some pieces of the box that had preceded it, the one that had been constructed when the first people settled down to make a village here. Every year, after the lottery, Mr. Summers began talking again about a new box, but every year the subject was allowed to fade off without anything's being done. The black box grew shabbier each year; by now it was no longer completely black but splintered badly along one side to show the original wood color, and in some places faded or stained.

Mr. Martin and his oldest son, Baxter, held the black box securely on the stool until Mr. Summers had stirred the papers thoroughly with his hand. Because so much of the ritual had been forgotten or discarded, Mr. Summers had been successful in having slips of paper substituted for the chips of wood that had been used for generations. Chips of wood, Mr. Summers had argued, had been all very well when the village was tiny, but now that the population was more than three hundred and likely to keep on growing, it was necessary to use something that would fit more easily into the black box. The night before the lottery, Mr. Summers and Mr. Graves made up the slips of paper and put them in the box, and it was then taken to the safe of Mr. Summers' coal company and locked up until Mr. Summers was ready to take it to the square next morning. The rest of the year, the box was put away, sometimes one place, sometimes another; it had spent one year in Mr. Graves's barn and another year underfoot in the post office, and sometimes it was set on a shelf in the Martin grocery and left there.

There was a great deal of fussing to be done before Mr. Summers declared the lottery open. There were the lists to make up——of heads of families, heads of households in each family, members of each household in each family. There was the proper swearing-in of Mr. Summers by the postmaster, as the official of the lottery; at one time, some people remembered, there had been a recital of some sort, performed by the official of the lottery, a perfunctory, tuneless chant that had been rattled off duly each year; some people believed that the official of the lottery used to stand just so when he said or sang it, others believed that he was supposed to walk among the people, but years and years ago this part of the ritual had been allowed to lapse. There had been, also, a ritual salute, which the official of the lottery had had to use in addressing each person who came up to draw from the box, but this also had changed with time, until now it was felt necessary only for the official to speak to each person approaching. Mr. Summers was very good at all this; in his clean white shirt and blue jeans, with one hand resting carelessly on the black box, he seemed very proper and important as he talked interminably to Mr. Graves and the Martins.

Just as Mr. Summers finally left off talking and turned to the assembled villagers, Mrs. Hutchinson came hurriedly along the path to the square, her sweater thrown over her shoulders, and slid into place in the back of the crowd. "Clean forgot what day it was," she said to Mrs. Delacroix, who stood next to her, and they both laughed softly. "Thought my old man was out back stacking wood," Mrs. Hutchinson went on, "and then I looked out the window and the kids was gone, and then I remembered it was the twenty-seventh and came a-running." She dried her hands on her apron, and Mrs. Delacroix said, "You're in time, though. They're still talking away up there."

Mrs. Hutchinson craned her neck to see through the crowd and found her husband and children standing near the front. She tapped Mrs. Delacroix on the arm as a farewell and began to make her way through the crowd. The people separated good-humoredly to let her through; two or three people said, in voices just loud enough to be heard across the crowd, "Here comes your Missus, Hutchinson," and "Bill, she made it after all." Mrs. Hutchinson reached her husband, and Mr. Summers, who had been waiting, said cheerfully, "Thought we were going to have to get on without you, Tessie." Mrs. Hutchinson said, grinning, "Wouldn't have me leave m'dishes in the sink, now, would you, Joe?," and soft laughter ran through the crowd as the people stirred back into position after Mrs. Hutchinson's arrival.

"Well, now," Mr. Summers said soberly, "guess we better get started, get this over with, so's we can go back to work. Anybody ain't here?"

"Dunbar," several people said. "Dunbar, Dunbar."

Mr. Summers consulted his list. "Clyde Dunbar," he said. "That's right. He's broke his leg, hasn't he? Who's drawing for him?"

"Me, I guess," a woman said, and Mr. Summers turned to look at her. "Wife draws for her husband," Mr. Summers said. "Don't you have a grown boy to do it for you, Janey?" Although Mr. Summers and everyone else in the village knew the answer perfectly well, it was the business of the official of the lottery to ask such questions formally. Mr. Summers waited with an expression of polite interest while Mrs. Dunbar answered.

"Horace's not but sixteen yet," Mrs. Dunbar said regretfully. "Guess I gotta fill in for the old man this year."

"Right," Mr. Summers said. He made a note on the list he was holding. Then he asked, "Watson boy drawing this year?"

A tall boy in the crowd raised his hand. "Here," he said. "I'm drawing for m'mother and me." He blinked his eyes nervously and ducked his head as several voices in the crowd said things like "Good fellow, Jack," and "Glad to see your mother's got a man to do it."

"Well," Mr. Summers said, "guess that's everyone. Old Man Warner make it?"

"Here," a voice said, and Mr. Summers nodded.

A sudden hush fell on the crowd as Mr. Summers cleared his throat and looked at the list. "All ready?" he called. "Now, I'll read the names—heads of families first—and the men come up and take a paper out of the box. Keep the paper folded in your hand without looking at it until everyone has had a turn. Everything clear?"

The people had done it so many times that they only half listened to the directions; most of them were quiet, wetting their lips, not looking around. Then Mr. Summers raised one hand high and said, "Adams." A man disengaged himself from the crowd and came forward. "Hi, Steve," Mr. Summers said, and Mr. Adams said, "Hi, Joe." They grinned at one another humorlessly and nervously. Then Mr. Adams reached into the black box and took out a folded paper. He held it firmly by one corner as he turned and went hastily back to his place in the crowd, where he stood a little apart from his family, not looking down at his hand.

"Allen," Mr. Summers said. "Anderson. . . . Bentham."

"Seems like there's no time at all between lotteries any more," Mrs. Delacroix said to Mrs. Graves in the back row. "Seems like we got through with the last one only last week."

"Time sure goes fast," Mrs. Graves said.

"Clark. . . . Delacroix."

"There goes my old man," Mrs. Delacroix said. She held her breath while her husband went forward.

"Dunbar," Mr. Summers said, and Mrs. Dunbar went steadily to the box while one of the women said, "Go on, Janey," and another said, "There she goes."

"We're next," Mrs. Graves said. She watched while Mr. Graves came around from the side of the box, greeted Mr. Summers gravely, and selected a slip of paper from the box. By now, all through the crowd there were men holding the small folded papers in their large hands, turning them over and over nervously. Mrs. Dunbar and her two sons stood together, Mrs. Dunbar holding the slip of paper.

"Harburt. . . . Hutchinson."

"Get up there, Bill," Mrs. Hutchinson said, and the people near her laughed.

"Jones."

"They do say," Mr. Adams said to Old Man Warner, who stood next to him, "that over in the north village they're talking of giving up the lottery."

Old Man Warner snorted. "Pack of crazy fools," he said. "Listening to the young folks, nothing's good enough for *them*. Next thing you know, they'll be wanting to go back to living in caves, nobody work any more, live *that* way for a while. Used to be a saying about 'Lottery in June, corn be heavy soon.' First thing you know, we'd all be eating stewed chickweed and acorns. There's *always* been a lottery," he added petulantly. "Bad enough to see young Joe Summers up there joking with everybody."

"Some places have already quit lotteries," Mrs. Adams said.

"Nothing but trouble in *that*," Old Man Warner said stoutly. "Pack of young fools."

"Martin." And Bobby Martin watched his father go forward. "Overdyke. . . . Percy."

"I wish they'd hurry," Mrs. Dunbar said to her older son. "I wish they'd hurry."

"They're almost through," her son said.

"You get ready to run tell Dad," Mrs. Dunbar said.

Mr. Summers called his own name and then stepped forward precisely and selected a slip from the box. Then he called, "Warner."

"Seventy-seventh year I been in the lottery," Old Man Warner said as he went through the crowd. "Seventy-seventh time."

"Watson." The tall boy came awkwardly through the crowd. Someone said, "Don't be nervous, Jack," and Mr. Summers said, "Take your time, son."

"Zanini."

After that, there was a long pause, a breathless pause, until Mr. Summers, holding his slip of paper in the air, said, "All right, fellows." For a minute, no one moved, and then all the slips of paper were opened. Suddenly, all the women began to speak at once, saying, "Who is it?," "Who's got it?," "Is it the Dunbars?," "Is it the Watsons?" Then the voices began to say, "It's Hutchinson. It's Bill," "Bill Hutchinson's got it."

"Go tell your father," Mrs. Dunbar said to her older son.

People began to look around to see the Hutchinsons. Bill Hutchinson was standing quiet, staring down at the paper in his hand. Suddenly, Tessie Hutchinson shouted to Mr. Summers, "You didn't give him time enough to take any paper he wanted. I saw you. It wasn't fair!"

"Be a good sport, Tessie," Mrs. Delacroix called, and Mrs. Graves said, "All of us took the same chance."

"Shut up, Tessie," Bill Hutchinson said.

"Well, everyone," Mr. Summers said, "that was done pretty fast, and now we've got to be hurrying a little more to get done in time." He consulted his next list. "Bill," he said, "you draw for the Hutchinson family. You got any other households in the Hutchinsons?"

"There's Don and Eva," Mrs. Hutchinson yelled. "Make *them* take their chance!"

"Daughters draw with their husbands' families, Tessie," Mr. Summers said gently. "You know that as well as anyone else."

"It wasn't *fair*," Tessie said.

"I guess not, Joe," Bill Hutchinson said regretfully. "My daughter draws with her husband's family, that's only fair. And I've got no other family except the kids."

"Then, as far as drawing for families is concerned, it's you," Mr. Summers said in explanation, "and as far as drawing for households is concerned, that's you, too. Right?"

"Right," Bill Hutchinson said.

"How many kids, Bill?" Mr. Summers asked formally.

"Three," Bill Hutchinson said. "There's Bill, Jr., and Nancy, and little Dave. And Tessie and me."

"All right, then," Mr. Summers said. "Harry, you got their tickets back?"

Mr. Graves nodded and held up the slips of paper. "Put them in the box, then," Mr. Summers directed. "Take Bill's and put it in."

"I think we ought to start over," Mrs. Hutchinson said, as

quietly as she could. "I tell you it wasn't *fair*. You didn't give him time enough to choose. *Every*body saw that."

Mr. Graves had selected the five slips and put them in the box, and he dropped all the papers but those onto the ground, where the breeze caught them and lifted them off.

"Listen, everybody," Mrs. Hutchinson was saying to the people around her.

"Ready, Bill?" Mr. Summers asked, and Bill Hutchinson, with one quick glance around at his wife and children, nodded.

"Remember," Mr. Summers said, "take the slips and keep them folded until each person has taken one. Harry, you help little Dave." Mr. Graves took the hand of the little boy, who came willingly with him up to the box. "Take a paper out of the box, Davy," Mr. Summers said. Davy put his hand into the box and laughed. "Take just *one* paper," Mr. Summers said. "Harry, you hold it for him." Mr. Graves took the child's hand and removed the folded paper from the tight fist and held it while little Dave stood next to him and looked up at him wonderingly.

"Nancy next," Mr. Summers said. Nancy was twelve, and her school friends breathed heavily as she went forward, switching her skirt, and took a slip daintily from the box. "Bill, Jr.," Mr. Summers said, and Billy, his face red and his feet over-large, nearly knocked the box over as he got a paper out. "Tessie," Mr. Summers said. She hesitated for a minute, looking around defiantly, and then set her lips and went up to the box. She snatched a paper out and held it behind her.

"Bill," Mr. Summers said, and Bill Hutchinson reached into the box and felt around, bringing his hand out at last with the slip of paper in it.

The crowd was quiet. A girl whispered, "I hope it's not Nancy," and the sound of the whisper reached the edges of the crowd.

"It's not the way it used to be," Old Man Warner said clearly. "People ain't the way they used to be."

"All right," Mr. Summers said. "Open the papers. Harry, you open little Dave's."

Mr. Graves opened the slip of paper and there was a general sigh through the crowd as he held it up and everyone could see that it was blank. Nancy and Bill, Jr., opened theirs at the same time, and both beamed and laughed, turning around to the crowd and holding their slips of paper above their heads.

"Tessie," Mr. Summers said. There was a pause, and then Mr. Summers looked at Bill Hutchinson, and Bill unfolded his paper and showed it. It was blank.

"It's Tessie," Mr. Summers said, and his voice was hushed. "Show us her paper, Bill."

Bill Hutchinson went over to his wife and forced the slip of paper out of her hand. It had a black spot on it, the black spot Mr. Summers had made the night before with the heavy pencil in the coal-company office. Bill Hutchinson held it up, and there was a stir in the crowd.

"All right, folks," Mr. Summers said. "Let's finish quickly."

Although the villagers had forgotten the ritual and lost the original black box, they still remembered to use stones. The pile of stones the boys had made earlier was ready; there were stones on the ground with the blowing scraps of paper that had come out of the box. Mrs. Delacroix selected a stone so large she had to pick it up with both hands and turned to Mrs. Dunbar. "Come on," she said. "Hurry up."

Mrs. Dunbar had small stones in both hands, and she said, gasping for breath, "I can't run at all. You'll have to go ahead and I'll catch up with you."

The children had stones already, and someone gave little Davy Hutchinson a few pebbles.

Tessie Hutchinson was in the center of a cleared space by now, and she held her hands out desperately as the villagers moved in on her. "It isn't fair," she said. A stone hit her on the side of the head.

Old Man Warner was saying, "Come on, come on, everyone." Steve Adams was in the front of the crowd of villagers, with Mrs. Graves beside him.

"It isn't fair, it isn't right," Mrs. Hutchinson screamed, and then they were upon her.

V

Epilogue

. . . *She set her foot upon the ship,*
No mariners could she behold,
But the sails were o the taffetie,
And the masts o the beaten gold.

She had not sailed a league, a league,
A league but barely three,
When dismal grew his countenance,
And drumlie grew his ee.

They had not sailed a league, a league,
A league but barely three,
Until she espied his cloven foot,
And she wept right bitterlie.

'O hold your tongue of your weeping,' says he,
'Of your weeping now let me be,
I will shew you how the lilies grow
On the banks of Italy.'

'O what hills are yon, yon pleasant hills,
That the sun shines sweetly on?'
'O yon are the hills of heaven,' he said,
'Where you will never win.'

'O whaten a mountain is yon,' she said,
'All so dreary wi frost and snow?'
'O yon is the mountain of hell,' he cried,
'Where you and I will go.'

He strack the tap-mast wi his hand,
The fore-mast wi his knee,
And he brake that gallant ship in twain,
And sank her in the sea.

from *James Harris, The Daemon Lover*
(Child Ballad No. 243)

THE HAUNTING
OF HILL HOUSE

For Leonard Brown

1

N O LIVE organism can continue for long to exist sanely under conditions of absolute reality; even larks and katy-dids are supposed, by some, to dream. Hill House, not sane, stood by itself against its hills, holding darkness within; it had stood so for eighty years and might stand for eighty more. Within, walls continued upright, bricks met neatly, floors were firm, and doors were sensibly shut; silence lay steadily against the wood and stone of Hill House, and whatever walked there, walked alone.

Dr. John Montague was a doctor of philosophy; he had taken his degree in anthropology, feeling obscurely that in this field he might come closest to his true vocation, the analysis of supernatural manifestations. He was scrupulous about the use of his title because, his investigations being so utterly unscien-tific, he hoped to borrow an air of respectability, even scholarly authority, from his education. It had cost him a good deal, in money and pride, since he was not a begging man, to rent Hill House for three months, but he expected absolutely to be compensated for his pains by the sensation following upon the publication of his definitive work on the causes and effects of psychic disturbances in a house commonly known as "haunted." He had been looking for an honestly haunted house all his life. When he heard of Hill House he had been at first doubtful, then hopeful, then indefatigable; he was not the man to let go of Hill House once he had found it.

Dr. Montague's intentions with regard to Hill House de-rived from the methods of the intrepid nineteenth-century ghost hunters; he was going to go and live in Hill House and see what happened there. It was his intention, at first, to follow the example of the anonymous Lady who went to stay at Bal-lechin House and ran a summer-long house party for skeptics and believers, with croquet and ghost-watching as the out-standing attractions, but skeptics, believers, and good croquet players are harder to come by today; Dr. Montague was forced to engage assistants. Perhaps the leisurely ways of Victorian life lent themselves more agreeably to the devices of psychic investigation, or perhaps the painstaking documentation of phenomena has largely gone out as a means of determining actuality; at any rate, Dr. Montague had not only to engage assistants but to search for them.

Because he thought of himself as careful and conscientious, he spent considerable time looking for his assistants. He combed the records of the psychic societies, the back files of sensational newspapers, the reports of parapsychologists, and assembled a list of names of people who had, in one way or another, at one time or another, no matter how briefly or dubiously, been involved in abnormal events. From his list he first eliminated the names of people who were dead. When he had then crossed off the names of those who seemed to him publicity-seekers, of subnormal intelligence, or unsuitable because of a clear tendency to take the center of the stage, he had a list of perhaps a dozen names. Each of these people, then, received a letter from Dr. Montague extending an invitation to spend all or part of a summer at a comfortable country house, old, but perfectly equipped with plumbing, electricity, central heating, and clean mattresses. The purpose of their stay, the letters stated clearly, was to observe and explore the various unsavory stories which had been circulated about the house for most of its eighty years of existence. Dr. Montague's letters did not say openly that Hill House was haunted, because Dr. Montague was a man of science and until he had actually experienced a psychic manifestation in Hill House he would not trust his luck too far. Consequently his letters had a certain ambiguous dignity calculated to catch at the imagination of a very special sort of reader. To his dozen letters, Dr. Montague had four replies, the other eight or so candidates having presumably moved and left no forwarding address, or possibly having lost interest in the supernormal, or even, perhaps, never having existed at all. To the four who replied, Dr. Montague wrote again, naming a specific day when the house would be officially regarded as ready for occupancy, and enclosing detailed directions for reaching it, since, as he was forced to explain, information about finding the house was extremely difficult to get, particularly from the rural community which surrounded it. On the day before he was to leave for Hill House, Dr. Montague was persuaded to take into his select company a representative of the family who owned the house, and a telegram arrived from one of his candidates, backing out with a clearly manufactured excuse. Another never came or wrote, perhaps because of some pressing personal problem which had intervened. The other two came.

2

Eleanor Vance was thirty-two years old when she came to Hill House. The only person in the world she genuinely hated, now that her mother was dead, was her sister. She disliked her brother-in-law and her five-year-old niece, and she had no friends. This was owing largely to the eleven years she had spent caring for her invalid mother, which had left her with some proficiency as a nurse and an inability to face strong sunlight without blinking. She could not remember ever being truly happy in her adult life; her years with her mother had been built up devotedly around small guilts and small reproaches, constant weariness, and unending despair. Without ever wanting to become reserved and shy, she had spent so long alone, with no one to love, that it was difficult for her to talk, even casually, to another person without self-consciousness and an awkward inability to find words. Her name had turned up on Dr. Montague's list because one day, when she was twelve years old and her sister was eighteen, and their father had been dead for not quite a month, showers of stones had fallen on their house, without any warning or any indication of purpose or reason, dropping from the ceilings, rolling loudly down the walls, breaking windows and pattering maddeningly on the roof. The stones continued intermittently for three days, during which time Eleanor and her sister were less un- nerved by the stones than by the neighbors and sightseers who gathered daily outside the front door, and by their mother's blind, hysterical insistence that all of this was due to malicious, backbiting people on the block who had had it in for her ever since she came. After three days Eleanor and her sister were re- moved to the house of a friend, and the stones stopped falling, nor did they ever return, although Eleanor and her sister and her mother went back to living in the house, and the feud with the entire neighborhood was never ended. The story had been forgotten by everyone except the people Dr. Montague consulted; it had certainly been forgotten by Eleanor and her sister, each of whom had supposed at the time that the other was responsible.

During the whole underside of her life, ever since her first memory, Eleanor had been waiting for something like Hill House. Caring for her mother, lifting a cross old lady from her chair to her bed, setting out endless little trays of soup and oatmeal, steeling herself to the filthy laundry, Eleanor had held fast to the belief that someday something would happen. She had accepted the invitation to Hill House by return mail, although her brother-in-law had insisted upon calling a couple of people to make sure that this doctor fellow was not aiming to introduce Eleanor to savage rites not unconnected with matters Eleanor's sister deemed it improper for an unmarried young woman to know. Perhaps, Eleanor's sister whispered in the privacy of the marital bedroom, perhaps Dr. Montague—if that really *was* his name, after all—perhaps this Dr. Montague *used* these women for some—well—*experiments. You* know—*experiments*, the way they do. Eleanor's sister dwelt richly upon experiments she had heard these doctors did. Eleanor had no such ideas, or, having them, was not afraid. Eleanor, in short, would have gone anywhere.

Theodora—that was as much name as she used; her sketches were signed "Theo" and on her apartment door and the window of her shop and her telephone listing and her pale stationery and the bottom of the lovely photograph of her which stood on the mantel, the name was always only Theodora—Theodora was not at all like Eleanor. Duty and conscience were, for Theodora, attributes which belonged properly to Girl Scouts. Theodora's world was one of delight and soft colors; she had come onto Dr. Montague's list because—going laughing into the laboratory, bringing with her a rush of floral perfume—she had somehow been able, amused and excited over her own incredible skill, to identify correctly eighteen cards out of twenty, fifteen cards out of twenty, nineteen cards out of twenty, held up by an assistant out of sight and hearing. The name of Theodora shone in the records of the laboratory and so came inevitably to Dr. Montague's attention. Theodora had been entertained by Dr. Montague's first letter and answered it out of curiosity (perhaps the wakened knowledge in Theodora which told her the names of symbols on cards held out of sight urged her on her way toward Hill House), and yet fully intended to decline the invitation. Yet— perhaps the stirring, urgent sense again—when Dr. Montague's confirming letter arrived, Theodora had been tempted and had somehow plunged blindly, wantonly, into a violent quarrel with the friend with whom she shared an apartment. Things were said on both sides which only time could eradicate; Theodora had deliberately and heartlessly smashed the lovely little figurine her friend had carved of her, and her friend had cruelly ripped to shreds the volume of Alfred de Musset which had been a birthday present from Theodora, taking particular pains with the page which bore Theodora's loving, teasing inscription. These acts were of course unforgettable, and before they could laugh over them together time would have to go by; Theodora had written that night, accepting Dr. Montague's invitation, and departed in cold silence the next day.

Luke Sanderson was a liar. He was also a thief. His aunt, who was the owner of Hill House, was fond of pointing out that her nephew had the best education, the best clothes, the best taste, and the worst companions of anyone she had ever known; she would have leaped at any chance to put him safely away for a few weeks. The family lawyer was prevailed upon to persuade Dr. Montague that the house could on no account be rented to him for his purposes without the confining presence of a member of the family during his stay, and perhaps at their first meeting the doctor perceived in Luke a kind of strength, or catlike instinct for self-preservation, which made him almost as anxious as Mrs. Sanderson to have Luke with him in the house. At any rate, Luke was amused, his aunt grateful, and Dr. Montague more than satisfied. Mrs. Sanderson told the family lawyer that at any rate there was really nothing in the house Luke could steal. The old silver there was of some value, she told the lawyer, but it represented an almost insuperable difficulty for Luke: it required energy to steal it and transform it into money. Mrs. Sanderson did Luke an injustice. Luke was not at all likely to make off with the family silver, or Dr.

Montague's watch, or Theodora's bracelet; his dishonesty was largely confined to taking petty cash from his aunt's pocket-book and cheating at cards. He was also apt to sell the watches and cigarette cases given him, fondly and with pretty blushes, by his aunt's friends. Someday Luke would inherit Hill House, but he had never thought to find himself living in it.

3

"I just don't think she should take the car, is all," Eleanor's brother-in-law said stubbornly.

"It's half my car," Eleanor said. "I helped pay for it."

"I just don't think she should take it, is all," her brother-in-law said. He appealed to his wife. "It isn't fair she should have the use of it for the whole summer, and us have to do without."

"Carrie drives it all the time, and I never even take it out of the garage," Eleanor said. "Besides, you'll be in the mountains all summer, and you can't use it *there*. Carrie, you know you won't use the car in the mountains."

"But suppose poor little Linnie got sick or something? And we needed a car to get her to a doctor?"

"It's half my car," Eleanor said. "I mean to take it."

"Suppose even *Carrie* got sick? Suppose we couldn't get a doctor and needed to go to a hospital?"

"I want it. I mean to take it."

"I don't think so." Carrie spoke slowly, deliberately. "We don't know where you're going, do we? You haven't seen fit to tell us very much about all this, have you? I don't think I can see my way clear to letting you borrow my car."

"It's half my car."

"No," Carrie said. "You may not."

"Right." Eleanor's brother-in-law nodded. "We need it, like Carrie says."

Carrie smiled slightly. "I'd never forgive myself, Eleanor, if I lent you the car and something happened. How do we know we can trust this doctor fellow? You're still a young woman, after all, and the car is worth a good deal of money."

"Well, now, Carrie, I *did* call Homer in the credit office, and he said this fellow was in good standing at some college or other—"

Carrie said, still smiling, "Of course, there is *every* reason to suppose that he is a decent man. But Eleanor does not choose to tell us where she is going, or how to reach her if we want the car back; something could happen, and we might never know. Even if Eleanor," she went on delicately, addressing her teacup, "even if *Eleanor* is prepared to run off to the ends of the earth at the invitation of any man, there is *still* no reason why she should be permitted to take my car with her."

"It's half my car."

"Suppose poor little Linnie got sick, up there in the mountains, with nobody around? No doctor?"

"In any case, Eleanor, I am sure that I am doing what Mother would have thought best. Mother had confidence in me and would certainly never have approved my letting you run wild, going off heaven knows where, in my car."

"Or suppose even *I* got sick, up there in—"

"I am sure Mother would have agreed with me, Eleanor."

"Besides," Eleanor's brother-in-law said, struck by a sudden idea, "how do we know she'd bring it back in good condition?"

There has to be a first time for everything, Eleanor told herself. She got out of the taxi, very early in the morning, trembling because by now, perhaps, her sister and her brother-in-law might be stirring with the first faint proddings of suspicion; she took her suitcase quickly out of the taxi while the driver lifted out the cardboard carton which had been on the front seat. Eleanor overtipped him, wondering if her sister and brother-in-law were following, were perhaps even now turning into the street and telling each other, "There she is, just as we thought, the thief, there she is"; she turned in haste to go into the huge city garage where their car was kept, glancing nervously toward the ends of the street. She crashed into a very little lady, sending packages in all directions, and saw with dismay a bag upset and break on the sidewalk, spilling out a broken piece of cheesecake, tomato slices, a hard roll. "Damn you damn you!" the little lady screamed, her face pushed up close to Eleanor's. "I was taking it home, damn you damn you!"

"I'm so sorry," Eleanor said; she bent down, but it did not seem possible to scoop up the fragments of tomato and cheesecake and shove them somehow back into the broken bag. The old lady was scowling down and snatching up her other packages before Eleanor could reach them, and at last Eleanor rose, smiling in convulsive apology. "I'm really so sorry," she said.

"Damn you," the little old lady said, but more quietly. "I was taking it home for my little lunch. And now, thanks to *you*—"

"Perhaps I could pay?" Eleanor took hold of her pocketbook, and the little lady stood very still and thought.

"I couldn't take money, just like that," she said at last. "I didn't buy the things, you see. They were left over." She snapped her lips angrily. "You should have seen the ham they had," she said, "but someone *else* got *that*. And the chocolate cake. And the potato salad. And the little candies in the little paper dishes. I was too late on *every*thing. And now . . ." She and Eleanor both glanced down at the mess on the sidewalk, and the little lady said, "So you see, I couldn't just take money, not money just from your hand, not for something that was left over."

"May I buy you something to replace this, then? I'm in a terrible hurry, but if we could find some place that's open—"

The little old lady smiled wickedly. "I've still got *this*, anyway," she said, and she hugged one package tight. "You may pay my taxi fare home," she said. "Then no one *else* will be likely to knock me down."

"Gladly," Eleanor said and turned to the taxi driver, who had been waiting, interested. "Can you take this lady home?" she asked.

"A couple of dollars will do it," the little lady said, "not including the tip for this gentleman, of course. Being as small as *I* am," she explained daintily, "it's quite a hazard, quite a hazard indeed, people knocking you down. Still, it's a genuine pleasure to find one as willing as you to make up for it. Sometimes the people who knock you down never turn once to look." With Eleanor's help she climbed into the taxi with her packages, and Eleanor took two dollars and a fifty-cent piece from her pocketbook and handed them to the little lady, who clutched them tight in her tiny hand.

"All right, sweetheart," the taxi driver said, "where do we go?"

The little lady chuckled. "I'll tell you after we start," she said, and then, to Eleanor, "Good luck to you, dearie. Watch out from now on how you go knocking people down."

"Good-by," Eleanor said, "and I'm really very sorry."

"That's fine, then," the little lady said, waving at her as the taxi pulled away from the curb. "I'll be praying for you, dearie."

Well, Eleanor thought, staring after the taxi, there's one person, anyway, who will be praying for me. One person anyway.

4

It was the first genuinely shining day of summer, a time of year which brought Eleanor always to aching memories of her early childhood, when it had seemed to be summer all the time; she could not remember a winter before her father's death on a cold wet day. She had taken to wondering lately, during these swift-counted years, what had been done with all those wasted summer days; how could she have spent them so wantonly? I am foolish, she told herself early every summer, I am very foolish; I am grown up now and know the values of things. Nothing is ever really wasted, she believed sensibly, even one's childhood, and then each year, one summer morning, the warm wind would come down the city street where she walked and she would be touched with the little cold thought: I have let more time go by. Yet this morning, driving the little car which she and her sister owned together, apprehensive lest they might still realize that she had come after all and just taken it away, going docilely along the street, following the lines of traffic, stopping when she was bidden and turning when she could, she smiled out at the sunlight slanting along the street and thought, I am going, I am going, I have finally taken a step.

Always before, when she had her sister's permission to drive the little car, she had gone cautiously, moving with extreme care to avoid even the slightest scratch or mar which might irritate her sister, but today, with her carton on the back seat and her suitcase on the floor, her gloves and pocketbook and light coat on the seat beside her, the car belonged entirely to her, a little contained world all her own; I am really going, she thought.

At the last traffic light in the city, before she turned to go onto the great highway out of town, she stopped, waiting, and slid Dr. Montague's letter out of her pocketbook. I will not even need a map, she thought; he must be a very careful man. ". . . Route 39 to Ashton," the letter said, "and then turn left onto Route 5 going west. Follow this for a little less than thirty miles, and you will come to the small village of Hillsdale. Go through Hillsdale to the corner with a gas station on the left and a church on the right, and turn left here onto what seems to be a narrow country road; you will be going up into the hills and the road is very poor. Follow this road to the end—about six miles—and you will come to the gates of Hill House. I am making these directions so detailed because it is inadvisable to stop in Hillsdale to ask your way. The people there are rude to strangers and openly hostile to anyone inquiring about Hill House.

"I am very happy that you will be joining us in Hill House, and will take great pleasure in making your acquaintance on Thursday the twenty-first of June. . . ."

The light changed; she turned onto the highway and was free of the city. No one, she thought, can catch me now; they don't even know which way I'm going.

She had never driven far alone before. The notion of dividing her lovely journey into miles and hours was silly; she saw it, bringing her car with precision between the line on the road and the line of trees beside the road, as a passage of moments, each one new, carrying her along with them, taking her down a path of incredible novelty to a new place. The journey itself was her positive action, her destination vague, unimagined, perhaps nonexistent. She meant to savor each turn of her traveling, loving the road and the trees and the houses and the small ugly towns, teasing herself with the notion that she might take it into her head to stop just anywhere and never leave again. She might pull her car to the side of the highway —though that was not allowed, she told herself; she would be punished if she really did—and leave it behind while she wandered off past the trees into the soft, welcoming country beyond. She might wander till she was exhausted, chasing butterflies or following a stream, and then come at nightfall to the hut of some poor woodcutter who would offer her shelter; she might make her home forever in East Barrington or Desmond or the incorporated village of Berk; she might never leave the road at all, but just hurry on and on until the wheels of the car were worn to nothing and she had come to the end of the world.

And, she thought, I might just go along to Hill House, where I am expected and where I am being given shelter and room and board and a small token salary in consideration of forsaking my commitments and involvements in the city and running away to see the world. I wonder what Dr. Montague is like. I wonder what Hill House is like. I wonder who else will be there.

She was well away from the city now, watching for the turning onto Route 39, that magic thread of road Dr. Montague had chosen for her, out of all the roads in the world, to bring her safely to him and to Hill House; no other road could lead her from where she was to where she wanted to be. Dr. Montague was confirmed, made infallible; under the sign which pointed the way to Route 39 was another sign saying: ASHTON, 121 MILES.

The road, her intimate friend now, turned and dipped, going around turns where surprises waited—once a cow, regarding her over a fence, once an incurious dog—down into hollows where small towns lay, past fields and orchards. On the main street of one village she passed a vast house, pillared and walled, with shutters over the windows and a pair of stone lions guarding the steps, and she thought that perhaps she might live there, dusting the lions each morning and patting their heads good night. Time is beginning this morning in June, she assured herself, but it is a time that is strangely new and of itself; in these few seconds I have lived a lifetime in a house with two lions in front. Every morning I swept the porch and dusted the lions, and every evening I patted their heads good night, and once a week I washed their faces and manes and paws with warm water and soda and cleaned between their teeth with a swab. Inside the house the rooms were tall and clear with shining floors and polished windows. A little dainty old lady took care of me, moving starchily with a silver tea service on a tray and bringing me a glass of elderberry wine each evening for my health's sake. I took my dinner alone in the long, quiet dining room at the gleaming table, and between the tall windows the white paneling of the walls shone in the candlelight; I dined upon a bird, and radishes from the garden, and homemade plum jam. When I slept it was under a canopy of white organdy, and a nightlight guarded me from the hall. People bowed to me on the streets of the town because everyone was very proud of my lions. When I died . . .

She had left the town far behind by now, and was going past dirty, closed lunch stands and torn signs. There had been a fair somewhere near here once, long ago, with motorcycle races; the signs still carried fragments of words. DARE, one of them read, and another, EVIL, and she laughed at herself, perceiving how she sought out omens everywhere; the word is DARE-DEVIL, Eleanor, daredevil drivers, and she slowed her car because she was driving too fast and might reach Hill House too soon.

At one spot she stopped altogether beside the road to stare in disbelief and wonder. Along the road for perhaps a quarter of a mile she had been passing and admiring a row of splendid tended oleanders, blooming pink and white in a steady row. Now she had come to the gateway they protected, and past the gateway the trees continued. The gateway was no more than a pair of ruined stone pillars, with a road leading away between them into empty fields. She could see that the oleander trees cut away from the road and ran up each side of a great square, and she could see all the way to the farther side of the square, which was a line of oleander trees seemingly going along a little river. Inside the oleander square there was nothing, no house, no building, nothing but the straight road going across and ending at the stream. Now what was here, she wondered, what was here, and is gone, or what was going to be here and never came? Was it going to be a house or a garden or an orchard; were they driven away forever or are they coming back? Oleanders are poisonous, she remembered; could they be here guarding something? Will I, she thought, will I get out of my car and go between the ruined gates and then, once I am in the magic oleander square, find that I have wandered into a fairyland, protected poisonously from the eyes of people passing? Once I have stepped between the magic gateposts, will I find myself through the protective barrier, the spell broken? I will go into a sweet garden, with fountains and low benches and roses trained over arbors, and find one path—jeweled, perhaps, with rubies and emeralds, soft enough for a king's daughter to walk upon with her little sandaled feet—and it will lead me directly to the palace which lies under a spell. I will walk up low stone steps past stone lions guarding and into a courtyard where a fountain plays and the queen waits, weeping, for the princess to return. She will drop her embroidery when she sees me, and cry out to the palace servants—stirring at last after their long sleep—to prepare a great feast, because the enchantment is ended and the palace is itself again. And we shall live happily ever after.

No, of course, she thought, turning to start her car again, once the palace becomes visible and the spell is broken, the *whole* spell will be broken and all this countryside outside the oleanders will return to its proper form, fading away, towns and signs and cows, into a soft green picture from a fairy tale. Then, coming down from the hills there will be a prince riding, bright in green and silver with a hundred bowmen riding behind him, pennants stirring, horses tossing, jewels flashing . . .

She laughed and turned to smile good-by at the magic oleanders. Another day, she told them, another day I'll come back and break your spell.

She stopped for lunch after she had driven a hundred miles and a mile. She found a country restaurant which advertised itself as an old mill and found herself seated, incredibly, upon a balcony over a dashing stream, looking down upon wet rocks and the intoxicating sparkle of moving water, with a cut-glass bowl of cottage cheese on the table before her, and corn sticks in a napkin. Because this was a time and a land where enchantments were swiftly made and broken she wanted to linger over her lunch, knowing that Hill House always waited for her at the end of her day. The only other people in the dining room were a family party, a mother and father with a small boy and girl, and they talked to one another softly and gently, and once the little girl turned and regarded Eleanor with frank curiosity and, after a minute, smiled. The lights from the stream below touched the ceiling and the polished tables and glanced along the little girl's curls, and the little girl's mother said, "She wants her cup of stars."

Eleanor looked up, surprised; the little girl was sliding back in her chair, sullenly refusing her milk, while her father frowned and her brother giggled and her mother said calmly, "She wants her cup of stars."

Indeed yes, Eleanor thought; indeed, so do I; a cup of stars, of course.

"Her little cup," the mother was explaining, smiling apologetically at the waitress, who was thunderstruck at the thought that the mill's good country milk was not rich enough for the little girl. "It has stars in the bottom, and she always drinks her milk from it at home. She calls it her cup of stars because she can see the stars while she drinks her milk." The waitress nodded, unconvinced, and the mother told the little girl, "You'll have your milk from your cup of stars tonight when we get home. But just for now, just to be a very good little girl, will you take a little milk from this glass?"

Don't do it, Eleanor told the little girl; insist on your cup of stars; once they have trapped you into being like everyone else you will never see your cup of stars again; don't do it; and the little girl glanced at her, and smiled a little subtle, dimpling, wholly comprehending smile, and shook her head stubbornly at the glass. Brave girl, Eleanor thought; wise, brave girl.

"You're spoiling her," the father said. "She ought not to be allowed these whims."

"Just this once," the mother said. She put down the glass of milk and touched the little girl gently on the hand. "Eat your ice cream," she said.

When they left, the little girl waved good-by to Eleanor, and Eleanor waved back, sitting in joyful loneliness to finish her coffee while the gay stream tumbled along below her. I have not very much farther to go, Eleanor thought; I am more than halfway there. Journey's end, she thought, and far back in her mind, sparkling like the little stream, a tag end of a tune danced through her head, bringing distantly a word or so; "In delay there lies no plenty," she thought, "in delay there lies no plenty."

She nearly stopped forever just outside Ashton, because she came to a tiny cottage buried in a garden. I could live there all alone, she thought, slowing the car to look down the winding garden path to the small blue front door with, perfectly, a white cat on the step. No one would ever find me there, either, behind all those roses, and just to make sure I would plant oleanders by the road. I will light a fire in the cool evenings and toast apples at my own hearth. I will raise white cats and sew white curtains for the windows and sometimes come out of my door to go to the store to buy cinnamon and tea and thread. People will come to me to have their fortunes told, and I will brew love potions for sad maidens; I will have a robin. . . . But the cottage was far behind, and it was time to look for her new road, so carefully charted by Dr. Montague.

"Turn left onto Route 5 going west," his letter said, and, as efficiently and promptly as though he had been guiding her from some spot far away, moving her car with controls in his hands, it was done; she was on Route 5 going west, and her journey was nearly done. In spite of what he said, though, she thought, I will stop in Hillsdale for a minute, just for a cup of coffee, because I cannot bear to have my long trip end so soon. It was not really disobeying, anyway; the letter said it was inadvisable to stop in Hillsdale to ask the way, not forbidden to stop for coffee, and perhaps if I don't mention Hill House I will not be doing wrong. Anyway, she thought obscurely, it's my last chance.

Hillsdale was upon her before she knew it, a tangled, disorderly mess of dirty houses and crooked streets. It was small; once she had come onto the main street she could see the corner at the end with the gas station and the church. There seemed to be only one place to stop for coffee, and that was an unattractive diner, but Eleanor was bound to stop in Hillsdale and so she brought her car to the broken curb in front of the diner and got out. After a minute's thought, with a silent nod to Hillsdale, she locked the car, mindful of her suitcase on the floor and the carton on the back seat. I will not spend long in Hillsdale, she thought, looking up and down the street, which managed, even in the sunlight, to be dark and ugly. A dog slept uneasily in the shade against a wall, a woman stood in a doorway across the street and looked at Eleanor, and two young boys lounged against a fence, elaborately silent. Eleanor, who was afraid of strange dogs and jeering women and young hoodlums, went quickly into the diner, clutching her pocket-book and her car keys. Inside, she found a counter with a chin-less, tired girl behind it, and a man sitting at the end eating. She wondered briefly how hungry he must have been to come in here at all, when she looked at the gray counter and the smeared glass bowl over a plate of doughnuts. "Coffee," she said to the girl behind the counter, and the girl turned wearily and tumbled down a cup from the piles on the shelves; I will have to drink this coffee because I said I was going to, Eleanor told herself sternly, but next time I will listen to Dr. Montague.

There was some elaborate joke going on between the man eating and the girl behind the counter; when she set Eleanor's coffee down she glanced at him and half-smiled, and he shrugged, and then the girl laughed. Eleanor looked up, but the girl was examining her fingernails and the man was wiping his plate with bread. Perhaps Eleanor's coffee was poisoned; it certainly looked it. Determined to plumb the village of Hills-dale to its lowest depths, Eleanor said to the girl, "I'll have one of those doughnuts too, please," and the girl, glancing side-ways at the man, slid one of the doughnuts onto a dish and set it down in front of Eleanor and laughed when she caught an-other look from the man.

"This is a pretty little town," Eleanor said to the girl. "What is it called?"

The girl stared at her; perhaps no one had ever before had the audacity to call Hillsdale a pretty little town; after a mo-ment the girl looked again at the man, as though calling for confirmation, and said, "Hillsdale."

"Have you lived here long?" Eleanor asked. I'm not going to mention Hill House, she assured Dr. Montague far away, I just want to waste a little time.

"Yeah," the girl said.

"It must be pleasant, living in a small town like this. I come from the city."

"Yeah?"

"Do you like it here?"

"It's all right," the girl said. She looked again at the man, who was listening carefully. "Not much to do."

"How large a town is it?"

"Pretty small. You want more coffee?" This was addressed to the man, who was rattling his cup against his saucer, and Eleanor took a first, shuddering sip of her own coffee and wondered how he could possibly want more.

"Do you have a lot of visitors around here?" she asked when the girl had filled the coffee cup and gone back to lounge against the shelves. "Tourists, I mean?"

"What for?" For a minute the girl flashed at her, from what might have been an emptiness greater than any Eleanor had ever known. "Why would anybody come *here*?" She looked sullenly at the man and added, "There's not even a movie."

"But the hills are so pretty. Mostly, with small out-of-the-way towns like this one, you'll find city people who have come and built themselves homes up in the hills. For privacy."

The girl laughed shortly. "Not *here* they don't."

"Or remodeling old houses—"

"Privacy," the girl said, and laughed again.

"It just seems surprising," Eleanor said, feeling the man looking at her.

"Yeah," the girl said. "If they'd put in a movie, even."

"I thought," Eleanor said carefully, "that I might even look around. Old houses are usually cheap, you know, and it's fun to make them over."

"Not around here," the girl said.

"Then," Eleanor said, "there are no old houses around here? Back in the hills?"

"Nope."

The man rose, taking change from his pocket, and spoke for the first time. "People *leave* this town," he said. "They don't *come* here."

When the door closed behind him the girl turned her flat eyes back to Eleanor, almost resentfully, as though Eleanor with her chatter had driven the man away. "He was right," she said finally. "They go away, the lucky ones."

"Why don't *you* run away?" Eleanor asked her, and the girl shrugged.

"Would I be any better off?" she asked. She took Eleanor's money without interest and returned the change. Then, with another of her quick flashes, she glanced at the empty plates at the end of the counter and almost smiled. "He comes in every day," she said. When Eleanor smiled back and started to speak, the girl turned her back and busied herself with the cups on the shelves, and Eleanor, feeling herself dismissed, rose gratefully from her coffee and took up her car keys and pocketbook. "Good-by," Eleanor said, and the girl, back still turned, said, "Good luck to you. I hope you find your house."

5

The road leading away from the gas station and the church was very poor indeed, deeply rutted and rocky. Eleanor's little car stumbled and bounced, reluctant to go farther into these unattractive hills, where the day seemed quickly drawing to an end under the thick, oppressive trees on either side. They do not really seem to have much traffic on this road, Eleanor thought wryly, turning the wheel quickly to avoid a particularly vicious rock ahead; six miles of this will not do the car any good; and for the first time in hours she thought of her sister and laughed. By now they would surely know that she had taken the car and gone, but they would not know where; they would be telling each other incredulously that they would never have suspected it of Eleanor. I would never have suspected it of myself, she thought, laughing still; everything is different, I am a new person, very far from home. "In delay there lies no plenty; . . . present mirth hath present laughter. . . ." And she gasped as the car cracked against a rock and reeled back across the road with an ominous scraping somewhere beneath, but then gathered itself together valiantly and resumed its dogged climb. The tree branches brushed against the windshield, and it grew steadily darker; Hill House likes to make an entrance, she thought; I wonder if the sun ever shines along here. At last, with one final effort, the car cleared a tangle of dead leaves and small branches across the road, and came into a clearing by the gate of Hill House.

Why am I here? she thought helplessly and at once; why am I here? The gate was tall and ominous and heavy, set strongly into a stone wall which went off through the trees. Even from the car she could see the padlock and the chain that was twisted around and through the bars. Beyond the gate she could see only that the road continued, turned, shadowed on either side by the still, dark trees.

Since the gate was so clearly locked—locked and double-locked and chained and barred; who, she wondered, wants so badly to get in?—she made no attempt to get out of her car, but pressed the horn, and the trees and the gate shuddered and withdrew slightly from the sound. After a minute she blew the horn again and then saw a man coming toward her from inside the gate; he was as dark and unwelcoming as the padlock, and before he moved toward the gate he peered through the bars at her, scowling.

"What *you* want?" His voice was sharp, mean.

"I want to come in, please. Please unlock the gate."

"Who say?"

"Why—" She faltered. "I'm supposed to come in," she said at last.

"What for?"

"I am expected." Or am I? she wondered suddenly; is this as far as I go?

"Who by?"

She knew, of course, that he was delighting in exceeding his authority, as though once he moved to unlock the gate he would lose the little temporary superiority he thought he had —and what superiority have I? she wondered; I am *outside* the gate, after all. She could already see that losing her temper, which she did rarely because she was so afraid of being in-effectual, would only turn him away, leaving her still outside the gate, railing futilely. She could even anticipate his inno-cence if he were reproved later for this arrogance—the mali-ciously vacant grin, the wide, blank eyes, the whining voice protesting that he *would* have let her in, he *planned* to let her in, but how could he be sure? He had his orders, didn't he? And he had to do what he was told? *He*'d be the one to get in trouble, wouldn't he, if he let in someone wasn't supposed to be inside? She could anticipate his shrug, and, picturing him, laughed, perhaps the worst thing she could have done.

Eying her, he moved back from the gate. "You better come back later," he said, and turned his back with an air of virtuous triumph.

"Listen," she called after him, still trying not to sound angry, "I am one of Doctor Montague's guests; he will be expecting me in the house—please *listen* to me!"

He turned and grinned at her. "They couldn't rightly be *expecting* you," he said, "seeing as you're the only one's *come*, so far."

"Do you mean that there's no one in the house?"

"No one *I* know of. Maybe my wife, getting it fixed up. So they couldn't be there exactly *expecting* you, now *could* they?"

She sat back against the car seat and closed her eyes. Hill House, she thought, you're as hard to get into as heaven.

"I suppose you know what you're *asking* for, coming here? I suppose they told you, back in the city? You *hear* anything about this place?"

"I heard that I was invited here as a guest of Doctor Montague's. When you open the gates I will go inside."

"I'll open them; I'm going to open them. I just want to be sure you know what's waiting for you in there. You ever been here before? One of the family, maybe?" He looked at her now, peering through the bars, his jeering face one more barrier, after padlock and chain. "I can't let you in till I'm *sure*, can I? What'd you say your name was?"

She sighed. "Eleanor Vance."

"Not one of the family then, I guess. You ever hear anything about this place?"

It's my chance, I suppose, she thought; I'm being given a last chance. I could turn my car around right here and now in front of these gates and go away from here, and no one would blame me. Anyone has a right to run away. She put her head out through the car window and said with fury, "My name is Eleanor Vance. I am expected in Hill House. Unlock those gates at once."

"All right, all *right*." Deliberately, making a wholly unnecessary display of fitting the key and turning it, he opened the padlock and loosened the chain and swung the gates just wide enough for the car to come through. Eleanor moved the car slowly, but the alacrity with which he leaped to the side of the road made her think for a minute that he had perceived the fleeting impulse crossing her mind; she laughed, and then stopped the car because he was coming toward her—safely, from the side.

"You won't like it," he said. "You'll be sorry I ever opened that gate."

"Out of the way, please," she said. "You've held me up long enough."

"You think they could get anyone else to open this gate? You think anyone else to stay around here that long, except me and my wife? You think we can't have things just about the way we want them, long as we stay around here and fix up the house and open the gates for all you city people think you know everything?"

"Please get away from my car." She dared not admit to herself that he frightened her, for fear that he might perceive it; his nearness, leaning against the side of the car, was ugly, and his enormous resentment puzzled her; she had certainly made him open the gate for her, but did he think of the house and gardens inside as his own? A name from Dr. Montague's letter came into her mind, and she asked curiously, "Are you Dudley, the caretaker?"

"Yes, I'm Dudley, the caretaker." He mimicked her. "Who else you think would be around here?"

The honest old family retainer, she thought, proud and loyal and thoroughly unpleasant. "You and your wife take care of the house all alone?"

"Who else?" It was his boast, his curse, his refrain.

She moved restlessly, afraid to draw away from him too obviously, and yet wanting, with small motions of starting the car, to make him stand aside. "I'm sure you'll be able to make us very comfortable, you and your wife," she said, putting a tone of finality into her voice. "Meanwhile, I'm very anxious to get to the house as soon as possible."

He snickered disagreeably. "*Me*, now," he said, "me, I don't hang around here after dark."

Grinning, satisfied with himself, he stood away from the car, and Eleanor was grateful, although awkward starting the car under his eye; perhaps he will keep popping out at me all along the drive, she thought, a sneering Cheshire Cat, yelling each time that I should be happy to find anyone willing to hang around this place, until dark, anyway. To show that she was not at all affected by the thought of the face of Dudley the caretaker between the trees she began to whistle, a little annoyed to find that the same tune still ran through her head. "Present mirth hath present laughter . . ." And she told herself crossly that she must really make an effort to think of something else; she was sure that the rest of the words must be most unsuitable, to hide so stubbornly from her memory, and probably wholly disreputable to be caught singing on her arrival at Hill House.

Over the trees, occasionally, between them and the hills, she caught glimpses of what must be the roofs, perhaps a tower, of Hill House. They made houses so oddly back when Hill House was built, she thought; they put towers and turrets and buttresses and wooden lace on them, even sometimes Gothic spires and gargoyles; nothing was ever left undecorated. Perhaps Hill House has a tower, or a secret chamber, or even a passageway going off into the hills and probably used by smugglers—although what could smugglers find to smuggle around these lonely hills? Perhaps I will encounter a devilishly handsome smuggler and . . .

She turned her car onto the last stretch of straight drive leading her directly, face to face, to Hill House and, moving without thought, pressed her foot on the brake to stall the car and sat, staring.

The house was vile. She shivered and thought, the words coming freely into her mind, Hill House is vile, it is diseased; get away from here at once.

2

No human eye can isolate the unhappy coincidence of line and place which suggests evil in the face of a house, and yet somehow a maniac juxtaposition, a badly turned angle, some chance meeting of roof and sky, turned Hill House into a place of despair, more frightening because the face of Hill House seemed awake, with a watchfulness from the blank windows and a touch of glee in the eyebrow of a cornice. Almost any house, caught unexpectedly or at an odd angle, can turn a deeply humorous look on a watching person; even a mischievous little chimney or a dormer like a dimple, can catch up a beholder with a sense of fellowship; but a house arrogant and hating, never off guard, can only be evil. This house, which seemed somehow to have formed itself, flying together into its own powerful pattern under the hands of its builders, fitting itself into its own construction of lines and angles, reared its great head back against the sky without concession to humanity. It was a house without kindness, never meant to be lived in, not a fit place for people or for love or for hope. Exorcism cannot alter the countenance of a house; Hill House would stay as it was until it was destroyed.

I should have turned back at the gate, Eleanor thought. The house had caught her with an atavistic turn in the pit of the stomach, and she looked along the lines of its roofs, fruitlessly endeavoring to locate the badness, whatever dwelt there; her hands turned nervously cold so that she fumbled, trying to take out a cigarette, and beyond everything else she was afraid, listening to the sick voice inside her which whispered, *Get away from here, get away.*

But this is what I came so far to find, she told herself; I can't go back. Besides, he would laugh at me if I tried to get back out through that gate.

Trying not to look up at the house—and she could not even have told its color, or its style, or its size, except that it was enormous and dark, looking down over her—she started the car again, and drove up the last bit of driveway directly to the steps, which led in a forthright, no-escape manner onto the veranda and aimed at the front door. The drive turned off on either side, to encircle the house, and probably later she could take her car around and find a building of some kind to put it in; now she felt uneasily that she did not care to cut off her means of departure too completely. She turned the car just enough to move it off to one side, out of the way of later arrivals—it would be a pity, she thought grimly, for anyone to get a first look at this house with anything so comforting as a human automobile parked in front of it—and got out, taking her suitcase and her coat. Well, she thought inadequately, here I am.

It was an act of moral strength to lift her foot and set it on the bottom step, and she thought that her deep unwillingness to touch Hill House for the first time came directly from the vivid feeling that it was waiting for her, evil, but patient. Journeys end in lovers meeting, she thought, remembering her song at last, and laughed, standing on the steps of Hill House, journeys end in lovers meeting, and she put her feet down firmly and went up to the veranda and the door. Hill House came around her in a rush; she was enshadowed, and the sound of her feet on the wood of the veranda was an outrage in the utter silence, as though it had been a very long time since feet stamped across the boards of Hill House. She brought her hand up to the heavy iron knocker that had a child's face, determined to make more noise and yet more, so that Hill House might be very sure she was there, and then the door opened without warning and she was looking at a woman who, if like ever merited like, could only be the wife of the man at the gate.

"Mrs. Dudley?" she said, catching her breath. "I'm Eleanor Vance. I'm expected."

Silently the woman stood aside. Her apron was clean, her hair was neat, and yet she gave an indefinable air of dirtiness, quite in keeping with her husband, and the suspicious sullenness of her face was a match for the malicious petulance of his. No, Eleanor told herself; it's partly because everything seems so dark around here, and partly because I expected that man's wife to be ugly. If I hadn't seen Hill House, would I be so unfair to these people? They only take care of it, after all.

The hall in which they stood was overfull of dark wood and weighty carving, dim under the heaviness of the staircase, which lay back from the farther end. Above there seemed to be another hallway, going the width of the house; she could see a wide landing and then, across the staircase well, doors closed along the upper hall. On either side of her now were great double doors, carved with fruit and grain and living things; all the doors she could see in this house were closed.

When she tried to speak, her voice was drowned in the dim stillness, and she had to try again to make a sound. "Can you take me to my room?" she asked at last, gesturing toward her suitcase on the floor and watching the wavering reflection of her hand going down and down into the deep shadows of the polished floor, "I gather I'm the first one here. You—you *did* say you were Mrs. Dudley?" I think I'm going to cry, she thought, like a child sobbing and wailing, *I don't like it here.* . . .

Mrs. Dudley turned and started up the stairs, and Eleanor took up her suitcase and followed, hurrying after anything else alive in this house. No, she thought, I don't like it here. Mrs. Dudley came to the top of the stairs and turned right, and Eleanor saw that with some rare perception the builders of the house had given up any attempt at style—probably after realizing what the house was going to be, whether they chose it or not—and had, on this second floor, set in a long, straight hall to accommodate the doors to the bedrooms; she had a quick impression of the builders finishing off the second and third stories of the house with a kind of indecent haste, eager to finish their work without embellishment and get out of there, following the simplest possible pattern for the rooms. At the left end of the hall was a second staircase, probably going from servants' rooms on the third floor down past the second to the service rooms below; at the right end of the hall another room had been set in, perhaps, since it was on the end, to get the maximum amount of sun and light. Except for a continuation of the dark woodwork, and what looked like a series of poorly executed engravings arranged with unlovely exactness along the hall in either direction, nothing broke the straightness of the hall except the series of doors, all closed.

Mrs. Dudley crossed the hall and opened a door, perhaps at random. "This is the blue room," she said.

From the turn in the staircase Eleanor assumed that the

room would be at the front of the house; sister Anne, sister Anne, she thought, and moved gratefully toward the light from the room. "How nice," she said, standing in the doorway, but only from the sense that she must say something; it was not nice at all, and only barely tolerable; it held enclosed the same clashing disharmony that marked Hill House throughout.

Mrs. Dudley turned aside to let Eleanor come in, and spoke, apparently to the wall. "I set dinner on the dining-room sideboard at six sharp," she said. "You can serve yourselves. I clear up in the morning. I have breakfast ready for you at nine. That's the way I agreed to do. I can't keep the rooms up the way you'd like, but there's no one else you could get that would help me. I don't wait on people. What I agreed to, it doesn't mean I wait on people."

Eleanor nodded, standing uncertainly in the doorway.

"I don't stay after I set out dinner," Mrs. Dudley went on. "Not after it begins to get dark. I leave before dark comes."

"I know," Eleanor said.

"We live over in the town, six miles away."

"Yes," Eleanor said, remembering Hillsdale.

"So there won't be anyone around if you need help."

"I understand."

"We couldn't even hear you, in the night."

"I don't suppose—"

"No one could. No one lives any nearer than the town. No one else will come any nearer than that."

"I know," Eleanor said tiredly.

"In the night," Mrs. Dudley said, and smiled outright. "In the dark," she said, and closed the door behind her.

Eleanor almost giggled, thinking of herself calling, "Oh, Mrs. Dudley, I need your help in the dark," and then she shivered.

2

She stood alone, beside her suitcase, her coat still hanging over her arm, thoroughly miserable, telling herself helplessly, Journeys end in lovers meeting, and wishing she could go home. Behind her lay the dark staircase and the polished hallway and the great front door and Mrs. Dudley and Dudley laughing at the gate and the padlocks and Hillsdale and the cottage of flowers and the family at the inn and the oleander garden and the house with the stone lions in front, and they had brought her, under Dr. Montague's unerring eye, to the blue room at Hill House. It's awful, she thought, unwilling to move, since motion might imply acceptance, a gesture of moving in, it's awful and I don't want to stay; but there was nowhere else to go; Dr. Montague's letter had brought her this far and could take her no farther. After a minute she sighed and shook her head and walked across to set her suitcase down on the bed.

Here I am in the blue room of Hill House, she said half aloud, although it was real enough, and beyond all question a blue room. There were blue dimity curtains over the two windows, which looked out over the roof of the veranda onto the lawn, and a blue figured rug on the floor, and a blue spread on the bed and a blue quilt at the foot. The walls, dark woodwork to shoulder height, were blue-figured paper above, with a design of tiny blue flowers, wreathed and gathered and delicate. Perhaps someone had once hoped to lighten the air of the blue room in Hill House with a dainty wallpaper, not seeing how such a hope would evaporate in Hill House, leaving only the faintest hint of its existence, like an almost inaudible echo of sobbing far away. . . . Eleanor shook herself, turning to see the room complete. It had an unbelievably faulty design which left it chillingly wrong in all its dimensions, so that the walls seemed always in one direction a fraction longer than the eye could endure, and in another direction a fraction less than the barest possible tolerable length; this is where they want me to *sleep*, Eleanor thought incredulously; what nightmares are waiting, shadowed, in those high corners—what breath of mindless fear will drift across my mouth . . . and shook herself again. *Really*, she told herself, *really*, Eleanor.

She opened her suitcase on the high bed and, slipping off her stiff city shoes with grateful relief, began to unpack, at the back of her mind the thoroughly female conviction that the best way to soothe a troubled mind is to put on comfortable shoes. Yesterday, packing her suitcase in the city, she had chosen clothes which she assumed would be suitable for wearing in an isolated country house; she had even run out at the last minute and bought—excited at her own daring—two pairs of slacks, something she had not worn in more years than she could remember. Mother would be *furious*, she had thought, packing the slacks down at the bottom of her suitcase so that she need not take them out, need never let anyone know she had them, in case she lost her courage. Now, in Hill House, they no longer seemed so new; she unpacked carelessly, setting dresses crookedly on hangers, tossing the slacks into the bottom drawer of the high marble-topped dresser, throwing her city shoes into a corner of the great wardrobe. She was bored already with the books she had brought; I am probably not going to stay anyway, she thought, and closed her empty suitcase and set it in the wardrobe corner; it won't take me five minutes to pack again. She discovered that she had been trying to put her suitcase down without making a sound and then realized that while she unpacked she had been in her stocking feet, trying to move as silently as possible, as though stillness were vital in Hill House; she remembered that Mrs. Dudley had also walked without sound. When she stood still in the middle of the room the pressing silence of Hill House came back all around her. I am like a small creature swallowed whole by a monster, she thought, and the monster feels my tiny little movements inside. "No," she said aloud, and the one word echoed. She went quickly across the room and pushed aside the blue dimity curtains, but the sunlight came only palely through the thick glass of the windows, and she could see only the roof of the veranda and a stretch of the lawn beyond. Somewhere down there was her little car, which could take her away again. Journeys end in lovers meeting, she thought; it was my own choice to come. Then she realized that she was afraid to go back across the room.

She was standing with her back to the window, looking from the door to the wardrobe to the dresser to the bed, telling herself that she was not afraid at all, when she heard, far below, the sounds of a car door slamming and then quick footsteps, almost dancing, up the steps and across the veranda, and then, shockingly, the crash of the great iron knocker coming down. Why, she thought, there are other people coming; I am not going to be here all alone. Almost laughing, she ran across the room and into the hall, to look down the staircase into the hallway below.

"Thank heaven you're here," she said, peering through the dimness, "thank heaven somebody's here." She realized without surprise that she was speaking as though Mrs. Dudley could not hear her, although Mrs. Dudley stood, straight and pale, in the hall. "Come on up," Eleanor said, "you'll have to carry your own suitcase." She was breathless and seemed unable to stop talking, her usual shyness melted away by relief. "My name's Eleanor Vance," she said, "and I'm so glad you're here."

"I'm Theodora. Just Theodora. This *bloody* house—"

"It's just as bad up here. Come on up. Make her give you the room next to mine."

Theodora came up the heavy stairway after Mrs. Dudley, looking incredulously at the stained-glass window on the landing, the marble urn in a niche, the patterned carpet. Her suitcase was considerably larger than Eleanor's, and considerably more luxurious, and Eleanor came forward to help her, glad that her own things were safely put away out of sight. "Wait till you see the bedrooms," Eleanor said. "Mine used to be the embalming room, I think."

"It's the home I've always dreamed of," Theodora said. "A little hideaway where I can be alone with my thoughts. Particularly if my thoughts happened to be about murder or suicide or—"

"Green room," Mrs. Dudley said coldly, and Eleanor sensed, with a quick turn of apprehension, that flippant or critical talk about the house bothered Mrs. Dudley in some manner; maybe she thinks it can hear us, Eleanor thought, and then was sorry she had thought it. Perhaps she shivered, because Theodora turned with a quick smile and touched her shoulder gently, reassuringly; she is charming, Eleanor thought, smiling back, not at all the sort of person who belongs in this dreary, dark place, but then, probably, I don't belong here either; I am not the sort of person for Hill House but I can't think of anybody who would be. She laughed then, watching Theodora's expression as she stood in the doorway of the green room.

"Good Lord," Theodora said, looking sideways at Eleanor. "How perfectly enchanting. A positive bower."

"I set dinner on the dining-room sideboard at six sharp," Mrs. Dudley said. "You can serve yourselves. I clear up in the morning. I have breakfast ready for you at nine. That's the way I agreed to do."

"You're frightened," Theodora said, watching Eleanor.

"I can't keep the rooms up the way you'd like, but there's no one else you could get that would help me. I don't wait on people. What I agreed to, it doesn't mean I wait on people."

"It was just when I thought I was all alone," Eleanor said.

"I don't stay after six. Not after it begins to get dark."

"I'm here now," Theodora said, "so it's all right."

"We have a connecting bathroom," Eleanor said absurdly. "The rooms are exactly alike."

Green dimity curtains hung over the windows in Theodora's room, the wallpaper was decked with green garlands, the bedspread and quilt were green, the marble-topped dresser and the huge wardrobe were the same. "I've never seen such awful places in my *life*," Eleanor said, her voice rising.

"Like the very best hotels," Theodora said, "or any good girl's camp."

"I leave before dark comes," Mrs. Dudley went on.

"No one can hear you if you scream in the night," Eleanor told Theodora. She realized that she was clutching at the doorknob and, under Theodora's quizzical eye, unclenched her fingers and walked steadily across the room. "We'll have to find some way of opening these windows," she said.

"So there won't be anyone around if you need help," Mrs. Dudley said. "We couldn't hear you, even in the night. No one could."

"All right now?" Theodora asked, and Eleanor nodded.

"No one lives any nearer than the town. No one else will come any nearer than that."

"You're probably just hungry," Theodora said. "And I'm starved myself." She set her suitcase on the bed and slipped off her shoes. "*Nothing*," she said, "upsets me more than being hungry; I snarl and snap and burst into tears." She lifted a pair of softly tailored slacks out of the suitcase.

"In the night," Mrs. Dudley said. She smiled. "In the dark," she said, and closed the door behind her.

After a minute Eleanor said, "She also walks without making a sound."

"Delightful old body." Theodora turned, regarding her

room. "I take it back, that about the best hotels," she said. "It's a little bit like a boarding school I went to for a while."

"Come and see mine," Eleanor said. She opened the bathroom door and led the way into her blue room. "I was all unpacked and thinking about packing again when you came."

"Poor baby. You're certainly starving. All *I* could think of when I got a look at the place from outside was what fun it would be to stand out there and watch it burn down. Maybe before we leave . . ."

"It was terrible, being here alone."

"You should have seen that boarding school of mine during vacations." Theodora went back into her own room and, with the sense of movement and sound in the two rooms, Eleanor felt more cheerful. She straightened her clothes on the hangers in the wardrobe and set her books evenly on the bed table. "You know," Theodora called from the other room, "it *is* kind of like the first day at school; everything's ugly and strange, and you don't know anybody, and you're afraid everyone's going to laugh at your clothes."

Eleanor, who had opened the dresser drawer to take out a pair of slacks, stopped and then laughed and threw the slacks on the bed.

"Did I understand correctly," Theodora went on, "that Mrs. Dudley is not going to come if we scream in the night?"

"It was not what she agreed to. Did you meet the amiable old retainer at the gate?"

"We had a lovely chat. He said I couldn't come in and I said I could and then I tried to run him down with my car but he jumped. Look, do you think we have to sit around here in our rooms and wait? I'd like to change into something comfortable —unless we dress for dinner, do you think?"

"I won't if you won't."

"I won't if *you* won't. They can't fight both of us. Anyway, let's get out of here and go exploring; I would very much like to get this roof off from over my head."

"It gets dark so early, in these hills, with all the trees . . ." Eleanor went to the window again, but there was still sunlight slanting across the lawn.

"It won't be really dark for nearly an hour. I want to go outside and roll on the grass."

Eleanor chose a red sweater, thinking that in this room in this house the red of the sweater and the red of the sandals bought to match it would almost certainly be utterly at war with each other, although they had been close enough yesterday in the city. Serves me right anyway, she thought, for wanting to wear such things; I never did before. But she looked oddly well, it seemed to her as she stood by the long mirror on the wardrobe door, almost comfortable. "Do you have any idea who else is coming?" she asked. "Or when?"

"Doctor Montague," Theodora said. "I thought he'd be here before anyone else."

"Have you known Doctor Montague long?"

"Never met him," Theodora said. "Have you?"

"Never. You almost ready?"

"All ready." Theodora came through the bathroom door into Eleanor's room; she is lovely, Eleanor thought, turning to look; I wish I were lovely. Theodora was wearing a vivid yellow shirt, and Eleanor laughed and said, "You bring more light into this room than the window."

Theodora came over and regarded herself approvingly in Eleanor's mirror. "I feel," she said, "that in this dreary place it is our duty to look as bright as possible. I approve of your red sweater; the two of us will be visible from one end of Hill House to the other." Still looking into the mirror, she asked, "I suppose Doctor Montague wrote to you?"

"Yes." Eleanor was embarrassed. "I didn't know, at first, whether it was a joke or not. But my brother-in-law checked up on him."

"You know," Theodora said slowly, "up until the last minute —when I got to the gates, I guess—I never really thought there *would* be a Hill House. You don't go around expecting things like this to happen."

"But some of us go around hoping," Eleanor said.

Theodora laughed and swung around before the mirror and caught Eleanor's hand. "Fellow babe in the woods," she said, "let's go exploring."

"We can't go far away from the house—"

"I promise not to go one step farther than you say. Do you think we have to check in and out with Mrs. Dudley?"

"She probably watches every move we make, anyway; it's probably part of what she agreed to."

"Agreed to with whom, I wonder? Count Dracula?"

"You think *he* lives in Hill House?"

"I think he spends all his week ends here; I swear I saw bats in the woodwork downstairs. Follow, follow."

They ran downstairs, moving with color and life against the dark woodwork and the clouded light of the stairs, their feet clattering, and Mrs. Dudley stood below and watched them in silence.

"We're going exploring, Mrs. Dudley," Theodora said lightly. "We'll be outside somewhere."

"But we'll be back soon," Eleanor added.

"I set dinner on the sideboard at six o'clock," Mrs. Dudley explained.

Eleanor, tugging, got the great front door open; it was just as heavy as it looked, and she thought, We will really have to find some easier way to get back in. "Leave this open," she said over her shoulder to Theodora. "It's terribly heavy. Get one of those big vases and prop it open."

Theodora wheeled one of the big stone vases from the corner of the hall, and they stood it in the doorway and rested the door against it. The fading sunlight outside was bright after the darkness of the house, and the air was fresh and sweet. Behind them Mrs. Dudley moved the vase again, and the big door slammed shut.

"Lovable old thing," Theodora said to the closed door. For a moment her face was thin with anger, and Eleanor thought, I hope she never looks at *me* like that, and was surprised, remembering that she was always shy with strangers, awkward and timid, and yet had come in no more than half an hour to think of Theodora as close and vital, someone whose anger would be frightening. "I think," Eleanor said hesitantly, and relaxed, because when she spoke Theodora turned and smiled again, "I think that during the daylight hours when Mrs. Dudley is around I shall find myself some absorbing occupation far, far from the house. Rolling the tennis court, perhaps. Or tending the grapes in the hothouse."

"Perhaps you could help Dudley with the gates."

"Or look for nameless graves in the nettlepatch."

They were standing by the rail of the veranda; from there they could see down the drive to the point where it turned among the trees again, and down over the soft curve of the hills to the distant small line which might have been the main highway, the road back to the cities from which they had come. Except for the wires which ran to the house from a spot among the trees, there was no evidence that Hill House belonged in any way to the rest of the world. Eleanor turned and followed the veranda; it went, apparently, all around the house. "Oh, look," she said, turning the corner.

Behind the house the hills were piled in great pressing masses, flooded with summer green now, rich, and still. "It's why they called it Hill House," Eleanor said inadequately.

"It's altogether Victorian," Theodora said. "They simply wallowed in this kind of great billowing overdone sort of thing and buried themselves in folds of velvet and tassels and purple plush. Anyone before them or after would have put this house right up there on *top* of those hills where it belongs, instead of snuggling it down here."

"If it were on top of the hill everyone could see it. I vote for keeping it well hidden where it is."

"All the time I'm here I'm going to be terrified," Theodora said, "thinking one of those hills will fall on us."

"They don't fall on you. They just slide down, silently and secretly, rolling over you while you try to run away."

"Thank you," Theodora said in a small voice. "What Mrs. Dudley has started you have completed nicely. I shall pack and go home at once."

Believing her for a minute, Eleanor turned and stared, and then saw the amusement on her face and thought, She's much braver than I am. Unexpectedly—although it was later to become a familiar note, a recognizable attribute of what was to mean "Theodora" in Eleanor's mind—Theodora caught at Eleanor's thought, and answered her. "Don't be so afraid all the time," she said and reached out to touch Eleanor's cheek with one finger. "We never know where our courage is coming from." Then, quickly, she ran down the steps and out onto the lawn between the tall grouped trees. "Hurry," she called back, "I want to see if there's a brook somewhere."

"We can't go too far," Eleanor said, following. Like two children they ran across the grass, both welcoming the sudden openness of clear spaces after even a little time in Hill House, their feet grateful for the grass after the solid floors; with an instinct almost animal, they followed the sound and smell of water. "Over here," Theodora said, "a little path."

It led them tantalizingly closer to the sound of the water, doubling back and forth through the trees, giving them occasional glimpses down the hill to the driveway, leading them around out of sight of the house across a rocky meadow, and always downhill. As they came away from the house and out of the trees to places where the sunlight could still find them Eleanor was easier, although she could see that the sun was dropping disturbingly closer to the heaped hills. She called to Theodora, but Theodora only called back, "Follow, follow," and ran down the path. Suddenly she stopped, breathless and tottering, on the very edge of the brook, which had leaped up before her almost without warning; Eleanor, coming more slowly behind, caught at her hand and held her back and then, laughing, they fell together against the bank which sloped sharply down to the brook.

"They like to surprise you around here," Theodora said, gasping.

"Serve you right if you went diving in," Eleanor said. "Running like that."

"It's pretty, isn't it?" The water of the brook moved quickly in little lighted ripples; on the other side the grass grew down to the edge of the water and yellow and blue flowers leaned their heads over; there was a rounded soft hill there, and perhaps more meadow beyond, and, far away, the great hills, still catching the light of the sun. "It's pretty," Theodora said with finality.

"I'm sure I've been here before," Eleanor said. "In a book of fairy tales, perhaps."

"I'm sure of it. Can you skip rocks?"

"This is where the princess comes to meet the magic golden fish who is really a prince in disguise—"

"He couldn't draw much water, that golden fish of yours; it can't be more than three inches deep."

"There are stepping stones to go across, and *little* fish swimming, tiny ones—minnows?"

"Princes in disguise, all of them." Theodora stretched in the sun on the bank, and yawned. "Tadpoles?" she suggested.

"Minnows. It's too late for tadpoles, silly, but I bet we can find frogs' eggs. I used to catch minnows in my hands and let them go."

"What a farmer's wife you might have made."

"This is a place for picnics, with lunch beside the brook and hard-boiled eggs."

Theodora laughed. "Chicken salad and chocolate cake."

"Lemonade in a Thermos bottle. Spilled salt."

Theodora rolled over luxuriously. "They're wrong about ants, you know. There were almost never ants. Cows, maybe, but I don't think I ever *did* see an ant on a picnic."

"Was there always a bull in a field? Did someone always say, 'But we can't go through that field; that's where the bull is'?"

Theodora opened one eye. "Did you use to have a comic uncle? Everyone always laughed, whatever he said? And he used to tell you not to be afraid of the bull—if the bull came after you all you had to do was grab the ring through his nose and swing him around your head?"

Eleanor tossed a pebble into the brook and watched it sink clearly to the bottom. "Did you have a lot of uncles?"

"Thousands. Do you?"

After a minute Eleanor said, "Oh, yes. Big ones and little ones and fat ones and thin ones—"

"Do you have an Aunt Edna?"

"Aunt Muriel."

"Kind of thin? Rimless glasses?"

"A garnet brooch," Eleanor said.

"Does she wear a kind of dark red dress to family parties?"

"Lace cuffs—"

"Then I think we must really be related," Theodora said. "Did you use to have braces on your teeth?"

"No. Freckles."

"I went to that private school where they made me learn to curtsy."

"I always had colds all winter long. My mother made me wear woollen stockings."

"*My* mother made my brother take me to dances, and I used to curtsy like mad. My brother still hates me."

"I fell down during the graduation procession."

"I forgot my lines in the operetta."

"I used to write poetry."

"Yes," Theodora said, "I'm positive we're cousins."

She sat up, laughing, and then Eleanor said, "Be quiet; there's something moving over there." Frozen, shoulders pressed together, they stared, watching the spot of hillside across the brook where the grass moved, watching something unseen move slowly across the bright green hill, chilling the sunlight and the dancing little brook. "What is it?" Eleanor said in a breath, and Theodora put a strong hand on her wrist.

"It's gone," Theodora said clearly, and the sun came back and it was warm again. "It was a rabbit," Theodora said.

"I couldn't see it," Eleanor said.

"I saw it the minute you spoke," Theodora said firmly. "It was a rabbit; it went the hill and out of sight."

"We've been away too long," Eleanor said and looked up anxiously at the sun touching the hilltops. She got up quickly and found that her legs were stiff from kneeling on the damp grass.

"Imagine two splendid old picnic-going girls like us," Theodora said, "afraid of a rabbit."

Eleanor leaned down and held out a hand to help her up. "We'd really better hurry back," she said and, because she did not herself understand her compelling anxiety, added, "The others might be there by now."

"We'll have to come back here for a picnic soon," Theodora said, following carefully up the path, which went steadily uphill. "We really must have a good old-fashioned picnic down by the brook."

"We can ask Mrs. Dudley to hard-boil some eggs." Eleanor stopped on the path, not turning. "Theodora," she said, "I don't think I can, you know. I don't think I really will be able to do it."

"Eleanor." Theodora put an arm across her shoulders. "Would you let them separate us now? Now that we've found out we're cousins?"

3

THE sun went down smoothly behind the hills, slipping almost eagerly, at last, into the pillowy masses. There were already long shadows on the lawn as Eleanor and Theodora came up the path toward the side veranda of Hill House, blessedly hiding its mad face in the growing darkness.

"There's someone waiting there," Eleanor said, walking more quickly, and so saw Luke for the first time. Journeys end in lovers meeting, she thought, and could only say inadequately, "Are you looking for us?"

He had come to the veranda rail, looking down at them in the dusk, and now he bowed with a deep welcoming gesture. " 'These being dead,' " he said, " 'then dead must I be.' Ladies, if you are the ghostly inhabitants of Hill House, I am here forever."

He's really kind of silly, Eleanor thought sternly, and Theodora said, "Sorry we weren't here to meet you; we've been exploring."

"A sour old beldame with a face of curds welcomed us, thank you," he said. " 'Howdy-do,' she told me, 'I hope I see you alive when I come back in the morning and your dinner's on the sideboard.' Saying which, she departed in a late-model convertible with First and Second Murderers."

"Mrs. Dudley," Theodora said. "First Murderer must be Dudley-at-the-gate; I suppose the other was Count Dracula. A wholesome family."

"Since we are listing our cast of characters," he said, "my name is Luke Sanderson."

Eleanor was startled into speaking. "Then you're one of the family? The people who own Hill House? Not one of Doctor Montague's guests?"

"I am one of the family; someday this stately pile will belong to me; until then, however, I am here as one of Doctor Montague's guests."

Theodora giggled. "*We*," she said, "are Eleanor and Theodora, two little girls who were planning a picnic down by the brook and got scared home by a rabbit."

"I go in mortal terror of rabbits," Luke agreed politely. "May I come if I carry the picnic basket?"

"You may bring your ukulele and strum to us while we eat chicken sandwiches. Is Doctor Montague here?"

"He's inside," Luke said, "gloating over his haunted house."

They were silent for a minute, wanting to move closer together, and then Theodora said thinly, "It doesn't sound so funny, does it, now it's getting dark?"

"Ladies, welcome." And the great front door opened. "Come inside. I am Doctor Montague."

2

The four of them stood, for the first time, in the wide, dark entrance hall of Hill House. Around them the house steadied and located them, above them the hills slept watchfully, small eddies of air and sound and movement stirred and waited and whispered, and the center of consciousness was somehow the small space where they stood, four separated people, and looked trustingly at one another.

"I am very happy that everyone arrived safely, and on time," Doctor Montague said. "Welcome, all of you, welcome to Hill House—although perhaps that sentiment ought to come more properly from you, my boy? In any case, welcome, welcome. Luke, my boy, can you make a martini?"

3

Dr. Montague raised his glass and sipped hopefully, and sighed. "Fair," he said. "Only fair, my boy. To our success at Hill House, however."

"How would one reckon success, exactly, in an affair like this?" Luke inquired curiously.

The doctor laughed. "Put it, then," he said, "that I hope that all of us will have an exciting visit and my book will rock my colleagues back on their heels. I cannot call your visit a vacation, although to some it might seem so, because I am hopeful of your working—although work, of course, depends largely upon what is to be done, does it not? Notes," he said with relief, as though fixing upon one unshakable solidity in a world of fog, "notes. We will take notes—to some, a not unbearable task."

"So long as no one makes any puns about spirits and spirits," Theodora said, holding out her glass to Luke to be filled.

"Spirits?" The doctor peered at her. "Spirits? Yes, indeed. Of course, none of *us* . . ." He hesitated, frowning. "Certainly not," he said and took three quick agitated sips at his cocktail.

"Everything's so strange," Eleanor said. "I mean, this morning I was wondering what Hill House would be like, and now I can't believe that it's real, and we're here."

They were sitting in a small room, chosen by the doctor, who had led them into it, down a narrow corridor, fumbling a little at first, but then finding his way. It was not a cozy room, certainly. It had an unpleasantly high ceiling, and a narrow tiled fireplace which looked chill in spite of the fire which Luke had lighted at once; the chairs in which they sat were rounded and slippery, and the light coming through the colored beaded shades of the lamps sent shadows into the corners. The overwhelming sense of the room was purple; beneath their feet the carpeting glowed in dim convoluted patterns, the walls were papered and gilt, and a marble cupid beamed fatuously down at them from the mantel. When they were silent for a moment the quiet weight of the house pressed down from all around them. Eleanor, wondering if she were really here at all, and not dreaming of Hill House from some safe spot impossibly remote, looked slowly and carefully around the room, telling herself that this was real, these things existed, from the tiles around the fireplace to the marble cupid; these people were going to be her friends. The doctor was round and rosy and bearded and looked as though he might be more suitably established before a fire in a pleasant little sitting room, with a cat on his knee and a rosy little wife to bring him jellied scones, and yet he was undeniably the Dr. Montague who had guided Eleanor here, a little man both knowledgeable and stubborn. Across the fire from the doctor was Theodora, who had gone unerringly to the most nearly comfortable chair, had wriggled herself into it somehow with her legs over the arm and her head tucked in against the back; she was like a cat, Eleanor thought, and clearly a cat waiting for its dinner. Luke was not still for a minute, but moved back and forth across the shadows, filling glasses, stirring the fire, touching the marble cupid; he was bright in the firelight, and restless. They were all silent, looking into the fire, lazy after their several journeys, and Eleanor thought, I am the fourth person in this room; I am one of them; I belong.

"Since we *are* all here," Luke said suddenly, as though there had been no pause in the conversation, "shouldn't we get acquainted? We know only names, so far. I know that it is Eleanor, here, who is wearing a red sweater, and consequently it must be Theodora who wears yellow—"

"Doctor Montague has a beard," Theodora said, "so you must be Luke."

"And you are Theodora," Eleanor said, "because *I* am Eleanor." An Eleanor, she told herself triumphantly, who belongs, who is talking easily, who is sitting by the fire with her friends.

"Therefore *you* are wearing the red sweater," Theodora explained to her soberly.

"I have no beard," Luke said, "so *he* must be Doctor Montague."

"*I* have a beard," Dr. Montague said, pleased, and looked around at them with a happy beam. "My wife," he told them, "*likes* a man to wear a beard. Many women, on the other hand, find a beard distasteful. A clean-shaven man—you'll excuse me, my boy—never looks fully dressed, my wife tells me." He held out his glass to Luke.

"Now that I know which of us is me," Luke said, "let me identify myself further. I am, in private life—assuming that this is public life and the rest of the world *is* actually private—let me see, a bullfighter. Yes. A bullfighter."

"I love my love with a B," Eleanor said in spite of herself, "because he is bearded."

"Very true." Luke nodded at her. "That makes me Doctor Montague. I live in Bangkok, and my hobby is bothering women."

"Not at all," Dr. Montague protested, amused. "I live in Belmont."

Theodora laughed and gave Luke that quick, understanding glance she had earlier given Eleanor. Eleanor, watching, thought wryly that it might sometimes be oppressive to be for long around one so immediately in tune, so perceptive, as Theodora. "I am by profession an artist's model," Eleanor said quickly, to silence her own thoughts. "I live a mad, abandoned life, draped in a shawl and going from garret to garret."

"Are you heartless and wanton?" Luke asked. "Or are you one of the fragile creatures who will fall in love with a lord's son and pine away?"

"Losing all your beauty and coughing a good deal?" Theodora added.

"I rather think I have a heart of gold," Eleanor said reflectively. "At any rate, my affairs are the talk of the cafés." Dear me, she thought. Dear me.

"Alas," Theodora said, "I am a lord's *daughter*. Ordinarily I go clad in silk and lace and cloth of gold, but I have borrowed my maid's finery to appear among you. I may of course become so enamored of the common life that I will never go back, and the poor girl will have to get herself new clothes. And you, Doctor Montague?"

He smiled in the firelight. "A pilgrim. A wanderer."

"Truly a congenial little group," Luke said approvingly. "Destined to be inseparable friends, in fact. A courtesan, a pilgrim, a princess, and a bullfighter. Hill House has surely never seen our like."

"I will give the honor to Hill House," Theodora said. "I have never seen *its* like." She rose, carrying her glass, and went to examine a bowl of glass flowers. "What did they *call* this room, do you suppose?"

"A parlor, perhaps," Dr. Montague said. "Perhaps a boudoir. I thought we would be more comfortable in here than in one of the other rooms. As a matter of fact, I think we ought to regard this room as our center of operations, a kind of common room; it may not be cheerful—"

"Of *course* it's cheerful," Theodora said stanchly. "There is nothing more exhilarating than maroon upholstery and oak paneling, and what is that in the corner there? A sedan chair?"

"Tomorrow you will see the *other* rooms," the doctor told her.

"If we are going to have this for a rumpus room," Luke said, "I propose we move in something to sit on. I cannot perch for long on anything here; I skid," he said confidentially to Eleanor.

"Tomorrow," the doctor said. "Tomorrow, as a matter of fact, we will explore the entire house and arrange things to please ourselves. And now, if you have all finished, I suggest that we determine what Mrs. Dudley has done about our dinner."

Theodora moved at once and then stopped, bewildered. "Someone is going to have to lead me," she said. "I can't possibly tell where the dining room is." She pointed. "*That* door leads to the long passage and then into the front hall," she said.

The doctor chuckled. "Wrong, my dear. That door leads to the conservatory." He rose to lead the way. "*I* have studied a map of the house," he said complacently, "and I believe that we have only to go through the door here, down the passage, into the front hall, and across the hall and through the billiard room to find the dining room. Not hard," he said, "once you get into practice."

"Why did they mix themselves up so?" Theodora asked. "Why so many little odd rooms?"

"Maybe they liked to hide from each other," Luke said.

"*I* can't understand why they wanted everything so dark," Theodora said. She and Eleanor were following Dr. Montague down the passage, and Luke came behind, lingering to look into the drawer of a narrow table, and wondering aloud to himself at the valance of cupid-heads and ribbon-bunches which topped the paneling in the dark hall.

"Some of these rooms are entirely inside rooms," the doctor said from ahead of them. "No windows, no access to the outdoors at all. However, a series of enclosed rooms is not altogether surprising in a house of this period, particularly when you recall that what windows they *did* have were heavily shrouded with hangings and draperies within, and shrubbery without. Ah." He opened the passage door and led them into the front hall. "Now," he said, considering the doorways opposite, two smaller doors flanking the great central double door; "Now," he said, and selected the nearest. "The house *does* have its little oddities," he continued, holding the door so that they might pass through into the dark room beyond. "Luke, come and hold this open so I can find the dining room." Moving cautiously, he crossed the dark room and opened a door, and they followed him into the pleasantest room they had seen so far, more pleasant, certainly, because of the lights and the sight and smell of food. "I congratulate myself," he said, rubbing his hands happily. "I have led you to civilization through the uncharted wastes of Hill House."

"We ought to make a practice of leaving every door wide open." Theodora glanced nervously over her shoulder. "I *hate* this wandering around in the dark."

"You'd have to prop them open with something, then," Eleanor said. "Every door in this house swings shut when you let go of it."

"Tomorrow," Dr. Montague said. "I will make a note. Door stops." He moved happily toward the sideboard, where Mrs. Dudley had set a warming oven and an impressive row of covered dishes. The table was set for four, with a lavish display of candles and damask and heavy silver.

"No stinting, I see," Luke said, taking up a fork with a gesture which would have confirmed his aunt's worst suspicions. "We get the company silver."

"I think Mrs. Dudley is proud of the house," Eleanor said.

"She doesn't intend to give us a poor table, at any rate," the doctor said, peering into the warming oven. "This is an excellent arrangement, I think. It gets Mrs. Dudley well away from here before dark and enables us to have our dinners without her uninviting company."

"Perhaps," Luke said, regarding the plate which he was filling generously, "perhaps I did good Mrs. Dudley—why *must* I continue to think of her, perversely, as *good* Mrs. Dudley?— perhaps I really did her an injustice. She said she hoped to find me alive in the morning, and our dinner was in the oven; now I suspect that she intended me to die of gluttony."

"What keeps her here?" Eleanor asked Dr. Montague. "Why do she and her husband stay on, alone in this house?"

"As I understand it, the Dudleys have taken care of Hill House ever since anyone can remember; certainly the Sandersons were happy enough to keep them on. But tomorrow—"

Theodora giggled. "Mrs. Dudley is probably the only true surviving member of the family to whom Hill House *really* belongs. *I* think she is only waiting until all the Sanderson heirs —that's you, Luke—die off in various horrible ways, and then she gets the house and the fortune in jewels buried in the cellar. Or maybe she and Dudley hoard their gold in the secret chamber, or there's oil under the house."

"There are no secret chambers in Hill House," the doctor said with finality. "Naturally, that possibility has been suggested before, and I think I may say with assurance that no such romantic devices exist here. But tomorrow—"

"In any case, oil is definitely old hat, nothing at all to discover on the property these days," Luke told Theodora. "The very least Mrs. Dudley could murder me for in cold blood is uranium."

"Or just the pure fun of it," Theodora said.

"Yes," Eleanor said, "but why are we here?"

For a long minute the three of them looked at her, Theodora and Luke curiously, the doctor gravely. Then Theodora said, "Just what *I* was going to ask. Why *are* we here? What *is* wrong with Hill House? What is going to happen?"

"Tomorrow—"

"No," Theodora said, almost petulantly. "We are three adult, intelligent people. We have all come a long way, Doctor Montague, to meet you here in Hill House; Eleanor wants to know why, and so do I."

"Me too," Luke said.

"Why did you bring us here, Doctor? Why are you here yourself? How did you hear about Hill House, and why does it have such a reputation and what really goes on here? What is going to *happen*?"

The doctor frowned unhappily. "I don't know," he said, and then, when Theodora made a quick, irritated gesture, he went on, "I know very little more about the house than you do, and naturally I intended to tell you everything I do know; as for what is going to *happen*, I will learn that when you do. But tomorrow is soon enough to talk about it, I think; daylight—"

"Not for me," Theodora said.

"I assure you," the doctor said, "that Hill House will be

quiet tonight. There is a pattern to these things, as though psychic phenomena were subject to laws of a very particular sort."

"I really think we ought to talk it over tonight," Luke said.

"We're not afraid," Eleanor added.

The doctor sighed again. "Suppose," he said slowly, "you heard the story of Hill House and decided not to stay. How would you leave, tonight?" He looked around at them again, quickly. "The gates are locked. Hill House has a reputation for insistent hospitality; it seemingly dislikes letting its guests get away. The last person who tried to leave Hill House in darkness —it was eighteen years ago, I grant you—was killed at the turn in the driveway, where his horse bolted and crushed him against the big tree. Suppose I tell you about Hill House, and one of you wants to leave? Tomorrow, at least, we could see that you got safely to the village."

"But we're not going to run away," Theodora said. "I'm not, and Eleanor isn't, and Luke isn't."

"Stoutly, upon the ramparts," Luke agreed.

"You are a mutinous group of assistants. After dinner, then. We will retire to our little boudoir for coffee and a little of the good brandy Luke has in his suitcase, and I will tell you all I know about Hill House. Now, however, let us talk about music, or painting, or even politics."

4

"I had not decided," the doctor said, turning the brandy in his glass, "how best to prepare the three of you for Hill House. I certainly could not write you about it, and I am most unwilling now to influence your minds with its complete history before you have had a chance to see for yourselves." They were back in the small parlor, warm and almost sleepy. Theodora had abandoned any attempt at a chair and had put herself down on the hearthrug, cross-legged and drowsy. Eleanor, wanting to sit on the hearthrug beside her, had not thought of it in time and had condemned herself to one of the slippery chairs, unwilling now to attract attention by moving and getting herself awkwardly down onto the floor. Mrs. Dudley's good dinner and an hour's quiet conversation had evaporated the faint air of unreality and constraint; they had begun to know one another, recognize individual voices and mannerisms, faces and laughter; Eleanor thought with a little shock of surprise that she had been in Hill House only for four or five hours, and smiled a little at the fire. She could feel the thin stem of her glass between her fingers, the stiff pressure of the chair against her back, the faint movements of air through the room which were barely perceptible in small stirrings of tassels and beads. Darkness lay in the corners, and the marble cupid smiled down on them with chubby good humor.

"What a time for a ghost story," Theodora said.

"If you please." The doctor was stiff. "We are not children trying to frighten one another," he said.

"Sorry." Theodora smiled up at him. "I'm just trying to get myself used to all of this."

"Let us," said the doctor, "exercise great caution in our language. Preconceived notions of ghosts and apparitions—"

"The disembodied hand in the soup," Luke said helpfully.

"My dear boy. *If* you please. I was trying to explain that our purpose here, since it is of a scientific and exploratory nature, ought not to he affected, perhaps even warped, by half-remembered spooky stories which belong more properly to a—let me see—a marshmallow roast." Pleased with himself, he looked around to be sure that they were all amused. "As a matter of fact, my researches over the past few years have led me to certain theories regarding psychic phenomena which I have now, for the first time, an opportunity of testing. Ideally, of course, you ought not to know anything about Hill House. You should be ignorant and receptive."

"And take notes," Theodora murmured.

"Notes. Yes, indeed. Notes. However, I realize that it is most impractical to leave you entirely without background information, largely because you are not people accustomed to meeting a situation without preparation." He beamed at them slyly. "You are three willful, spoiled children who are prepared to nag me for your bedtime story." Theodora giggled, and the doctor nodded at her happily. He rose and moved to stand by the fire in an unmistakable classroom pose; he seemed to feel the lack of a blackboard behind him, because once or twice he half turned, hand raised, as though looking for chalk to illustrate a point. "Now," he said, "we will take up the history of Hill House." I wish I had a notebook and a pen, Eleanor thought, just to make him feel at home. She glanced at Theodora and Luke and found both their faces fallen instinctively into a completely rapt classroom look; high earnestness, she thought; we have moved into another stage of our adventure.

"You will recall," the doctor began, "the houses described in Leviticus as 'leprous,' *tsaraas*, or Homer's phrase for the underworld: *aidao domos*, the house of Hades; I need not remind you, I think, that the concept of certain houses as unclean or forbidden—perhaps sacred—is as old as the mind of man. Certainly there are spots which inevitably attach to themselves an atmosphere of holiness and goodness; it might not then be too fanciful to say that some houses are born bad. Hill House, whatever the cause, has been unfit for human habitation for upwards of twenty years. What it was like before then, whether its personality was molded by the people who lived here, or the things they did, or whether it was evil from its start are all questions I cannot answer. Naturally I hope that we will all know a good deal more about Hill House before we leave. No one knows, even, why some houses are called haunted."

"What else *could* you call Hill House?" Luke demanded.

"Well—disturbed, perhaps. Leprous. Sick. Any of the popular euphemisms for insanity; a deranged house is a pretty conceit. There are popular theories, however, which discount the eerie, the mysterious; there are people who will tell you that the disturbances I am calling 'psychic' are actually the result of subterranean waters, or electric currents, or hallucinations caused by polluted air; atmospheric pressure, sun spots, earth tremors all have their advocates among the skeptical. People," the doctor said sadly, "are always so anxious to get things out into the open where they can put a name to them, even a meaningless name, so long as it has something of a scientific ring." He sighed, relaxing, and gave them a little quizzical smile. "A haunted house," he said. "Everyone laughs. I found myself telling my colleagues at the university that I was going camping this summer."

"I told people I was participating in a scientific experiment,"

Theodora said helpfully. "Without telling them where or what, of course."

"Presumably your friends feel less strongly about scientific experiments than mine. Yes." The doctor sighed again. "Camping. At my age. And yet *that* they believed. Well." He straightened up again and fumbled at his side, perhaps for a yardstick. "I first heard about Hill House a year ago, from a former tenant. He began by assuring me that he had left Hill House because his family objected to living so far out in the country, and ended by saying that in his opinion the house ought to be burned down and the ground sowed with salt. I learned of other people who had rented Hill House, and found that none of them had stayed more than a few days, certainly never the full terms of their leases, giving reasons that ranged from the dampness of the location—not at all true, by the way; the house is very dry—to a pressing need to move elsewhere, for business reasons. That is, every tenant who has left Hill House hastily has made an effort to supply a rational reason for leaving, and yet every one of them has left. I tried, of course, to learn more from these former tenants, and yet in no case could I persuade them to discuss the house; they all seemed most unwilling to give me information and were, in fact, reluctant to recall the details of their several stays. In only one opinion were they united. Without exception, every person who has spent any length of time in this house urged me to stay as far away from it as possible. Not one of the former tenants could bring himself to admit that Hill House was haunted, but when I visited Hillsdale and looked up the newspaper records—"

"Newspapers?" Theodora asked. "Was there a scandal?"

"Oh, yes," the doctor said. "A perfectly splendid scandal, with a suicide and madness and lawsuits. *Then* I learned that the local people had no doubts about the house. I heard a dozen different stories, of course—it is really *unbelievably* difficult to get accurate information about a haunted house; it would astonish you to know what I have gone through to learn only as much as I have—and as a result I went to Mrs. Sanderson, Luke's aunt, and arranged to rent Hill House. She was most frank about its undesirability—"

"It's harder to burn down a house than you think," Luke said.

"—but agreed to allow me a short lease to carry out my researches, on condition that a member of the family be one of my party."

"They hope," Luke said solemnly, "that I will dissuade you from digging up the lovely old scandals."

"There. Now I have explained how I happen to be here, and why Luke has come. As for you two ladies, we all know by now that you are here because I wrote you, and you accepted my invitation. I hoped that each of you might, in her own way, intensify the forces at work in the house; Theodora has shown herself possessed of some telepathic ability, and Eleanor has in the past been intimately involved in poltergeist phenomena—"

"*I?*"

"Of course." The doctor looked at her curiously. "Many years ago, when you were a child. The stones—"

Eleanor frowned, and shook her head. Her fingers trembled around the stem of her glass, and then she said, "That was the neighbors. My mother said the neighbors did that. People are always jealous."

"Perhaps so." The doctor spoke quietly and smiled at Eleanor. "The incident has been forgotten long ago, of course; I only mentioned it because that is why I wanted you in Hill House."

"When *I* was a child," Theodora said lazily, "—'many years ago,' Doctor, as you put it so tactfully—I was whipped for throwing a brick through a greenhouse roof. I remember I thought about it for a long time, remembering the whipping but remembering also the lovely crash, and after thinking about it very seriously I went out and did it again."

"I don't remember very well," Eleanor said uncertainly to the doctor.

"But *why*?" Theodora asked. "I mean, I can accept that Hill House is supposed to be haunted, and you want us here, Doctor Montague, to help keep track of what happens—and I bet besides that you wouldn't at all like being here *alone*—but I just don't understand. It's a horrible old house, and if I rented it I'd scream for my money back after one fast look at the front hall, but what's *here*? What really frightens people so?"

"I will not put a name to what has no name," the doctor said. "I don't know."

"They never even told me what was going on," Eleanor said urgently to the doctor. "My mother said it was the neighbors, they were always against us because she wouldn't mix with them. My mother—"

Luke interrupted her, slowly and deliberately. "I think," he said, "that what we all want is facts. Something we can understand and put together."

"First," the doctor said, "I am going to ask you all a question. Do you want to leave? Do you advise that we pack up now and leave Hill House to itself, and never have anything more to do with it?"

He looked at Eleanor, and Eleanor put her hands together tight; it is another chance to get away, she was thinking, and she said, "No," and glanced with embarrassment at Theodora. "I was kind of a baby this afternoon," she explained. "I did let myself get frightened."

"She's not telling all the truth," Theodora said loyally. "She wasn't any more frightened than I was; we scared each other to death over a rabbit."

"Horrible creatures, rabbits," Luke said.

The doctor laughed. "I suppose we were all nervous this afternoon, anyway. It is a rude shock to turn that corner and get a clear look at Hill House."

"I thought he was going to send the car into a tree," Luke said.

"I am really very brave now, in a warm room with a fire and company," Theodora said.

"I don't think we could leave now if we wanted to." Eleanor had spoken before she realized clearly what she was going to say, or what it was going to sound like to the others; she saw that they were staring at her, and laughed and added lamely, "Mrs. Dudley would never forgive us." She wondered if they really believed that that was what she had meant to say, and thought, Perhaps it has us now, this house, perhaps it will not let us go.

"Let us have a little more brandy," the doctor said, "and I will tell you the story of Hill House." He returned to his classroom position before the fireplace and began slowly, as one giving an account of kings long dead and wars long done with; his voice was carefully unemotional. "Hill House was built eighty-odd years ago," he began. "It was built as a home for his family by a man named Hugh Crain, a country home where he hoped to see his children and grandchildren live in comfortable luxury, and where he fully expected to end his days in quiet. Unfortunately Hill House was a sad house almost from the beginning; Hugh Crain's young wife died minutes before she first was to set eyes on the house, when the carriage bringing her here overturned in the driveway, and the lady was brought—ah, *lifeless*, I believe is the phrase they use —into the home her husband had built for her. He was a sad and bitter man, Hugh Crain, left with two small daughters to bring up, but he did not leave Hill House."

"Children grew up here?" Eleanor asked incredulously.

The doctor smiled. "The house is dry, as I said. There were no swamps to bring them fevers, the country air was thought to be beneficial to them, and the house itself was regarded as luxurious. I have no doubt that two small children could play here, lonely perhaps, but not unhappy."

"I hope they went wading in the brook," Theodora said. She stared deeply into the fire. "Poor little things. I hope someone let them run in that meadow and pick wildflowers."

"Their father married again," the doctor went on. "Twice more, as a matter of fact. He seems to have been—unlucky in his wives. The second Mrs. Crain died of a fall, although I have been unable to ascertain how or why. Her death seems to have been as tragically unexpected as her predecessor's. The third Mrs. Crain died of what they used to call consumption, some-where in Europe; there is, somewhere in the library, a collec-tion of postcards sent to the two little girls left behind in Hill House from their father and their stepmother traveling from one health resort to another. The little girls were left here with their governess until their stepmother's death. After that Hugh Crain declared his intention of closing Hill House and remaining abroad, and his daughters were sent to live with a cousin of their mother's, and there they remained until they were grown up."

"I hope Mama's cousin was a little jollier than old Hugh,"

Theodora said, still staring darkly into the fire. "It's not nice to think of children growing up like mushrooms, in the dark."

"They felt differently," the doctor said. "The two sisters spent the rest of their lives quarreling over Hill House. After all his high hopes of a dynasty centered here, Hugh Crain died somewhere in Europe, shortly after his wife, and Hill House was left jointly to the two sisters, who must have been quite young ladies by then; the older sister had, at any rate, made her debut into society."

"And put up her hair, and learned to drink champagne and carry a fan . . ."

"Hill House was empty for a number of years, but kept always in readiness for the family; at first in expectation of Hugh Crain's return, and then, after his death, for either of the sisters who chose to live there. Somewhere during this time it was apparently agreed between the two sisters that Hill House should become the property of the older; the younger sister had married—"

"Aha," Theodora said. "The *younger* sister married. Stole her sister's beau, I've no doubt."

"It was said that the older sister was crossed in love," the doctor agreed, "although that is said of almost any lady who prefers, for whatever reason, to live alone. At any rate, it was the older sister who came back here to live. She seems to have resembled her father strongly; she lived here alone for a number of years, almost in seclusion, although the village of Hillsdale knew her. Incredible as it may sound to you, she genuinely loved Hill House and looked upon it as her family home. She eventually took a girl from the village to live with her, as a kind of companion; so far as I can learn there seems to have been no strong feeling among the villagers about the house then, since old Miss Crain—as she was inevitably known —hired her servants in the village, and it was thought a fine thing for her to take the village girl as a companion. Old Miss Crain was in constant disagreement with her sister over the house, the younger sister insisting that she had given up her claim on the house in exchange for a number of family heirlooms, some of considerable value, which her sister then refused to give her. There were some jewels, several pieces of antique furniture, and a set of gold-rimmed dishes, which seemed to irritate the younger sister more than anything else. Mrs. Sanderson let me rummage through a box of family papers, and so I have seen some of the letters Miss Crain received from her sister, and in all of them those dishes stand out as the recurrent sore subject. At any rate, the older sister died of pneumonia here in the house, with only the little companion to help her—there were stories later of a doctor called too late, of the old lady lying neglected upstairs while the younger woman dallied in the garden with some village lout, but I suspect that these are only scandalous inventions; I certainly cannot find that anything of the sort was widely believed at the time, and in fact most of the stories seem to stem directly from the poisonous vengefulness of the younger sister, who never rested in her anger."

"I don't like the younger sister," Theodora said. "First she stole her sister's lover, and then she tried to steal her sister's dishes. No, I don't like her."

"Hill House has an impressive list of tragedies connected with it, but then, most old houses have. People have to live and die *somewhere*, after all, and a house can hardly stand for eighty years without seeing some of its inhabitants die within its walls. After the death of the older sister, there was a lawsuit over the house. The companion insisted that the house was left to her, but the younger sister and her husband maintained most violently that the house belonged legally to them and claimed that the companion had tricked the older sister into signing away property which she had always intended leaving to her sister. It was an unpleasant business, like all family quarrels, and as in all family quarrels incredibly harsh and cruel things were said on either side. The companion swore in court—and here, I think, is the first hint of Hill House in its true personality —that the younger sister came into the house at night and stole things. When she was pressed to enlarge upon this accusation, she became very nervous and incoherent, and finally, forced to give some evidence for her charge, said that a silver service was missing, and a valuable set of enamels, in addition to the famous set of gold-rimmed dishes, which would actually be a very difficult thing to steal, when you think about it. For her part, the younger sister went so far as to mention murder and demand an investigation into the death of old Miss Crain, bringing up the first hints of the stories of neglect and mismanagement. I cannot discover that these suggestions were ever taken seriously. There is no record whatever of any but the most formal notice of the older sister's death, and certainly the villagers would have been the first to wonder if there had been any oddness about the death. The companion won her case at last, and could, in my opinion, have won a case for slander besides, and the house became legally hers, although the younger sister never gave up trying to get it. She kept after the unfortunate companion with letters and threats, made the wildest accusations against her everywhere, and in the local police records there is listed at least one occasion when the companion was forced to apply for police protection to prevent her enemy from attacking her with a broom. The companion went in terror, seemingly; her house burgled at night—she never stopped insisting that they came and stole things—and I read one pathetic letter in which she complained that she had not spent a peaceful night in the house since the death of her benefactor. Oddly enough, sympathy around the village was almost entirely with the younger sister, perhaps because the companion, once a village girl, was now lady of the manor. The villagers believed—and still believe, I think—that the younger sister was defrauded of her inheritance by a scheming young woman. They did not believe that she would murder her friend, you see, but they were delighted to believe that she was dishonest, certainly because they were capable of dishonesty themselves when opportunity arose. Well, gossip is always a bad enemy. When the poor creature killed herself—"

"Killed herself?" Eleanor, shocked into speech, half rose. "She had to kill herself?"

"You mean, was there another way of escaping her tormentor? She certainly did not seem to think so. It was accepted locally that she had chosen suicide because her guilty conscience drove her to it. I am more inclined to believe that she was one of those tenacious, unclever young women who can hold on desperately to what they believe is their own but cannot withstand, mentally, a constant nagging persecution; she had certainly no weapons to fight back against the younger sister's campaign of hatred, her own friends in the village had been turned against her, and she seems to have been maddened by the conviction that locks and bolts could not keep out the enemy who stole into her house at night—"

"She should have gone away," Eleanor said. "Left the house and run as far as she could go."

"In effect, she did. I really think the poor girl was hated to death; she hanged herself, by the way. Gossip says she hanged herself from the turret on the tower, but when you have a house like Hill House with a tower and a turret, gossip would hardly allow you to hang yourself anywhere else. After her death, the house passed legally into the hands of the Sanderson family, who were cousins of hers and in no way as vulnerable to the persecutions of the younger sister, who must have been a little demented herself by that time. I heard from Mrs. Sanderson that when the family—it would have been her husband's parents—first came to see the house, the younger sister showed up to abuse them, standing on the road to howl at them as they went by, and found herself packed right off to the local police station. And that seems to be the end of the younger sister's part in the story: from the day the first Sanderson sent her packing to the brief notice of her death a few years later, she seems to have spent her time brooding silently over her wrongs, but far away from the Sandersons. Oddly enough, in all her ranting, she insisted always on one point—she had not, would not, come into this house at night, to steal or for any other reason."

"Was anything ever really stolen?" Luke asked.

"As I told you, the companion was finally pressed into saying that one or two things seemed to be missing, but could not say for sure. As you can imagine, the story of the nightly intruder did a good deal to enhance Hill House's further reputation. Moreover, the Sandersons did not live here at all. They spent a few days in the house, telling the villagers that they were preparing it for their immediate occupancy, and then abruptly cleared out, closing the house the way it stood. They told around the village that urgent business took them to live in the city, but the villagers thought they knew better. No one has lived in the house since for more than a few days at a time. It has been on the market, for sale or rent, ever since. Well, that is a long story. I need more brandy."

"Those two poor little girls," Eleanor said, looking into the fire. "I can't forget them, walking through these dark rooms, trying to play dolls, maybe, in here or those bedrooms upstairs."

"And so the old house has just been sitting here." Luke put out a tentative finger and touched the marble cupid gingerly. "Nothing in it touched, nothing used, nothing here wanted by anyone any more, just sitting here thinking."

"And waiting," Eleanor said.

"And waiting," the doctor confirmed. "Essentially," he went on slowly, "the evil is the house itself, I think. It has enchained and destroyed its people and their lives, it is a place of contained ill will. Well. Tomorrow you will see it all. The Sandersons put in electricity and plumbing and a telephone when they first thought to live here, but otherwise nothing has been changed."

"Well," Luke said after a little silence, "I'm sure we will all be very comfortable here."

5

Eleanor found herself unexpectedly admiring her own feet. Theodora dreamed over the fire just beyond the tips of her toes, and Eleanor thought with deep satisfaction that her feet were handsome in their red sandals; what a complete and separate thing I am, she thought, going from my red toes to the top of my head, individually an I, possessed of attributes belonging only to me. I have red shoes, she thought—that goes with being Eleanor; I dislike lobster and sleep on my left side and crack my knuckles when I am nervous and save buttons. I am holding a brandy glass which is mine because I am here and I am using it and I have a place in this room. I have red shoes and tomorrow I will wake up and I will still be here.

"I have red shoes," she said very softly, and Theodora turned and smiled up at her.

"I *had* intended—" and the doctor looked around at them with bright, anxious optimism—"I *had* intended to ask if you all played bridge?"

"Of course," Eleanor said. I play bridge, she thought; I used to have a cat named Dancer; I can swim.

"I'm afraid not," Theodora said, and the other three turned and regarded her with frank dismay.

"Not at all?" the doctor asked.

"I've been playing bridge twice a week for eleven years," Eleanor said, "with my mother and her lawyer and his wife— I'm *sure* you must play as well as *that*."

"Maybe you could teach me?" Theodora asked. "I'm quick at learning games."

"Oh, dear," the doctor said, and Eleanor and Luke laughed.

"We'll do something else instead," Eleanor said; I can play bridge, she thought; I like apple pie with sour cream, and I drove here by myself.

"Backgammon," the doctor said with bitterness.

"I play a fair game of chess," Luke said to the doctor, who cheered at once.

Theodora set her mouth stubbornly. "I didn't suppose we came here to play *games*," she said.

"Relaxation," the doctor said vaguely, and Theodora turned with a sullen shrug and stared again into the fire.

"I'll get the chessmen, if you'll tell me where," Luke said, and the doctor smiled.

"Better let me go," he said. "I've studied a floor plan of the house, remember. If we let you go off wandering by yourself we'd very likely never find you again." As the door closed behind him Luke gave Theodora a quick curious glance and then came over to stand by Eleanor. "You're not nervous, are you? Did that story frighten you?"

Eleanor shook her head emphatically, and Luke said, "You looked pale."

"I probably ought to be in bed," Eleanor said. "I'm not used to driving as far as I did today."

"Brandy," Luke said. "It will make you sleep better. You too," he said to the back of Theodora's head.

"Thank you," Theodora said coldly, not turning. "I rarely have trouble sleeping."

Luke grinned knowingly at Eleanor, and then turned as the doctor opened the door. "My wild imagination," the doctor said, setting down the chess set. "What a house this is."

"Did something happen?" Eleanor asked.

The doctor shook his head. "We probably ought to agree, now, not to wander around the house alone," he said.

"What happened?" Eleanor asked.

"My own imagination," the doctor said firmly. "This table all right, Luke?"

"It's a lovely old chess set," Luke said. "I wonder how the younger sister happened to overlook it."

"I can tell you one thing," the doctor said, "if it *was* the younger sister sneaking around this house at night, she had nerves of iron. It watches," he added suddenly. "The house. It watches every move you make." And then, "My own imagination, of course."

In the light of the fire Theodora's face was stiff and sulky; she likes attention, Eleanor thought wisely and, without thinking, moved and sat on the floor beside Theodora. Behind her she could hear the gentle sound of chessmen being set down on a board and the comfortable small movements of Luke and the doctor taking each other's measure, and in the fire there were points of flame and little stirrings. She waited a minute for Theodora to speak, and then said agreeably, "Still hard to believe you're really here?"

"I had no idea it would be so dull," Theodora said.

"We'll find plenty to do in the morning," Eleanor said.

"At home there would be people around, and lots of talking and laughing and lights and excitement—"

"I suppose I don't need such things," Eleanor said, almost apologetically. "There never was much excitement for me. I had to stay with Mother, of course. And when she was asleep I kind of got used to playing solitaire or listening to the radio. I never could bear to read in the evenings because I had to read aloud to her for two hours every afternoon. Love stories"— and she smiled a little, looking into the fire. But that's not all, she thought, astonished at herself, that doesn't tell what it was like, even if I wanted to tell; why am I talking?

"I'm terrible, aren't I?" Theodora moved quickly and put her hand over Eleanor's. "I sit here and grouch because there's nothing to amuse me; I'm very selfish. Tell me how horrible I am." And in the firelight her eyes shone with delight.

"You're horrible," Eleanor said obediently; Theodora's

hand on her own embarrassed her. She disliked being touched, and yet a small physical gesture seemed to be Theodora's chosen way of expressing contrition, or pleasure, or sympathy; I wonder if my fingernails are clean, Eleanor thought, and slid her hand away gently.

"I am horrible," Theodora said, good-humored again. "I'm horrible and beastly and no one can stand me. There. Now tell me about yourself."

"I'm horrible and beastly and no one can stand me."

Theodora laughed. "Don't make fun of me. You're sweet and pleasant and everyone likes you very much; Luke has fallen madly in love with you, and I am jealous. Now I want to know more about you. Did you really take care of your mother for many years?"

"Yes," Eleanor said. Her fingernails *were* dirty, and her hand was badly shaped and people made jokes about love because sometimes it was funny. "Eleven years, until she died three months ago."

"Were you sorry when she died? Should I say how sorry *I* am?"

"No. She wasn't very happy."

"And neither were you?"

"And neither was I."

"But what about now? What did you do afterward, when you were free at last?"

"I sold the house," Eleanor said. "My sister and I each took whatever we wanted from it, small things; there was really nothing much except little things my mother had saved—my father's watch, and some old jewelry. Not at all like the sisters of Hill House."

"And you sold everything else?"

"Everything. Just as soon as I could."

"And then of course you started a gay, mad fling that brought you inevitably to Hill House?"

"Not exactly." Eleanor laughed.

"But all those wasted years! Did you go on a cruise, look for exciting young men, buy new clothes . . . ?"

"Unfortunately," Eleanor said dryly, "there was not at all that much money. My sister put her share into the bank for her little girl's education. I did buy some clothes, to come to Hill

House." People like answering questions about themselves, she thought; what an odd pleasure it is. I would answer anything right now.

"What will you do when you go back? Do you have a job?"

"No, no job right now. I don't know what I'm going to do."

"I know what *I'll* do." Theodora stretched luxuriously. "I'll turn on every light in our apartment and just bask."

"What is your apartment like?"

Theodora shrugged. "Nice," she said. "We found an old place and fixed it up ourselves. One big room, and a couple of small bedrooms, nice kitchen—we painted it red and white and made over a lot of old furniture we dug up in junk shops —one really nice table, with a marble top. We both love doing over old things."

"Are you married?" Eleanor asked.

There was a little silence, and then Theodora laughed quickly and said, "No."

"Sorry," Eleanor said, horribly embarrassed. "I didn't mean to be curious."

"You're funny," Theodora said and touched Eleanor's cheek with her finger. There are lines by my eyes, Eleanor thought, and turned her face away from the fire. "Tell me where you live," Theodora said.

Eleanor thought, looking down at her hands which were badly shaped. We could have afforded a laundress, she thought; it wasn't fair. My hands are awful. "I have a little place of my own," she said slowly. "An apartment, like yours, only I live alone. Smaller than yours, I'm sure. I'm still furnishing it— buying one thing at a time, you know, to make sure I get everything absolutely right. White curtains. I had to look for weeks before I found my little stone lions on each corner of the mantel, and I have a white cat and my books and records and pictures. Everything has to be exactly the way I want it, because there's only me to use it; once I had a blue cup with stars painted on the inside; when you looked down into a cup of tea it was full of stars. I want a cup like that."

"Maybe one will turn up someday, in my shop," Theodora said. "Then I can send it to you. Someday you'll get a little package saying 'To Eleanor with love from her friend Theodora,' and it will be a blue cup full of stars."

"I would have stolen those gold-rimmed dishes," Eleanor said, laughing.

"Mate," Luke said, and the doctor said, "Oh dear, oh dear."

"Blind luck," Luke said cheerfully. "Have you ladies fallen asleep there by the fire?"

"Just about," Theodora said. Luke came across the room and held out a hand to each of them to help them up, and Eleanor, moving awkwardly, almost fell; Theodora rose in a quick motion and stretched and yawned. "Theo is sleepy," she said.

"I'll have to lead you upstairs," the doctor said. "Tomorrow we must really start to learn our way around. Luke, will you screen the fire?"

"Had we better make sure that the doors are locked?" Luke asked. "I imagine that Mrs. Dudley locked the back door when she left, but what about the others?"

"I hardly think we'll catch anyone breaking in," Theodora said. "Anyway, the little companion used to lock her doors, and what good did it do her?"

"Suppose we want to break out?" Eleanor asked.

The doctor glanced quickly at Eleanor and then away. "I see no need for locking doors," he said quietly.

"There is certainly not much danger of burglars from the village," Luke said.

"In any case," the doctor said, "I will not sleep for an hour or so yet; at my age an hour's reading before bedtime is essential, and I wisely brought *Pamela* with me. If any of you has trouble sleeping, I will read aloud to you. I never yet knew anyone who could not fall asleep with Richardson being read aloud to him." Talking quietly, he led them down the narrow hallway and through the great front hall and to the stairs. "I have often planned to try it on very small children," he went on.

Eleanor followed Theodora up the stairs; she had not realized until now how worn she was, and each step was an effort. She reminded herself naggingly that she was in Hill House, but even the blue room meant only, right now, the bed with the blue coverlet and the blue quilt. "On the other hand," the doctor continued behind her, "a Fielding novel comparable in length, although hardly in subject matter, would never do for very young children. I even have doubts about Sterne—"

Theodora went to the door of the green room and turned and smiled. "If you feel the least bit nervous," she said to Eleanor, "run right into my room."

"I will," Eleanor said earnestly. "Thank you; good night."

"—and certainly not Smollett. Ladies, Luke and I are here, on the other side of the stairway—"

"What color are your rooms?" Eleanor asked, unable to resist.

"Yellow," the doctor said, surprised.

"Pink," Luke said with a dainty gesture of distaste.

"We're blue and green down here," Theodora said.

"I will be awake, reading," the doctor said. "I will leave my door ajar, so I will certainly hear any sound. Good night. Sleep well."

"Good night," Luke said. "Good night, all."

As she closed the door of the blue room behind her Eleanor thought wearily that it might be the darkness and oppression of Hill House that tired her so, and then it no longer mattered. The blue bed was unbelievably soft. Odd, she thought sleepily, that the house should be so dreadful and yet in many respects so physically comfortable—the soft bed, the pleasant lawn, the good fire, the cooking of Mrs. Dudley. The company too, she thought, and then thought, Now I can think about them; I am all alone. Why is Luke here? But why am *I* here? Journeys end in lovers meeting. They all saw that I was afraid.

She shivered and sat up in bed to reach for the quilt at the foot. Then, half amused and half cold, she slipped out of bed and went, barefoot and silent, across the room to turn the key in the lock of the door; they won't know I locked it, she thought, and went hastily back to bed. With the quilt pulled up around her she found herself looking with quick apprehension at the window, shining palely in the darkness, and then at the door. I wish I had a sleeping pill to take, she thought, and looked again over her shoulder, compulsively, at the window, and then again at the door, and thought, Is it moving? But I locked it; is it moving?

I think, she decided concretely, that I would like this better if I had the blankets over my head. Hidden deep in the bed under the blankets, she giggled and was glad none of the others could hear her. In the city she never slept with her head under the covers; I have come all this way today, she thought.

Then she slept, secure; in the next room Theodora slept, smiling, with her light on. Farther down the hall the doctor, reading *Pamela*, lifted his head occasionally to listen, and once went to his door and stood for a minute, looking down the hall, before going back to his book. A nightlight shone at the top of the stairs over the pool of blackness which was the hall. Luke slept, on his bedside table a flashlight and the lucky piece he always carried with him. Around them the house brooded, settling and stirring with a movement that was almost like a shudder.

Six miles away Mrs. Dudley awakened, looked at her clock, thought of Hill House, and shut her eyes quickly. Mrs. Gloria Sanderson, who owned Hill House and lived three hundred miles away from it, closed her detective story, yawned, and reached up to turn off her light, wondering briefly if she had remembered to put the chain on the front door. Theodora's friend slept; so did the doctor's wife and Eleanor's sister. Far away, in the trees over Hill House, an owl cried out, and toward morning a thin, fine rain began, misty and dull.

4

ELEANOR awakened to find the blue room gray and colorless in the morning rain. She found that she had thrown the quilt off during the night and had finished sleeping in her usual manner, with her head on the pillow. It was a surprise to find that she had slept until after eight, and she thought that it was ironic that the first good night's sleep she had had in years had come to her in Hill House. Lying in the blue bed, looking up into the dim ceiling with its remote carved pattern, she asked herself, half asleep still, What did I do; did I make a fool of myself? Were they laughing at me?

Thinking quickly over the evening before, she could remember only that she had—must have—seemed foolishly, childishly contented, almost happy; had the others been amused to see that she was so simple? I said silly things, she told herself, and of course they noticed. Today I will be more reserved, less openly grateful to all of them for having me.

Then, awakening completely, she shook her head and sighed. You are a very silly baby, Eleanor, she told herself, as she did every morning.

The room came clearly alive around her; she was in the blue room at Hill House, the dimity curtains were moving slightly at the window, and the wild splashing in the bathroom must be Theodora, awake, sure to be dressed and ready first, certain to be hungry. "Good morning," Eleanor called, and Theodora answering, gasping, "Good morning—through in a minute— I'll leave the tub filled for you—are you starving? Because I am." Does she think I wouldn't bathe unless she left a full tub for me? Eleanor wondered, and then was ashamed; I came here to stop thinking things like that, she told herself sternly and rolled out of bed and went to the window. She looked out across the veranda roof to the wide lawn below, with its bushes and little clumps of trees wound around with mist. Far down at the end of the lawn was the line of trees which marked the path to the creek, although the prospect of a jolly picnic on the grass was not, this morning, so appealing. It was clearly going to be wet all day, but it was a summer rain, deepening the green of the grass and the trees, sweetening and cleaning the air. It's charming, Eleanor thought, surprised at herself; she wondered if she was the first person ever to find Hill House charming and then thought, chilled, Or do they *all* think so, the *first* morning? She shivered, and found herself at the same time unable to account for the excitement she felt, which made it difficult to remember why it was so odd to wake up happy in Hill House.

"I'll *starve* to death." Theodora pounded on the bathroom door, and Eleanor snatched at her robe and hurried. "Try to look like a stray sunbeam," Theodora called out from her room. "It's such a dark day we've got to be a little brighter than usual."

Sing before breakfast you'll cry before night, Eleanor told herself, because she had been singing softly, "In delay there lies no plenty. . . ."

"I thought *I* was the lazy one," Theodora said complacently through the door, "but you're much, *much* worse. Lazy hardly *begins* to describe you. You *must* be clean enough now to come and have breakfast."

"Mrs. Dudley sets out breakfast at nine. What will she think when we show up bright and smiling?"

"She will sob with disappointment. Did anyone scream for her in the night, do you suppose?"

Eleanor regarded a soapy leg critically. "I slept like a log," she said.

"So did I. If you are not ready in three minutes I will come in and drown you. I want my *breakfast*."

Eleanor was thinking that it had been a very long time since she had dressed to look like a stray sunbeam, or been so hungry for breakfast, or arisen so aware, so conscious of herself, so deliberate and tender in her attentions; she even brushed her teeth with a niceness she could not remember ever feeling before. It is all the result of a good night's sleep, she thought; since Mother died I must have been sleeping even more poorly than I realized.

"Aren't you ready *yet*?"

"Coming, coming," Eleanor said, and ran to the door, remembered that it was still locked, and unlocked it softly. Theodora was waiting for her in the hall, vivid in the dullness in gaudy plaid; looking at Theodora, it was not possible for Eleanor to believe that she ever dressed or washed or moved or ate or slept or talked without enjoying every minute of what she was doing; perhaps Theodora never cared at all what other people thought of her.

"Do you realize that we may be another hour or so just *finding* the dining room?" Theodora said. "But maybe they have left us a map—did you know that Luke and the doctor have been up for hours? I was talking to them from the window."

They have started without me, Eleanor thought; tomorrow I will wake up earlier and be there to talk from the window too. They came to the foot of the stairs, and Theodora crossed the great dark hall and put her hand confidently to a door. "Here," she said, but the door opened into a dim, echoing room neither of them had seen before. "Here," Eleanor said, but the door she chose led onto the narrow passage to the little parlor where last night they had sat before a fire.

"It's across the hall from *that*," Theodora said, and turned, baffled. "*Damn* it," she said, and put her head back and shouted. "Luke? Doctor?"

Distantly they heard an answering shout, and Theodora moved to open another door. "If they think," she said over her shoulder, "that they are going to keep me forever in this filthy hall, trying one door after another to get to my breakfast—"

"That's the right one, I think," Eleanor said, "with the dark room to go through, and then the dining room beyond."

Theodora shouted again, blundered against some light piece of furniture, cursed, and then the door beyond was opened and the doctor said, "Good morning."

"Foul, filthy house," Theodora said, rubbing her knee. "Good morning."

"You will never believe this now, of course," the doctor said, "but three minutes ago these doors were wide open. We left them open so you could find your way. We sat here and watched them swing shut just before you called. Well. Good morning."

"Kippers," Luke said from the table. "Good morning. I hope you ladies *are* the kipper kind."

They had come through the darkness of one night, they had

met morning in Hill House, and they were a family, greeting one another with easy informality and going to the chairs they had used last night at dinner, their own places at the table.

"A fine big breakfast is what Mrs. Dudley certainly agreed to set out at nine," Luke said, waving a fork. "We had begun to wonder if you were the coffee-and-a-roll-in-bed types."

"We would have been here much sooner in any other house," Theodora said.

"Did you really leave all the doors open for us?" Eleanor asked.

"That's how we knew you were coming," Luke told her. "We saw the doors swing shut."

"Today we will nail all the doors open," Theodora said. "I am going to pace this house until I can find food ten times out of ten. I slept with my light on all night," she confided to the doctor, "but nothing happened at all."

"It was all very quiet," the doctor said.

"Did you watch over us all night?" Eleanor asked.

"Until about three, when *Pamela* finally put me to sleep. There wasn't a sound until the rain started sometime after two. One of you ladies called out in her sleep once—"

"That must have been me," Theodora said shamelessly. "Dreaming about the wicked sister at the gates of Hill House."

"I dreamed about her too," Eleanor said. She looked at the doctor and said suddenly, "It's *embarrassing*. To think about being afraid, I mean."

"We're all in it together, you know," Theodora said.

"It's worse if you try not to show it," the doctor said.

"Stuff yourself very full of kippers," Luke said. "Then it will be impossible to feel anything at all."

Eleanor felt, as she had the day before, that the conversation was being skillfully guided away from the thought of fear, so very present in her own mind. Perhaps she was to be allowed to speak occasionally for all of them so that, quieting her, they quieted themselves and could leave the subject behind them; perhaps, vehicle for every kind of fear, she contained enough for all. They are like children, she thought crossly, daring each other to go first, ready to turn and call names at whoever comes last; she pushed her plate away from her and sighed.

"Before I go to sleep *tonight*," Theodora was saying to the doctor, "I want to be sure that I have seen every inch of this house. No more lying there wondering what is over my head or under me. And we have to open some windows and keep the doors open and stop feeling our way around."

"Little signs," Luke suggested. "Arrows pointing, reading THIS WAY OUT."

"Or DEAD END," Eleanor said.

"Or WATCH OUT FOR FALLING FURNITURE," Theodora said. "*We*'ll make them," she said to Luke.

"First we all explore the house," Eleanor said, too quickly perhaps, because Theodora turned and looked at her curiously. "I don't want to find myself left behind in an attic or something," Eleanor added uncomfortably.

"No one wants to leave you behind anywhere," Theodora said.

"Then *I* suggest," Luke said, "that we first of all finish off the coffee in the pot, and then go nervously from room to room, endeavoring to discover some rational plan to this house, and leaving doors open as we go. I never thought," he said, shaking his head sadly, "that I would stand to inherit a house where I had to put up signs to find my way around."

"We need to find out what to call the rooms," Theodora said. "Suppose I told you, Luke, that I would meet you clandestinely in the second-best drawing room—how would you ever know where to find me?"

"You could keep whistling till I got there," Luke offered.

Theodora shuddered. "You would hear me whistling, and calling you, while you wandered from door to door, never opening the right one, and I would be inside, not able to find any way to get out—"

"And nothing to eat," Eleanor said unkindly.

Theodora looked at her again. "And nothing to eat," she agreed after a minute. Then, "It's the crazy house at the carnival," she said. "Rooms opening out of each other and doors going everywhere at once and swinging shut when you come, and I bet that somewhere there are mirrors that make you look all sideways and an air hose to blow up your skirts, and something that comes out of a dark passage and laughs in your face—" She was suddenly quiet and picked up her cup so quickly that her coffee spilled.

"Not as bad as all that," the doctor said easily. "Actually, the ground floor is laid out in what I might almost call concentric circles of rooms; at the center is the little parlor where we sat last night; around it, roughly, are a series of rooms—the billiard room, for instance, and a dismal little den entirely furnished in rose-colored satin—"

"Where Eleanor and I will go each morning with our needlework."

"—and surrounding these—I call them the inside rooms because they are the ones with no direct way to the outside; they have no windows, you remember—surrounding these are the ring of outside rooms, the drawing room, the library, the conservatory, the—"

"No," Theodora said, shaking her head. "I am still lost back in the rose-colored satin."

"And the veranda goes all around the house. There are doors opening onto the veranda from the drawing room, and the conservatory, and one sitting room. There is also a passage—"

"Stop, stop." Theodora was laughing, but she shook her head. "It's a filthy, *rotten* house."

The swinging door in the corner of the dining room opened, and Mrs. Dudley stood, one hand holding the door open, looking without expression at the breakfast table. "I clear off at ten," Mrs. Dudley said.

"Good morning, Mrs. Dudley," Luke said.

Mrs. Dudley turned her eyes to him. "I clear off at ten," she said. "The dishes are supposed to be back on the shelves. I take them out again for lunch. I set out lunch at one, but first the dishes have to be back on the shelves."

"Of course, Mrs. Dudley." The doctor rose and put down his napkin. "Everybody ready?" he asked.

Under Mrs. Dudley's eye Theodora deliberately lifted her cup and finished the last of her coffee, then touched her mouth with her napkin and sat back. "Splendid breakfast," she said conversationally. "Do the dishes belong to the house?"

"They belong on the shelves," Mrs. Dudley said.

"And the glassware and the silver and the linen? Lovely old things."

"The linen," Mrs. Dudley said, "belongs in the linen drawers in the dining room. The silver belongs in the silver chest. The glasses belong on the shelves."

"We must be quite a bother to you," Theodora said.

Mrs. Dudley was silent. Finally she said, "I clear up at ten. I set out lunch at one."

Theodora laughed and rose. "On," she said, "on, on. Let us go and open doors."

They began reasonably enough with the dining-room door, which they propped open with a heavy chair. The room beyond was the game room; the table against which Theodora had stumbled was a low inlaid chess table ("Now, I could not have overlooked that last night," the doctor said irritably), and at one end of the room were card tables and chairs, and a tall cabinet where the chessmen had been, with croquet balls and the cribbage board.

"Jolly spot to spend a carefree hour," Luke said, standing in the doorway regarding the bleak room. The cold greens of the table tops were reflected unhappily in the dark tiles around the fireplace; the inevitable wood paneling was, here, not at all enlivened by a series of sporting prints which seemed entirely devoted to various methods of doing wild animals to death, and over the mantel a deer-head looked down upon them in patent embarrassment.

"This is where they came to enjoy themselves," Theodora said, and her voice echoed shakily from the high ceiling. "They came here," she explained, "to relax from the oppressive atmosphere of the rest of the house." The deer-head looked down on her mournfully. "Those two little girls," she said. "Can we *please* take down that *beast* up there?"

"I think it's taken a fancy to you," Luke said. "It's never taken its eyes off you since you came in. Let's get out of here."

They propped the door open as they left, and came out into the hall, which shone dully under the light from the open rooms. "When we find a room with a window," the doctor remarked, "we will open it; until then, let us be content with opening the front door."

"You keep thinking of the little children," Eleanor said to

Theodora, "but I can't forget that lonely little companion, walking around these rooms, wondering who else was in the house."

Luke tugged the great front door open and wheeled the big vase to hold it; "Fresh air," he said thankfully. The warm smell of rain and wet grass swept into the hall, and for a minute they stood in the open doorway, breathing air from outside Hill House. Then the doctor said, "Now *here* is something none of you anticipated," and he opened a small door tucked in beside the tall front door and stood back, smiling. "The library," he said. "In the tower."

"I can't go in there," Eleanor said, surprising herself, but she could not. She backed away, overwhelmed with the cold air of mold and earth which rushed at her. "My mother—" she said, not knowing what she wanted to tell them, and pressed herself against the wall.

"Indeed?" said the doctor, regarding her with interest. "Theodora?" Theodora shrugged and stepped into the library; Eleanor shivered. "Luke?" said the doctor, but Luke was already inside. From where she stood Eleanor could see only a part of the circular wall of the library, with a narrow iron staircase going up and perhaps, since it was the tower, up and up and up; Eleanor shut her eyes, hearing the doctor's voice distantly, hollow against the stone of the library walls.

"Can you see the little trapdoor up there in the shadows?" he was asking. "It leads out onto a little balcony, and of course that's where she is commonly supposed to have hanged herself —the girl, you remember. A most suitable spot, certainly; more suitable for suicides I would think, than for books. She is supposed to have tied the rope onto the iron railing and then just stepped—"

"Thanks," Theodora said from within. "I can visualize it perfectly, thank you. For myself, I would probably have anchored the rope onto the deer head in the game room, but I suppose she had some sentimental attachment to the tower; what a nice word 'attachment' is in that context, don't you think?"

"Delicious." It was Luke's voice, louder; they were coming out of the library and back to the hall where Eleanor waited. "I think that I will make this room into a night club. I will put the orchestra up there on the balcony, and dancing girls will come down that winding iron staircase; the bar—"

"Eleanor," Theodora said, "are you all right now? It's a perfectly awful room, and you were right to stay out of it."

Eleanor stood away from the wall; her hands were cold and she wanted to cry, but she turned her back to the library door, which the doctor propped open with a stack of books. "I don't think I'll do much reading while I'm here," she said, trying to speak lightly. "Not if the books smell like the library."

"I hadn't noticed a smell," the doctor said. He looked inquiringly at Luke, who shook his head. "Odd," the doctor went on, "and just the kind of thing we're looking for. Make a note of it, my dear, and try to describe it exactly."

Theodora was puzzled. She stood in the hallway, turning, looking back of her at the staircase and then around again at the front door. "Are there two front doors?" she asked. "Am I just mixed up?"

The doctor smiled happily; he had clearly been hoping for some such question. "This is the only front door," he said. "It is the one you came in yesterday."

Theodora frowned. "Then why can't Eleanor and I see the tower from our bedroom windows? Our rooms look out over the front of the house, and yet—"

The doctor laughed and clapped his hands. "At last," he said. "Clever Theodora. This is why I wanted you to see the house by day. Come, sit on the stairs while I tell you."

Obediently they settled on the stairs, looking up at the doctor, who took on his lecturing stance and began formally, "One of the peculiar traits of Hill House is its design—"

"Crazy house at the carnival."

"Precisely. Have you not wondered at our *extreme* difficulty in finding our way around? An ordinary house would not have had the four of us in such confusion for so long, and yet time after time we choose the wrong doors, the room we want eludes us. Even I have had my troubles." He sighed and nodded. "I daresay," he went on, "that old Hugh Crain expected that someday Hill House might become a showplace, like the Winchester House in California or the many octagon houses; he designed Hill House himself, remember, and, I have told you before, he was a strange man. Every angle"—and the doctor gestured toward the doorway—"every angle is slightly wrong. Hugh Crain must have detested other people and their sensible squared-away houses, because he made his house to suit his mind. Angles which you assume are the right angles you are accustomed to, and have every right to expect are true, are actually a fraction of a degree off in one direction or another. I am sure, for instance, that you believe that the stairs you are sitting on are level, because you are not prepared for stairs which are not level—"

They moved uneasily, and Theodora put out a quick hand to take hold of the balustrade, as though she felt she might be falling.

"—are actually on a very slight slant toward the central shaft; the doorways are all a very little bit off center—that may be, by the way, the reason the doors swing shut unless they are held; I wondered this morning whether the approaching footsteps of you two ladies upset the delicate balance of the doors. Of course the result of all these tiny aberrations of measurement adds up to a fairly large distortion in the house as a whole. Theodora cannot see the tower from her bedroom window because the tower actually stands at the corner of the house. From Theodora's bedroom window it is completely invisible, although from here it seems to be directly outside her room. The window of Theodora's room is actually fifteen feet to the left of where we are now."

Theodora spread her hands helplessly. "Golly," she said.

"I see," Eleanor said. "The veranda roof is what misleads us. I can look out my window and see the veranda roof and because I came directly into the house and up the stairs I assumed that the front door was right below, although really—"

"You see only the veranda roof," the doctor said. "The front door is far away; it and the tower are visible from the nursery, which is the big room at the end of the hallway; we will see it later today. It is"—and his voice was saddened—"a masterpiece of architectural misdirection. The double stairway at Chambord—"

"Then everything is a little bit off center?" Theodora asked uncertainly. "That's why it all feels so disjointed?"

"What happens when you go back to a real house?" Eleanor asked. "I mean—a—well—a *real* house?"

"It must be like coming off shipboard," Luke said. "After being here for a while your sense of balance could be so distorted that it would take you a while to lose your sea legs, or your Hill House legs. Could it be," he asked the doctor, "that what people have been assuming were supernatural manifestations were really only the result of a slight loss of balance in the people who live here? The inner ear," he told Theodora wisely.

"It must certainly affect people in some way," the doctor said. "We have grown to trust blindly in our senses of balance and reason, and I can see where the mind might fight wildly to preserve its own familiar stable patterns against all evidence that it was leaning sideways." He turned away. "We have marvels still before us," he said, and they came down from the stairway and followed him, walking gingerly, testing the floors as they moved. They went down the narrow passage to the little parlor where they had sat the night before, and from there, leaving doors propped open behind them, they moved into the outer circle of rooms, which looked out onto the veranda. They pulled heavy draperies away from windows and the light from outside came into Hill House. They passed through a music room where a harp stood sternly apart from them, with never a jangle of strings to mark their footfalls. A grand piano stood tightly shut, with a candelabra above, no candle ever touched by flame. A marble-topped table held wax flowers under glass, and the chairs were twig-thin and gilded. Beyond this was the conservatory, with tall glass doors showing them the rain outside, and ferns growing damply around and over wicker furniture. Here it was uncomfortably moist, and they left it quickly, to come through an arched doorway into the drawing room and stand, aghast and incredulous.

"It's not there," Theodora said, weak and laughing. "I don't believe it's there." She shook her head. "Eleanor, do you see it too?"

"How . . . ?" Eleanor said helplessly.

"I thought you would be pleased." The doctor was complacent.

One entire end of the drawing room was in possession of a marble statuary piece; against the mauve stripes and flowered carpet it was huge and grotesque and somehow whitely naked; Eleanor put her hands over her eyes, and Theodora clung to her. "I thought it might be intended for Venus rising from the waves," the doctor said.

"Not at all," said Luke, finding his voice, "it's Saint Francis curing the lepers."

"No, no," Eleanor said. "One of them is a dragon."

"It's none of that," said Theodora roundly; "it's a family portrait, you sillies. Composite. *Any*one would know it at once; that figure in the center, that tall, undraped—good heavens!—masculine one, that's old Hugh, patting himself on the back because he built Hill House, and his two attendant nymphs are his daughters. The one on the right who seems to be brandishing an ear of corn is actually telling about her lawsuit, and the other one, the little one on the end, is the companion, and the one on the *other* end—"

"Is Mrs. Dudley, done from life," Luke said.

"And that grass stuff they're all standing on is really supposed to be the dining-room carpet, grown up a little. Did anyone else notice that dining-room carpet? It looks like a field of hay, and you can feel it tickling your ankles. In back, that kind of overspreading apple-tree kind of thing, *that*'s—"

"A symbol of the protection of the house, surely," Dr. Montague said.

"I'd hate to think it might fall on us," Eleanor said. "Since the house is so unbalanced, Doctor, isn't there some chance of that?"

"I have read that the statue was carefully, and at great expense, constructed to offset the uncertainty of the floor on which it stands. It was put in, at any rate, when the house was built, and it has not fallen yet. It is possible, you know, that Hugh Crain admired it, even found it lovely."

"It is also possible that he used it to scare his children with," Theodora said. "What a pretty room this would be without it." She turned, swinging. "A dancing room," she said, "for ladies in full skirts, and room enough for a full country dance. Hugh Crain, will you take a turn with me?" and she curtsied to the statue.

"I believe he's going to accept," Eleanor said, taking an involuntary step backward.

"Don't let him tread on your toes," the doctor said, and laughed. "Remember what happened to Don Juan."

Theodora touched the statue timidly, putting her finger against the outstretched hand of one of the figures. "Marble is always a shock," she said. "It never feels like you think it's going to. I suppose a lifesize statue looks enough like a real person to make you expect to feel skin." Then, turning again, and shimmering in the dim room, she waltzed alone, turning to bow to the statue.

"At the end of the room," the doctor said to Eleanor and Luke, "under those draperies, are doors leading onto the veranda; when Theodora is heated from dancing she may step out into the cooler air." He went the length of the room to pull aside the heavy blue draperies and opened the doors. Again the smell of the warm rain came in, and a burst of wind, so that a little breath seemed to move across the statue, and light touched the colored walls.

"Nothing in this house moves," Eleanor said, "until you look away, and then you just catch something from the corner of your eye. Look at the little figurines on the shelves; when we all had our backs turned they were dancing with Theodora."

"*I* move," Theodora said, circling toward them.

"Flowers under glass," Luke said. "Tassels. I am beginning to fancy this house."

Theodora pulled at Eleanor's hair. "Race you around the veranda," she said and darted for the doors. Eleanor, with no time for hesitation or thought, followed, and they ran out onto the veranda. Eleanor, running and laughing, came around a curve of the veranda to find Theodora going in another door, and stopped, breathless. They had come to the kitchen, and Mrs. Dudley, turning away from the sink, watched them silently.

"Mrs. Dudley," Theodora said politely, "we've been exploring the house."

Mrs. Dudley's eyes moved to the clock on the shelf over the stove. "It is half-past eleven," she said. "I—"

"—set lunch on at one," Theodora said. "We'd like to look over the kitchen, if we may. We've seen all the other downstairs rooms, I think."

Mrs. Dudley was still for a minute and then, moving her head acquiescently, turned and walked deliberately across the kitchen to a farther doorway. When she opened it they could see the back stairs beyond, and Mrs. Dudley turned and closed the door behind her before she started up. Theodora cocked her head at the doorway and waited a minute before she said, "I wonder if Mrs. Dudley has a soft spot in her heart for me, I really do."

"I suppose she's gone up to hang herself from the turret," Eleanor said. "Let's see what's for lunch while we're here."

"Don't joggle anything," Theodora said. "You know perfectly well that the dishes belong on the shelves. Do you think that woman really means to make us a soufflé? Here is certainly a soufflé dish, and eggs and cheese—"

"It's a nice kitchen," Eleanor said. "In my mother's house the kitchen was dark and narrow, and nothing you cooked there ever had any taste or color."

"What about your own kitchen?" Theodora asked absently. "In your little apartment? Eleanor, look at the doors."

"I can't make a soufflé," Eleanor said.

"Look, Eleanor. There's the door onto the veranda, and another that opens onto steps going down—to the cellar, I guess—and another over there going onto the veranda again, and the one she used to go upstairs, and another one over there—"

"To the veranda again," Eleanor said, opening it. "Three doors going out onto the veranda from one kitchen."

"And the door to the butler's pantry and on into the dining room. Our good Mrs. Dudley likes doors, doesn't she? She can certainly"—and their eyes met—"get out fast in any direction if she wants to."

Eleanor turned abruptly and went back to the veranda. "I wonder if she had Dudley cut extra doors for her. I wonder how she likes working in a kitchen where a door in back of her might open without her knowing it. I wonder, actually, just what Mrs. Dudley is in the habit of meeting in her kitchen so that she wants to make sure that she'll find a way out no matter which direction she runs. I wonder—"

"Shut up," Theodora said amiably. "A nervous cook can't make a good soufflé, anyone knows that, and she's probably listening on the stairs. Let us choose one of her doors and leave it open behind us."

Luke and the doctor were standing on the veranda, looking

out over the lawn; the front door was oddly close, beyond them. Behind the house, seeming almost overhead, the great hills were muted and dull in the rain. Eleanor wandered along the veranda, thinking that she had never before known a house so completely surrounded. Like a very tight belt; she thought; would the house fly apart if the veranda came off? She went what she thought must be the great part of the circle around the house, and then she saw the tower. It rose up before her suddenly, almost without warning, as she came around the curve of the veranda. It was made of gray stone, grotesquely solid, jammed hard against the wooden side of the house, with the insistent veranda holding it there. Hideous, she thought, and then thought that if the house burned away someday the tower would still stand, gray and forbidding over the ruins, warning people away from what was left of Hill House, with perhaps a stone fallen here and there, so owls and bats might fly in and out and nest among the books below. Halfway up windows began, thin angled slits in the stone, and she wondered what it would be like, looking down from them, and wondered that she had not been able to enter the tower. I will never look down from those windows, she thought, and tried to imagine the narrow iron stairway going up and around inside. High on top was a conical wooden roof, topped by a wooden spire. It must have been laughable in any other house, but here in Hill House it belonged, gleeful and expectant, awaiting perhaps a slight creature creeping out from the little window onto the slanted roof, reaching up to the spire, knotting a rope. . . .

"You'll fall," Luke said, and Eleanor gasped; she brought her eyes down with an effort and found that she was gripping the veranda rail tightly and leaning far backward. "Don't trust your balance in my charming Hill House," Luke said, and Eleanor breathed deeply, dizzy, and staggered. He caught her and held her while she tried to steady herself in the rocking world where the trees and the lawn seemed somehow tilted sideways and the sky turned and swung.

"Eleanor?" Theodora said nearby, and she heard the sound of the doctor's feet running along the veranda. "This damnable house," Luke said. "You have to watch it every minute."

"Eleanor?" said the doctor.

"I'm all right," Eleanor said, shaking her head and standing unsteadily by herself. "I was leaning back to see the top of the tower and I got dizzy."

"She was standing almost sideways when I caught her," Luke said.

"I've had that feeling once or twice this morning," Theodora said, "as though I was walking up the wall."

"Bring her back inside," the doctor said. "It's not so bad when you're *inside* the house."

"I'm really all right," Eleanor said, very much embarrassed, and she walked with deliberate steps along the veranda to the front door, which was closed. "I thought we left it open," she said with a little shake in her voice, and the doctor came past her and pushed the heavy door open again. Inside, the hall had returned to itself; all the doors they had left open were neatly closed. When the doctor opened the door into the game room they could see beyond him that the doors to the dining room were closed, and the little stool they had used to prop one door open was neatly back in place against the wall. In the boudoir and the drawing room, the parlor and the conservatory, the doors and windows were closed, the draperies pulled together, and the darkness back again.

"It's Mrs. Dudley," Theodora said, trailing after the doctor and Luke, who moved quickly from one room to the next, pushing doors wide open again and propping them, sweeping drapes away from windows and letting in the warm, wet air. "Mrs. Dudley did it yesterday, as soon as Eleanor and I were out of the way, because she'd rather shut them herself than come along and find them shut by themselves because the doors belong shut and the windows belong shut and the dishes belong—" She began to laugh foolishly, and the doctor turned and frowned at her with irritation.

"Mrs. Dudley had better learn her place," he said. "I will nail these doors open if I have to." He turned down the passageway to their little parlor and sent the door swinging open with a crash. "Losing my temper will not help," he said, and gave the door a vicious kick.

"Sherry in the parlor before lunch," Luke said amiably. "Ladies, enter."

2

"Mrs. Dudley," the doctor said, putting down his fork, "an admirable soufflé."

Mrs. Dudley turned to regard him briefly and went into the kitchen with an empty dish.

The doctor sighed and moved his shoulders tiredly. "After my vigil last night, I feel the need of a rest this afternoon, and you," he said to Eleanor, "would do well to lie down for an hour. Perhaps a regular afternoon rest might be more comfortable for all of us."

"I see," said Theodora, amused. "I must take an afternoon nap. It may look funny when I go home again, but I can always tell them that it was part of my schedule at Hill House."

"Perhaps we will have trouble sleeping at night," the doctor said, and a little chill went around the table, darkening the light of the silver and the bright colors of the china, a little cloud that drifted through the dining room and brought Mrs. Dudley after it.

"It's five minutes of two," Mrs. Dudley said.

3

Eleanor did not sleep during the afternoon, although she would have liked to; instead, she lay on Theodora's bed in the green room and watched Theodora do her nails, chatting lazily, unwilling to let herself perceive that she had followed Theodora into the green room because she had not dared to be alone.

"I love decorating myself," Theodora said, regarding her hand affectionately. "I'd like to paint myself all over."

Eleanor moved comfortably. "Gold paint," she suggested, hardly thinking. With her eyes almost closed she could see Theodora only as a mass of color sitting on the floor.

"Nail polish and perfume and bath salts," Theodora said, as one telling the cities of the Nile. "Mascara. You don't think half enough of such things, Eleanor."

Eleanor laughed and closed her eyes altogether. "No time," she said.

"Well," Theodora said with determination, "by the time I'm through with you, you will be a different person; I dislike being with women of no color." She laughed to show that she was teasing, and then went on, "I think I will put red polish on your toes."

Eleanor laughed too and held out her bare foot. After a minute, nearly asleep, she felt the odd cold little touch of the brush on her toes, and shivered.

"Surely a famous courtesan like yourself is accustomed to the ministrations of handmaidens," Theodora said. "Your feet are dirty."

Shocked, Eleanor sat up and looked; her feet *were* dirty, and her nails were painted bright red. "It's *horrible*," she said to Theodora, "it's *wicked*," wanting to cry. Then, helplessly, she began to laugh at the look on Theodora's face. "I'll go and wash my feet," she said.

"Golly." Theodora sat on the floor beside the bed, staring. "Look," she said. "My feet are dirty, too, baby, honest. *Look*."

"Anyway," Eleanor said, "I hate having things done to me."

"You're about as crazy as anyone *I* ever saw," Theodora said cheerfully.

"I don't like to feel helpless," Eleanor said. "My mother—"

"Your mother would have been delighted to see you with your toenails painted red," Theodora said. "They look nice."

Eleanor looked at her feet again. "It's wicked," she said inadequately. "I mean—on *my* feet. It makes me feel like I look like a fool."

"You've got foolishness and wickedness somehow mixed up." Theodora began to gather her equipment together. "Anyway, I won't take it off and we'll both watch to see whether Luke and the doctor look at your feet first."

"No matter what I try to say, you make it sound foolish," Eleanor said.

"Or wicked." Theodora looked up at her gravely. "I have a hunch," she said, "that you ought to go home, Eleanor."

Is she laughing at me? Eleanor wondered; has she decided that I am not fit to stay? "I don't want to go," she said, and Theodora looked at her again quickly and then away, and touched Eleanor's toes softly. "The polish is dry," she said.

"I'm an idiot. Just something frightened me for a minute."
She stood up and stretched. "Let's go look for the others," she
said.

4

Luke leaned himself wearily against the wall of the upstairs
hall, his head resting against the gold frame of an engraving of
a ruin. "I keep thinking of this house as my own future property," he said, "more now than I did before; I keep telling myself that it will belong to me someday, and I keep asking myself
why." He gestured at the length of the hall. "If I had a passion
for doors," he said, "or gilded clocks, or miniatures; if I
wanted a Turkish corner of my own, I would very likely regard
Hill House as a fairyland of beauty."

"It's a handsome house," the doctor said stanchly. "It must
have been thought of as elegant when it was built." He started
off down the hall, to the large room on the end which had
once been the nursery. "Now," he said, "we shall see the tower
from a window"—and shivered as he passed through the door.
Then he turned and looked back curiously. "Could there be a
draft across that doorway?"

"A draft? In Hill House?" Theodora laughed. "Not unless
you could manage to make one of those doors stay open."

"Come here one at a time, then," the doctor said, and Theodora moved forward, grimacing as she passed the doorway.

"Like the doorway of a tomb," she said. "It's warm enough
inside, though."

Luke came, hesitated in the cold spot, and then moved
quickly to get out of it, and Eleanor, following, felt with incredulity the piercing cold that struck her between one step
and the next; it was like passing through a wall of ice, she
thought, and asked the doctor, "What is it?"

The doctor was patting his hands together with delight.
"You can keep your Turkish corners, my boy," he said. He
reached out a hand and held it carefully over the location of
the cold. "They *cannot* explain this," he said. "The very
essence of the tomb, as Theodora points out. The cold spot in
Borley Rectory only dropped eleven degrees," he went on

complacently. "This, I should think, is considerably colder. The heart of the house."

Theodora and Eleanor had moved to stand closer together; although the nursery was warm, it smelled musty and close, and the cold crossing the doorway was almost tangible, visible as a barrier which must be crossed in order to get out. Beyond the windows the gray stone of the tower pressed close; inside, the room was dark and the line of nursery animals painted along the wall seemed somehow not at all jolly, but as though they were trapped, or related to the dying deer in the sporting prints of the game room. The nursery, larger than the other bedrooms, had an indefinable air of neglect found nowhere else in Hill House, and it crossed Eleanor's mind that even Mrs. Dudley's diligent care might not bring her across that cold barrier any oftener than necessary.

Luke had stepped back across the cold spot and was examining the hall carpet, then the walls, patting at the surfaces as though hoping to discover some cause for the odd cold. "It *couldn't* be a draft," he said, looking up at the doctor. "Unless they've got a direct air line to the North Pole. Everything's solid, anyway."

"I wonder who slept in the nursery," the doctor said irrelevantly. "Do you suppose they shut it up, once the children were gone?"

"Look," Luke said, pointing. In either corner of the hall, over the nursery doorway, two grinning heads were set; meant, apparently, as gay decorations for the nursery entrance, they were no more jolly or carefree than the animals inside. Their separate stares, captured forever in distorted laughter, met and locked at the point of the hall where the vicious cold centered. "When you stand where they can look at you," Luke explained, "they freeze you."

Curiously, the doctor stepped down the hall to join him, looking up. "Don't leave us alone in here," Theodora said, and ran out of the nursery, pulling Eleanor through the cold, which was like a fast slap, or a close cold breath. "A fine place to chill our beer," she said, and put out her tongue at the grinning faces.

"I must make a full account of this," the doctor said happily.

"It doesn't seem like an *impartial* cold," Eleanor said, awkward because she was not quite sure what she meant. "I felt it as *deliberate*, as though something wanted to give me an unpleasant shock."

"It's because of the faces, I suppose," the doctor said; he was on his hands and knees, feeling along the floor. "Measuring tape and thermometer," he told himself, "chalk for an outline; perhaps the cold intensifies at night? Everything is worse," he said, looking at Eleanor, "if you think something is looking at you."

Luke stepped through the cold, with a shiver, and closed the door to the nursery; he came back to the others in the hall with a kind of leap, as though he thought he could escape the cold by not touching the floor. With the nursery door closed they realized all at once how much darker it had become, and Theodora said restlessly, "Let's get downstairs to our parlor; I can feel those hills pushing in."

"After five," Luke said. "Cocktail time. I suppose," he said to the doctor, "you will trust me to mix you a cocktail again tonight?"

"Too much vermouth," the doctor said, and followed them lingeringly, watching the nursery door over his shoulder.

5

"I propose," the doctor said, setting down his napkin, "that we take our coffee in our little parlor. I find that fire very cheerful."

Theodora giggled. "Mrs. Dudley's gone, so let's race around fast and get all those doors and windows open and take everything down from the shelves—"

"The house seems different when she's not in it," Eleanor said.

"Emptier." Luke looked at her and nodded; he was arranging the coffee cups on a tray, and the doctor had already gone on, doggedly opening doors and propping them. "Each night I realize suddenly that we four are alone here."

"Although Mrs. Dudley's not much good as far as company is concerned; it's funny," Eleanor said, looking down at the dinner table. "I dislike Mrs. Dudley as much as any of you, but my mother would *never* let me get up and leave a table looking like this until morning."

"If she wants to leave before dark she has to clear away in the morning," Theodora said without interest. "*I*'m certainly not going to do it."

"It's not nice to walk away and leave a dirty table."

"You couldn't get them back on the right shelves anyway, and she'd have to do it all over again just to get your finger-marks off things."

"If I just took the silverware and let it soak—"

"No," Theodora said, catching her hand. "Do you want to go out into that kitchen all alone, with all those doors?"

"No," Eleanor said, setting down the handful of forks she had gathered. "I guess I don't, really." She lingered to look uneasily at the table, at the crumpled napkins and the drop of wine spilled by Luke's place, and shook her head. "I don't know what my mother would say, though."

"Come on," Theodora said. "They've left lights for us."

The fire in the little parlor was bright, and Theodora sat down beside the coffee tray while Luke brought brandy from the cupboard where he had carefully set it away the night before. "We must be cheerful at all costs," he said. "I'll challenge you again tonight, Doctor."

Before dinner they had ransacked the other downstairs rooms for comfortable chairs and lamps, and now their little parlor was easily the pleasantest room in the house. "Hill House has really been very kind to us," Theodora said, giving Eleanor her coffee, and Eleanor sat down gratefully in a pillowy, over-stuffed chair. "No dirty dishes for Eleanor to wash, a pleasant evening in good company, and perhaps the sun shining again tomorrow."

"We must plan our picnic," Eleanor said.

"I am going to get fat and lazy in Hill House," Theodora went on. Her insistence on naming Hill House troubled Eleanor. It's as though she were saying it deliberately, Eleanor thought, telling the house she knows its name, calling the house to tell it where we are; is it bravado? "Hill House, Hill House, Hill House," Theodora said softly, and smiled across at Eleanor.

"Tell me," Luke said politely to Theodora, "since you *are* a princess, tell me about the political situation in your country."

"Very unsettled," Theodora said. "I ran away because my father, who is of course the king, insists that I marry Black Michael, who is the pretender to the throne. I, of course, cannot endure the sight of Black Michael, who wears one gold earring and beats his grooms with a riding crop."

"A most unstable country," Luke said. "How did you ever manage to get away?"

"I fled in a hay wagon, disguised as a milkmaid. They never thought to look for me there, and I crossed the border with papers I forged myself in a woodcutter's hut."

"And Black Michael will no doubt take over the country now in a *coup d'état*?"

"Undoubtedly. And he can have it."

It's like waiting in a dentist's office, Eleanor thought, watching them over her coffee cup; waiting in a dentist's office and listening to other patients make brave jokes across the room, all of you certain to meet the dentist sooner or later. She looked up suddenly, aware of the doctor near her, and smiled uncertainly.

"Nervous?" the doctor asked, and Eleanor nodded.

"Only because I wonder what's going to happen," she said.

"So do I." The doctor moved a chair and sat down beside her. "You have the feeling that something—whatever it is—is going to happen soon?"

"Yes. Everything seems to be waiting."

"And *they*"—the doctor nodded at Theodora and Luke, who were laughing at each other—"*they* meet it in *their* way; I wonder what it will do to all of us. I would have said a month ago that a situation like this would never really come about, that we four would sit here together, in this house." *He* does not name it, Eleanor noticed. "I've been waiting for a long time," he said.

"You think we are right to stay?"

"Right?" he said. "I think we are all incredibly silly to stay. I think that an atmosphere like this one can find out the flaws and faults and weaknesses in all of us, and break us apart in a matter of days. We have only one defense, and that is running away. At least it can't *follow* us, can it? When we feel ourselves endangered we can leave, just as we came. And," he added dryly, "just as fast as we can go."

"But we are forewarned," Eleanor said, "and there are four of us together."

"I have already mentioned this to Luke and Theodora," he said. "Promise me absolutely that you will leave, as fast as you can, if you begin to feel the house catching at you."

"I promise," Eleanor said, smiling. He is trying to make me feel braver, she thought, and was grateful. "It's all right, though," she told him. "Really, it's all right."

"I will feel no hesitation about sending you away," he said, rising, "if it seems to be necessary. Luke?" he said. "Will the ladies excuse us?"

While they set up the chessboard and men Theodora wandered, cup in hand, around the room, and Eleanor thought, She moves like an animal, nervous and alert; she can't sit still while there is any scent of disturbance in the air; we are all uneasy. "Come and sit by me," she said, and Theodora came, moving with grace, circling to a resting spot. She sat down in the chair the doctor had left, and leaned her head back tiredly; how lovely she is, Eleanor thought, how thoughtlessly, luckily lovely. "Are you tired?"

Theodora turned her head, smiling. "I can't stand waiting much longer."

"I was just thinking how relaxed you looked."

"And *I* was just thinking of—when was it? day before yesterday?—and wondering how I could have brought myself to leave there and come here. Possibly I'm homesick."

"Already?"

"Did you ever think about being homesick? If your home was Hill House would you be homesick for it? Did those two little girls cry for their dark, grim house when they were taken away?"

"I've never been away from anywhere," Eleanor said carefully, "so I suppose I've never been homesick."

"How about now? Your little apartment?"

"Perhaps," Eleanor said, looking into the fire, "I haven't had it long enough to believe it's my own."

"I want my own bed," Theodora said, and Eleanor thought,

She is sulking again; when she is hungry or tired or bored she turns into a baby. "I'm sleepy," Theodora said.

"It's after eleven," Eleanor said, and as she turned to glance at the chess game the doctor shouted with joyful triumph, and Luke laughed.

"Now, sir," the doctor said. "*Now*, sir."

"Fairly beaten, I admit," Luke said. He began to gather the chessmen and set them back into their box. "Any reason why I can't take a drop of brandy upstairs with me? To put myself to sleep, or give myself Dutch courage, or some such reason. Actually"—and he smiled over at Theodora and Eleanor—"I plan to stay up and read for a while."

"Are you still reading *Pamela*?" Eleanor asked the doctor.

"Volume two. I have three volumes to go, and then I shall begin *Clarissa Harlowe*, I think. Perhaps Luke would care to borrow—"

"No, thanks," Luke said hastily. "I have a suitcase full of mystery stories."

The doctor turned to look around. "Let me see," he said, "fire screened, lights out. Leave the doors for Mrs. Dudley to close in the morning."

Tiredly, following one another, they went up the great stairway, turning out lights behind them. "Has everyone got a flashlight, by the way?" the doctor asked, and they nodded, more intent upon sleep than the waves of darkness which came after them up the stairs of Hill House.

"Good night, everyone," Eleanor said, opening the door to the blue room.

"Good night," Luke said.

"Good night," Theodora said.

"Good night," the doctor said. "Sleep tight."

6

"Coming, mother, coming," Eleanor said, fumbling for the light. "It's all right, I'm coming." *Eleanor*, she heard, *Eleanor*. "Coming, coming," she shouted irritably, "just a *minute*, I'm *coming*."

"Eleanor?"

Then she thought, with a crashing shock which brought her awake, cold and shivering, out of bed and awake: *I am in Hill House*.

"What?" she cried out. "What? Theodora?"

"Eleanor? In here."

"Coming." No time for the light; she kicked a table out of the way, wondering at the noise of it, and struggled briefly with the door of the connecting bathroom. That is not the table falling, she thought; my mother is knocking on the wall. It was blessedly light in Theodora's room, and Theodora was sitting up in bed, her hair tangled from sleep and her eyes wide with the shock of awakening; I must look the same way, Eleanor thought, and said, "I'm here, what *is* it?"—and then heard, clearly for the first time, although she had been hearing it ever since she awakened. "What *is* it?" she whispered.

She sat down slowly on the foot of Theodora's bed, wondering at what seemed calmness in herself. Now, she thought, now. It is only a noise, and terribly cold, terribly, terribly cold. It is a noise down the hall, far down at the end, near the nursery door, and terribly cold; *not* my mother knocking on the wall.

"Something is knocking on the doors," Theodora said in a tone of pure rationality.

"That's all. And it's down near the other end of the hall. Luke and the doctor are probably there already, to see what is going on." Not at all like my mother knocking on the wall; I was dreaming again.

"Bang bang," Theodora said.

"Bang," Eleanor said, and giggled. I am calm, she thought, but so very cold; the noise is only a kind of banging on the doors, one after another; is this what I was so afraid about? "Bang" is the best word for it; it sounds like something children do, not mothers knocking against the wall for help, and anyway Luke and the doctor are there; is this what they mean by cold chills going up and down your back? Because it is not pleasant; it starts in your stomach and goes in waves around and up and down again like something alive. Like something alive. Yes. Like something alive.

"Theodora," she said, and closed her eyes and tightened her

teeth together and wrapped her arms around herself, "it's getting closer."

"Just a noise," Theodora said, and moved next to Eleanor and sat tight against her. "It has an echo."

It sounded, Eleanor thought, like a hollow noise, a hollow bang, as though something were hitting the doors with an iron kettle, or an iron bar, or an iron glove. It pounded regularly for a minute, and then suddenly more softly, and then again in a quick flurry, seeming to be going methodically from door to door at the end of the hall. Distantly she thought she could hear the voices of Luke and the doctor, calling from somewhere below, and she thought, *Then they are not up here with us at all*, and heard the iron crashing against what must have been a door very close.

"Maybe it will go on down the other side of the hall," Theodora whispered, and Eleanor thought that the oddest part of this indescribable experience was that Theodora should be having it too. "No," Theodora said, and they heard the crash against the door across the hall. It was louder, it was deafening, it struck against the door next to them (did it move back and forth across the hall? did it go on feet along the carpet? did it lift a hand to the door?), and Eleanor threw herself away from the bed and ran to hold her hands against the door. "Go away," she shouted wildly. "Go away, go away!"

There was complete silence, and Eleanor thought, standing with her face against the door, Now I've done it; it was looking for the room with someone inside.

The cold crept and pinched at them, filling and overflowing the room. Anyone would have thought that the inhabitants of Hill House slept sweetly in this quiet, and then, so suddenly that Eleanor wheeled around, the sound of Theodora's teeth chattering, and Eleanor laughed. "You big baby," she said.

"I'm cold," Theodora said. "Deadly cold."

"So am I." Eleanor took the green quilt and threw it around Theodora, and took up Theodora's warm dressing gown and put it on. "You warmer now?"

"Where's Luke? Where's the doctor?"

"I don't know. Are you warmer now?"

"No." Theodora shivered.

"In a minute I'll go out in the hall and call them; are you—"

It started again, as though it had been listening, waiting to hear their voices and what they said, to identify them, to know how well prepared they were against it, waiting to hear if they were afraid. So suddenly that Eleanor leaped back against the bed and Theodora gasped and cried out, the iron crash came against their door, and both of them lifted their eyes in horror, because the hammering was against the upper edge of the door, higher than either of them could reach, higher than Luke or the doctor could reach, and the sickening, degrading cold came in waves from whatever was outside the door.

Eleanor stood perfectly still and looked at the door. She did not quite know what to do, although she believed that she was thinking coherently and was not unusually frightened, not more frightened, certainly, than she had believed in her worst dreams she could be. The cold troubled her even more than the sounds; even Theodora's warm robe was useless against the icy little curls of fingers on her back. The intelligent thing to do, perhaps, was to walk over and open the door; that, perhaps, would belong with the doctor's views of pure scientific inquiry. Eleanor knew that, even if her feet would take her as far as the door, her hand would not lift to the doorknob; impartially, remotely, she told herself that no one's hand would touch that knob; it's not the work hands were made for, she told herself. She had been rocking a little, each crash against the door pushing her a little backward, and now she was still because the noise was fading. "I'm going to complain to the janitor about the radiators," Theodora said from behind her. "Is it stopping?"

"No," Eleanor said, sick. "No."

It had found them. Since Eleanor would not open the door, it was going to make its own way in. Eleanor said aloud, "Now I know why people scream, because I think I'm going to," and Theodora said, "I will if you will," and laughed, so that Eleanor turned quickly back to the bed and they held each other, listening in silence. Little pattings came from around the doorframe, small seeking sounds, feeling the edges of the door, trying to sneak a way in. The doorknob was fondled, and Eleanor, whispering, asked, "Is it locked?" and Theodora nodded and then, wide-eyed, turned to stare at the connecting bathroom door. "Mine's locked too," Eleanor said against her ear, and Theodora closed her eyes in relief. The little sticky sounds moved on around the doorframe and then, as though a fury caught whatever was outside, the crashing came again, and Eleanor and Theodora saw the wood of the door tremble and shake, and the door move against its hinges.

"You can't get in," Eleanor said wildly, and again there was a silence, as though the house listened with attention to her words, understanding, cynically agreeing, content to wait. A thin little giggle came, in a breath of air through the room, a little mad rising laugh, the smallest whisper of a laugh, and Eleanor heard it all up and down her back, a little gloating laugh moving past them around the house, and then she heard the doctor and Luke calling from the stairs and, mercifully, it was over.

When the real silence came, Eleanor breathed shakily and moved stiffly. "We've been clutching each other like a couple of lost children," Theodora said and untwined her arms from around Eleanor's neck. "You're wearing my bathrobe."

"I forgot mine. Is it really over?"

"For tonight, anyway." Theodora spoke with certainty. "Can't you tell? Aren't you warm again?"

The sickening cold was gone, except for a reminiscent little thrill of it down Eleanor's back when she looked at the door. She began to pull at the tight knot she had put in the bathrobe cord, and said, "Intense cold is one of the symptoms of shock."

"Intense shock is one of the symptoms I've got," Theodora said. "Here come Luke and the doctor." Their voices were outside in the hall, speaking quickly, anxiously, and Eleanor dropped Theodora's robe on the bed and said, "For heaven's sake, don't let them knock on that door—one more knock would finish me"—and ran into her own room to get her own robe. Behind her she could hear Theodora telling them to wait a minute, and then going to unlock the door, and then Luke's voice saying pleasantly to Theodora, "Why, you look as though you'd seen a ghost."

When Eleanor came back she noticed that both Luke and the doctor were dressed, and it occurred to her that it might be a sound idea from now on; if that intense cold was going to come back at night it was going to find Eleanor sleeping in a wool suit and a heavy sweater, and she didn't care what Mrs. Dudley was going to say when she found that at least one of the lady guests was lying in one of the clean beds in heavy shoes and wool socks. "Well," she asked, "how do you gentlemen like living in a haunted house?"

"It's perfectly fine," Luke said, "perfectly fine. It gives me an excuse to have a drink in the middle of the night." He had the brandy bottle and glasses, and Eleanor thought that they must make a companionable little group, the four of them, sitting around Theodora's room at four in the morning, drinking brandy. They spoke lightly, quickly, and gave one another fast, hidden, little curious glances, each of them wondering what secret terror had been tapped in the others, what changes might show in face or gesture, what unguarded weakness might have opened the way to ruin.

"Did anything happen in here while we were outside?" the doctor asked.

Eleanor and Theodora looked at each other and laughed, honestly at last, without any edge of hysteria or fear. After a minute Theodora said carefully, "Nothing in particular. Someone knocked on the door with a cannon ball and then tried to get in and eat us, and started laughing its head off when we wouldn't open the door. But nothing really out of the way."

Curiously, Eleanor went over and opened the door. "I thought the whole door was going to shatter," she said, bewildered, "and there isn't even a scratch on the wood, nor on any of the other doors; they're perfectly smooth."

"How nice that it didn't mar the woodwork," Theodora said, holding her brandy glass out to Luke. "I couldn't bear it if this dear old house got hurt." She grinned at Eleanor. "Nellie here was going to scream."

"So were you."

"Not at all; I only said so to keep you company. Besides, Mrs. Dudley already said she wouldn't come. And where were *you*, our manly defenders?"

"We were chasing a dog," Luke said. "At least, some animal like a dog." He stopped, and then went on reluctantly. "We followed it outside."

Theodora stared, and Eleanor said, "You mean it was *inside?*"

"I saw it run past my door," the doctor said, "just caught a glimpse of it, slipping along. I woke Luke and we followed it down the stairs and out into the garden and lost it somewhere back of the house."

"The front door was open?"

"No," Luke said. "The front door was closed. So were all the other doors. We checked."

"We've been wandering around for quite a while," the doctor said. "We never dreamed that you ladies were awake until we heard your voices." He spoke gravely. "There is one thing we have not taken into account," he said.

They looked at him, puzzled, and he explained, checking on his fingers in his lecture style. "First," he said, "Luke and I were awakened earlier than you ladies, clearly; we have been up and about, outside and in, for better than two hours, led on what you perhaps might allow me to call a wild-goose chase. Second, neither of us"—he glanced inquiringly at Luke as he spoke—"heard any sound up here until your voices began. It was perfectly quiet. That is, the sound which hammered on your door was not audible to us. When we gave up our vigil and decided to come upstairs we apparently drove away whatever was waiting outside your door. Now, as we sit here together, all is quiet."

"I still don't see what you mean," Theodora said, frowning.

"We must take precautions," he said.

"Against what? How?"

"When Luke and I are called outside, and you two are kept imprisoned inside, doesn't it begin to seem"—and his voice was very quiet—"doesn't it begin to seem that the intention is, somehow, to separate us?"

5

LOOKING at herself in the mirror, with the bright morning sunlight freshening even the blue room of Hill House, Eleanor thought, It is my second morning in Hill House, and I am unbelievably happy. Journeys end in lovers meeting; I have spent an all but sleepless night, I have told lies and made a fool of myself, and the very air tastes like wine. I have been frightened half out of my foolish wits, but I have somehow earned this joy; I have been waiting for it for so long. Abandoning a lifelong belief that to name happiness is to dissipate it, she smiled at herself in the mirror and told herself silently, You are happy, Eleanor, you have finally been given a part of your measure of happiness. Looking away from her own face in the mirror, she thought blindly, Journeys end in lovers meeting, lovers meeting.

"Luke?" It was Theodora, calling outside in the hall. "You carried off one of my stockings last night, and you are a thieving cad, and I hope Mrs. Dudley can hear me."

Eleanor could hear Luke, faintly, answering; he protested that a gentleman had a right to keep the favors bestowed upon him by a lady, and he was absolutely certain that Mrs. Dudley could hear every word.

"Eleanor?" Now Theodora pounded on the connecting door. "Are you awake? May I come in?"

"Come, of course," Eleanor said, looking at her own face in the mirror. You deserve it, she told herself, you have spent your life earning it. Theodora opened the door and said happily, "How pretty you look this morning, my Nell. This curious life agrees with you."

Eleanor smiled at her; the life clearly agreed with Theodora too.

"We ought by rights to be walking around with dark circles under our eyes and a look of wild despair," Theodora said, putting an arm around Eleanor and looking into the mirror beside her, "and look at us—two blooming, fresh young lovelies."

"I'm thirty-four years old," Eleanor said, and wondered what obscure defiance made her add two years.

"And you look about fourteen," Theodora said. "Come along; we've earned our breakfast."

Laughing, they raced down the great staircase and found their way through the game room and into the dining room. "Good morning," Luke said brightly. "And how did everyone sleep?"

"Delightfully, thank you," Eleanor said. "Like a baby."

"There may have been a little noise," Theodora said, "but one has to expect that in these old houses. Doctor, what do we do this morning?"

"Hm?" said the doctor, looking up. He alone looked tired, but his eyes were lighted with the same brightness they found, all, in one another; it is excitement, Eleanor thought; we are all enjoying ourselves.

"Ballechin House," the doctor said, savoring his words. "Borley Rectory. Glamis Castle. It is incredible to find oneself experiencing it, absolutely incredible. I could *not* have believed it. I begin to understand, dimly, the remote delight of your true medium. I think I shall have the marmalade, if you would be so kind. Thank you. My wife will never believe me. Food has a new flavor—do you find it so?"

"It isn't just that Mrs. Dudley has surpassed herself, then; I was wondering," Luke said.

"I've been trying to remember," Eleanor said. "About last night, I mean. I can remember *knowing* that I was frightened, but I can't imagine actually *being* frightened—"

"I remember the cold," Theodora said, and shivered.

"I think it's because it was so unreal by any pattern of thought I'm used to; I mean, it just didn't make *sense*." Eleanor stopped and laughed, embarrassed.

"I agree," Luke said. "I found myself this morning *telling* myself what had happened last night; the reverse of a bad dream, as a matter of fact, where you keep telling yourself that it *didn't* really happen."

"I thought it was exciting," Theodora said.

The doctor lifted a warning finger. "It is still perfectly possible that it is all caused by subterranean waters."

"Then more houses ought to be built over secret springs," Theodora said.

The doctor frowned. "This excitement troubles me," he said. "It is intoxicating, certainly, but might it not also be dangerous? An effect of the atmosphere of Hill House? The first sign that we have—as it were—fallen under a spell?"

"Then I will be an enchanted princess," Theodora said.

"And yet," Luke said, "if last night is a true measure of Hill House, we are not going to have much trouble; we were frightened, certainly, and found the experience unpleasant while it was going on, and yet I cannot remember that I felt in any *physical* danger; even Theodora telling that whatever was outside her door was coming to eat her did not really sound—"

"I know what she meant," Eleanor said, "because I thought it was exactly the right word. The sense was that it wanted to consume us, take us into itself, make us a part of the house, maybe—oh, dear. I thought I knew what I was saying, but I'm doing it very badly."

"No physical danger exists," the doctor said positively. "No ghost in all the long histories of ghosts has ever hurt anyone physically. The only damage done is by the victim to himself. One cannot even say that the ghost attacks the mind, because the mind, the conscious, thinking mind, is invulnerable; in all our conscious minds, as we sit here talking, there is not one iota of belief in ghosts. Not one of us, even after last night, can say the word 'ghost' without a little involuntary smile. No, the menace of the supernatural is that it attacks where modern minds are weakest, where we have abandoned our protective armor of superstition and have no substitute defense. Not one of us thinks rationally that what ran through the garden last night was a ghost, and what knocked on the door was a ghost, and yet there was certainly *something* going on in Hill House last night, and the mind's instinctive refuge—self-doubt—is eliminated. We cannot say, 'It was my imagination,' because three other people were there too."

"I could say," Eleanor put in, smiling, "'All three of you are in my imagination; none of this is real.'"

"If I thought you could really believe that," the doctor said gravely, "I would turn you out of Hill House this morning. You would be venturing far too close to the state of mind which would welcome the perils of Hill House with a kind of sisterly embrace."

"He means he would think you were batty, Nell dear."

"Well," Eleanor said, "I expect I would be. If I had to take sides with Hill House against the rest of you, I would expect you to send me away." Why me, she wondered, why me? Am I the public conscience? Expected always to say in cold words what the rest of them are too arrogant to recognize? Am I supposed to be the weakest, weaker than Theodora? Of all of us, she thought, I am surely the one least likely to turn against the others.

"Poltergeists are another thing altogether," the doctor said, his eyes resting briefly on Eleanor. "They deal entirely with the physical world; they throw stones, they move objects, they smash dishes; Mrs. Foyster at Borley Rectory was a long-suffering woman, but she finally lost her temper entirely when her best teapot was hurled through the window. Poltergeists, however, are rock-bottom on the supernatural social scale; they are destructive, but mindless and will-less; they are merely undirected force. Do you recall," he asked with a little smile, "Oscar Wilde's lovely story, 'The Canterville Ghost'?"

"The American twins who routed the fine old English ghost," Theodora said.

"Exactly. I have always liked the notion that the American twins were actually a poltergeist phenomenon; certainly poltergeists can overshadow any more interesting manifestation. Bad ghosts drive out good." And he patted his hands happily. "They drive out everything else, too," he added. "There is a manor in Scotland, infested with poltergeists, where as many as seventeen spontaneous fires have broken out in one day; poltergeists like to turn people out of bed violently by tipping the bed end over end, and I remember the case of a minister who was forced to leave his home because he was tormented, day after day, by a poltergeist who hurled at his head hymn books stolen from a rival church."

Suddenly, without reason, laughter trembled inside Eleanor; she wanted to run to the head of the table and hug the doctor, she wanted to reel, chanting, across the stretches of the lawn, she wanted to sing and to shout and to fling her arms and move in great emphatic, possessing circles around the rooms of Hill House; I am here, I am here, she thought. She shut her eyes quickly in delight and then said demurely to the doctor, "And what do we do today?"

"You're still like a pack of children," the doctor said, smiling too. "Always asking me what to do today. Can't you amuse yourselves with your toys? Or with each other? *I* have work to do."

"All I *really* want to do"—and Theodora giggled—"is slide down that banister." The excited gaiety had caught her as it had Eleanor.

"Hide and seek," Luke said.

"Try not to wander around alone too much," the doctor said. "I can't think of a good reason why not, but it does seem sensible."

"Because there are bears in the woods," Theodora said.

"And tigers in the attic," Eleanor said.

"And an old witch in the tower, and a dragon in the drawing room."

"I am quite serious," the doctor said, laughing.

"It's ten o'clock. I clear—"

"Good morning, Mrs. Dudley," the doctor said, and Eleanor and Theodora and Luke leaned back and laughed helplessly.

"I clear at ten o'clock."

"We won't keep you long. About fifteen minutes, please, and then you can clear the table."

"I clear breakfast at ten o'clock. I set on lunch at one. Dinner I set on at six. It's ten o'clock."

"Mrs. Dudley," the doctor began sternly, and then, noticing Luke's face tight with silent laughter, lifted his napkin to cover his eyes, and gave in. "You may clear the table, Mrs. Dudley," the doctor said brokenly.

Happily, the sound of their laughter echoing along the halls of Hill House and carrying to the marble group in the drawing room and the nursery upstairs and the odd little top to the tower, they made their way down the passage to their parlor and fell, still laughing, into chairs. "We must not make fun of Mrs. Dudley," the doctor said and leaned forward, his face in his hands and his shoulders shaking.

They laughed for a long time, speaking now and then in

half-phrases, trying to tell one another something, pointing at one another wildly, and their laughter rocked Hill House until, weak and aching, they lay back, spent, and regarded one another. "Now—" the doctor began, and was stopped by a little giggling burst from Theodora.

"Now," the doctor said again, more severely, and they were quiet. "I want more coffee," he said, appealing. "Don't we all?"

"You mean go right in there and ask Mrs. Dudley?" Eleanor asked.

"Walk right up to her when it isn't one o'clock or six o'clock and just *ask* her for some coffee?" Theodora demanded.

"Roughly, yes," the doctor said. "Luke, my boy, I have observed that you are already something of a favorite with Mrs. Dudley—"

"And how," Luke inquired with amazement, "did you ever manage to observe anything so unlikely? Mrs. Dudley regards me with the same particular loathing she gives a dish not properly on its shelf; in Mrs. Dudley's eyes—"

"You are, after all, the heir to the house," the doctor said coaxingly. "Mrs. Dudley must feel for you as an old family retainer feels for the young master."

"In Mrs. Dudley's eyes I am something lower than a dropped fork. I beg of you, if you are contemplating asking the old fool for something, send Theo, or our charming Nell. *They* are not afraid—"

"Nope," Theodora said. "You can't send a helpless female to face down Mrs. Dudley. Nell and I are here to be protected, not to man the battlements for you cowards."

"The doctor—"

"Nonsense," the doctor said heartily. "You certainly wouldn't think of asking *me*, an older man; anyway, you *know* she adores you."

"Insolent graybeard," Luke said. "Sacrificing me for a cup of coffee. Do not be surprised, and I say it darkly, do not be surprised if you lose your Luke in this cause; perhaps Mrs. Dudley has not yet had her own midmorning snack, and she is perfectly capable of a *filet de Luke à la meunière*, or perhaps *dieppoise*, depending upon her mood; if I do not return"—and he shook his finger warningly under the doctor's nose—"I entreat you to regard your lunch with the gravest suspicion."

Bowing extravagantly, as befitted one off to slay a giant, he closed the door behind him.

"Lovely Luke." Theodora stretched luxuriously.

"Lovely Hill House," Eleanor said. "Theo, there is a kind of little summerhouse in the side garden, all overgrown; I noticed it yesterday. Can we explore it this morning?"

"Delighted," Theodora said. "I would not like to leave one inch of Hill House uncherished. Anyway, it's too nice a day to stay inside."

"We'll ask Luke to come too," Eleanor said. "And you, Doctor?"

"My notes—" the doctor began, and then stopped as the door opened so suddenly that in Eleanor's mind was only the thought that Luke had not dared face Mrs. Dudley after all, but had stood, waiting, pressed against the door; then, looking at his white face and hearing the doctor say with fury, "I broke my own first rule; I sent him alone," she found herself only asking urgently, "Luke? Luke?"

"It's all right." Luke even smiled. "But come into the long hallway."

Chilled by his face and his voice and his smile, they got up silently and followed him through the doorway into the dark long hallway which led back to the front hall. "Here," Luke said, and a little winding shiver of sickness went down Eleanor's back when she saw that he was holding a lighted match up to the wall.

"It's—writing?" Eleanor asked, pressing closer to see.

"Writing," Luke said. "I didn't even notice it until I was coming back. Mrs. Dudley said no," he added, his voice tight.

"My flash." The doctor took his flashlight from his pocket, and under its light, as he moved slowly from one end of the hall to the other, the letters stood out clearly. "Chalk," the doctor said, stepping forward to touch a letter with the tip of his finger. "Written in chalk."

The writing was large and straggling and ought to have looked, Eleanor thought, as though it had been scribbled by bad boys on a fence. Instead, it was incredibly real, going in broken lines over the thick paneling of the hallway. From one end of the hallway to the other the letters went, almost too large to read, even when she stood back against the opposite wall.

"Can you read it?" Luke asked softly, and the doctor, moving his flashlight, read slowly: HELP ELEANOR COME HOME.

"No." And Eleanor felt the words stop in her throat; she had seen her name as the doctor read it. It is me, she thought. It is my name standing out there so clearly; I should not be on the walls of this house. "Wipe it off, *please*," she said, and felt Theodora's arm go around her shoulders. "It's *crazy*," Eleanor said, bewildered.

"Crazy is the word, all right," Theodora said strongly. "Come back inside, Nell, and sit down. Luke will get something and wipe it off."

"But it's *crazy*," Eleanor said, hanging back to see her name on the wall. "*Why—?*"

Firmly the doctor put her through the door into the little parlor and closed it; Luke had already attacked the message with his handkerchief. "Now you listen to me," the doctor said to Eleanor. "Just because your name—"

"That's it," Eleanor said, staring at him. "It knows my name, doesn't it? It knows *my* name."

"Shut up, will you?" Theodora shook her violently. "It could have said any of us; it knows *all* our names."

"Did you write it?" Eleanor turned to Theodora. "Please tell me—I won't be angry or anything, just so I can know that—maybe it was only a joke? To frighten me?" She looked appealingly at the doctor.

"You know that none of us wrote it," the doctor said.

Luke came in, wiping his hands on his handkerchief, and Eleanor turned hopefully. "Luke," she said, "you wrote it, didn't you? When you went out?"

Luke stared, and then came to sit on the arm of her chair. "Listen," he said, "you want me to go writing your name everywhere? Carving your initials on trees? Writing 'Eleanor, Eleanor' on little scraps of paper?" He gave her hair a soft little pull. "I've got more sense," he said. "Behave yourself."

"Then why me?" Eleanor said, looking from one of them to another; I am outside, she thought madly, I am the one chosen, and she said quickly, beggingly, "Did I do something to attract attention, more than anyone else?"

"No more than usual, dear," Theodora said. She was standing by the fireplace, leaning on the mantel and tapping her fingers, and when she spoke she looked at Eleanor with a bright smile. "Maybe you wrote it yourself."

Angry, Eleanor almost shouted. "You think I *want* to see my name scribbled all over this foul house? You think *I* like the idea that I'm the center of attention? *I*'m not the spoiled baby, after all—*I* don't like being singled out—"

"Asking for help, did you notice?" Theodora said lightly. "Perhaps the spirit of the poor little companion has found a means of communication at last. Maybe she was only waiting for some drab, timid—"

"Maybe it was only addressed to me because no possible appeal for help could get through that iron selfishness of yours; maybe I might have more sympathy and understanding in one minute than—"

"And maybe, of course, you wrote it to yourself," Theodora said again.

After the manner of men who see women quarreling, the doctor and Luke had withdrawn, standing tight together in miserable silence; now, at last, Luke moved and spoke. "That's enough, Eleanor," he said, unbelievably, and Eleanor whirled around, stamping. "How dare you?" she said, gasping. "How *dare* you?"

And the doctor laughed, then, and she stared at him and then at Luke, who was smiling and watching her. What is wrong with me? she thought. Then—but they think Theodora did it on purpose, made me mad so I wouldn't be frightened; how shameful to be maneuvered that way. She covered her face and sat down in her chair.

"Nell, dear," Theodora said, "I *am* sorry."

I must say something, Eleanor told herself; I must show them that I am a good sport, after all; a good sport; let them think that I am ashamed of myself. "*I*'m sorry," she said. "I was frightened."

"Of course you were," the doctor said, and Eleanor thought, How simple he is, how transparent; he believes every silly thing he has ever heard. He thinks, even, that Theodora shocked me out of hysteria. She smiled at him and thought, Now I am back in the fold.

"I really thought you were going to start shrieking," Theodora said, coming to kneel by Eleanor's chair. "*I* would have, in your place. But we can't afford to have you break up, you know."

We can't afford to have anyone but Theodora in the center of the stage, Eleanor thought; if Eleanor is going to be the outsider, she is going to be it all alone. She reached out and patted Theodora's head and said, "Thanks. I guess I was kind of shaky for a minute."

"I wondered if you two were going to come to blows," Luke said, "until I realized what Theodora was doing."

Smiling down into Theodora's bright, happy eyes, Eleanor thought, But that isn't what Theodora was doing at all.

2

Time passed lazily at Hill House. Eleanor and Theodora, the doctor and Luke, alert against terror, wrapped around by the rich hills and securely set into the warm, dark luxuries of the house, were permitted a quiet day and a quiet night—enough, perhaps, to dull them a little. They took their meals together, and Mrs. Dudley's cooking stayed perfect. They talked together and played chess; the doctor finished *Pamela* and began on *Sir Charles Grandison*. A compelling need for occasional privacy led them to spend some hours alone in their separate rooms, without disturbance. Theodora and Eleanor and Luke explored the tangled thicket behind the house and found the little summerhouse, while the doctor sat on the wide lawn, writing, within sight and hearing. They found a walled-in rose garden, grown over with weeds, and a vegetable garden tenderly nourished by the Dudleys. They spoke often of arranging their picnic by the brook. There were wild strawberries near the summerhouse, and Theodora and Eleanor and Luke brought back a handkerchief full and lay on the lawn near the doctor, eating them, staining their hands and their mouths; like children, the doctor told them, looking up with amusement from his notes. Each of them had written—carelessly, and with little attention to detail—an account of what they thought they had seen and heard so far in Hill House, and the doctor had put the papers away in his portfolio. The next morning—their third morning in Hill House—the doctor, aided by Luke, had spent a loving and maddening hour on the floor of the upstairs hall, trying, with chalk and measuring tape, to determine the precise dimensions of the cold spot, while Eleanor and Theodora sat cross-legged on the hall floor, noting down the doctor's measurements and playing tic-tac-toe. The doctor was considerably hampered in his work by the fact that, his hands repeatedly chilled by the extreme cold, he could not hold either the chalk or the tape for more than a minute at a time. Luke, inside the nursery doorway, could hold one end of the tape until his hand came into the cold spot, and then his fingers lost strength and relaxed helplessly. A thermometer, dropped into the center of the cold spot, refused to register any change at all, but continued doggedly maintaining that the temperature there was the same as the temperature down the rest of the hall, causing the doctor to fume wildly against the statisticians of Borley Rectory, who had caught an eleven-degree drop. When he had defined the cold spot as well as he could, and noted his results in his notebook, he brought them downstairs for lunch and issued a general challenge to them, to meet him at croquet in the cool of the afternoon.

"It seems foolish," he explained, "to spend a morning as glorious as this has been looking at a frigid place on a floor. We must plan to spend more time outside"—and was mildly surprised when they laughed.

"Is there still a world somewhere?" Eleanor, asked wonderingly. Mrs. Dudley had made them a peach shortcake, and she looked down at her plate and said, "I am sure Mrs. Dudley goes somewhere else at night, and she brings back heavy cream each morning, and Dudley comes up with groceries every afternoon, but as far as I can remember there is no other place than this."

"We are on a desert island," Luke said.

"I can't picture any world but Hill House," Eleanor said.

"Perhaps," Theodora said, "we should make notches on a stick, or pile pebbles in a heap, one each day, so we will know how long we have been marooned."

"How pleasant not to have any word from outside." Luke helped himself to an enormous heap of whipped cream. "No letters, no newspapers; anything might be happening."

"Unfortunately—" the doctor said, and then stopped. "I beg your pardon," he went on. "I meant only to say that word *will* be reaching us from outside, and of course it is not unfortunate at all. Mrs. Montague—my wife, that is—will be here on Saturday."

"But when is Saturday?" Luke asked. "Delighted to see Mrs. Montague, of course."

"Day after tomorrow." The doctor thought. "Yes," he said after a minute, "I believe that the day after tomorrow is Saturday. We will know it is Saturday, of course," he told them with a little twinkle, "because Mrs. Montague will be here."

"I hope she is not holding high hopes of things going bump in the night," Theodora said. "Hill House has fallen far short of its original promise, I think. Or perhaps Mrs. Montague will be greeted with a volley of psychic experiences."

"Mrs. Montague," the doctor said, "will be perfectly ready to receive them."

"I wonder," Theodora said to Eleanor as they left the lunch table under Mrs. Dudley's watchful eye, "why everything *has* been so quiet. I think this waiting is nerve-racking, almost worse than having something happen."

"It's not us doing the waiting," Eleanor said. "It's the house. I think it's biding its time."

"Waiting until we feel secure, maybe, and then it will pounce."

"I wonder how long it can wait." Eleanor shivered and started up the great staircase. "I am almost tempted to write a letter to my sister. You know—'Having a perfectly *splendid* time here in jolly old Hill House. . . .'"

" 'You really must plan to bring the whole family next summer,' " Theodora went on. " 'We sleep under blankets every night. . . .'"

" 'The air is so bracing, particularly in the upstairs hall. . . .'"

" 'You go around all the time just glad to be alive. . . .'"

" 'There's something going on every minute. . . .'"

" 'Civilization seems so far away. . . .'"

Eleanor laughed. She was ahead of Theodora, at the top of the stairs. The dark hallway was a little lightened this afternoon, because they had left the nursery door open and the sunlight came through the windows by the tower and touched the doctor's measuring tape and chalk on the floor. The light reflected from the stained-glass window on the stair landing and made shattered fragments of blue and orange and green on the dark wood of the hall. "I'm going to sleep," she said. "I've never been so lazy in my life."

"I'm going to lie on my bed and dream about streetcars," Theodora said.

It had become Eleanor's habit to hesitate in the doorway of her room, glancing around quickly before she went inside; she told herself that this was because the room was so exceedingly blue and always took a moment to get used to. When she came inside she went across to open the window, which she always found closed; today she was halfway across the room before she heard Theodora's door slam back, and Theodora's smothered "Eleanor!" Moving quickly, Eleanor ran into the hall and to Theodora's doorway, to stop, aghast, looking over Theodora's shoulder. "What *is* it?" she whispered.

"What does it *look* like?" Theodora's voice rose crazily. "What does it *look* like, you fool?"

And I won't forgive her *that* either, Eleanor thought concretely through her bewilderment. "It looks like paint," she said hesitantly. "Except"—realizing—"except the smell is awful."

"It's blood," Theodora said with finality. She clung to the door, swaying as the door moved, staring. "Blood," she said. "All over. Do you see it?"

"Of course I see it. And it's not *all* over. Stop making such a fuss." Although, she thought conscientiously, Theodora was making very little of a fuss, actually. One of these times, she thought, one of us *is* going to put her head back and really howl, and I hope it won't be me, because I'm trying to guard against it; it *will* be Theodora who . . . And then, cold, she asked, "Is that more writing on the wall?"—and heard Theodora's wild laugh, and thought, Maybe it will be me, after all, and I can't afford to. I must be steady, and she closed her eyes and found herself saying silently, O stay and hear, your true love's coming, that can sing both high and low. Trip no further, pretty sweeting; journeys end in lovers meeting . . .

"Yes indeed, dear," Theodora said. "I don't know how you managed it."

Every wise man's son doth know. "Be sensible," Eleanor said. "Call Luke. And the doctor."

"Why?" Theodora asked. "Wasn't it to be just a little private surprise for me? A secret just for the two of us?" Then, pulling away from Eleanor, who tried to hold her from going farther into the room, she ran to the great wardrobe and threw open the door and, cruelly, began to cry. "My clothes," she said. "My clothes."

Steadily Eleanor turned and went to the top of the stairs. "Luke," she called, leaning over the banisters. "Doctor." Her voice was not loud, and she had tried to keep it level, but she heard the doctor's book drop to the floor and then the pounding of feet as he and Luke ran for the stairs. She watched them, seeing their apprehensive faces, wondering at the uneasiness which lay so close below the surface in all of them, so that each of them seemed always waiting for a cry for help from one of the others; intelligence and understanding are really no protection at all, she thought. "It's Theo," she said as they came to the top of the stairs. "She's hysterical. Someone —something—has gotten red paint in her room, and she's crying over her clothes." Now I could not have put it more fairly than that, she thought, turning to follow them. Could I have put it more fairly than that? she asked herself, and found that she was smiling.

Theodora was still sobbing wildly in her room and kicking at the wardrobe door, in a tantrum that might have been laughable if she had not been holding her yellow shirt, matted and stained; her other clothes had been torn from the hangers and lay trampled and disordered on the wardrobe floor, all of them smeared and reddened. "What is it?" Luke asked the doctor, and the doctor, shaking his head, said, "I would swear that it was blood, and yet to get so much blood one would almost have to . . ." and then was abruptly quiet.

All of them stood in silence for a moment and looked at HELP ELEANOR COME HOME ELEANOR written in shaky red letters on the wallpaper over Theodora's bed.

This time I am ready, Eleanor told herself, and said, "You'd better get her out of here; bring her into my room."

"My clothes are ruined," Theodora said to the doctor. "Do you see my clothes?"

The smell was atrocious, and the writing on the wall had dripped and splattered. There was a line of drops from the wall to the wardrobe—perhaps what had first turned Theodora's attention that way—and a great irregular stain on the green rug. "It's disgusting," Eleanor said. "Please get Theo into my room."

Luke and the doctor between them persuaded Theodora through the bathroom and into Eleanor's room, and Eleanor, looking at the red paint (It must be paint, she told herself; it's simply got to be paint; what else *could* it be?), said aloud, "But *why?*"—and stared up at the writing on the wall. Here lies one, she thought gracefully, whose name was writ in blood; is it possible that I am not quite coherent at this moment?

"Is she all right?" she asked, turning as the doctor came back into the room.

"She will be in a few minutes. We'll have to move her in with you for a while, I should think; I can't imagine her wanting to sleep in *here* again." The doctor smiled a little wanly. "It will be a long time, I think, before she opens another door by herself."

"I suppose she'll have to wear my clothes."

"I suppose she will, if you don't mind." The doctor looked at her curiously. "This message troubles you less than the other?"

"It's too silly," Eleanor said, trying to understand her own feelings. "I've been standing here looking at it and just wondering *why*. I mean, it's like a joke that didn't come off; I was supposed to be *much* more frightened than this, I think, and I'm not because it's simply *too* horrible to be real. And I keep remembering Theo putting red polish . . ." She giggled, and the doctor looked at her sharply, but she went on, "It might as *well* be paint, don't you see?" I can't stop talking, she thought; what do *I* have to explain in all this? "Maybe I can't take it seriously," she said, "after the sight of Theo screaming over her poor clothes and accusing me of writing my name all over her wall. Maybe I'm getting used to her blaming me for everything."

"Nobody's blaming you for anything," the doctor said, and Eleanor felt that she had been reproved.

"I hope my clothes will be good enough for her," she said tartly.

The doctor turned, looking around the room; he touched one finger gingerly to the letters on the wall and moved Theodora's yellow shirt with his foot. "Later," he said absently. "Tomorrow, perhaps." He glanced at Eleanor and smiled. "I can make an exact sketch of this," he said.

"I can help you," Eleanor said. "It makes me sick, but it doesn't frighten me."

"Yes," the doctor said. "I think we'd better close up the room for now, however; we don't want Theodora blundering in here again. Then later, at my leisure, I can study it. Also," he said with a flash of amusement, "I would not like to have Mrs. Dudley coming in here to straighten up."

Eleanor watched silently while he locked the hall door from inside the room, and then they went through the bathroom and he locked the connecting door into Theodora's green room. "I'll see about moving in another bed," he said, and then, with some awkwardness, "You've kept your head well, Eleanor; it's a help to me."

"I told you, it makes me sick but it doesn't frighten me," she said, pleased, and turned to Theodora. Theodora was lying on Eleanor's bed, and Eleanor saw with a queasy turn that Theodora had gotten red on her hands and it was rubbing off onto Eleanor's pillow. "Look," she said harshly, coming over to Theodora, "you'll have to wear my clothes until you get new ones, or until we get the others cleaned."

"Cleaned?" Theodora rolled convulsively on the bed and pressed her stained hands against her eyes. "*Cleaned?*"

"For heaven's sake," Eleanor said, "let me wash you off." She thought, without trying to find a reason, that she had never felt such uncontrollable loathing for any person before, and she went into the bathroom and soaked a towel and came back to scrub roughly at Theodora's hands and face. "You're filthy with the stuff," she said, hating to touch Theodora.

Suddenly Theodora smiled at her. "I don't really think you did it," she said, and Eleanor turned to see that Luke was behind her, looking down at them. "What a fool I am," Theodora said to him, and Luke laughed.

"You will be a delight in Nell's red sweater," he said.

She is wicked, Eleanor thought, beastly and soiled and dirty. She took the towel into the bathroom and left it to soak in cold water; when she came out Luke was saying, ". . . another bed in here; you girls are going to share a room from now on."

"Share a room and share our clothes," Theodora said. "We're going to be practically twins."

"Cousins," Eleanor said, but no one heard her.

3

"It was the custom, rigidly adhered to," Luke said, turning the brandy in his glass, "for the public executioner, before a quartering, to outline his knife strokes in chalk upon the belly of his victim—for fear of a slip, you understand."

I would like to hit her with a stick, Eleanor thought, looking down on Theodora's head beside her chair; I would like to batter her with rocks.

"An exquisite refinement, exquisite. Because of course the chalk strokes would have been almost unbearable, excruciating, if the victim were ticklish."

I hate her, Eleanor thought, she sickens me; she is all washed and clean and wearing my red sweater.

"When the death was by hanging in chains, however, the executioner . . ."

"Nell?" Theodora looked up at her and smiled. "I really am sorry, you know," she said.

I would like to watch her dying, Eleanor thought, and smiled back and said, "Don't be silly."

"Among the Sufis there is a teaching that the universe has never been created and consequently cannot be destroyed. I have spent the afternoon," Luke announced gravely, "browsing in our little library."

The doctor sighed. "No chess tonight, I think," he said to Luke, and Luke nodded. "It has been an exhausting day," the doctor said, "and I think you ladies should retire early."

"Not until I am well dulled with brandy," Theodora said firmly.

"Fear," the doctor said, "is the relinquishment of logic, the *willing* relinquishing of reasonable patterns. We yield to it or we fight it, but we cannot meet it halfway."

"I was wondering earlier," Eleanor said, feeling she had somehow an apology to make to all of them. "I thought I was altogether calm, and yet now I know I was terribly afraid." She frowned, puzzled, and they waited for her to go on. "When I *am* afraid, I can see perfectly the sensible, beautiful not-afraid side of the world, I can see chairs and tables and windows staying the same, not affected in the least, and I can see things like the careful woven texture of the carpet, not even moving. But when I am afraid I no longer exist in any relation to these things. I suppose because things are *not* afraid."

"I think we are only afraid of ourselves," the doctor said slowly.

"No," Luke said. "Of seeing ourselves clearly and without disguise."

"Of knowing what we really want," Theodora said. She pressed her cheek against Eleanor's hand and Eleanor, hating the touch of her, took her hand away quickly.

"I am always afraid of being alone," Eleanor said, and wondered, Am *I* talking like this? Am I saying something I will regret bitterly tomorrow? Am I making more guilt for myself? "Those letters spelled out *my* name, and none of you know what that feels like—it's so *familiar*." And she gestured to them, almost in appeal. "Try to *see*," she said. "It's my own dear name, and it belongs to me, and something is using it and writing it and calling me with it and my own *name* . . ." She stopped and said, looking from one of them to another, even down onto Theodora's face looking up at her, "Look. There's only one of me, and it's all I've got. I *hate* seeing myself dissolve and slip and separate so that I'm living in one half, my mind, and I see the other half of me helpless and frantic and driven and I can't stop it, but I know I'm not really going to be hurt and yet time is so long and even a second goes on and on and I could stand any of it if I could only surrender—"

"*Surrender?*" said the doctor sharply, and Eleanor stared.

"Surrender?" Luke repeated.

"I don't know," Eleanor said, perplexed. I was just talking along, she told herself, I was saying something—what was I just saying?

"She has done this before," Luke said to the doctor.

"I know," said the doctor gravely, and Eleanor could feel them all looking at her. "I'm sorry," she said. "Did I make a fool of myself? It's probably because I'm tired."

"Not at all," the doctor said, still grave. "Drink your brandy."

"Brandy?" And Eleanor looked down, realizing that she held a brandy glass. "What did I *say?*" she asked them.

Theodora chuckled. "Drink," she said. "You need it, my Nell."

Obediently Eleanor sipped at her brandy, feeling clearly its sharp burn, and then said to the doctor, "I must have said something silly, from the way you're all staring at me."

The doctor laughed. "Stop trying to be the center of attention."

"Vanity," Luke said serenely.

"Have to be in the limelight," Theodora said, and they smiled fondly, all looking at Eleanor.

4

Sitting up in the two beds beside each other, Eleanor and Theodora reached out between and held hands tight; the room was brutally cold and thickly dark. From the room next door, the room which until that morning had been Theodora's, came the steady low sound of a voice babbling, too low for words to be understood, too steady for disbelief. Holding hands so hard that each of them could feel the other's bones, Eleanor and Theodora listened, and the low, steady sound went on and on, the voice lifting sometimes for an emphasis on a mumbled word, falling sometimes to a breath, going on and on. Then, without warning, there was a little laugh, the small gurgling laugh that broke through the babbling, and rose as it laughed, on up and up the scale, and then broke off suddenly in a little painful gasp, and the voice went on.

Theodora's grasp loosened, and tightened, and Eleanor, lulled for a minute by the sounds, started and looked across to where Theodora ought to be in the darkness, and then thought, screamingly, Why is it dark? *Why is it dark?* She rolled and clutched Theodora's hand with both of hers, and tried to speak and could not, and held on, blindly, and frozen, trying to stand her mind on its feet, trying to reason again. We left the light on, she told herself, so why is it dark? Theodora, she tried to whisper, and her mouth could not move; Theodora, she tried to ask, why is it dark? and the voice went on, babbling, low and steady, a little liquid gloating sound. She thought she might be able to distinguish words if she lay perfectly still, if she lay perfectly still, and listened, and listened and heard the voice going on and on, never ceasing, and she hung desperately to Theodora's hand and felt an answering weight on her own hand.

Then the little gurgling laugh came again, and the rising mad sound of it drowned out the voice, and then suddenly absolute silence. Eleanor took a breath, wondering if she could speak now, and then she heard a little soft cry which broke her heart, a little infinitely sad cry, a little sweet moan of wild sadness. It is a *child*, she thought with disbelief, a child is crying somewhere, and then, upon that thought, came the wild shrieking voice she had never heard before and yet knew she had heard always in her nightmares. "Go away!" it screamed. "Go away, go away, don't hurt me," and, after, sobbing, "Please don't hurt me. Please let me go home," and then the little sad crying again.

I can't stand it, Eleanor thought concretely. This is monstrous, this is cruel, they have been hurting a child and I won't let anyone hurt a child, and the babbling went on, low and steady, on and on and on, the voice rising a little and falling a little, going on and on.

Now, Eleanor thought, perceiving that she was lying sideways on the bed in the black darkness, holding with both hands to Theodora's hand, holding so tight she could feel the fine bones of Theodora's fingers, now, I will not endure this. They think to scare me. Well, they have. I am scared, but more than that, I am a person, I am human, I am a walking reasoning humorous human being and I will take a lot from this lunatic filthy house but I will not go along with hurting a child, no, I will not; I will by God get my mouth to open right now and I will yell I will I will yell "STOP IT," she shouted, and the lights were on the way they had left them and Theodora was sitting up in bed, startled and disheveled.

"What?" Theodora was saying. "What, Nell? What?"

"God God," Eleanor said, flinging herself out of bed and across the room to stand shuddering in a corner, "God God— whose hand was I holding?"

6

I AM learning the pathways of the heart, Eleanor thought quite seriously, and then wondered what she could have meant by thinking any such thing. It was afternoon, and she sat in the sunlight on the steps of the summerhouse beside Luke; these are the silent pathways of the heart, she thought. She knew that she was pale, and still shaken, with dark circles under her eyes, but the sun was warm and the leaves moved gently overhead, and Luke beside her lay lazily against the step. "Luke," she asked, going slowly for fear of ridicule, "why do people want to talk to each other? I mean, what are the things people always want to find out about other people?"

"What do you want to know about me, for instance?" He laughed. She thought, But why not ask what *he* wants to know about *me*; he is so extremely vain—and laughed in turn and said, "What can I *ever* know about you, beyond what I see?" *See* was the least of the words she might have chosen, but the safest. Tell me something that only I will ever know, was perhaps what she wanted to ask him, or, What will you give me to remember you by?—or, even, Nothing of the least importance has ever belonged to me; can you help? Then she wondered if she had been foolish, or bold, amazed at her own thoughts, but he only stared down at the leaf he held in his hands and frowned a little, as one who devotes himself completely to an absorbing problem.

He is trying to phrase everything to make as good an impression as possible, she thought, and I will know how he holds me by what he answers; how is he anxious to appear to me? Does he think that I will be content with small mysticism, or will he exert himself to seem unique? Is he going to be gallant? That would be humiliating, because then he would show that he knows that gallantry enchants me; will he be mysterious? Mad? And how am I to receive this, which I perceive already will be a confidence, even if it is not true? Grant that Luke take me at my worth, she thought, or at least let me not see the difference. Let him be wise, or let me be blind; don't

359

let me, she hoped concretely, don't let me know too surely what he thinks of me.

Then he looked at her briefly and smiled what she was coming to know as his self-deprecatory smile; did Theodora, she wondered, and the thought was unwelcome, did Theodora know him as well as this?

"I never had a mother," he said, and the shock was enormous. Is *that* all he thinks of me, his estimate of what I want to hear of him; will I enlarge this into a confidence making me worthy of great confidences? Shall I sigh? Murmur? Walk away? "No one ever loved me because I belonged," he said. "I suppose you can understand that?"

No, she thought, you are not going to catch me so cheaply; I do not understand words and will not accept them in trade for my feelings; this man is a parrot. I will tell him that I can never understand such a thing, that maudlin self-pity does not move directly at my heart; I will not make a fool of myself by encouraging him to mock me. "I understand, yes," she said.

"I thought you might," he said, and she wanted, quite honestly, to slap his face. "I think you must be a very fine person, Nell," he said, and then spoiled it by adding, "warmhearted, and honest. Afterwards, when you go home . . ." His voice trailed off, and she thought, Either he is beginning to tell me something extremely important, or he is killing time until this conversation can gracefully be ended. He would not speak in this fashion without a reason; he does not willingly give himself away. Does he think that a human gesture of affection might seduce me into hurling myself madly at him? Is he afraid that I cannot behave like a lady? What does he know about me, about how I think and feel; does he feel sorry for me? "Journeys end in lovers meeting," she said.

"Yes," he said. "I never had a mother, as I told you. Now I find that everyone else has had something that I missed." He smiled at her. "I am entirely selfish," he said ruefully, "and always hoping that someone will tell me to behave, someone will make herself responsible for me and make me be grown-up."

He is altogether selfish, she thought in some surprise, the only man I have ever sat and talked to alone, and I am impatient; he is simply not very interesting. "Why don't you grow up by yourself?" she asked him, and wondered how many people—how many women—had already asked him that.

"You're clever." And how many times had he answered that way?

This conversation must be largely instinctive, she thought with amusement, and said gently, "You must be a very lonely person." All I want is to be cherished, she thought, and here I am talking gibberish with a selfish man. "You must be very lonely indeed."

He touched her hand, and smiled again. "You were so lucky," he told her. "You had a mother."

2

"I found it in the library," Luke said. "I swear I found it in the library."

"Incredible," the doctor said.

"Look," Luke said. He set the great book on the table and turned to the title page. "He made it himself—look, the title's been lettered in ink: MEMORIES, *for* SOPHIA ANNE LESTER CRAIN; *A Legacy for Her Education and Enlightenment During Her Lifetime From Her Affectionate and Devoted Father*, HUGH DESMOND LESTER CRAIN; *Twenty-first June, 1881*."

They pressed around the table, Theodora and Eleanor and the doctor, while Luke lifted and turned the first great page of the book. "You see," Luke said, "his little girl is to learn humility. He has clearly cut up a number of fine old books to make this scrapbook, because I seem to recognize several of the pictures, and they are all glued in."

"The vanity of human accomplishment," the doctor said sadly. "Think of the books Hugh Crain hacked apart to make this. Now here is a Goya etching; a horrible thing for a little girl to meditate upon."

"Underneath he has written," Luke said, "under this ugly picture: 'Honor thy father and thy mother, Daughter, authors of thy being, upon whom a heavy charge has been laid, that they lead their child in innocence and righteousness along the fearful narrow path to everlasting bliss, and render her up at last to her God a pious and a virtuous soul; reflect, Daughter, upon the joy in Heaven as the souls of these tiny creatures wing upward, released before they have learned aught of sin or faithlessness, and make it thine unceasing duty to remain as pure as these.'"

"Poor baby," Eleanor said, and gasped as Luke turned the page; Hugh Crain's second moral lesson derived from a color plate of a snake pit, and vividly painted snakes writhed and twisted along the page, above the message, neatly printed, and touched with gold: "Eternal damnation is the lot of mankind; neither tears, nor reparation, can undo Man's heritage of sin. Daughter, hold apart from this world, that its lusts and ingratitudes corrupt thee not; Daughter, preserve thyself."

"Next comes hell," Luke said. "Don't look if you're squeamish."

"I think I will skip hell," Eleanor said, "but read it to me."

"Wise of you," the doctor said. "An illustration from Foxe; one of the less attractive deaths, I have always thought, although who can fathom the ways of martyrs?"

"See this, though," Luke said. "He's burnt away a corner of the page, and here is what he says: 'Daughter, could you but hear for a moment the agony, the screaming, the dreadful crying out and repentance, of those poor souls condemned to everlasting flame! Could thine eyes be seared, but for an instant, with the red glare of wasteland burning always! Alas, wretched beings, in undying pain! Daughter, your father has this minute touched the corner of his page to his candle, and seen the frail paper shrivel and curl in the flame; consider, Daughter, that the heat of this candle is to the everlasting fires of Hell as a grain of sand to the reaching desert, and, as this paper burns in its slight flame so shall your soul burn forever, in fire a thousandfold more keen.'"

"I'll bet he read it to her every night before she went to sleep," Theodora said.

"Wait," Luke said. "You haven't seen Heaven yet—even *you* can look at this one, Nell. It's Blake, and a bit stern, I think, but obviously better than Hell. Listen—'Holy, holy, holy! In the pure light of heaven the angels praise Him and one another unendingly. Daughter, it is Here that I will seek thee.'"

"What a labor of love it is," the doctor said. "Hours of time just planning it, and the lettering is so dainty, and the gilt—"

"Now the seven deadly sins," Luke said, "and I think the old boy drew them himself."

"He really put his heart into gluttony," Theodora said. "I'm not sure I'll ever be hungry again."

"Wait till lust," Luke told her. "The old fellow outdid himself."

"I don't really want to look at any more of it, I think," Theodora said. "I'll sit over here with Nell, and if you come across any particularly edifying moral precepts you think would do me good, read them aloud."

"*Here* is lust," Luke said. "Was ever woman in this humor wooed?"

"Good heavens," said the doctor. "Good heavens."

"He *must* have drawn it himself," Luke said.

"For a *child?*" The doctor was outraged.

"Her very own scrapbook. Note Pride, the very image of our Nell here."

"What?" said Eleanor, starting up.

"Teasing," the doctor said placatingly. "Don't come look, my dear; he's teasing you."

"Sloth, now," Luke said.

"Envy," said the doctor. "How the poor child dared transgress . . ."

"The last page is the very nicest, I think. This, ladies, is Hugh Crain's blood. Nell, do you want to see Hugh Crain's blood?"

"No, thank you."

"Theo? No? In any case, I insist, for the sake of your two consciences, in reading what Hugh Crain has to say in closing his book: 'Daughter: sacred pacts are signed in blood, and I have here taken from my own wrist the vital fluid with which I bind you. Live virtuously, be meek, have faith in thy Redeemer, and in me, thy father, and I swear to thee that we will be joined together hereafter in unending bliss. Accept these precepts from thy devoted father, who in humbleness of spirit has made this book. May it serve its purpose well, my feeble effort, and preserve my Child from the pitfalls of this world and bring her safe to her father's arms in Heaven.' And signed: 'Thy everloving father, in this world and the next, author of thy being and guardian of thy virtue; in meekest love, Hugh Crain.'"

Theodora shuddered. "How he must have enjoyed it," she said, "signing his name in his own blood; I can see him laughing his head off."

"Not healthy, not at all a healthy work for a man," the doctor said.

"But she must have been very small when her father left the house," Eleanor said. "I wonder if he ever did read it to her."

"I'm sure he did, leaning over her cradle and spitting out the words so they would take root in her little mind. Hugh Crain," Theodora said, "you were a dirty old man, and you made a dirty old house and if you can still hear me from anywhere I would like to tell you to your face that I genuinely hope you will spend eternity in that foul horrible picture and never stop burning for a minute." She made a wild, derisive gesture around the room, and for a minute, still remembering, they were all silent, as though waiting for an answer, and then the coals in the fire fell with a little crash, and the doctor looked at his watch and Luke rose.

"The sun is over the yardarm," the doctor said happily.

3

Theodora curled by the fire, looking up wickedly at Eleanor; at the other end of the room the chessmen moved softly, jarring with little sounds against the table, and Theodora spoke gently, tormentingly. "Will you have him at your little apartment, Nell, and offer him to drink from your cup of stars?"

Eleanor looked into the fire, not answering. I have been so silly, she thought, I have been a fool.

"Is there room enough for two? Would he come if you asked him?"

Nothing could be worse than this, Eleanor thought; I have been a fool.

"Perhaps he has been longing for a tiny home—something smaller, of course, than Hill House; perhaps he will come home with you."

A fool, a ludicrous fool.

"Your white curtains—your tiny stone lions—"

Eleanor looked down at her, almost gently. "But I *had* to

come," she said, and stood up, turning blindly to get away. Not hearing the startled voices behind her, not seeing where or how she went, she blundered somehow to the great front door and out into the soft warm night. "I *had* to come," she said to the world outside.

Fear and guilt are sisters; Theodora caught her on the lawn. Silent, angry, hurt, they left Hill House side by side, walking together, each sorry for the other. A person angry, or laughing, or terrified, or jealous, will go stubbornly on into extremes of behavior impossible at another time; neither Eleanor nor Theodora reflected for a minute that it was imprudent for them to walk far from Hill House after dark. Each was so bent upon her own despair that escape into darkness was vital, and, containing themselves in that tight, vulnerable, impossible cloak which is fury, they stamped along together, each achingly aware of the other, each determined to be the last to speak.

Eleanor spoke first, finally; she had hurt her foot against a rock and tried to be too proud to notice it, but after a minute, her foot paining, she said, in a voice tight with the attempt to sound level, "I can't imagine why you think you have any right to interfere in my affairs," her language formal to prevent a flood of recrimination, or undeserved reproach (were they not strangers? cousins?). "I am sure that nothing I do is of any interest to you."

"That's right," Theodora said grimly. "Nothing that you do is of any interest to me."

We are walking on either side of a fence, Eleanor thought, but I have a right to live too, and I wasted an hour with Luke at the summerhouse trying to prove it. "I hurt my foot," she said.

"I'm sorry." Theodora sounded genuinely grieved. "You know what a beast he is." She hesitated. "A rake," she said finally, with a touch of amusement.

"I'm sure it's nothing to me *what* he is." And then, because they were women quarreling, "As if *you* cared, anyway."

"He shouldn't be allowed to get away with it," Theodora said.

"Get away with *what*?" Eleanor asked daintily.

"You're making a fool of yourself," Theodora said.

"Suppose I'm not, though? You'd mind terribly if you turned out to be wrong this time, wouldn't you?"

Theodora's voice was wearied, cynical. "If I'm wrong," she said, "I will bless you with all my heart. Fool that you are."

"You could hardly say anything else."

They were moving along the path toward the brook. In the darkness their feet felt that they were going downhill, and each privately and perversely accused the other of taking, deliberately, a path they had followed together once before in happiness.

"Anyway," Eleanor said, in a reasonable tone, "it doesn't mean anything to you, no matter what happens. Why should you care whether I make a fool of myself?"

Theodora was silent for a minute, walking in the darkness, and Eleanor was suddenly absurdly sure that Theodora had put out a hand to her, unseen. "Theo," Eleanor said awkwardly, "I'm no good at talking to people and saying things."

Theodora laughed. "What *are* you good at?" she demanded. "Running away?"

Nothing irrevocable had yet been spoken, but there was only the barest margin of safety left them; each of them moving delicately along the outskirts of an open question, and, once spoken, such a question—as "Do you love me?"—could never be answered or forgotten. They walked slowly, meditating, wondering, and the path sloped down from their feet and they followed, walking side by side in the most extreme intimacy of expectation; their feinting and hesitation done with, they could only await passively for resolution. Each knew, almost within a breath, what the other was thinking and wanting to say; each of them almost wept for the other. They perceived at the same moment the change in the path and each knew then the other's knowledge of it; Theodora took Eleanor's arm and, afraid to stop, they moved on slowly, close together, and ahead of them the path widened and blackened and curved.

Eleanor caught her breath, and Theodora's hand tightened, warning her to be quiet. On either side of them the trees, silent, relinquished the dark color they had held, paled, grew transparent and stood white and ghastly against the black sky. The grass was colorless, the path wide and black; there was nothing else. Eleanor's teeth were chattering, and the nausea of fear almost doubled her; her arm shivered under Theodora's holding hand, now almost a clutch, and she felt every slow step as a willed act, a precise mad insistence upon the putting of one foot down after the other as the only sane choice. Her eyes hurt with tears against the screaming blackness of the path and the shuddering whiteness of the trees, and she thought, with a clear intelligent picture of the words in her mind, burning, Now I am really afraid.

They moved on, the path unrolling ahead of them, the white trees unchanging on either side and, above all, the black sky lying thick overhead; their feet were shimmering white where they touched the path; Theodora's hand was pale and luminous. Ahead of them the path curved out of sight, and they walked slowly on, moving their feet precisely because it was the only physical act possible to them, the only thing left to keep them from sinking into the awful blackness and whiteness and luminous evil glow. Now I am really afraid, Eleanor thought in words of fire; remotely she could still feel Theodora's hand on her arm, but Theodora was distant, locked away; it was bitterly cold, with no human warmth near. Now I am really afraid, Eleanor thought, and put her feet forward one after another, shivering as they touched the path, shivering with mindless cold.

The path unwound; perhaps it was taking them somewhere, willfully, since neither of them could step off it and go knowingly into the annihilation of whiteness that was the grass on either side. The path curved, black and shining, and they followed. Theodora's hand tightened, and Eleanor caught her breath on a little sob—had something moved, ahead, something whiter than the white trees, beckoning? Beckoning, fading into the trees, watching? Was there movement beside them, imperceptible in the soundless night; did some footstep go invisibly along with them in the white grass? Where were they?

The path led them to its destined end and died beneath their feet. Eleanor and Theodora looked into a garden, their eyes blinded with the light of sun and rich color; incredibly, there was a picnic party on the grass in the garden. They could hear the laughter of the children and the affectionate, amused voices of the mother and father; the grass was richly, thickly green, the flowers were colored red and orange and yellow, the sky was blue and gold, and one child wore a scarlet jumper and raised its voice again in laughter, tumbling after a puppy over the grass. There was a checked tablecloth spread out, and, smiling, the mother leaned over to take up a plate of bright fruit; then Theodora screamed.

"Don't look back," she cried out in a voice high with fear, "don't look back—don't look—run!"

Running, without knowing why she ran, Eleanor thought that she would catch her foot in the checked tablecloth; she was afraid she might stumble over the puppy; but as they ran across the garden there was nothing except weeds growing blackly in the darkness, and Theodora, screaming still, trampled over the bushes where there had been flowers and stumbled, sobbing, over half-buried stones and what might have been a broken cup. Then they were beating and scratching wildly at the white stone wall where vines grew blackly, screaming still and begging to be let out, until a rusted iron gate gave way and they ran, crying and gasping and somehow holding hands, across the kitchen garden of Hill House, and crashed through a back door into the kitchen to see Luke and the doctor hurrying to them. "What happened?" Luke said, catching at Theodora. "Are you all right?"

"We've been nearly crazy," the doctor said, worn. "We've been out looking for you for hours."

"It was a picnic," Eleanor said. She had fallen into a kitchen chair and she looked down at her hands, scratched and bleeding and shaking without her knowledge. "We tried to get out," she told them, holding her hands out for them to see. "It was a picnic. The children . . ."

Theodora laughed in a little continuing cry, laughing on and on thinly, and said through her laughter, "I looked back —I went and looked behind us . . ." and laughed on.

"The children . . . and a puppy . . ."

"Eleanor." Theodora turned wildly and put her head against Eleanor. "Eleanor," she said. "Eleanor."

And, holding Theodora, Eleanor looked up at Luke and the doctor, and felt the room rock madly, and time, as she had always known time, stop.

7

O N the afternoon of the day that Mrs. Montague was expected, Eleanor went alone into the hills above Hill House, not really intending to arrive at any place in particular, not even caring where or how she went, wanting only to be secret and out from under the heavy dark wood of the house. She found a small spot where the grass was soft and dry and lay down, wondering how many years it had been since she had lain on soft grass to be alone to think. Around her the trees and wild flowers, with that oddly courteous air of natural things suddenly interrupted in their pressing occupations of growing and dying, turned toward her with attention, as though, dull and imperceptive as she was, it was still necessary for them to be gentle to a creation so unfortunate as not to be rooted in the ground, forced to go from one place to another, heart-breakingly mobile. Idly Eleanor picked a wild daisy, which died in her fingers, and, lying on the grass, looked up into its dead face. There was nothing in her mind beyond an overwhelming wild happiness. She pulled at the daisy, and wondered, smiling at herself, What am I going to do? What *am* I going to do?

2

"Put the bags down in the hall, Arthur," Mrs. Montague said. "Wouldn't you think there'd be someone here to help us with this door? They'll *have* to get someone to take the bags upstairs. John? John?"

"My dear, my dear." Dr. Montague hurried into the hallway, carrying his napkin, and kissed his wife obediently on the cheek she held out for him. "How nice that you got here; we'd given you up."

"I *said* I'd be here today, didn't I? Did you ever know me *not* to come when I said I would? I brought Arthur."

"Arthur," the doctor said without enthusiasm.

"Well, *some*body had to drive," Mrs. Montague said. "I imagine you expected that I would drive myself all the way out here? Because you know perfectly well that I get tired. How do you do."

The doctor turned, smiling on Eleanor and Theodora, with Luke behind them, clustered uncertainly in the doorway. "My dear," he said, "these are my friends who have been staying in Hill House with me these past few days. Theodora. Eleanor Vance. Luke Sanderson."

Theodora and Eleanor and Luke murmured civilly, and Mrs. Montague nodded and said, "I see you didn't bother to wait dinner for us."

"We'd given you up," the doctor said.

"I believe that I told you that I would be here today. Of course, it is *perfectly* possible that I am mistaken, but it is *my* recollection that I said I would be here today. I'm sure I will get to know all your names very soon. This gentleman is Arthur Parker; he drove me here because I dislike driving myself. Arthur, these are John's friends. Can anybody do something about our suitcases?"

The doctor and Luke approached, murmuring, and Mrs. Montague went on, "I am to be in your most haunted room, of course. Arthur can go anywhere. That blue suitcase is mine, young man, and the small attaché case; they will go in your most haunted room."

"The nursery, I think," Dr. Montague said when Luke looked at him inquiringly. "I believe the nursery is one source of disturbance," he told his wife, and she sighed irritably.

"It does seem to me that you could be more methodical," she said. "You've been here nearly a week and I suppose you've done *nothing* with planchette? Automatic writing? I don't imagine either of these young women has mediumistic gifts? Those are Arthur's bags right there. He brought his golf clubs, just in case."

"Just in case of what?" Theodora asked blankly, and Mrs. Montague turned to regard her coldly.

"Please don't let me interrupt your dinner," she said finally.

"There's a definite cold spot just outside the nursery door," the doctor told his wife hopefully.

"Yes, dear, very nice. Isn't that young man going to take Arthur's bags upstairs? You do seem to be in a good deal of confusion here, don't you? After nearly a week I certainly thought you'd have things in some kind of order. Any figures materialize?"

"There have been decided manifestations—"

"Well, I'm here now, and we'll get things going right. Where is Arthur to put the car?"

"There's an empty stable in back of the house where we have put our other cars. He can take it around in the morning."

"Nonsense. I do not believe in putting things off, John, as you know perfectly well. Arthur will have plenty to do in the morning without adding tonight's work. He must move the car at once."

"It's dark outside," the doctor said hesitantly.

"John, you astound me. Is it your belief that I do *not* know whether it is dark outside at night? The car has lights, John, and that young man can go with Arthur to show him the way."

"Thank you," said Luke grimly, "but we have a positive policy against going outside after dark. Arthur may, of course, if he cares to, but I will not."

"The young ladies," the doctor said, "had a shocking—"

"Young man's a coward," Arthur said. He had concluded his fetching of suitcases and golf bags and hampers from the car and now stood beside Mrs. Montague, looking down on Luke; Arthur's face was red and his hair was white, and now, scorning Luke, he bristled. "Ought to be ashamed of yourself, fellow, in front of the women."

"The women are just as much afraid as I am," Luke said primly.

"Indeed, indeed." Dr. Montague put his hand on Arthur's arm soothingly. "After you've been here for a while, Arthur, you'll understand that Luke's attitude is sensible, not cowardly. We make a point of staying together after dark."

"I must say, John, I never expected to find you all so *nervous*," Mrs. Montague said. "I deplore fear in these matters." She tapped her foot irritably. "You know perfectly well, John, that those who have passed beyond *expect* to see us happy and smiling; they *want* to know that we are thinking of them lovingly. The spirits dwelling in this house may be actually *suffering* because they are aware that you are afraid of them."

"We can talk about it later," the doctor said wearily. "Now, how about dinner?"

"Of course." Mrs. Montague glanced at Theodora and Eleanor. "What a pity that we had to interrupt you," she said.

"Have you had dinner?"

"Naturally we have not had dinner, John. I *said* we would be here for dinner, didn't I? Or am I mistaken again?"

"At any rate, I told Mrs. Dudley that you would be here," the doctor said, opening the door which led to the game room and on into the dining room. "She left us a splendid feast."

Poor Dr. Montague, Eleanor thought, standing aside to let the doctor take his wife into the dining room; he is so uncomfortable; I wonder how long she is going to stay.

"I wonder how long she is going to stay?" Theodora whispered in her ear.

"Maybe her suitcase is filled with ectoplasm," Eleanor said hopefully.

"And how long will you be able to stay?" Dr. Montague asked, sitting at the head of the dinner table with his wife cozily beside him.

"Well, dear," Mrs. Montague said, tasting daintily of Mrs. Dudley's caper sauce "—you have found a fair cook, have you not?—you *know* that Arthur has to get back to his school; Arthur is a headmaster," she explained down the table, "and he has generously canceled his appointments for Monday. So we had better leave Monday afternoon and then Arthur can be there for classes on Tuesday."

"A lot of happy schoolboys Arthur no doubt left behind," Luke said softly to Theodora, and Theodora said, "But today is only Saturday."

"I do not mind this cooking at all," Mrs. Montague said. "John, I will speak to your cook in the morning."

"Mrs. Dudley is an admirable woman," the doctor said carefully.

"Bit fancy for *my* taste," Arthur said. "I'm a meat-and-potatoes man, myself," he explained to Theodora. "Don't drink, don't smoke, don't read trash. Bad example for the fellows at the school. They look up to one a bit, you know."

"I'm sure they must all model themselves on you," Theodora said soberly.

"Get a bad hat now and then," Arthur said, shaking his head. "No taste for sports, you know. Moping in corners. Crybabies. Knock *that* out of them fast enough." He reached for the butter.

Mrs. Montague leaned forward to look down the table at Arthur. "Eat lightly, Arthur," she advised. "We have a busy night ahead of us."

"What on earth do you plan to do?" the doctor asked.

"I'm sure that *you* would never dream of going about these things with any system, but you will have to admit, John, that in this area I have simply more of an instinctive understanding; women do, you know, John, at least *some* women." She paused and regarded Eleanor and Theodora speculatively. "Neither of *them*, I daresay. Unless, of course, I am mistaken again? You are very fond of pointing out my errors, John."

"My dear—"

"I *cannot* abide a slipshod job in anything. Arthur will patrol, of course. I brought Arthur for that purpose. It is so rare," she explained to Luke, who sat on her other side, "to find persons in the educational field who are interested in the other world; you will find Arthur surprisingly well informed. I will recline in your haunted room with only a nightlight burning, and will endeavor to get in touch with the elements disturbing this house. I never sleep when there are troubled spirits about," she told Luke, who nodded, speechless.

"Little sound common sense," Arthur said. "Got to go about these things in the right way. Never pays to aim too low. Tell my fellows that."

"I think perhaps after dinner we will have a little session with planchette," Mrs. Montague said. "Just Arthur and I, of course; the rest of you, I can see, are not ready yet; you would only drive away the spirits. We will need a quiet room—"

"The library," Luke suggested politely.

"The library? I think it might do; books are frequently very good carriers, you know. Materializations are often best produced in rooms where there are books. I cannot think of any time when materialization was in any way hampered by the presence of books. I suppose the library has been dusted? Arthur sometimes sneezes."

"Mrs. Dudley keeps the entire house in perfect order," the doctor said.

"I really will speak to Mrs. Dudley in the morning. You will show us the library, then, John, and that young man will bring down my case; not the large suitcase, mind, but the small attaché case. Bring it to me in the library. We will join you later; after a session with planchette I require a glass of milk and perhaps a small cake; crackers will do if they are not too heavily salted. A few minutes of quiet conversation with congenial people is also very helpful, particularly if I am to be receptive during the night; the mind is a precise instrument and cannot be tended too carefully. Arthur?" She bowed distantly to Eleanor and Theodora and went out, escorted by Arthur, Luke, and her husband.

After a minute Theodora said, "I think I am going to be simply crazy about Mrs. Montague."

"I don't know," Eleanor said. "Arthur is rather more to my taste. And Luke *is* a coward, I think."

"Poor Luke," Theodora said. "He never had a mother." Looking up, Eleanor found that Theodora was regarding her with a curious smile, and she moved away from the table so quickly that a glass spilled.

"We shouldn't be alone," she said, oddly breathless. "We've got to find the others." She left the table and almost ran from the room, and Theodora ran after her, laughing, down the corridor and into the little parlor, where Luke and the doctor stood before the fire.

"Please, sir," Luke was saying meekly, "who is planchette?"

The doctor sighed irritably. "Imbeciles," he said, and then, "Sorry. The whole idea annoys me, but if *she* likes it . . ." He turned and poked the fire furiously. "Planchette," he went on after a moment, "is a device similar to the Ouija Board, or perhaps I might explain better by saying that it is a form of automatic writing; a method of communicating with—ah—intangible beings, although to *my* way of thinking the only intangible beings who ever get in touch through one of those things are the imaginations of the people running it. Yes. Well. Planchette is a little piece of light wood, usually heart-shaped or triangular. A pencil is set into the narrow end, and at the other end is a pair of wheels, or feet which will slip easily over paper. Two people place fingers on it, ask it questions, and the object moves, pushed by what force we will not here discuss, and writes answers. The Ouija Board, as I say, is very similar, except that the object moves on a board pointing to separate letters. An ordinary wineglass will do the same thing; I have seen it tried with a child's wheeled toy, although I will admit that it looked silly. Each person uses the tips of the fingers of one hand, keeping the other hand free to note down questions and answers. The answers are invariably, I believe, meaningless, although of course my wife will tell you different. Balderdash." And he went at the fire again. "Schoolgirls," he said. "Superstition."

3

"Planchette has been very kind tonight," Mrs. Montague said. "John, there are definitely foreign elements present in this house."

"Quite a splendid sitting, really," Arthur said. He waved a sheaf of paper triumphantly.

"We've gotten a good deal of information for you," Mrs. Montague said. "Now. Planchette was quite insistent about a nun. Have you learned anything about a nun, John?"

"In Hill House? Not likely."

"Planchette felt very strongly about a nun, John. Perhaps something of the sort—a dark, vague figure, even—has been seen in the neighborhood? Villagers terrified when staggering home late at night?"

"The figure of a nun is a fairly common—"

"John, *if* you please. I assume you are suggesting that I am mistaken. Or perhaps it is your intention to point out that *planchette* may be mistaken? I assure you—and you must believe planchette, even if *my* word is not good enough for you—that a nun was most specifically suggested."

"I am only trying to say, my dear, that the wraith of a nun is far and away the most common form of appearance. There has never been such a thing connected with Hill House, but in almost every—"

"John, *if* you *please*. I assume I may continue? Or is planchette to be dismissed without a hearing? Thank you."

Mrs. Montague composed herself. "Now, then. There is also a name, spelled variously as Helen, or Helene, or Elena. Who might that be?"

"My dear, many people have lived—"

"Helen brought us a warning against a mysterious monk. Now when a monk and a nun *both* turn up in one house—"

"Expect the place was built on an older site," Arthur said. "Influences prevailing, you know. Older influences hanging around," he explained more fully.

"It sounds very much like broken vows, does it not? Very much."

"Had a lot of that back then, you know. Temptation, probably."

"I hardly think—" the doctor began.

"I daresay she was walled up alive," Mrs. Montague said. "The nun, I mean. They always did that, you know. You've no idea the messages I've gotten from nuns walled up alive."

"There is *no* case on record of *any* nun *ever* being—"

"John. May I point out to you once more that I *myself* have had messages from nuns walled up alive? Do you think I am telling you a fib, John? Or do you suppose that a nun would deliberately *pretend* to have been walled up alive when she was not? Is it possible that I am mistaken once more, John?"

"Certainly not, my dear." Dr. Montague sighed wearily.

"With one candle and a crust of bread," Arthur told Theodora. "Horrible thing to do, when you think about it."

"No nun was ever walled up alive," the doctor said sullenly. He raised his voice slightly. "It is a legend. A story. A libel circulated—"

"All right, John. We won't quarrel over it. You may believe whatever you choose. Just understand, however, that sometimes purely materialistic views must give way before *facts*. Now it is a proven fact that among the visitations troubling this house are a nun and a—"

"What else was there?" Luke asked hastily. "I am *so* interested in hearing what—ah—planchette had to say."

Mrs. Montague waggled a finger roguishly. "Nothing about *you*, young man. Although one of the ladies present may hear something of interest."

Impossible woman, Eleanor thought; impossible, vulgar,

possessive woman. "Now, Helen," Mrs. Montague went on, "wants us to search the cellar for an old well."

"Don't tell me *Helen* was *buried* alive," the doctor said.

"I hardly think so, John. I am sure that she would have mentioned it. As a matter of fact, Helen was most unclear about just what we *were* to find in the well. I doubt, however, that it will be treasure. One so rarely meets with *real* treasure in a case of this kind. More likely evidence of the missing nun."

"More likely eighty years of rubbish."

"John, I can*not* understand this skepticism in you, of all people. After all, you did come to this house to collect evidence of supernatural activity, and now, when I bring you a full account of the *causes*, and an indication of where to start looking, you are positively scornful."

"We have no authority to dig up the cellar."

"Arthur could—" Mrs. Montague began hopefully, but the doctor said with firmness, "No. My lease of the house specifically forbids me to tamper with the house itself. There will be no digging of cellars, no tearing out of woodwork, no ripping up of floors. Hill House is still a valuable property, and we are students, not vandals."

"I should think you'd want to know the *truth*, John."

"There is nothing I should like to know more." Dr. Montague stamped across the room to the chessboard and took up a knight and regarded it furiously. He looked as though he were doggedly counting to a hundred.

"Dear me, how patient one must be sometimes." Mrs. Montague sighed. "But I do want to read you the little passage we received toward the end. Arthur, do you have it?"

Arthur shuffled through his sheaf of papers. "It was just after the message about the flowers you are to send to your aunt," Mrs. Montague said. "Planchette has a control named Merrigot," she explained, "and Merrigot takes a genuine personal interest in Arthur; brings him word from relatives, and so on."

"Not a fatal illness, you understand," Arthur said gravely. "Have to send flowers, of course, but Merrigot is most reassuring."

"Now." Mrs. Montague selected several pages, and turned

them over quickly; they were covered with loose, sprawling penciled words, and Mrs. Montague frowned, running down the pages with her finger. "Here," she said. "Arthur, you read the questions and I'll read the answers; that way, it will sound more natural."

"Off we go," Arthur said brightly, and leaned over Mrs. Montague's shoulder. "Now—let me see—start right about here?"

"With 'Who are you?'"

"Righto. Who are you?"

"Nell," Mrs. Montague read in her sharp voice, and Eleanor and Theodora and Luke and the doctor turned, listening.

"Nell who?"

"Eleanor Nellie Nell Nell. They sometimes do that," Mrs. Montague broke off to explain. "They repeat a word over and over to make sure it comes across all right."

Arthur cleared his throat. "What do you want?" he read.

"Home."

"Do you want to go home?" And Theodora shrugged comically at Eleanor.

"Want to be home."

"What are you doing here?"

"Waiting."

"Waiting for what?"

"Home." Arthur stopped, and nodded profoundly. "There it is again," he said. "Like a word, and use it over and over, just for the sound of it."

"Ordinarily we never ask *why*," Mrs. Montague said, "because it tends to confuse planchette. However, this time we were bold, and came right out and asked. Arthur?"

"Why?" Arthur read.

"Mother," Mrs. Montague read. "So you see, this time we were right to ask, because planchette was perfectly free with the answer."

"Is Hill House your home?" Arthur read levelly.

"Home," Mrs. Montague responded, and the doctor sighed.

"Are you suffering?" Arthur read.

"No answer here." Mrs. Montague nodded reassuringly. "Sometimes they dislike admitting to pain; it tends to discourage those of us left behind, you know. Just like Arthur's aunt, for instance, will *never* let on that she is sick, but Merrigot always lets us know, and it's even worse when they've passed over."

"Stoical," Arthur confirmed, and read, "Can we help you?"

"No," Mrs. Montague read.

"Can we do anything at all for you?"

"No. Lost. Lost. Lost." Mrs. Montague looked up. "You see?" she asked. "One word, over and over again. They *love* to repeat themselves. I've had one word go on to cover a whole page sometimes."

"What do you want?" Arthur read.

"Mother," Mrs. Montague read back.

"Why?"

"Child."

"Where is your mother?"

"Home."

"Where is your home?"

"Lost. Lost. Lost. And after that," Mrs. Montague said, folding the paper briskly, "there was nothing but gibberish."

"*Never* known planchette so cooperative," Arthur said confidingly to Theodora. "Quite an experience, really."

"But why pick on Nell?" Theodora asked with annoyance. "Your fool planchette has no right to send messages to people without permission or—"

"You'll never get results by abusing planchette," Arthur began, but Mrs. Montague interrupted him, swinging to stare at Eleanor. "*You're* Nell?" she demanded, and turned on Theodora. "We thought *you* were Nell," she said.

"So?" said Theodora impudently.

"It doesn't affect the messages, of course," Mrs. Montague said, tapping her paper irritably, "although I *do* think we might have been correctly introduced. I am sure that *planchette* knew the difference between you, but I certainly do not care to be misled."

"Don't feel neglected," Luke said to Theodora. "We will bury you alive."

"When I get a message from that thing," Theodora said, "I expect it to be about hidden treasure. None of this nonsense about sending flowers to my aunt."

They are all carefully avoiding looking at me, Eleanor

thought; I have been singled out again, and they are kind enough to pretend it is nothing; "Why do you think all that was sent to me?" she asked, helpless.

"Really, child," Mrs. Montague said, dropping the papers on the low table, "I couldn't *begin* to say. Although you *are* rather more than a child, aren't you? Perhaps you are more receptive psychically than you realize, although"—and she turned away indifferently—"how you *could* be, a week in this house and not picking up the simplest message from beyond . . . That fire wants stirring."

"Nell doesn't want messages from beyond," Theodora said comfortingly, moving to take Eleanor's cold hand in hers. "Nell wants her warm bed and a little sleep."

Peace, Eleanor thought concretely; what I want in all this world is peace, a quiet spot to lie and think, a quiet spot up among the flowers where I can dream and tell myself sweet stories.

4

"I," Arthur said richly, "shall make my headquarters in the small room just this side of the nursery, well within shouting distance. I shall have with me a drawn revolver—do not take alarm, ladies; I am an excellent shot—and a flashlight, in addition to a most piercing whistle. I shall have no difficulty summoning the rest of you in case I observe anything worth your notice, or I require—ah—company. You may all sleep quietly, I assure you."

"Arthur," Mrs. Montague explained, "will patrol the house. Every hour, regularly, he will make a round of the upstairs rooms; I think he need hardly bother with the downstairs rooms tonight, since *I* shall be up here. We have done this before, many times. Come along, everyone." Silently they followed her up the staircase, watching her little affectionate dabs at the stair rail and the carvings on the walls. "It is such a blessing," she said once, "to know that the beings in this house are only waiting for an opportunity to tell their stories and free themselves from the burden of their sorrow. Now. Arthur will first of all inspect the bedrooms. Arthur?"

"With apologies, ladies, with apologies," Arthur said,

opening the door of the blue room, which Eleanor and Theodora shared. "A dainty spot," he said plummily, "fit for two
such charming ladies; I shall, if you like, save you the trouble
of glancing into the closet and under the bed." Solemnly they
watched Arthur go down onto his hands and knees and look
under the beds and then rise, dusting his hands. "Perfectly
safe," he said.

"Now, where am I to be?" Mrs. Montague asked. "Where
did that young man put my bags?"

"Directly at the end of the hall," the doctor said. "We call it
the nursery."

Mrs. Montague, followed by Arthur, moved purposefully
down the hall, passed the cold spot in the hall, and shivered. "I
will certainly need extra blankets," she said. "Have that young
man bring extra blankets from one of the other rooms."
Opening the nursery door, she nodded and said, "The bed
looks quite fresh, I must admit, but has the room been aired?"

"I told Mrs. Dudley," the doctor said.

"It smells musty. Arthur, you will have to open that window,
in spite of the cold."

Drearily the animals on the nursery wall looked down on
Mrs. Montague. "Are you sure . . ." The doctor hesitated,
and glanced up apprehensively at the grinning faces over the
nursery door. "I wonder if you ought to have someone in here
with you," he said.

"My dear." Mrs. Montague, good-humored now in the
presence of those who had passed beyond, was amused. "How
many hours—how many, *many* hours—have I sat in purest
love and understanding, alone in a room and yet never alone?
My dear, how can I make you perceive that there is no danger
where there is nothing but love and sympathetic understanding? I am here to *help* these unfortunate beings—I am
here to extend the hand of heartfelt fondness, and let them
know that there are still *some* who remember, who will listen
and weep for them; their loneliness is over, and I—"

"Yes," the doctor said, "but leave the door open."

"Unlocked, if you insist." Mrs. Montague was positively
magnanimous.

"I shall be only down the hall," the doctor said. "I can

hardly offer to patrol, since that will be Arthur's occupation, but if you need anything I can hear you."

Mrs. Montague laughed and waved her hand at him. "These others need your protection so much more than I," she said. "I will do what I can, of course. But they are so very, *very* vulnerable, with their hard hearts and their unseeing eyes."

Arthur, followed by a Luke looking very much amused, returned from checking the other bedrooms on the floor and nodded briskly at the doctor. "All clear," he said. "Perfectly safe for you to go to bed now."

"Thank you," the doctor told him soberly and then said to his wife, "Good night. Be careful."

"Good night," Mrs. Montague said, and smiled around at all of them. "Please don't be afraid," she said. "No matter what happens, remember that I am here."

"Good night," Theodora said, and "Good night," said Luke, and with Arthur behind them assuring them that they might rest quietly, and not to worry if they heard shots, and he would start his first patrol at midnight, Eleanor and Theodora went into their own room, and Luke on down the hall to his. After a moment the doctor, turning reluctantly away from his wife's closed door, followed.

"Wait," Theodora said to Eleanor, once in their room. "Luke said they want us down the hall; don't get undressed and be quiet." She opened the door a crack and whispered over her shoulder, "I swear that old biddy's going to blow this house wide open with that perfect love business; if I ever saw a place that had no use for perfect love, it's Hill House. Now. Arthur's closed his door. Quick. Be quiet."

Silently, making no sound on the hall carpeting, they hurried in their stocking feet down the hall to the doctor's room. "Hurry," the doctor said, opening the door just wide enough for them to come in, "be quiet."

"It's not safe," Luke said, closing the door to a crack and coming back to sit on the floor, "that man's going to shoot somebody."

"I don't like it," the doctor said, worried. "Luke and I will stay up and watch, and I want you two ladies in here where we can keep an eye on you. Something's going to happen," he said. "I don't like it."

"I just hope she didn't go and make anything mad, with her planchette," Theodora said. "Sorry, Doctor Montague. I don't intend to speak rudely of your wife."

The doctor laughed, but stayed with his eye to the door. "She originally planned to come for our entire stay," he said, "but she had enrolled in a course in yoga and could not miss her meetings. She is an excellent woman in most respects," he added, looking earnestly around at them. "She is a good wife, and takes very good care of me. She does things splendidly, really. Buttons on my shirts." He smiled hopefully. "This"— and he gestured in the direction of the hall—"*this* is practically her only vice."

"Perhaps she feels she is helping you with your work," Eleanor said.

The doctor grimaced, and shivered; at that moment the door swung wide and then crashed shut, and in the silence outside they could hear slow rushing movements as though a very steady, very strong wind were blowing the length of the hall. Glancing at one another, they tried to smile, tried to look courageous under the slow coming of the unreal cold and then, through the noise of wind, the knocking on the doors downstairs. Without a word Theodora took up the quilt from the foot of the doctor's bed and folded it around Eleanor and herself, and they moved close together, slowly in order not to make a sound. Eleanor, clinging to Theodora, deadly cold in spite of Theodora's arms around her, thought, It knows my name, it knows my name this time. The pounding came up the stairs, crashing on each step. The doctor was tense, standing by the door, and Luke moved over to stand beside him. "It's nowhere near the nursery," he said to the doctor, and put his hand out to stop the doctor from opening the door.

"How weary one gets of this constant pounding," Theodora said ridiculously. "Next summer, I must really go somewhere else."

"There are disadvantages everywhere," Luke told her. "In the lake regions you get mosquitoes."

"Could we have exhausted the repertoire of Hill House?" Theodora asked, her voice shaking in spite of her light tone. "Seems like we've had this pounding act before; is it going to start everything all over again?" The crashing echoed along the hall, seeming to come from the far end, the farthest from the nursery, and the doctor, tense against the door, shook his head anxiously. "I'm going to have to go out there," he said. "She might be frightened," he told them.

Eleanor, rocking to the pounding, which seemed inside her head as much as in the hall, holding tight to Theodora, said, "They know where we are," and the others, assuming that she meant Arthur and Mrs. Montague, nodded and listened. The knocking, Eleanor told herself, pressing her hands to her eyes and swaying with the noise, will go on down the hall, it will go on and on to the end of the hall and turn and come back again, it will just go on and on the way it did before and then it will stop and we will look at each other and laugh and try to remember how cold we were, and the little swimming curls of fear on our backs; after a while it will stop.

"It never hurt *us*," Theodora was telling the doctor, across the noise of the pounding. "It won't hurt *them*."

"I only hope she doesn't try to *do* anything about it," the doctor said grimly; he was still at the door, but seemingly unable to open it against the volume of noise outside.

"I feel positively like an old hand at this," Theodora said to Eleanor. "Come closer, Nell; keep warm," and she pulled Eleanor even nearer to her under the blanket, and the sickening, still cold surrounded them.

Then there came, suddenly, quiet, and the secret creeping silence they all remembered; holding their breaths, they looked at one another. The doctor held the doorknob with both hands, and Luke, although his face was white and his voice trembled, said lightly, "Brandy, anyone? My passion for spirits—"

"No." Theodora giggled wildly. "Not that pun," she said.

"Sorry. You won't believe me," Luke said, the brandy decanter rattling against the glass as he tried to pour, "but I no longer think of it as a pun. That is what living in a haunted house does for a sense of humor." Using both hands to carry the glass, he came to the bed where Theodora and Eleanor huddled under the blanket, and Theodora brought out one hand and took the glass. "Here," she said, holding it to Eleanor's mouth. "Drink."

Sipping, not warmed, Eleanor thought, We are in the eye of

the storm; there is not much more time. She watched Luke carefully carry a glass of brandy over to the doctor and hold it out, and then, without comprehending, watched the glass slip through Luke's fingers to the floor as the door was shaken, violently and silently. Luke pulled the doctor back, and the door was attacked without sound, seeming almost to be pulling away from its hinges, almost ready to buckle and go down, leaving them exposed. Backing away, Luke and the doctor waited, tense and helpless.

"It can't get in," Theodora was whispering over and over, her eyes on the door, "it can't get in, don't let it get in, it can't get in—" The shaking stopped, the door was quiet, and a little caressing touch began on the doorknob, feeling intimately and softly and then, because the door was locked, patting and fondling the doorframe, as though wheedling to be let in.

"It knows we're here," Eleanor whispered, and Luke, looking back at her over his shoulder, gestured furiously for her to be quiet.

It is so cold, Eleanor thought childishly; I will never be able to sleep again with all this noise coming from inside my head; how can these others hear the noise when it is coming from inside my head? I am disappearing inch by inch into this house, I am going apart a little bit at a time because all this noise is breaking me; why are the *others* frightened?

She was aware, dully, that the pounding had begun again, the metallic overwhelming sound of it washed over her like waves; she put her cold hands to her mouth to feel if her face was still there; I have had enough, she thought, I am too cold.

"At the nursery door," Luke said tensely, speaking clearly through the noise. "At the nursery door; don't." And he put out a hand to stop the doctor.

"Purest love," Theodora said madly, "purest love." And she began to giggle again.

"If they don't open the doors—" Luke said to the doctor. The doctor stood now with his head against the door, listening, with Luke holding his arm to keep him from moving.

Now we are going to have a new noise, Eleanor thought, listening to the inside of her head; it is changing. The pounding had stopped, as though it had proved ineffectual, and there was now a swift movement up and down the hall, as of an animal pacing back and forth with unbelievable impatience, watching first one door and then another, alert for a movement inside, and there was again the little babbling murmur which Eleanor remembered; Am I doing it? she wondered quickly, is that me? And heard the tiny laughter beyond the door, mocking her.

"Fe-fi-fo-fum," Theodora said under her breath, and the laughter swelled and became a shouting; it's inside my head, Eleanor thought, putting her hands over her face, it's inside my head and it's getting out, getting out, getting out—

Now the house shivered and shook, the curtains dashing against the windows, the furniture swaying, and the noise in the hall became so great that it pushed against the walls; they could hear breaking glass as the pictures in the hall came down, and perhaps the smashing of windows. Luke and the doctor strained against the door, as though desperately holding it shut, and the floor moved under their feet. We're going, we're going, Eleanor thought, and heard Theodora say, far away, "The house is coming down." She sounded calm, and beyond fear. Holding to the bed, buffeted and shaken, Eleanor put her head down and closed her eyes and bit her lips against the cold and felt the sickening drop as the room fell away beneath her and then right itself and then turned, slowly, swinging. "God almighty," Theodora said, and a mile away at the door Luke caught the doctor and held him upright.

"Are you all right?" Luke called, back braced against the door, holding the doctor by the shoulders. "Theo, are you all right?"

"Hanging on," Theodora said. "I don't know about Nell."

"Keep her warm," Luke said, far away. "We haven't seen it all yet." His voice trailed away; Eleanor could hear and see him far away in the distant room where he and Theodora and the doctor still waited; in the churning darkness where she fell endlessly nothing was real except her own hands white around the bedpost. She could see them, very small, and see them tighten when the bed rocked and the wall leaned forward and the door turned sideways far away. Somewhere there was a great, shaking crash as some huge thing came headlong; it must be the tower, Eleanor thought, and I supposed it would stand for years; we are lost, lost; the house is destroying itself. She heard the laughter over all, coming thin and lunatic, rising in its little crazy tune, and thought, No; it is over for me. It is too much, she thought, I will relinquish my possession of this self of mine, abdicate, give over willingly what I never wanted at all; whatever it wants of me it can have.

"I'll come," she said aloud, and was speaking up to Theodora, who leaned over her. The room was perfectly quiet, and between the still curtains at the window she could see the sunlight. Luke sat in a chair by the window; his face was bruised and his shirt was torn, and he was still drinking brandy. The doctor sat back in another chair; his hair freshly combed, looking neat and dapper and self-possessed. Theodora, leaning over Eleanor, said, "She's all right, I think," and Eleanor sat up and shook her head, staring. Composed and quiet, the house lifted itself primly around her, and nothing had been moved.

"How . . ." Eleanor said, and all three of them laughed.

"Another day," the doctor said, and in spite of his appearance his voice was wan. "Another night," he said.

"As I tried to say earlier," Luke remarked, "living in a haunted house plays hell with a sense of humor; I really did not intend to make a forbidden pun," he told Theodora.

"How—are they?" Eleanor asked, the words sounding unfamiliar and her mouth stiff.

"Both sleeping like babies," the doctor said. "Actually," he said, as though continuing a conversation begun while Eleanor slept, "I cannot believe that my wife stirred up that storm, but I do admit that one more word about pure love . . ."

"What happened?" Eleanor asked; I must have been gritting my teeth all night, she thought, the way my mouth feels.

"Hill House went dancing," Theodora said, "taking us along on a mad midnight fling. At least, I *think* it was dancing; it might have been turning somersaults."

"It's almost nine," the doctor said. "When Eleanor is ready . . ."

"Come along, baby," Theodora said. "Theo will wash your face for you and make you all neat for breakfast."

8

"DID anyone tell them that Mrs. Dudley clears at ten?"
Theodora looked into the coffee pot speculatively.

The doctor hesitated. "I hate to wake them after such a night."

"But Mrs. Dudley clears at ten."

"They're coming," Eleanor said. "I can hear them on the stairs." I can hear everything, all over the house, she wanted to tell them.

Then, distantly, they could all hear Mrs. Montague's voice, raised in irritation and Luke, realizing, said, "Oh, Lord—they can't find the dining room," and hurried out to open doors.

"—properly aired." Mrs. Montague's voice preceded her, and she swept into the dining room, tapped the doctor curtly on the shoulder by way of greeting and seated herself with a general nod to the others. "I must say," she began at once, "that I think you might have called us for breakfast. I suppose everything is cold? Is the coffee bearable?"

"Good morning," Arthur said sulkily, and sat down himself with an air of sullen ill temper. Theodora almost upset the coffee pot in her haste to set a cup of coffee before Mrs. Montague.

"It *seems* hot enough," Mrs. Montague said. "I shall speak to your Mrs. Dudley this morning in any case. That room must be aired."

"And your night?" the doctor asked timidly. "Did you spend a—ah—profitable night?"

"If by profitable you meant comfortable, John, I wish you would say so. No, in answer to your most civil inquiry, I did *not* spend a comfortable night. I did not sleep a wink. That room is unendurable."

"Noisy old house, isn't it?" Arthur said. "Branch kept tapping against my window all night; nearly drove me crazy, tapping and tapping."

"Even with the windows open that room is stuffy. Mrs. Dudley's coffee is not as poor as her housekeeping. Another cup, if you please. I am astonished, John, that you put me in a room not properly aired; if there is to be any communication with those beyond, the air circulation, at least, ought to be adequate. I smelled dust all night."

"Can't understand *you*," Arthur said to the doctor, "letting yourself get all nervy about this place. Sat there all night long with my revolver and not a mouse stirred. Except for that infernal branch tapping on the window. Nearly drove me crazy," he confided to Theodora.

"We will not give up hope, of course." Mrs. Montague scowled at her husband. "Perhaps tonight there may be some manifestations."

2

"Theo?" Eleanor put down her notepad, and Theodora, scribbling busily, looked up with a frown. "I've been thinking about something."

"I *hate* writing these notes; I feel like a damn fool trying to write this crazy stuff."

"I've been wondering."

"Well?" Theodora smiled a little. "You look so serious," she said. "Are you coming to some great decision?"

"Yes," Eleanor said, deciding. "About what I'm going to do afterwards. After we all leave Hill House."

"Well?"

"I'm coming with you," Eleanor said.

"Coming where with me?"

"Back with you, back home. I"—and Eleanor smiled wryly —"am going to follow you home."

Theodora stared. "Why?" she asked blankly.

"I never had anyone to care about," Eleanor said, wondering where she had heard someone say something like this before. "I want to be someplace where I belong."

"I am not in the habit of taking home stray cats," Theodora said lightly.

Eleanor laughed too. "I *am* a kind of stray cat, aren't I?"

"Well." Theodora took her pencil again. "You have your own home," she said. "You'll be glad enough to get back to it when the time comes, Nell my Nellie. I suppose we'll all be glad to get back home. What are you saying about those noises last night? *I* can't describe them."

"I'll come, you know," Eleanor said. "I'll just come."

"Nellie, Nellie." Theodora laughed again. "Look," she said. "This is just a summer, just a few weeks' visit to a lovely old summer resort in the country. You have your life back home, I have *my* life. When the summer is over, we go back. We'll write each other, of course, and maybe visit, but Hill House is not forever, you know."

"I can get a job; I won't be in your way."

"I don't understand." Theodora threw down her pencil in exasperation. "Do you *always* go where you're not wanted?"

Eleanor smiled placidly. "I've never been wanted *anywhere*," she said.

3

"It's all so motherly," Luke said. "Everything so soft. Everything so padded. Great embracing chairs and sofas which turn out to be hard and unwelcome when you sit down, and reject you at once—"

"Theo?" Eleanor said softly, and Theodora looked at her and shook her head in bewilderment.

"—and hands everywhere. Little soft glass hands, curving out to you, beckoning—"

"Theo?" Eleanor said.

"No," Theodora said. "I won't have you. And I don't want to talk about it any more."

"Perhaps," Luke said, watching them, "the single most repulsive aspect is the emphasis upon the globe. I ask you to regard impartially the lampshade made of tiny pieces of broken glass glued together, or the great round balls of the lights upon the stairs or the fluted iridescent candy jar at Theo's elbow. In the dining room there is a bowl of particularly filthy yellow glass resting upon the cupped hands of a child, and an Easter egg of sugar with a vision of shepherds dancing inside. A bosomy lady supports the stair-rail on her head, and under glass in the drawing room—"

"Nellie, leave me alone. Let's walk down to the brook or something."

"—a child's face, done in cross-stitch. Nell, don't look so apprehensive; Theo has only suggested that you walk down to the brook. If you like, I will go along."

"Anything," Theodora said.

"To frighten away rabbits. If you like, I will carry a stick. If you like, I will not come at all. Theo has only to say the word."

Theodora laughed. "Perhaps Nell would rather stay here and write on walls."

"So unkind," Luke said. "Callous of you, Theo."

"I want to hear more about the shepherds dancing in the Easter egg," Theodora said.

"A world contained in sugar. Six very tiny shepherds dancing, and a shepherdess in pink and blue reclining upon a mossy bank enjoying them; there are flowers and trees and sheep, and an old goatherd playing pipes. I would like to have been a goatherd, I think."

"If you were not a bullfighter," Theodora said.

"If I were not a bullfighter. Nell's affairs are the talk of the cafés, you will recall."

"Pan," Theodora said. "You should live in a hollow tree, Luke."

"Nell," Luke said, "you are not listening."

"I think you frighten her, Luke."

"Because Hill House will be mine someday, with its untold treasures and its cushions? I am not gentle with a house, Nell; I might take a fit of restlessness and smash the sugar Easter egg, or shatter the little child hands or go stomping and shouting up and down the stairs striking at glued-glass lamps with a cane and slashing at the bosomy lady with the staircase on her head; I might—"

"You see? You do frighten her."

"I believe I do," Luke said. "Nell, I am only talking nonsense."

"I don't think he even owns a cane," Theodora said.

"As a matter of fact, I do. Nell, I am *only* talking nonsense. What is she thinking about, Theo?"

Theodora said carefully, "She wants me to take her home with me after we leave Hill House, and I won't do it."

Luke laughed. "Poor silly Nell," he said. "Journeys end in lovers meeting. Let's go down to the brook."

*

"A mother house," Luke said, as they came down the steps from the veranda to the lawn, "a housemother, a headmistress, a housemistress. I am sure I will be a very poor housemaster, like our Arthur, when Hill House belongs to me."

"I can't understand anyone wanting to own Hill House," Theodora said, and Luke turned and looked back with amusement at the house.

"You never know what you are going to want until you see it clearly," he said. "If I never had a chance of owning it I might feel very differently. What do people really want with each other, as Nell asked me once; what use are other people?"

"It was my fault my mother died," Eleanor said. "She knocked on the wall and called me and called me and I never woke up. I ought to have brought her the medicine; I always did before. But this time she called me and I never woke up."

"You should have forgotten all that by now," Theodora said.

"I've wondered ever since if I did wake up. If I did wake up and hear her, and if I just went back to sleep. It would have been easy, and I've wondered about it."

"Turn here," Luke said. "If we're going to the brook."

"You worry too much, Nell. You probably just *like* thinking it was your fault."

"It was going to happen sooner or later, in any case," Eleanor said. "But of course no matter when it happened, it was going to be my fault."

"If it hadn't happened you would never have come to Hill House."

"We go single file along here," Luke said. "Nell, go first."

Smiling, Eleanor went on ahead, kicking her feet comfortably along the path. Now I know where I am going, she thought; I told her about my mother so *that's* all right; I will find a little house, or maybe an apartment like hers. I will see her every day, and we will go searching together for lovely things—gold-trimmed dishes, and a white cat, and a sugar Easter egg, and a cup of stars. I will not be frightened or alone any more; I will call myself just *Eleanor*. "Are you two talking about me?" she asked over her shoulder.

After a minute Luke answered politely, "A struggle between

good and evil for the soul of Nell. I suppose I will have to be God, however."

"But of course she can*not* trust either of us," Theodora said, amused.

"Not me, certainly," Luke said.

"Besides, Nell," Theodora said, "we were not talking about you at all. As though I were the games mistress," she said, half angry, to Luke.

I have waited such a long time, Eleanor was thinking; I have finally earned my happiness. She came, leading them, to the top of the hill and looked down to the slim line of trees they must pass through to get to the brook. They are lovely against the sky, she thought, so straight and free; Luke was wrong about the softness everywhere, because the trees are hard like wooden trees. They are still talking about me, talking about how I came to Hill House and found Theodora and now I will not let her go. Behind her she could hear the murmur of their voices, edged sometimes with malice, sometimes rising in mockery, sometimes touched with a laughter almost of kinship, and she walked on dreamily, hearing them come behind. She could tell when they entered the tall grass a minute after she did, because the grass moved hissingly beneath their feet and a startled grasshopper leaped wildly away.

I could help her in her shop, Eleanor thought; she loves beautiful things and I would go with her to find them. We could go anywhere we pleased, to the edge of the world if we liked, and come back when we wanted to. He is telling her now what he knows about me: that I am not easily taken in, that I had an oleander wall around me, and she is laughing because I am not going to be lonely any more. They are very much alike and they are very kind; I would not really have expected as much from them as they are giving me; I was very right to come because journeys end in lovers meeting.

She came under the hard branches of the trees and the shadows were pleasantly cool after the hot sun on the path; now she had to walk more carefully because the path led downhill and there were sometimes rocks and roots across her way. Behind her their voices went on, quick and sharp, and then more slowly and laughing; I will not look back, she thought happily, because then they would know what I am thinking; we will talk about it together someday, Theo and I, when we have plenty of time. How strange I feel, she thought, coming out of the trees onto the last steep part of the path going down to the brook; I am caught in a kind of wonder, I am still with joy. I will not look around until I am next to the brook, where she almost fell the day we came; I will remind her about the golden fish in the brook and about our picnic.

She sat down on the narrow green bank and put her chin on her knees; I will not forget this one moment in my life, she promised herself, listening to their voices and their footsteps coming slowly down the hill. "Hurry up," she said, turning her head to look for Theodora. "I—" and was silent. There was no one on the hill, nothing but the footsteps coming clearly along the path and the faint mocking laughter.

"Who—?" she whispered. "Who?"

She could see the grass go down under the weight of the footsteps. She saw another grasshopper leap wildly away, and a pebble jar and roll. She heard clearly the brush of footsteps on the path and then, standing back hard against the bank, heard the laughter very close; "Eleanor, Eleanor," and she heard it inside and outside her head; this was a call she had been listening for all her life. The footsteps stopped and she was caught in a movement of air so solid that she staggered and was held. "Eleanor, Eleanor," she heard through the rushing of air past her ears, "Eleanor, Eleanor," and she was held tight and safe. It is not cold at all, she thought, it is not cold at all. She closed her eyes and leaned back against the bank and thought, Don't let me go, and then, Stay, stay, as the firmness which held her slipped away, leaving her and fading; "Eleanor, Eleanor," she heard once more and then she stood beside the brook, shivering as though the sun had gone, watching without surprise the vacant footsteps move across the water of the brook, sending small ripples going, and then over onto the grass on the other side, moving slowly and caressingly up and over the hill.

Come back, she almost said, standing shaking by the brook, and then she turned and ran madly up the hill, crying as she ran and calling, "Theo? Luke?"

She found them in the little group of trees, leaning against a tree trunk and talking softly and laughing; when she ran to them they turned, startled, and Theodora was almost angry. "What on earth do you want this time?" she said.

"I waited for you by the brook—"

"We decided to stay here where it was cool," Theodora said. "We thought you heard us calling you. Didn't we, Luke?"

"Oh, yes," said Luke, embarrassed. "We were sure you heard us calling."

"Anyway," Theodora said, "we were going to come along in a minute. Weren't we, Luke?"

"Yes," said Luke, grinning. "Oh, yes."

4

"Subterranean waters," the doctor said, waving his fork.

"Nonsense. Does Mrs. Dudley do all your cooking? The asparagus is more than passable. Arthur, let that young man help you to asparagus."

"My dear." The doctor looked fondly upon his wife. "It has become our custom to rest for an hour or so after lunch; if you—"

"Certainly not. I have far too much to do while I am here. I must speak to your cook, I must see that my room is aired, I must ready planchette for another session this evening; Arthur must clean his revolver."

"Mark of a fighting man," Arthur conceded. "Firearms always in good order."

"*You* and *these* young people may rest, of course. Perhaps you do not feel the urgency which I do, the terrible compulsion to aid whatever poor souls wander restlessly here; perhaps you find me foolish in my sympathy for them, perhaps I am even ludicrous in your eyes because I can spare a tear for a lost abandoned soul, left without any helping hand; pure love—"

"Croquet?" Luke said hastily. "Croquet, perhaps?" He looked eagerly from one to another. "Badminton?" he suggested. "Croquet?"

"Subterranean waters?" Theodora added helpfully.

"No fancy sauces for *me*," Arthur said firmly. "Tell my fellows it's the mark of a cad." He looked thoughtfully at Luke.

"Mark of a cad. Fancy sauces, women waiting on you. *My* fellows wait on themselves. Mark of a man," he said to Theodora.

"And what else do you teach them?" Theodora asked politely.

"Teach? You mean—do they learn anything, my fellows? You mean—algebra, like? Latin? Certainly." Arthur sat back, pleased. "Leave all that kind of thing to the teachers," he explained.

"And how many fellows are there in your school?" Theodora leaned forward, courteous, interested, making conversation with a guest, and Arthur basked; at the head of the table Mrs. Montague frowned and tapped her fingers impatiently.

"How many? How many. Got a crack tennis team, you know." He beamed on Theodora. "Crack. Absolutely top-hole. Not counting milksops?"

"Not counting," said Theodora, "milksops."

"Oh. Tennis. Golf. Baseball. Track. Cricket." He smiled slyly. "Didn't guess we played cricket, did you? Then there's swimming, and volleyball. Some fellows go out for everything, though," he told her anxiously. "All-around types. Maybe seventy, altogether."

"Arthur?" Mrs. Montague could contain herself no longer. "No shop talk, now. You're on vacation, remember."

"Yes, silly of me." Arthur smiled fondly. "Got to check the weapons," he explained.

"It's two o'clock," Mrs. Dudley said in the doorway. "I clear off at two."

5

Theodora laughed, and Eleanor, hidden deep in the shadows behind the summerhouse, put her hands over her mouth to keep from speaking to let them know she was there; I've got to find out, she was thinking, I've got to find out.

"It's called 'The Grattan Murders,'" Luke was saying. "Lovely thing. I can even sing it if you prefer."

"Mark of a cad." Theodora laughed again. "Poor Luke; I would have said 'scoundrel.'"

"If you would rather be spending this brief hour with Arthur . . ."

"Of course I would rather be with Arthur. An educated man is always an enlivening companion."

"Cricket," Luke said. "Never would have thought we played cricket, would you?"

"Sing, sing," Theodora said, laughing.

Luke sang, in a nasal monotone, emphasizing each word distinctly:

> "The first was young Miss Grattan,
> She tried not to let him in;
> He stabbed her with a corn knife,
> That's how his crimes begin.
>
> "The next was Grandma Grattan,
> So old and tired and gray;
> She fit off her attacker
> Until her strength give way.
>
> "The next was Grandpa Grattan,
> A-settin' by the fire;
> He crept up close behind him
> And strangled him with a wire.
>
> "The last was Baby Grattan
> All in his trundle bed;
> He stove him in the short ribs
> Until that child was dead.
>
> "And spit tobacco juice
> All on his golden head."

When he finished there was a moment's silence, and then Theodora said weakly, "It's lovely, Luke. Perfectly beautiful. I will never hear it again without thinking of you."

"I plan to sing it to Arthur," Luke said. When are they going to talk about me? Eleanor wondered in the shadows. After a minute Luke went on idly, "I wonder what the doctor's book will be like, when he writes it? Do you suppose he'll put us in?"

"You will probably turn up as an earnest young psychic

researcher. And I will be a lady of undeniable gifts but dubious reputation."

"I wonder if Mrs. Montague will have a chapter to herself."

"And Arthur. And Mrs. Dudley. I hope he doesn't reduce us all to figures on a graph."

"I wonder, I wonder," said Luke. "It's warm this afternoon," he said. "What could we do that is cool?"

"We could ask Mrs. Dudley to make lemonade."

"You know what I want to do?" Luke said. "I want to explore. Let's follow the brook up into the hills and see where it comes from; maybe there's a pond somewhere and we can go swimming."

"Or a waterfall; it looks like a brook that runs naturally from a waterfall."

"Come on, then." Listening behind the summerhouse, Eleanor heard their laughter and the sound of their feet running down the path to the house.

6

"Here's an interesting thing, here," Arthur's voice said in the manner of one endeavoring valiantly to entertain, "here in this book. Says how to make candles out of ordinary children's crayons."

"Interesting." The doctor sounded weary. "If you will excuse me, Arthur, I have all these notes to write up."

"Sure, Doctor. All got our work to do. Not a sound." Eleanor, listening outside the parlor door, heard the small irritating noises of Arthur settling down to be quiet. "Not much to do around here, is there?" Arthur said. "How d'you pass the time generally?"

"Working," the doctor said shortly.

"You writing down what happens in the house?"

"Yes."

"You got me in there?"

"No."

"Seems like you ought to put in our notes from planchette. What are you writing now?"

"Arthur. Can you read, or something?"

"Sure. Never meant to make a nuisance of myself." Eleanor

heard Arthur take up a book, and put it down, and light a cigarette, and sigh, and stir, and finally say, "Listen, isn't there anything to *do* around here? Where *is* everybody?"

The doctor spoke patiently, but without interest. "Theodora and Luke have gone to explore the brook, I think. And I suppose the others are around somewhere. As a matter of fact, I believe my wife was looking for Mrs. Dudley."

"Oh." Arthur sighed again. "Might as well read, I guess," he said, and then, after a minute, "Say, Doctor. I don't like to bother you, but listen to what it says here in this book. . . ."

7

"No," Mrs. Montague said, "I do *not* believe in throwing young people together promiscuously, Mrs. Dudley. If my husband had consulted *me* before arranging this fantastic house party—"

"Well, now." It was Mrs. Dudley's voice, and Eleanor, pressed against the dining-room door, stared and opened her mouth wide against the wooden panels of the door. "I always say, Mrs. Montague, that you're only young once. Those young people are enjoying themselves, and it's only natural for the young."

"But living under one roof—"

"It's not as though they weren't grown up enough to know right from wrong. That pretty Theodora lady is old enough to take care of herself, I'd think, no matter how gay Mr. Luke."

"I need a dry dishtowel, Mrs. Dudley, for the silverware. It's a shame, I think, the way children grow up these days knowing everything. There should be more mysteries for them, more things that belong rightly to grownups, that they have to wait to find out."

"Then they find them out the hard way." Mrs. Dudley's voice was comfortable and easy. "Dudley brought in these tomatoes from the garden this morning," she said. "They did well this year."

"Shall I start on them?"

"No, oh, no. You sit down over there and rest; you've done enough. I'll put on the water and we'll have a nice cup of tea."

8

"Journeys end in lovers meeting," Luke said, and smiled across the room at Eleanor. "Does that blue dress on Theo really belong to you? I've never seen it before."

"I am Eleanor," Theodora said wickedly, "because I have a beard."

"You were wise to bring clothes for two," Luke told Eleanor. "Theo would never have looked half so well in my old blazer."

"I am Eleanor," Theo said, "because I am wearing blue. I love my love with an E because she is ethereal. Her name is Eleanor, and she lives in expectation."

She is being spiteful, Eleanor thought remotely; from a great distance, it seemed, she could watch these people and listen to them. Now she thought, Theo is being spiteful and Luke is trying to be nice; Luke is ashamed of himself for laughing at me and he is ashamed of Theo for being spiteful. "Luke," Theodora said, with a half-glance at Eleanor, "come and sing to me again."

"Later," Luke said uncomfortably. "The doctor has just set up the chessmen." He turned away in some haste.

Theodora, piqued, leaned her head against the back of her chair and closed her eyes, clearly determined not to speak. Eleanor sat, looking down at her hands, and listened to the sounds of the house. Somewhere upstairs a door swung quietly shut; a bird touched the tower briefly and flew off. In the kitchen the stove was settling and cooling, with little soft creakings. An animal—a rabbit—moved through the bushes by the summerhouse. She could even hear, with her new awareness of the house, the dust drifting gently in the attics, the wood aging. Only the library was closed to her; she could not hear the heavy breathing of Mrs. Montague and Arthur over their planchette, nor their little excited questions; she could not hear the books rotting or rust seeping into the circular iron stairway to the tower. In the little parlor she could hear, without raising her eyes, Theodora's small irritated tappings and the quiet sound of the chessmen being set down. She heard when the library door slammed open, and then the sharp angry sound of footsteps coming to the little parlor, and then all of them turned as Mrs. Montague opened the door and marched in.

"I must say," said Mrs. Montague on a sharp, explosive breath, "I really must *say* that this is the most *infuriating*—"

"My dear." The doctor rose, but Mrs. Montague waved him aside angrily. "If you had the *decency*—" she said.

Arthur, coming behind her sheepishly, moved past her and, almost slinking, settled in a chair by the fire. He shook his head warily when Theodora turned to him.

"The common *decency*. After all, John, I *did* come all this way, and so did Arthur, just to help out and I certainly must say that I never expected to meet with such cynicism and incredulity from *you*, of all people, and *these*—" She gestured at Eleanor and Theodora and Luke. "All I ask, all I *ask*, is some small minimum of trust, just a little bit of sympathy for all I am trying to do, and instead you disbelieve, you scoff, you mock and jeer." Breathing heavily, red-faced, she shook her finger at the doctor. "Planchette," she said bitterly, "will not speak to me tonight. Not *one single word* have I had from planchette, as a direct result of your sneering and your skepticism; planchette may very possibly not speak to me for a matter of weeks—it has happened before, I can tell you; it has happened before, when I subjected it to the taunts of unbelievers; I have known planchette to be silent for weeks, and the very *least* I could have expected, coming here as I did with none but the finest motives, was a little respect." She shook her finger at the doctor, wordless for the moment.

"My dear," the doctor said, "I am certain that none of us would knowingly have interfered."

"Mocking and jeering, were you not? Skeptical, with planchette's very words before your eyes? Those young people pert and insolent?"

"Mrs. Montague, really . . ." said Luke, but Mrs. Montague brushed past him and sat herself down, her lips tight and her eyes blazing. The doctor sighed, started to speak, and then stopped. Turning away from his wife, he gestured Luke back to the chess table. Apprehensively, Luke followed, and Arthur, wriggling in his chair, said in a low voice to Theodora, "Never seen her so upset, you know. Miserable experience, waiting for planchette. So easily offended, of course. Sensitive to atmosphere." Seeming to believe that he had satisfactorily explained the situation, he sat back and smiled timidly.

Eleanor was hardly listening, wondering dimly at the movement in the room. Someone was walking around, she thought without interest; Luke was walking back and forth in the room, talking softly to himself; surely an odd way to play chess? Humming? Singing? Once or twice she almost made out a broken word, and then Luke spoke quietly; he was at the chess table where he belonged, and Eleanor turned and looked at the empty center of the room, where someone was walking and singing softly, and then she heard it clearly:

> Go walking through the valley,
> Go walking through the valley,
> Go walking through the valley,
> As we have done before. . . .

Why, I know that, she thought, listening, smiling, to the faint melody; we used to play that game; I remember that.

"It's simply that it's a most delicate and intricate piece of machinery," Mrs. Montague was saying to Theodora; she was still angry, but visibly softening under Theodora's sympathetic attention. "The slightest air of disbelief offends it, naturally. How would *you* feel if people refused to believe in *you*?"

> Go in and out the windows,
> Go in and out the windows,
> Go in and out the windows,
> As we have done before. . . .

The voice was light, perhaps only a child's voice, singing sweetly and thinly, on the barest breath, and Eleanor smiled and remembered, hearing the little song more clearly than Mrs. Montague's voice continuing about planchette.

> Go forth and face your lover,
> Go forth and face your lover,
> Go forth and face your lover,
> As we have done before. . . .

She heard the little melody fade, and felt the slight movement of air as the footsteps came close to her, and something almost brushed her face; perhaps there was a tiny sigh against her cheek, and she turned in surprise. Luke and the doctor bent over the chessboard, Arthur leaned confidingly close to Theodora, and Mrs. Montague talked.

None of them heard it, she thought with joy; nobody heard it but me.

9

ELEANOR closed the bedroom door softly behind her, not wanting to awaken Theodora, although the noise of a door closing would hardly disturb anyone, she thought, who slept so soundly as Theodora; I learned to sleep very lightly, she told herself comfortingly, when I was listening for my mother. The hall was dim, lighted only by the small nightlight over the stairs, and all the doors were closed. Funny, Eleanor thought, going soundlessly in her bare feet along the hall carpet, it's the only house I ever knew where you don't have to worry about making noise at night, or at least about anyone knowing it's you. She had awakened with the thought of going down to the library, and her mind had supplied her with a reason: I cannot sleep, she explained to herself, and so I am going downstairs to get a book. If anyone asks me where I am going, it is down to the library to get a book because I cannot sleep.

It was warm, drowsily, luxuriously warm. She went barefoot and in silence down the great staircase and to the library door before she thought, But I can't go in there; I'm not allowed in there—and recoiled in the doorway before the odor of decay, which nauseated her. "Mother," she said aloud, and stepped quickly back. "Come along," a voice answered distinctly upstairs, and Eleanor turned, eager, and hurried to the staircase. "Mother?" she said softly, and then again, "Mother?" A little soft laugh floated down to her, and she ran, breathless, up the stairs and stopped at the top, looking to right and left along the hallway at the closed doors.

"You're here somewhere," she said, and down the hall the little echo went, slipping in a whisper on the tiny currents of air. "Somewhere," it said. "Somewhere."

Laughing, Eleanor followed, running soundlessly down the hall to the nursery doorway; the cold spot was gone, and she laughed up at the two grinning faces looking down at her. "Are you in here?" she whispered outside the door, "are you in here?" and knocked, pounding with her fists.

"Yes?" It was Mrs. Montague, inside, clearly just awakened. "Yes? Come in, whatever you are."

No, no, Eleanor thought, hugging herself and laughing silently, not in there, not with Mrs. Montague, and slipped away down the hall, hearing Mrs. Montague behind her calling, "I am your friend; I intend you no harm. Come in and tell me what is troubling you."

She won't open her door, Eleanor thought wisely; she is not afraid but she won't open her door, and knocked, pounding, against Arthur's door and heard Arthur's awakening gasp.

Dancing, the carpet soft under her feet, she came to the door behind which Theodora slept; faithless Theo, she thought, cruel, laughing Theo, wake up, wake up, wake up, and pounded and slapped the door, laughing, and shook the door-knob and then ran swiftly down the hall to Luke's door and pounded; wake up, she thought, wake up and be faithless. None of them will open their doors, she thought; they will sit inside, with the blankets pressed around them, shivering and wondering what is going to happen to them next; wake up, she thought, pounding on the doctor's door; I dare you to open your door and come out to see me dancing in the hall of Hill House.

Then Theodora startled her by calling out wildly, "Nell? Nell? Doctor, Luke, Nell's not here!"

Poor house, Eleanor thought, I had forgotten Eleanor; now they will have to open their doors, and she ran quickly down the stairs, hearing behind her the doctor's voice raised anxiously, and Theodora calling, "Nell? Eleanor?" What fools they are, she thought; now I will have to go into the library. "Mother, Mother," she whispered, "Mother," and stopped at the library door, sick. Behind her she could hear them talking upstairs in the hall; funny, she thought, I can feel the whole house, and heard even Mrs. Montague protesting, and Arthur, and then the doctor, clearly. "We've got to look for her; everyone please hurry."

Well, I can hurry too, she thought, and ran down the corridor to the little parlor, where the fire flickered briefly at her when she opened the door, and the chessmen sat where Luke and the doctor had left their game. The scarf Theodora had been wearing lay across the back of her chair; I can take care of *that* too, Eleanor thought, her maid's pathetic finery, and put one end of it between her teeth and pulled, tearing, and then dropped it when she heard them behind her on the stairs. They were coming down all together, anxious, telling one another where to look first, now and then calling, "Eleanor? Nell?"

"Coming? Coming?" she heard far away, somewhere else in the house, and she heard the stairs shake under their feet and a cricket stir on the lawn. Daring, gay, she ran down the corridor again to the hall and peeked out at them from the doorway. They were moving purposefully, all together, straining to stay near one another, and the doctor's flashlight swept the hall and stopped at the great front door, which was standing open wide. Then, in a rush, calling "Eleanor, *Eleanor*," they ran all together across the hall and out the front door, looking and calling, the flashlight moving busily. Eleanor clung to the door and laughed until tears came into her eyes; what fools they are, she thought; we trick them so easily. They are so slow, and so deaf and so *heavy*; they trample over the house, poking and peering and rough. She ran across the hall and through the game room and into the dining room and from there into the kitchen, with its doors. It's good here, she thought, I can go in any direction when I hear them. When they came back into the front hall, blundering and calling her, she darted quickly out onto the veranda into the cool night. She stood with her back against the door, the little mists of Hill House curling around her ankles, and looked up at the pressing, heavy hills. Gathered comfortably into the hills, she thought, protected and warm; Hill House is lucky.

"Eleanor?" They were very close, and she ran along the veranda and darted into the drawing room; "Hugh Crain," she said, "will you come and dance with me?" She curtsied to the huge leaning statue, and its eyes flickered and shone at her; little reflected lights touched the figurines and the gilded chairs, and she danced gravely before Hugh Crain, who watched her, gleaming. "Go in and out the windows," she sang, and felt her hands taken as she danced. "Go in and out the windows," and she danced out onto the veranda and around the house. Going around and around and around the house, she thought, and none of them can see me. She touched a kitchen door as she passed, and six miles away Mrs. Dudley shuddered in her sleep. She came to the tower, held so tightly in the embrace of the house, in the straining grip of the house, and walked slowly past its gray stones, not allowed to touch even the outside. Then she turned and stood before the great doorway; the door was closed again, and she put out her hand and opened it effortlessly. Thus I enter Hill House, she told herself, and stepped inside as though it were her own. "Here I am," she said aloud. "I've been all around the house, in and out the windows, and I danced—"

"Eleanor?" It was Luke's voice, and she thought, Of all of them I would least like to have Luke catch me; don't let him see me, she thought beggingly, and turned and ran, without stopping, into the library.

And here I am, she thought. Here I am inside. It was not cold at all, but deliciously, fondly warm. It was light enough for her to see the iron stairway curving around and around up to the tower, and the little door at the top. Under her feet the stone floor moved caressingly, rubbing itself against the soles of her feet, and all around the soft air touched her, stirring her hair, drifting against her fingers, coming in a light breath across her mouth, and she danced in circles. No stone lions for me, she thought, no oleanders; I have broken the spell of Hill House and somehow come inside. I am home, she thought, and stopped in wonder at the thought. I am home, I am home, she thought; now to climb.

Climbing the narrow iron stairway was intoxicating—going higher and higher, around and around, looking down, clinging to the slim iron railing, looking far far down onto the stone floor. Climbing, looking down, she thought of the soft green grass outside and the rolling hills and the rich trees. Looking up, she thought of the tower of Hill House rising triumphantly between the trees, tall over the road which wound through Hillsdale and past a white house set in flowers and past the magic oleanders and past the stone lions and on, far, far away, to a little lady who was going to pray for her. Time is ended now, she thought, all *that* is gone and left behind, and that poor little lady, praying still, for me.

"Eleanor!"

For a minute she could not remember who they were (had they been guests of hers in the house of the stone lions? Dining at her long table in the candlelight? Had she met them at the inn, over the tumbling stream? Had one of them come riding down a green hill, banners flying? Had one of them run beside her in the darkness? and then she remembered, and they fell into place where they belonged) and she hesitated, clinging to the railing. They were so small, so ineffectual. They stood far below on the stone floor and pointed at her; they called to her, and their voices were urgent and far away.

"Luke," she said, remembering. They could hear her, because they were quiet when she spoke. "Doctor Montague," she said. "Mrs. Montague. Arthur." She could not remember the other, who stood silent and a little apart.

"Eleanor," Dr. Montague called, "turn around very carefully and come slowly down the steps. Move very, very slowly, Eleanor. Hold on to the railing all the time. Now turn and come down."

"What on earth is the creature doing?" Mrs. Montague demanded. Her hair was in curlers, and her bathrobe had a dragon on the stomach. "Make her come down so we can go back to bed. Arthur, make her come down at once."

"See here," Arthur began, and Luke moved to the foot of the stairway and started up.

"For God's sake be careful," the doctor said as Luke moved steadily on. "The thing is rotted away from the wall."

"It won't hold both of you," Mrs. Montague said positively. "You'll have it down on our heads. Arthur, move over here near the door."

"Eleanor," the doctor called, "can you turn around and start down slowly?"

Above her was only the little trapdoor leading out onto the turret; she stood on the little narrow platform at the top and pressed against the trapdoor, but it would not move. Futilely she hammered against it with her fists, thinking wildly, Make it open, make it open, or they'll catch me. Glancing over her shoulder, she could see Luke climbing steadily, around and around. "Eleanor," he said, "stand still. Don't move," and he sounded frightened.

I can't get away, she thought, and looked down; she saw

one face clearly, and the name came into her mind. "Theo-dora," she said.

"Nell, do as they tell you. Please."

"Theodora? I can't get out; the door's been nailed shut."

"Damn right it's been nailed shut," Luke said. "And lucky for you, too, my girl." Climbing, coming very slowly, he had almost reached the narrow platform. "Stay perfectly still," he said.

"Stay perfectly still, Eleanor," the doctor said.

"Nell," Theodora said. "*Please* do what they say."

"Why?" Eleanor looked down and saw the dizzy fall of the tower below her, the iron stairway clinging to the tower walls, shaking and straining under Luke's feet, the cold stone floor, the distant, pale, staring faces. "How can I get down?" she asked helplessly. "Doctor—how can I get down?"

"Move very slowly," he said. "Do what Luke tells you."

"Nell," Theodora said, "don't be frightened. It will be all right, really."

"Of course it will be all right," Luke said grimly. "Probably it will only be *my* neck that gets broken. Hold on, Nell; I'm coming onto the platform. I want to get past you so you can go down ahead of me." He seemed hardly out of breath, in spite of climbing, but his hand trembled as he reached out to take hold of the railing, and his face was wet. "Come on," he said sharply.

Eleanor hung back. "The last time you told me to go ahead you never followed," she said.

"Perhaps I will just push you over the edge," Luke said. "Let you smash down there on the floor. Now behave yourself and move slowly; get past me and start down the stairs. And just hope," he added furiously, "that I can resist the tempta-tion to give you a shove."

Meekly she came along the platform and pressed herself against the hard stone wall while Luke moved cautiously past her. "Start down," he said. "I'll be right behind you."

Precariously, the iron stairway shaking and groaning with every step, she felt her way. She looked at her hand on the railing, white because she was holding so tight, and at her bare feet going one at a time, step by step, moving with extreme care, but never looked down again to the stone floor. Go down very slowly, she told herself over and over, not thinking of more than the steps which seemed almost to bend and buckle beneath her feet, go down very very very slowly. "Steady," Luke said behind her. "Take it easy, Nell, nothing to be afraid of, we're almost there."

Involuntarily, below her, the doctor and Theodora held out their arms, as though ready to catch her if she fell, and once when Eleanor stumbled and missed a step, the handrail wavering as she clung to it, Theodora gasped and ran to hold the end of the stairway. "It's all right, my Nellie," she said over and over, "it's all right, it's all right."

"Only a little farther," the doctor said.

Creeping, Eleanor slid her feet down, one step after another, and at last, almost before she could believe it, stepped off onto the stone floor. Behind her the stairway rocked and clanged as Luke leaped down the last few steps and walked steadily across the room to fall against a chair and stop, head down and trembling still. Eleanor turned and looked up to the infinitely high little spot where she had been standing, at the iron stairway, warped and crooked and swaying against the tower wall, and said in a small voice, "I ran up. I ran up all the way."

Mrs. Montague moved purposefully forward from the doorway where she and Arthur had been sheltering against the probable collapse of the stairway. "Does anybody agree with me," she asked with great delicacy, "in thinking that this young woman has given us quite enough trouble tonight? *I*, for one, would like to go back to bed, and so would Arthur."

"Hill House—" the doctor began.

"This childish nonsense has almost certainly destroyed any chance of manifestations *tonight*, I can tell you. I certainly do not look to see any of our friends from beyond after *this* ridiculous performance, so if you will all excuse me—and if you are *sure* that you are finished with your posturing and performing and waking up busy people—I will say good night. Arthur." Mrs. Montague swept out, dragon rampant, quivering with indignation.

"Luke was scared," Eleanor said, looking at the doctor and at Theodora.

"Luke was most certainly scared," he agreed from behind

her. "Luke was so scared he almost didn't get himself down from there. Nell, what an imbecile you are."

"I would be inclined to agree with Luke." The doctor was displeased, and Eleanor looked away, looked at Theodora, and Theodora said, "I suppose you *had* to do it, Nell?"

"I'm all right," Eleanor said, and could not longer look at any of them. She looked, surprised, down at her own bare feet, realizing suddenly that they had carried her, unfeeling, down the iron stairway. She thought, looking at her feet, and then raised her head. "I came down to the library to get a book," she said.

2

It was humiliating, disastrous. Nothing was said at breakfast, and Eleanor was served coffee and eggs and rolls just like the others. She was allowed to linger over her coffee with the rest of them, observe the sunlight outside, comment upon the good day ahead; for a few minutes she might have been persuaded to believe that nothing had happened. Luke passed her the marmalade, Theodora smiled at her over Arthur's head, the doctor bade her good morning. Then, after breakfast, after Mrs. Dudley's entrance at ten, they came without comment, following one another silently, to the little parlor, and the doctor took his position before the fireplace. Theodora was wearing Eleanor's red sweater.

"Luke will bring your car around," the doctor said gently. In spite of what he was saying, his eyes were considerate and friendly. "Theodora will go up and pack for you."

Eleanor giggled. "She can't. She won't have anything to wear."

"Nell—" Theodora began, and stopped and glanced at Mrs. Montague, who shrugged her shoulders and said, "I examined the room. *Naturally*. I can't imagine why none of *you* thought to do it."

"I was going to," the doctor said apologetically. "But I thought—"

"You *always* think, John, and that's your trouble. *Naturally* I examined the room at once."

"Theodora's room?" Luke asked. "I wouldn't like to go in there again."

Mrs. Montague sounded surprised. "I can't think why not," she said, "There's nothing wrong with it."

"I went in and looked at my clothes," Theodora said to the doctor. "They're perfectly fine."

"The room needs dusting, *naturally*, but what can you expect if you lock the door and Mrs. Dudley cannot—"

The doctor's voice rose over his wife's. "—cannot tell you how sorry I am," he was saying. "If there is ever anything I can do . . ."

Eleanor laughed. "But I can't leave," she said, wondering where to find words to explain.

"You have been here quite long enough," the doctor said.

Theodora stared at her. "I don't need your clothes," she said patiently. "Didn't you just hear Mrs. Montague? I don't need your clothes, and even if I *did* I wouldn't wear them now; Nell, you've got to go away from here."

"But I can't leave," Eleanor said, laughing still because it was so perfectly impossible to explain.

"Madam," Luke said somberly, "you are no longer welcome as my guest."

"Perhaps Arthur *had* better drive her back to the city. Arthur could see that she gets there safely."

"Gets where?" Eleanor shook her head at them, feeling her lovely heavy hair around her face. "Gets where?" she asked happily.

"Why," the doctor said, "home, of course," and Theodora said, "Nell, your own little place, your own apartment, where all your things are," and Eleanor laughed.

"I haven't any apartment," she said to Theodora. "I made it up. I sleep on a cot at my sister's, in the baby's room. I haven't any home, no place at all. And I can't go back to my sister's because I stole her car." She laughed, hearing her own words, so inadequate and so unutterably sad. "I haven't any home," she said again, and regarded them hopefully. "No home. Everything in all the world that belongs to me is in a carton in the back of my car. That's all I have, some books and things I had when I was a little girl, and a watch my mother gave me. So you see there's no place you can send me."

I could, of course, go on and on, she wanted to tell them, seeing always their frightened, staring faces. I could go on and on, leaving my clothes for Theodora; I could go wandering and homeless, errant, and I would always come back here. It would be simpler to let me stay, more sensible, she wanted to tell them, happier.

"I want to stay here," she said to them.

"I've already spoken to the sister," Mrs. Montague said importantly. "I must say, she asked first about the car. A vulgar person; I told her she need have no fear. You were very wrong, John, to let her steal her sister's car and come here."

"My dear," Dr. Montague began and stopped, spreading his hands helplessly.

"At any rate, she is expected. The sister was most annoyed at me because they had planned to go off on their vacation today, although why she should be annoyed at *me* . . ." Mrs. Montague scowled at Eleanor. "I do think someone ought to see her safely into their hands," she said.

The doctor shook his head. "It would be a mistake," he said slowly. "It would be a mistake to send one of us with her. She must be allowed to forget everything about this house as soon as she can; we cannot prolong the association. Once away from here, she will be herself again; can you find your way home?" he asked Eleanor, and Eleanor laughed.

"I'll go and get that packing done," Theodora said. "Luke, check her car and bring it around; she's only got one suitcase."

"Walled up alive." Eleanor began to laugh again at their stone faces. "Walled up alive," she said. "I want to stay here."

3

They made a solid line along—the steps of Hill House, guarding the door. Beyond their heads she could see the windows looking down, and to one side the tower waited confidently. She might have cried if she could have thought of any way of telling them why; instead, she smiled brokenly up at the house, looking at her own window, at the amused, certain face of the house, watching her quietly. The house was waiting now, she thought, and it was waiting for her; no one else could satisfy it. "The house wants me to stay," she told the doctor, and he stared at her. He was standing very stiff and with great dignity, as though he expected her to choose him instead of the house, as though, having brought her here, he thought that by unwinding his directions he could send her back again. His back was squarely turned to the house, and, looking at him honestly, she said, "I'm sorry. I'm terribly sorry, really."

"You'll go to Hillsdale," he said levelly; perhaps he was afraid of saying too much, perhaps he thought that a kind word, or a sympathetic one, might rebound upon himself and bring her back. The sun was shining on the hills and the house and the garden and the lawn and the trees and the brook; Eleanor took a deep breath and turned, seeing it all. "In Hillsdale turn onto Route Five going east; at Ashton you will meet Route Thirty-nine, and that will take you home. For your own safety," he added with a kind of urgency, "for your own safety, my dear; believe me, if I had foreseen this—"

"I'm really terribly sorry," she said.

"We can't take chances, you know, *any* chances. I am only beginning to perceive what a terrible risk I was asking of you all. Now . . ." He sighed and shook his head. "You'll remember?" he asked. "To Hillsdale, and then Route Five—"

"Look." Eleanor was quiet for a minute, wanting to tell them all exactly how it was. "I wasn't afraid," she said at last. "I really wasn't afraid. I'm fine now. I was—happy." She looked earnestly at the doctor. "*Happy*," she said. "I don't know what to say," she said, afraid again that she was going to cry. "I don't want to go away from here."

"There might be a next time," the doctor said sternly. "Can't you understand that we *cannot* take that chance?"

Eleanor faltered. "Someone is praying for me," she said foolishly. "A lady I met a long time ago."

The doctor's voice was gentle, but he tapped his foot impatiently. "You will forget all of this quite soon," he said. "You must forget everything about Hill House. I was so wrong to bring you here," he said.

"How long *have* we been here?" Eleanor asked suddenly.

"A little over a week. Why?"

"It's the only time anything's ever happened to me. I liked it."

"That," said the doctor, "is why you are leaving in such a hurry."

Eleanor closed her eyes and sighed, feeling and hearing and smelling the house; a flowering bush beyond the kitchen was heavy with scent, and the water in the brook moved sparkling over the stones. Far away, upstairs, perhaps in the nursery, a little eddy of wind gathered itself and swept along the floor, carrying dust. In the library the iron stairway swayed, and light glittered on the marble eyes of Hugh Crain; Theodora's yellow shirt hung neat and unstained, Mrs. Dudley was setting the lunch table for five. Hill House watched, arrogant and patient. "I won't go away," Eleanor said up to the high windows.

"You *will* go away," the doctor said, showing his impatience at last. "Right now."

Eleanor laughed, and turned, holding out her hand. "Luke," she said, and he came toward her, silent. "Thank you for bringing me down last night," she said. "That was wrong of me. I know it now, and you were very brave."

"I was indeed," Luke said. "It was an act of courage far surpassing any other in *my* life. And I am glad to see you going, Nell, because I would certainly never do it again."

"Well, it seems to *me*," Mrs. Montague said, "if you're going you'd better get on with it. I've no quarrel with saying good-by, although I personally feel that you've all got an exaggerated view of this place, but I *do* think we've got better things to do than stand here arguing when we all know you've *got* to go. You'll be a time as it is, getting back to the city, and your sister waiting to go on her vacation."

Arthur nodded. "Tearful farewells," he said. "Don't hold with them, myself."

Far away, in the little parlor, the ash dropped softly in the fireplace. "John," Mrs. Montague said, "possibly it *would* be better if Arthur—"

"No," the doctor said strongly. "Eleanor has to go back the way she came."

"And who do I thank for a lovely time?" Eleanor asked.

The doctor took her by the arm and, with Luke beside her, led her to her car and opened the door for her. The carton was still on the back seat, her suitcase was on the floor, her coat and pocketbook on the seat; Luke had left the motor running. "Doctor," Eleanor said, clutching at him, "Doctor."

"I'm sorry," he said. "Good-by."

"Drive carefully," Luke said politely.

"You can't just *make* me go," she said wildly. "You *brought* me here."

"And I am sending you away," the doctor said. "We won't forget you, Eleanor. But right now the only important thing for *you* is to forget Hill House and all of us. Good-by."

"Good-by," Mrs. Montague said firmly from the steps, and Arthur said, "Good-by, have a good trip."

Then Eleanor, her hand on the door of the car, stopped and turned. "Theo?" she said inquiringly, and Theodora ran down the steps to her.

"I thought you weren't going to say good-by to me," she said. "Oh, Nellie, my Nell—be happy; please be happy. Don't *really* forget me; someday things really *will* be all right again, and you'll write me letters and I'll answer and we'll visit each other and we'll have fun talking over the crazy things we did and saw and heard in Hill House—oh, Nellie! I thought you weren't going to say good-by to me."

"Good-by," Eleanor said to her.

"Nellie," Theodora said timidly, and put out a hand to touch Eleanor's cheek, "listen—maybe someday we can meet here again? And have our picnic by the brook? We never had our picnic," she told the doctor, and he shook his head, looking at Eleanor.

"Good-by," Eleanor said to Mrs. Montague, "good-by, Arthur. Good-by, Doctor. I hope your book is very successful. Luke," she said, "good-by. And good-by."

"Nell," Theodora said, "please be careful."

"Good-by," Eleanor said, and slid into the car; it felt unfamiliar and awkward; I am too used already to the comforts of Hill House, she thought, and reminded herself to wave a hand from the car window. "Good-by," she called, wondering if there had ever been another word for her to say, "good-by, good-by." Clumsily, her hands fumbling, she released the brake and let the car move slowly.

They waved back at her dutifully, standing still, watching her. They will watch me down the drive as far as they can see, she thought; it is only civil for them to look at me until I am out of sight; so now I am going. Journeys end in lovers meeting. But I *won't* go, she thought, and laughed aloud to herself; Hill

House is not as easy as *they* are; just by telling me to go away they can't make me leave, not if Hill House means me to stay. "Go away, Eleanor," she chanted aloud, "go away, Eleanor, we don't want you any more, not in *our* Hill House, go away, Eleanor, you can't stay *here*; but I can," she sang, "but I can; *they* don't make the rules around *here*. They can't turn me out or shut me out or laugh at me or hide from me; I won't go, and Hill House belongs to *me*."

With what she perceived as quick cleverness she pressed her foot down hard on the accelerator; they can't run fast enough to catch me this time, she thought, but by now they must be beginning to realize; I wonder who notices first? Luke, almost certainly. I can hear them calling now, she thought, and the little footsteps running through Hill House and the soft sound of the hills pressing closer. I am really doing it, she thought, turning the wheel to send the car directly at the great tree at the curve of the driveway, I am really doing it, I am doing this all by myself, now, at last; this is me, I am really really really doing it by myself.

In the unending, crashing second before the car hurled into the tree she thought clearly, *Why* am I doing this? Why am I doing this? Why don't they stop me?

4

Mrs. Sanderson was enormously relieved to hear that Dr. Montague and his party had left Hill House; she would have turned them out, she told the family lawyer, if Dr. Montague had shown any sign of wanting to stay. Theodora's friend, mollified and contrite, was delighted to see Theodora back so soon; Luke took himself off to Paris, where his aunt fervently hoped he would stay for a while. Dr. Montague finally retired from active scholarly pursuits after the cool, almost contemptuous reception of his preliminary article analyzing the psychic phenomena of Hill House. Hill House itself, not sane, stood against its hills, holding darkness within; it had stood so for eighty years and might stand for eighty more. Within, its walls continued upright, bricks met neatly, floors were firm, and doors were sensibly shut; silence lay steadily against the wood and stone of Hill House, and whatever walked there, walked alone.

WE HAVE ALWAYS LIVED
IN THE CASTLE

For Pascal Covici

1

M Y NAME is Mary Katherine Blackwood. I am eighteen years old, and I live with my sister Constance. I have often thought that with any luck at all I could have been born a werewolf, because the two middle fingers on both my hands are the same length, but I have had to be content with what I had. I dislike washing myself, and dogs, and noise. I like my sister Constance, and Richard Plantagenet, and *Amanita phalloides*, the death-cup mushroom. Everyone else in my family is dead.

The last time I glanced at the library books on the kitchen shelf they were more than five months overdue, and I wondered whether I would have chosen differently if I had known that these were the last books, the ones which would stand forever on our kitchen shelf. We rarely moved things; the Blackwoods were never much of a family for restlessness and stirring. We dealt with the small surface transient objects, the books and the flowers and the spoons, but underneath we had always a solid foundation of stable possessions. We always put things back where they belonged. We dusted and swept under tables and chairs and beds and pictures and rugs and lamps, but we left them where they were; the tortoiseshell toilet set on our mother's dressing table was never off place by so much as a fraction of an inch. Blackwoods had always lived in our house, and kept their things in order; as soon as a new Blackwood wife moved in, a place was found for her belongings, and so our house was built up with layers of Blackwood property weighting it, and keeping it steady against the world.

It was on a Friday in late April that I brought the library books into our house. Fridays and Tuesdays were terrible days, because I had to go into the village. Someone had to go to the library, and the grocery; Constance never went past her own garden, and Uncle Julian could not. Therefore it was not pride that took me into the village twice a week, or even stubbornness, but only the simple need for books and food. It may have been pride that brought me into Stella's for a cup of coffee before I started home; I told myself it was pride and would not avoid going into Stella's no matter how much I wanted to be at home, but I knew, too, that Stella would see me pass if I did not go in, and perhaps think I was afraid, and that thought I could not endure.

"Good morning, Mary Katherine," Stella always said, reaching over to wipe the counter with a damp rag, "how are you today?"

"Very well, thank you."

"And Constance Blackwood, is she well?"

"Very well, thank you."

"And how is *he*?"

"As well as can be expected. Black coffee, please."

If anyone else came in and sat down at the counter I would leave my coffee without seeming hurried, and leave, nodding goodbye to Stella. "Keep well," she always said automatically as I went out.

I chose the library books with care. There were books in our house, of course; our father's study had books covering two walls, but I liked fairy tales and books of history, and Constance liked books about food. Although Uncle Julian never took up a book, he liked to see Constance reading in the evenings while he worked at his papers, and sometimes he turned his head to look at her and nod.

"What are you reading, my dear? A pretty sight, a lady with a book."

"I'm reading something called *The Art of Cooking*, Uncle Julian."

"Admirable."

We never sat quietly for long, of course, with Uncle Julian in the room, but I do not recall that Constance and I have ever opened the library books which are still on our kitchen shelf. It was a fine April morning when I came out of the library; the sun was shining and the false glorious promises of spring were everywhere, showing oddly through the village grime. I remember that I stood on the library steps holding my books and looking for a minute at the soft hinted green in the branches against the sky and wishing, as I always did, that I could walk home across the sky instead of through the village. From the library steps I could cross the street directly and walk on the other side along to the grocery, but that meant that I must pass the general store and the men sitting in front. In this village the men stayed young and did the gossiping and the women aged with grey evil weariness and stood silently waiting for the men to get up and come home. I could leave the library and walk up the street on this side until I was opposite the grocery and then cross; that was preferable, although it took me past the post office and the Rochester house with the piles of rusted tin and the broken automobiles and the empty gas tins and the old mattresses and plumbing fixtures and wash tubs that the Harler family brought home and—I genuinely believe—loved.

The Rochester house was the loveliest in town and had once had a walnut-panelled library and a second-floor ballroom and a profusion of roses along the veranda; our mother had been born there and by rights it should have belonged to Constance. I decided as I always did that it would be safer to go past the post office and the Rochester house, although I disliked seeing the house where our mother was born. This side of the street was generally deserted in the morning, since it was shady, and after I went into the grocery I would in any case have to pass the general store to get home, and passing it going and coming was more than I could bear.

Outside the village, on Hill Road and River Road and Old Mountain, people like the Clarkes and the Carringtons had built new lovely homes. They had to come through the village to get to Hill Road and River Road because the main street of the village was also the main highway across the state, but the Clarke children and the Carrington boys went to private schools and the food in the Hill Road kitchens came from the towns and the city; mail was taken from the village post office by car along along the River Road and up to Old Mountain, but the Mountain people mailed their letters in the towns and the River Road people had their hair cut in the city.

I was always puzzled that the people of the village, living in their dirty little houses on the main highway or out on Creek Road, smiled and nodded and waved when the Clarkes and the Carringtons drove by; if Helen Clarke came into Elbert's Grocery to pick up a can of tomato sauce or a pound of coffee her cook had forgotten everyone told her "Good morning," and said the weather was better today. The Clarke's house is newer but no finer than the Blackwood house. Our father brought home the first piano ever seen in the village. The Carringtons own the paper mill but the Blackwoods own all the land between the highway and the river. The Shepherds of Old Mountain gave the village its town hall, which is white and peaked and set in a green lawn with a cannon in front. There was some talk once of putting in zoning laws in the village and tearing down the shacks on Creek Road and building up the whole village to match the town hall, but no one ever lifted a finger; maybe they thought the Blackwoods might take to attending town meetings if they did. The villagers get their hunting and fishing licenses in the town hall, and once a year the Clarkes and the Carringtons and the Shepherds attend town meeting and solemnly vote to get the Harler junk yard off Main Street and take away the benches in front of the general store, and each year the villagers gleefully outvote them. Past the town hall, bearing to the left, is Blackwood Road, which is the way home. Blackwood Road goes in a great circle around the Blackwood land and along every inch of Blackwood Road is a wire fence built by our father. Not far past the town hall is the big black rock which marks the entrance to the path where I unlock the gate and lock it behind me and go through the woods and am home.

The people of the village have always hated us.

I played a game when I did the shopping. I thought about the children's games where the board is marked into little spaces and each player moves according to a throw of the dice; there were always dangers, like "lose one turn" and "go back four spaces" and "return to start," and little helps, like "advance three spaces" and "take an extra turn." The library was my start and the black rock was my goal. I had to move down one side of Main Street, cross, and then move up the other side until I reached the black rock, when I would win. I began well, with a good safe turn along the empty side of Main Street, and perhaps this would turn out to be one of the very good days; it was like that sometimes, but not often on spring mornings. If it was a very good day I would later make an offering of jewelry out of gratitude.

I walked quickly when I started, taking a deep breath to go

on with and not looking around; I had the library books and my shopping bag to carry and I watched my feet moving one after the other; two feet in our mother's old brown shoes. I felt someone watching me from inside the post office—we did not accept mail, and we did not have a telephone; both had become unbearable six years before—but I could bear a quick stare from the office; that was old Miss Dutton, who never did her staring out in the open like other folks, but only looked out between blinds or from behind curtains. I never looked at the Rochester house. I could not bear to think of our mother being born there. I wondered sometimes if the Harler people knew that they lived in a house which should have belonged to Constance; there was always so much noise of crashing tinware in their yard that they could not hear me walking. Perhaps the Harlers thought that the unending noise drove away demons, or perhaps they were musical and found it agreeable; perhaps the Harlers lived inside the way they did outside, sitting in old bathtubs and eating their dinner off broken plates set on the skeleton of an old Ford car, rattling cans as they ate, and talking in bellows. A spray of dirt always lay across the sidewalk where the Harlers lived.

Crossing the street (lose one turn) came next, to get to the grocery directly opposite. I always hesitated, vulnerable and exposed, on the side of the road while the traffic went by. Most Main Street traffic was going through, cars and trucks passing through the village because the highway did, so the drivers hardly glanced at me; I could tell a local car by the quick ugly glance from the driver and I wondered, always, what would happen if I stepped down from the curb onto the road; would there be a quick, almost unintended swerve toward me? Just to scare me, perhaps, just to see me jump? And then the laughter, coming from all sides, from behind the blinds in the post office, from the men in front of the general store, from the women peering out of the grocery doorway, all of them watching and gloating, to see Mary Katherine Blackwood scurrying out of the way of a car. I sometimes lost two or even three turns because I waited so carefully for the road to clear in both directions before I crossed.

In the middle of the street I came out of the shade and into the bright, misleading sunshine of April; by July the surface of the road would be soft in the heat and my feet would stick, making the crossing more perilous (Mary Katherine Blackwood, her foot caught in the tar, cringing as a car bore down on her; go back, all the way, and start over), and the buildings would be uglier. All of the village was of a piece, a time, and a style; it was as though the people needed the ugliness of the village, and fed on it. The houses and the stores seemed to have been set up in contemptuous haste to provide shelter for the drab and the unpleasant, and the Rochester house and the Blackwood house and even the town hall had been brought here perhaps accidentally from some far lovely country where people lived with grace. Perhaps the fine houses had been captured—perhaps as punishment for the Rochesters and the Blackwoods and their secret bad hearts?—and were held prisoner in the village; perhaps their slow rot was a sign of the ugliness of the villagers. The row of stores along Main Street was unchangingly grey. The people who owned the stores lived above them, in a row of second-story apartments, and the curtains in the regular line of second-story windows were pale and without life; whatever planned to be colorful lost its heart quickly in the village. The blight on the village never came from the Blackwoods; the villagers belonged here and the village was the only proper place for them.

I always thought about rot when I came toward the row of stores; I thought about burning black painful rot that ate away from inside, hurting dreadfully. I wished it on the village.

I had a shopping list for the grocery; Constance made it out for me every Tuesday and Friday before I left home. The people of the village disliked the fact that we always had plenty of money to pay for whatever we wanted; we had taken our money out of the bank, of course, and I knew they talked about the money hidden in our house, as though it were great heaps of golden coins and Constance and Uncle Julian and I sat in the evenings, our library books forgotten, and played with it, running our hands through it and counting and stacking and tumbling it, jeering and mocking behind locked doors. I imagine that there were plenty of rotting hearts in the village coveting our heaps of golden coins but they were cowards and they were afraid of Blackwoods. When I took my grocery list out of my shopping bag I took out the purse too so that Elbert in the grocery would know that I had brought money and he could not refuse to sell to me.

It never mattered who was in the grocery. I was always served at once; Mr. Elbert or his pale greedy wife always came right away from wherever they were in the store to get me what I wanted. Sometimes, if their older boy was helping out in school vacation, they hurried to make sure that he was not the one who waited on me and once when a little girl—a child strange to the village, of course—came close to me in the grocery Mrs. Elbert pulled her back so roughly that she screamed and then there was a long still minute while everyone waited before Mrs. Elbert took a breath and said, "Anything else?" I always stood perfectly straight and stiff when the children came close, because I was afraid of them. I was afraid that they might touch me and the mothers would come at me like a flock of taloned hawks; that was always the picture I had in my mind—birds descending, striking, gashing with razor claws. Today I had a great many things to buy for Constance, and it was a relief to see that there were no children in the store and not many women; take an extra turn, I thought, and said to Mr. Elbert, "Good morning."

He nodded to me; he could not go entirely without greeting me and yet the women in the store were watching. I turned my back to them, but I could feel them standing behind me, holding a can or a half-filled bag of cookies or a head of lettuce, not willing to move until I had gone out through the door again and the wave of talk began and they were swept back into their own lives. Mrs. Donell was back there somewhere; I had seen her as I came in, and I wondered as I had before if she came on purpose when she knew I was coming, because she always tried to say something; she was one of the few who spoke.

"A roasting chicken," I said to Mr. Elbert, and across the store his greedy wife opened the refrigerated case and took out a chicken and began to wrap it. "A small leg of lamb," I said, "my Uncle Julian always fancies a roasted lamb in the first spring days." I should not have said it, I knew, and a little gasp went around the store like a scream. I could make them run like rabbits, I thought, if I said to them what I really wanted to, but they would only gather again outside and watch for me there. "Onions," I said politely to Mr. Elbert, "coffee, bread, flour. Walnuts," I said, "and sugar; we are very low on sugar." Somewhere behind me there was a little horrified laugh, and Mr. Elbert glanced past me, briefly, and then to the items he was arranging on the counter. In a minute Mrs. Elbert would bring my chicken and my meat, wrapped, and set them down by the other things; I need not turn around until I was ready to go. "Two quarts of milk," I said. "A half pint of cream, a pound of butter." The Harrises had stopped delivering dairy goods to us six years ago and I brought milk and butter home from the grocery now. "And a dozen eggs." Constance had forgotten to put eggs on the list, but there had been only two at home. "A box of peanut brittle," I said; Uncle Julian would clatter and crunch over his papers tonight, and go to bed sticky.

"The Blackwoods always did set a fine table." That was Mrs. Donell, speaking clearly from somewhere behind me, and someone giggled and someone else said "Shh." I never turned; it was enough to feel them all there in back of me without looking into their flat grey faces with the hating eyes. I wish you were all dead, I thought, and longed to say it out loud. Constance said, "Never let them see that you care," and "If you pay any attention they'll only get worse," and probably it was true, but I wished they were dead. I would have liked to come into the grocery some morning and see them all, even the Elberts and the children, lying there crying with the pain and dying. I would then help myself to groceries, I thought, stepping over their bodies, taking whatever I fancied from the shelves, and go home, with perhaps a kick for Mrs. Donell while she lay there. I was never sorry when I had thoughts like this; I only wished they would come true. "It's wrong to hate them," Constance said, "it only weakens *you*," but I hated them anyway, and wondered why it had been worth while creating them in the first place.

Mr. Elbert put all my groceries together on the counter and waited, looking past me into the distance. "That's all I want today," I told him, and without looking at me he wrote the prices on a slip and added, then passed the slip to me so I could make sure he had not cheated me. I always made a point of checking his figures carefully, although he never made a mistake; there were not many things I could do to get back at them, but I did what I could. The groceries filled my shopping bag and another bag besides, but there was no way of getting them home except by carrying them. No one would ever offer to help me, of course, even if I would let them.

Lose two turns. With my library books and my groceries, going slowly, I had to walk down the sidewalk past the general store and into Stella's. I stopped in the doorway of the grocery, feeling around inside myself for some thought to make me safe. Behind me the little stirrings and coughings began. They were getting ready to talk again, and across the width of the store the Elberts were probably rolling their eyes at each other in relief. I froze my face hard. Today I was going to think about taking our lunch out into the garden, and while I kept my eyes open just enough to see where I was walking— our mother's brown shoes going up and down—in my mind I was setting the table with a green cloth and bringing out yellow dishes and strawberries in a white bowl. Yellow dishes, I thought, feeling the eyes of the men looking at me as I went by, and Uncle Julian shall have a nice soft egg with toast broken into it, and I will remember to ask Constance to put a shawl across his shoulders because it is still very early spring. Without looking I could see the grinning and the gesturing; I wished they were all dead and I was walking on their bodies. They rarely spoke directly to me, but only to each other. "That's one of the Blackwood girls," I heard one of them say in a high mocking voice, "one of the Blackwood girls from Blackwood Farm." "Too bad about the Blackwoods," someone else said, just loud enough, "too bad about those poor girls." "Nice farm out there," they said, "nice land to farm. Man could get rich, farming the Blackwood land. If he had a million years and three heads, and didn't care what grew, a man could get rich. Keep their land pretty well locked up, the Blackwoods do." "Man could get rich." "Too bad about the Blackwood girls." "Never can tell what'll grow on Blackwood land."

I am walking on their bodies, I thought, we are having lunch in the garden and Uncle Julian is wearing his shawl. I always held my groceries carefully along here, because one terrible morning I had dropped the shopping bag and the eggs broke and the milk spilled and I gathered up what I could while they shouted, telling myself that whatever I did I would not run away, shovelling cans and boxes and spilled sugar wildly back into the shopping bag, telling myself not to run away.

In front of Stella's there was a crack in the sidewalk that looked like a finger pointing; the crack had always been there. Other landmarks, like the handprint Johnny Harris made in the concrete foundation of the town hall and the Mueller boy's initials on the library porch, had been put in in times that I remembered; I was in the third grade at the school when the town hall was built. But the crack in the sidewalk in front of Stella's had always been there, just as Stella's had always been there. I remember roller-skating across the crack, and being careful not to step on it or it would break our mother's back, and riding a bicycle past here with my hair flying behind; the villagers had not openly disliked us then although our father said they were trash. Our mother told me once that the crack was here when she was a girl in the Rochester house, so it must have been here when she married our father and went to live on Blackwood Farm, and I suppose the crack was there, like a finger pointing, from the time when the village was first put together out of old grey wood and the ugly people with their evil faces were brought from some impossible place and set down in the houses to live.

Stella bought the coffee urn and put in the marble counter with the insurance money when her husband died, but otherwise there had been no change in Stella's since I could remember; Constance and I had come in here to spend pennies after school and every afternoon we picked up the newspaper to take home for our father to read in the evening; we no longer bought newspapers, but Stella still sold them, along with magazines and penny candy and grey postcards of the town hall.

"Good morning, Mary Katherine," Stella said when I sat down at the counter and put my groceries on the floor; I sometimes thought when I wished all the village people dead that I might spare Stella because she was the closest to kind that any of them could be, and the only one who managed to keep hold of any color at all. She was round and pink and when she put on a bright print dress it stayed looking bright for a little while before it merged into the dirty grey of the rest. "How are you today?" she asked.

"Very well, thank you."

"And Constance Blackwood, is she well?"

"Very well, thank you."

"And how is *he*?"

"As well as can be expected. Black coffee, please." I really preferred sugar and cream in my coffee, because it is such bitter stuff, but since I only came here out of pride I needed to accept only the barest minimum for token.

If anyone came into Stella's while I was there I got up and left quietly, but some days I had bad luck. This morning she had only set my coffee down on the counter when there was a shadow against the doorway, and Stella looked up, and said, "Good morning, Jim." She went down to the other end of the counter and waited, expecting him to sit down there so I could leave without being noticed, but it was Jim Donell and I knew at once that today I had bad luck. Some of the people in the village had real faces that I knew and could hate individually; Jim Donell and his wife were among these, because they were deliberate instead of just hating dully and from habit like the others. Most people would have stayed down at the end of the counter where Stella waited, but Jim Donell came right to the end where I was sitting and took the stool next to me, as close to me as he could come because, I knew, he wanted this morning to be bad luck for me.

"They tell me," he said, swinging to sit sideways on his stool and look at me directly, "they tell me you're moving away."

I wished he would not sit so close to me; Stella came toward us on the inside of the counter and I wished she would ask him to move so I could get up and leave without having to struggle around him. "They tell me you're moving away," he said solemnly.

"No," I said, because he was waiting.

"Funny," he said, looking from me to Stella and then back. "I could have swore someone told me you'd be going soon."

"No," I said.

"Coffee, Jim?" Stella asked.

"Who do you think would of started a story like that, Stella? Who do you think would want to tell me they're moving away when they're not doing any such thing?" Stella shook her head at him, but she was trying not to smile. I saw that my hands were tearing at the paper napkin in my lap, ripping off a little corner, and I forced my hands to be still and made a rule for myself: Whenever I saw a tiny scrap of paper I was to remember to be kinder to Uncle Julian.

"Can't ever tell how gossip gets around," Jim Donell said. Perhaps someday soon Jim Donell would die; perhaps there was already a rot growing inside him that was going to kill him. "Did you ever hear anything like the gossip in this town?" he asked Stella.

"Leave her alone, Jim," Stella said.

Uncle Julian was an old man and he was dying, dying regrettably, more surely than Jim Donell and Stella and anyone else. The poor old Uncle Julian was dying and I made a firm rule to be kinder to him. We would have a picnic lunch on the lawn. Constance would bring his shawl and put it over his shoulders, and I would lie on the grass.

"I'm not bothering anybody, Stell. Am I bothering anybody? I'm just asking Miss Mary Katherine Blackwood here how it happens everyone in town is saying she and her big sister are going to be leaving us soon. Moving away. Going somewheres else to live." He stirred his coffee; from the corner of my eye I could see the spoon going around and around and around, and I wanted to laugh. There was something so simple and silly about the spoon going around while Jim Donell talked; I wondered if he would stop talking if I reached out and took hold of the spoon. Very likely he would, I told myself wisely, very likely he would throw the coffee in my face.

"Going somewheres else," he said sadly.

"Cut it out," Stella said.

I would listen more carefully when Uncle Julian told his story. I was already bringing peanut brittle; that was good.

"Here I was all upset," Jim Donell said, "thinking the town would be losing one of its fine old families. That would be really too bad." He swung the other way around on the stool because someone else was coming through the doorway; I was looking at my hands in my lap and of course would not turn around to see who was coming, but then Jim Donell said "Joe," and I knew it was Dunham, the carpenter; "Joe, you ever hear anything like this? Here all over town they're saying that the Blackwoods are moving away, and now Miss Mary

Katherine Blackwood sits right here and speaks up and tells me they're not."

There was a little silence. I knew that Dunham was scowling, looking at Jim Donell and at Stella and at me, thinking over what he had heard, sorting out the words and deciding what each one meant. "That so?" he said at last.

"Listen, you two," Stella said, but Jim Donell went right on, talking with his back to me, and his legs stretched out so I could not get past him and outside. "I was saying to people only this morning it's too bad when the old families go. Although you could rightly say a good number of the Blackwoods are gone already." He laughed, and slapped the counter, with his hand. "Gone already," he said again. The spoon in his cup was still, but he was talking on. "A village loses a lot of style when the fine old people go. Anyone would think," he said slowly, "that they wasn't wanted."

"That's right," Dunham said, and he laughed.

"The way they live up in their fine old private estate, with their fences and their private path and their stylish way of living." He always went on until he was tired. When Jim Donell thought of something to say he said it as often and in as many ways as possible, perhaps because he had very few ideas and had to wring each one dry. Besides, each time he repeated himself he thought it was funnier; I knew he might go on like this until he was really sure that no one was listening any more, and I made a rule for myself: Never think anything more than once, and I put my hands quietly in my lap. I am living on the moon, I told myself, I have a little house all by myself on the moon.

"Well," Jim Donell said; he smelled, too. "I can always tell people I used to know the Blackwoods. They never did anything to *me* that I can remember, always perfectly polite to *me*. Not," he said, and laughed, "that I ever got invited to take my dinner with them, nothing like that."

"That's enough right there," Stella said, and her voice was sharp. "You go pick on someone else, Jim Donell."

"Was I picking on anyone? You think I *wanted* to be asked to dinner? You think I'm *crazy?*"

"Me," Dunham said, "I can always tell people I fixed their broken step once and never got paid for it." That was true.

Constance had sent me out to tell him that we wouldn't pay carpenter's prices for a raw board nailed crookedly across the step when what he was supposed to do was build it trim and new. When I went out and told him we wouldn't pay he grinned at me and spat, and picked up his hammer and pried the board loose and threw it on the ground. "Do it yourself," he said to me, and got into his truck and drove away. "Never did get paid for it," he said now.

"That must of been an oversight, Joe. You just go right up and speak to Miss Constance Blackwood and she'll see you get what's coming to you. Just if you get invited to dinner, Joe, you just be sure and say no thank you to Miss Blackwood."

Dunham laughed. "Not me," he said. "I fixed their step for them and never did get paid for it."

"Funny," Jim Donell said, "them getting the house fixed up and all, and planning to move away all the time."

"Mary Katherine," Stella said, coming down inside the counter to where I was sitting, "you go along home. Just get up off that stool and go along home. There won't be any peace around here until you go."

"Now, *that's* the truth," Jim Donell said. Stella looked at him, and he moved his legs and let me pass. "You just say the word, Miss Mary Katherine, and we'll all come out and help you pack. Just you say the word, Merricat."

"And you can tell your sister from me—" Dunham started to say, but I hurried, and by the time I got outside all I could hear was the laughter, the two of them and Stella.

I liked my house on the moon, and I put a fireplace in it and a garden outside (what would flourish, growing on the moon? I must ask Constance) and I was going to have lunch outside in my garden on the moon. Things on the moon were very bright, and odd colors; my little house would be blue. I watched my small brown feet go in and out, and let the shopping bag swing a little by my side; I had been to Stella's and now I needed only to pass the town hall, which would be empty except for the people who made out dog licenses and the people who counted traffic fines from the drivers who followed the highway into the village and on through, and the people who sent out notices about water and sewage and garbage and forbade other people to burn leaves or to fish;

these would all be buried somewhere deep inside the town hall, working busily together; I had nothing to fear from them unless I fished out of season. I thought of catching scarlet fish in the rivers on the moon and saw that the Harris boys were in their front yard, clamoring and quarrelling with half a dozen other boys. I had not been able to see them until I came past the corner by the town hall, and I could still have turned back and gone the other way, up the main highway to the creek, and then across the creek and home along the other half of the path to our house, but it was late, and I had the groceries, and the creek was nasty to wade in our mother's brown shoes, and I thought, I am living on the moon, and I walked quickly. They saw me at once, and I thought of them rotting away and curling in pain and crying out loud; I wanted them doubled up and crying on the ground in front of me.

"Merricat," they called, "Merricat, Merricat," and moved all together to stand in a line by the fence.

I wondered if their parents taught them, Jim Donell and Dunham and dirty Harris leading regular drills of their children, teaching them with loving care, making sure they pitched their voices right; how else could so many children learn so thoroughly?

> Merricat, said Connie, would you like a cup of tea?
> Oh no, said Merricat, you'll poison me.
> Merricat, said Connie, would you like to go to sleep?
> Down in the boneyard ten feet deep!

I was pretending that I did not speak their language; on the moon we spoke a soft, liquid tongue, and sang in the starlight, looking down on the dead dried world; I was almost halfway past the fence.

"Merricat, Merricat!"

"Where's old Connie—home cooking dinner?"

"Would you like a cup of tea?"

It was strange to be inside myself, walking steadily and rigidly past the fence, putting my feet down strongly but without haste that they might have noticed, to be inside and know that they were looking at me; I was hiding very far inside but I could hear them and see them still from one corner of my eye. I wished they were all lying there dead on the ground.

"Down in the boneyard ten feet deep."

"Merricat!"

Once when I was going past, the Harris boys' mother came out onto the porch, perhaps to see what they were all yelling so about. She stood there for a minute watching and listening and I stopped and looked at her, looking into her flat dull eyes and knowing I must not speak to her and knowing I would. "Can't you make them stop?" I asked her that day, wondering if there was anything in this woman I could speak to, if she had ever run joyfully over grass, or had watched flowers, or known delight or love. "Can't you make them stop?"

"Kids," she said, not changing her voice or her look or her air of dull enjoyment, "don't call the lady names."

"Yes, ma," one of the boys said soberly.

"Don't go near no fence. Don't call no lady names."

And I walked on, while they shrieked and shouted and the woman stood on the porch and laughed.

> Merricat, said Connie, would you like a cup of tea?
> Oh, no, said Merricat, you'll poison me.

Their tongues will burn, I thought, as though they had eaten fire. Their throats will burn when the words come out, and in their bellies they will feel a torment hotter than a thousand fires.

"Goodbye, Merricat," they called as I went by the end of the fence, "don't hurry back."

"Goodbye, Merricat, give our love to Connie."

"Goodbye, Merricat," but I was at the black rock and there was the gate to our path.

2

I HAD to put down the shopping bag to open the lock on the gate; it was a simple padlock and any child could have broken it, but on the gate was a sign saying PRIVATE NO TRESPASSING and no one could go past that. Our father had put up the signs and the gates and the locks when he closed off the path; before, everyone used the path as a short-cut from the village to the highway four-corners where the bus stopped; it saved them perhaps a quarter of a mile to use our path and walk past our front door. Our mother disliked the sight of anyone who wanted to walking past our front door, and when our father brought her to live in the Blackwood house, one of the first things he had to do was close off the path and fence in the entire Blackwood property, from the highway to the creek. There was another gate at the other end of the path, although I rarely went that way, and that gate too had a padlock and a sign saying PRIVATE NO TRESPASSING. "The highway's built for common people," our mother said, "and my front door is private."

Anyone who came to see us, properly invited, came up the main drive which led straight from the gateposts on the highway up to our front door. When I was small I used to lie in my bedroom at the back of the house and imagine the driveway and the path as a crossroad meeting before our front door, and up and down the driveway went the good people, the clean and rich ones dressed in satin and lace, who came rightfully to visit, and back and forth along the path, sneaking and weaving and sidestepping servilely, went the people from the village. They can't get in, I used to tell myself over and over, lying in my dark room with the trees patterned in shadow on the ceiling, they can't ever get in any more; the path is closed forever. Sometimes I stood inside the fence, hidden by the bushes, and watched people walking on the highway to get from the village to the four corners. As far as I knew, no one from the village had ever tried to use the path since our father locked the gates.

When I had moved the shopping bag inside, I carefully locked the gate again, and tested the padlock to make sure it held. Once the padlock was securely fastened behind me I was safe. The path was dark, because once our father had given up any idea of putting his land to profitable use he had let the trees and bushes and small flowers grow as they chose, and except for one great meadow and the gardens our land was heavily wooded, and no one knew its secret ways but me. When I went along the path, going easily now because I was home, I knew each step and every turn. Constance could put names to all the growing things, but I was content to know them by their way and place of growing, and their unfailing offers of refuge. The only prints on the path were my own, going in and out to the village. Past the turn I might find a mark of Constance's foot, because she sometimes came that far to wait for me, but most of Constance's prints were in the garden and in the house. Today she had come to the end of the garden, and I saw her as soon as I came around the turn; she was standing with the house behind her, in the sunlight, and I ran to meet her.

"Merricat," she said, smiling at me, "look how far I came today."

"It's too far," I said. "First thing I know you'll be following me into the village."

"I might, at that," she said.

Even though I knew she was teasing me I was chilled, but I laughed. "You wouldn't like it much," I told her. "Here, lazy, take some of these packages. Where's my cat?"

"He went off chasing butterflies because you were late. Did you remember eggs? I forgot to tell you."

"Of course. Let's have lunch on the lawn."

When I was small I thought Constance was a fairy princess. I used to try to draw her picture, with long golden hair and eyes as blue as the crayon could make them, and a bright pink spot on either cheek; the pictures always surprised me, because she *did* look like that; even at the worst time she was pink and white and golden, and nothing had ever seemed to dim the brightness of her. She was the most precious person in my world, always. I followed her across the soft grass, past the flowers she tended, into our house, and Jonas, my cat, came out of the flowers and followed me.

Constance waited inside the tall front door while I came up

the steps behind her, and then I put my packages down on the table in the hall and locked the door. We would not use it again until afternoon, because almost all of our life was lived toward the back of the house, on the lawn and the garden where no one else ever came. We left the front of the house turned toward the highway and the village, and went our own ways behind its stern, unwelcoming face. Although we kept the house well, the rooms we used together were the back ones, the kitchen and the back bedrooms and the little warm room off the kitchen where Uncle Julian lived; outside was Constance's chestnut tree and the wide, lovely reach of lawn and Constance's flowers and then, beyond, the vegetable garden Constance tended and, past that, the trees which shaded the creek. When we sat on the back lawn no one could see us from anywhere.

I remembered that I was to be kinder to Uncle Julian when I saw him sitting at his great old desk in the kitchen corner playing with his papers. "Will you let Uncle Julian have peanut brittle?" I asked Constance.

"After his lunch," Constance said. She took the groceries carefully from the bags; food of any kind was precious to Constance, and she always touched foodstuffs with quiet respect. I was not allowed to help; I was not allowed to prepare food, nor was I allowed to gather mushrooms, although I sometimes carried vegetables in from the garden, or apples from the old trees. "We'll have muffins," Constance said, almost singing because she was sorting and putting away the food. "Uncle Julian will have an egg, done soft and buttery, and a muffin and a little pudding."

"Pap," said Uncle Julian.

"Merricat will have something lean and rich and salty."

"Jonas will catch me a mouse," I said to my cat on my knee.

"I'm always so happy when you come home from the village," Constance said; she stopped to look and smile at me. "Partly because you bring home food, of course. But partly because I miss you."

"I'm always happy to get home from the village," I told her.

"Was it very bad?" She touched my cheek quickly with one finger.

"You don't want to know about it."

"Someday I'll go." It was the second time she had spoken of going outside, and I was chilled.

"Constance," Uncle Julian said. He lifted a small scrap of paper from his desk and studied it, frowning. "I do not seem to have any information on whether your father took his cigar in the garden as usual that morning."

"I'm sure he did," Constance said. "That cat's been fishing in the creek," she told me. "He came in all mud." She folded the grocery bag and put it with the others in the drawer, and set the library books on the shelf where they were going to stay forever. Jonas and I were expected to stay in our corner, out of the way, while Constance worked in the kitchen, and it was a joy to watch her, moving beautifully in the sunlight, touching foods so softly. "It's Helen Clarke's day," I said. "Are you frightened?"

She turned to smile at me. "Not a bit," she said. "I'm getting better all the time, I think. And today I'm going to make little rum cakes."

"And Helen Clarke will scream and gobble them."

Even now, Constance and I still saw some small society, visiting acquaintances who drove up the driveway to call. Helen Clarke took her tea with us on Fridays, and Mrs. Shepherd or Mrs. Rice or old Mrs. Crowley stopped by occasionally on a Sunday after church to tell us we would have enjoyed the sermon. They came dutifully, although we never returned their calls, and stayed a proper few minutes and sometimes brought flowers from their gardens, or books, or a song that Constance might care to try over on her harp; they spoke politely and with little runs of laughter, and never failed to invite us to their houses although they knew we would never come. They were civil to Uncle Julian, and patient with his talk, they offered to take us for drives in their cars, they referred to themselves as our friends. Constance and I always spoke well of them to each other, because they believed that their visits brought us pleasure. They never walked on the path. If Constance offered them a cutting from a rosebush, or invited them to see a happy new arrangement of colors, they went into the garden, but they never offered to step beyond their defined areas; they walked along the garden and got into their cars by the front door and drove away down the driveway and out through the big gates. Several times Mr. and Mrs. Carrington had come to see how we were getting along, because Mr. Carrington had been a very good friend of our father's. They never came inside or took any refreshment, but they drove to the front steps and sat in their car and talked for a few minutes. "How are you getting along?" they always asked, looking from Constance to me and back; "how are you managing all by yourselves? Is there anything you need, anything we can do? How are you getting along?" Constance always invited them in, because we had been brought up to believe that it was discourteous to keep guests talking outside, but the Carringtons never came into the house. "I wonder," I said, thinking about them, "whether the Carringtons would bring me a horse if I asked them. I could ride it in the long meadow."

Constance turned and looked at me for a minute, frowning a little. "You will not ask them," she said at last. "We do not ask from anyone. Remember that."

"I was teasing," I said, and she smiled again. "I really only want a winged horse, anyway. We could fly you to the moon and back, my horse and I."

"I remember when you used to want a griffin," she said. "Now, Miss Idleness, run out and set the table."

"They quarrelled hatefully that last night," Uncle Julian said. "'I won't have it,' she said, 'I won't stand for it, John Blackwood,' and 'We have no choice,' he said. I listened at the door, of course, but I came too late to hear what they quarrelled about; I suppose it was money."

"They didn't often quarrel," Constance said.

"They were almost invariably civil to one another, Niece, if that is what you mean by not quarrelling; a most unsatisfactory example for the rest of us. My wife and I preferred to shout."

"It hardly seems like six years, sometimes," Constance said. I took the yellow tablecloth and went outside to the lawn to start the table; behind me I heard her saying to Uncle Julian, "Sometimes I feel I would give anything to have them all back again."

When I was a child I used to believe that someday I would grow up and be tall enough to touch the tops of the windows in our mother's drawing room. They were summer windows, because the house was really intended to be only a summer house and our father had only put in a heating system because there was no other house for our family to move to in the winters; by rights we should have had the Rochester house in the village, but that was long lost to us. The windows in the drawing room of our house reached from the floor to the ceiling, and I could never touch the top; our mother used to tell visitors that the light blue silk drapes on the windows had been made up fourteen feet long. There were two tall windows in the drawing room and two tall windows in the dining room across the hall, and from the outside they looked narrow and thin and gave the house a gaunt high look. Inside, however, the drawing room was lovely. Our mother had brought golden-legged chairs from the Rochester house, and her harp was here, and the room shone in reflections from mirrors and sparkling glass. Constance and I only used the room when Helen Clarke came for tea, but we kept it perfectly. Constance stood on a stepladder to wash the tops of the windows, and we dusted the Dresden figurines on the mantel, and with a cloth on the end of a broom I went around the wedding-cake trim at the tops of the walls, staring up into the white fruit and leaves, brushing away at cupids and ribbon knots, dizzy always from looking up and walking backward, and laughing at Constance when she caught me. We polished the floors and mended tiny tears in the rose brocade on the sofas and chairs. There was a golden valance over each high window, and golden scrollwork around the fireplace, and our mother's portrait hung in the drawing room; "I cannot bear to see my lovely room untidy," our mother used to say, and so Constance and I had never been allowed in here, but now we kept it shining and silky.

Our mother had always served tea to her friends from a low table at one side of the fireplace, so that was where Constance always set her table. She sat on the rose sofa with our mother's portrait looking down on her, and I sat in my small chair in the corner and watched. I was allowed to carry cups and saucers and pass sandwiches and cakes, but not to pour tea. I disliked eating anything while people were looking at me, so I had my tea afterwards, in the kitchen. That day, which was the last time Helen Clarke ever came for tea, Constance had set the table as usual, with the lovely thin rose-colored cups our mother had always used, and two silver dishes, one with small sandwiches and one with the very special rum cakes; two rum cakes were waiting for me in the kitchen, in case Helen Clarke ate all of these. Constance sat quietly on the sofa; she never fidgeted, and her hands were neatly in her lap. I waited by the window, watching for Helen Clarke, who was always precisely on time. "Are you frightened?" I asked Constance once, and she said, "No, not at all." Without turning I could hear from her voice that she was quiet.

I saw the car turn into the driveway and then saw that there were two people in it instead of one; "Constance," I said, "she's brought someone else."

Constance was still for a minute, and then she said quite firmly, "I think it will be all right."

I turned to look at her, and she was quiet. "I'll send them away," I said. "She knows better than this."

"No," Constance said. "I really think it will be all right. You watch me."

"But I won't *have* you frightened."

"Sooner or later," she said, "sooner or later I will have to take a first step."

I was chilled. "I want to send them away."

"No," Constance said. "Absolutely not."

The car stopped in front of the house, and I went into the hall to open the front door, which I had unlocked earlier because it was not courteous to unlock the door in a guest's face. When I came onto the porch I saw that it was not quite as bad as I had expected; it was not a stranger Helen Clarke had with her, but little Mrs. Wright, who had come once before and been more frightened than anyone else. She would not be too much for Constance, but Helen Clarke ought not to have brought her without telling me.

"Good afternoon, Mary Katherine," Helen Clarke said, coming around the car and to the steps, "isn't this a lovely spring day? How is dear Constance? I brought Lucille." She was going to handle it brazenly, as though people brought almost-strangers every day to see Constance, and I disliked having to smile at her. "You remember Lucille Wright?" she asked me, and poor little Mrs. Wright said in a small voice that she had so wanted to come again. I held the front door open and they came into the hall. They had not worn coats because it was such a fine day, but Helen Clarke had the common sense to delay a minute anyway; "Tell dear Constance we've come," she said to me, and I knew she was giving me time to tell Constance who was here, so I slipped into the drawing room, where Constance sat quietly, and said, "It's Mrs. Wright, the frightened one."

Constance smiled. "Kind of a weak first step," she said. "It's going to be fine, Merricat."

In the hall Helen Clarke was showing off the staircase to Mrs. Wright, telling the familiar story about the carving and the wood brought from Italy; when I came out of the drawing room she glanced at me and then said, "This staircase is one of the wonders of the county, Mary Katherine. Shame to keep it hidden from the world. Lucille?" They moved into the drawing room.

Constance was perfectly composed. She rose and smiled and said she was glad to see them. Because Helen Clarke was ungraceful by nature, she managed to make the simple act of moving into a room and sitting down a complex ballet for three people; before Constance had quite finished speaking Helen Clarke jostled Mrs. Wright and sent Mrs. Wright sideways like a careening croquet ball off into the far corner of the room where she sat abruptly and clearly without intention upon a small and uncomfortable chair. Helen Clarke made for the sofa where Constance sat, nearly upsetting the tea table, and although there were enough chairs in the room and another sofa, she sat finally uncomfortably close to Constance, who detested having anyone near her but me. "Now," Helen Clarke said, spreading, "it's good to see you again."

"So kind of you to have us," Mrs. Wright said, leaning forward. "Such a lovely staircase."

"You look well, Constance. Have you been working in the garden?"

"I couldn't help it, on a day like this." Constance laughed; she was doing very well. "It's so exciting," she said across to Mrs. Wright. "Perhaps you're a gardener, too? These first bright days are so exciting for a gardener."

She was talking a little too much and a little too fast, but no one noticed it except me.

"I do love a garden," Mrs. Wright said in a little burst. "I do so love a garden."

"How is Julian?" Helen Clarke asked before Mrs. Wright had quite finished speaking. "How is old Julian?"

"Very well, thank you. He is expecting to join us for a cup of tea this afternoon."

"Have you met Julian Blackwood?" Helen Clarke asked Mrs. Wright, and Mrs. Wright, shaking her head, began, "I would love to meet him, of course; I have heard so much—" and stopped.

"He's a touch . . . eccentric," Helen Clarke said, smiling at Constance as though it had been a secret until now. I was thinking that if eccentric meant, as the dictionary said it did, *deviating from regularity*, it was Helen Clarke who was far more eccentric than Uncle Julian, with her awkward movements and her unexpected questions, and her bringing strangers here to tea; Uncle Julian lived smoothly, in a perfectly planned pattern, rounded and sleek. She ought not to call people things they're not, I thought, remembering that I was to be kinder to Uncle Julian.

"Constance, you've always been one of my closest friends," she was saying now, and I wondered at her; she really could not see how Constance withdrew from such words. "I'm going to give you just a word of advice, and remember, it comes from a friend."

I must have known what she was going to say, because I was chilled; all this day had been building up to what Helen Clarke was going to say right now. I sat low in my chair and looked hard at Constance, wanting her to get up and run away, wanting her not to hear what was just about to be said, but Helen Clarke went on, "It's spring, you're young, you're lovely, you have a right to be happy. Come back into the world."

Once, even a month ago when it was still winter, words like that would have made Constance draw back and run away; now, I saw that she was listening and smiling, although she shook her head.

"You've done penance long enough," Helen Clarke said.

"I would so like to give a little luncheon—" Mrs. Wright began.

"You've forgotten the milk; I'll get it." I stood up and spoke directly to Constance and she looked around at me, almost surprised.

"Thank you, dear," she said.

I went out of the drawing room and into the hall and started toward the kitchen; this morning the kitchen had been bright and happy and now, chilled, I saw that it was dreary. Constance had looked as though suddenly, after all this time of refusing and denying, she had come to see that it might be possible, after all, to go outside. I realized now that this was the third time in one day that the subject had been touched, and three times makes it real. I could not breathe; I was tied with wire, and my head was huge and going to explode; I ran to the back door and opened it to breathe. I wanted to run; if I could have run to the end of our land and back I would have been all right, but Constance was alone with them in the drawing room and I had to hurry back. I had to content myself with smashing the milk pitcher which waited on the table; it had been our mother's and I left the pieces on the floor so Constance would see them. I took down the second-best milk pitcher, which did not match the cups; I was allowed to pour milk, so I filled it and took it to the drawing room.

"—do with Mary Katherine?" Constance was saying, and then she turned and smiled at me in the doorway. "Thank you, dear," she said, and glanced at the milk pitcher and at me. "Thank you," she said again, and I put the pitcher down on the tray.

"Not too much at first," Helen Clarke said. "That *would* look odd, I grant you. But a call or two on old friends, perhaps a day in the city shopping—no one would recognize you in the city, you know."

"A little luncheon?" Mrs. Wright said hopefully.

"I'll have to think." Constance made a little, laughing, bewildered gesture, and Helen Clarke nodded.

"You'll need some clothes," she said.

I came from my place in the corner to take a cup of tea from Constance and carry it over to Mrs. Wright, whose hand trembled when she took it. "Thank you, my dear," she said. I could see the tea trembling in the cup; it was only her second visit here, after all.

"Sugar?" I asked her; I couldn't help it, and besides, it was polite.

"Oh, no," she said. "No, thank you. No sugar."

I thought, looking at her, that she had dressed to come here today; Constance and I never wore black but Mrs. Wright had perhaps thought it was appropriate, and today she wore a plain black dress with a necklace of pearls. She had worn black the other time, too, I recalled; always in good taste, I thought, except in our mother's drawing room. I went back to Constance and took up the plate of rum cakes and brought them to Mrs. Wright; that was not kind either, and she should have had the sandwiches first, but I wanted her to be unhappy, dressed in black in our mother's drawing room. "My sister made these this morning," I said.

"Thank you," she said. Her hand hesitated over the plate and then she took a rum cake and set it carefully on the edge of her saucer. I thought that Mrs. Wright was being almost hysterically polite, and I said, "Do take two. Everything my sister cooks is delicious."

"No," she said. "Oh, no. Thank you."

Helen Clarke was eating sandwiches, reaching down past Constance to take one after another. She wouldn't behave like this anywhere else, I thought, only here. She never cares what Constance thinks or I think of her manners; she only supposes we are so very glad to see her. Go away, I told her in my mind. Go away, go away. I wondered if Helen Clarke saved particular costumes for her visits to our house. "This," I could imagine her saying, turning out her closet, "no sense in throwing *this* away, I can keep it for visiting dear Constance." I began dressing Helen Clarke in my mind, putting her in a bathing suit on a snow bank, setting her high in the hard branches of a tree in a dress of flimsy pink ruffles that caught and pulled and tore; she was tangled in the tree and screaming and I almost laughed.

"Why not ask some people here?" Helen Clarke was saying to Constance. "A few old friends—there are many people who have wanted to keep in touch with you, Constance dear—a few old friends some evening. For dinner? No," she said, "perhaps not for dinner. Perhaps not, not at first."

"I myself—" Mrs. Wright began again; she had set her cup of tea and the little rum cake carefully on the table next to her.

"Although why not for dinner?" Helen Clarke said. "After all, you have to take the plunge sometime."

I was going to have to say something. Constance was not looking at me, but only at Helen Clarke. "Why not invite some good people from the village?" I asked loudly.

"Good heavens, Mary Katherine," Helen Clarke said. "You really startled me." She laughed. "I don't recall that the Blackwoods ever mingled socially with the villagers," she said.

"They hate us," I said.

"*I* don't listen to their gossip, and I hope you don't. And, Mary Katherine, you know as well as I do that nine-tenths of that feeling is nothing but your imagination, and if you'd go halfway to be friendly there'd never be a word said against you. Good heavens. I grant you there might have been a little feeling once, but on your side it's just been exaggerated out of all proportion."

"People *will* gossip," Mrs. Wright said reassuringly.

"I've been saying right along that I was a close friend of the Blackwoods and not the least bit ashamed of it, either. You want to come to people of your *own* kind, Constance. They don't talk about *us*."

I wished they would be more amusing; I thought that now Constance was looking a little tired. If they would leave soon I would brush Constance's hair until she fell asleep.

"Uncle Julian is coming," I said to Constance. I could hear the soft sound of the wheel chair in the hall and I got up to open the door.

Helen Clarke said, "Do you suppose that people would really be afraid to visit here?" and Uncle Julian stopped in the doorway. He had put on his dandyish tie for company at tea, and washed his face until it was pink. "Afraid?" he said. "To visit here?" He bowed to Mrs. Wright from his chair and then to Helen Clarke. "Madam," he said, and "Madam." I knew that he could not remember either of their names, or whether he had ever seen them before.

"You look well, Julian," Helen Clarke said.

"Afraid to visit here? I apologize for repeating your words, madam, but I am astonished. My niece, after all, was acquitted of murder. There could be no possible danger in visiting here *now*."

Mrs. Wright made a little convulsive gesture toward her cup of tea and then set her hands firmly in her lap.

"It could be said that there is danger everywhere," Uncle Julian said. "Danger of poison, certainly. My niece can tell you of the most unlikely perils—garden plants more deadly than snakes and simple herbs that slash like knives through the lining of your belly, madam. My niece—"

"Such a lovely garden," Mrs. Wright said earnestly to Constance. "I'm sure I don't know how you do it."

Helen Clarke said firmly, "Now, that's all been forgotten long ago, Julian. No one ever thinks about it any more."

"Regrettable," Uncle Julian said. "A most fascinating case, one of the few genuine mysteries of our time. Of my time, particularly. My life work," he told Mrs. Wright.

"Julian," Helen Clarke said quickly; Mrs. Wright seemed mesmerized. "There is such a thing as good taste, Julian."

"Taste, madam? Have you ever tasted arsenic? I assure you that there is one moment of utter incredulity before the mind can accept—"

A moment ago poor little Mrs. Wright would probably have bitten her tongue out before she mentioned the subject, but now she said, hardly breathing, "You mean you remember?"

"Remember." Uncle Julian sighed, shaking his head happily. "Perhaps," he said with eagerness, "perhaps you are not familiar with the story? Perhaps I might—"

"Julian," Helen Clarke said, "Lucille does not want to hear it. You should be ashamed to ask her."

I thought that Mrs. Wright very much did want to hear it, and I looked at Constance just as she glanced at me; we were both very sober, to suit the subject, but I knew she was as full of merriment as I; it was good to hear Uncle Julian, who was so lonely most of the time.

And poor, poor Mrs. Wright, tempted at last beyond endurance, was not able to hold it back any longer. She blushed deeply, and faltered, but Uncle Julian was a tempter and Mrs. Wright's human discipline could not resist forever. "It happened right in this house," she said like a prayer.

We were all silent, regarding her courteously, and she whispered, "I *do* beg your pardon."

"Naturally, in this house," Constance said. "In the dining room. We were having dinner."

"A family gathering for the evening meal," Uncle Julian said, caressing his words. "Never supposing it was to be our last."

"Arsenic in the sugar," Mrs. Wright said, carried away, hopelessly lost to all decorum.

"I used that sugar." Uncle Julian shook his finger at her. "I used that sugar myself, on my blackberries. Luckily," and he smiled blandly, "fate intervened. Some of us, that day, she led inexorably through the gates of death. Some of us, innocent and unsuspecting, took, unwillingly, that one last step to oblivion. Some of us took very little sugar."

"I never touch berries," Constance said; she looked directly at Mrs. Wright and said soberly, "I rarely take sugar on anything. Even now."

"It counted strongly against her at the trial," Uncle Julian said. "That she used no sugar, I mean. But my niece has never cared for berries. Even as a child it was her custom to refuse berries."

"Please," Helen Clarke said loudly, "it's *outrageous*, it really is; I can't bear to hear it talked about. Constance—Julian—what will Lucille think of you?"

"No, really," Mrs. Wright said, lifting her hands.

"I won't sit here and listen to another word," Helen Clarke said. "Constance must start thinking about the future; this dwelling on the past is not wholesome; the poor darling has suffered enough."

"Well, I miss them all, of course," Constance said. "Things have been much different with all of them gone, but I'm sure I don't think of myself as suffering."

"In some ways," Uncle Julian sailed on, "a piece of extraordinarily good fortune for me. I am a survivor of the most sensational poisoning case of the century. I have all the newspaper clippings. I knew the victims, the accused, intimately, as only a relative living in the very house *could* know them. I have exhaustive notes on all that happened. I have never been well since."

"I said I didn't want to talk about it," Helen Clarke said.

Uncle Julian stopped. He looked at Helen Clarke, and then at Constance. "Didn't it really happen?" he asked after a minute, fingers at his mouth.

"Of course it really happened." Constance smiled at him.

"I have the newspaper clippings," Uncle Julian said uncertainly. "I have my notes," he told Helen Clarke, "I have written down everything."

"It was a terrible thing." Mrs. Wright was leaning forward earnestly and Uncle Julian turned to her.

"Dreadful," he agreed. "Frightful, madam." He maneuvered his wheel chair so his back was to Helen Clarke. "Would you like to view the dining room?" he asked. "The fatal board? I did not give evidence at the trial, you understand; my health was not equal, then or now, to the rude questions of strangers." He gave a little flick of his head in Helen Clarke's direction. "I wanted badly to take the witness stand. I flatter myself that I would not have appeared to disadvantage. But of course she was acquitted after all."

"Certainly she was acquitted," Helen Clarke said vehemently. She reached for her huge pocketbook and took it up onto her lap and felt in it for her gloves. "No one ever thinks about it any more." She caught Mrs. Wright's eye and prepared to rise.

"The dining room . . . ?" Mrs. Wright said timidly. "Just a glance?"

"Madam." Uncle Julian contrived a bow from his wheel chair, and Mrs. Wright hurried to reach the door and open it for him. "Directly across the hall," Uncle Julian said, and she followed. "I admire a decently curious woman, madam; I could see at once that you were devoured with a passion to view the scene of the tragedy; it happened in this very room, and we still have our dinner in here every night."

We could hear him clearly; he was apparently moving around our dining-room table while Mrs. Wright watched him from the doorway. "You will perceive that our table is round. It is overlarge now for the pitiful remnant of our family, but we have been reluctant to disturb what is, after all, a monument of sorts; at one time, a picture of this room would have commanded a large price from any of the newspapers. We were a large family once, you recall, a large and happy family. We had small disagreements, of course, we were not all of us over-blessed with patience; I might almost say that there were quarrels. Nothing serious; husband and wife, brother and sister, did not always see eye to eye."

"Then why did she—"

"Yes," Uncle Julian said, "that is perplexing, is it not? My brother, as head of the family, sat naturally at the head of the table, there, with the windows at his back and the decanter before him. John Blackwood took pride in his table, his family, his position in the world."

"She never even met him," Helen Clarke said. She looked angrily at Constance. "I remember your father well."

Faces fade away out of memory, I thought. I wondered if I would recognize Mrs. Wright if I saw her in the village. I wondered if Mrs. Wright in the village would walk past me, not seeing; perhaps Mrs. Wright was so timid that she never looked up at faces at all. Her cup of tea and her little rum cake still sat on the table, untouched.

"*And* I was a good friend of your mother's, Constance. That's why I feel able to speak to you openly, for your own good. Your mother would have wanted—"

"—my sister-in-law, who was, madam, a delicate woman. You will have noticed her portrait in the drawing room, and the exquisite line of the jawbone under the skin. A woman born for tragedy, perhaps, although inclined to be a little silly. On her right at this table, myself, younger then, and not an invalid; I have only been helpless since that night. Across from me, the boy Thomas—did you know I once had a nephew, that my brother had a son? Certainly, you would have read about him. He was ten years old and possessed many of his father's more forceful traits of character."

"He used the most sugar," Mrs. Wright said.

"Alas," Uncle Julian said. "Then, on either side of my brother, his daughter Constance and my wife Dorothy, who had done me the honor of casting in her lot with mine, although I do not think that she anticipated anything so severe as arsenic on her blackberries. Another child, my niece Mary Katherine, was not at table."

"She was in her room," Mrs. Wright said.

"A great child of twelve, sent to bed without her supper. But she need not concern us."

I laughed, and Constance said to Helen Clarke, "Merricat was always in disgrace. I used to go up the back stairs with a tray of dinner for her after my father had left the dining room. She was a wicked, disobedient child," and she smiled at me.

"An unhealthy environment," Helen Clarke said. "A child should be punished for wrongdoing, but she should be made to feel that she is still loved. *I* would never have tolerated the child's wildness. And now we really *must* . . ." She began to put on her gloves again.

"—spring lamb roasted, with a mint jelly made from Constance's garden mint. Spring potatoes, new peas, a salad, again from Constance's garden. I remember it perfectly, madam. It is still one of my favorite meals. I have also, of course, made very thorough notes of everything about that meal and, in fact, that entire day. You will see at once how the dinner revolves around my niece. It was early summer, her garden was doing well—the weather was lovely that year, I recall; we have not seen such another summer since, or perhaps I am only getting older. We relied upon Constance for various small delicacies which only she could provide; I am of course not referring to arsenic."

"Well, the blackberries were the important part." Mrs. Wright sounded a little hoarse.

"What a mind you have, madam! So precise, so unerring. I can see that you are going to ask me why she should conceivably have used arsenic. My niece is not capable of such subtlety, and her lawyer luckily said so at the trial. Constance can put her hand upon a bewildering array of deadly substances without ever leaving home; she could feed you a sauce of poison hemlock, a member of the parsley family which produces immediate paralysis and death when eaten. She might have made a marmalade of the lovely thornapple or the baneberry, she might have tossed the salad with *Holcus lanatus*, called velvet grass, and rich in hydrocyanic acid. I have notes on all these, madam. Deadly nightshade is a relative of the tomato;

would we, any of us, have had the prescience to decline if Constance served it to us, spiced and made into pickle? Or consider just the mushroom family, rich as that is in tradition and deception. We were all fond of mushrooms—my niece makes a mushroom omelette you must taste to believe, madam—and the common death cup—"

"She should not have been doing the cooking," said Mrs. Wright strongly.

"Well, of course, there is the root of our trouble. Certainly she should not have been doing the cooking if her intention was to destroy all of us with poison; we would have been blindly unselfish to encourage her to cook under such circumstances. But she was acquitted. Not only of the deed, but of the intention."

"What was wrong with Mrs. Blackwood doing her own cooking?"

"Please." Uncle Julian's voice had a little shudder in it, and I knew the gesture he was using with it even though he was out of my sight. He would have raised one hand, fingers spread, and he would be smiling at her over his fingers; it was a gallant, Uncle Julian, gesture; I had seen him use it with Constance. "I personally preferred to chance the arsenic," Uncle Julian said.

"We must go home," Helen Clarke said. "I don't know what's come over Lucille. I *told* her before we came not to mention this subject."

"I am going to put up wild strawberries this year," Constance said to me. "I noticed a considerable patch of them near the end of the garden."

"It's terribly tactless of her, and she's keeping *me* waiting."

"—the sugar bowl on the sideboard, the heavy silver sugar bowl. It is a family heirloom; my brother prized it highly. You will be wondering about that sugar bowl, I imagine. Is it still in use? you are wondering; has it been cleaned? you may very well ask; was it thoroughly washed? I can reassure you at once. My niece Constance washed it before the doctor or the police had come, and you will allow that it was not a felicitous moment to wash a sugar bowl. The other dishes used at dinner were still on the table, but my niece took the sugar bowl to the kitchen, emptied it, and scrubbed it thoroughly with boiling water. It was a curious act."

"There was a spider in it," Constance said to the teapot. We used a little rose-covered sugar bowl for the lump sugar for tea.

"—there was a spider in it, she said. That was what she told the police. That was why she washed it."

"Well," Mrs. Wright said, "it does seem as though she might have thought of a better reason. Even if it *was* a real spider—I mean, you don't wash—I mean, you just take the spider *out*."

"What reason would *you* have given, madam?"

"Well, I've never killed anybody, so I don't know—I mean, I don't know what I'd say. The first thing that came into my head, I suppose. I mean, she must have been upset."

"I assure you the pangs were fearful; you say you have never tasted arsenic? It is not agreeable. I am extremely sorry for all of them. I myself lingered on in great pain for several days; Constance would, I am sure, have demonstrated only the deepest sympathy for me, but by then, of course, she was largely unavailable. They arrested her at once."

Mrs. Wright sounded more forceful, almost unwillingly eager. "I've always thought, ever since we moved up here, that it would be a wonderful chance to meet you people and *really* find out what happened, because of course there's always that one question, the one nobody has ever been able to answer; of course I hardly expected to *talk* to you about it, but look." There was the sound of a dining-room chair being moved; Mrs. Wright had clearly decided to settle down. "First," she said, "she bought the arsenic."

"To kill rats," Constance said to the teapot, and then turned and smiled at me.

"To kill rats," Uncle Julian said. "The only other popular use for arsenic is in taxidermy, and my niece could hardly pretend a working knowledge of that subject."

"She cooked the dinner, she set the table."

"I confess I am surprised at that woman," Helen Clarke said. "She seems such a quiet little body."

"It was Constance who saw them dying around her like flies —I do beg your pardon—and never called a doctor until it was too late. She washed the sugar bowl."

"There was a spider in it," Constance said.

"She told the police those people deserved to die."

"She was excited, madam. Perhaps the remark was misconstrued. My niece is not hard-hearted; besides, she thought at the time that I was among them and although I deserve to die—we all do, do we not?—I hardly think that my niece is the one to point it out."

"She told the police that it was all her fault."

"Now there," Uncle Julian said, "I think she made a mistake. It was certainly true that she thought at first that her cooking had caused all this, but in taking full blame I think that she was over-eager. I would have advised her against any such attitude had I been consulted; it smacks of self-pity."

"But the great, the unanswered question, is *why*? Why did she do it? I mean, unless we agree that Constance was a homicidal maniac—"

"You have met her, madam."

"I have what? Oh, my goodness yes. I completely forgot. I cannot seem to remember that that pretty young girl is actually—well. Your mass murderer must have a reason, Mr. Blackwood, even if it is only some perverted, twisted—oh, dear. She is such a charming girl, your niece; I cannot remember when I have taken to anyone as I have to her. But if she *is* a homicidal maniac—"

"I'm leaving." Helen Clarke stood up and slammed her pocketbook emphatically under her arm. "Lucille," she said, "I am leaving. We have overstayed all limits of decency; it's after five o'clock."

Mrs. Wright scurried out of the dining room, distraught. "I'm so sorry," she said. "We were chatting and I lost track of time. Oh, dear." She ran to her chair to gather up her pocketbook.

"You haven't even touched your tea," I said, wanting to see her blush.

"Thank you," she said; she looked down at her teacup and blushed. "It was delicious."

Uncle Julian stopped his wheel chair in the center of the room and folded his hands happily before him. He looked at Constance and then raised his eyes to gaze on a corner of the ceiling, sober and demure.

"Julian, goodbye," Helen Clarke said shortly. "Constance, I'm sorry we stayed so long; it was inexcusable. Lucille?"

Mrs. Wright looked like a child who knows it is going to be punished, but she had not forgotten her manners. "Thank you," she said to Constance, putting her hand out and then taking it back again quickly. "I had a very nice time. Goodbye," she said to Uncle Julian. They went into the hall and I followed, to lock the door after they had gone. Helen Clarke started the car before poor Mrs. Wright had quite finished getting herself inside, and the last I heard of Mrs. Wright was a little shriek as the car started down the driveway. I was laughing when I came back into the drawing room, and I went over and kissed Constance. "A very nice tea party," I said.

"That *impossible* woman." Constance put her head back against the couch and laughed. "Ill bred, pretentious, stupid. Why she keeps coming I'll never know."

"She wants to reform you." I took up Mrs. Wright's teacup and her rum cake and brought them over to the tea tray. "Poor little Mrs. Wright," I said.

"You were teasing her, Merricat."

"A little bit, maybe. I can't help it when people are frightened; I always want to frighten them more."

"Constance?" Uncle Julian turned his wheel chair to face her. "How was I?"

"Superb, Uncle Julian." Constance stood up and went over to him and touched his old head lightly. "You didn't need your notes at all."

"It really happened?" he asked her.

"It certainly did. I'll take you in to your room and you can look at your newspaper clippings."

"I think not right now. It has been a superlative afternoon, but I think I am a little tired. I will rest till dinner."

Constance pushed the wheel chair down the hall and I followed with the tea tray. I was allowed to carry dirty dishes but not to wash them, so I set the tray on the kitchen table and watched while Constance stacked the dishes by the sink to wash later, swept up the broken milk pitcher on the floor, and took out the potatoes to start for dinner. Finally I had to ask her; the thought had been chilling me all afternoon. "Are you going to do what she said?" I asked her. "What Helen Clarke said?"

She did not pretend not to understand. She stood there looking down at her hands working, and smiled a little. "I don't know," she said.

3

A CHANGE was coming, and nobody knew it but me. Constance suspected, perhaps; I noticed that she stood occasionally in her garden and looked not down at the plants she was tending, and not back at our house, but outward, toward the trees which hid the fence, and sometimes she looked long and curiously down the length of the driveway, as though wondering how it would feel to walk along it to the gates. I watched her. On Saturday morning, after Helen Clarke had come to tea, Constance looked at the driveway three times. Uncle Julian was not well on Saturday morning, after tiring himself at tea, and stayed in his bed in his warm room next to the kitchen, looking out of the window beside his pillow, calling now and then to make Constance notice him. Even Jonas was fretful—he was running up a storm, our mother used to say— and could not sleep quietly; all during those days when the change was coming Jonas stayed restless. From a deep sleep he would start suddenly, lifting his head as though listening, and then, on his feet and moving in one quick ripple, he ran up the stairs and across the beds and around through the doors in and out and then down the stairs and across the hall and over the chair in the dining room and around the table and through the kitchen and out into the garden where he would slow, sauntering, and then pause to lick a paw and flick an ear and take a look at the day. At night we could hear him running, feel him cross our feet as we lay in bed, running up a storm.

All the omens spoke of change. I woke up on Saturday morning and thought I heard them calling me; they want me to get up, I thought before I came fully awake and remembered that they were dead; Constance never called me to wake up. When I dressed and came downstairs that morning she was waiting to make my breakfast, and I told her, "I thought I heard them calling me this morning."

"Hurry with your breakfast," she said. "It's another lovely day."

After breakfast on the good mornings when I did not have to go into the village I had my work to do. Always on Wednesday mornings I went around the fence. It was necessary for me to check constantly to be sure that the wires were not broken and the gates were securely locked. I could make the repairs myself, winding the wire back together where it had torn, tightening loose strands, and it was a pleasure to know, every Wednesday morning, that we were safe for another week.

On Sunday mornings I examined my safeguards, the box of silver dollars I had buried by the creek, and the doll buried in the long field, and the book nailed to the tree in the pine woods; so long as they were where I had put them nothing could get in to harm us. I had always buried things, even when I was small; I remember that once I quartered the long field and buried something in each quarter to make the grass grow higher as I grew taller, so I would always be able to hide there. I once buried six blue marbles in the creek bed to make the river beyond run dry. "Here is treasure for you to bury," Constance used to say to me when I was small, giving me a penny, or a bright ribbon; I had buried all my baby teeth as they came out one by one and perhaps someday they would grow as dragons. All our land was enriched with my treasures buried in it, thickly inhabited just below the surface with my marbles and my teeth and my colored stones, all perhaps turned to jewels by now, held together under the ground in a powerful taut web which never loosened, but held fast to guard us.

On Tuesdays and Fridays I went into the village, and on Thursday, which was my most powerful day, I went into the big attic and dressed in their clothes.

Mondays we neatened the house, Constance and I, going into every room with mops and dustcloths, carefully setting the little things back after we had dusted, never altering the perfect line of our mother's tortoise-shell comb. Every spring we washed and polished the house for another year, but on Mondays we neatened; very little dust fell in their rooms, but even that little could not be permitted to stay. Sometimes Constance tried to neaten Uncle Julian's room, but Uncle Julian disliked being disturbed and kept his things in their own places, and Constance had to be content with washing his medicine glasses and changing his bed. I was not allowed in Uncle Julian's room.

On Saturday mornings I helped Constance. I was not

allowed to handle knives, but when she worked in the garden
I cared for her tools, keeping them bright and clean, and I carried great baskets of flowers, sometimes, or vegetables which
Constance picked to make into food. The entire cellar of our
house was filled with food. All the Blackwood women had
made food and had taken pride in adding to the great supply
of food in our cellar. There were jars of jam made by great-
grandmothers, with labels in thin pale writing, almost unread-
able by now, and pickles made by great-aunts and vegetables
put up by our grandmother, and even our mother had left
behind her six jars of apple jelly. Constance had worked all her
life at adding to the food in the cellar, and her rows and rows
of jars were easily the handsomest, and shone among the
others. "You bury food the way I bury treasure," I told her
sometimes, and she answered me once: "The food comes from
the ground and can't be permitted to stay there and rot; *something* has to be done with it." All the Blackwood women had
taken the food that came from the ground and preserved it,
and the deeply colored rows of jellies and pickles and bottled
vegetables and fruit, maroon and amber and dark rich green
stood side by side in our cellar and would stand there forever,
a poem by the Blackwood women. Each year Constance and
Uncle Julian and I had jam or preserve or pickle that Constance had made, but we never touched what belonged to the
others; Constance said it would kill us if we ate it.

This Saturday morning I had apricot jam on my toast, and I
thought of Constance making it and putting it away carefully
for me to eat on some bright morning, never dreaming that a
change would be coming before the jar was finished.

"Lazy Merricat," Constance said to me, "stop dreaming
over your toast; I want you in the garden on this lovely day."

She was arranging Uncle Julian's tray, putting his hot milk
into a jug painted with yellow daisies, and trimming his toast
so it would be tiny and hot and square; if anything looked
large, or difficult to eat, Uncle Julian would leave it on the
plate. Constance always took Uncle Julian's tray in to him in
the morning because he slept painfully and sometimes lay
awake in the darkness waiting for the first light and the comfort of Constance with his tray. Some nights, when his heart
hurt him badly, he might take one more pill than usual, and

then lie all morning drowsy and dull, unwilling to sip from his hot milk, but wanting to know that Constance was busy in the kitchen next door to his bedroom, or in the garden where he could see her from his pillow. On his very good mornings she brought him into the kitchen for his breakfast, and he would sit at his old desk in the corner, spilling crumbs among his notes, studying his papers while he ate. "If I am spared," he always said to Constance, "I will write the book myself. If not, see that my notes are entrusted to some worthy cynic who will not be too concerned with the truth."

I wanted to be kinder to Uncle Julian, so this morning I hoped he would enjoy his breakfast and later come out into the garden in his wheel chair and sit in the sun. "Maybe there will be a tulip open today," I said, looking out through the open kitchen door into the bright sunlight.

"Not until tomorrow, I think," said Constance, who always knew. "Wear your boots if you wander today; it will still be quite wet in the woods."

"There's a change coming," I said.

"It's spring, silly," she said, and took up Uncle Julian's tray. "Don't run off while I'm gone; there's work to be done."

She opened Uncle Julian's door and I heard her say good morning to him. When he said good morning back his voice was old and I knew that he was not well. Constance would have to stay near him all day.

"Is your father home yet, child?" he asked her.

"No, not today," Constance said. "Let me get your other pillow. It's a lovely day."

"He's a busy man," Uncle Julian said. "Bring me a pencil, my dear; I want to make a note of that. He's a very busy man."

"Take some hot milk; it will make you warm."

"You're not Dorothy. You're my niece Constance."

"Drink."

"Good morning, Constance."

"Good morning, Uncle Julian."

I decided that I would choose three powerful words, words of strong protection, and so long as these great words were never spoken aloud no change would come. I wrote the first word—*melody*—in the apricot jam on my toast with the handle of a spoon and then put the toast in my mouth and ate it very quickly. I was one-third safe. Constance came out of Uncle Julian's room carrying the tray.

"He's not well this morning," she said. "He left most of his breakfast and he's very tired."

"If I had a winged horse I could fly him to the moon; he would be more comfortable there."

"Later I'll take him out into the sunshine, and perhaps make him a little eggnog."

"Everything's safe on the moon."

She looked at me distantly. "Dandelion greens," she said. "And radishes. I thought of working in the vegetable garden this morning, but I don't want to leave Uncle Julian. I hope that the carrots . . ." She tapped her fingers on the table, thinking. "Rhubarb," she said.

I carried my breakfast dishes over to the sink and set them down; I was deciding on my second magic word, which I thought might very well be *Gloucester*. It was strong, and I thought it would do, although Uncle Julian might take it into his head to say almost anything and no word was truly safe when Uncle Julian was talking.

"Why not make a pie for Uncle Julian?"

Constance smiled. "You mean, why not make a pie for Merricat? Shall I make a rhubarb pie?"

"Jonas and I dislike rhubarb."

"But it has the prettiest colors of all; nothing is so pretty on the shelves as rhubarb jam."

"Make it for the shelves, then. Make me a dandelion pie."

"Silly Merricat," Constance said. She was wearing her blue dress, the sunlight was patterned on the kitchen floor, and color was beginning to show in the garden outside. Jonas sat on the step, washing, and Constance began to sing as she turned to wash the dishes. I was two-thirds safe, with only one magic word to find.

Later Uncle Julian still slept and Constance thought to take five minutes and run down to the vegetable garden to gather what she could; I sat at the kitchen table listening for Uncle Julian so I could call Constance if he awakened, but when she came back he was still quiet. I ate tiny sweet raw carrots while Constance washed the vegetables and put them away. "We will have a spring salad," she said.

"We eat the year away. We eat the spring and the summer and the fall. We wait for something to grow and then we eat it."

"Silly Merricat," Constance said.

At twenty minutes after eleven by the kitchen clock she took off her apron, glanced in at Uncle Julian, and went, as she always did, upstairs to her room to wait until I called her. I went to the front door and unlocked it and opened it just as the doctor's car turned into the drive. He was in a hurry, always, and he stopped his car quickly and ran up the steps; "Good morning, Miss Blackwood," he said, going past me and down the hall, and by the time he had reached the kitchen he had his coat off and was ready to put it over the back of one of the kitchen chairs. He went directly to Uncle Julian's room without a glance at me or at the kitchen, and then when he opened Uncle Julian's door he was suddenly still, and gentle. "Good morning, Mr. Blackwood," he said, his voice easy, "how are things today?"

"Where's the old fool?" Uncle Julian said, as he always did. "Why didn't Jack Mason come?"

Dr. Mason was the one Constance called the night they all died.

"Dr. Mason couldn't make it today," the doctor said, as he always did. "I'm Dr. Levy. I've come to see you instead."

"Rather have Jack Mason."

"I'll do the best I can."

"Always said I'd outlive the old fool." Uncle Julian laughed thinly. "Why are you pretending with me? Jack Mason died three years ago."

"Mr. Blackwood," the doctor said, "it is a pleasure to have you as a patient." He closed the door very quietly. I thought of using *digitalis* as my third magic word, but it was too easy for someone to say, and at last I decided on *Pegasus*. I took a glass from the cabinet, and said the word very distinctly into the glass, then filled it with water and drank. Uncle Julian's door opened, and the doctor stood in the doorway for a minute.

"Remember, now," he said. "And I'll see you next Saturday."

"Quack," Uncle Julian said.

The doctor turned, smiling, and then the smile disappeared and he began to hurry again. He took up his coat and went off down the hall. I followed him and by the time I came to the front door he was already going down the steps. "Goodbye, Miss Blackwood," he said, not looking around, and got into his car and started at once, going faster and faster until he reached the gates and turned onto the highway. I locked the front door and went to the foot of the stairs. "Constance?" I called.

"Coming," she said from upstairs. "Coming, Merricat."

Uncle Julian was better later in the day, and sat out in the warm afternoon sun, hands folded in his lap, half-dreaming. I lay near him on the marble bench our mother had liked to sit on, and Constance knelt in the dirt, both hands buried as though she were growing, kneading the dirt and turning it, touching the plants on their roots.

"It was a fine morning," Uncle Julian said, his voice going on and on, "a fine bright morning, and none of them knew it was their last. She was downstairs first, my niece Constance. I woke up and heard her moving in the kitchen—I slept upstairs then, I could still go upstairs, and I slept with my wife in our room—and I thought, this is a fine morning, never dreaming then that it was their last. Then I heard my nephew—no, it was my brother; my brother came downstairs first after Constance. I heard him whistling. Constance?"

"Yes?"

"What was the tune my brother used to whistle, and always off-key?"

Constance thought, her hands in the ground, and hummed softly, and I shivered.

"Of course. I never had a head for music; I could remember what people looked like and what they said and what they did but I could never remember what they sang. It was my brother who came downstairs after Constance, never caring of course if he woke people with his noise and his whistling, never thinking that perhaps I might still be asleep, although as it happened I was already awake." Uncle Julian sighed, and lifted his head to look curiously, once, around the garden. "He never knew it was his last morning on earth. He might have been quieter, I think, if he did know. I heard him in the kitchen with Constance and I said to my wife—she was awake, too; his noise had awakened her—I said to my wife, you had better get dressed; we live here with my brother and his wife, after all, and we must remember to show them that we are friendly and eager to help out wherever we can; dress and go down to Constance in the kitchen. She did as she was told; our wives always did as they were told, although my sister-in-law lay in bed late that morning; perhaps *she* had a premonition and wanted to take her earthly rest while she could. I heard them all. I heard the boy go downstairs. I thought of dressing; Constance?"

"Yes, Uncle Julian?"

"I could still dress myself in those days, you know, although that *was* the last day. I could still walk around by myself, and dress myself, and feed myself, and I had no pain. I slept well in those days as a strong man should. I was not young, but I was strong and I slept well and I could still dress myself."

"Would you like a rug over your knees?"

"No, my dear, I thank you. You have been a good niece to me, although there are some grounds for supposing you an undutiful daughter. My sister-in-law came downstairs before I did. We had pancakes for breakfast, tiny thin hot pancakes, and my brother had two fried eggs and my wife—although I did not encourage her to eat heavily, since we were living with my brother—took largely of sausage. Homemade sausage, made by Constance. Constance?"

"Yes, Uncle Julian?"

"I think if I had known it was her last breakfast I would have permitted her more sausage. I am surprised, now I think of it, that no one suspected it was their last morning; they might not have grudged my wife more sausage *then*. My brother sometimes remarked upon what we ate, my wife and I; he was a just man, and never stinted his food, so long as we did not take too much. He watched my wife take sausage that morning, Constance. I saw him watching her. We took little enough from him, Constance. He had pancakes and fried eggs and sausage but I felt that he was going to speak to my wife; the boy ate hugely. I am pleased that the breakfast was particularly good that day."

"I could make you sausage next week, Uncle Julian; I think homemade sausage would not disagree with you if you had very little."

"My brother never grudged our food if we did not take too much. My wife helped to wash the dishes."

"I was very grateful to her."

"She might have done more, I think now. She entertained my sister-in-law, and she saw to our clothes, and she helped with the dishes in the mornings, but I believe that my brother thought that she might have done more. He went off after breakfast to see a man on business."

"He wanted an arbor built; it was his plan to start a grape arbor."

"I am sorry about that; we might now be eating jam from our own grapes. I was always better able to chat after he was gone; I recall that I entertained the ladies that morning, and we sat here in the garden. We talked about music; my wife was quite musical although she had never learned to play. My sister-in-law had a delicate touch; it was always said of her that she had a delicate touch, and she played in the evenings usually. Not that evening, of course. She was not able to play that evening. In the morning we thought she would play in the evening as usual. Do you recall that I was very entertaining in the garden that morning, Constance?"

"I was weeding the vegetables," Constance said. "I could hear you all laughing."

"I was quite entertaining; I am happy for that now." He was quiet for a minute, folding and refolding his hands. I wanted to be kinder to him, but I could not fold his hands for him, and there was nothing I could bring him, so I lay still and listened to him talk. Constance frowned, staring at a leaf, and the shadows moved softly across the lawn.

"The boy was off somewhere," Uncle Julian said at last in his sad old voice. "The boy had gone off somewhere—was he fishing, Constance?"

"He was climbing the chestnut tree."

"I remember. Of course. I remember all of it very clearly, my dear, and I have it all down in my notes. It was the last morning of all and I would not like to forget. He was climbing the chestnut tree, shouting down to us from very high in the tree, and dropping twigs until my sister-in-law spoke sharply to him. She disliked the twigs falling into her hair, and my wife disliked it too, although she would never have been the first to speak. I think my wife was civil to your mother, Constance. I would hate to think not; we lived in my brother's house and ate his food. I know my brother was home for lunch."

"We had a rarebit," Constance said. "I had been working with the vegetables all morning and I had to make something quickly for lunch."

"It was a rarebit we had. I have often wondered why the arsenic was never put into the rarebit. It is an interesting point, and one I shall bring out forcefully in my book. Why was the arsenic not put into the rarebit? They would have lost some hours of life on that last day, but it would all have been over with that much sooner. Constance, if there is one dish you prepare which I strongly dislike, it is a rarebit. I have never cared for rarebit."

"I know, Uncle Julian. I never serve it to you."

"It would have been most suitable for the arsenic. I had a salad instead, I recall. There was an apple pudding for dessert, left over from the night before."

"The sun is going down." Constance rose and brushed the dirt from her hands. "You'll be chilly unless I take you indoors."

"It would have been far more suitable in the rarebit, Constance. Odd that the point was never brought out at the time. Arsenic is tasteless, you know, although I swear a rarebit is not. Where am I going?"

"You are going indoors. You will rest in your room for an hour until your dinner, and after dinner I will play for you, if you like."

"I cannot afford the time, my dear. I have a thousand details to remember and note down, and not a minute to waste. I would hate to lose any small thing from their last day; my book must be complete. I think, on the whole, it was a pleasant day for all of them; and of course it is much better that they never supposed it was to be their last. I think I am chilly, Constance."

"You will be tucked away in your room in a minute."

I came slowly behind them, unwilling to leave the darkening garden; Jonas came after me, moving toward the light in the house. When Jonas and I came inside Constance was just closing the door to Uncle Julian's room, and she smiled at me. "He's practically asleep already," she said softly.

"When I'm as old as Uncle Julian will you take care of me?" I asked her.

"If I'm still around," she said, and I was chilled. I sat in my corner holding Jonas and watched her move quickly and silently around our bright kitchen. In a few minutes she would ask me to set the table for the three of us in the dining room, and then after dinner it would be night and we would sit warmly together in the kitchen where we were guarded by the house and no one from outside could see so much as a light.

4

On Sunday morning the change was one day nearer. I was resolute about not thinking my three magic words and would not let them into my mind, but the air of change was so strong that there was no avoiding it; change lay over the stairs and the kitchen and the garden like fog. I would not forget my magic words; they were MELODY GLOUCESTER PEGASUS, but I refused to let them into my mind. The weather was uneasy on Sunday morning and I thought that perhaps Jonas would succeed after all in running up a storm; the sun shone into the kitchen but there were clouds moving quickly across the sky and a sharp little breeze that came in and out of the kitchen while I had my breakfast.

"Wear your boots if you wander today," Constance told me.

"I don't expect that Uncle Julian will sit outdoors today; it will be far too cool for him."

"Pure spring weather," Constance said, and smiled out at her garden.

"I love you, Constance," I said.

"I love you too, silly Merricat."

"Is Uncle Julian better?"

"I don't think so. He had his tray while you were still asleep, and I thought he seemed very tired. He said he had an extra pill during the night. I think perhaps he is getting worse."

"Are you worried about him?"

"Yes. Very."

"Will he die?"

"Do you know what he said to me this morning?" Constance turned, leaning against the sink, and looked at me with sadness. "He thought I was Aunt Dorothy, and he held my hand and said, 'It's terrible to be old, and just lie here wondering when it will happen.' He almost frightened me."

"You should have let me take him to the moon," I said.

"I gave him his hot milk and then he remembered who I was."

I thought that Uncle Julian was probably really very happy, with both Constance and Aunt Dorothy to take care of him, and I told myself that long thin things would remind me to be kinder to Uncle Julian; this was to be a day of long thin things, since there had already been a hair in my toothbrush, and a fragment of a string was caught on the side of my chair and I could see a splinter broken off the back step. "Make him a little pudding," I said.

"Perhaps I will." She took out the long thin slicing knife and set it on the sink. "Or a cup of cocoa. And dumplings with his chicken tonight."

"Do you need me?"

"No, my Merricat. Run along, and wear your boots."

The day outside was full of changing light, and Jonas danced in and out of shadows as he followed me. When I ran Jonas ran, and when I stopped and stood still he stopped and glanced at me and then went briskly off in another direction, as though we were not acquainted, and then he sat down and waited for me to run again. We were going to the long field which today looked like an ocean, although I had never seen an ocean; the grass was moving in the breeze and the cloud shadows passed back and forth and the trees in the distance moved. Jonas disappeared into the grass, which was tall enough for me to touch with my hands while I walked, and he made small crooked movements of his own; for a minute the grass would all bend together under the breeze and then there would be a hurrying pattern across it where Jonas was running. I started at one corner and walked diagonally across the long field toward the opposite corner, and in the middle I came directly to the rock covering the spot where the doll was buried; I could always find it although much of my buried treasure was forever lost. The rock was undisturbed and so the doll was safe. I am walking on buried treasure, I thought, with the grass brushing against my hands and nothing around me but the reach of the long field with the grass blowing and the pine woods at the end; behind me was the house, and far off to my left, hidden by trees and almost out of sight, was the wire fence our father had built to keep people out.

When I left the long field I went between the four apple trees we called our orchard, and along the path toward the creek. My box of silver dollars buried by the creek was safe. Near the creek, well hidden, was one of my hiding places, which I had made carefully and used often. I had torn away two or three low bushes and smoothed the ground; all around were more bushes and tree branches, and the entrance was covered by a branch which almost touched the ground. It was not really necessary to be so secret, since no one ever came looking for me here, but I liked to lie inside with Jonas and know that I could never be found. I used leaves and branches for a bed, and Constance had given me a blanket. The trees around and overhead were so thick that it was always dry inside and on Sunday morning I lay there with Jonas, listening to his stories. All cat stories start with the statement: "My mother, who was the first cat, told me this," and I lay with my head close to Jonas and listened. There was no change coming, I thought here, only spring; I was wrong to be so frightened. The days would get warmer, and Uncle Julian would sit in the sun, and Constance would laugh when she worked in the garden, and it would always be the same. Jonas went on and on ("And then we sang! And then we sang!") and the leaves moved overhead and it would always be the same.

I found a nest of baby snakes near the creek and killed them all; I dislike snakes and Constance had never asked me not to. I was on my way back to the house when I found a very bad omen, one of the worst. My book nailed to a tree in the pine woods had fallen down. I decided that the nail had rusted away and the book—it was a little notebook of our father's, where he used to record the names of people who owed him money, and people who ought, he thought, to do favors for him—was useless now as protection. I had wrapped it very thoroughly in heavy paper before nailing it to the tree, but the nail had rusted and it had fallen. I thought I had better destroy it, in case it was now actively bad, and bring something else out to the tree, perhaps a scarf of our mother's, or a glove. It was really too late, although I did not know it then; he was already on his way to the house. By the time I found the book he had probably already left his suitcase in the post office and was asking directions. All Jonas and I knew then was that we were hungry, and we ran together back to the house, and came with the breeze into the kitchen.

"Did you really forget your boots?" Constance said. She tried to frown and then laughed. "Silly Merricat."

"Jonas had no boots. It's a wonderful day."

"Perhaps tomorrow we'll go to gather mushrooms."

"Jonas and I are hungry *today*."

By then he was already walking through the village toward the black rock, with all of them watching him and wondering and whispering as he passed.

It was the last of our slow lovely days, although, as Uncle Julian would have pointed out, we never suspected it then. Constance and I had lunch, giggling and never knowing that while we were happy he was trying the locked gate, and peering down the path, and wandering the woods, shut out for a time by our father's fence. The rain started while we sat in the kitchen, and we left the kitchen door open so we could watch the rain slanting past the doorway and washing the garden; Constance was pleased, the way any good gardener is pleased with rain. "We'll see color out there soon," she said.

"We'll always be here together, won't we, Constance?"

"Don't you ever want to leave here, Merricat?"

"Where could we go?" I asked her. "What place would be better for us than this? Who wants us, outside? The world is full of terrible people."

"I wonder sometimes." She was very serious for a minute, and then she turned and smiled at me. "Don't you worry, my Merricat. Nothing bad will happen."

That must have been just about the minute he found the entrance and started up the driveway, hurrying in the rain, because I had only a minute or two left before I saw him. I might have used that minute or two for so many things: I might have warned Constance, somehow, or I might have thought of a new, safer, magic word, or I might have pushed the table across the kitchen doorway; as it happened, I played with my spoon, and looked at Jonas, and when Constance shivered I said, "I'll get your sweater for you." That was what brought me into the hall as he was coming up the steps. I saw him through the dining-room window and for a minute, chilled, I could not breathe. I knew the front door was locked; I thought of that first. "Constance," I said softly, not moving, "there's one outside. The kitchen door, quickly." I thought she had heard me, because I heard her move in the kitchen, but Uncle Julian had called at that moment, and she went in to him, leaving the heart of our house unguarded. I ran to the front door and leaned against it and heard his steps outside. He knocked, quietly at first and then firmly, and I leaned against the door, feeling the knocks hit at me, knowing how close he was. I knew already that he was one of the bad ones; I had seen his face briefly and he was one of the bad ones, who go around and around the house, trying to get in, looking in the windows, puffing and poking and stealing souvenirs.

He knocked again, and then called out, "Constance? Constance?"

Well, they always knew her name. They knew her name and Uncle Julian's name and how she wore her hair and the color of the three dresses she had to wear in court and how old she was and how she talked and moved and when they could they looked close in her face to see if she was crying. "I want to talk to Constance," he said outside, the way they always did.

It had been a long time since any of them came, but I had not forgotten how they made me feel. At first, they were always there, waiting for Constance, just wanting to see her. "Look," they said, nudging each other and pointing, "there she is, that one, that's the one, Constance." "Doesn't *look* like a murderess, does she?" they told each other; "listen, see if you can get a picture of her when she shows again." "Let's just take some of these flowers," they said comfortably to each other; "get a rock or something out of the garden, we can take it home to show the kids."

"Constance?" he said outside. "Constance?" He knocked again. "I want to talk to Constance," he said, "I have something important to say to her."

They always had something important they wanted to tell Constance, whether they were pushing at the door or yelling outside or calling on the telephone or writing the terrible terrible letters. Sometimes they wanted Julian Blackwood, but they never asked for me. I had been sent to bed without my supper, I had not been allowed in the courtroom, no one had taken my picture. While they were looking at Constance in the courtroom I had been lying on the cot at the orphanage, staring at the ceiling, wishing they were all dead, waiting for Constance to come and take me home.

"Constance, *can* you hear me?" he called outside. "Please listen for just a minute."

I wondered if he could hear me breathing on the inside of the door; I knew what he would do next. First he would back away from the house, sheltering his eyes from the rain, and look up at the windows upstairs, hoping to see a face looking down. Then he would start toward the side of the house, following the walk which was only supposed to be used by Constance and me. When he found the side door, which we never opened, he would knock there, calling Constance. Sometimes they went away when no one answered at either the front door or the side; the ones who were faintly embarrassed at being here at all and wished they had not bothered to come in the first place because there was really nothing to see and they could have saved their time or gone somewhere else—they usually hurried off when they found they were not going to get in to see Constance, but the stubborn ones, the ones I wished would die and lie there dead on the driveway, went around and around the house, trying every door and tapping on the windows. "We got a *right* to see her," they used to shout, "she killed all those people, didn't she?" They drove cars up to the steps and parked there. Most of them locked their cars carefully, making sure all the windows were shut, before they came to pound at the house and call to Constance. They had picnics on the lawn and took pictures of each other standing in front of the house and let their dogs run in the garden. They wrote their names on the walls and on the front door.

"Look," he said outside, "you've *got* to let me in."

I heard him go down the steps and knew he was looking up. The windows were all locked. The side door was locked. I knew better than to try to look out through the narrow glass panels on either side of the door; they always noticed even the slightest movement, and if I had even barely touched the dining-room drapes he would have been running at the house, shouting, "There she is, there she is." I leaned against the front door and thought about opening it and finding him dead on the driveway.

He was looking up at a blank face of a house looking down because we always kept the shades drawn on the upstairs windows; he would get no answer there and I had to find Constance a sweater before she shivered any more. It was safe to go upstairs, but I wanted to be back with Constance while he was waiting outside, so I ran up the stairs and snatched a sweater from the chair in Constance's room and ran downstairs and down the hall into the kitchen and he was sitting at the table in my chair,

"I had three magic words," I said, holding the sweater. "Their names were MELODY GLOUCESTER PEGASUS, and we were safe until they were said out loud."

"Merricat," Constance said; she turned and looked at me, smiling. "It's our cousin, our cousin Charles Blackwood. I knew him at once; he looks like Father."

"Well, Mary," he said. He stood up; he was taller now that he was inside, bigger and bigger as he came closer to me. "Got a kiss for your cousin Charles?"

Behind him the kitchen door was open wide; he was the first one who had ever gotten inside and Constance had let him in. Constance stood up; she knew better than to touch me but she said "Merricat, Merricat" gently and held out her arms to me. I was held tight, wound round with wire, I couldn't breathe, and I had to run. I threw the sweater on the floor and went out the door and down to the creek where I always went. Jonas found me after a while and we lay there together, protected from the rain by the trees crowding overhead, dim and rich in the kind of knowing, possessive way trees have of pressing closer. I looked back at the trees and listened to the soft sound of the water. There was no cousin, no Charles Blackwood, no intruder inside. It was because the book had fallen from the tree; I had neglected to replace it at once and our wall of safety had cracked. Tomorrow I would find some powerful thing and nail it to the tree. I fell asleep listening to Jonas, just as the shadows were coming down. Sometime during the night Jonas left me to go hunting, and I woke a little when he came back, pressing against me to get warm. "Jonas," I said, and he purred comfortably. When I woke up the early morning mists were wandering lightly along the creek, curling around my face and touching me. I lay there laughing, feeling the almost imaginary brush of the mist across my eyes, and looking up into the trees.

5

WHEN I came into the kitchen, still trailing mist from the creek, Constance was arranging Uncle Julian's breakfast tray. Uncle Julian was clearly feeling well this morning, since Constance was giving him tea instead of hot milk; he must have awakened early and asked for tea. I went to her and put my arms around her and she turned and hugged me.

"Good morning, my Merricat," she said.

"Good morning, my Constance. Is Uncle Julian better today?"

"Much, much better. And the sun is going to shine after yesterday's rain. And I am going to make a chocolate mousse for your dinner, my Merricat."

"I love you, Constance."

"And I love you. Now what will you have for breakfast?"

"Pancakes. Little tiny hot ones. And two fried eggs. Today my winged horse is coming and I am carrying you off to the moon and on the moon we will eat rose petals."

"Some rose petals are poisonous."

"Not on the moon. Is it true that you can plant a leaf?"

"Some leaves. Furred leaves. You can put them in water and they grow roots and then you plant them and they grow into a plant. The kind of a plant they were when they started, of course, not just any plant."

"I'm sorry about that. Good morning, Jonas. You are a furred leaf, I think."

"Silly Merricat."

"I like a leaf that grows into a different plant. All furry."

Constance was laughing. "Uncle Julian will never get his breakfast if I listen to you," she said. She took up the tray and went into Uncle Julian's room. "Hot tea coming," she said.

"Constance, my dear. A glorious morning, I think. A splendid day to work."

"And to sit in the sun."

Jonas sat in the sunlit doorway, washing his face. I was hungry; perhaps it would be kind to Uncle Julian today if I put a

476

feather on the lawn at the spot where Uncle Julian's chair would go; I was not allowed to bury things in the lawn. On the moon we wore feathers in our hair, and rubies on our hands. On the moon we had gold spoons.

"Perhaps today is a good day to begin a new chapter. Constance?"

"Yes, Uncle Julian?"

"Do you think I should begin chapter forty-four today?"

"Of course."

"Some of the early pages need a little brushing up. A work like this is never done."

"Shall I brush your hair?"

"I think I will brush it myself this morning, thank you. A man's head should be his own responsibility, after all. I have no jam."

"Shall I get you some?"

"No, because I see that I have somehow eaten all my toast. I fancy a broiled liver for my lunch, Constance."

"You shall have it. Shall I take your tray?"

"Yes, thank you. And I will brush my hair."

Constance came back into the kitchen and set down the tray. "And now for you, my Merricat," she said.

"And Jonas."

"Jonas had his breakfast long ago."

"Will you plant a leaf for me?"

"One of these days." She turned her head and listened. "He is still asleep," she said.

"Who is still asleep? Will I watch it grow?"

"Cousin Charles is still asleep," she said, and the day fell apart around me. I saw Jonas in the doorway and Constance by the stove but they had no color. I could not breathe, I was tied around tight, everything was cold.

"He was a ghost," I said.

Constance laughed, and it was a sound very far away. "Then a ghost is sleeping in Father's bed," she said. "And ate a very hearty dinner last night. While you were gone," she said.

"I dreamed that he came. I fell asleep on the ground and dreamed that he came, but then I dreamed him away." I was held tight; when Constance believed me I could breathe again.

"We talked for a long time last night."

"Go and look," I said, not breathing, "go and look; he isn't there."

"Silly Merricat," she said.

I could not run; I had to help Constance. I took my glass and smashed it on the floor. "Now he'll go away," I said.

Constance came to the table and sat down across from me, looking very serious. I wanted to go around the table and hug her, but she still had no color. "My Merricat," she said slowly, "Cousin Charles is here. He is our cousin. As long as his father was alive—that was Arthur Blackwood, Father's brother— Cousin Charles could not come to us, or try to help us, because his father would not allow him. His father," she said, and smiled a little, "thought very badly of us. He refused to take care of you during the trial, did you know that? And he never let our names be mentioned in his house."

"Then why do you mention his name in our house?"

"Because I am trying to explain. As soon as his father died Cousin Charles hurried here to help us."

"How can he help us? We're very happy, aren't we, Constance?"

"Very happy, Merricat. But please be pleasant to Cousin Charles."

I could breathe a little; it was going to be all right. Cousin Charles was a ghost, but a ghost that could be driven away. "He'll go away," I said.

"I don't suppose he plans to stay forever," Constance said. "He only came for a visit, after all."

I would have to find something, a device, to use against him. "Has Uncle Julian seen him?"

"Uncle Julian knows he is here, but Uncle Julian was too unwell last night to leave his room. He had his dinner on a tray, only a little soup. I was glad he asked for tea this morning."

"Today we neaten the house."

"Later, after Cousin Charles is awake. And I'd better sweep up that broken glass before he comes down."

I watched her while she swept up the glass; today would be a glittering day, full of tiny sparkling things. There was no point in hurrying with my breakfast, because today I could not go out until we had neatened the house, so I lingered, drinking milk slowly and watching Jonas. Before I was finished Uncle Julian called Constance to come and help him into his chair, and she brought him into the kitchen and put him by his table and his papers.

"I really think I shall commence chapter forty-four," he said, patting his hands together. "I shall commence, I think, with a slight exaggeration and go on from there into an outright lie. Constance, my dear?"

"Yes, Uncle Julian?"

"I am going to say that my wife was beautiful."

Then we were all silent for a minute, puzzled by the sound of a foot stepping upstairs where there had always been silence before. It was unpleasant, this walking overhead. Constance always stepped lightly, and Uncle Julian never walked; this footstep was heavy and even and bad.

"That is Cousin Charles," Constance said, looking up.

"Indeed," said Uncle Julian. He carefully arranged a paper before him and took up a pencil. "I am anticipating considerable pleasure from the society of my brother's son," he said. "Perhaps he can fill in some details on the behavior of his family during the trial. Although, I confess, I have somewhere set down notes on a possible conversation they might have had . . ." He turned to one of his notebooks. "This will delay chapter forty-four, I suspect."

I took Jonas and went to my corner, and Constance went into the hall to meet Charles when he came down the stairs. "Good morning, Cousin Charles," she said.

"Good morning, Connie." It was the same voice as he had used last night. I got further into my corner as she brought him into the kitchen, and Uncle Julian touched his papers and turned to face the doorway.

"Uncle Julian. I am pleased to meet you at last."

"Charles. You are Arthur's son, but you resemble my brother John, who is dead."

"Arthur's dead, too. That's why I'm here."

"He died wealthy, I trust? I was the only brother with no knack for money."

"As a matter of fact, Uncle Julian, my father left nothing."

"A pity. *His* father left a considerable sum. It came to a

considerable sum, even divided among the three of us. I always knew my share would melt away, but I had not suspected it of my brother Arthur. Perhaps your mother was an extravagant woman? I do not remember her very clearly. I recall that when my niece Constance wrote to her uncle during the trial, it was his wife who answered, requesting that the family connection be severed."

"I wanted to come before, Uncle Julian."

"I daresay. Youth is always curious. And a woman of such notoriety as your cousin Constance would present a romantic figure to a young man. Constance?"

"Yes, Uncle Julian?"

"Have I had my breakfast?"

"Yes."

"I will have another cup of tea, then. This young man and I have a great deal to discuss."

I still could not see him clearly, perhaps because he was a ghost, perhaps because he was so very big. His great round face, looking so much like our father's, turned from Constance to Uncle Julian and back, smiling and opening its mouth to talk. I moved as far into my corner as I could, but finally the big face turned at me.

"Why, there's Mary," it said. "Good morning, Mary."

I put my face down to Jonas.

"Shy?" he asked Constance. "Never mind. Kids always take to me."

Constance laughed. "We don't see many strangers," she said. She was not at all awkward or uncomfortable; it was as though she had been expecting all her life that Cousin Charles would come, as though she had planned exactly what to do and say, almost as though in the house of her life there had always been a room kept for Cousin Charles.

He stood up and came closer to me. "That's a handsome cat," he said. "Does it have a name?"

Jonas and I looked at him and then I thought that Jonas's name might be the safest thing to speak to him first. "Jonas," I said.

"Jonas? Is he your special pet?"

"Yes," I said. We looked at him, Jonas and I, not daring to

blink or turn away. The big white face was close, still looking like our father, and the big mouth was smiling.

"We're going to be good friends, you and Jonas and I," he said.

"What will you have for breakfast?" Constance asked him, and she smiled at me because I had told him Jonas's name.

"Whatever you're serving," he said, turning away from me at last.

"Merricat had pancakes."

"Pancakes would be great. A good breakfast in charming company on a beautiful day; what more could I ask?"

"Pancakes," observed Uncle Julian, "are an honored dish in this family, although I rarely take them myself; my health permits only the lightest and daintiest foods. Pancakes were served for breakfast on that last—"

"Uncle Julian," Constance said, "your papers are spilling on the floor."

"Let me get them, sir." Cousin Charles kneeled to gather the papers and Constance said, "After breakfast you'll see my garden."

"A chivalrous young man," Uncle Julian said, accepting his papers from Charles. "I thank you; I am not able myself to leap across a room and kneel on the floor and I am gratified to find someone who can. I believe that you are a year or so older than my niece?"

"I'm thirty-two," Charles said.

"And Constance is approximately twenty-eight. We long ago gave up the practice of birthdays, but twenty-eight should be about right. Constance, I should not be talking so on an empty stomach. Where is my breakfast?"

"You finished it an hour ago, Uncle Julian. I am making you a cup of tea, and pancakes for Cousin Charles."

"Charles is intrepid. Your cooking, although it is of a very high standard indeed, has certain disadvantages."

"I'm not afraid to eat anything Constance cooks," Charles said.

"Really?" said Uncle Julian. "I congratulate you. I was referring to the effect a weighty meal like pancakes is apt to have on a delicate stomach. I suppose *your* reference was to arsenic."

"Come and have your breakfast," Constance said.

I was laughing, although Jonas hid my face. It took Charles a good half-minute to pick up his fork, and he kept smiling at Constance. Finally, knowing that Constance and Uncle Julian and Jonas and I were watching him, he cut off a small piece of pancake and brought it to his mouth, but could not bring himself to put it inside. Finally he set the fork with the piece of pancake down on his plate and turned to Uncle Julian. "You know, I was thinking," he said. "Maybe while I'm here there are things I could do for you—dig in the garden, maybe, or run errands. I'm pretty good at hard work."

"You had dinner here last night and woke up alive this morning," Constance said; I was laughing but she suddenly looked almost cross.

"What?" Charles said. "Oh." He looked down at his fork as though he had forgotten it and at last he picked it up and put the piece of pancake into his mouth very quickly, and chewed it and swallowed it and looked up at Constance. "Delicious," he said, and Constance smiled.

"Constance?"

"Yes, Uncle Julian?"

"I think I shall not, after all, begin chapter forty-four this morning. I think I shall go back to chapter seventeen, where I recall that I made some slight mention of your cousin and his family, and their attitude during the trial. Charles, you are a clever young man. I am eager to hear your story."

"It was all so long ago," Charles said.

"You should have kept notes," Uncle Julian said.

"I mean," Charles said, "can't it all be forgotten? There's no point in keeping those memories alive."

"Forgotten?" Uncle Julian said. "Forgotten?"

"It was a sad and horrible time and it's not going to do Connie here any good at all to keep talking about it."

"Young man, you are speaking slightingly, I believe, of my work. A man does not take his work lightly. A man has his work to do, and he does it. Remember that, Charles."

"I'm just saying that I don't want to talk about Connie and that bad time."

"I shall be forced to invent, to fictionalize, to imagine."

"I refuse to discuss it any further."

"Constance?"

"Yes, Uncle Julian?" Constance looked very serious.

"It *did* happen? I remember that it happened," said Uncle Julian, fingers at his mouth.

Constance hesitated, and then she said, "Of course it did, Uncle Julian."

"My notes . . ." Uncle Julian's voice trailed off, and he gestured at his papers.

"Yes, Uncle Julian. It was real."

I was angry because Charles ought to be kind to Uncle Julian. I remembered that today was to be a day of sparkles and light, and I thought that I would find something bright and pretty to put near Uncle Julian's chair.

"Constance?"

"Yes?"

"May I go outside? Am I warm enough?"

"I think so, Uncle Julian." Constance was sorry, too. Uncle Julian was shaking his head back and forth sadly and he had put down his pencil. Constance went into Uncle Julian's room and brought out his shawl, which she put around his shoulders very gently. Charles was eating his pancakes bravely now, and did not look up; I wondered if he cared that he had not been kind to Uncle Julian.

"Now you will go outside," Constance said quietly to Uncle Julian, "and the sun will be warm and the garden will be bright and you will have broiled liver for your lunch."

"Perhaps not," Uncle Julian said. "Perhaps I had better have just an egg."

Constance wheeled him gently to the door and eased his chair carefully down the step. Charles looked up from his pancakes but when he started to rise to help her she shook her head. "I'll put you in your special corner," she said to Uncle Julian, "where I can see you every minute and five times an hour I'll wave hello to you."

We could hear her talking all the time she was wheeling Uncle Julian to his corner. Jonas left me and went to sit in the doorway and watch them, "Jonas?" Charles said, and Jonas turned toward him. "Cousin Mary doesn't like me," Charles said to Jonas. I disliked the way he was talking to Jonas and I disliked the way Jonas appeared to be listening to him. "How can I make Cousin Mary like me?" Charles said, and Jonas looked quickly at me and then back to Charles. "Here I've come to visit my two dear cousins," Charles said, "my two dear cousins and my old uncle whom I haven't seen for years, and my Cousin Mary won't even be polite to me. What do you think, Jonas?"

There were sparkles at the sink where a drop of water was swelling to fall. Perhaps if I held my breath until the drop fell Charles would go away, but I knew that was not true; holding my breath was too easy.

"Oh, well," Charles said to Jonas, "*Constance* likes me, and I guess that's all that matters."

Constance came to the doorway, waited for Jonas to move, and when he did not, stepped over him. "More pancakes?" she said to Charles.

"No, thanks. I'm trying to get acquainted with my little cousin."

"It won't be long before she's fond of you." Constance was looking at me. Jonas had fallen to washing himself, and I thought at last of what to say.

"Today we neaten the house," I said.

Uncle Julian slept all morning in the garden. Constance went often to the back bedroom windows to look down on him while we worked and stood sometimes, with the dustcloth in her hands, as though she were forgetting to come back and dust our mother's jewel box that held our mother's pearls, and her sapphire ring, and her brooch with diamonds. I looked out the window only once, to see Uncle Julian with his eyes closed and Charles standing nearby. It was ugly to think of Charles walking among the vegetables and under the apple trees and across the lawn where Uncle Julian slept.

"We'll let Father's room go this morning," Constance said, "because Charles is living there." Some time later she said, as though she had been thinking about it, "I wonder if it would be right for me to wear Mother's pearls. I have never worn pearls."

"They've always been in the box," I said. "You'd have to take them out."

"It's not likely that anyone would care," Constance said.

"*I* would care, if you looked more beautiful."

Constance laughed, and said, "I'm silly now. Why should I want to wear pearls?"

"They're better off in the box where they belong."

Charles had closed the door of our father's room so I could not look inside, but I wondered if he had moved our father's things, or put a hat or a handkerchief or a glove on the dresser beside our father's silver brushes. I wondered if he had looked into the closet or into the drawers. Our father's room was in the front of the house, and I wondered if Charles had looked down from the windows and out over the lawn and the long driveway to the road, and wanted to be on that road and away home.

"How long did it take Charles to get here?" I asked Constance.

"Four or five hours, I think," she said. "He came by bus to the village, and had to walk from there."

"Then it will take him four or five hours to get home again?"

"I suppose so. When he goes."

"But first he will have to walk back to the village?"

"Unless you take him on your winged horse."

"I don't have any winged horse," I said.

"Oh, Merricat," Constance said. "Charles is *not* a bad man."

There were sparkles in the mirrors and inside our mother's jewel box the diamonds and the pearls were shining in the darkness. Constance made shadows up and down the hall when she went to the window to look down on Uncle Julian and outside the new leaves moved quickly in the sunlight. Charles had only gotten in because the magic was broken; if I could re-seal the protection around Constance and shut Charles out he would have to leave the house. Every touch he made on the house must be erased.

"Charles is a ghost," I said, and Constance sighed.

I polished the doorknob to our father's room with my dustcloth, and at least one of Charles' touches was gone.

When we had neatened the upstairs rooms we came downstairs together, carrying our dustcloths and the broom and dustpan and mop like a pair of witches walking home. In the drawing room we dusted the golden-legged chairs and the harp, and everything sparkled at us, even the blue dress in the portrait of our mother. I dusted the wedding cake trim with a cloth on the end of a broom, staggering, and looking up and pretending that the ceiling was the floor and I was sweeping, hovering busily in space looking down at my broom, weightless and flying until the room swung dizzily and I was again on the floor looking up.

"Charles has not yet seen this room," Constance said. "Mother was so proud of it; I ought to have showed it to him right away."

"May I have sandwiches for my lunch? I want to go down to the creek."

"Sooner or later you're going to have to sit at the table with him, Merricat."

"Tonight at dinner. I promise."

We dusted the dining room and the silver tea service and the high wooden backs of the chairs. Constance went every few minutes into the kitchen to look out the back door and check on Uncle Julian, and once I heard her laugh and call, "Watch out for the mud down there," and I knew she was talking to Charles.

"Where did you let Charles sit last night at dinner?" I asked her once.

"In Father's chair," she said, and then, "He has a perfect right to sit there. He's a guest, and he even *looks* like Father."

"Will he sit there tonight?"

"Yes, Merricat."

I dusted our father's chair thoroughly, although it was small use if Charles was to sit there again tonight. I would have to clean all the silverware.

When we had finished neatening the house we came back to the kitchen. Charles was sitting at the kitchen table smoking his pipe and looking at Jonas, who was looking back at him. The pipe smoke was disagreeable in our kitchen, and I disliked having Jonas look at Charles. Constance went on out the back door to get Uncle Julian, and we could hear him say, "Dorothy? I was not asleep, Dorothy."

"Cousin Mary doesn't like me," Charles said again to Jonas. "I wonder if Cousin Mary knows how I get even with people who don't like me? Can I help you with that chair, Constance? Have a nice nap, Uncle?"

Constance made sandwiches for Jonas and me, and we ate them in a tree; I sat in a low fork and Jonas sat on a small branch near me, watching for birds.

"Jonas," I told him, "you are not to listen any more to Cousin Charles," and Jonas regarded me in wide-eyed astonishment, that I should attempt to make decisions for him. "Jonas," I said, "he is a ghost," and Jonas closed his eyes and turned away.

It was important to choose the exact device to drive Charles away. An imperfect magic, or one incorrectly used, might only bring more disaster upon our house. I thought of my mother's jewels, since this was a day of sparkling things, but they might not be strong on a dull day, and Constance would be angry if I took them out of the box where they belonged, when she herself had decided against it. I thought of books, which are always strongly protective, but my father's book had fallen from the tree and let Charles in; books, then, were perhaps powerless against Charles. I lay back against the tree trunk and thought of magic; if Charles had not gone away before three days I would smash the mirror in the hall.

He sat across from me at dinner, in our father's chair, with his big white face blotting out the silver on the sideboard behind him. He watched while Constance cut up Uncle Julian's chicken and put it correctly on the plate, and he watched when Uncle Julian took the first bite and turned it over and over in his mouth.

"Here is a biscuit, Uncle Julian," Constance said. "Eat the soft inside."

Constance had forgotten and put dressing on my salad, but I would not have eaten anyway with that big white face watching. Jonas, who was not allowed chicken, sat on the floor beside my chair.

"Does he always eat with you?" Charles asked once, nodding his head at Uncle Julian.

"When he's well enough," Constance said.

"I wonder how you stand it," Charles said.

"I tell you, John," Uncle Julian said suddenly to Charles, "investments are not what they were when Father made his money. He was a shrewd man, but he never understood that times change."

"Who's he talking to?" Charles asked Constance.

"He thinks you are his brother John."

Charles looked at Uncle Julian for a long minute, and then shook his head and returned to his chicken.

"That was my dead wife's chair on your left, young man," Uncle Julian said. "I well recall the last time she sat there; we—"

"None of that," Charles said, and shook his finger at Uncle Julian; he had been holding his chicken in his hands to eat it, and his finger sparkled with grease. "We're not going to talk about it any more, Uncle."

Constance was pleased with me because I had come to the table and when I looked at her she smiled at me. She knew that I disliked eating when anyone was watching me, and she would save my plate and bring it to me later in the kitchen; she did not remember, I saw, that she had put dressing on my salad.

"Noticed this morning," Charles said, taking up the platter of chicken and looking into it carefully, "that there was a broken step out back. How about I fix it for you one of these days? I might as well earn my keep."

"It would be very kind of you," Constance said. "That step has been a nuisance for a long time."

"And I want to run into the village to get some pipe tobacco, so I can pick up anything you need there."

"But I go to the village on Tuesday," I said, startled.

"You do?" He looked at me across the table, big white face turned directly at me. I was quiet; I remembered that walking to the village was the first step on Charles' way home.

"Merricat, dear, I think if Charles doesn't mind it might be a good idea. I never feel quite comfortable when you're away in the village." Constance laughed. "I'll give you a list, Charles, and the money, and you shall be the grocery boy."

"You keep the money in the house?"

"Of course."

"Doesn't sound very wise."

"It's in Father's safe."

"Even so."

"I assure you, sir," Uncle Julian said, "I made a point of examining the books thoroughly before committing myself. I cannot have been deceived."

"So I'm taking little Cousin Mary's job away from her," Charles said, looking at me again. "You'll have to find something else for her to do, Connie."

I had made sure of what to say to him before I came to the table. "The *Amanita phalloides*," I said to him, "holds three different poisons. There is amanitin, which works slowly and is most potent. There is phalloidin, which acts at once, and there is phallin, which dissolves red corpuscles, although it is the least potent. The first symptoms do not appear until seven to twelve hours after eating, in some cases not before twenty-four or even forty hours. The symptoms begin with violent stomach pains, cold sweat, vomiting—"

"Listen," Charles said. He put down his chicken. "You stop that," he said.

Constance was laughing. "Oh, Merricat," she said, laughing through the words, "you *are* silly. I taught her," she told Charles, "there are mushrooms by the creek and in the fields and I made her learn the deadly ones. Oh, Merricat."

"Death occurs between five and ten days after eating," I said.

"I don't think that's very funny," Charles said.

"Silly Merricat," Constance said.

6

THE house was not secure just because Charles had gone out of it and into the village; for one thing, Constance had given him a key to the gates. There had originally been a key for each of us; our father had a key, and our mother, and the keys were kept on a rack beside the kitchen door. When Charles started out for the village Constance gave him a key, perhaps our father's key, and a shopping list, and the money to pay for what he bought.

"You shouldn't keep money in the house like this," he said, holding it tight in his hand for a minute before he reached into a back pocket and took out a wallet. "Women alone like you are, you shouldn't keep money in the house."

I was watching him from my corner of the kitchen but I would not let Jonas come to me while Charles was in the house. "Are you sure you put everything down?" he asked Constance. "Hate to make two trips."

I waited until Charles was well along, perhaps almost to the black rock, and then I said, "He forgot the library books."

Constance looked at me for a minute. "Miss Wickedness," she said. "You wanted him to forget."

"How could he know about the library books? He doesn't belong in this house; he has nothing to do with our books."

"Do you know," Constance said, looking into a pot on the stove, "I think that soon we will be picking lettuce; the weather has stayed so warm."

"On the moon," I said, and then stopped.

"On the moon," Constance said, turning to smile at me, "you have lettuce all year round, perhaps?"

"On the moon we have everything. Lettuce, and pumpkin pie and *Amanita phalloides*. We have cat-furred plants and horses dancing with their wings. All the locks are solid and tight, and there are no ghosts. On the moon Uncle Julian would be well and the sun would shine every day. You would wear our mother's pearls and sing, and the sun would shine all the time."

"I wish I could go to your moon. I wonder if I should start the gingerbread now; it will be cold if Charles is late."

"I'll be here to eat it," I said.

"But Charles said he loved gingerbread."

I was making a little house at the table, out of the library books, standing one across two set on edge. "Old witch," I said, "you have a gingerbread house."

"I do not," Constance said. "I have a lovely house where I live with my sister Merricat."

I laughed at her; she was worrying at the pot on the stove and she had flour on her face. "Maybe he'll never come back," I said.

"He has to; I'm making gingerbread for him."

Since Charles had taken my occupation for Tuesday morning I had nothing to do. I wondered about going down to the creek, but I had no reason to suppose that the creek would even be there, since I never visited it on Tuesday mornings; would the people in the village be waiting for me, glancing from the corners of their eyes to see if I was coming, nudging one another, and then turn in astonishment when they saw Charles? Perhaps the whole village would falter and slow, bewildered at the lack of Miss Mary Katherine Blackwood? I giggled, thinking of Jim Donell and the Harris boys peering anxiously up the road to see if I was coming.

"What's funny?" Constance asked, turning to see.

"I was thinking that you might make a gingerbread man, and I could name him Charles and eat him."

"Oh, Merricat, *please*."

I could tell that Constance was going to be irritable, partly because of me and partly because of the gingerbread, so I thought it wiser to run away. Since it was a free morning, and I was uneasy at going out of doors, it might be a good time to search out a device to use against Charles, and I started upstairs; the smell of baking gingerbread followed me almost halfway to the top. Charles had left his door open, not wide, but enough for me to get a hand inside.

When I pushed a little the door opened wide and I looked in at our father's room, which now belonged to Charles. Charles had made his bed, I noticed; his mother must have taught him.

His suitcase was on a chair, but it was closed; there were things belonging to Charles on the dresser where our father's possessions had always been kept; I saw Charles' pipe, and a handkerchief, things that Charles had touched and used dirtying our father's room. One drawer of the dresser was a little open, and I thought again of Charles picking over our father's clothes. I walked very softly across the room because I did not want Constance to hear me from downstairs, and looked into the open drawer. I thought that Charles would not be pleased to know that I had caught him looking at our father's things, and something from this drawer might be extraordinarily powerful, since it would carry a guilt of Charles. I was not surprised to find that he had been looking at our father's jewelry; inside the drawer was a leather box which held, I knew, a watch and chain made of gold, and cuff links, and a signet ring. I would not touch our mother's jewelry, but Constance had not said anything about our father's jewelry, had not even come into this room to neaten, so I thought I could open the box and take something out. The watch was inside, in a small private box of its own, resting on a satin lining and not ticking, and the watch chain was curled beside it. I would not touch the ring; the thought of a ring around my finger always made me feel tied tight, because rings had no openings to get out of, but I liked the watch chain, which twisted and wound around my hand when I picked it up. I put the jewelry box carefully back inside the drawer and closed the drawer and went out of the room and closed the door after me, and took the watch chain into my room, where it curled again into a sleeping gold heap on the pillow.

I had intended to bury it, but I was sorry when I thought how long it had been there in the darkness in the box in our father's drawer, and I thought that it had earned a place up high, where it could sparkle in the sunlight, and I decided to nail it to the tree where the book had come down. While Constance made gingerbread in the kitchen, and Uncle Julian slept in his room, and Charles walked in and out of the village stores, I lay on my bed and played with my golden chain.

"That's my brother's gold watch chain," Uncle Julian said, leaning forward curiously. "I thought he was buried in it."

Charles' hand was shaking as he held it out; I could see it shaking against the yellow of the wall behind him. "In a tree," he said, and his voice was shaking too. "I found it nailed to a tree, for God's sake. What kind of a house *is* this?"

"It's not important," Constance said. "Really, Charles, it's not important."

"Not important? Connie, this thing's made of *gold*."

"But no one wants it."

"One of the links is smashed," Charles said, mourning over the chain. "I could have worn it; what a hell of a way to treat a valuable thing. We could have sold it," he said to Constance.

"But why?"

"I certainly did think he was buried in it," Uncle Julian said. "He was never a man to give things away easily. I suppose he never knew they kept it from him."

"It's worth money," Charles said, explaining carefully to Constance. "This is a gold watch chain, worth possibly a good deal of money. Sensible people don't go around nailing this kind of valuable thing to trees."

"Lunch will be cold if you stand there worrying."

"I'll take it up and put it back in the box where it belongs," Charles said. No one but me noticed that he knew where it had been kept. "Later," he said, looking at me, "we'll find out how it got on the tree."

"Merricat put it there," Constance said. "Please do come to lunch."

"How do you know? About Mary?"

"She always does." Constance smiled at me. "Silly Merricat."

"Does she indeed?" said Charles. He came slowly over to the table, looking at me.

"He was a man very fond of his person," Uncle Julian said. "Given to adorning himself, and not overly clean."

It was quiet in the kitchen; Constance was in Uncle Julian's room, putting him to bed for his afternoon nap. "Where would poor Cousin Mary go if her sister turned her out?" Charles asked Jonas, who listened quietly. "What would poor Cousin Mary do if Constance and Charles didn't love her?"

*

I cannot think why it seemed to me that I might simply ask Charles to go away. Perhaps I thought that he had to be asked politely just once; perhaps the idea of going away had just not come into his mind and it was necessary to put it there. I decided that asking Charles to go away was the next thing to do, before he was everywhere in the house and could never be eradicated. Already the house smelled of him, of his pipe and his shaving lotion, and the noise of him echoed in the rooms all day long; his pipe was sometimes on the kitchen table and his gloves or his tobacco pouch or his constant boxes of matches were scattered through our rooms. He walked into the village each afternoon and brought back newspapers which he left lying anywhere, even in the kitchen where Constance might see them. A spark from his pipe had left a tiny burn on the rose brocade of a chair in the drawing room; Constance had not yet noticed it and I thought not to tell her because I hoped that the house, injured, would reject him by itself.

"Constance," I asked her on a bright morning; Charles had been in our house for three days then, I thought; "Constance, has he said anything yet about leaving?"

She was increasingly cross with me when I wanted Charles to leave; always before Constance had listened and smiled and only been angry when Jonas and I had been wicked, but now she frowned at me often, as though I somehow looked different to her. "I've told you," she said to me, "I've told you and told you that I won't hear any more silliness about Charles. He is our cousin and he has been invited to visit us and he will probably go when he is ready."

"He makes Uncle Julian sicker."

"He's only trying to keep Uncle Julian from thinking about sad things all the time. And I agree with him. Uncle Julian should be cheerful."

"Why should he be cheerful if he's going to die?"

"I haven't been doing my duty," Constance said.

"I don't know what that means."

"I've been hiding here," Constance said slowly, as though she were not at all sure of the correct order of the words. She stood by the stove in the sunlight with color in her hair and eyes and not smiling, and she said slowly, "I have let Uncle Julian spend all his time living in the past and particularly re-living that one dreadful day. I have let you run wild; how long has it been since you combed your hair?"

I could not allow myself to be angry, and particularly not angry with Constance, but I wished Charles dead. Constance needed guarding more than ever before and if I became angry and looked aside she might very well be lost. I said very cautiously, "On the moon . . ."

"On the moon," Constance said, and laughed unpleasantly. "It's all been my fault," she said. "I didn't realize how wrong I was, letting things go on and on because I wanted to hide. It wasn't fair to you or to Uncle Julian."

"And Charles is also mending the broken step?"

"Uncle Julian should be in a hospital, with nurses to take care of him. And you—" She opened her eyes wide suddenly, as though seeing her old Merricat again, and then she held out her arms to me. "Oh, Merricat," she said, and laughed a little. "Listen to me scolding you; how silly I am."

I went to her and put my arms around her. "I love you, Constance."

"You're a good child, Merricat," she said.

That was when I left her and went outside to talk to Charles. I knew I would dislike talking to Charles, but it was almost too late to ask him politely and I thought I should ask him once. Even the garden had become a strange landscape with Charles' figure in it; I could see him standing under the apple trees and the trees were crooked and shortened beside him. I came out the kitchen door and walked slowly toward him. I was trying to think charitably of him, since I would never be able to speak kindly until I did, but whenever I thought of his big white face grinning at me across the table or watching me whenever I moved I wanted to beat at him until he went away, I wanted to stamp on him after he was dead, and see him lying dead on the grass. So I made my mind charitable toward Charles and came up to him slowly.

"Cousin Charles?" I said, and he turned to look at me. I thought of seeing him dead. "Cousin Charles?"

"Well?"

"I have decided to ask you please to go away."

"All right," he said. "You asked me."

"Please will you go away?"

"No," he said.

I could not think of anything further to say. I saw that he was wearing our father's gold watch chain, even with the crooked link, and I knew without seeing that our father's watch was in his pocket. I thought that tomorrow he would be wearing our father's signet ring, and I wondered if he would make Constance put on our mother's pearls.

"You stay away from Jonas," I said.

"As a matter of fact," he said, "come about a month from now, I wonder who *will* still be here? You," he said, "or me?"

I ran back into the house and straight up to our father's room, where I hammered with a shoe at the mirror over the dresser until it cracked across. Then I went into my room and rested my head on the window sill and slept.

I was remembering these days to be kinder to Uncle Julian. I was sorry because he was spending more and more time in his room, taking both his breakfast and his lunch on a tray and only eating his dinners in the dining room under the despising eye of Charles.

"Can't you feed him or something?" Charles asked Constance. "He's got food all over himself."

"I didn't mean to," Uncle Julian said, looking at Constance.

"Ought to wear a baby bib," Charles said, laughing.

While Charles sat in the kitchen in the mornings eating hugely of ham and potatoes and fried eggs and hot biscuits and doughnuts and toast, Uncle Julian drowsed in his room over his hot milk and sometimes when he called to Constance, Charles said, "Tell him you're busy; you don't have to go running every time he wets his bed; he just likes being waited on."

I always had my breakfast earlier than Charles on those sunny mornings, and if he came down before I finished I would take my plate out and sit on the grass under the chestnut tree. Once I brought Uncle Julian a new leaf from the chestnut tree and put it on his window sill. I stood outside in the sunlight and looked in at him lying still in the dark room and tried to think of ways I might be kinder. I thought of him lying there alone dreaming old Uncle Julian dreams, and I went into the kitchen and said to Constance, "Will you make Uncle Julian a little soft cake for his lunch?"

"She's too busy now," Charles said with his mouth full. "Your sister works like a slave."

"Will you?" I asked Constance.

"I'm sorry," Constance said. "I have so much to do."

"But Uncle Julian is going to die."

"Constance is too busy," Charles said. "Run along and play."

I followed Charles one afternoon when he went to the village. I stopped by the black rock, because it was not one of my days for going into the village, and watched Charles go down the main street. He stopped and talked for a minute to Stella, who was standing in the sunlight outside her shop, and he bought a paper; when I saw him sit down on the benches with the other men I turned and went back to our house. If I went into the village shopping again Charles would be one of the men who watched me going past. Constance was working in her garden and Uncle Julian slept in his chair in the sun, and when I sat quietly on my bench Constance asked, not looking up at me, "Where have you been, Merricat?"

"Wandering. Where is my cat?"

"I think," Constance said, "that we are going to have to forbid your wandering. It's time you quieted down a little."

"Does 'we' mean you and Charles?"

"Merricat." Constance turned toward me, sitting back against her feet and folding her hands before her. "I never realized until lately how wrong I was to let you and Uncle Julian hide here with me. We should have faced the world and tried to live normal lives; Uncle Julian should have been in a hospital all these years, with good care and nurses to watch him. We should have been living like other people. You should . . ." She stopped, and waved her hands helplessly. "You should have boy friends," she said finally, and then began to laugh because she sounded funny even to herself.

"I have Jonas," I said, and we both laughed and Uncle Julian woke up suddenly and laughed a thin old cackle.

"You are the silliest person I ever saw," I told Constance, and went off to look for Jonas. While I was wandering Charles came back to our house; he brought a newspaper and a bottle of wine for his dinner and our father's scarf which I had used to tie shut the gate, because Charles had a key.

"I could have worn this scarf," he said irritably, and I heard him from the vegetable garden where I had found Jonas sleeping in a tangle of young lettuce plants. "It's an expensive thing, and I like the colors."

"It belonged to Father," Constance said.

"That reminds me," Charles said. "One of these days I'd like to look over the rest of his clothes." He was quiet for a minute; I thought he was probably sitting down on my bench. Then he went on, very lightly. "Also," he said, "while I'm here, I ought to go over your father's papers. There might be something important."

"Not *my* papers," Uncle Julian said. "That young man is not to put a finger on *my* papers."

"I haven't even seen your father's study," Charles said.

"We don't use it. Nothing in there is ever touched."

"Except the safe, of course," Charles said.

"Constance?"

"Yes, Uncle Julian?"

"I want you to have my papers afterwards. No one else is to touch my papers, do you hear me?"

"Yes, Uncle Julian."

I was not allowed to open the safe where Constance kept our father's money. I was allowed to go into the study, but I disliked it and never even touched the doorknob. I hoped Constance would not open the study for Charles; he already had our father's bedroom, after all, and our father's watch and his gold chain and his signet ring. I was thinking that being a demon and a ghost must be very difficult, even for Charles; if he ever forgot, or let his disguise drop for a minute, he would be recognized at once and driven away; he must be extremely careful to use the same voice every time, and present the same face and the same manner without a slip; he must be constantly on guard against betraying himself. I wondered if he would turn back to his true form when he was dead. When it grew cooler and I knew that Constance would be taking Uncle Julian indoors I left Jonas asleep on the lettuce plants and came back into the house. When I came into the kitchen Uncle Julian was poking furiously at the papers on his table, trying to get them into a small heap, and Constance was peeling potatoes. I could hear Charles moving around upstairs, and for a minute the kitchen was warm and glowing and bright.

"Jonas is asleep in the lettuce," I said.

"There is nothing I like more than cat fur in my salad," Constance said amiably.

"It is time that I had a box," Uncle Julian announced. He sat back and looked angrily at his papers. "They must all be put into a box, this very minute. Constance?"

"Yes, Uncle Julian; I can find you a box."

"If I put all my papers in a box and put the box in my room, then that dreadful young man cannot touch them. He *is* a dreadful young man, Constance."

"Really, Uncle Julian, Charles is very kind."

"He is dishonest. His father was dishonest. Both my brothers were dishonest. If he tries to take my papers you must stop him; I cannot permit tampering with my papers and I will not tolerate intrusion. You must tell him this, Constance. He is a bastard."

"Uncle Julian—"

"In a purely metaphorical sense, I assure you. Both my brothers married women of very strong will. That is merely a word used—among men, my dear; I apologize for submitting you to such a word—to categorize an undesirable fellow."

Constance turned without speaking and opened the door which led to the cellar stairs and to the rows and rows of food preserved at the very bottom of our house. She went quietly down the stairs, and we could hear Charles moving upstairs and Constance moving downstairs.

"William of Orange was a bastard," Uncle Julian said to himself; he took up a bit of paper and made a note. Constance came back up the cellar stairs with a box which she brought to Uncle Julian. "Here is a clean box," she said.

"What for?" Uncle Julian asked.

"To put your papers in."

"That young man is not to touch my papers, Constance. I will not have that young man going through my papers."

"This is all my fault," Constance said, turning to me. "He should be in a hospital."

"I will put my papers in that box, Constance, my dear, if you will be kind enough to hand it to me."

"He has a happy time," I said to Constance.

"I should have done everything differently."

"It would certainly not be kind to put Uncle Julian in a hospital."

"But I'll have to if I—" and Constance stopped suddenly, and turned back to the sink and the potatoes. "Shall I put walnuts in the applesauce?" she asked.

I sat very quietly, listening to what she had almost said. Time was running shorter, tightening around our house, crushing me. I thought it might be time to smash the big mirror in the hall, but then Charles' feet were coming heavily down the stairs and through the hall and into the kitchen.

"Well, well, everybody's here," he said. "What's for dinner?"

That evening Constance played for us in the drawing room, the tall curve of her harp making shadows against our mother's portrait and the soft notes falling into the air like petals. She played "Over the Sea to Skye" and "Flow Gently, Sweet Afton" and "I Saw a Lady," and other songs our mother used to play, but I never remember that our mother's fingers touched the strings so lightly with such a breath of melody. Uncle Julian kept himself awake, listening and dreaming, and even Charles did not quite dare to put his feet on the furniture in the drawing room, although the smoke from his pipe drifted against the wedding cake ceiling and he moved restlessly while Constance played.

"A delicate touch," Uncle Julian said once. "All the Blackwood women had a gifted touch."

Charles stopped by the fireplace to knock his pipe against the grate. "Pretty," he said, taking down one of the Dresden figurines. Constance stopped playing and he turned to look at her. "Valuable?"

"Not particularly," Constance said. "My mother liked them."

Uncle Julian said, "My particular favorite was always 'Bluebells of Scotland'; Constance, my dear, would you—"

"No more now," Charles said. "Now Constance and I want to talk, Uncle. We've got plans to make."

7

THURSDAY was my most powerful day. It was the right day
to settle with Charles. In the morning Constance decided
to make spice cookies for dinner; that was too bad, because if
any of us had known we could have told her not to bother,
that Thursday was going to be the last day. Even Uncle Julian
did not suspect, however; he felt a little stronger on Thursday
morning and late in the morning Constance brought him into
the kitchen which smelled richly of spice cookies and he continued putting his papers into the box. Charles had taken a
hammer and found nails and a board and was pounding away
mercilessly at the broken step; from the kitchen window I
could see that he was doing it very badly and I was pleased; I
wished the hammer to pound his thumb. I stayed in the
kitchen until I was certain that they would all keep where they
were for a while and then I went upstairs and into our father's
room, walking softly so Constance would not know I was
there. The first thing to do was stop our father's watch which
Charles had started. I knew he was not wearing it to mend the
broken step because he was not wearing the chain, and I found
the watch and the chain and our father's signet ring on our
father's dresser with Charles' tobacco pouch and four books of
matches. I was not allowed to touch matches but in any case I
would not have touched Charles' matches. I took up the
watch and listened to it ticking because Charles had started it;
I could not turn it all the way back to where it had formerly
been because he had kept it going for two or three days, but I
twisted the winding knob backward until there was a small
complaining crack from the watch and the ticking stopped.
When I was sure that he could never start it ticking again I put
it back gently where I had found it; one thing, at least, had
been released from Charles' spell and I thought that I had at
last broken through his tight skin of invulnerability. I need not
bother about the chain, which was broken, and I disliked the
ring. Eliminating Charles from everything he had touched
was almost impossible, but it seemed to me that if I altered our
father's room, and perhaps later the kitchen and the drawing

room and the study, and even finally the garden, Charles would be lost, shut off from what he recognized, and would have to concede that this was not the house he had come to visit and so would go away. I altered our father's room very quickly, and almost without noise.

During the night I had gone out in the darkness and brought in a large basket filled with pieces of wood and broken sticks and leaves and scraps of glass and metal from the field and the wood. Jonas came back and forth with me, amused at our walking silently while everyone slept. When I altered our father's room I took the books from the desk and blankets from the bed, and I put my glass and metal and wood and sticks and leaves into the empty places. I could not put the things which had been our father's into my own room, so I carried them softly up the stairs to the attic where everything else of theirs was kept. I poured a pitcher of water onto our father's bed; Charles could not sleep there again. The mirror over the dresser was already smashed; it would not reflect Charles. He would not be able to find books or clothes and would be lost in a room of leaves and broken sticks. I tore down the curtains and threw them on the floor; now Charles would have to look outside and see the driveway going away and the road beyond.

I looked at the room with pleasure. A demon-ghost would not easily find himself here. I was back in my own room, lying on the bed and playing with Jonas when I heard Charles down below in the garden shouting to Constance. "This is too much," he was saying, "simply too much."

"What now?" Constance asked; she had come to the kitchen door and I could hear Uncle Julian somewhere below saying, "Tell that young fool to stop his bellowing."

I looked out quickly; the broken step had clearly been too much for Charles because the hammer and the board lay on the ground and the step was still broken; Charles was coming up the path from the creek and he was carrying something; I wondered what he had found now.

"Did you ever hear of anything like this?" he was saying; even though he was close now he was still shouting. "Look at this, Connie, just *look* at it."

"I suppose it belongs to Merricat," Constance said.

"It does *not* belong to Merricat, or anything like it. This is *money*."

"I remember," Constance said. "Silver dollars. I remember when she buried them."

"There must be twenty or thirty dollars here; this is outrageous."

"She likes to bury things."

Charles was still shouting, shaking my box of silver dollars back and forth violently. I wondered if he would drop it; I would like to have seen Charles on the ground, scrabbling after my silver dollars.

"It's not her money," he was shouting, "she has no right to hide it."

I wondered how he had happened to find the box where I had buried it; perhaps Charles and money found each other no matter how far apart they were, or perhaps Charles was engaged in systematically digging up every inch of our land. "This is terrible," he was shouting, "terrible; she has no right."

"No harm is done," Constance said. I could see that she was puzzled and somewhere inside the kitchen Uncle Julian was pounding and calling her.

"How do you know there isn't more?" Charles held the box out accusingly. "How do you know that crazy kid hasn't buried thousands of dollars all over, where we'll *never* find it?"

"She likes to bury things," Constance said. "Coming, Uncle Julian."

Charles followed her inside, still holding the box tenderly. I supposed I could bury the box again after he had gone, but I was not pleased. I came to the top of the stairs and watched Charles proceeding down the hall to the study; he was clearly going to put my silver dollars into our father's safe. I ran down the stairs quickly and quietly and out through the kitchen. "Silly Merricat," Constance said to me as I passed; she was putting spice cookies in long rows to cool.

I was thinking of Charles. I could turn him into a fly and drop him into a spider's web and watch him tangled and helpless and struggling, shut into the body of a dying buzzing fly; I could wish him dead until he died. I could fasten him to a tree and keep him there until he grew into the trunk and bark grew over his mouth. I could bury him in the hole where my box of silver dollars had been so safe until he came; if he was under the ground I could walk over him stamping my feet.

He had not even bothered to fill in the hole. I could imagine him walking here and noticing the spot where the ground was disturbed, stopping to poke in it and then digging wildly with both his hands, scowling and finally greedy and shocked and gasping when he found my box of silver dollars. "Don't blame *me*," I said to the hole; I would have to find something else to bury here and I wished it could be Charles.

The hole would hold his head nicely. I laughed when I found a round stone the right size, and scratched a face on it and buried it in the hole. "Goodbye, Charles," I said. "Next time don't go around taking other people's things."

I stayed by the creek for an hour or so; I was staying by the creek when Charles finally went upstairs and into the room which was no longer his and no longer our father's. I thought for one minute that Charles had been in my shelter, but nothing was disturbed, as it would have been if Charles had come scratching around. He had been near enough to bother me, however, so I cleared out the grass and leaves I usually slept on, and shook out my blanket, and put in everything fresh. I washed the flat rock where I sometimes ate my meals, and put a better branch across the entrance. I wondered if Charles would come back looking for more silver dollars and I wondered if he would like my six blue marbles. I was finally hungry and went back to our house, and there in the kitchen was Charles, still shouting.

"I can't *believe* it," he was saying, quite shrill by now, "I simply can't *believe* it."

I wondered how long Charles was going to go on shouting. He made a black noise in our house and his voice was getting thinner and higher; perhaps if he shouted long enough he would squeak. I sat on the kitchen step next to Jonas and thought that perhaps Constance might laugh out loud if Charles squeaked at her. It never happened, however, because as soon as he saw that I was sitting on the step he was quiet for a minute and then when he spoke he had brought his voice down and made it slow.

"So you're back," he said. He did not move toward me but

I felt his voice as though he were coming closer. I did not look at him; I looked at Jonas, who was looking at him.

"I haven't quite decided what I'm going to do with you," he said. "But whatever I do, you'll remember it."

"Don't bully her, Charles," Constance said. I did not like her voice either because it was strange and I knew she was uncertain. "It's all my fault, anyway." That was her new way of thinking.

I thought I would help Constance, perhaps make her laugh. "*Amanita pantherina*," I said, "highly poisonous. *Amanita rubescens*, edible and good. The *Cicuta maculata* is the water hemlock, one of the most poisonous of wild plants if taken internally. The *Apocynum cannabinum* is not a poisonous plant of the first importance, but the snakeberry—"

"Stop it," Charles said, still quiet.

"Constance," I said, "we came home for lunch, Jonas and I."

"First you will have to explain to Cousin Charles," Constance said, and I was chilled.

Charles was sitting at the kitchen table, with his chair pushed back and turned a little to face me in the doorway. Constance stood behind him, leaning against the sink. Uncle Julian sat at his table, stirring papers. There were rows and rows of spice cookies cooling and the kitchen still smelled of cinnamon and nutmeg. I wondered if Constance would give Jonas a spice cookie with his supper but of course she never did because that was the last day.

"Now listen," Charles said. He had brought down a handful of sticks and dirt, perhaps to prove to Constance that they had really been in his room, or perhaps because he was going to clean it away handful by handful; the sticks and dirt looked wrong on the kitchen table and I thought that perhaps one reason Constance looked so sad was the dirt on her clean table. "Now listen," Charles said.

"I cannot work in here if that young man is going to talk all the time," Uncle Julian said. "Constance, tell him he must be quiet for a little while."

"You, too," Charles said in that soft voice. "I have put up with enough from both of you. One of you fouls my room and goes around burying money and the other one can't even remember my name."

"Charles," I said to Jonas. I was the one who buried money, certainly, so I was not the one who could not remember his name; poor old Uncle Julian could not bury anything and could not remember Charles' name. I would remember to be kinder to Uncle Julian. "Will you give Uncle Julian a spice cookie for his dinner?" I asked Constance. "And Jonas one too?"

"Mary Katherine," Charles said, "I am going to give you one chance to explain. Why did you make that mess in my room?"

There was no reason to answer him. He was not Constance, and anything I said to him might perhaps help him to get back his thin grasp on our house. I sat on the door step and played with Jonas's ears, which flicked and snapped when I tickled them.

"Answer me," Charles said.

"How often must I tell you, John, that I know nothing whatsoever about it?" Uncle Julian slammed his hand down onto his papers and scattered them. "It is a quarrel between the women and none of my affair. I do not involve myself in my wife's petty squabbles and I strongly advise you to do the same. It is not fitting for men of dignity to threaten and reproach because women have had a falling out. You lose stature, John, you lose stature."

"Shut up," Charles said; he was shouting again and I was pleased. "Constance," he said, lowering his voice a little, "this is terrible. The sooner you're out of it the better."

"—will not be told to shut up by my own brother. We will leave your house, John, if that is really your desire. I ask you, however, to reflect. My wife and I—"

"It's my fault, all of it," Constance said. I thought she was going to cry. It was unthinkable for Constance to cry again after all these years, but I was held tight, I was chilled, and I could not move to go over to her.

"You are evil," I said to Charles. "You are a ghost and a demon."

"What the *hell*?" Charles said.

"Don't pay any attention," Constance told him. "Don't listen to Merricat's nonsense."

"You are a very selfish man, John, perhaps even a scoundrel, and overly fond of the world's goods; I sometimes wonder, John, if you are every bit the gentleman."

"It's a crazy house," Charles said with conviction. "Constance, this is a crazy house."

"I'll clean your room, right away. Charles, please don't be angry." Constance looked at me wildly, but I was held tight and could not see her.

"Uncle Julian." Charles got up and went over to where Uncle Julian sat at his table.

"Don't you touch my papers," Uncle Julian said, trying to cover them with his hands. "You get away from my papers, you bastard."

"What?" said Charles.

"I apologize," Uncle Julian said to Constance. "Not language fitting for your ears, my dear. Just tell this young bastard to stay away from my papers."

"Look," Charles said to Uncle Julian, "I tell you I've had enough of this. I am not going to touch your silly papers and I am not your brother John."

"Of course you are not my brother John; you are not tall enough by half an inch. You are a young bastard and I desire that you return to your father, who, to my shame, is my brother Arthur, and tell him I said so. In the presence of your mother, if you choose; she is a strong-willed woman but lacks family feeling. She desired that the family connection be severed. I have consequently no objection to your repeating my high language in her presence."

"That has all been forgotten, Uncle Julian; Constance and I—"

"I think you have forgotten *yourself*, young man, to take such a tone to me. I am pleased that you are repentant, but you have taken far too much of my time. Please be extremely quiet now."

"Not until I have finished with your niece Mary Katherine."

"My niece Mary Katherine has been a long time dead, young man. She did not survive the loss of her family; I supposed you knew that."

"What?" Charles turned furiously to Constance.

"My niece Mary Katherine died in an orphanage, of neglect, during her sister's trial for murder. But she is of very little consequence to my book, and so we will have done with her."

"She is sitting right here." Charles waved his hands, and his face was red.

"Young man." Uncle Julian put down his pencil and half-turned to face Charles. "I have pointed out to you, I believe, the importance of my work. You choose constantly to interrupt me. I have had enough. You must either be quiet or you must leave this room."

I was laughing at Charles and even Constance was smiling. Charles stood staring at Uncle Julian, and Uncle Julian, going through his papers, said to himself, "Damned impertinent puppy," and then, "Constance?"

"Yes, Uncle Julian?"

"Why have my papers been put into this box? I shall have to take them all out again and rearrange them. Has that young man been near my papers? Has he?"

"No, Uncle Julian."

"He takes a great deal upon himself, I think. When is he going away?"

"I'm not going away," Charles said. "I am going to stay."

"Impossible," Uncle Julian said. "We have not the room. Constance?"

"Yes, Uncle Julian?"

"I would like a chop for my lunch. A nice little chop, neatly broiled. Perhaps a mushroom."

"Yes," Constance said with relief, "I should start lunch." As though she were happy to be doing it at last she came to the table to brush away the dirt and leaves that Charles had left there. She brushed them into a paper bag and threw the bag into the wastebasket, and then she came back with a cloth and scrubbed the table. Charles looked at her and at me and at Uncle Julian. He was clearly baffled, unable to grasp his fingers tightly around anything he saw or heard; it was a joyful sight, to see the first twistings and turnings of the demon caught, and I was very proud of Uncle Julian. Constance smiled down at Charles, happy that no one was shouting any more; she was not going to cry now and perhaps she too was getting a quick glimpse of a straining demon because she said, "You look tired, Charles. Go and rest till lunch."

"Go and rest where?" he said and he was still angry. "I am not going to stir out of here until something is done about that girl."

"Merricat? Why should anything be done? I said I would clean your room."

"Aren't you even going to punish her?"

"Punish me?" I was standing then, shivering against the door frame. "Punish me? You mean send me to bed without my dinner?"

And I ran. I ran until I was in the field of grass, in the very center where it was safe, and I sat there, the grass taller than my head and hiding me. Jonas found me, and we sat there together where no one could ever see us.

After a very long time I stood up again because I knew where I was going. I was going to the summerhouse. I had not been near the summerhouse for six years, but Charles had blackened the world and only the summerhouse would do. Jonas would not follow me; he disliked the summerhouse and when he saw me turning onto the overgrown path which led there he went another way as though he had something important to do and would meet me somewhere later. No one had ever liked the summerhouse very much, I remembered. Our father had planned it and had intended to lead the creek near it and build a tiny waterfall, but something had gotten into the wood and stone and paint when the summerhouse was built and made it bad. Our mother had once seen a rat in the doorway looking in and nothing after that could persuade her there again, and where our mother did not go, no one else went.

I had never buried anything around here. The ground was black and wet and nothing buried would have been quite comfortable. The trees pressed too closely against the sides of the summerhouse, and breathed heavily on its roof, and the poor flowers planted here once had either died or grown into huge tasteless wild things. When I stood near the summerhouse and looked at it I thought it the ugliest place I had ever seen; I remembered that our mother had quite seriously asked to have it burned down.

Inside was all wet and dark. I disliked sitting on the stone floor but there was no other place; once, I recalled, there had been chairs here and perhaps even a low table but these were gone now, carried off or rotted away. I sat on the floor and placed all of them correctly in my mind, in the circle around the dining-room table. Our father sat at the head. Our mother sat at the foot. Uncle Julian sat on one hand of our mother, and our brother Thomas on the other; beside my father sat our Aunt Dorothy and Constance. I sat between Constance and Uncle Julian, in my rightful, my own and proper, place at the table. Slowly I began to listen to them talking.

"—to buy a book for Mary Katherine. Lucy, should not Mary Katherine have a new book?"

"Mary Katherine should have anything she wants, my dear. Our most loved daughter must have anything she likes."

"Constance, your sister lacks butter. Pass it to her at once, please."

"Mary Katherine, we love you."

"You must never be punished. Lucy, you are to see to it that our most loved daughter Mary Katherine is never punished."

"Mary Katherine would never allow herself to do anything wrong; there is never any need to punish her."

"I have heard, Lucy, of disobedient children being sent to their beds without dinner as a punishment. That must not be permitted with our Mary Katherine."

"I quite agree, my dear. Mary Katherine must never be punished. Must never be sent to bed without her dinner. Mary Katherine will never allow herself to do anything inviting punishment."

"Our beloved, our dearest Mary Katherine must be guarded and cherished. Thomas, give your sister your dinner; she would like more to eat."

"Dorothy—Julian. Rise when our beloved daughter rises."

"Bow all your heads to our adored Mary Katherine."

8

I HAD to go back for dinner; it was vital that I sit at the dinner table with Constance and Uncle Julian and Charles. It was unthinkable that they should sit there, eating their dinner and talking and passing food to one another, and see my place empty. As Jonas and I came along the path and through the garden in the gathering darkness I looked at the house with all the richness of love I contained; it was a good house, and soon it would be cleaned and fair again. I stopped for a minute, looking, and Jonas brushed my leg and spoke softly, in curiosity.

"I'm looking at our house," I told him and he stood quietly beside me, looking up with me. The roof pointed firmly against the sky, and the walls met one another compactly, and the windows shone darkly; it was a good house, and nearly clean. There was light from the kitchen window and from the windows of the dining room; it was time for their dinner and I must be there. I wanted to be inside the house, with the door shut behind me.

When I opened the kitchen door to go inside I could feel at once that the house still held anger, and I wondered that anyone could keep one emotion so long; I could hear his voice clearly from the kitchen, going on and on.

"—*must* be done about her," he was saying, "things simply can*not* continue like this."

Poor Constance, I thought, having to listen and listen and watch the food getting cold. Jonas ran ahead of me into the dining room, and Constance said, "Here she is."

I stood in the dining-room doorway and looked carefully for a minute. Constance was wearing pink, and her hair was combed back nicely; she smiled at me when I looked at her, and I knew she was tired of listening. Uncle Julian's wheel chair was pushed up tight against the table and I was sorry to see that Constance had tucked his napkin under his chin; it was too bad that Uncle Julian should not be allowed to eat freely. He was eating meat loaf, and peas which Constance had preserved one fragrant summer day; Constance had cut the meat loaf into small pieces and Uncle Julian mashed meat loaf and peas with the back of his spoon and stirred them before trying to get them into his mouth. He was not listening, but the voice went on and on.

"So you decided to come back again, did you? And high time, too, young lady; your sister and I have been trying to decide how to teach you a lesson."

"Wash your face, Merricat," Constance said gently. "And comb your hair; we do not want you untidy at table, and your Cousin Charles is already angry with you."

Charles pointed his fork at me. "I may as well tell you, Mary, that your tricks are over for good. Your sister and I have decided that we have had just exactly enough of hiding and destroying and temper."

I disliked having a fork pointed at me and I disliked the sound of the voice never stopping; I wished he would put food on the fork and put it into his mouth and strangle himself.

"Run along, Merricat," Constance said, "your dinner will be cold." She knew I would not eat dinner sitting at that table and she would bring me my dinner in the kitchen afterward, but I thought that she did not want to remind Charles of that and so give him one more thing to talk about. I smiled at her and went into the hall, with the voice still talking behind me. There had not been this many words sounded in our house for a long time, and it was going to take a while to clean them out. I walked heavily going up the stairs so they could hear that I was surely going up, but when I reached the top I went as softly as Jonas behind me.

Constance had cleaned the room where he was living. It looked very empty, because all she had done was take things out; she had nothing to put back because I had carried all of it to the attic. I knew the dresser drawers were empty, and the closet, and the bookshelves. There was no mirror, and a broken watch and a smashed chain lay alone on the dresser top. Constance had taken away the wet bedding, and I supposed she had dried and turned the mattress, because the bed was made up again. The long curtains were gone, perhaps to be washed. He had been lying on the bed, because it was disarranged, and his pipe, still burning, lay on the table beside the bed; I supposed that he had been lying here when Constance called him to dinner, and I wondered if he had looked around

and around the altered room, trying to find something familiar, hoping that perhaps the angle of the closet door or the
light on the ceiling would bring everything back to him again.
I was sorry that Constance had to turn the mattress alone; usually I helped her but perhaps he had come and offered to do it
for her. She had even brought him a clean saucer for his pipe;
our house did not have ashtrays and when he kept trying to
find places to put down his pipe Constance had brought a
set of chipped saucers from the pantry shelf and given them
to him to hold his pipe. The saucers were pink, with gold
leaves around the rim; they were from a set older than any I
remembered.

"Who used them?" I asked Constance, when she brought
them into the kitchen. "Where are their cups?"

"I've never seen them used; they come from a time before I
was in the kitchen. Some great-grandmother brought them
with her dowry and they were used and broken and replaced
and finally put away on the top shelf of the pantry; there are
only these saucers and three dinner plates."

"They belong in the pantry," I said. "Not put around the
house."

Constance had given them to Charles and now they were
scattered, instead of spending their little time decently put
away on a shelf. There was one in the drawing room and one
in the dining room and one, I supposed, in the study. They
were not fragile, because the one now in the bedroom had not
cracked although the pipe on it was burning. I had known all
day that I would find something here; I brushed the saucer
and the pipe off the table into the wastebasket and they fell
softly onto the newspapers he had brought into the house.

I was wondering about my eyes; one of my eyes—the left—
saw everything golden and yellow and orange, and the other
eye saw shades of blue and grey and green; perhaps one eye
was for daylight and the other was for night. If everyone in the
world saw different colors from different eyes there might be a
great many new colors still to be invented. I had reached the
staircase to go downstairs before I remembered and had to go
back to wash, and comb my hair. "What took you so long?" he
asked when I sat down at the table. "What have you been doing
up there?"

"Will you make me a cake with pink frosting?" I asked Constance. "With little gold leaves around the edge? Jonas and I are going to have a party."

"Perhaps tomorrow," Constance said.

"We are going to have a long talk after dinner," Charles said.

"*Solanum dulcamara*," I told him.

"What?" he said.

"Deadly nightshade," Constance said. "Charles, please let it wait."

"I've had enough," he said,

"Constance?"

"Yes, Uncle Julian?"

"I have cleaned my plate." Uncle Julian found a morsel of meat loaf on his napkin and put it into his mouth. "What do I have now?"

"Perhaps a little more, Uncle Julian? It is a pleasure to see you so hungry."

"I feel considerably better tonight. I have not felt so hearty for days."

I was pleased that Uncle Julian was well and I knew he was happy because he had been so discourteous to Charles. While Constance was cutting up another small piece of meat loaf Uncle Julian looked at Charles with an evil shine in his old eyes, and I knew he was going to say something wicked. "Young man," he began at last, but Charles turned his head suddenly to look into the hall.

"I smell smoke," Charles said.

Constance paused and lifted her head and turned to the kitchen door. "The stove?" she said and got up quickly to go into the kitchen.

"Young man—"

"There is certainly smoke." Charles went to look into the hall. "I smell it out here," he said. I wondered whom he thought he was talking to; Constance was in the kitchen and Uncle Julian was thinking about what he was going to say, and I had stopped listening. "There *is* smoke," Charles said.

"It's not the stove." Constance stood in the kitchen doorway and looked at Charles.

Charles turned and came closer to me. "If this is anything you've done . . ." he said.

I laughed because it was clear that Charles was afraid to go upstairs and follow the smoke; then Constance said, "Charles —your pipe—" and he turned and ran up the stairs. "I've asked him and asked him," Constance said.

"Would it start a fire?" I asked her, and then Charles screamed from upstairs, screamed, I thought, with the exact sound of a bluejay in the woods. "That's Charles," I said politely to Constance, and she hurried to go into the hall and look up. "What *is* it?" she asked, "Charles, what *is* it?"

"Fire," Charles said, crashing down the stairs, "Run, run; the whole damn house is on fire," he screamed into Constance's face, "and you haven't got a *phone*."

"My papers," Uncle Julian said. "I shall collect my papers and remove them to a place of safety." He pushed against the edge of the table to move his chair away. "Constance?"

"Run," Charles said, at the front door now, wrenching at the lock, "*run*, you fool."

"I have not done much running in the past few years, young man. I see no cause for this hysteria; there is time to gather my papers."

Charles had the front door open now, and turned on the doorsill to call to Constance. "Don't try to carry the safe," he said, "put the money in a bag. I'll be back as fast as I can get help. Don't panic." He ran, and we could hear him screaming "Fire! Fire! Fire!" as he ran toward the village.

"Good heavens," Constance said, almost amused. Then she took Uncle Julian's chair to help him into his room and I went into the hall and looked upstairs. Charles had left the door to our father's room standing open and I could see the movement of fire inside. Fire burns upward, I thought; it will burn their things in the attic. Charles had left the front door open too, and a line of smoke reached down the stairs and drifted outside. I did not see any need to move quickly or to run shrieking around the house because the fire did not seem to be hurrying itself. I wondered if I could go up the stairs and shut the door to our father's room and keep the fire inside, belonging entirely to Charles, but when I started up the stairs I saw a finger of flame reach out to touch the hall carpet and some heavy object fell crashing in our father's room. There would be nothing of Charles in there now; even his pipe must have been consumed.

"Uncle Julian is gathering his papers," Constance said, coming into the hall to stand beside me. She had Uncle Julian's shawl over her arm.

"We will have to go outside," I said. I knew that she was frightened, so I said, "We can stay on the porch, behind the vines, in the darkness."

"We neatened it just the other day," she said. "It has no *right* to burn." She began to shiver as though she were angry, and I took her by the hand and brought her through the open front door and just as we turned back for another look the lights came into the driveway with the disgusting noise of sirens and we were held in the doorway in the light. Constance put her face against me to hide, and then there was Jim Donell, the first one to leap from the fire engine and run up the steps. "Out of the way," he said, and pushed past us and into our house. I took Constance along the porch to the corner where the vines grew thick, and she moved into the corner and pressed against the vines. I held her hand tight, and together we watched the great feet of the men stepping across our doorsill, dragging their hoses, bringing filth and confusion and danger into our house. More lights moved into the driveway and up to the steps, and the front of the house was white and pale and uncomfortable at being so clearly visible; it had never been lighted before. The noise was too much for me to hear all together, but somewhere in the noise was Charles' voice, still going on and on. "Get the safe in the study," he said a thousand times.

Smoke squeezed out the front door, coming between the big men pushing in. "Constance," I whispered, "Constance, don't watch them."

"Can they see me?" she whispered back. "Is anyone looking?"

"They're all watching the fire. Be very quiet."

I looked carefully out between the vines. There was a long row of cars, and the village fire engine, all parked as close to the house as they could get, and everyone in the village was there, looking up and watching. I saw faces laughing, and faces that looked frightened, and then someone called out, very near to us, "What about the women, and the old man? Anyone see them?"

"They had plenty of warning," Charles shouted from somewhere, "they're all right."

Uncle Julian could manage his chair well enough to get out the back door, I thought, but it did not seem that the fire was going near the kitchen or Uncle Julian's room; I could see the hoses and hear the men shouting, and they were all on the stairs and in the front bedrooms upstairs. I could not get through the front door, and even if I could leave Constance there was no way to go around to the back door without going down the steps in the light with all of them watching. "Was Uncle Julian frightened?" I whispered to Constance.

"I think he was annoyed," she said. A few minutes later she said, "It will take a great deal of scrubbing to get that hall clean again," and sighed. I was pleased that she thought of the house and forgot the people outside.

"Jonas?" I said to her; "where is he?"

I could see her smile a little in the darkness of the vines. "He was annoyed, too," she said. "He went out the back door when I took Uncle Julian in to get his papers."

We were all right. Uncle Julian might very well forget that there was a fire at all if he became interested in his papers, and Jonas was almost certainly watching from the shadow of the trees. When they had finished putting out Charles' fire I would take Constance back inside and we could start to clean our house again. Constance was quieter, although more and more cars came down the driveway and the unending pattern of feet went back and forth across our doorsill. Except for Jim Donell, who wore a hat proclaiming him "Chief," it was impossible to identify any one person, any more than it was possible to put a name to any of the faces out in front of our house, looking up and laughing at the fire.

I tried to think clearly. The house was burning; there was fire inside our house, but Jim Donell and the other, anonymous, men in hats and raincoats were curiously able to destroy the fire which was running through the bones of our house. It was Charles' fire. When I listened particularly for the fire I could hear it, a singing hot noise upstairs, but over and around it, smothering it, were the voices of the men inside and the voices of the people watching outside and the distant sound of cars on the driveway. Next to me Constance was standing quietly, sometimes looking at the men going into the house, but more often covering her eyes with her hands; she was excited, I thought, but not in any danger. Every now and then it was possible to hear one voice raised above the others; Jim Donell shouted some word of instruction, or someone in the crowd called out. "Why not let it burn?" a woman's voice came loudly, laughing, and "Get the safe out of the study downstairs"; that was Charles, safely in the crowd out front.

"Why not let it burn?" the woman called insistently, and one of the dark men going in and out of our front door turned and waved and grinned. "We're the firemen," he called back, "we *got* to put it out."

"Let it burn," the woman called.

Smoke was everywhere, thick and ugly. Sometimes when I looked out the faces of the people were clouded with smoke, and it came out the front door in frightening waves. Once there was a crash from inside the house and voices speaking quickly and urgently, and the faces outside turned up happily in the smoke, mouths open. "Get the safe," Charles called out wildly, "two or three of you men get the safe out of the study; the whole house is going."

"Let it burn," the woman called.

I was hungry and I wanted my dinner, and I wondered how long they could make the fire last before they put it out and went away and Constance and I could go back inside. One or two of the village boys had edged onto the porch dangerously close to where we stood, but they only looked inside, not at the porch, and tried to stand on their toes and see past the fireman and the hoses. I was tired and I wished it would all be over. I realized then that the light was lessening, the faces on the lawn less distinct, and a new tone came into the noise; the voices inside were surer, less sharp, almost pleased, and the voices outside were lower, and disappointed.

"It's going out," someone said.

"Under control," another voice added.

"Did a lot of damage, though." There was laughter. "Sure made a mess of the old place."

"Should of burned it down years ago."

"And them in it."

They mean us, I thought, Constance and me.

"Say—anybody *seen* them?"

"No such luck. Firemen threw them out."

"Too bad."

The light was almost gone. The people outside stood now in shadows, their faces narrowed and dark, with only the headlights of the cars to light them; I saw the flash of a smile, and somewhere else a hand raised to wave, and the voices went on regretfully.

"Just about over."

"Pretty good fire."

Jim Donell came through the front door. Everyone knew him because of his size and his hat saying CHIEF. "Say, Jim," someone called, "why don't you let it burn?"

He lifted both his hands to make everyone be quiet. "Fire's all out, folks," he said.

Very carefully he put up his hands and took off his hat saying CHIEF and while everyone watched he walked slowly down the steps and over to the fire engine and set his hat down on the front seat. Then he bent down, searching thoughtfully, and finally, while everyone watched, he took up a rock. In complete silence he turned slowly and then raised his arm and smashed the rock through one of the great tall windows of our mother's drawing room. A wall of laughter rose and grew behind him and then, first the boys on the steps and then the other men and at last the women and the smaller children, they moved like a wave at our house.

"Constance," I said, "Constance," but she had her hands over her eyes.

The other of the drawing-room windows crashed, this time from inside, and I saw that it had been shattered by the lamp which always stood by Constance's chair in the drawing room.

Above it all, most horrible, was the laughter. I saw one of the Dresden figurines thrown and break against the porch rail, and the other fell unbroken and rolled along the grass. I heard

Constance's harp go over with a musical cry, and a sound which I knew was a chair being smashed against the wall.

"Listen," said Charles from somewhere, "will a couple of you guys help me with this safe?"

Then, through the laughter, someone began, "Merricat, said Constance, would you like a cup of tea?" It was rhythmic and insistent. I am on the moon, I thought, please let me be on the moon. Then I heard the sound of dishes smashing and at that minute realized that we stood outside the tall windows of the dining room and they were coming very close.

"Constance," I said, "we have to run."

She shook her head, her hands over her face.

"They'll find us in a minute. Please, Constance dearest; run with me."

"I can't," she said, and from just inside the dining-room window a shout went up: "Merricat, said Constance, would you like to go to sleep?" and I pulled Constance away a second before the window went; I thought a chair had been thrown through it, perhaps the dining-room chair where our father used to sit and Charles used to sit. "Hurry," I said, no longer able to be quiet in all that noise, and pulling Constance by the hand I ran toward the steps. As we came into the light she threw Uncle Julian's shawl across her face to hide it.

A little girl ran out of the front door carrying something, and her mother, behind her, caught her by the back of the dress and slapped her hands. "Don't you put that stuff in your mouth," the mother screamed, and the little girl dropped a handful of Constance's spice cookies.

"Merricat, said Constance, would you like a cup of tea?"

"Merricat, said Constance, would you like to go to sleep?"

"Oh, no, said Merricat, you'll poison me."

We had to get down the steps and into the woods to be safe; it was not far but the headlights of the cars shone across the lawn. I wondered if Constance would slip and fall, running through the light, but we had to get to the woods and there was no other way. We hesitated near the steps, neither one of us quite daring to go farther, but the windows were broken and inside they were throwing our dishes and our glasses and our silverware and even the pots Constance used in cooking; I wondered if my stool in the corner of the kitchen had been smashed yet. While we stood still for a last minute, a car came up the driveway, and another behind it; they swung to a stop in front of the house, sending more light onto the lawn. "What the holy devil is going *on* here?" Jim Clarke said, rolling out of the first car, and Helen Clarke, on the other side, opened her mouth and stared. Shouting and pushing, and not seeing us at all, Jim Clarke made his way through our door and into our house, "What the holy goddam devil is going *on* here?" he kept saying and outside Helen Clarke never saw us, but only stared at our house. "Crazy fools," Jim Clarke yelled inside, "crazy drunken fools." Dr. Levy came out of the second car and hurried toward the house. "Has everyone gone crazy in here?" Jim Clarke was saying from inside, and there was a shout of laughter, "Would you like a cup of tea?" someone inside screamed, and they laughed. "Ought to bring it down brick by brick," someone said inside.

The doctor came up the steps running, and pushed us aside without looking. "Where is Julian Blackwood?" he asked a woman in the doorway, and the woman said, "Down in the boneyard ten feet deep."

It was time; I took Constance tightly by the hand, and we started carefully down the steps. I would not run yet because I was afraid that Constance might fall, so I brought her slowly down the steps; no one could see us yet except Helen Clarke and she stared at the house. Behind us I heard Jim Clarke shouting; he was trying to make the people leave our house, and before we reached the bottom step there were voices behind us.

"There they are," someone shouted and I think it was Stella. "There they are, there they are, there they are," and I started to run but Constance stumbled and then they were all around us, pushing and laughing and trying to get close to see. Constance held Uncle Julian's shawl across her face so they could not look at her, and for a minute we stood very still, pressed together by the feeling of people all around us.

"Put them back in the house and start the fire all over again."

"We fixed things up nice for you girls, just like you always wanted it."

"Merricat, said Constance, would you like a cup of tea?"

For one terrible minute I thought that they were going to join hands and dance around us, singing. I saw Helen Clarke far away, pressed hard against the side of her car; she was crying and saying something and even though I could not hear her through the noise I knew she was saying "I want to go home, please, I want to go home."

"Merricat, said Constance, would you like to go to sleep?"

They were trying not to touch us; whenever I turned they fell back a little; once, between two shoulders I saw Harler of the junk yard wandering across the porch of our house, picking up things and setting them to one side in a pile. I moved a little, holding Constance's hand tight, and as they fell back we ran suddenly, going toward the trees, but Jim Donell's wife and Mrs. Mueller came in front of us, laughing and holding out their arms, and we stopped. I turned, and gave Constance a little pull, and we ran, but Stella and the Harris boys crossed in front of us, laughing, and the Harris boys shouting "Down in the boneyard ten feet deep," and we stopped. Then I turned toward the house, running again with Constance pulled behind me, and Elbert the grocer and his greedy wife were there, holding their hands to halt us, almost dancing together, and we stopped. I went then to the side, and Jim Donell stepped in front of us, and we stopped.

"Oh, no, said Merricat, you'll poison me," Jim Donell said politely, and they came around us again, circling and keeping carefully out of reach. "Merricat, said Constance, would you like to go to sleep?" Over it all was the laughter, almost drowning the singing and the shouting and the howling of the Harris boys.

"Merricat, said Constance, would you like a cup of tea?"

Constance held to me with one hand and with the other hand she kept Uncle Julian's shawl across her face. I saw an opening in the circle around us, and ran again for the trees, but all the Harris boys were there, one on the ground with laughter, and we stopped. I turned again and ran for the house but Stella came forward and we stopped. Constance was stumbling, and I wondered if we were going to fall onto the ground in front of them, lying there where they might step on us in their dancing, and I stood still; I could not possibly let Constance fall in front of them.

"That's all now," Jim Clarke said from the porch. His voice was not loud, but they all heard. "That's enough," he said. There was a small polite silence, and then someone said, "Down in the boneyard ten feet deep," and the laughter rose.

"Listen to me," Jim Clarke said, raising his voice, "listen to me. Julian Blackwood is dead."

Then they were quiet at last. After a minute Charles Blackwood said from the crowd around us, "Did she kill him?" They went back from us, moving slowly in small steps, withdrawing, until there was a wide clear space around us and Constance standing clearly with Uncle Julian's shawl across her face. "Did she kill him?" Charles Blackwood asked again.

"She did not," said the doctor, standing in the doorway of our house. "Julian died as I have always known he would; he has been waiting a long time."

"Now go quietly," Jim Clarke said. He began to take people by the shoulders, pushing a little at their backs, turning them, toward their cars and the driveway. "Go quickly," he said, "There has been a death in this house."

It was so quiet, in spite of many people moving across the grass and going away, that I heard Helen Clarke say, "Poor Julian."

I took a cautious step toward the darkness, pulling Constance a little so that she followed me. "Heart," the doctor said on the porch, and I went another step. No one turned to look at us. Car doors slammed softly and motors started. I looked back once. A little group was standing around the doctor on the steps. Most of the lights were turned away, heading down the driveway. When I felt the shadows of the trees fall on us, I moved quickly; one last step and we were inside. Pulling Constance, I hurried under the trees, in the darkness; when I felt my feet leave the grass of the lawn and touch the soft mossy ground of the path through the woods and knew that the trees had closed in around us I stopped and put my arms around Constance. "It's all over," I told her, and held her tight. "It's all right," I said, "all right now."

I knew my way in the darkness or in the light. I thought once how good it was that I had straightened my hiding place and freshened it, so it would now be pleasant for Constance. I would cover her with leaves, like children in a story, and keep her safe and warm. Perhaps I would sing to her or tell her stories; I would bring her bright fruits and berries and water in a leaf cup. Someday we would go to the moon. I found the entrance to my hiding place and led Constance in and took her to the corner where there was a fresh pile of leaves and a blanket. I pushed her gently until she sat down and I took Uncle Julian's shawl away from her and covered her with it. A little purr came from the corner and I knew that Jonas had been waiting here for me.

I put branches across the entrance; even if they came with lights they would not see us. It was not entirely dark; I could see the shadow that was Constance and when I put my head back I saw two or three stars, shining from far away between the leaves and the branches and down onto my head.

One of our mother's Dresden figurines is broken, I thought, and I said aloud to Constance, "I am going to put death in all their food and watch them die."

Constance stirred, and the leaves rustled. "The way you did before?" she asked.

It had never been spoken of between us, not once in six years.

"Yes," I said after a minute, "the way I did before."

9

S OMETIME during the night an ambulance came and took Uncle Julian away, and I wondered if they missed his shawl, which was wound around Constance as she slept. I saw the ambulance lights turning into the driveway, with the small red light on top, and I heard the distant sounds of Uncle Julian's leaving, the voices speaking gently because they were in the presence of the dead, and the doors opening and closing. They called to us two or three times, perhaps to ask if they might have Uncle Julian, but their voices were subdued and no one came into the woods. I sat by the creek, wishing that I had been kinder to Uncle Julian. Uncle Julian had believed that I was dead, and now he was dead himself; bow your heads to our beloved Mary Katherine, I thought, or you will be dead.

The water moved sleepily in the darkness and I wondered what kind of a house we would have now. Perhaps the fire had destroyed everything and we would go back tomorrow and find that the past six years had been burned and they were waiting for us, sitting around the dining-room table waiting for Constance to bring them their dinner. Perhaps we would find ourselves in the Rochester house, or living in the village or on a houseboat on the river or in a tower on top of a hill; perhaps the fire might be persuaded to reverse itself and abandon our house and destroy the village instead; perhaps the villagers were all dead now. Perhaps the village was really a great game board, with the squares neatly marked out, and I had been moved past the square which read "Fire; return to Start," and was now on the last few squares, with only one move to go to reach home.

Jonas's fur smelled of smoke. Today was Helen Clarke's day to come to tea, but there would be no tea today, because we would have to neaten the house, although it was not the usual day for neatening the house. I wished that Constance had made sandwiches for us to bring down to the creek, and I wondered if Helen Clarke would try to come to tea even though the house was not ready. I decided that from now on I would not be allowed to hand tea cups.

When it first began to get light I heard Constance stirring on the leaves and I went into my hiding place to be near her when she awakened. When she opened her eyes she looked first at the trees above her, and then at me and smiled.

"We are on the moon at last," I told her, and she smiled.

"I thought I dreamed it all," she said.

"It really happened," I said.

"Poor Uncle Julian."

"They came in the night and took him away, and we stayed here on the moon."

"I'm glad to be here," she said. "Thank you for bringing me."

There were leaves in her hair and dirt on her face and Jonas, who had followed me into my hiding place, stared at her in surprise; he had never seen Constance with a dirty face before. For a minute she was quiet, no longer smiling, looking back at Jonas, realizing that she was dirty, and then she said, "Merricat, what are we going to do?"

"First we must neaten the house, even though it is not the usual day."

"The house," she said. "Oh, Merricat."

"I had no dinner last night," I told her.

"Oh, *Merricat*." She sat up and untangled herself quickly from Uncle Julian's shawl and the leaves; "Oh, Merricat, poor baby," she said. "We'll hurry," and she scrambled to her feet.

"First you had better wash your face."

She went to the creek and wet her handkerchief and scrubbed at her face while I shook out Uncle Julian's shawl and folded it, thinking how strange and backward everything was this morning; I had never touched Uncle Julian's shawl before. I already saw that the rules were going to be different, but it was odd to be folding Uncle Julian's shawl. Later, I thought, I would come back here to my hiding place and clean it, and put in fresh leaves.

"Merricat, you'll starve."

"We have to watch," I said, taking her hand to slow her. "We have to go very quietly and carefully; some of them may still be around waiting."

I went first down the path, walking silently, with Constance and Jonas behind me. Constance could not step as silently as I could, but she made very little sound and of course Jonas made no sound at all. I took the path that would bring us out of the woods at the back of the house, near the vegetable garden, and when I came to the edge of the woods I stopped and held Constance back while we looked carefully to see if there were any of them left. For one first minute we saw only the garden and the kitchen door, looking just as always, and then Constance gasped and said, "Oh, *Merricat*," with a little moan, and I held myself very still, because the top of our house was gone.

I remembered that I had stood looking at our house with love yesterday, and I thought how it had always been so tall, reaching up into the trees. Today the house ended above the kitchen doorway in a nightmare of black and twisted wood; I saw part of a window frame still holding broken glass and I thought: that was my window; I looked out that window from my room.

There was no one there, and no sound. We moved together very slowly toward the house, trying to understand its ugliness and ruin and shame. I saw that ash had drifted among the vegetable plants; the lettuce would have to be washed before I could eat it, and the tomatoes. No fire had come this way, but everything, the grass and the apple trees and the marble bench in Constance's garden, had an air of smokiness and everything was dirty. As we came closer to the house we saw more clearly that the fire had not reached the ground floor, but had had to be content with the bedrooms and the attic. Constance hesitated at the kitchen door, but she had opened it a thousand times before and it ought surely to recognize the touch of her hand, so she took the latch and lifted it. The house seemed to shiver when she opened the door, although one more draft could hardly chill it now. Constance had to push at the door to make it open, but no burned timber crashed down, and there was not, as I half thought there might be, a sudden rushing falling together, as a house, seemingly solid but really made only of ash, might dissolve at a touch.

"My kitchen," Constance said. "My kitchen."

She stood in the doorway, looking. I thought that we had somehow not found our way back correctly through the night, that we had somehow lost ourselves and come back through the wrong gap in time, or the wrong door, or the wrong fairy tale. Constance put her hand against the door frame to steady herself, and said again, "My kitchen, Merricat."

"My stool is still there," I said.

The obstacle which made the door hard to open was the kitchen table, turned on its side. I set it upright, and we went inside. Two of the chairs had been smashed, and the floor was horrible with broken dishes and glasses and broken boxes of food and paper torn from the shelves. Jars of jam and syrup and catsup had been shattered against the walls. The sink where Constance washed her dishes was filled with broken glass, as though glass after glass had been broken there methodically, one after another. Drawers of silverware and cooking ware had been pulled out and broken against the table and the walls, and silverware that had been in the house for generations of Blackwood wives was lying bent and scattered on the floor. Tablecloths and napkins hemmed by Blackwood women, and washed and ironed again and again, mended and cherished, had been ripped from the dining-room sideboard and dragged across the kitchen. It seemed that all the wealth and hidden treasure of our house had been found out and torn and soiled; I saw broken plates which had come from the top shelves in the cupboard, and our little sugar bowl with roses lay almost at my feet, handles gone. Constance bent down and picked up a silver spoon. "This was our grandmother's wedding pattern," she said, and set the spoon on the table. Then she said, "The preserves," and turned to the cellar door; it was closed and I hoped that perhaps they had not seen it, or had perhaps not had time to go down the stairs. Constance picked her way carefully across the floor and opened the cellar door and looked down. I thought of the jars and jars so beautifully preserved lying in broken sticky heaps in the cellar, but Constance went down a step or two and said, "No, it's all right; nothing here's been touched." She closed the cellar door again and made her way across to the sink to wash her hands and dry them on a dishtowel from the floor. "First, your breakfast," she said.

Jonas sat on the doorstep in the growing sunlight looking at the kitchen with astonishment; once he raised his eyes to me and I wondered if he thought that Constance and I had made this mess. I saw a cup not broken, and picked it up and set it on the table, and then thought to look for more things which might have escaped. I remembered that one of our mother's Dresden figurines had rolled safely onto the grass and I wondered if it had hidden successfully and preserved itself; I would look for it later.

Nothing was orderly, nothing was planned; it was not like any other day. Once Constance went into the cellar and came back with her arms full. "Vegetable soup," she said, almost singing, "and strawberry jam, and chicken soup, and pickled beef." She set the jars on the kitchen table and turned slowly, looking down at the floor. "There," she said at last, and went to a corner, to pick up a small saucepan. Then on a sudden thought she set down the saucepan and made her way into the pantry. "Merricat," she called with laughter, "they didn't find the flour in the barrel. Or the salt. Or the potatoes."

They found the sugar, I thought. The floor was gritty, and almost alive under my feet, and I thought of course; of course they would go looking for the sugar and have a lovely time; perhaps they had thrown handfuls of sugar at one another, screaming, "Blackwood sugar, Blackwood sugar, want a taste?"

"They got to the pantry shelves," Constance went on, "the cereals and the spices and the canned food."

I walked slowly around the kitchen, looking at the floor. I thought that they had probably tumbled things by the armload, because cans of food were scattered and bent as though they had been tossed into the air, and the boxes of cereal and tea and crackers had been trampled under foot and broken open. The tins of spices were all together, thrown into a corner unopened; I thought I could still smell the faint spicy scent of Constance's cookies and then saw some of them, crushed on the floor.

Constance came out of the pantry carrying a loaf of bread. "Look what they didn't find," she said, "and there are eggs and milk and butter in the cooler." Since they had not found the cellar door they had not found the cooler just inside, and I was pleased that they had not discovered eggs to mix into the mess on the floor.

At one time I found three unbroken chairs and set them where they belonged around the table. Jonas sat in my corner, on my stool, watching us. I drank chicken soup from a cup without a handle, and Constance washed a knife to spread butter on the bread. Although I did not perceive it then, time and the orderly pattern of our old days had ended; I do not know when I found the three chairs and when I ate buttered bread, whether I had found the chairs and then eaten bread, or whether I had eaten first, or even done both at once. Once Constance turned suddenly and put down her knife; she started for the closed door to Uncle Julian's room and then turned back, smiling a little. "I thought I heard him waking," she said, and sat down again.

We had not yet been out of the kitchen. We still did not know how much house was left to us, or what we might find waiting beyond the closed doors into the dining room and the hall. We sat quietly in the kitchen, grateful for the chairs and the chicken soup and the sunlight coming through the doorway, not yet ready to go further.

"What will they do with Uncle Julian?" I asked.

"They will have a funeral," Constance said with sadness. "Do you remember the others?"

"I was in the orphanage."

"They let me go to the funerals of the others. I can remember. They will have a funeral for Uncle Julian, and the Clarkes will go, and the Carringtons, and certainly little Mrs. Wright. They will tell each other how sorry they are. They will look to see if we are there."

I felt them looking to see if we were there, and I shivered.

"They will bury him with the others."

"I would like to bury something for Uncle Julian," I said.

Constance was quiet, looking at her fingers which lay still and long on the table. "Uncle Julian is gone, and the others," she said. "Most of our house is gone, Merricat; we are all that is left."

"Jonas."

"Jonas. We are going to lock ourselves in more securely than ever."

"But today is the day Helen Clarke comes to tea."

"No," she said. "Not again. Not here."

As long as we sat quietly together in the kitchen it was possible to postpone seeing the rest of the house. The library books were still on their shelf, untouched, and I supposed that no one had wanted to touch books belonging to the library; there was a fine, after all, for destroying library property.

Constance, who was always dancing, seemed now unwilling to move; she sat on at the kitchen table with her hands spread before her, not looking around at the destruction, and almost dreaming, as though she never believed that she had wakened this morning at all. "We must neaten the house," I said to her uneasily, and she smiled across at me.

When I felt that I could not wait for her any longer I said, "I'm going to look," and got up and went to the dining-room door. She watched me, not moving. When I opened the door to the dining room there was a shocking smell of wetness and burned wood and destruction, and glass from the tall windows lay across the floor and the silver tea service had been swept off the sideboard and stamped into grotesque, unrecognizable shapes. Chairs were broken here, too; I remembered that they had taken up chairs and hurled them at windows and walls. I went through the dining room and into the front hall. The front door stood wide open and early sunlight lay in patterns along the floor of the hall, touching broken glass and torn cloth; after a minute I recognized the cloth as the drawing-room draperies which our mother had once had made up four-teen feet long. No one was outside; I stood in the open doorway and saw that the lawn was marked with the tires of cars and the feet which had danced, and where the hoses had gone there were puddles and mud. The front porch was lit-tered, and I remembered the neat pile of partly broken furni-ture which Harler the junk dealer had set together last night. I wondered if he planned to come today with a truck and gather up everything he could, or if he had only put the pile together because he loved great piles of broken things and could not re-sist stacking junk wherever he found it. I waited in the door-way to be sure that no one was watching, and then I ran down the steps across the grass and found our mother's Dresden fig-urine unbroken where it had hidden against the roots of a bush; I thought to take it to Constance.

She was still sitting quietly at the kitchen table, and when I put the Dresden figurine down before her she looked for a minute and then took it in her hands and held it against her cheek. "It was all my fault," she said. "Somehow it was all my fault."

"I love you, Constance," I said.

"And I love you, Merricat."

"And will you make that little cake for Jonas and me? Pink frosting, with gold leaves around the edge?"

She shook her head, and for a minute I thought she was not going to answer me, and then she took a deep breath, and stood up. "First," she said, "I'm going to clean this kitchen."

"What are you going to do with that?" I asked her, touching the Dresden figurine with the very tip of my finger.

"Put it back where it belongs," she said, and I followed her as she opened the door to the hall and made her way down the hall to the drawing-room doorway. The hall was less littered than the rooms, because there had been less in it to smash, but there were fragments carried from the kitchen, and we stepped on spoons and dishes which had been thrown here. I was shocked when we came into the drawing room to see our mother's portrait looking down on us graciously while her drawing room lay destroyed around her. The white wedding cake trim was blackened with smoke and soot and would never be clean again; I disliked seeing the drawing room even more than the kitchen or the dining room, because we had always kept it so tidy, and our mother had loved this room. I wondered which of them had pushed over Constance's harp and I remembered that I had heard it cry out as it fell. The rose brocade on the chairs was torn and dirty, smudged with the marks of wet feet that had kicked at the chairs and stamped on the sofa. The windows were broken here too, and with the drapes torn down we were clearly visible from outside.

"I think I can close the shutters," I said, as Constance hesitated in the doorway, unwilling to come further into the room. I stepped out onto the porch through the broken window, thinking that no one had ever come this way before, and found that I could unhook the shutters easily. The shutters were as tall as the windows; originally it was intended that a man with a ladder would close the shutters when the summers were ended and the family went away to a city house, but so many years had passed since the shutters were closed that the hooks had rusted and I needed only to shake the heavy shutters to pull the hooks away from the house. I swung the shutters closed, but I could only reach the lower bolt to hold them; there were two more bolts high above my head; perhaps some night I might come out here with a ladder, but the lower bolt would have to hold them now. After I had closed the shutters on both tall drawing-room windows I went along the porch and in, formally, through the front door and into the drawing room where Constance stood in dimness now, without the sunlight. Constance went to the mantel and set the Dresden figurine in its place below the portrait of our mother and for one quick minute the great shadowy room came back together again, as it should be, and then fell apart forever.

We had to walk carefully because of the broken things on the floor. Our father's safe lay just inside the drawing-room door, and I laughed and even Constance smiled, because it had not been opened and it had clearly not been possible to carry it any farther than this. "Foolishness," Constance said, and touched the safe with her toe.

Our mother had always been pleased when people admired her drawing room, but now no one could come to the windows and look in, and no one would ever see it again. Constance and I closed the drawing-room door behind us and never opened it afterwards. Constance waited just inside the front door while I went onto the porch again and closed the shutters over the tall dining-room windows, and then I came inside and we shut and locked the front door and we were safe. The hall was dark, with two narrow lines of sunlight coming through the two narrow glass panels set on either side of the door; we could look outside through the glass, but no one could see in, even by putting their eyes up close, because the hall inside was dark. Above us the stairs were black and led into blackness or burned rooms with, incredibly, tiny spots of sky showing through. Until now, the roof had always hidden us from the sky, but I did not think that there was any way we could be vulnerable from above, and closed my mind against the thought of silent winged creatures coming out of the trees above to perch on the broken burnt rafters of our house, peering down. I thought it might be wise to barricade the stairs by putting something—a broken chair, perhaps—across. A mattress, soaked and dirty, lay halfway down the stairs; this was where they had stood with the hoses and fought the fire back and out. I stood at the foot of the stairs, looking up, wondering where our house had gone, the walls and the floors and the beds and the boxes of things in the attic; our father's watch was burned away, and our mother's tortoise-shell dressing set. I could feel a breath of air on my cheek; it came from the sky I could see, but it smelled of smoke and ruin. Our house was a castle, turreted and open to the sky.

"Come back to the kitchen," Constance said. "I can't stay out here."

Like children hunting for shells, or two old ladies going through dead leaves looking for pennies, we shuffled along the kitchen floor with our feet, turning over broken trash to find things which were still whole, and useful. When we had been along and across and diagonally through the kitchen we had gathered together a little pile of practical things on the kitchen table, and there was quite enough for the two of us. There were two cups with handles, and several without, and half a dozen plates, and three bowls. We had been able to rescue all the cans of food undamaged, and the cans of spice went neatly back onto their shelf. We found most of the silverware and straightened most of it as well as we could and put it back into its proper drawers. Since every Blackwood bride had brought her own silverware and china and linen into the house we had always had dozens of butter knives and soup ladles and cake servers; our mother's best silverware had been in a tarnish-proof box in the dining-room sideboard, but they had found it and scattered it on the floor.

One of our whole cups was green with a pale yellow inside, and Constance said that one could be mine. "I never saw anyone use it before," she said. "I suppose a grandmother or a great-great-aunt brought that set to the house as her wedding china. There once were plates to match." The cup which Constance chose was white with orange flowers, and one of the plates matched that. "I remember when we used those dishes," Constance said; "they were the everyday china when I was very small. The china we used for best then was white, with gold edges. Then Mother bought new best china and the white and gold china was used for everyday and these flowered dishes went onto the pantry shelf with the other half-broken sets. These last few years I have always used Mother's everyday china, except when Helen Clarke came to tea. We will take our meals like ladies," she said, "using cups with handles."

When we had taken out everything we wanted and could use, Constance got the heavy broom and swept all the rubble into the dining room. "Now we won't have to look at it," she said. She swept the hall clear so we could go from the kitchen to the front door without passing through the dining room, and then we closed all the doors to the dining room and never opened them again. I thought of the Dresden figurine standing small and courageous under our mother's portrait in the dark drawing room and I remembered that we would never dust it again. Before Constance swept away the torn cloth that had been the drawing-room drapes I asked her to cut me off a piece of the cord which had once drawn them open and shut, and she cut me a piece with a gold tassel on the end; I wondered if it might be the right thing to bury for Uncle Julian.

When we had finished and Constance had scrubbed the kitchen floor our house looked clean and new; from the front door to the kitchen door everything was clear and swept. So many things were gone from the kitchen that it looked bare, but Constance put our cups and plates and bowls on a shelf, and found a pan to give Jonas milk, and we were quite safe. The front door was locked, and the kitchen door was locked and bolted, and we were sitting at the kitchen table drinking milk from our two cups and Jonas was drinking from his pan when a knocking started on the front door. Constance ran to the cellar, and I stopped just long enough to be sure that the kitchen door was bolted, and then followed her. We sat on the cellar stairs in the darkness, and listened. Far away, at the front door, the knocking went on and on, and then a voice called, "Constance? Mary Katherine?"

"It's Helen Clarke," Constance said in a whisper.

"Do you think she has come for her tea?"

"No. Never again."

As we had both known she would, she came around the house, calling us. When she knocked on the kitchen door we held our breath, neither of us moving, because the top half of the kitchen door was glass, and we knew she could see in, but we were safely on the cellar stairs and she could not open the door.

"Constance? Mary Katherine? Are you *in* there?" She shook the door handle as people do when they want a door to open and think to catch it unaware and slip in before the lock can hold. "Jim," she said, "I *know* they're in there. I can see something cooking on the stove. You've got to open the door," she said, raising her voice. "Constance, come and talk to me; I want to see you. Jim," she said, "they're in there and they can hear me, I know it."

"I'm sure they can hear you," Jim Clarke said. "They can probably hear you in the village."

"But I'm sure they misunderstood the people last night; I'm sure Constance was upset, and I *must* tell them that nobody meant any harm. Constance, listen to me, please. We want you and Mary Katherine to come to our house until we can decide what to do with you. Everything's all right, really it is; we're going to forget all about it."

"Do you think she will push over the house?" I whispered to Constance, and Constance shook her head wordlessly.

"Jim, do you think you could break down the door?"

"Certainly not. Leave them alone, Helen, they'll come out when they're ready."

"But Constance takes these things so *seriously*. I'm sure she's frightened now."

"Leave them alone."

"They cannot be left alone, that is absolutely the worst possible thing for them. I want them out of there and home with me where I can take care of them."

"They don't seem to want to come," Jim Clarke said.

"Constance? Constance? I know you're in there; come and open the door."

I was thinking that we might very well put a cloth or a piece of cardboard over the window in the kitchen door; it simply would not do to have Helen Clarke constantly peering in to watch pots cooking on the stove. We could pin the curtains together across the kitchen windows, and perhaps if the windows were all covered we could sit quietly at the table when Helen Clarke came pounding outside and not have to hide on the cellar stairs.

"Let's leave," Jim Clarke said. "They're not going to answer you."

"But I want to take them home with me."

"We did what we could. We'll come back another time, when they'll feel more like seeing you."

"Constance? Constance, *please* answer me."

Constance sighed, and tapped her fingers irritably and almost noiselessly on the stair rail. "I wish she'd hurry," she said into my ear, "my soup is going to boil over."

Helen Clarke called again and again, going back around the house to their car, calling "Constance? Constance?" as though we might be somewhere in the woods, up a tree perhaps, or under the lettuce leaves, or waiting to spring out at her from behind a bush. When we heard their car start, distantly, we came up out of the cellar and Constance turned off her soup and I went along the hall to the front door to be sure they had gone and that the door was safely locked. I saw their car turn out of the driveway and thought I could still hear Helen Clarke calling "Constance? Constance?"

"She certainly wanted her tea," I said to Constance when I came back to the kitchen.

"We have only two cups with handles," Constance said. "She will never take tea here again."

"It's a good thing Uncle Julian's gone, or one of us would have to use a broken cup. Are you going to neaten Uncle Julian's room?"

"Merricat." Constance turned from the stove to look at me. "What are we going to do?"

"We've neatened the house. We've had food. We've hidden from Helen Clarke. What *are* we going to do?"

"Where are we going to sleep? How are we going to know what time it is? What will we wear for clothes?"

"Why do we need to know what time it is?"

"Our food won't last forever, even the preserves."

"We can sleep in my hiding place by the creek."

"No. That's all right for hiding, but you must have a real bed."

"I saw a mattress on the stairs. From my own old bed, perhaps. We can pull it down and clean it and dry it in the sun. One corner is burned."

"Good," said Constance. We went together to the stairs and took hold of the mattress awkwardly; it was unpleasantly wet and dirty. We dragged it, pulling together, along the hall, with little scraps of wood and glass coming with it, and got it across Constance's clean kitchen floor to the kitchen door. Before unlocking the door I looked out carefully, and even when the door was opened I went out first to look around in every direction, but it was safe. We dragged the mattress out onto the lawn, and put it in the sun near our mother's marble bench.

"Uncle Julian used to sit right here," I said.

"It would be a good day, today, for Uncle Julian to sit in the sun."

"I hope he was warm when he died. Perhaps he remembered the sun for a minute."

"I had his shawl; I hope he didn't wish for it. Merricat, I am going to plant something here, where he used to sit."

"I am going to bury something for him. What will you plant?"

"A flower." Constance leaned, and touched the grass softly. "Some kind of a yellow flower."

"It's going to look funny, right in the middle of the lawn."

"We'll know why its there, and no one else will ever see it."

"And I will bury something yellow, to keep Uncle Julian warm."

"First, however, my lazy Merricat, you will get a pot of water and scrub that mattress clean. And I will wash the kitchen floor again."

We were going to be very happy, I thought. There were a great many things to do, and a whole new pattern of days to arrange, but I thought we were going to be very happy. Constance was pale, and still saddened by what they had done to her kitchen, but she had scrubbed every shelf, and washed the table again and again, and washed the windows and the floor. Our dishes were bravely on their shelf, and the cans and unbroken boxes of food we had rescued made a substantial row in the pantry.

"I could train Jonas to bring back rabbits for stew," I told her, and she laughed, and Jonas looked back at her blandly.

"That cat is so used to living on cream and rum cakes and

buttered eggs that I doubt if he could catch a grasshopper," she said.

"I don't think I could care for a grasshopper stew."

"At any rate, right *now* I am making an onion pie."

While Constance washed the kitchen I found a heavy cardboard carton which I took apart carefully, and so had several large pieces of cardboard to cover the glass window in the kitchen door. The hammer and the nails were in the tool shed where Charles Blackwood had put them after trying to mend the broken step, and I nailed cardboard across the kitchen door until the glass was completely covered and no one could see in. I nailed more cardboard across the two kitchen windows, and the kitchen was dark, but safe. "It would be safer to let the kitchen windows get dirty," I told Constance, but she was shocked, and said, "I wouldn't live in a house with dirty windows."

When we had finished the kitchen was very clean but could not sparkle because there was so little light, and I knew that Constance was not pleased. She loved sunshine and brightness and cooking in a light lovely kitchen. "We can keep the door open," I said, "if we watch carefully all the time. We'll hear if any cars stop in front of the house. When I can," I said, "I will try to think of a way to build barricades along the sides of the house so no one will be able to come around here to the back."

"I am sure Helen Clarke will try again."

"At any rate she cannot look in now."

The afternoon was drawing in; even with the door open the sunlight came only a short way across the floor, and Jonas came to Constance at the stove, asking for his supper. The kitchen was warm and comfortable and familiar and clean. It would be nice to have a fireplace in here, I thought; we could sit beside a fire, and then I thought no, we have already had a fire.

"I will go and make sure that the front door is locked," I said.

The front door was locked and no one was outside. When I came back into the kitchen Constance said, "Tomorrow I will clean Uncle Julian's room. We have so little house left that it should all be very clean."

"Will you sleep in there? In Uncle Julian's bed?"

"No, Merricat. I want you to sleep in there. It's the only bed we have."

"I am not allowed in Uncle Julian's room."

She was quiet for a minute, looking at me curiously, and then asked, "Even though Uncle Julian's gone, Merricat?"

"Besides, I found the mattress, and cleaned it, and it came from my bed. I want it on the floor in my corner."

"Silly Merricat. Anyway, I'm afraid we'll both have the floor tonight. The mattress will not dry before tomorrow, and Uncle Julian's bed is not clean."

"I can bring branches from my hiding place, and leaves."

"On my clean kitchen floor?"

"I'll get the blanket, though, and Uncle Julian's shawl."

"You're going out? Now? All that way?"

"No one's outside," I said. "It's almost dark and I can go very safely. If anyone comes, close the door and lock it; if I see that the door is closed I will wait by the creek until I can come safely home. And I will take Jonas for protection."

I ran all the way to the creek, but Jonas was faster, and was waiting for me when I got to my hiding place. It was good to run, and good to come back again to our house and see the kitchen door standing open and the warm light inside. When Jonas and I came in I shut the door and bolted it and we were ready for the night.

"It's a good dinner," Constance said, warm and happy from cooking. "Come and sit down, Merricat." With the door shut she had had to turn on the ceiling light, and our dishes on the table were neatly set. "Tomorrow I will try to polish the silverware," she said, "and we must bring in things from the garden."

"The lettuce is full of ashes."

"Tomorrow, too," Constance said, looking at the black squares of cardboard which covered the windows, "I am going to try to think of some kind of curtains to hide your cardboard."

"Tomorrow I will barricade the sides of the house. Tomorrow Jonas will catch us a rabbit. Tomorrow I will guess for you what time it is."

Far away, in the front of the house, a car stopped, and we were silent, looking at one another; now, I thought, now we will know how safe we are, and I got up and made sure that the kitchen door was bolted; I could not see out through the cardboard and I was sure that they could not see in. The knocking started at the front door, but there was no time to make sure that the front door was locked. They knocked only for a moment, as though certain that we would not be in the front of the house, and then we heard them stumbling in the darkness as they tried to find their way around the side of the house to the back. I heard Jim Clarke's voice, and another which I remembered was the voice of Dr. Levy.

"Can't see a thing," Jim Clarke said. "Black as sin out here."

"There's a crack of light at one of the windows."

Which one, I wondered; which window still showed a crack?

"They're in there, all right," Jim Clarke said. "No place else they could be."

"I just want to know if they're hurt, or sick; don't like to think of them shut up in there needing help."

"I'm supposed to bring them home with me," Jim Clarke said.

They came to the back door; their voices were directly outside, and Constance reached out her hand across the table to me; if it seemed that they might be able to look in we could run together for the cellar. "Damn place is all boarded up," Jim Clarke said, and I thought, good, oh, that's good. I had forgotten that there would be real boards in the tool shed; I never thought of anything but cardboard which is much too weak.

"Miss Blackwood?" the doctor called, and one of them knocked on the door. "Miss Blackwood? It's Dr. Levy."

"And Jim Clarke. Helen's husband. Helen's very worried about you."

"Are you hurt? Sick? Do you need help?"

"Helen wants you to come to our house; she's waiting there for you."

"Listen," the doctor said, and I thought he had his face up very close to the glass, almost touching it. He talked in a very friendly voice, and quietly. "Listen, no one's going to hurt you. We're your friends. We came all the way over here to help you and make sure you were all right and we don't want to bother you. As a matter of fact, we promise not to bother you at all, ever again, if you'll just once say that you're well and safe. Just one word."

"You can't just let people go on worrying and worrying about you," Jim Clarke said.

"Just one word," the doctor said. "All you have to do is say you're all right."

They waited; I could feel them pressing their faces close to the glass, longing to see inside. Constance looked at me across the table and smiled a little, and I smiled back; our safeguards were good and they could not see in.

"Listen," the doctor said, and he raised his voice a little; "listen, Julian's funeral is tomorrow. We thought you'd want to know."

"There are a lot of flowers already," Jim Clarke said. "You'd be really pleased to see all the flowers. We sent flowers, and the Wrights, and the Carringtons. I think you'd feel a little different about your friends if you could see the flowers we all sent Julian."

I wondered why we would feel different if we saw who sent Uncle Julian flowers. Certainly Uncle Julian buried in flowers, swarmed over by flowers, would not resemble the Uncle Julian we had seen every day. Perhaps masses of flowers would warm Uncle Julian dead; I tried to think of Uncle Julian dead and could only remember him asleep. I thought of the Clarkes and the Carringtons and the Wrights pouring armfuls of flowers down onto poor old Uncle Julian, helplessly dead.

"You're not gaining anything by driving away your friends, you know. Helen said to tell you—"

"Listen." I could feel them pushing against the door. "No one's going to bother you. Just tell us, are you all right?"

"We're not going to keep coming, you know. There's a limit to how much friends can take."

Jonas yawned. In silence Constance turned, slowly and carefully, back to face her place at the table, and took up a buttered biscuit and took a tiny silent bite. I wanted to laugh, and put my hands over my mouth; Constance eating a biscuit silently was funny, like a doll pretending to eat.

"*Damn* it," Jim Clarke said. He knocked on the door. "*Damn* it," he said.

"For the last time," the doctor said, "we know you're in there; for the last time will you just—"

"Oh, come away," Jim Clarke said, "It's not worth all the yelling."

"Listen," the doctor said, and I thought he had his mouth against the door, "one of these days you're going to *need* help. You'll be sick, or hurt. You'll *need* help. *Then* you'll be quick enough to—"

"Leave them be," Jim Clarke said. "Come on."

I heard their footsteps going around the side of the house and wondered if they were tricking us, pretending to walk away and then coming silently back to stand without sound outside the door, waiting. I thought of Constance silently eating a biscuit inside and Jim Clarke silently listening outside and a little cold chill went up my back; perhaps there would never be noise in the world again. Then the car started at the front of the house and we heard it drive away and Constance put her fork down on her plate with a little crash and I breathed again and said, "Where have they got Uncle Julian, do you suppose?"

"At that same place," Constance said absently, "in the city. Merricat," she said, looking up suddenly.

"Yes, Constance?"

"I want to say I'm sorry. I was wicked last night."

I was still and cold, looking at her and remembering.

"I was very wicked," she said. "I never should have reminded you of why they all died."

"Then don't remind me now." I could not move my hand to reach over and take hers.

"I wanted you to forget about it. I never wanted to speak about it, ever, and I'm sorry I did."

"I put it in the sugar."

"I know. I knew then."

"You never used sugar."

"No."

"So I put it in the sugar."

Constance sighed. "Merricat," she said, "we'll never talk about it again. Never."

I was chilled, but she smiled at me kindly and it was all right.

"I love you, Constance," I said.

"And I love you, my Merricat."

Jonas sat on the floor and slept on the floor and I thought it ought not to be so difficult for me. Constance should have had leaves and soft moss under her blanket but we could not dirty the kitchen floor again. I put my blanket in the corner near my stool because it was the place I knew best, and Jonas got up onto the stool and sat there, looking down on me. Constance lay on the floor near the stove; it was dark, but I could see the paleness of her face across the kitchen. "Are you comfortable?" I asked her, and she laughed.

"I've spent a lot of time in this kitchen," she said, "but I never before tried lying on its floor. I've taken such good care of it that it has to make me welcome, I think."

"Tomorrow we bring in lettuce."

10

SLOWLY the pattern of our days grew, and shaped itself into a happy life. In the mornings when I awakened I would go at once down the hall to make sure the front door was locked. We were most active in the very early morning because no one was ever around. We had not realized that, with the gates opened and the path exposed to public use, the children would come; one morning I stood beside the front door, looking out through the narrow pane of glass, and saw children playing on our front lawn. Perhaps the parents had sent them to explore the way and make sure it was navigable, or perhaps children can never resist playing anywhere; they seemed a little uneasy playing in front of our house, and their voices were subdued. I thought that perhaps they were only pretending to play, because they were children and were supposed to play, but perhaps they were actually sent here to look for us, thinly disguised as children. They were not really convincing, I decided as I watched them; they moved gracelessly, and never once glanced, that I could see, at our house. I wondered how soon they would creep onto the porch, and press their small faces against the shutters, trying to see through cracks. Constance came up behind me and looked out over my shoulder. "They are the children of the strangers," I told her. "They have no faces."

"They have eyes."

"Pretend they are birds. They can't see us. They don't know it yet, they don't want to believe it, but they won't ever see us again."

"I suppose that now they've come once, they'll come again."

"All the strangers will come, but they can't see inside. And now may I please have my breakfast?"

The kitchen was always dark in the mornings until I unbolted the kitchen door and opened it to let the sunlight in. Then Jonas went to sit on the step and bathe and Constance sang while she made our breakfast. After breakfast I sat on the step with Jonas while Constance washed the kitchen.

Barricading the sides of the house had been easier than I expected; I managed it in one night with Constance holding a flashlight for me. At either side of our house there was a spot where the trees and bushes grew close to the house, sheltering the back and narrowing the path which was the only way around. I brought piece after piece from the pile of junk Mr. Harler had made on our front porch, and heaped the broken boards and furniture across the narrowest spot. It would not really keep anyone out, of course; the children could climb over it easily, but if anyone did try to get past there would be enough noise and falling of broken boards to give us plenty of time to close and bolt the kitchen door. I had found some boards around the tool shed, and nailed them rudely across the glass of the kitchen door, but I disliked putting them across the sides of the house as a barricade, where anyone might see them and know how clumsily I built. Perhaps, I told myself, I might try my hand at mending the broken step.

"What are you laughing about now?" Constance asked me.

"I am thinking that we are on the moon, but it is not quite as I supposed it would be."

"It is a very happy place, though." Constance was bringing breakfast to the table: scrambled eggs and toasted biscuits and blackberry jam she had made some golden summer. "We ought to bring in as much food as we can," she said. "I don't like to think of the garden waiting there for us to come and gather growing things. And I'd feel much better if we had more food put securely away in the house."

"I will go on my winged horse and bring you cinnamon and thyme, emeralds and clove, cloth of gold and cabbages."

"And rhubarb."

We were able to leave the kitchen door open when we went down to the vegetable garden, because we could see clearly whether anyone was approaching my barricades and run back to the house if we needed to. I carried the basket and we brought back lettuce, still grey with ash, and radishes, and tomatoes and cucumbers and, later, berries, and melons. Usually I ate fruit and vegetables still moist from the ground and the air, but I disliked eating anything while it was still dirty with the ash from our burned house. Most of the dirt and the soot had blown away and the air around the garden was fresh and clean, but the smoke was in the ground and I thought it would always be there.

As soon as we were safely settled Constance had opened Uncle Julian's room and cleaned it. She brought out the sheets from Uncle Julian's bed, and the blankets, and washed them in the kitchen sink and set them outside to dry in the sunlight. "What are you going to do with Uncle Julian's papers?" I asked her, and she rested her hands against the edge of the sink, hesitating.

"I suppose I'll keep them all in the box," she said at last. "I suppose I'll put the box down in the cellar."

"And preserve it?"

"And preserve it. He would like to think that his papers were treated respectfully. And I would not want Uncle Julian to suspect that his papers were not preserved."

"I had better go and see that the front door is locked."

The children were often outside on our front lawn, playing their still games and not looking at our house, moving awkwardly in little dashing runs, and slapping one another without cause. Whenever I checked to make sure that the front door was locked I looked out to see if the children were there. Very often I saw people walking on our path now, using it to go from one place to another, and putting their feet down where once only my feet had gone; I thought they used the path without wanting to, as though each of them had to travel it once to show that it could be done, but I thought that only a few, the defiant hating ones, came by more than once.

I dreamed away the long afternoon while Constance cleaned Uncle Julian's room; I sat on the doorsill with Jonas asleep beside me, and looked out on the quiet safe garden.

"Look, Merricat," Constance said, coming to me with an armful of clothes, "look, Uncle Julian had two suits, and a top-coat and a hat."

"He walked upright once; he told us so himself."

"I can just barely remember him, years ago, going off one day to buy a suit, and I suppose it was one of these suits he bought; they are neither of them much worn."

"What would he have been wearing on the last day with them? What tie did he have on at dinner? He would surely like to have it remembered."

She looked at me for a minute, not smiling. "It would hardly have been one of these; when I came to get him afterwards, at the hospital, he was wearing pajamas and a robe."

"Perhaps he should have one of these suits now."

"He was probably buried in an old suit of Jim Clarke's." Constance started for the cellar, and then stopped. "Merricat?"

"Yes, Constance?"

"Do you realize that these things of Uncle Julian's are the only clothes left in our house? All of mine burned, and all of yours."

"And everything of theirs in the attic."

"I have only this pink dress I have on."

I looked down. "And I am wearing brown."

"And yours needs washing, and mending; how *can* you tear your clothes so, my Merricat?"

"I shall weave a suit of leaves. At once. With acorns for buttons."

"Merricat, be serious. We will have to wear Uncle Julian's clothes."

"I am not allowed to touch Uncle Julian's things. I shall have a lining of moss, for cold winter days, and a hat made of bird feathers."

"That may be all very well for the moon, Miss Foolishness. On the moon you may wear a suit of fur like Jonas, for all of me. But right here in our house you are going to be clothed in one of your Uncle Julian's old shirts, and perhaps his trousers too."

"Or Uncle Julian's bathrobe and pajamas, I suppose. No; I am not allowed to touch Uncle Julian's things; I will wear leaves."

"But you are allowed. I tell you that you are allowed."

"No."

She sighed. "Well," she said, "you'll probably see me wearing them." Then she stopped, and laughed, and looked at me, and laughed again.

"Constance?" I said.

She put Uncle Julian's clothes over the back of a chair, and, still laughing, went into the pantry and opened one of the drawers. I remembered what she was after and I laughed too.

Then she came back and put an armload of tablecloths down beside me.

"These will do you very nicely, elegant Merricat. Look; how will you feel in this, with a border of yellow flowers? Or this handsome red and white check? The damask, I am afraid, is too stiff for comfort, and besides it has been darned."

I stood up and held the red and white checked tablecloth against me. "You can cut a hole for my head," I said; I was pleased.

"I have no sewing things. You will simply have to tie it around your waist with a cord or let it hang like a toga."

"I will use the damask for a cloak; who else wears a damask cloak?"

"Merricat, oh, Merricat." Constance dropped the tablecloth she was holding and put her arms around me. "What have I done to my baby Merricat?" she said. "No house. No food. And dressed in a tablecloth; what have I *done?*"

"Constance," I said, "I love you, Constance."

"Dressed in a tablecloth like a rag doll."

"Constance. We are going to be very happy, Constance."

"Oh, Merricat," she said, holding me.

"Listen to me, Constance. We are going to be very happy."

I dressed at once, not wanting to give Constance more time to think. I chose the red and white check, and when Constance had cut a hole for my head I took my gold cord with the tassel that Constance had cut from the drawing-room drapes and tied it around me for a belt and looked, I thought, very fine. Constance was sad at first, and turned away sadly when she saw me, and scrubbed furiously at the sink to get my brown dress clean, but I liked my robe, and danced in it, and before long she smiled again and then laughed at me.

"Robinson Crusoe dressed in the skins of animals," I told her. "He had no gay cloths with a gold belt."

"I must say you never looked so bright before."

"You will be wearing the skins of Uncle Julian; I prefer my tablecloth."

"I believe the one you are wearing now was used for summer breakfasts on the lawn many years ago. Red and white check would never be used in the dining room, of course."

"Some days I shall be a summer breakfast on the lawn, and some days I shall be a formal dinner by candlelight, and some days I shall be—"

"A very dirty Merricat. You have a fine gown, but your face is dirty. We have lost almost everything, young lady, but at least we still have clean water and a comb."

One thing was most lucky about Uncle Julian's room: I persuaded Constance to bring out his chair and wheel it through the garden to reinforce my barricade. It looked strange to see Constance wheeling the empty chair, and for a minute I tried to see Uncle Julian again, riding with his hands in his lap, but all that remained of Uncle Julian's presence were the worn spots on the chair, and a handkerchief tucked under the cushion. The chair would be powerful in my barricade, however, staring out always at intruders with a blank menace of dead Uncle Julian. I was troubled to think that Uncle Julian might vanish altogether, with his papers in a box and his chair on the barricade and his toothbrush thrown away and even the smell of Uncle Julian gone from his room, but when the ground was soft Constance planted a yellow rosebush at Uncle Julian's spot on the lawn, and one night I went down to the creek and buried Uncle Julian's initialled gold pencil by the water, so the creek would always speak his name. Jonas took to going into Uncle Julian's room, where he had never gone before, but I did not go inside.

Helen Clarke came to our door twice more, knocking and calling and begging us to answer, but we sat quietly, and when she found that she could not come round the house because of my barricade she told us from the front door that she would not come back, and she did not. One evening, perhaps the evening of the day Constance planted Uncle Julian's rosebush, we heard a very soft knock at our front door while we sat at the table eating dinner. It was far too soft a knock for Helen Clarke, and I left the table and hurried silently down the hall to be sure that the front door was locked, and Constance followed me, curious. We pressed silently against the door and listened.

"Miss Blackwood?" someone said outside, in a low voice; I

wondered if he suspected we were so close to him. "Miss Constance? Miss Mary Katherine?"

It was not quite dark outside, but inside where we stood we could only see one another dimly, two white faces against the door. "Miss Constance?" he said again. "Listen."

I thought that he was moving his head from side to side to make sure that he was not seen. "Listen," he said, "I got a chicken here."

He tapped softly on the door. "I hope you can hear me," he said. "I got a chicken here. My wife fixed it, roasted it nice, and there's some cookies and a pie. I hope you can hear me."

I could see that Constance's eyes were wide with wonder. I stared at her and she stared at me.

"I sure hope you can hear me, Miss Blackwood. I broke one of your chairs and I'm sorry." He tapped against the door again, very softly. "Well," he said. "I'll just set this basket down on your step here. I hope you heard me. Goodbye."

We listened to quiet footsteps going away, and after a minute Constance said, "What shall we do? Shall we open the door?"

"Later," I said. "I'll come when it's really dark."

"I wonder what kind of pie it is. Do you think it's as good as my pies?"

We finished our dinner and waited until I was sure that no one could possibly see the front door opening, and then we went down the hall and I unlocked the door and looked outside. The basket sat on the doorstep, covered with a napkin. I brought it inside and locked the door while Constance took the basket from me and carried it to the kitchen. "Blueberry," she said when I came. "Quite good, too; it's still warm."

She took out the chicken, wrapped in a napkin, and the little package of cookies, touching each lovingly and with gentleness. "Everything's still warm," she said. "She must have baked them right after dinner, so he could bring them right over. I wonder if she made two pies, one for the house. She wrapped everything while it was still warm and told him to bring them over. These cookies are not crisp enough."

"I'll take the basket back and leave it on the porch, so he'll know we found it."

"No, no." Constance caught me by the arm. "Not until I've washed the napkins; what would she think of me?"

Sometimes they brought bacon, home-cured, or fruit, or their own preserves, which were never as good as the preserves Constance made. Mostly they brought roasted chicken; sometimes a cake or a pie, frequently cookies, sometimes a potato salad or coleslaw. Once they brought a pot of beef stew, which Constance took apart and put back together again according to her own rules for beef stew, and sometimes there were pots of baked beans or macaroni. "We are the biggest church supper they ever had," Constance said once, looking at a loaf of homemade bread I had just brought inside.

These things were always left on the front doorstep, always silently and in the evenings. We thought that the men came home from work and the women had the baskets ready for them to carry over; perhaps they came in darkness not to be recognized, as though each of them wanted to hide from the others, and bringing us food was somehow a shameful thing to do in public. There were many women cooking, Constance said. "Here is one," she explained to me once, tasting a bean, "who uses ketchup, and too much of it; and the last one used more molasses." Once or twice there was a note in the basket: "This is for the dishes," or "We apologize about the curtains," or "Sorry for your harp." We always set the baskets back where we had found them, and never opened the front door until it was completely dark and we were sure that no one was near. I always checked carefully afterwards to make certain that the front door was locked.

I discovered that I was no longer allowed to go to the creek; Uncle Julian was there, and it was much too far from Constance. I never went farther away than the edge of the woods, and Constance went only as far as the vegetable garden. I was not allowed to bury anything more, nor was I allowed to touch stone. Every day I looked over the boards across the kitchen windows and when I found small cracks I nailed on more boards. Every morning I checked at once to make sure the front door was locked, and every morning Constance washed the kitchen. We spent a good deal of time at the front door, particularly during the afternoons, when most people came by; we sat, one on either side of the front door, looking out through the narrow glass panels which I had covered almost entirely with cardboard so that we had each only a small peephole and no one could possibly see inside. We watched the children playing, and the people walking past, and we heard their voices and they were all strangers, with their wide staring eyes and their evil open mouths. One day a group came by bicycle; there were two women and a man, and two children. They parked their bicycles in our driveway and lay down on our front lawn, pulling at the grass and talking while they rested. The children ran up and down our driveway and over and around the trees and bushes. This was the day that we learned that the vines were growing over the burned roof of our house, because one of the women glanced sideways at the house and said that the vines almost hid the marks of burning. They rarely turned squarely to look at our house face to face, but looked from the corners of their eyes or from over a shoulder or through their fingers. "It used to be a lovely old house, I hear," said the woman sitting on our grass. "I've heard that it was quite a local landmark at one time."

"Now it looks like a tomb," the other woman said.

"Shh," the first woman said, and gestured toward the house with her head. "I heard," she said loudly, "that they had a staircase which was very fine. Carved in Italy, I heard."

"They can't hear you," the other woman said, amused. "And who cares if they do, anyway?"

"Shhh."

"No one knows for sure if there's anyone inside or not. The local people tell some tall tales."

"Shh. Tommy," she called to one of the children, "don't you go near those steps."

"Why?" said the child, backing away.

"Because the ladies live in there, and they don't like it."

"Why?" said the child, pausing at the foot of the steps and giving a quick look backward at our front door.

"The ladies don't like little boys," the second woman said; she was one of the bad ones; I could see her mouth from the side and it was the mouth of a snake.

"What would they do to me?"

"They'd hold you down and make you eat candy full of

poison; I heard that dozens of bad little boys have gone too near that house and never been seen again. They catch little boys and they—"

"Shh. *Honestly*, Ethel."

"Do they like little girls?" The other child drew near.

"They hate little boys *and* little girls. The difference is, they *eat* the little girls."

"Ethel, stop. You're terrifying the children. It isn't true, darlings; she's only teasing you."

"They never come out except at night," the bad woman said, looking evilly at the children, "and then when it's dark they go hunting little children."

"Just the same," the man said suddenly, "I don't want to see the kids going too near that house."

Charles Blackwood came back only once. He came in a car with another man late one afternoon when we had been watching for a long time. All the strangers had gone, and Constance had just stirred and said, "Time to put on the potatoes," when the car turned into the driveway and she settled back to watch again. Charles and the other man got out of the car in front of the house and walked directly to the foot of the steps, looking up, although they could not see us inside. I remembered the first time Charles had come and stood looking up at our house in just the same manner, but this time he would never get in. I reached up and touched the lock on the front door to make sure it was fastened, and on the other side of the doorway Constance turned and nodded to me; she knew, too, that Charles would never get in again.

"See?" Charles said, outside, at the foot of our steps. "There's the house, just like I said. It doesn't look as bad as it did, now the vines have grown so. But the roof's been burned away, and the place was gutted inside."

"Are the ladies in there?"

"Sure." Charles laughed, and I remembered his laughter and his big staring white face and from inside the door I wished him dead. "They're in there all right," he said. "And so is a whole damn fortune."

"You *know* that?"

"They've got money in there's never even been counted. They've got it buried all over, and a safe full, and God knows where else they've hidden it. They never come out, just hide away inside with all that money."

"Look," the other man said, "they know you, don't they?"

"Sure. I'm their cousin. I came here on a visit once."

"You think there's any chance you might get one of them to talk to you? Maybe come to the window or something, so I could get a picture?"

Charles thought. He looked at the house and at the other man, and thought. "If you sell this, to the magazine or somewhere, do I get half?"

"Sure, it's a promise."

"I'll try it," Charles said. "You get back behind the car, out of sight. They certainly won't come out if they see a stranger." The other man went back to the car and took out a camera and settled himself on the other side of the car where we could not see him. "Okay," he called, and Charles started up the steps to our front door.

"Connie?" he called. "Hey, Connie? It's Charles; I'm back."

I looked at Constance and thought she had never seen Charles so truly before.

"Connie?"

She knew now that Charles was a ghost and a demon, one of the strangers.

"Let's forget all that happened," Charles said. He came close to the door and spoke pleasantly, with a little pleading tone. "Let's be friends again."

I could see his feet. One of them was tapping and tapping on the floor of our porch. "I don't know what you've got against me," he said, "and I've been waiting and waiting for you to let me know I could come back again. If I did anything to offend you, I'm really sorry."

I wished Charles could see inside, could see us sitting on the floor on either side of the front door, listening to him and looking at his feet, while he talked beggingly to the door three feet above our heads.

"Open the door," he said very softly. "Connie, will you open the door for me, for Cousin Charles?"

Constance looked up to where his face must be and smiled unpleasantly. I thought it must be a smile she had been saving for Charles if he ever came back again.

"I went to see old Julian's grave this morning," Charles said. "I came back to visit old Julian's grave and to see you once more." He waited a minute and then said with a little break in his voice, "I put a couple of flowers—*you* know—on the old fellow's grave; he was a fine old guy, and he was always pretty good to me."

Beyond Charles' feet I saw the other man coming out from behind the car with his camera. "Look," he called, "you're wasting your breath. And I haven't got all day."

"Don't you understand?" Charles had turned away from the door, but his voice still had the little break in it. "I've *got* to see her once more. I was the cause of it all."

"What?"

"Why do you suppose two old maids shut themselves up in a house like this? God knows," Charles said, "I didn't mean it to turn out this way."

I thought Constance was going to speak then, or at least laugh out loud, and I reached across and touched her arm, warning her to be quiet, but she did not turn her head to me.

"If I could just *talk* to her," Charles said. "You can get some pictures of the house, anyway, with me standing here. Or knocking at the door; I could be knocking frantically at the door."

"You could be stretched across the doorsill dying of a broken heart, for all of me," the other man said. He went to the car and put his camera inside. "Waste of time."

"And all that money. Connie," Charles called loudly, "will you for heaven's sake open that door?"

"You know," the other man said from the car, "I'll just bet you're never going to see those silver dollars again."

"Connie," Charles said, "you don't know what you're doing to me; I never deserved to be treated like this. *Please*, Connie."

"You want to walk back to town?" the other man said. He closed the car door.

Charles turned away from the door and then turned back.

"All right, Connie," he said, "this is it. If you let me go this time, you'll never see me again. I mean it, Connie."

"I'm leaving," the other man said from the car.

"I mean it, Connie, I really do." Charles started down the steps, talking over his shoulder. "Take a last look," he said. "I'm going. One word could make me stay."

I did not think he was going to go in time. I honestly did not know whether Constance was going to be able to contain herself until he got down the steps and safely into the car. "Goodbye, Connie," he said from the foot of the steps and then turned away and went slowly toward the car. He looked for a minute as though he might wipe his eyes or blow his nose, but the other man said, "Hurry *up*," and Charles looked back once more, raised his hand sadly, and got into the car. Then Constance laughed, and I laughed, and for a minute I saw Charles in the car turn his head quickly, as though he had heard us laughing, but the car started, and drove off down the driveway, and we held each other in the dark hall and laughed, with the tears running down our cheeks and echoes of our laughter going up the ruined stairway to the sky.

"I am so happy," Constance said at last, gasping. "Merricat, I am so happy."

"I told you that you would like it on the moon."

The Carringtons stopped their car in front of our house one Sunday after church and sat quietly in the car looking at our house, as though supposing that we would come out if there was anything the Carringtons could do for us. Sometimes I thought of the drawing room and the dining room, forever closed away, with our mother's lovely broken things lying scattered, and the dust sifting gently down to cover them; we had new landmarks in the house, just as we had a new pattern for our days. The crooked, broken-off fragment which was all that was left of our lovely stairway was something we passed every day and came to know as intimately as we had once known the stairs themselves. The boards across the kitchen windows were ours, and part of our house, and we loved them. We were very happy, although Constance was always in terror lest one of our two cups should break, and one of us have to use a cup without a handle. We had our well-known and familiar places: our chairs at the table, and our beds, and our places beside the front door. Constance washed the red and white tablecloth and the shirts of Uncle Julian's which she wore, and while they were hanging in the garden to dry I wore a tablecloth with a yellow border, which looked very handsome with my gold belt. Our mother's old brown shoes were safely put away in my corner of the kitchen, since in the warm summer days I went barefoot like Jonas. Constance disliked picking many flowers, but there was always a bowl on the kitchen table with roses or daisies, although of course she never picked a rose from Uncle Julian's rosebush.

I sometimes thought of my six blue marbles, but I was not allowed to go to the long field now, and I thought that perhaps my six blue marbles had been buried to protect a house which no longer existed and had no connection with the house where we lived now, and where we were very happy. My new magical safeguards were the lock on the front door, and the boards over the windows, and the barricades along the sides of the house. In the evenings sometimes we saw movement in the darkness on the lawn, and heard whispers.

"Don't; the ladies might be watching."

"You think they can see in the dark?"

"I heard they see everything that goes on."

Then there might be laughter, drifting away into the warm darkness.

"They will soon be calling this Lover's Lane," Constance said.

"After Charles, no doubt."

"The least Charles could have done," Constance said, considering seriously, "was shoot himself through the head in the driveway."

We learned, from listening, that all the strangers could see from outside, when they looked at all, was a great ruined structure overgrown with vines, barely recognizable as a house. It was the point halfway between the village and the highway, the middle spot on the path, and no one ever saw our eyes looking out through the vines.

"You can't go on those steps," the children warned each other; "if you do, the ladies will get you."

Once a boy, dared by the others, stood at the foot of the steps facing the house, and shivered and almost cried and almost ran away, and then called out shakily, "Merricat, said Constance, would you like a cup of tea?" and then fled, followed by all the others. That night we found on the doorsill a basket of fresh eggs and a note reading, "He didn't mean it, please."

"Poor child," Constance said, putting the eggs into a bowl to go into the cooler. "He's probably hiding under the bed right now."

"Perhaps he had a good whipping to teach him manners."

"We will have an omelette for breakfast."

"I wonder if I *could* eat a child if I had the chance."

"I doubt if I could cook one," said Constance.

"Poor strangers," I said. "They have so much to be afraid of."

"Well," Constance said, "I am afraid of spiders."

"Jonas and I will see to it that no spider ever comes near you. Oh, Constance," I said, "we are so happy."

OTHER STORIES
AND SKETCHES

I

Uncollected

Janice

First, to me on the phone, in a half-amused melancholy: "Guess I'm not going back to school . . ."

"Why not, Jan?"

"Oh, my *mother*. She says we can't afford it." How can I reproduce the uncaring inflections of Janice's voice, saying conversationally that what she wanted she could not have? "So I guess I'm not going back."

"I'm so sorry, Jan."

But then, struck by another thought: "Y'know *what*?"

"What?"

"Darn near killed myself this afternoon."

"Jan! How?"

Almost whimsical, indifferent: "Locked myself in the garage and turned on the car motor."

"But why?"

"I dunno. 'Cause I couldn't go back, I suppose."

"What happened?"

"Oh, the fellow that was cutting our lawn heard the motor and came and got me. I was pretty near out."

"But that's terrible, Jan. What ever possessed—"

"Oh, well. Say—" changing again, "—going to Sally's tonight?" . . .

And, later, that night at Sally's where Janice was not the center of the group, but sat talking to me and to Bob: "Nearly killed myself this afternoon, Bob."

"What!"

Lightly: "Nearly killed myself. Locked myself in the garage with the car motor running."

"But why, Jan?"

"I guess because they wouldn't let me go back to school."

"Oh, I'm sorry about that, Jan. But what about this afternoon? What did you do?"

"Man cutting the grass got me out."

Sally coming over: "What's this, Jan?"

"Oh, I'm not going back to school."

Myself, cutting in: "How did it feel to be dying, Jan?"

Laughing "Gee, funny. All black." Then, to Sally's incredulous stare: "Nearly killed myself this afternoon, Sally . . ."

1938

A Cauliflower in Her Hair

M R. AND MRS. GARLAND and their daughter Virginia lived in a pleasant house in a pretty town and every night at seven they ate the agreeable dinner cooked by Agnes, the maid who cooked well and dusted adequately and made beds abominably. Mr. and Mrs. Garland belonged to two country clubs and Mr. Garland had a mustache; Mrs. Garland had given up evening gowns in favor of dinner dresses and had two fur coats, a leopard and an inferior mink. Virginia was in first year high school and went out with the captain of the basketball team. Every Saturday night Mr. Garland shook hands with this young man and they chatted jovially about the war until Virginia came down the stairs wearing her mother's perfume. Virginia was fifteen years old, Mr. Garland was thirty-nine, and Mrs. Garland was forty-one.

One evening at dinner—it would have been about twenty minutes past seven—Virginia remarked: "Mother, Millie said she'd be around tonight. Can I skip helping Agnes with the dishes?"

"What is Millie?" Mr. Garland inquired, regarding the cauliflower Agnes was offering, "a cow?"

Virginia giggled. "She looks a little bit like one," she said. "Only she isn't. She's Millie, from school, She's coming over and we're going to do algebra."

"Millie can wait while you help Agnes," Mrs. Garland said. She looked at Virginia to make Virginia realize that Agnes must be kept in good humor. "It doesn't take ten minutes, and Millie can wait."

"I'll entertain Millie," Mr. Garland said helpfully, "Millie and I will do all your algebra. Used to be quite a hand at algebra," he told Mrs. Garland solemnly.

"You're still quite a hand at talk," Mrs. Garland said. "Take some cauliflower before it gets too cold. Agnes has to have some too, you know."

"Millie hasn't been in school long," Virginia said. "She didn't come until the second semester and I'm helping her catch up."

"Very kind of you," Mr. Garland said.

The doorbell rang, and Virginia dropped her napkin. "When she says early she means early," she said.

"That would be Millie?" Mr. Garland inquired.

Virginia answered the door and Mr. and Mrs. Garland could hear her voice for a minute in the hall. Then she came back into the dining room, leading Millie. Millie was pretty and stupid-looking, and she had heavy black eyelashes and wore a great deal of lipstick.

"This is my mother and father," Virginia said, sliding into her chair, "this is Millie. Pull up a chair, Millie."

Mrs. Garland frowned slightly. "Have you had your dinner, Millie?"

"Yes," Millie said. She looked at Virginia and giggled. "I ought to wait in the living room," she said, "but Ginny said to come right on in."

"Of course," Mr. Garland said, "have some cauliflower?"

Millie giggled again, staring at Mr. Garland.

"If you don't care to eat it," Mr. Garland said, "you could wear it in your hair."

"My father never takes anything seriously," Virginia said to Millie. "He's like that all the time, don't mind him."

"Maybe you'll have some dessert with us, Millie?" Mrs. Garland said.

"No, thank you," Millie said.

"If you eat anything," Mr. Garland scowled ferociously at Millie, "you'll have to wash dishes. Anyone eats in this house, right after dinner they have to go out in the kitchen and wash dishes."

"Charles!" Mrs. Garland said. "You'll frighten the child."

"Millie isn't scared of anything, Mother," Virginia said, "Millie and I can do anything."

"I'll bet Millie can do anything," Mr. Garland said. Mrs. Garland looked up.

"Virginia," she said finally, "since you and Millie have to do algebra I'll explain to Agnes and she won't mind if you don't help her."

"Hallelujah," Virginia said. "Come on, Millie. Be excused, Mother?"

Mrs. Garland nodded and Virginia slid off her chair and ran out of the dining room, waving Millie to follow her.

Mr. and Mrs. Garland were quiet for a little while after Virginia and Millie had left the room, until finally Mrs. Garland remarked: "She doesn't seem like an awfully *nice* girl, does she, this Millie?"

"I don't know," Mr. Garland said, putting down his coffee cup, "she looked all right to me."

Mr. and Mrs. Garland were sitting quietly in the living room some time later, Mrs. Garland doing needlepoint—she was making a footstool—and Mr. Garland reading the *Saturday Evening Post*, when Virginia and Millie, heralded by a clatter of feet from upstairs, burst into the room.

"Mother," Virginia cried as she came, "Mother, we finished our homework and can we go down and get a soda, Mother?"

Mrs. Garland thought. "I suppose so," she said slowly, "only hurry back."

"Wait," Mr. Garland said reaching into his pocket, "bring back some ice cream and we'll all have some. Mother and I would like some ice cream."

"I don't think . . ." Mrs. Garland said.

Virginia rushed over and grabbed the money from her father's hand. "Back in two seconds," she said, and she and Millie ran out again.

"They do rush around so, don't they," Mrs. Garland said, turning back to her needlework.

"They're young," Mr. Garland said, "let them have their fun."

"I don't think we should encourage Millie as a friend for Virginia," Mrs. Garland said, "she doesn't seem to be quite a *nice* girl."

"She seems all right to me," Mr. Garland said.

Millie and Virginia put the ice cream in dishes and brought it in to Mr. and Mrs. Garland. Mr. Garland received his with disgust. "Why should Millie," he inquired, "get away with so much and only leave this little bit for me?"

Millie giggled. "I don't have one bit more than you do, Mr. Garland."

"I dished it out myself," Virginia said.

"You certainly do, Millie," Mr. Garland went on, "I got robbed." He went over to Millie to compare dishes and sat down next to her on the couch. "Now I'm going to sit right down here," he said, "and watch every bit you eat, and count how much you have, and then you'll be sorry you didn't let me have more."

Millie giggled again. "Stop, Mr. Garland," she said, "I'm choking."

"Charles," Mrs. Garland said, "you're spoiling the girl's good time."

"No, Mrs. Garland," Millie said, "I think Mr. Garland's awfully funny."

"Now I'm funny," Mr. Garland said. "First you rob me of my ice cream and then you think I'm funny. Just a silly old man, I guess."

"You're not an old man," Millie said.

"He's old enough not to act like a clown," Mrs. Garland said sharply.

"I don't think you're old at all," Millie protested, "really, I think you're young."

Mr. Garland eyed Millie. "How young would you say?" he demanded.

Millie giggled.

"My father's always like that," Virginia said to Millie. "He's always fooling people."

"Wouldn't go out with a guy my age, would you, Millie?" Mr. Garland said.

Millie looked up at him. "I couldn't say," she said.

"Now don't tease me," Mr. Garland said.

Mrs. Garland rose, put down her sewing, and went to the door. In the doorway she stopped for a minute. "Virginia," she said, without turning around, "I want to speak to you for a minute, please."

Virginia got up and followed her mother out of the room. "Be right with you, Millie," she said.

When Virginia was gone Millie turned around to Mr. Garland. "Is Mrs. Garland mad about something I said or something?" she asked.

"Don't pay any attention to her," Mr. Garland said. He touched the flower in Millie's hair. "Pretty flower," he said.

"My boy friend gave it to me," Millie said.

"Got a boy friend?" Mr. Garland said. "Does he take you out and show you a good time?"

Millie giggled. "He sure does," she said.

"Where does he take you?" Mr. Garland asked. "Ever take you to this place downtown, this club they call The Blue Lantern?"

"I've been there," Millie said.

Mr. Garland got up and walked across the room to get a cigarette and, as an afterthought, offered one to Millie.

"*She* coming back?" Millie asked, her hand out.

"Mrs. Garland? Not for a minute or two, probably." Millie took the cigarette and Mr. Garland lit it for her.

"She doesn't like me," Millie said, leaning back.

"I shouldn't think so," Mr. Garland said.

"But Virginia's a swell kid," Millie said. Mr. Garland laughed, and Millie looked up at him. "What did I *say?*" she asked.

Virginia came into the doorway and stopped for a minute.

"Millie," she said, and Millie juggled Mr. Garland's hand insistently to make him take her cigarette. "Millie," Virginia said, "Mother wants to know if we will run down and get her a couple of things at the store. Want to go?"

Millie hesitated, and Mrs. Garland came into the doorway behind Virginia. "Charles," she said, "I told Virginia that if she and Millie went down to the store for me like good children you'd give them each a dime."

"We'll get a soda," Virginia said.

"After all that ice cream?" Mrs. Garland asked tolerantly. "You'd like to have a dime, wouldn't you, Millie?"

Millie hesitated. "Come *on*, Millie," Virginia said impatiently. "Daddy, give us a dime."

Mr. Garland looked at his wife, and reached into his pocket and took out a quarter. "Here," he said.

Virginia came over and took the quarter and then grabbed Millie's arm and started her toward the door.

Mrs. Garland sat down and picked up her sewing again. "Charles," she said, "don't you think the children are having too much ice cream?"

Behold the Child Among His Newborn Blisses

IT WAS late on Saturday morning and the doctor's office was nearly empty. Two mothers sat quietly, one holding a little girl in a pink bonnet and dress, the other watching tolerantly while her little boy charged around the room, pulling a series of wooden ducks on wheels. From far within the doctor's office a baby screamed violently. Neither of the mothers paid the slightest attention. They had been waiting together for about fifteen minutes before the little girl on her mother's lap got the hiccups. Her mother blushed, patted the little girl's back, and finally turned her over onto her stomach on the couch. "Stay there, darling," she said, "and the nasty old hiccups will go away so quick you won't know you had them." She smiled at the other mother.

"They get them, don't they," the other mother said sympathetically.

"She gets them all the time," the little girl's mother said. "She just doesn't have a minute's peace with them."

"This one," the other mother gestured at the little boy, "he used to get them all the time, too."

"Terrible," the little girl's mother said.

"He outgrew them," the little boy's mother said, pleased.

The outer door opened and stayed open, letting in a draft. The little girl's mother, glaring at the doorway, picked up a pink sweater and threw it over the little girl, who was still lying on her stomach. The little boy's mother called: "Thomas, stay away from the door, dear, you'll catch your death of cold."

An enormous middle-aged woman backed in through the doorway, holding her hand out before her and calling "Come on, honey, come on into the nice office. Come on, Girlie honey."

"Would you mind closing that door?" the little girl's mother said angrily, "there are children in here."

"I've got to get him to come in, don't I?" the big woman said. "Just a minute." She began to snap her fingers, calling again, "Girlie honey, come on in—you've got to come in and see the nice doctor."

The little girl's mother looked at the little boy's mother, who shrugged and sighed. Then they both sat back furiously and watched their own children. The big woman was slowly backing into the room, still snapping her fingers and coaxing. Finally a boy of about ten appeared in the doorway, looking around watchfully and holding one hand behind him. Both the mothers smiled automatically; in the doctor's office it is manners to smile at someone else's children. The boy was reassured and came a step into the room. The big woman moved slowly forward and then caught him. "There," she said, "now you'll see, he isn't going to hurt you a bit."

"Would you *please* close that door?" the little girl's mother demanded.

The big woman said apologetically: "I just had to get him to come in. He's scared." She kicked the door shut. "He's never been to the doctor before."

"Never?" the little boy's mother asked incredulously.

"No." The big woman, still holding the boy, went over to an upholstered chair and sat down, putting the boy on her knee. He had one hand bandaged in a huge white handkerchief. "That's why he's scared, I guess."

"Hasn't he even had any whooping-cough inoculations?" the little girl's mother asked.

"Or diphtheria?" the little boy's mother added.

"Or his weight?" the little girl's mother insisted. "Don't you watch his weight?"

"He's good and healthy, he is," the big woman said. "He never needed to go to a doctor before."

The little boy on the floor had abandoned the ducks and was standing close to the big woman, watching the boy on her knee. They regarded one another steadily, almost without curiosity. "You want to get down?" the big woman said to the boy on her knee. "Girlie, you want down?" The boy shook his head. "I guess he's kind of shy of you at first," the big woman said to the little boy standing watching. "He doesn't always take to strangers right away."

The little boy's mother leaned forward. "Hello," she said to the boy, "aren't you a big boy?" The boy turned his eyes on her. "You're a *big* boy, aren't you?" she said. "Can't you talk to me?" He turned his eyes back to the little boy watching him, and the little boy's mother laughed embarrassedly. "I guess he is sort of shy," she said.

"He hardly ever talks anyway," the big woman said.

"How old is he?" the little girl's mother asked.

"He's ten, going on eleven."

"Ten," the little girl's mother repeated speculatively.

"*This* one," the little boy's mother said, "is five."

"Well," the big woman said. She turned to the boy on her knee. "This little man here is only five years old, Girlie. Imagine!"

"I'm five," the little boy said.

The boy on the big woman's knee stirred. "So'm I," he said.

The big woman laughed. "See," she said, "he can talk."

"Do you call him Girlie?" the little boy asked. "Is that boy's name Girlie?"

"It sure is," the big woman said, "it's Girlie all right."

"Why is his name Girlie? Is he a girl?"

The big woman laughed. "I'll tell you," she said, "when he was born he didn't cry a sound, and his old man said he couldn't be a real man, so quiet, and so that's why we call him Girlie."

"Is he a girl, though?" the little boy persisted.

The big woman laughed again. "I guess he doesn't know himself, sometimes," she said. "Do you, Girlie?"

Girlie moved suddenly. He twisted out of the big woman's arms and charged at the little boy, knocking him down. "Girlie," he said. "Boy."

The little boy began to cry even before his mother reached him and snatched him up. "Well!" she said, "a big boy like that!"

"Good lord!" the little girl's mother said, horrified. "A terrible thing to do!"

The little boy's mother turned on Girlie, who stood in the middle of the floor grinning hopefully. "You bad bad boy," she said. "You awful boy!"

"Play," Girlie said, "play with Girlie."

"Can't you even say you're sorry?" the little boy's mother said, and she turned to the big woman. "Doesn't he even say he's sorry when he does a thing like that?"

"Now wait a minute," the big woman said soothingly, "Girlie didn't mean to hurt the little fellow. He just wanted to play. I guess he's just about as sorry as anybody, and he didn't mean to do anyone any harm or start any fuss. He's a good boy, Girlie is."

"Well, he shouldn't do a thing like that to a child littler than he is," the little boy's mother said.

"Good heavens no!" the little girl's mother said. "First thing you know he'd do the same thing to *anyone*, babies even." She picked up the little girl and held her protectingly on her lap, and the little girl hiccuped reproachfully.

"Girlie," the big woman said. He turned to her. "Now you shouldn't have done that, Girlie. That was dirty, Girlie, *dirty*. That was a dirty thing to do, *dirty*."

Girlie hung his head. "Dirty," he said.

"There," the big woman turned to the little boy's mother. "Now he's sorry. He knows now it was bad."

"Well, he should learn to behave better with children littler than he is," the little boy's mother said. She took the little boy and went across the room to a chair near the little girl's mother. "Did you ever!" she said.

"Never!" the little girl's mother said.

"Thomas dear," the little boy's mother said loudly, "are you all right now? Did he hurt you badly, darling?"

Thomas had stopped crying and was looking at Girlie. He squirmed. "I want to go play with that Girlie boy, Mother," he said.

"Thomas!" his mother said. Thomas wriggled out of her arms and stood on the floor. "Stay over here, dear," she said.

Thomas looked at Girlie. "Hello, Girlie," he said. "Come on and play with these chickens."

"Ducks, dear," his mother said. She hesitated and then smiled condescendingly on the big woman.

"Ducks," Thomas said. He picked up the string attached to the ducks on wheels. "Look at me, Girlie," he said, "look at me pull the ducks."

"Ducks," Girlie said questioningly. He looked at the big woman. "Ducks?" he repeated.

"Sure," the big woman said. "Those are ducks, Girlie."

"Ducks," Girlie said.

"How old did you say he was?" the little girl's mother asked the big woman.

"Ten going on eleven," the big woman said. "He's a good boy."

"*This* one never cries," the little boy's mother said. "He's happy as a lark, the whole day long. Except when he's hurt, of course," she added reflectively.

"You say he's *never* been to the doctor before?" the little girl's mother asked.

"Hasn't ever needed to go to a doctor," the big woman said. "Now, though, he's got something wrong with his hand."

"Thomas," the little boy's mother said instantly, "come back over here, dear."

"He cut it on something," the big woman said. "It's been paining him."

The door to the doctor's office opened and a woman came out carrying the baby that had been screaming. She smiled miserably at the other mothers and went to the chair where she had left the baby's coat and hat. When she set the baby down it stopped screaming and, fist in its mouth, looked at the other children.

"Poor darling," the little girl's mother said. "Injection?"

The baby's mother nodded. "Third," she said. "Whooping cough."

"Terrible," the little girl's mother said. "We've had ours. Boy or girl?"

"Girl," the baby's mother said.

"This too," the little girl's mother said. "How old?"

"Twenty-seven weeks," the baby's mother said. "Yours?"

"Thirty-five," the little girl's mother said.

"Oh." The baby's mother smiled commiseratingly. "Almost time for the diphtheria."

"Next visit," the little girl's mother said. "Creep yet?"

"Up on her hands and knees," the baby's mother said. She had the baby dressed by that time and had picked up her own coat. "Well," she said.

"Sorry for the noise."

"That's all right," the little girl's mother said.

"Too bad," the little boy's mother said.

"They all yell," the big woman said.

The baby's mother gave her a startled look and went out, carrying the baby carefully.

The doctor appeared in the office door. "Well," he said, smiling broadly, "if it isn't Thomas; how are you, little man?"

"Say hello to the doctor, Thomas," the little boy's mother said.

"Hello," Thomas said, but the doctor was looking at the little girl. "Coming along fine, I see," he said. "Well, who's next?"

The little girl's mother looked at the little boy's mother. "I guess she is," the little boy's mother said, pointing at the big woman.

"Oh, no," the big woman said, "you two were here—"

"Go ahead," the little girl's mother said, "I've got to wait here for my husband anyway."

"We're in no hurry at all," the little boy's mother said. "You go right on in."

"Well, then," the big woman said. She reached out suddenly and grabbed Girlie's arm. "Come along, Girlie."

"Well," the doctor said, looking down at Girlie, "what seems to be the matter with this fine young man?"

He disappeared into his office. The big woman hesitated in the doorway, wanting to speak to the two other mothers, who were watching their children again. "Look," the big woman said slowly, "he's a good boy, Girlie. He's a good boy," she went on earnestly, turning to the little girl's mother. "He's not awfully bright, this Girlie isn't, but he's a *good* boy."

The door closed behind her. The little girl's mother put the little girl back down on the couch. "Those nasty old hiccups are all gone at last," she said.

The little boy's mother did not look up. She was staring at her son. "Thomas," she said. He turned. "Come here, dear," she said.

Thomas walked over to his mother, pulling the ducks on the string.

"And the way that creature *stared* at those ducks," the little girl's mother said, "and keeping the door open all that time."

"Thomas," the little boy's mother said softly, "do you know

what you were playing with? Do you know what Mother had to sit here and watch you playing with? Do you know that boy was an idiot?"

"No," Thomas said.

"Do you know what an idiot is, Thomas?" the little boy's mother almost whispered. "Do you know what you were playing with?"

Thomas was watching his mother curiously. Her lips were tight and she was breathing quickly. "You heard what his own mother said about him?" she demanded, her voice rising.

Thomas shook his head. Because he was not expecting punishment his mother's slap caught him sharply in the face. Afraid even to cry, he still stood staring.

"His own mother said he was dirty, that's what she said he was," the little boy's mother said. "This lady here heard his own mother say he was dirty and she saw you playing with him right in front of your mother. A dirty little idiot!"

The little girl's mother had turned her eyes down to her own daughter and was playing with a ruffle on the pink dress. Thomas looked at her quickly and back at his mother. Then he began to cry.

1944

It Isn't the Money I Mind

I<small>T WAS</small> a sunny afternoon and the Park was nearly full. Old men and women sat on the benches; mothers sat idly beside baby carriages or watched children run shrieking over the grass. There were a lot of dogs walking up and down the paths on leashes or lying next to the benches. Except for the children, there was little conversation and not much noise.

A man came into the Park from one of the side entrances. He stopped just inside the entrance to pat a dog on the head and speak to the owner, and then walked on slowly, looking for a place to sit down. He was middle-aged, partly bald, and, judging by his clothes, not very well off. As he walked he watched the people in the Park with a bright interest, stopping to listen to an argument between a mother and child, and later to pick up a ball for a group of older boys. One of them said, "Throw it back here, Mister," and held out his hands. The man threw the ball clumsily and it bounced twice before the boy scooped it up. The boy said, "Thanks," and turned and threw it easily far across the grass to another boy. The man watched for a minute and then walked on. Finally he stopped in front of a bench with an empty place at one end. Next to it sat a woman with a baby carriage. "May I sit here?" he asked. She looked up and said, "It's not taken," and the man sat down. He sighed and sat still for a minute before reaching into his pocket for a cigarette.

The woman looked at him irritably and then turned away. A baby was lying in the carriage on its stomach, asleep, wearing only a diaper. The baby's back was brown, except for a sharp white edge where the diaper began. The woman was tirelessly rocking the carriage back and forth.

"Will the smoke bother the baby?" the man asked.

"I just got her to sleep," the woman said. "Just about anything wakes her."

The man leaned over and dropped the cigarette onto the ground and put his foot on it. "She looks like a fine, healthy baby," he said.

The woman smiled. "She's only six months old," she said, "and never even had a cold."

"A fine baby," the man said. "You see so many around here looking pale and white."

"They're not healthy," the woman said. "Some of the children in this park are really unhealthy."

"It's hard for children in the city."

"Their mothers should keep them out of the Park if they have things other children can catch," the woman said.

While he was talking, the man had been fingering his billfold, riffling through the papers in it absent-mindedly. Now he pulled one out—a magazine clipping. "Want to see my little girl?" he asked.

The woman reached out with the hand that was not rocking the carriage. "Of course," she said. "I could tell from the way you talked that you had one of your own."

The clipping was of a little blond girl of about six, with a pretty, adult face and a lot of makeup. "She's lovely," the woman said. "She has such a sweet face."

"She's a nice kid," the man said. He hesitated. "Know who she is?" he asked finally.

The woman shook her head.

"Her name's Angela Foster, now."

"Of course," the woman said. "In the movies!"

"That's right." The man took the clipping and looked at it fondly. "It used to be Martin—that's my name. Her mother changed it. Angela Martin's not good for the movies," he said.

"What a lucky little girl!" the woman said, reaching over to adjust the hood of the carriage. "In the movies!"

"She'll be a second Shirley Temple someday," the man said. "She's got talent—everything."

"You must be very proud of her."

"I'll tell you," the man began carefully, "I'm proud of her, of course. And it isn't the money I mind, either. She's making plenty right now and I don't grudge it to her. But it's like this. Before her mother took her out to Hollywood, I was always kicking about the dancing lessons and the singing lessons and the costumes and the late nights when her dancing class gave a recital. And now I know I just didn't have sense enough to see the baby had talent."

"It's hard to tell," the woman said. "All children have a natural sense of rhythm. Even at six months—"

"It isn't the money I mind," the man said again. "I don't think a six-year-old girl *should* have to support her father."

"Well, there's a lot of luck connected with it," the woman said.

"I saw this article about her in a movie magazine," the man went on. "It said she was five years old, but she must be six now. And she's already getting fan mail."

"Really?" the woman said.

"I thought of writing to her and asking for a picture," the man said. "Her own father."

"I'm sure you'll be very proud of her," the woman said. He reached into his pocket again for his cigarettes, and she frowned and shook her head. The man rose.

"I'll just finish my walk while I smoke this," he said. He smiled at the woman and leaned over the carriage for a minute. "Such a pretty baby," he said. He bowed slightly to the woman and went rapidly down the path.

When the man got around the next turn, he began to walk more slowly. A little boy just learning to walk staggered out from a bench and grabbed him by the leg. The man said, "Where you going, Champ?," turned the little boy around, and started him back to his mother. The man stopped for a minute to watch a checker game and then went on again, only to stop a minute later and help a little girl of about two push her stroller around a difficult turn. The man called her "honey." Her mother, who was standing nearby, thanked him and he said, "Lovely little girl." The mother smiled and went on, pulling the little girl and talking to her as she went.

The broad circle the man had been making had by now taken him back in the direction he had come from. As he passed the group of boys playing ball, he saw the ball strike a tree and bounce in his direction. He scooped it up awkwardly and, holding it in his hand, walked over to the boys. They were waiting impatiently for the ball, and as he stepped across a low railing and handed the ball to the nearest, he smiled apologetically and said, "Don't have the muscle I used to."

"Thanks," the boy said. He threw the ball and the boys began to scatter. One of them caught the ball and threw it to another. The man said, "Bud," and the nearest boy turned around. The man, taking out his billfold, said, "Know who this is?" He pulled forth a newspaper clipping and held it out to the boy.

The boy glanced over his shoulder at his friends and then went over to the man. "Sure," he said, looking at the clipping, but without making any attempt to hold it. "Nicky Lopez. The middleweight challenger."

A couple of the boys nearby had also turned when the man called and now they came slowly over. "Nicky Lopez," one of them said. "Let's see Nicky Lopez." The man handed him the clipping and he looked at it and said professionally, "There's a guy that can fight."

"He's pretty good," another of the boys said, taking the clipping in turn.

"I used to manage Nicky," the man said, watching the boys' heads turn slowly toward him. "Yeah," he said reminiscently, "I used to manage Nicky, until the syndicate got him away from me." He looked around at the boys and then went on, "It isn't the money I mind, you understand, but I sure hated to lose that boy."

1945

The Third Baby's the Easiest

EVERYONE says the third baby is the easiest one to have, and now I know why. It's the easiest because it's the funniest, because you've been there twice, and you know. You know, for instance, how you're going to look in a maternity dress about the seventh month, and you know how to release the footbrake on a baby carriage without fumbling amateurishly, and you know how to tie your shoes before and do knee-chests after, and while you're not exactly casual, you're a little bit off-hand about the whole thing. Sentimental people keep insisting that women go on to have a third baby because they love babies, and cynical people seem to maintain that a woman with two healthy, active children around the house will do *any*thing for ten quiet days in the hospital; my own position is somewhere between the two, but agree that the third is the easiest. The whole event is far too recent for me to be deluded.

Because it *was* my third I was saved a lot of unnecessary discomfort. No one sent me any dainty pink sweaters, for instance. We only received one pair of booties, and those were a pair of rosebud-covered white ones that someone had sent my first child when he was born and which I had given, still in their original pink tissue paper, to a friend when *her* first child was born; she had subsequently sent them to her cousin in Texas for a second baby, and the cousin sent them back East on the occasion of a mutual friend's twins; the mutual friend gave them to me, with a card saying "Love to Baby" and the pink tissue paper hardly ruffled. I have them carefully set aside, because I know someone who is having a baby in June.

I borrowed back my baby carriage from my next-door neighbor, took the crib down out of the attic, washed my way through the chest of baby shirts and woolen shawls, briefed the two incumbent children far enough ahead of time, and spent a loving and painstaking month packing my suitcase. This time I knew exactly what I was taking with me to the hospital, but assembling it took time and eventually required an emergency trip to New York from our home in Vermont. I packed it, though, finally: a yellow nightgown trimmed with lace, a white nightgown that tied at the throat with a blue bow, two of the fanciest bed-jackets I could find—that was what I went to New York for—and then, two pounds of homemade fudge, as many mystery stories as I could cram in, and a bag of apples. Almost at the last minute I added a box of pralines, a bottle of expensive cologne, and my toothbrush. I have heard of people who take their own satin sheets to the hospital but that has always seemed to me a waste of good suitcase space.

My doctor was very pleasant and my friends were very thoughtful; for the last two weeks before I went to the hospital almost everyone I know called me almost once a day and said, "Haven't you gone *yet?*" My mother- and father-in-law settled on a weekend to visit us when, according to the best astronomical figuring, I should have had a two-weeks-old baby ready to show them; they arrived, were entertained with some restraint on my part, and left, eying me with disfavor and some suspicion. My mother sent me a telegram from California saying, "Is everything all right? Shall I come? Where is baby?" My children were sullen, my husband was embarrassed.

Everything was, as I say, perfectly normal, up to and including the frightful moment when I leaped out of bed at two in the morning as though there had been a pea under the mattress; when I turned on the light my husband said sleepily, "Having baby?"

"I really don't know," I said nervously. I was looking for the clock, which I hide at night so that in the morning when the alarm rings I will have to wake up looking for it. It was hard to find it without the alarm ringing.

"Shall I wake up?" my husband asked without any sign of pleased anticipation.

"I can't find the *clock*," I said.

"Clock?" my husband said. "Clock. Wake me five minutes apart." I unlocked the suitcase and took out a mystery story, and sat down in the armchair with a blanket over me. After a few minutes the cat, who usually sleeps on the foot of my son's bed, wandered in and settled down on a corner of the blanket by my feet. She slept as peacefully as my husband did most of the night, except that now and then she raised her head to regard me with a look of silent contempt.

Because we live in a small country town and our hospital is

five miles away I had an uneasy feeling that I ought to allow plenty of time, particularly since neither of us has ever learned to drive and consequently I must call our local taxi to take me to the hospital. At seven-thirty I called my doctor and we chatted agreeably for a few minutes, and I said I would just give the children their breakfast and wash up the dishes and then run over to the hospital, and he said that would be just fine and he'd plan to meet me later, then; the unspoken conviction between us was that I ought to be back in the fields before sundown.

I went into the kitchen and proceeded methodically to work, humming cheerfully and stopping occasionally to grab the back of a chair and hold my breath. My husband told me later that he found his cup and saucer (the one with "Father" written on it) in the oven, but I am inclined to believe that he was too upset to be a completely reliable reporter. My own recollection is of doing everything the way I have a thousand times before—school-morning short-cuts so familiar that I am hardly aware, usually, of doing them at all. The frying pan, for instance. My single immediate object was a cup of coffee, and I decided to heat up the coffee left from the night before, rather than take the time to make fresh; it seemed brilliantly logical to heat it in the frying pan because anyone knows that a broad shallow container will heat liquid faster than a tall narrow one, like the coffee pot. I will not try to deny, however, that it *looked* funny.

By the time the children came down everything seemed to be moving along handsomely; my son grimly got two glasses and filled them with fruit juice for his sister and himself. He offered me one, but I had no desire to eat, or in fact to do anything which might upset my precarious balance between two, and three, children, or to interrupt my morning's work for more than coffee, which I was still doggedly making in the frying pan. My husband came downstairs, sat in his usual place, said good-morning to the children, accepted the glass of fruit juice my son poured for him, and asked me brightly, "How do you feel?"

"Splendid," I said, making an enormous smile for all of them. "I'm doing wonderfully well."

"Good," he said. "How soon do you think we ought to leave?"

"Around noon, probably," I said. "Everything is fine, really."

My husband asked politely, "May I help you with breakfast?"

"No indeed," I said. I stopped to catch my breath and smiled reassuringly. "I feel *so* well," I said.

"Would you be offended," he said, still very politely, "if I took this egg out of my glass?"

"Certainly not," I said. "I'm sorry, I can't think how it got there."

"It's nothing at all," my husband said. "I was just thirsty."

They were all staring at me oddly, and I kept giving them my reassuring smile; I *did* feel splendid; my months of waiting were nearly over, my careful preparations had finally been brought to a purpose, tomorrow I would be wearing my yellow nightgown. "I'm so pleased," I said.

I was slightly dizzy, perhaps. And there *were* pains, but they were authentic ones, not the feeble imitations I had been dreaming up the past few weeks. I patted my son on the head. "Well," I said, in the tone I had used perhaps five hundred times in the last months. "Well, do we want a little boy or a little boy?"

"Won't you sit down?" my husband said. He had the air of a man who expects that an explanation will somehow be given him for a series of extraordinary events in which he is unwillingly involved. "I think you ought to sit down," he added urgently.

It was about then that I realized that he was right. I ought to sit down. As a matter of fact, I ought to go to the hospital, right now, immediately. I dropped my reassuring smile and the fork I had been carrying around with me.

"I'd better hurry," I said inadequately.

My husband called the taxi and brought down my suitcase. The children were going to stay with friends, and one of the things I had planned to do was drop them off on my way to the hospital; now, however, I felt vitally that I had not the time. I began to talk fast.

"You'll have to take care of the children," I told my husband. "See that . . ." I stopped. I remember thinking with incredible clarity and speed. "See that they finish their breakfast," I said. Pajamas on the line, I thought, school, cats, toothbrushes. Milkman. Overalls to be mended; laundry. "I ought to make a list," I said vaguely. "Leave a note for the milkman tomorrow night. Soap, too. We need soap."

"Yes, dear," my husband kept saying. "Yes dear yes dear."

The taxi arrived and suddenly I was saying good-by to the children. "See you later," my son said casually. "Have a good time."

"Bring me a present," my daughter added.

"Don't worry about a thing," my husband said.

"Now, don't you worry," I told him. "There's nothing to worry about."

"Everything will be *fine*," I said. "Don't worry."

I waited for a good moment and then scrambled into the taxi without grace; I did not dare risk my reassuring smile on the taxi driver but I nodded to him briskly.

"I'll be with you in an hour," my husband said nervously. "And don't worry."

"Everything will be fine," I said. "Don't worry."

"Nothing to worry about," the taxi driver said to my husband, and we started off, my husband standing at the curb wringing his hands and the taxi tacking insanely from side to side of the road to avoid even the slightest bump.

I sat very still in the back seat, trying not to breathe. I had one arm lovingly around my suitcase, which held my yellow nightgown, and I tried to light a cigarette without using any muscles except those in my hands and my neck, and still not let go of my suitcase.

"Going to be a beautiful day," I said to the taxi driver at last. We had a twenty-minute trip ahead of us at least—much longer, if he continued his zigzag path. "Pretty warm for the time of year."

"Pretty warm yesterday, too," the taxi driver said.

"It *was* warm yesterday," I conceded, and stopped to catch my breath. The driver, who was obviously avoiding looking at me in the mirror, said a little bit hysterically, "Probably be warm tomorrow, too."

I waited for a minute, and then I was able to say, dubiously, "I don't know as it will stay warm *that* long. Might cool off by tomorrow."

"Well," the taxi driver said, "it was sure warm *yesterday*."

"Yesterday," I said. "Yes, that was a warm day."

"Going to be nice today, too," the taxi driver said. I clutched my suitcase tighter and made some small sound—more like a yelp than anything else—and the taxi veered madly off to the left and then began to pick up speed with enthusiasm.

"Very warm indeed," the driver babbled, leaning forward against the wheel. "Warmest day I ever saw for the time of year. Usually this time of year it's colder. Yesterday it was *terribly*—"

"It was not," I said. "It was freezing. I can see the tower of the hospital."

"I remember thinking how warm it was," the driver said. He turned into the hospital drive. "It was so warm I noticed it right away. 'This is a warm day,' I thought, that's how warm it was."

We pulled up with a magnificent flourish at the hospital entrance, and the driver skittered out of the front seat and came around and opened the door and took my arm.

"My wife had five," he said. "I'll take the suitcase, Miss. Five, and never a minute's trouble with any of them."

He rushed me in through the door and up to the desk. "Here," he said to the desk clerk. "Pay me later," he said to me, and fled.

"Name?" the desk clerk said to me politely, her pencil poised.

"Name," I said vaguely. I remembered, and told her.

"Age?" she asked. "Sex? Occupation?"

"Writer," I said.

"Housewife," she said.

"Writer," I said.

"I'll just put down housewife," she said. "Doctor? How many children?"

"Two," I said. "Up to now."

"Normal pregnancy?" she said. "Blood test? X-ray?"

"Look—" I said.

"Husband's name?" she said. "Address? Occupation?"

"Just put down housewife," I said. "I don't remember *his* name, really."

"Legitimate?"

"What?" I said.

"Is your husband the father of this child? Do you have a husband?"

"Please," I said plaintively, "can I go on upstairs?"

"Well, *really*," she said, and sniffed. "You're *only* having a baby."

She waved delicately to a nurse, who took me by the same arm everybody else had been using that morning, and in the elevator this nurse was very nice. She asked me twice how I was feeling and said "Maternity?" to me politely as we left the elevator; I was carrying my own suitcase by then.

Two more nurses joined us upstairs; we made light conversation while I got into the hospital nightgown. The nurses had all been to some occupational party the night before and one of them had been simply a riot; she was still being a riot while I undressed, because every now and then one of the two other nurses would turn around to me and say, "Isn't she a riot, honestly?"

I made a few remarks, just to show that I too was lighthearted and not at all nervous; I commented laughingly on the hospital nightgown, and asked with amusement tinged with foreboding what was the apparatus they were wheeling in on the tray.

My doctor arrived about half an hour later; he had obviously had three cups of coffee and a good cigar; he patted me on the shoulder and said, "How do we feel?"

"Pretty well," I said, with an uneasy giggle that ended in a squawk. "How long do you suppose it will be before—"

"We don't need to worry about *that* for a while yet," the doctor said. He laughed pleasantly, and nodded to the nurses. They all bore down on me at once. One of them smoothed my pillow, one of them held my hand, and the third one stroked my forehead and said, "After all, you're *only* having a baby."

"Call me if you want me," the doctor said to the nurses as he left. "I'll be downstairs in the coffee shop."

"*I'll* call you if I need you," I told him ominously, and one of the nurses said in a honeyed voice, "Now, look, we don't want our husband to get all worried."

I opened one eye; my husband was sitting, suddenly, beside

the bed. He looked as though he were trying not to scream. "They *told* me to come in here," he said. "I was trying to find the waiting room."

"The other end of the hall," I told him grimly. I pounded on the bell and the nurse came running. "Get him out of here," I said, waving my head at my husband.

"They *told* me—" my husband began, looking miserably at the nurse.

"It's al-l-l-l-l right," the nurse said. She began to stroke my forehead again. "Hubby belongs right here."

"Either he goes or I go," I said.

The door slammed open and the doctor came in. "Heard you were here," he said jovially, shaking my husband's hand. "Look a little pale."

My husband smiled weakly.

"Never lost a father yet," the doctor said, and slapped him on the back. He turned to me. "How do we feel?" he said.

"Terrible," I said, and the doctor laughed again. "Just on my way downstairs," he said to my husband. "Come along?"

No one seemed, actually, to go or come that morning; I would open my eyes and they were there, open my eyes again and they were gone. This time, when I opened my eyes, a pleasant-faced nurse was standing beside me; she was swabbing my arm with a piece of cotton. Although I am ordinarily timid about hypodermics I welcomed this one with what was almost a genuine echo of my old reassuring smile. "Well, well," I said to the nurse. "Sure glad to see *you*."

"Sissy," she said distinctly, and jabbed me in the arm.

"How soon will this wear off?" I asked her with deep suspicion; I am always afraid with nurses that they feel that the psychological effect of a hypodermic is enough, and that I am actually being inoculated with some useless, although probably harmless, concoction.

"You won't even notice," she said enigmatically, and left.

The hypodermic hit me suddenly, and I began to giggle about five minutes after she left. I was alone in the room, lying there giggling to myself, when I opened my eyes and there was a woman standing beside the bed. She was human, not a nurse; she was wearing a baggy blue bathrobe. "I'm across the hall," she said. "I been hearing you."

"I was laughing," I said, with vast dignity.

"I heard you," she said. "Tomorrow it might be me, maybe."

"You here for a baby?"

"Someday," she said gloomily. "I was here two weeks ago, I was having pains. I come in the morning and that night they said to me, 'Go home, wait a while longer.' So I went home, and I come again three days later, I was having pains. And they said to me, 'Go home, wait a while longer.' And so yesterday I come again, I was having pains. So far they let me stay."

"That's too bad," I said.

"I got my mother there," she said. "She takes care of everything and sees the meals made, but she's beginning to think I got her there with false pretenses."

"That's too bad," I said. I began to pound the wall with my fists.

"Stop that," she said. "Somebody'll hear you. This is my third. The first two—nothing."

"This is *my* third," I said. "I don't care who hears me."

"My kids," she said. "Every time I come home they say to me, 'Where's the baby?' My mother too. My husband, he keeps driving me over and driving me back."

"They kept telling me the third was the easiest," I said. I began to giggle again.

"There you go," she said. "Laughing your head off. I wish *I* had something to laugh at."

She waved her hand at me and turned and went mournfully through the door. I opened my same weary eye and my husband was sitting comfortably in his chair. "I said," he was saying loudly, "I said, 'Do you mind if I read?'" He had the *New York Times* on his knee.

"Look," I said. "Do I have anything to read? Here I am, with nothing to do and no one to talk to and you sit there and read the *New York Times* right in front of me and here I am, with nothing—"

"How do we feel?" the doctor asked. He was suddenly much taller than before and the walls of the room were rocking distinctly.

"Doctor," I said, and I believe that my voice was a little louder than I intended it should be. "You better give me—"

He patted me on the hand and it was my husband instead of the doctor. "Stop yelling," he said.

"I'm *not* yelling," I said. "I don't like this any more. I've changed my mind, I don't want any baby, I want to go home and forget the whole thing."

"I know *just* how you feel," he said.

My only answer was a word which certainly I knew that I *knew*, although I had never honestly expected to hear it spoken in my own ladylike voice.

"Stop yelling," my husband said urgently. "*Please* stop saying that."

I had the idea that I was perfectly conscious, and I looked at him with dignity. "Who is doing this," I asked. "You or me?"

"It's all right," the doctor said. "We're on our way." The walls were moving along on either side of me and the woman in the blue bathrobe was waving from a doorway.

"She loved me for the dangers I had passed," I said to the doctor, "and I loved her that she did pity them."

"It's all right, I tell you," the doctor said. "Hold your breath."

"Did he finish his *New York Times*?"

"Hours ago," the doctor said.

"What's he reading now?" I asked.

"The *Tribune*," the doctor said. "Hold your breath."

It was so unbelievably bright that I closed my eyes. "Such a lovely time," I said to the doctor. "Thank you so much for asking me, I can't tell you how I've enjoyed it. Next time you must come to our—"

"It's a girl," the doctor said.

"Sarah," I said politely, as though I were introducing them. I still thought I was perfectly conscious, and then I was. My husband was sitting beside the bed, smiling cheerfully.

"What happened to *you*?" I asked him. "No *Wall Street Journal*?"

"It's a girl," he said.

"I know," I said. "I was there."

I was in a pleasant, clean room. There was no doubt that it was all over; I could see my feet under the bedspread.

"It's a girl," I said to my husband.

The door opened and the doctor came in. "Well," he said. "How do we feel?"

"Fine," I said. "It's a girl."

"I know," he said.

The door was still open and a face peered around it. My husband, the doctor, and I, all turned happily to look. It was the woman in the blue bathrobe.

"Had it yet?" I asked her.

"No," she said. "You?"

"Yep," I said. "You going home again?"

"Listen," she said. "I been thinking. Home, the kids all yelling and my mother looking sad like she's disappointed in me. Like I did something. My husband, every time he sees me jump he reaches for the car keys. My sister, she calls me every day and if I answer, the phone she hangs up. Here, I get three meals a day I don't cook, I know all the nurses and I meet a lot of people going in and out. I figure I'd be a *fool* to go home. What was it, boy or girl?"

"Girl," I said.

"Girl," she said. "They say the third's the easiest."

1949

The Summer People

THE Allisons' country cottage, seven miles from the nearest town, was set prettily on a hill; from three sides it looked down on soft trees and grass that seldom, even at midsummer, lay still and dry. On the fourth side was the lake, which touched against the wooden pier the Allisons had to keep repairing, and which looked equally well from the Allisons' front porch, their side porch or any spot on the wooden staircase leading from the porch down to the water. Although the Allisons loved their summer cottage, looked forward to arriving in the early summer and hated to leave in the fall, they had not troubled themselves to put in any improvements, regarding the cottage itself and the lake as improvement enough for the life left to them. The cottage had no heat, no running water except the precarious supply from the backyard pump, and no electricity. For seventeen summers, Janet Allison had cooked on a kerosene stove, heating all their water; Robert Allison had brought buckets full of water daily from the pump and read his paper by kerosene light in the evenings; and they had both, sanitary city people, become stolid and matter-of-fact about their backhouse. In the first two years they had gone through all the standard vaudeville and magazine jokes about backhouses and by now, when they no longer had frequent guests to impress, they had subsided to a comfortable security which made the backhouse, as well as the pump and the kerosene, an indefinable asset to their summer life.

In themselves, the Allisons were ordinary people. Mrs. Allison was fifty-eight years old and Mr. Allison sixty; they had seen their children outgrow the summer cottage and go on to families of their own and seashore resorts; their friends were either dead or settled in comfortable year-round houses, their nieces and nephews vague. In the winter they told one another they could stand their New York apartment while waiting for the summer; in the summer they told one another that the winter was well worth while, waiting to get to the country.

Since they were old enough not to be ashamed of regular habits, the Allisons invariably left their summer cottage the

Tuesday after Labor Day, and were as invariably sorry when the months of September and early October turned out to be pleasant and almost insufferably barren in the city; each year they recognized that there was nothing to bring them back to New York, but it was not until this year that they overcame their traditional inertia enough to decide to stay in the cottage after Labor Day.

"There isn't really anything to take us back to the city," Mrs. Allison told her husband seriously, as though it were a new idea, and he told her, as though neither of them had ever considered it, "We might as well enjoy the country as long as possible."

Consequently, with much pleasure and a slight feeling of adventure, Mrs. Allison went into their village the day after Labor Day and told those natives with whom she had dealings, with a pretty air of breaking away from tradition, that she and her husband had decided to stay at least a month longer at their cottage.

"It isn't as though we had anything to take us back to the city," she said to Mr. Babcock, her grocer. "We might as well enjoy the country while we can."

"Nobody ever stayed at the lake past Labor Day before," Mr. Babcock said. He was putting Mrs. Allison's groceries into a large cardboard carton, and he stopped for a minute to look reflectively into a bag of cookies. "Nobody," he added.

"But the city!" Mrs. Allison always spoke of the city to Mr. Babcock as though it were Mr. Babcock's dream to go there. "It's so hot—you've really no idea. We're always sorry when we leave."

"Hate to leave," Mr. Babcock said. One of the most irritating native tricks Mrs. Allison had noticed was that of taking a trivial statement and rephrasing it downward, into an even more trite statement. "I'd hate to leave myself," Mr. Babcock said, after deliberation, and both he and Mrs. Allison smiled. "But I never heard of anyone ever staying out at the lake after Labor Day before."

"Well, we're going to give it a try," Mrs. Allison said, and Mr. Babcock replied gravely, "Never know till you try."

Physically, Mrs. Allison decided, as she always did when leaving the grocery after one of her inconclusive conversations with Mr. Babcock, physically, Mr. Babcock could model for a statue of Daniel Webster, but mentally . . . it was horrible to think into what old New England Yankee stock had degenerated. She said as much to Mr. Allison when she got into the car, and he said, "It's generations of inbreeding. That and the bad land."

Since this was their big trip into town, which they made only once every two weeks to buy things they could not have delivered, they spent all day at it, stopping to have a sandwich in the newspaper and soda shop, and leaving packages heaped in the back of the car. Although Mrs. Allison was able to order groceries delivered regularly, she was never able to form any accurate idea of Mr. Babcock's current stock by telephone, and her lists of odds and ends that might be procured was always supplemented, almost beyond their need, by the new and fresh local vegetables Mr. Babcock was selling temporarily, or the packaged candy which had just come in. This trip Mrs. Allison was tempted, too, by the set of glass baking dishes that had found themselves completely by chance in the hardware and clothing and general store, and which had seemingly been waiting there for no one but Mrs. Allison, since the country people, with their instinctive distrust of anything that did not look as permanent as trees and rocks and sky, had only recently begun to experiment in aluminum baking dishes instead of ironware, and had, apparently within the memory of local inhabitants, discarded stoneware in favor of iron.

Mrs. Allison had the glass baking dishes carefully wrapped, to endure the uncomfortable ride home over the rocky road that led up to the Allisons' cottage, and while Mr. Charley Walpole, who, with his younger brother Albert, ran the hardware-clothing-general store (the store itself was called Johnson's, because it stood on the site of the old Johnson cabin, burned fifty years before Charley Walpole was born), laboriously unfolded newspapers to wrap around the dishes, Mrs. Allison said, informally, "Course, I *could* have waited and gotten those dishes in New York, but we're not going back so soon this year."

"Heard you was staying on," Mr. Charley Walpole said. His old fingers fumbled maddeningly with the thin sheets of news-

paper, carefully trying to isolate only one sheet at a time, and
he did not look up at Mrs. Allison as he went on, "Don't know
about staying on up there to the lake. Not after Labor Day."

"Well, you know," Mrs. Allison said, quite as though he deserved an explanation, "it just seemed to us that we've been
hurrying back to New York every year, and there just wasn't
any need for it. You know what the city's like in the fall." And
she smiled confidingly up at Mr. Charley Walpole.

Rhythmically he wound string around the package. He's
giving me a piece long enough to save, Mrs. Allison thought,
and she looked away quickly to avoid giving any sign of impatience. "I feel sort of like we belong here, more," she said.
"Staying on after everyone else has left." To prove this, she
smiled brightly across the store at a woman with a familiar
face, who might have been the woman who sold berries to the
Allisons one year, or the woman who occasionally helped in
the grocery and was probably Mr. Babcock's aunt.

"Well," Mr. Charley Walpole said. He shoved the package a
little across the counter, to show that it was finished and that
for a sale well made, a package well wrapped, he was willing to
accept pay. "Well," he said again. "Never been summer people
before, at the lake after Labor Day."

Mrs. Allison gave him a five-dollar bill, and he made change
methodically, giving great weight even to the pennies. "Never
after Labor Day," he said, and nodded at Mrs. Allison, and
went soberly along the store to deal with two women who
were looking at cotton house dresses.

As Mrs. Allison passed on her way out she heard one of the
women say acutely, "Why is one of them dresses one dollar
and thirty-nine cents and this one here is only ninety-eight?"

"They're great people," Mrs. Allison told her husband as
they went together down the sidewalk after meeting at the
door of the hardware store. "They're so solid, and so reasonable, and so *honest*."

"Makes you feel good, knowing there are still towns like
this," Mr. Allison said.

"You know, in New York," Mrs. Allison said, "I might have
paid a few cents less for these dishes, but there wouldn't have
been anything sort of personal in the transaction."

"Staying on to the lake?" Mrs. Martin, in the newspaper and sandwich shop, asked the Allisons. "Heard you was staying on."

"Thought we'd take advantage of the lovely weather this year," Mr. Allison said.

Mrs. Martin was a comparative newcomer to the town; she had married into the newspaper and sandwich shop from a neighboring farm, and had stayed on after her husband's death. She served bottled soft drinks, and fried egg and onion sandwiches on thick bread, which she made on her own stove at the back of the store. Occasionally when Mrs. Martin served a sandwich it would carry with it the rich fragrance of the stew or the pork chops cooking alongside for Mrs. Martin's dinner.

"I don't guess anyone's ever stayed out there so long before," Mrs. Martin said. "Not after Labor Day, anyway."

"I guess Labor Day is when they usually leave," Mr. Hall, the Allisons' nearest neighbor, told them later, in front of Mr. Babcock's store, where the Allisons were getting into their car to go home. "Surprised you're staying on."

"It seemed a shame to go so soon," Mrs. Allison said. Mr. Hall lived three miles away; he supplied the Allisons with butter and eggs, and occasionally, from the top of their hill, the Allisons could see the lights in his house in the early evening before the Halls went to bed.

"They usually leave Labor Day," Mr. Hall said.

The ride home was long and rough; it was beginning to get dark, and Mr. Allison had to drive very carefully over the dirt road by the lake. Mrs. Allison lay back against the seat, pleasantly relaxed after a day of what seemed whirlwind shopping compared with their day-to-day existence; the new glass baking dishes lurked agreeably in her mind, and the half bushel of red eating apples, and the package of colored thumbtacks with which she was going to put up new shelf edging in the kitchen. "Good to get home," she said softly as they came in sight of their cottage, silhouetted above them against the sky.

"Glad we decided to stay on," Mr. Allison agreed.

Mrs. Allison spent the next morning lovingly washing her baking dishes, although in his innocence Charley Walpole had neglected to notice the chip in the edge of one; she decided, wastefully, to use some of the red eating apples in a pie for dinner, and, while the pie was in the oven and Mr. Allison was down getting the mail, she sat out on the little lawn the Allisons had made at the top of the hill, and watched the changing lights on the lake, alternating gray and blue as clouds moved quickly across the sun.

Mr. Allison came back a little out of sorts; it always irritated him to walk the mile to the mailbox on the state road and come back with nothing, even though he assumed that the walk was good for his health. This morning there was nothing but a circular from a New York department store, and their New York paper, which arrived erratically by mail from one to four days later than it should, so that some days the Allisons might have three papers and frequently none. Mrs. Allison, although she shared with her husband the annoyance of not having mail when they so anticipated it, pored affectionately over the department store circular, and made a mental note to drop in at the store when she finally went back to New York, and check on the sale of wool blankets; it was hard to find good ones in pretty colors nowadays. She debated saving the circular to remind herself, but after thinking about getting up and getting into the cottage to put it away safely somewhere, she dropped it into the grass beside her chair and lay back, her eyes half closed.

"Looks like we might have some rain," Mr. Allison said, squinting at the sky.

"Good for the crops," Mrs. Allison said laconically, and they both laughed.

The kerosene man came the next morning while Mr. Allison was down getting the mail; they were getting low on kerosene and Mrs. Allison greeted the man warmly; he sold kerosene and ice, and, during the summer, hauled garbage away for the summer people. A garbage man was only necessary for improvident city folk; country people had no garbage.

"I'm glad to see you," Mrs. Allison told him. "We were getting pretty low."

The kerosene man, whose name Mrs. Allison had never learned, used a hose attachment to fill the twenty-gallon tank which supplied light and heat and cooking facilities for the Allisons; but today, instead of swinging down from his truck and unhooking the hose from where it coiled affectionately around the cab of the truck, the man stared uncomfortably at Mrs. Allison, his truck motor still going.

"Thought you folks'd be leaving," he said.

"We're staying on another month," Mrs. Allison said brightly. "The weather was so nice, and it seemed like—"

"That's what they told me," the man said. "Can't give you no oil, though."

"What do you mean?" Mrs. Allison raised her eyebrows. "We're just going to keep on with our regular—"

"After Labor Day," the man said. "I don't get so much oil myself after Labor Day."

Mrs. Allison reminded herself, as she had frequently to do when in disagreement with her neighbors, that city manners were no good with country people; you could not expect to overrule a country employee as you could a city worker, and Mrs. Allison smiled engagingly as she said, "But can't you get extra oil, at least while we stay?"

"You see," the man said. He tapped his finger exasperatingly against the car wheel as he spoke. "You see," he said slowly, "I order this oil. I order it down from maybe fifty, fifty-five miles away. I order back in June, how much I'll need for the summer. Then I order again . . . oh, about November. Round about now it's starting to get pretty short." As though the subject were closed, he stopped tapping his finger and tightened his hands on the wheel in preparation for departure.

"But can't you give us *some*?" Mrs. Allison said. "Isn't there anyone else?"

"Don't know as you could get oil anywheres else right now," the man said consideringly. "*I* can't give you none." Before Mrs. Allison could speak, the truck began to move; then it stopped for a minute and he looked at her through the back window of the cab. "Ice?" he called. "I could let you have some ice."

Mrs. Allison shook her head; they were not terribly low on ice, and she was angry. She ran a few steps to catch up with the truck, calling, "Will you try to get us some? Next week?"

"Don't see's I can," the man said. "After Labor Day, it's harder." The truck drove away, and Mrs. Allison, only comforted by the thought that she could probably get kerosene from Mr. Babcock, or, at worst, the Halls, watched it go with anger. "Next summer," she told herself. "Just let *him* try coming around next summer!"

There was no mail again, only the paper, which seemed to be coming doggedly on time, and Mr. Allison was openly cross when he returned. When Mrs. Allison told him about the kerosene man he was not particularly impressed.

"Probably keeping it all for a high price during the winter," he commented. "What's happened to Anne and Jerry, do you think?"

Anne and Jerry were their son and daughter, both married, one living in Chicago, one in the Far West; their dutiful weekly letters were late; so late, in fact, that Mr. Allison's annoyance at the lack of mail was able to settle on a legitimate grievance. "Ought to realize how we wait for their letters," he said. "Thoughtless, selfish children. Ought to know better."

"Well, dear," Mrs. Allison said placatingly. Anger at Anne and Jerry would not relieve her emotions toward the kerosene man. After a few minutes she said, "Wishing won't bring the mail, dear. I'm going to go call Mr. Babcock and tell him to send up some kerosene with my order."

"At least a postcard," Mr. Allison said as she left.

As with most of the cottage's inconveniences, the Allisons no longer noticed the phone particularly, but yielded to its eccentricities without conscious complaint. It was a wall phone, of a type still seen in only few communities; in order to get the operator, Mrs. Allison had first to turn the sidecrank and ring once. Usually it took two or three tries to force the operator to answer, and Mrs. Allison, making any kind of telephone call, approached the phone with resignation and a sort of desperate patience. She had to crank the phone three times this morning before the operator answered, and then it was still longer before Mr. Babcock picked up the receiver at his phone in the corner of the grocery behind the meat table. He said "Store?" with the rising inflection that seemed to indicate suspicion of anyone who tried to communicate with him by means of this unreliable instrument.

"This is Mrs. Allison, Mr. Babcock. I thought I'd give you my order a day early because I wanted to be sure and get some—"

"What say, Mrs. Allison?"

Mrs. Allison raised her voice a little; she saw Mr. Allison, out on the lawn, turn in his chair and regard her sympathetically. "I said, Mr. Babcock, I thought I'd call in my order early so you could send me—"

"Mrs. Allison?" Mr. Babcock said. "You'll come and pick it up?"

"Pick it up?" In her surprise Mrs. Allison let her voice drop back to its normal tone and Mr. Babcock said loudly, "What's that, Mrs. Allison?"

"I thought I'd have you send it out as usual," Mrs. Allison said.

"Well, Mrs. Allison," Mr. Babcock said, and there was a pause while Mrs. Allison waited, staring past the phone over her husband's head out into the sky. "Mrs. Allison," Mr. Babcock went on finally, "I'll tell you, my boy's been working for me went back to school yesterday and now I got no one to deliver. I only got a boy delivering summers, you see."

"I thought you *always* delivered," Mrs. Allison said.

"Not after Labor Day, Mrs. Allison," Mr. Babcock said firmly. "You never been here after Labor Day before, so's you wouldn't know, of course."

"Well," Mrs. Allison said helplessly. Far inside her mind she was saying, over and over, can't use city manners on country folk, no use getting mad.

"Are you *sure*?" she asked finally. "Couldn't you just send out an order today, Mr. Babcock?"

"Matter of fact," Mr. Babcock said, "I guess I couldn't, Mrs. Allison. It wouldn't hardly pay, delivering, with no one else out at the lake."

"What about Mr. Hall?" Mrs. Allison asked suddenly, "the people who live about three miles away from us out here? Mr. Hall could bring it out when he comes."

"Hall?" Mr. Babcock said. "John Hall? They've gone to visit her folks upstate, Mrs. Allison."

"But they bring all our butter and eggs," Mrs. Allison said, appalled.

"Left yesterday," Mr. Babcock said. "Probably didn't think you folks would stay on up there."

"But I told Mr. Hall . . ." Mrs. Allison started to say, and then stopped. "I'll send Mr. Allison in after some groceries tomorrow," she said.

"You got all you need till then," Mr. Babcock said, satisfied; it was not a question, but a confirmation.

After she hung up, Mrs. Allison went slowly out to sit again in her chair next to her husband. "He won't deliver," she said. "You'll have to go in tomorrow. We've got just enough kerosene to last till you get back."

"He should have told us sooner," Mr. Allison said.

It was not possible to remain troubled long in the face of the day; the country had never seemed more inviting, and the lake moved quietly below them, among the trees, with the almost incredible softness of a summer picture. Mrs. Allison sighed deeply, in the pleasure of possessing for themselves that sight of the lake, with the distant green hills beyond, the gentleness of the small wind through the trees.

The weather continued fair; the next morning Mr. Allison, duly armed with a list of groceries, with "kerosene" in large letters at the top, went down the path to the garage, and Mrs. Allison began another pie in her new baking dishes. She had mixed the crust and was starting to pare the apples when Mr. Allison came rapidly up the path and flung open the screen door into the kitchen.

"Damn car won't start," he announced, with the end-of-the-tether voice of a man who depends on a car as he depends on his right arm.

"What's wrong with it?" Mrs. Allison demanded, stopping with the paring knife in one hand and an apple in the other. "It was all right on Tuesday."

"Well," Mr. Allison said between his teeth, "it's not all right on Friday."

"Can you fix it?" Mrs. Allison asked.

"No," Mr. Allison said, "I can not. Got to call someone, I guess."

"Who?" Mrs. Allison asked.

"Man runs the filling station, I guess." Mr. Allison moved purposefully toward the phone. "He fixed it last summer one time."

A little apprehensive, Mrs. Allison went on paring apples

absentmindedly, while she listened to Mr. Allison with the phone, ringing, waiting, finally giving the number to the operator, then waiting again and giving the number again, giving the number a third time, and then slamming down the receiver.

"No one there," he announced as he came into the kitchen.

"He's probably gone out for a minute," Mrs. Allison said nervously; she was not quite sure what made her so nervous, unless it was the probability of her husband's losing his temper completely. "He's there alone, I imagine, so if he goes out there's no one to answer the phone."

"That must be it," Mr. Allison said with heavy irony. He slumped into one of the kitchen chairs and watched Mrs. Allison paring apples. After a minute, Mrs. Allison said soothingly, "Why don't you go down and get the mail and then call him again?"

Mr. Allison debated and then said, "Guess I might as well." He rose heavily and when he got to the kitchen door he turned and said, "But if there's no mail—" and leaving an awful silence behind him, he went off down the path.

Mrs. Allison hurried with her pie. Twice she went to the window to glance at the sky to see if there were clouds coming up. The room seemed unexpectedly dark, and she herself felt in the state of tension that preceded a thunderstorm, but both times when she looked the sky was clear and serene, smiling indifferently down on the Allisons' summer cottage as well as on the rest of the world. When Mrs. Allison, her pie ready for the oven, went a third time to look outside, she saw her husband coming up the path; he seemed more cheerful, and when he saw her, he waved eagerly and held a letter in the air.

"From Jerry," he called as soon as he was close enough for her to hear him, "at last—a letter!" Mrs. Allison noticed with concern that he was no longer able to get up the gentle slope of the path without breathing heavily; but then he was in the doorway, holding out the letter. "I saved it till I got here," he said.

Mrs. Allison looked with an eagerness that surprised her on the familiar handwriting of her son; she could not imagine why the letter excited her so, except that it was the first they had received in so long; it would be a pleasant, dutiful letter, full of the doings of Alice and the children, reporting progress with his job, commenting on the recent weather in Chicago, closing with love from all; both Mr. and Mrs. Allison could, if they wished, recite a pattern letter from either of their children.

Mr. Allison slit the letter open with great deliberation, and then he spread it out on the kitchen table and they leaned down and read it together.

"*Dear Mother and Dad*," it began, in Jerry's familiar, rather childish, handwriting, "*Am glad this goes to the lake as usual we always thought you came back too soon and ought to stay up there as long as you could. Alice says that now that you're not as young as you used to be and have no demands on your time, fewer friends, etc., in the city, you ought to get what fun you can while you can. Since you two are both happy up there, it's a good idea for you to stay.*"

Uneasily Mrs. Allison glanced sideways at her husband; he was reading intently, and she reached out and picked up the empty envelope, not knowing exactly what she wanted from it. It was addressed quite as usual, in Jerry's handwriting, and was postmarked "Chicago." Of course it's postmarked Chicago, she thought quickly, why would they want to postmark it anywhere else? When she looked back down at the letter, her husband had turned the page, and she read on with him: "*—and of course if they get measles, etc., now, they will be better off later. Alice is well, of course; me too. Been playing a lot of bridge lately with some people you don't know, named Carruthers. Nice young couple, about our age. Well, will close now as I guess it bores you to hear about things so far away. Tell Dad old Dickson, in our Chicago office, died. He used to ask about Dad a lot. Have a good time up at the lake, and don't bother hurrying back. Love from all of us, Jerry.*"

"Funny," Mr. Allison commented.

"It doesn't sound like Jerry," Mrs. Allison said in a small voice, "He never wrote anything like . . ." She stopped.

"Like what?" Mr. Allison demanded. "Never wrote anything like what?"

Mrs. Allison turned the letter over, frowning. It was impossible to find any sentence, any word, even, that did not sound like Jerry's regular letters. Perhaps it was only that the letter was so late, or the unusual number of dirty fingerprints on the envelope.

"I don't *know*," she said impatiently.

"Going to try that phone call again," Mr. Allison said.

Mrs. Allison read the letter twice more, trying to find a phrase that sounded wrong. Then Mr. Allison came back and said, very quietly, "Phone's dead."

"What?" Mrs. Allison said, dropping the letter.

"Phone's dead," Mr. Allison said.

The rest of the day went quickly; after a lunch of crackers and milk, the Allisons went to sit outside on the lawn, but their afternoon was cut short by the gradually increasing storm clouds that came up over the lake to the cottage, so that it was as dark as evening by four o'clock. The storm delayed, however, as though in loving anticipation of the moment it would break over the summer cottage, and there was an occasional flash of lightning, but no rain. In the evening Mr. and Mrs. Allison, sitting close together inside their cottage, turned on the battery radio they had brought with them from New York. There were no lamps lighted in the cottage, and the only light came from the lightning outside and the small square glow from the dial of the radio.

The slight framework of the cottage was not strong enough to withstand the city noises, the music and the voices, from the radio, and the Allisons could hear them far off echoing across the lake, the saxophones in the New York dance band wailing over the water, the flat voice of the girl vocalist going inexorably out into the clean country air. Even the announcer, speaking glowingly of the virtues of razor blades, was no more than an inhuman voice sounding out from the Allisons' cottage and echoing back, as though the lake and the hills and the trees were returning it unwanted.

During one pause between commercials, Mrs. Allison turned and smiled weakly at her husband. "I wonder if we're supposed to . . . *do* anything," she said.

"No," Mr. Allison said consideringly. "I don't think so. Just wait."

Mrs. Allison caught her breath quickly, and Mr. Allison said, under the trivial melody of the dance band beginning again. "The car had been tampered with, you know. Even I could see that."

Mrs. Allison hesitated a minute and then said very softly, "I suppose the phone wires were cut."

"I imagine so," Mr. Allison said.

After a while, the dance music stopped and they listened attentively to a news broadcast, the announcer's rich voice telling them breathlessly of a marriage in Hollywood, the latest baseball scores, the estimated rise in food prices during the coming week. He spoke to them, in the summer cottage, quite as though they still deserved to hear news of a world that no longer reached them except through the fallible batteries on the radio, which were already beginning to fade, almost as though they still belonged, however tenuously, to the rest of the world.

Mrs. Allison glanced out the window at the smooth surface of the lake, the black masses of the trees, and the waiting storm, and said conversationally, "I feel better about that letter of Jerry's."

"I knew when I saw the light down at the Hall place last night," Mr. Allison said.

The wind, coming up suddenly over the lake, swept around the summer cottage and slapped hard at the windows. Mr. and Mrs. Allison involuntarily moved closer together, and with the first sudden crash of thunder, Mr. Allison reached out and took his wife's hand. And then, while the lightning flashed outside, and the radio faded and sputtered, the two old people huddled together in their summer cottage and waited.

1950

Island

M RS. MONTAGUE's son had been very good to her, with the kind affection and attention to her well-being that is seldom found toward mothers in sons with busy wives and growing families of their own; when Mrs. Montague lost her mind, her son came into his natural role of guardian. There had always been a great deal of warm feeling between Mrs. Montague and her son, and although they lived nearly a thousand miles apart by now, Henry Paul Montague was careful to see that his mother was well taken care of; he ascertained, minutely, that the monthly bills for her apartment, her food, her clothes, and her companion were large enough to ensure that Mrs. Montague was getting the best of everything; he wrote to her weekly, tender letters in longhand inquiring about her health; when he came to New York he visited her promptly, and always left an extra check for the companion, to make sure that any small things Mrs. Montague lacked would be given her. The companion, Miss Oakes, had been with Mrs. Montague for six years, and in that time their invariable quiet routine had been broken only by the regular visits from Mrs. Montague's son, and by Miss Oakes's annual six-weeks' leave, during which Mrs. Montague was cared for no less scrupulously by a carefully chosen substitute.

Between such disturbing occasions, Mrs. Montague lived quietly and expensively in her handsome apartment, following with Miss Oakes a life of placid regularity, which it required all of Miss Oakes's competence to engineer, and duly reported on to Mrs. Montague's son. "I *do* think we're very lucky, dear," was Miss Oakes's frequent comment, "to have a good son like Mr. Montague to take care of us so well."

To which Mrs. Montague's usual answer was, "Henry Paul was a good boy."

Mrs. Montague usually spent the morning in bed, and got up for lunch; after the effort of bathing and dressing and eating she was ready for another rest and then her walk, which occurred regularly at four o'clock, and which was followed by dinner sent up from the restaurant downstairs, and, shortly after, by Mrs. Montague's bedtime. Although Miss Oakes did not leave the apartment except in an emergency, she had a great deal of time to herself and her regular duties were not harsh, although Mrs. Montague was not the best company in the world. Frequently Miss Oakes would look up from her magazine to find Mrs. Montague watching her curiously; sometimes Mrs. Montague, in a spirit of petulant stubbornness, would decline all food under any persuasion until it was necessary for Miss Oakes to call in Mrs. Montague's doctor for Mrs. Montague to hear a firm lecture on her duties as a patient. Once Mrs. Montague had tried to run away, and had been recaptured by Miss Oakes in the street in front of the apartment house, going vaguely through the traffic; and always, constantly, Mrs. Montague was trying to give things to Miss Oakes, many of which, in absolute frankness, it cost Miss Oakes a pang to refuse.

Miss Oakes had not been born to the luxury which Mrs. Montague had known all her life; Miss Oakes had worked hard and never had a fur coat; no matter how much she tried Miss Oakes could not disguise the fact that she relished the food sent up from the restaurant downstairs, delicately cooked and prettily served; Miss Oakes was persuaded that she disdained jewelry, and she chose her clothes hurriedly and inexpensively, under the eye of an impatient, badly dressed salesgirl in a department store. No matter how agonizingly Miss Oakes debated under the insinuating lights of the budget dress department, the clothes she carried home with her turned out to be garish reds and yellows in the daylight, inexactly striped or dotted, badly cut. Miss Oakes sometimes thought longingly of the security of her white uniforms, neatly stacked in her dresser drawer, but Mrs. Montague was apt to go into a tantrum at any outward show of Miss Oakes's professional competence, and Miss Oakes dined nightly on the agreeable food from the restaurant downstairs in her red and yellow dresses, with her colorless hair drawn ungracefully to a bun in back, her ringless hands moving appreciatively among the plates. Mrs. Montague, who ordinarily spilled food all over herself, chose her dresses from a selection sent every three or four months from an exclusive dress shop near by; all information as to size and color was predigested in the shop, and the soft-voiced saleslady brought only dresses absolutely right for Mrs. Montague. Mrs. Montague usually chose two dresses each time, and they went, neatly hung on sacheted hangers, to live softly in Mrs. Montague's closet along with other dresses just like them, all in soft blues and grays and mauves.

"We *must* try to be more careful of our pretty clothes," Miss Oakes would say, looking up from her dinner to find Mrs. Montague, almost deliberately, it seemed sometimes, emptying her spoonful of oatmeal down the front of her dress. "Dear, we really *must* try to be more careful; remember what our nice son has to pay for those dresses."

Mrs. Montague stared vaguely sometimes, holding her spoon; sometimes she said, "I want my pudding now; I'll be careful with my pudding." Now and then, usually when the day had gone badly and Mrs. Montague was overtired, or cross for one reason or another, she might turn the dish of oatmeal over onto the tablecloth, and then, frequently, Miss Oakes was angry, and Mrs. Montague was deprived of her pudding and sat blankly while Miss Oakes moved her own dishes to a coffee table and called the waiter to remove the dinner table with its mess of oatmeal.

It was in the late spring that Mrs. Montague was usually at her worst; then, for some reason, it seemed that the stirring of green life, even under the dirty city traffic, communicated a restlessness and longing to her that she felt only spasmodically the rest of the year; around April or May, Miss Oakes began to prepare for trouble, for runnings-away and supreme oatmeal overturnings. In summer, Mrs. Montague seemed happier, because it was possible to walk in the park and feed the squirrels; in the fall, she quieted, in preparation for the long winter when she was almost dormant, like an animal, rarely speaking, and suffering herself to be dressed and undressed without rebellion; it was the winter that Miss Oakes most appreciated, although as the months moved on into spring Miss Oakes began to think more often of giving up her position, her pleasant salary, the odorous meals from the restaurant downstairs.

It was in the spring that Mrs. Montague so often tried to give things to Miss Oakes; one afternoon when their walk was dubious because of the rain, Mrs. Montague had gone as of habit to the hall closet and taken out her coat, and now sat in her armchair with the rich dark mink heaped in her lap, smoothing the fur as though she held a cat. "Pretty," Mrs. Montague was saying, "pretty, pretty."

"We're very lucky to have such lovely things," Miss Oakes said. Because it was her practice to keep busy always, never to let her knowledgeable fingers rest so long as they might be doing something useful, she was knitting a scarf. It was only half-finished, but already Miss Oakes was beginning to despair of it; the yarn, in the store and in the roll, seemed a soft tender green, but knit up into the scarf it assumed a gaudy chartreuse character that made its original purpose—to embrace the firm fleshy neck of Henry Paul Montague—seem faintly improper; when Miss Oakes looked at the scarf impartially it irritated her, as did almost everything she created.

"Think of the money," Miss Oakes said, "that goes into all those beautiful things, just because your son is so generous and kind."

"I will give you this fur," Mrs. Montague said suddenly. "Because you have no beautiful things of your own."

"Thank you, dear," Miss Oakes said. She worked busily at her scarf for a minute and then said, "It's not being very grateful for nice things like that, dear, to want to give them away."

"It wouldn't look nice on you," Mrs. Montague said, "it would look awful. You're not very pretty."

Miss Oakes was silent again for a minute, and then she said, "Well, dear, shall we see if it's still raining?" With great deliberation she put down the knitting and walked over to the window. When she pulled back the lace curtain and the heavy dark-red drape she did so carefully, because the curtain and the drape were not precisely her own, but were of service to her, and pleasant to her touch, and expensive. "It's almost stopped," she said brightly. She squinted her eyes and looked up at the sky. "I *do* believe it's going to clear up," she went on, as though her brightness might create a sun of reflected brilliance. "In about fifteen minutes . . ." She let her voice trail off, and smiled at Mrs. Montague with vast anticipation.

"I don't want to go for any walk," Mrs. Montague said sullenly. "Once when we were children we used to take off all our clothes and run out in the rain."

Miss Oakes returned to her chair and took up her knitting. "We can start to get ready in a few minutes," she promised.

"I couldn't do that *now*, of course," Mrs. Montague said. "I want to color."

She slid out of her chair, dropping the mink coat into a heap on the floor, and went slowly, with her faltering walk, across the room to the card table where her coloring book and box of crayons lay. Miss Oakes sighed, set her knitting down, and walked over to pick up the mink coat; she draped it tenderly over the back of the chair, and went back and picked up her knitting again.

"Pretty, pretty," Mrs. Montague crooned over her coloring, "Pretty blue, pretty water, pretty, pretty."

Miss Oakes allowed a small smile to touch her face as she regarded the scarf; it was a bright color, perhaps too bright for a man no longer very young, but it was gay and not really *unusually* green. His birthday was three weeks off; the card in the box would say "To remind you of your loyal friend and admirer, Polly Oakes." Miss Oakes sighed quickly.

"I want to go for a *walk*," Mrs. Montague said abruptly.

"Just a minute, dear," Miss Oakes said. She put the knitting down again and smiled at Mrs. Montague. "I'll help you," Miss Oakes said, and went over to assist Mrs. Montague in the slow task that getting out of a straight chair always entailed. "Why, look at you," Miss Oakes said, regarding the coloring book over Mrs. Montague's head. She laughed. "You've gone and made the whole thing blue, you silly child." She turned back a page. "And here," she said, and laughed again. "Why does the man have a blue face? And the little girl in the picture —she mustn't be blue, dear, her face should be pink and her hair should be—oh, yellow, for instance. Not *blue*."

Mrs. Montague put her hands violently over the picture. "Mine," she said. "Get away, this is mine."

"I'm sorry," Miss Oakes said smoothly, "I wasn't laughing at you, dear. It was just funny to see a man with a blue face." She helped Mrs. Montague out of the chair and escorted her across the room to the mink coat. Mrs. Montague stood stiffly while Miss Oakes put the coat over her shoulders and helped her arms into the sleeves, and when Miss Oakes came around in front of her to button the coat at the neck Mrs. Montague turned down the corners of her mouth and said sullenly into Miss Oakes's face, so close to hers, "You don't know what things *are*, really."

"Perhaps I don't," Miss Oakes said absently. She surveyed Mrs. Montague, neatly buttoned into the mink coat, and then took Mrs. Montague's rose-covered hat from the table in the hall and set it on Mrs. Montague's head, with great regard to the correct angle and the neatness of the roses. "Now we look so pretty," Miss Oakes said. Mrs. Montague stood silently while Miss Oakes went to the hall closet and took out her own serviceable blue coat. She shrugged herself into it, settled it with a brisk tug at the collar, and pulled on her hat with a quick gesture from back to front that landed the hatbrim at exactly the usual angle over her eye. It was not until she was escorting Mrs. Montague to the door that Miss Oakes gave one brief, furtive glance at the hall mirror, as one who does so from a nervous compulsion rather than any real desire for information.

Miss Oakes enjoyed walking down the hall; its carpets were so thick that even the stout shoes of Miss Oakes made no sound. The elevator was self-service, and Miss Oakes, with superhuman control, allowed it to sweep soundlessly down to the main floor, carrying with it Miss Oakes herself, and Mrs. Montague, who sat docilely on the velvet-covered bench and stared at the paneling as though she had never seen it before. When the elevator door opened and they moved out into the lobby Miss Oakes knew that the few people who saw them—the girl at the switchboard, the doorman, another tenant coming to the elevator—recognized Mrs. Montague as the rich old lady who lived high upstairs, and Miss Oakes as the infinitely competent companion, without whose unswerving assistance Mrs. Montague could not live for ten minutes. Miss Oakes walked sturdily and well through the lobby, her firm hand guiding soft little Mrs. Montague; the lobby floor was pale carpeting on which their feet made no sound, and the lobby walls were painted an expensive color so neutral as to be almost invisible; as Miss Oakes went with Mrs. Montague through the lobby it was as though they walked upon clouds, through the noncommittal areas of infinite space. The doorway was their aim, and the doorman, dressed in gray, opened the way for them with a flourish and a "Good afternoon" which began by being directed at Mrs. Montague, as the employer, and ended by addressing Miss Oakes, as the person who would be expected to answer.

"Good afternoon, George," Miss Oakes said, with a stately smile, and passed on through the doorway, leading Mrs. Montague. Once outside on the sidewalk, Miss Oakes steered Mrs. Montague quickly to the left, since, allowed her head, Mrs. Montague might as easily have turned unexpectedly to the right, although they always turned to the left, and so upset Miss Oakes's walk for the day. With slow steps they moved into the current of people walking up the street, Miss Oakes watching ahead to avoid Mrs. Montague's walking into strangers, Mrs. Montague with her face turned up to the gray sky.

"It's a *lovely* day," Miss Oakes said. "Pleasantly cool after the rain."

They had gone perhaps half a block when Mrs. Montague, by a gentle pressure against Miss Oakes's arm, began to direct them toward the inside of the sidewalk and the shop windows; Miss Oakes, resisting at first, at last allowed herself to be reluctantly influenced and they crossed the sidewalk to stand in front of the window to a stationery store.

They stopped here every day, and, as she said every day, Mrs. Montague murmured softly, "*Look* at all the lovely things." She watched with amusement a plastic bird, colored bright red and yellow, which methodically dipped its beak into a glass of water and withdrew it; while they stood watching the bird lowered its head and touched the water, hesitated, and then rose.

"Does it stop when we're not here?" Mrs. Montague asked, and Miss Oakes laughed, and said, "It never stops. It goes on while we're eating and while we're sleeping and all the time."

Mrs. Montague's attention had wandered to the open pages of a diary, spread nakedly to the pages dated June 14–June 15. Mrs. Montague, looking at the smooth unwritten paper, caught her breath. "I'd like to have *that*," she said, and Miss Oakes, as she answered every day, said, "What would you write in it, dear?"

The thing that always caught Mrs. Montague next was a softly curved blue bowl which stood in the center of the window display; Mrs. Montague pored lovingly and speechlessly over this daily, trying to touch it through the glass of the window.

"Come *on* dear," Miss Oakes said finally, with an almost-impatient tug at Mrs. Montague's arm. "We'll never get our walk finished if you don't come *on*."

Docilely Mrs. Montague followed. "Pretty," she whispered, "pretty, pretty."

She opened her eyes suddenly and was aware that she saw. The sky was unbelievably, steadily blue, and the sand beneath her feet was hot; she could see the water, colored more deeply than the sky, but faintly greener. Far off was the line where the sky and water met, and it was infinitely pure.

"Pretty," she said inadequately, and was aware that she spoke. She was walking on the sand, and with a sudden impatient gesture she stopped and slipped off her shoes, standing first on one foot and then on the other. This encouraged her to look down at herself; she was very tall, high above her shoes on the sand, and when she moved it was freely and easily except for the cumbering clothes, the heavy coat and the hat, which sat on her head with a tangible, oppressive weight. She threw the hat onto the hot lovely sand, and it looked so offensive, lying with its patently unreal roses against the smooth clarity of the sand, that she bent quickly and covered the hat with handfuls of sand; the coat was more difficult to cover, and the sand ran delicately between the hairs of the short dark fur; before she had half covered the coat she decided to put the rest of her clothes with it, and did so, slipping easily out of the straps and buttons and catches of many garments, which she remembered as difficult to put on. When all her clothes were buried she looked with satisfaction down at her strong white legs, and thought, aware that she was thinking it: they are almost the same color as the sand. She began to run freely, with the blue ocean and the bluer sky on her right, the trees on her left, and the moving sand underfoot; she ran until she came back to the place where a corner of her coat still showed through the sand. When she saw it she stopped again and said, "Pretty, pretty," and leaned over and took a handful of sand and let it run through her fingers.

Far away, somewhere in the grove of trees that centered the island she could hear the parrot calling. "Eat, eat," it shrieked, and then something indistinguishable, and then, "Eat, eat."

An idea came indirectly and subtly to her mind; it was the idea of food, for a minute unpleasant and as though it meant a disagreeable sensation, and then glowingly happy. She turned and ran—it was impossible to move slowly on the island, with the clear hot air all around her, and the ocean stirring constantly, pushing at the island, and the unbelievable blue sky above—and when she came into the sudden warm shade of the trees she ran from one to another, putting her hand for a minute on each.

"Hello," the parrot gabbled, "Hello, who's there, eat?" She could see it flashing among the trees, no more than a saw-toothed voice and a flash of ugly red and yellow.

The grass was green and rich and soft, and she sat down by the little brook where the food was set out. Today there was a great polished wooden bowl, soft to the touch, full of purple grapes; the sun that came unevenly between the trees struck a high shine from the bowl, and lay flatly against the grapes, which were dusty with warmth, and almost black. There was a shimmering glass just full of dark red wine; there was a flat blue plate filled with little cakes; she touched one and it was full of cream, and heavily iced with soft chocolate. There were pomegranates, and cheese, and small, sharp-flavored candies. She lay down beside the food, and closed her eyes against the heavy scent from the grapes.

"Eat, eat," the parrot screamed from somewhere over her head. She opened her eyes lazily and looked up, to see the flash of red and yellow in the trees. "Be still, you noisy beast," she said, and smiled to herself because it was not important, actually, whether the parrot were quiet or not. Later, after she had slept, she ate some of the grapes and the cheese, and several of the rich little cakes. While she ate the parrot came cautiously closer, begging for food, sidling up near to the dish of cakes and then moving quickly away.

"Beast," she said pleasantly to the parrot, "greedy beast."

When she was sure she was quite through with the food, she put one of the cakes on a green leaf and set it a little bit away from her for the parrot. It came up to the cake slowly and fearfully, watching on either side for some sudden prohibitive movement; when it finally reached the cake it hesitated, and then dipped its head down to bury its beak in the soft frosting; it lifted its head, paused to look around, and then lowered its beak to the cake again. The gesture was familiar, and she laughed, not knowing why.

She was faintly aware that she had slept again, and awakened wanting to run, to go out into the hot sand on the beach and run shouting around the island. The parrot was gone, its cake a mess of crumbs and frosting on the ground. She ran out onto the beach, and the water was there, and the sky. For a few minutes she ran, going down to the water and then swiftly back before it could touch her bare feet, and then she dropped luxuriously onto the sand and lay there. After a while she began to draw a picture in the sand; it was a round face with dots for eyes and nose and a line for a mouth. "Henry Paul," she said, touching the face caressingly with her fingers, and then, laughing, she leaped to her feet and began to run again, around the island. When she passed the face drawn on the sand she put one bare foot on it and ground it away. "Eat, eat," she could hear the parrot calling from the trees; the parrot was afraid of the hot sand and the water and stayed always in the trees near the food. Far off, across the water, she could see the sweet, the always comforting, line of the horizon.

When she was tired with running she lay down again on the sand. For a little while she played idly, writing words on the sand and then rubbing them out with her hand; once she drew a crude picture of a doorway and punched her fist through it.

Finally she lay down and put her face down to the sand. It was hot, hotter than anything else had ever been, and the soft grits of the sand slipped into her mouth, where she could taste them, deliciously hard and grainy against her teeth; they were in her eyes, rich and warm; the sand was covering her face and the blue sky was gone from above her and the sand was cooler, then grayer, covering her face, and cold.

*

"*Nearly* home," Miss Oakes said brightly, as they turned the last corner of their block. "It's been a *nice* walk, hasn't it?"

She tried, unsuccessfully, to guide Mrs. Montague quickly past the bakery, but Mrs. Montague's feet, moving against Miss Oakes's pressure from habit, brought them up to stand in front of the bakery window.

"I don't know *why* they leave those fly-specked éclairs out here," Miss Oakes said irritably. "There's nothing *less* appetizing. *Look* at that cake; the cream is positively *curdled*."

She moved her arm insinuatingly within Mrs. Montague's; "In a few minutes we'll be home," she said softly, "and then we can have our nice cocktail, and rest for a few minutes, and then dinner."

"Pretty," Mrs. Montague said at the cakes. "I want some."

Miss Oakes shuddered violently. "Don't even *say* it," she implored. "Just *look* at that stuff. You'd be sick for a week."

She moved Mrs. Montague along, and they came, moving quicker than they had when they started, back to their own doorway where the doorman in gray waited for them. He opened the door and said, beginning with Mrs. Montague and finishing with Miss Oakes, "Have a nice walk?"

"Very pleasant, thank you," Miss Oakes said agreeably. They passed through the doorway and into the lobby where the open doors of the elevator waited for them. "Dinner soon," Miss Oakes said as they went across the lobby.

Miss Oakes was careful, on their own floor, to see that Mrs. Montague found the right doorway; while Miss Oakes put the key in the door Mrs. Montague stood waiting without expression.

Mrs. Montague moved forward automatically when the door was opened, and Miss Oakes caught her arm, saying shrilly, "Don't *step* on it!" Mrs. Montague stopped, and waited, while Miss Oakes picked up the dinner menu from the floor just inside the door; it had been slipped under the door while they were out.

Once inside, Miss Oakes removed Mrs. Montague's rosy hat and the mink coat, and Mrs. Montague took the mink coat in her arms and sat down in her chair with it, smoothing the fur. Miss Oakes slid out of her own coat and hung it neatly in the closet, and then came into the living room, carrying the dinner menu.

"Chicken liver omelette," Miss Oakes read as she walked. "The last time it was a trifle underdone; I could *mention* it, of course, but they never seem to pay much attention. Roast turkey. Filet mignon. I *really* do think a nice little piece of . . ." she looked up at Mrs. Montague and smiled. "Hungry?" she suggested.

"No," Mrs. Montague said. "I've had enough."

"Nice oatmeal?" Miss Oakes said. "If you're *very* good you can have ice cream tonight."

"Don't want ice cream," Mrs. Montague said.

Miss Oakes sighed, and then said "Well . . ." placatingly. She returned to the menu. "French-fried potatoes," she said. "They're *very* heavy on the stomach, but I do have my heart set on a nice little piece of steak and some french-fried potatoes. It sounds just *right* tonight."

"Shall I give you this coat?" Mrs. Montague asked suddenly.

Miss Oakes stopped on her way to the phone and patted Mrs. Montague lightly on the shoulder. "You're very generous, dear," she said, "but of course you don't really want to give me your beautiful coat. What would your dear son say?"

Mrs. Montague ran her hand over the fur of the coat affectionately. Then she stood up, slowly, and the coat slid to the floor.

"I'm going to color," she announced.

Miss Oakes turned back from the phone to pick up the coat and put it over the back of the chair. "All right," she said. She went to the phone, sat so she could keep an eye on Mrs. Montague while she talked, and said into the phone "Room service."

Mrs. Montague moved across the room and sat down at the card table. Reflectively she turned the pages of the coloring book, found a picture that pleased her, and opened the crayon box. Miss Oakes hummed softly into the phone. "Room service?" she said finally. "I want to order dinner sent up to Mrs. Montague's suite, please." She looked over the phone at Mrs. Montague and said, "You all right, dear?"

Without turning, Mrs. Montague moved her shoulders

impatiently, and selected a crayon from the box. She examined the point of it with great care while Miss Oakes said, "I want one very sweet martini, please. And Mrs. Montague's prune juice." She picked up the menu and wet her lips, then said, "One crab-meat cocktail. And tonight will you see that Mrs. Montague has milk with her oatmeal; you sent cream last night. Yes, milk, please. You'd think they'd know by *now*," she added to Mrs. Montague over the top of the phone. "Now let me see," she said, into the phone again, her eyes on the menu.

Disregarding Miss Oakes, Mrs. Montague had begun to color. Her shoulders bent low over the book, a vague smile on her old face, she was devoting herself to a picture of a farm-yard; a hen and three chickens strutted across the foreground of the picture, a barn surrounded by trees was the background. Mrs. Montague had laboriously colored the hen and the three chickens, the barn and the trees a rich blue, and now, with alternate touches of the crayons, was engaged in putting a red and yellow blot far up in the blue trees.

1950

The Night We All Had Grippe

W E ARE all of us, in our family, very fond of puzzles. I do Double-Crostics and read mystery stories, my husband does baseball box scores and figures out batting averages, our son Laurie is addicted to the kind of puzzle which begins, "There are fifty-four items in this picture beginning with the letter C," our older daughter Jannie does children's jigsaws, and Sally, the baby, can put together an intricate little arrangement of rings and bars which has had the rest of us stopped for two months. We are none of us, however, capable of solving the puzzles we work up for ourselves in the oddly diffuse patterns of our several lives (who is, now I think of it?); and along with such family brain-teasers as, "Why is there a pair of roller skates in Mommy's desk?" and, "What is *really* in the back of Laurie's closet?" and, "Why doesn't Daddy wear the nice shirts Jannie picked out for Father's Day?" we are all of us still wondering nervously about what might be called The Great Grippe Mystery. As a matter of fact, I should be extremely grateful if anyone could solve it for us, because we are certainly very short of blankets, and it's annoying not to have *any* kind of answer. Here, in rough outline, is our puzzle:

Our house is large, and the second floor has four bedrooms and a bathroom, all opening out onto a long narrow hall which we have made even narrower by lining it with bookcases so that every inch of hall which is not doorway is books. As is the case with most houses, both the front door and the back door are downstairs on the first floor. The front bedroom, which is my husband's and mine, is the largest and lightest, and has a double bed. The room next down the hall belongs to the girls, and contains a crib and a single, short bed. Laurie's room, across the hall, has a double-decker bed and he sleeps on the top half. The guest room, at the end of the hall, has a double bed. The double bed in our room is made up with white sheets and cases, the baby's crib has pink linen, and Jannie's bed has yellow. Laurie's bed has green linen and the guest room has blue. The bottom half of Laurie's bed is never made up, unless company is going to use it immediately, because the dog, whose name is Toby, traditionally spends a large part of his time there and regards it as his bed. There is no bed table on the distaff side of the double bed in our room. One side of the bed in the guest room is pushed against the wall. No one can fit into the baby's crib except the baby; the ladder to the top half of Laurie's double-decker is very shaky and stands in a corner of the room; the children reach the top half of the bed by climbing up over the footboard. All three of the children are accustomed to having a glass of apple juice, to which they are addicted, by their bedsides at night. My husband invariably keeps a glass of water by *his* bedside. Laurie uses a green glass, Jannie uses a red glass, the baby uses one of those little flowered cheese glasses, and my husband uses a tin glass because he has broken so many ordinary glasses trying to find them in the dark.

I do not take cough drops or cough medicine in any form.

The baby customarily sleeps with half a dozen cloth books, an armless doll, and a small cardboard suitcase which holds the remnants of half a dozen decks of cards. Jannie is very partial to a pink baby blanket, which has shrunk from many washings. The girls' room is very warm, the guest room moderately so; our room is chilly, and Laurie's room is quite cold. We are all of us, including the dog, notoriously easy and heavy sleepers; my husband never eats coffeecake.

My husband caught the grippe first, on a Friday, and snarled and shivered and complained until I prevailed upon him to go to bed. By Friday night both Laurie and the baby were feverish, and on Saturday Jannie and I began to cough and sniffle. In our family we take ill in different manners; my husband is extremely annoyed at the whole procedure, and is convinced that his being sick is somebody else's fault, Laurie tends to become a little lightheaded and strew handkerchiefs around his room, Jannie coughs and coughs and coughs, the baby turns bright red, and I suffer in stoical silence, so long as everyone knows clearly that I am sick. We are each of us privately convinced that our own ailment is far more severe than anyone else's. At any rate, on Saturday night I put all the children into their beds, gave each of them half an aspirin and the usual fruit juice, covered them warmly, and then settled my husband down for the night with his glass of water and his cigarettes and matches and ash tray; he had decided to sleep in the guest room because it was warmer. At about ten o'clock I checked to see that all the children were covered and asleep and that Toby was in his place on the bottom half of the double-decker. I then took two sleeping pills and went to sleep in my own bed in my own room. Because my husband was in the guest room I slept on his side of the bed, next to the bed table. I put my cigarettes and matches on the end table next to the ash tray, along with a small glass of brandy, which I find more efficacious than cough medicine.

I woke up some time later to find Jannie standing beside the bed. "Can't sleep," she said. "Want to come in *your* bed."

"Come along," I said. "Bring your own pillow."

She went and got her pillow and her small pink blanket and her glass of fruit juice, which she put on the floor next to the bed, since she had gotten the side without any end table. She put her pillow down, rolled herself in her pink blanket, and fell asleep. I went back to sleep, but some time later the baby came in, asking sleepily, "Where's Jannie?"

"She's here," I said. "Are you coming in bed with us?"

"Yes," said the baby.

"Go and get your pillow, then," I said. She returned with her pillow, her books, her doll, her suitcase, and her fruit juice, which she put on the floor next to Jannie's. Then she crowded in comfortably next to Jannie and fell asleep. Eventually the pressure of the two of them began to force me uneasily toward the edge of the bed, so I rolled out wearily, took my pillow and my small glass of brandy and my cigarettes and matches and my ash tray and went into the guest room, where my husband was asleep. I pushed at him and he snarled, but finally moved over to the side next to the wall, and I put my cigarettes and matches and my brandy and my ash tray on the end table next to *his* cigarettes and matches and ash tray and tin glass of water and put my pillow on the bed and fell asleep. Shortly after this he woke me and asked me to let him get out of the bed, since it was too hot in that room to sleep and he was going back to his own bed.

He took his pillow and his cigarettes and matches and his

ash tray and his tin glass of water and went padding off down the hall. In a few minutes Laurie came into the guest room where I had just fallen asleep again; he was carrying his pillow and his glass of fruit juice. "Too cold in my room," he said, and I moved out of the way and let him get into the bed on the side next to the wall. After a few minutes the dog came in, whining nervously, and came up onto the bed and curled himself up around Laurie, and I had to get out or be smothered. I gathered together what of my possessions I could, and made my way into my own room, where my husband was asleep with Jannie on one side and the baby on the other. Jannie woke up when I came in and said, "Own bed," so I helped her carry her pillow and her fruit juice and her pink blanket back to her own bed.

The minute Jannie got out of our bed the baby rolled over and turned sideways, so there was no room for me. I could not get into the crib and I could not climb into the top half of the double-decker so since the dog was in the guest room I went and took the blanket off the crib and got into the bottom half of the double-decker, setting my brandy and my cigarettes and matches and my ash tray on the floor next to the bed. Shortly after that Jannie, who apparently felt left out, came in with her pillow and her pink blanket and her fruit juice and got up into the top half of the double-decker, leaving her fruit juice on the floor next to my brandy.

At about six in the morning the dog wanted to get out, or else he wanted his bed back, because he came and stood next to me and howled. I got up and went downstairs, sneezing, and let him out, and then decided that since it had been so cold anyway in the bottom half of the double-decker I might as well stay downstairs and heat up some coffee and have that much warmth, at least. While I was waiting for the coffee to heat, Jannie came to the top of the stairs and asked if I would bring *her* something hot, and I heard Laurie stirring in the guest room, so I heated some milk and put it into a jug and decided that while I was at it I might just as well give every-body something hot, so I set out enough cups for everyone and brought out a coffeecake and put it on the tray and added some onion rolls for my husband, who does not eat coffeecake. When I brought the tray upstairs Laurie and Jannie were both in the guest room, giggling, so I put the tray down in there and heard Baby waking from our room in the front. I went to get her and she was sitting up in the bed talking to her father, who was only very slightly awake. "Play card?" she was asking brightly, and she opened her suitcase and dealt him onto the pillow next to his nose four diamonds to the ace jack and the seven of clubs.

I asked my husband if he would like some coffee and he said it was terribly cold. I suggested that he come down into the guest room, where it was warmer. He and the baby followed me down to the guest room and my husband and Laurie got into the bed and the rest of us sat on the foot of the bed and I poured the coffee and the hot milk and gave the children coffeecake and my husband the onion rolls. Jannie decided to take her milk and coffeecake back into her own bed and since she had mislaid her pillow she took one from the guest room bed. Baby of course followed her, going first back into our room to pick up *her* pillow. My husband fell asleep again while I was pouring his coffee, and Laurie set his hot milk precariously on the headboard of the bed and asked me to get his pillow from wherever it was, so I went into the double-decker and got him the pillow from the top, which turned out to be Jannie's, and her pink blanket was with it.

I took my coffeecake and my coffee into my own bed and had just settled down when Laurie came in to say cloudily that Daddy had kicked him out of bed and could he stay in here? I said of course and he said he would get a pillow and he came back in a minute with the one from the bottom half of the doubler-decker, which was mine. He went to sleep right away, and then the baby came in to get her books and her suitcase and decided to stay with her milk and her coffeecake so I left and went into the guest room and made my husband move over and sat *there* and had my coffee. Meanwhile Jannie had moved into the top half of the double-decker, looking for her pillow, and had taken instead the pillow from baby's bed and my glass of brandy and had settled down there to listen to Laurie's radio. I went downstairs to let the dog in and he came upstairs and got into his bed on the bottom half of the double-decker and while I was gone my husband had moved back over onto the accessible side of the guest-room bed so I went into Jannie's bed, which is rather too short, and I brought a pillow from the guest room, and my coffee.

At about nine o'clock the Sunday papers came and I went down to get them, and at about nine-thirty everyone woke up. My husband had moved back into his own bed when Laurie and Baby vacated it for their own beds, Laurie driving Jannie into the guest room when he took back the top half of the double-decker, and my husband woke up at nine-thirty and found himself wrapped in Jannie's pink blanket, sleeping on Laurie's green pillow and with a piece of coffeecake and Baby's fruit-juice glass, not to mention the four diamonds to the ace jack and the seven of clubs. Laurie in the top half of the double-decker had my glass of brandy and my cigarettes and matches and the baby's pink pillow. The dog had my white pillow and my ash tray. Jannie in the guest room had one white pillow and one blue pillow and two glasses of fruit juice and my husband's cigarettes and matches and ash tray and Laurie's hot milk, besides her own hot milk and coffeecake and her father's onion rolls. The baby in her crib had her father's tin glass of water and her suitcase and books and doll and a blue pillow from the guest room, but no blanket.

The puzzle, is, of course, what became of the blanket from Baby's bed? I took it off her crib and put it on the bottom half of the double-decker, but the dog did not have it when he woke up, and neither did any of the other beds. It was a blue-patterned patchwork blanket, and has not been seen since, and I would most particularly like to know where it got to. As I say, we are very short of blankets.

1952

A Visit

or, The Lovely House

FOR DYLAN THOMAS

T HE house in itself was, even before anything had happened there, as lovely a thing as she had ever seen. Set
among its lavish grounds, with a park and a river and a wooded
hill surrounding it, and carefully planned and tended gardens
close upon all sides, it lay upon the hills as though it were
something too precious to be seen by everyone; Margaret's
very coming there had been a product of such elaborate
arrangement, and such letters to and fro, and such meetings
and hopings and wishings, that when she alighted with Carla
Rhodes at the doorway of Carla's home, she felt that she too
had come home, to a place striven for and earned. Carla
stopped before the doorway and stood for a minute, looking
first behind her, at the vast reaching gardens and the green
lawn going down to the river, and the soft hills beyond, and
then at the perfect grace of the house, showing so clearly the
long-boned structure within, the curving staircases and the
arched doorways and the tall thin lines of steadying beams, all
of it resting back against the hills, and up, past rows of
windows and the flying lines of the roof, on, to the tower—
Carla stopped, and looked, and smiled, and then turned and
said, "Welcome, Margaret."

"It's a lovely house," Margaret said, and felt that she had
much better have said nothing.

The doors were opened and Margaret, touching as she
went the warm head of a stone faun beside her, passed inside.
Carla, following, greeted the servants by name, and was welcomed with reserved pleasure; they stood for a minute on the
rose-and-white tiled floor. "Again, welcome, Margaret," Carla
said.

Far ahead of them the great stairway soared upward, held to
the hall where they stood by only the slimmest of carved
balustrades; on Margaret's left hand a tapestry moved softly as

the door behind was closed. She could see the fine threads of the weave, and the light colors, but she could not have told the picture unless she went far away, perhaps as far away as the staircase, and looked at it from there; perhaps, she thought, from halfway up the stairway this great hall, and perhaps the whole house, is visible, as a complete body of story together, all joined and in sequence. Or perhaps I shall be allowed to move slowly from one thing to another, observing each, or would that take all the time of my visit?

"I never saw anything so lovely," she said to Carla, and Carla smiled.

"Come and meet my mama," Carla said.

They went through doors at the right, and Margaret, before she could see the light room she went into, was stricken with fear at meeting the owners of the house and the park and the river, and as she went beside Carla she kept her eyes down.

"Mama," said Carla, "this is Margaret, from school."

"Margaret," said Carla's mother, and smiled at Margaret kindly. "We are very glad you were able to come."

She was a tall lady wearing pale green and pale blue, and Margaret said as gracefully as she could, "Thank you, Mrs. Rhodes; I am very grateful for having been invited."

"Surely," said Mrs. Rhodes softly, "surely my daughter's friend Margaret from school should be welcome here; surely we should be grateful that she has come."

"Thank you, Mrs. Rhodes," Margaret said, not knowing how she was answering, but knowing that she was grateful.

When Mrs. Rhodes turned her kind eyes on her daughter, Margaret was at last able to look at the room where she stood next to her friend; it was a pale-green and a pale-blue long room with tall windows that looked out onto the lawn and the sky, and thin colored china ornaments on the mantel. Mrs. Rhodes had left her needlepoint when they came in and from where Margaret stood she could see the pale sweet pattern from the underside; all soft colors it was, melting into one another endlessly, and not finished. On the table near by were books, and one large book of sketches that were most certainly Carla's; Carla's harp stood next to the windows, and beyond one window were marble steps outside, going shallowly down to a fountain, where water moved in the sunlight. Margaret thought of her own embroidery—a pair of slippers she was working for her friend—and knew that she should never be able to bring it into this room, where Mrs. Rhodes's long white hands rested on the needlepoint frame, soft as dust on the pale colors.

"Come," said Carla, taking Margaret's hand in her own, "Mama has said that I might show you some of the house."

They went out again into the hall, across the rose and white tiles which made a pattern too large to be seen from the floor, and through a doorway where tiny bronze fauns grinned at them from the carving. The first room that they went into was all gold, with gilt on the window frames and on the legs of the chairs and tables, and the small chairs standing on the yellow carpet were made of gold brocade with small gilded backs, and on the wall were more tapestries showing the house as it looked in the sunlight with even the trees around it shining, and these tapestries were let into the wall and edged with thin gilded frames.

"There is so much tapestry," Margaret said.

"In every room," Carla agreed. "Mama has embroidered all the hangings for her own room, the room where she writes her letters. The other tapestries were done by my grandmamas and my great-grandmamas and my great-great-grandmamas."

The next room was silver, and the small chairs were of silver brocade with narrow silvered backs, and the tapestries on the walls of this room were edged with silver frames and showed the house in moonlight, with the white light shining on the stones and the windows glittering.

"Who uses these rooms?" Margaret asked.

"No one," Carla said.

They passed then into a room where everything grew smaller as they looked at it: the mirrors on both sides of the room showed the door opening and Margaret and Carla coming through, and then, reflected, a smaller door opening and a small Margaret and a smaller Carla coming through, and then, reflected again, a still smaller door and Margaret and Carla, and so on, endlessly, Margaret and Carla diminishing and reflecting. There was a table here and nesting under it another lesser table, and under that another one, and another under that one, and on the greatest table lay a carved wooden bowl holding within it another carved wooden bowl, and another within that, and another within that one. The tapestries in this room were of the house reflected in the lake, and the tapestries themselves were reflected, in and out, among the mirrors on the wall, with the house in the tapestries reflected in the lake.

This room frightened Margaret rather, because it was so difficult for her to tell what was in it and what was not, and how far in any direction she might easily move, and she backed out hastily, pushing Carla behind her. They turned from here into another doorway which led them out again into the great hall under the soaring staircase, and Carla said, "We had better go upstairs and see your room; we can see more of the house another time. We have *plenty* of time, after all," and she squeezed Margaret's hand joyfully.

They climbed the great staircase, and passed, in the hall upstairs, Carla's room, which was like the inside of a shell in pale colors, with lilacs on the table, and the fragrance of the lilacs followed them as they went down the halls.

The sound of their shoes on the polished floor was like rain, but the sun came in on them wherever they went. "Here," Carla said, opening a door, "is where we have breakfast when it is warm; here," opening another door, "is the passage to the room where Mama does her letters. And that—" nodding "—is the stairway to the tower, and *here* is where we shall have dances when my brother comes home."

"A real tower?" Margaret said.

"And *here*," Carla said, "is the old schoolroom, and my brother and I studied here before he went away, and I stayed on alone studying here until it was time for me to come to school and meet *you*."

"Can we go up into the tower?" Margaret asked.

"Down here, at the end of the hall," Carla said, "is where all my grandpapas and my grandmamas and my great-great-grandpapas and grandmamas live." She opened the door to the long gallery, where pictures of tall old people in lace and pale waistcoats leaned down to stare at Margaret and Carla. And then, to a walk at the top of the house, where they leaned over and looked at the ground below and the tower above, and Margaret looked at the gray stone of the tower and wondered who lived there, and Carla pointed out where the river ran far below, far away, and said they should walk there tomorrow.

"When my brother comes," she said, "he will take us boating on the river."

In her room, unpacking her clothes, Margaret realized that her white dress was the only one possible for dinner, and thought that she would have to send home for more things; she had intended to wear her ordinary gray downstairs most evenings before Carla's brother came, but knew she could not when she saw Carla in light blue, with pearls around her neck. When Margaret and Carla came into the drawing room before dinner Mrs. Rhodes greeted them very kindly, and asked had Margaret seen the painted room or the room with the tiles?

"We had no time to go near that part of the house at all," Carla said.

"After dinner, then," Mrs. Rhodes said, putting her arm affectionately around Margaret's shoulders, "we will go and see the painted room and the room with the tiles, because they are particular favorites of mine."

"Come and meet my papa," Carla said.

The door was just opening for Mr. Rhodes, and Margaret, who felt almost at ease now with Mrs. Rhodes, was frightened again of Mr. Rhodes, who spoke loudly and said, "So this is m'girl's friend from school? Lift up your head, girl, and let's have a look at you." When Margaret looked up blindly, and smiled weakly, he patted her cheek and said, "We shall have to make you look bolder before you leave us," and then he tapped his daughter on the shoulder and said she had grown to a monstrous fine girl.

They went in to dinner, and on the walls of the dining room were tapestries of the house in the seasons of the year, and the dinner service was white china with veins of gold running through it, as though it had been mined and not moulded. The fish was one Margaret did not recognize, and Mr. Rhodes very generously insisted upon serving her himself without smiling at her ignorance. Carla and Margaret were each given a glassful of pale spicy wine.

"When my brother comes," Carla said to Margaret, "we will not dare be so quiet at table." She looked across the white cloth to Margaret, and then to her father at the head, to her mother at the foot, with the long table between them, and said, "My brother can make us laugh all the time."

"Your mother will not miss you for these summer months?" Mrs. Rhodes said to Margaret.

"She has my sisters, ma'am," Margaret said, "and I have been away at school for so long that she has learned to do without me."

"We mothers never learn to do without our daughters," Mrs. Rhodes said, and looked fondly at Carla. "Or our sons," she added with a sigh.

"When my brother comes," Carla said, "you will see what this house can be like with life in it."

"When does he come?" Margaret asked.

"One week," Mr. Rhodes said, "three days, and four hours."

When Mrs. Rhodes rose, Margaret and Carla followed her, and Mr. Rhodes rose gallantly to hold the door for them all.

That evening Carla and Margaret played and sang duets, although Carla said that their voices together were too thin to be appealing without a deeper voice accompanying, and that when her brother came they should have some splendid trios. Mrs. Rhodes complimented their singing, and Mr. Rhodes fell asleep in his chair.

Before they went upstairs Mrs. Rhodes reminded herself of her promise to show Margaret the painted room and the room with the tiles, and so she and Margaret and Carla, holding their long dresses up away from the floor in front so that their skirts whispered behind them, went down a hall and through a passage and down another hall, and through a room filled with books and then through a painted door into a tiny octagonal room where each of the sides was paneled and painted, with pink and blue and green and gold small pictures of shepherds and nymphs, lambs and fauns, playing on the broad green lawns by the river, with the house standing lovely behind them. There was nothing else in the little room, because seemingly the paintings were furniture enough for one room, and Margaret felt surely that she could stay happily and watch the small painted people playing, without ever seeing anything more of the house. But Mrs. Rhodes led her on, into the room of the tiles, which was not exactly a room at all, but had one side all glass window looking out onto the same lawn of the pictures in the octagonal room. The tiles were set into the floor of this room, in tiny bright spots of color which showed, when you stood back and looked at them, that they were again a picture of the house, only now the same materials that made the house made the tiles, so that the tiny windows were tiles of glass, and the stones of the tower were chips of gray stone, and the bricks of the chimneys were chips of brick.

Beyond the tiles of the house Margaret, lifting her long skirt as she walked, so that she should not brush a chip of the tower out of place, stopped and said, "What is *this*?" And stood back to see, and then knelt down and said, "*What* is this?"

"Isn't she enchanting?" said Mrs. Rhodes, smiling at Margaret, "I've always loved her."

"I was wondering what Margaret would say when she saw it," said Carla, smiling also.

It was a curiously made picture of a girl's face, with blue-chip eyes and a red-chip mouth, staring blindly from the floor, with long light braids made of yellow stone chips going down evenly on either side of her round cheeks.

"She is pretty," said Margaret, stepping back to see her better. "What does it say underneath?"

She stepped back again, holding her head up and back to read the letters, pieced together with stone chips and set unevenly in the floor. "Here was Margaret," it said, "who died for love."

2

There was, of course, not time to do everything. Before Margaret had seen half the house, Carla's brother came home. Carla came running up the great staircase one afternoon calling "Margaret, Margaret, he's come," and Margaret, running down to meet her, hugged her and said, "I'm so glad."

He had certainly come, and Margaret, entering the drawing room shyly behind Carla, saw Mrs. Rhodes with tears in her eyes and Mr. Rhodes standing straighter and prouder than before, and Carla said, "Brother, here is Margaret."

He was tall and haughty in uniform, and Margaret wished she had met him a little later, when she had perhaps been to her room again, and perhaps tucked up her hair. Next to him stood his friend, a captain, small and dark and bitter, and smiling bleakly upon the family assembled. Margaret smiled back timidly at them both, and stood behind Carla.

Everyone then spoke at once. Mrs. Rhodes said "We've missed you so," and Mr. Rhodes said "Glad to have you back, m'boy," and Carla said "We shall have such times—I've promised Margaret—" and Carla's brother said "So this is Margaret?" and the dark captain said "I've been wanting to come."

It seemed that they all spoke at once, every time; there would be a long waiting silence while all of them looked around with joy at being together, and then suddenly everyone would have found something to say. It was so at dinner: Mrs. Rhodes said "You're not eating enough," and "You used to be more fond of pomegranates," and Carla said "We're to go boating," and "We'll have a dance, won't we?" and "Margaret and I insist upon a picnic," and "I saved the river for my brother to show to Margaret." Mr. Rhodes puffed and laughed and passed the wine, and Margaret hardly dared lift her eyes. The black captain said "Never realized what an attractive old place it could be, after all," and Carla's brother said "There's much about the house I'd like to show Margaret."

After dinner they played charades, and even Mrs. Rhodes did Achilles with Mr. Rhodes, holding his heel and both of them laughing and glancing at Carla and Margaret and the captain. Carla's brother leaned on the back of Margaret's chair and once she looked up at him and said, "No one ever calls you by name. Do you actually have a name?"

"Paul," he said.

The next morning they walked on the lawn, Carla with the captain and Margaret with Paul. They stood by the lake, and Margaret looked at the pure reflection of the house and said, "It almost seems as though we could open a door and go in."

"There," said Paul, and he pointed with his stick at the front entrance. "There is where we shall enter, and it will swing open for us with an underwater crash."

"Margaret," said Carla, laughing, "you say odd things, sometimes. If you tried to go into *that* house, you'd be in the lake."

"Indeed, and not like it much, at all," the captain added.

"Or would you have the side door?" asked Paul, pointing with his stick.

"I think I prefer the front door," said Margaret.

"But you'd be drowned," Carla said. She took Margaret's arm as they started back toward the house, and said, "We'd make a scene for a tapestry right now, on the lawn before the house."

"Another tapestry?" said the captain, and grimaced.

They played croquet, and Paul hit Margaret's ball toward a wicket, and the captain accused her of cheating prettily. And they played word games in the evening, and Margaret and Paul won, and everyone said Margaret was so clever. And they walked endlessly on the lawns before the house, and looked into the still lake, and watched the reflection of the house in the water, and Margaret chose a room in the reflected house for her own, and Paul said she should have it.

"That's the room where Mama writes her letters," said Carla, looking strangely at Margaret.

"Not in our house in the lake," said Paul.

"And I suppose if you like it she would lend it to you while you stay," Carla said.

"Not at all," said Margaret amiably. "I think I should prefer the tower anyway."

"Have you seen the rose garden?" Carla asked.

"Let me take you there," said Paul.

Margaret started across the lawn with him, and Carla called to her, "Where are you off to now, Margaret?"

"Why, to the rose garden," Margaret called back, and Carla said, staring, "You are really very odd, sometimes, Margaret. And it's growing colder, far too cold to linger among the roses," and so Margaret and Paul turned back.

Mrs. Rhodes's needlepoint was coming on well. She had filled in most of the outlines of the house, and was setting in the windows. After the first small shock of surprise, Margaret no longer wondered that Mrs. Rhodes was able to set out the house so well without a pattern or a plan; she did it from memory and Margaret, realizing this for the first time, thought "How amazing," and then "But of course; how else *would* she do it?"

To see a picture of the house, Mrs. Rhodes needed only

to lift her eyes in any direction, but, more than that, she had of course never used any other model for her embroidery; she had of course learned the faces of the house better than the faces of her children. The dreamy life of the Rhodeses in the house was most clearly shown Margaret as she watched Mrs. Rhodes surely and capably building doors and windows, carvings and cornices, in her embroidered house, smiling tenderly across the room to where Carla and the captain bent over a book together, while her fingers almost of themselves turned the edge of a carving Margaret had forgotten or never known about until, leaning over the back of Mrs. Rhodes's chair, she saw it form itself under Mrs. Rhodes's hands.

The small thread of days and sunlight, then, that bound Margaret to the house, was woven here as she watched. And Carla, lifting her head to look over, might say, "Margaret, do come and look, here. Mother is always at her work, but my brother is rarely home."

They went for a picnic, Carla and the captain and Paul and Margaret, and Mrs. Rhodes waved to them from the doorway as they left, and Mr. Rhodes came to his study window and lifted his hand to them. They chose to go to the wooded hill beyond the house, although Carla was timid about going too far away—"I always like to be where I can see the roofs, at least," she said—and sat among the trees, on moss greener than Margaret had ever seen before, and spread out a white cloth and drank red wine.

It was a very proper forest, with neat trees and the green moss, and an occasional purple or yellow flower growing discreetly away from the path. There was no sense of brooding silence, as there sometimes is with trees about, and Margaret realized, looking up to see the sky clearly between the branches, that she had seen this forest in the tapestries in the breakfast room, with the house shining in the sunlight beyond.

"Doesn't the river come through here somewhere?" she asked, hearing, she thought, the sound of it through the trees. "I feel so comfortable here among these trees, so at home."

"It is possible," said Paul, "to take a boat from the lawn in front of the house and move without sound down the river, through the trees, past the fields and then, for some reason, around past the house again. The river, you see, goes almost around the house in a great circle. We are very proud of that."

"The river *is* near by," said Carla. "It goes almost completely around the house."

"Margaret," said the captain. "You must not look rapt on a picnic unless you are contemplating nature."

"I was, as a matter of fact," said Margaret. "I was contemplating a caterpillar approaching Carla's foot."

"Will you come and look at the river?" said Paul, rising and holding his hand out to Margaret. "I think we can see much of its great circle from near here."

"Margaret," said Carla as Margaret stood up. "You are *always* wandering off."

"I'm coming right back," Margaret said, with a laugh. "It's only to look at the river."

"Don't be away long," Carla said, "We must be getting back before dark."

The river as it went through the trees was shadowed and cool, broadening out into pools where only the barest movement disturbed the ferns along its edge, and where small stones made it possible to step out and see the water all around, from a precarious island, and where without sound a leaf might be carried from the limits of sight to the limits of sight, moving swiftly but imperceptibly and turning a little as it went.

"Who lives in the tower, Paul?" asked Margaret, holding a fern and running it softly over the back of her hand. "I know someone lives there, because I saw someone moving at the window once."

"Not *lives* there," said Paul, amused. "Did you think we kept a political prisoner locked away?"

"I thought it might be the birds, at first," Margaret said, glad to be describing this to someone.

"No," said Paul, still amused. "There's an aunt, or a great-aunt, or perhaps even a great-great-great-aunt. She doesn't live there, at all, but goes there because she says she cannot *endure* the sight of tapestry." He laughed. "She has filled the tower with books, and a huge old cat, and she may practice alchemy there, for all anyone knows. The reason you've never seen her would be that she has one of her spells of hiding away. Sometimes she is downstairs daily."

"Will I ever meet her?" Margaret asked wonderingly.

"Perhaps," Paul said. "She might take it into her head to come down formally one night to dinner. Or she might wander carelessly up to you where you sat on the lawn, and introduce herself. Or you might never see her, at that."

"Suppose I went up to the tower?"

Paul glanced at her strangely. "I suppose you could, if you wanted to," he said. "*I've* been there."

"Margaret," Carla called through the woods. "Margaret, we shall be late if you do not give up brooding by the river."

All this time, almost daily, Margaret was seeing new places in the house: the fan room, where the most delicate filigree fans had been set into the walls with their fine ivory sticks painted in exquisite miniature; the small room where incredibly perfect wooden and glass and metal fruits and flowers and trees stood on glittering glass shelves, lined up against the windows. And daily she passed and repassed the door behind which lay the stairway to the tower, and almost daily she stepped carefully around the tiles on the floor which read "Here was Margaret, who died for love."

It was no longer possible, however, to put off going to the tower. It was no longer possible to pass the doorway several times a day and do no more than touch her hand secretly to the panels, or perhaps set her head against and listen, to hear if there were footsteps going up or down, or a voice calling her. It was not possible to pass the doorway once more, and so in the early morning Margaret set her hand firmly to the door and pulled it open, and it came easily, as though relieved that at last, after so many hints and insinuations, and so much waiting and such helpless despair, Margaret had finally come to open it.

The stairs beyond, gray stone and rough, were, Margaret thought, steep for an old lady's feet, but Margaret went up effortlessly, though timidly. The stairway turned around and around, going up to the tower, and Margaret followed, setting her feet carefully upon one step after another, and holding her hands against the warm stone wall on either side, looking forward and up, expecting to be seen or spoken to before she reached the top; perhaps, she thought once, the walls of the tower were transparent and she was clearly, ridiculously visible from the outside, and Mrs. Rhodes and Carla, on the lawn—if indeed they ever looked upward to the tower—might watch her and turn to one another with smiles, saying "There is Margaret, going up to the tower at last," and, smiling, nod to one another.

The stairway ended, as she had not expected it would, in a heavy wooden door, which made Margaret, standing on the step below to find room to raise her hand and knock, seem smaller, and even standing at the top of the tower she felt that she was not really tall.

"Come in," said the great-aunt's voice, when Margaret had knocked twice; the first knock had been received with an expectant silence, as though inside someone had said inaudibly, "Is that someone knocking at *this* door?" and then waited to be convinced by a second knock—and Margaret's knuckles hurt from the effort of knocking to be heard through a heavy wooden door. She opened the door awkwardly from below— how much easier this all would be, she thought, if I knew the way—went in, and said politely, before she looked around, "I'm Carla's friend. They said I might come up to the tower to see it, but of course if you would rather I went away I shall." She had planned to say this more gracefully, without such an implication that invitations to the tower were issued by the downstairs Rhodeses, but the long climb and her being out of breath forced her to say everything at once, and she had really no time for the sounding periods she had composed.

In any case the great-aunt said politely—she was sitting at the other side of the round room, against a window, and she was not very clearly visible—"I am amazed that they told you about me at all. However, since you are here I cannot pretend that I really object to having you; you may come in and sit down."

Margaret came obediently into the room and sat clown on the stone bench which ran all the way around the tower room, under the windows which of course were on all sides and open to the winds, so that the movement of the air through the tower room was insistent and constant, making talk difficult and even distinguishing objects a matter of some effort.

As though it were necessary to establish her position in the house emphatically and immediately, the old lady said, with a gesture and a grin, "My tapestries," and waved at the windows. She seemed to be not older than a great-aunt, although perhaps too old for a mere aunt, but her voice was clearly able to carry through the sound of the wind in the tower room and she seemed compact and strong beside the window, not at all as though she might be dizzy from looking out, or tired from the stairs.

"May I look out the window?" Margaret asked, almost of the cat, which sat next to her and regarded her without friendship, but without, as yet, dislike.

"Certainly," said the great-aunt. "Look out the windows, by all means."

Margaret turned on the bench and leaned her arms on the wide stone ledge of the window, but she was disappointed. Although the tops of the trees did not reach halfway up the tower, she could see only branches and leaves below and no sign of the wide lawns or the roofs of the house or the curve of the river.

"I hoped I could see the way the river went, from here."

"The river doesn't *go* from here," said the old lady, and laughed.

"I mean," Margaret said, "they told me that the river went around in a curve, almost surrounding the house."

"Who told you?" said the old lady.

"Paul."

"I see," said the old lady. "*He's* back, is he?"

"He's been here for several days, but he's going away again soon."

"And what's *your* name?" asked the old lady, leaning forward.

"Margaret."

"I see," said the old lady again. "That's my name, too," she said.

Margaret thought that "How nice" would be an inappropriate reply to this, and something like "Is it?" or "Just imagine" or "What a coincidence" would certainly make her feel more foolish than she believed she really was, so she smiled uncertainly at the old lady and dismissed the notion of saying "What a lovely name."

"He should have come and gone sooner," the old lady went on, as though to herself. "Then we'd have it all behind us."

"Have all *what* behind us?" Margaret asked, although she felt that she was not really being included in the old lady's conversation with herself, a conversation that seemed—and probably was—part of a larger conversation which the old lady had with herself constantly and on larger subjects than the matter of Margaret's name, and which even Margaret, intruder as she was, and young, could not be allowed to interrupt for very long. "Have all *what* behind us?" Margaret asked insistently.

"I say," said the old lady, turning to look at Margaret, "he should have come and gone already, and we'd all be well out of it by now."

"I see," said Margaret. "Well, I don't think he's going to be here much longer. He's talking of going." In spite of herself, her voice trembled a little. In order to prove to the old lady that the trembling in her voice was imaginary, Margaret said almost defiantly, "It will be very lonely here after he has gone."

"We'll be well out of it, Margaret, you and I," the old lady said. "Stand away from the window, child, you'll be wet."

Margaret realized with this that the storm which had—she knew now—been hanging over the house for long sunny days had broken, suddenly, and that the wind had grown louder and was bringing with it through the windows of the tower long stinging rain. There were drops on the cat's black fur, and Margaret felt the side of her face wet. "Do your windows close?" she asked. "If I could help you—?"

"*I* don't mind the rain," the old lady said. "It wouldn't be the first time it's rained around the tower."

"*I* don't mind it," Margaret said hastily, drawing away from the window. She realized that she was staring back at the cat, and added nervously, "Although, of course, getting wet is—" She hesitated and the cat stared back at her without expression. "I mean," she said apologetically, "some people don't *like* getting wet."

The cat deliberately turned its back on her and put its face closer to the window.

"What were you saying about Paul?" Margaret asked the old lady, feeling somehow that there might he a thin thread of reason tangling the old lady and the cat and the tower and the rain, and even, with abrupt clarity, defining Margaret herself and the strange hesitation which had caught at her here in the tower. "He's going away soon, you know."

"It would have been better if it were over with by now," the old lady said. "These things don't take really long, you know, and the sooner the better, *I* say."

"I suppose *that's* true," Margaret said intelligently.

"After all," said the old lady dreamily, with raindrops in her hair, "we don't always see ahead, into things that are going to happen."

Margaret was wondering how soon she might politely go back downstairs and dry herself off, and she meant to say politely only so long as the old lady seemed to be talking, however remotely, about Paul. Also, the rain and the wind were coming through the window onto Margaret in great driving gusts, as though Margaret and the old lady and the books and the cat would be washed away, and the top of the tower cleaned of them.

"I *would* help you if I could," the old lady said earnestly to Margaret, raising her voice almost to a scream to be heard over the wind and the rain. She stood up to approach Margaret, and Margaret, thinking she was about to fall, reached out a hand to catch her. The cat stood up and spat, the rain came through the window in a great sweep, and Margaret, holding the old lady's hands, heard through the sounds of the wind the equal sounds of all the voices in the world, and they called to her saying "Good-by, good-by," and "All is lost," and another voice saying "I will always remember you," and still another called, "It is so dark." And, far away from the others, she could hear a voice calling, "Come back, come back." Then the old lady pulled her hands away from Margaret and the voices were gone. The cat shrank back and the old lady looked coldly at Margaret and said, "As I was saying, I would help you if I *could*."

"I'm so sorry," Margaret said weakly. "I thought you were going to fall."

"Good-by," said the old lady.

3

At the ball Margaret wore a gown of thin blue lace that belonged to Carla, and yellow roses in her hair, and she carried one of the fans from the fan room, a daintily painted ivory thing which seemed indestructible, since she dropped it twice, and which had a tiny picture of the house painted on its ivory sticks, so that when the fan was closed the house was gone. Mrs. Rhodes had given it to her to carry, and had given Carla another, so that when Margaret and Carla passed one another dancing, or met by the punch bowl or in the halls, they said happily to one another, "Have you still got your fan? I gave mine to someone to hold for a minute; I showed mine to everyone. Are you still carrying your fan? I've got *mine*."

Margaret danced with strangers and with Paul, and when she danced with Paul they danced away from the others, up and down the long gallery hung with pictures, in and out between the pillars which led to the great hall opening into the room of the tiles. Near them danced ladies in scarlet silk, and green satin, and white velvet, and Mrs. Rhodes, in black with diamonds at her throat and on her hands, stood at the top of the room and smiled at the dancers, or went on Mr. Rhodes's arm to greet guests who came laughingly in between the pillars looking eagerly and already moving in time to the music as they walked. One lady wore white feathers in her hair, curling down against her shoulder; another had a pink scarf over her arms, and it floated behind her as she danced. Paul was in his haughty uniform, and Carla wore red roses in her hair and danced with the captain.

"Are you really going tomorrow?" Margaret asked Paul once during the evening; she knew that he was, but somehow asking the question—which she had done several times before —established a communication between them, of his right to go and her right to wonder, which was sadly sweet to her.

"I *said* you might meet the great-aunt," said Paul, as

though in answer; Margaret followed his glance, and saw the old lady of the tower. She was dressed in yellow satin, and looked very regal and proud as she moved through the crowd of dancers, drawing her skirt aside if any of them came too close to her. She was coming toward Margaret and Paul where they sat on small chairs against the wall, and when she came close enough she smiled, looking at Paul, and said to him, holding out her hands, "I am very glad to see you, my dear."

Then she smiled at Margaret and Margaret smiled back, very glad that the old lady held out no hands to her.

"Margaret told me you were here," the old lady said to Paul, "and I came down to see you once more."

"I'm very glad you did," Paul said. "I wanted to see you so much that I almost came to the tower."

They both laughed and Margaret, looking from one to the other of them, wondered at the strong resemblance between them. Margaret sat very straight and stiff on her narrow chair, with her blue lace skirt falling charmingly around her and her hands folded neatly in her lap, and listened to their talk. Paul had found the old lady a chair and they sat with their heads near together, looking at one another as they talked, and smiling.

"You look very fit," the old lady said. "Very fit indeed." She sighed.

"You look wonderfully well," Paul said.

"Oh, well," said the old lady. "I've aged. I've aged, I know it."

"So have I," said Paul.

"Not noticeably," said the old lady, shaking her head and regarding him soberly for a minute. "*You* never will, I suppose."

At that moment the captain came up and bowed in front of Margaret, and Margaret, hoping that Paul might notice, got up to dance with him.

"I saw you sitting there alone," said the captain, "and I seized the precise opportunity I have been awaiting all evening."

"Excellent military tactics," said Margaret, wondering if these remarks had not been made a thousand times before, at a thousand different balls.

"I could be a splendid tactician," said the captain gallantly, as though carrying on his share of the echoing conversation, the words spoken under so many glittering chandeliers, "if my objective were always so agreeable to me."

"I saw you dancing with Carla," said Margaret.

"Carla," he said, and made a small gesture that somehow showed Carla as infinitely less than Margaret. Margaret knew that she had seen him make the same gesture to Carla, probably with reference to Margaret. She laughed.

"I forget what I'm supposed to say now," she told him.

"You're supposed to say," he told her seriously, "'And do you really leave us so soon?'"

"And do you really leave us so soon?" said Margaret obediently.

"The sooner to return," he said, and tightened his arm around her waist. Margaret said, it being her turn, "We shall miss you very much."

"*I* shall miss *you*," he said, with a manly air of resignation.

They danced two waltzes, after which the captain escorted her handsomely back to the chair from which he had taken her, next to which Paul and the old lady continued in conversation, laughing and gesturing. The captain bowed to Margaret deeply, clicking his heels.

"May I leave you alone for a minute or so?" he asked. "I believe Carla is looking for me."

"I'm perfectly all right here," Margaret said. As the captain hurried away she turned to hear what Paul and the old lady were saying.

"I remember, I remember," said the old lady laughing, and she tapped Paul on the wrist with her fan. "I never imagined there would be a time when I should find it funny."

"But it *was* funny," said Paul.

"We were so young," the old lady said. "I can hardly remember."

She stood up abruptly, bowed to Margaret, and started back across the room among the dancers. Paul followed her as far as the doorway and then left her to come back to Margaret. When he sat down next to her he said, "So you met the old lady?"

"I went to the tower," Margaret said.

"She told me," he said absently, looking down at his gloves. "Well," he said finally, looking up with an air of cheerfulness. "Are they *never* going to play a waltz?"

Shortly before the sun came up over the river the next morning they sat at breakfast, Mr. and Mrs. Rhodes at the ends of the table, Carla and the captain, Margaret and Paul. The red roses in Carla's hair had faded and been thrown away, as had Margaret's yellow roses, but both Carla and Margaret still wore their ball gowns, which they had been wearing for so long that the soft richness of them seemed natural, as though they were to wear nothing else for an eternity in the house, and the gay confusion of helping one another dress, and admiring one another, and straightening the last folds to hang more gracefully, seemed all to have happened longer ago than memory, to be perhaps a dream that might never have happened at all, as perhaps the figures in the tapestries on the walls of the dining room might remember, secretly, an imagined process of dressing themselves and coming with laughter and light voices to sit on the lawn where they were woven. Margaret, looking at Carla, thought that she had never seen Carla so familiarly as in this soft white gown, with her hair dressed high on her head—had it really been curled and pinned that way? Or had it always, forever, been so?—and the fan in her hand—had she not always had that fan, held just so?—and when Clara turned her head slightly on her long neck she captured the air of one of the portraits in the long gallery. Paul and the captain were still somehow trim in their uniforms; they were leaving at sunrise.

"Must you really leave this morning?" Margaret whispered to Paul.

"You are all kind to stay up and say good-by," said the captain, and he leaned forward to look down the table at Margaret, as though it were particularly kind of her.

"Every time my son leaves me," said Mrs. Rhodes, "it is as though it were the first time."

Abruptly, the captain turned to Mrs. Rhodes and said, "I noticed this morning that there was a bare patch on the grass before the door. Can it be restored?"

"I had not known," Mrs. Rhodes said, and she looked nervously at Mr. Rhodes, who put his hand quietly on the table and said, "We hope to keep the house in good repair so long as we are able."

"But the broken statue by the lake?" said the captain. "And the tear in the tapestry behind your head?"

"It is wrong of you to notice these things," Mrs. Rhodes said, gently.

"What can I do?" he said to her. "It is impossible not to notice these things. The fish are dying, for instance. There are no grapes in the arbor this year. The carpet is worn to thread near your embroidery frame," he bowed to Mrs. Rhodes, "and in the house itself—" bowing to Mr. Rhodes "—there is a noticeable crack over the window of the conservatory, a crack in the solid stone. Can you repair that?"

Mr. Rhodes said weakly, "It is very wrong of you to notice these things. Have you neglected the sun, and the bright perfection of the drawing room? Have you been recently to the gallery of portraits? Have you walked on the green portions of the lawn, or only watched for the bare places?"

"The drawing room is shabby," said the captain softly. "The green brocade sofa is torn a little near the arm. The carpet has lost its luster. The gilt is chipped on four of the small chairs in the gold room, the silver paint scratched in the silver room. A tile is missing from the face of Margaret, who died for love, and in the great gallery the paint has faded slightly on the portrait of—" bowing again to Mr. Rhodes "—your great-great-great grandfather, sir."

Mr. Rhodes and Mrs. Rhodes looked at one another, and then Mrs. Rhodes said, "Surely it is not necessary to reproach *us* for these things?"

The captain reddened and shook his head.

"My embroidery is very nearly finished," Mrs. Rhodes said. "I have only to put the figures into the foreground."

"*I* shall mend the brocade sofa," said Carla.

The captain glanced once around the table, and sighed. "I must pack," he said. "We cannot delay our duties even though we have offended lovely women." Mrs. Rhodes, turning coldly away from him, rose and left the table, with Carla and Margaret following.

Margaret went quickly to the tile room, where the white

face of Margaret who died for love stared eternally into the sky beyond the broad window. There was indeed a tile missing from the wide white cheek, and the broken spot looked like a tear, Margaret thought; she knelt down and touched the tile face quickly to be sure that it was not a tear.

Then she went slowly back through the lovely rooms; across the broad rose-and-white tiled hall, and into the drawing room, and stopped to close the tall doors behind her.

"There really is a tile missing," she said.

Paul turned and frowned; he was standing alone in the drawing room, tall and bright in his uniform, ready to leave. "You are mistaken," he said. "It is not possible that anything should be missing."

"I saw it."

"It is not *true*, you know," he said. He was walking quickly up and down the room, slapping his gloves on his wrist, glancing nervously, now and then, at the door, at the tall windows opening out onto the marble stairway. "The house is the same as ever," he said. "It does not change."

"But the worn carpet . . ." It was under his feet as he walked.

"Nonsense," he said violently. "Don't you think I'd know my own house? I care for it constantly, even when *they* forget; without this house I could not exist; do you think it would begin to crack while I am here?"

"How can you keep it from aging? Carpets *will* wear, you know, and unless they are replaced . . ."

"Replaced?" He stared as though she had said something evil. "What could replace anything in this house?" He touched Mrs. Rhodes's embroidery frame, softly. "All *we* can do is add to it."

There was a sound outside; it was the family coming down the great stairway to say good-by. He turned quickly and listened, and it seemed to be the sound he had been expecting. "I will always remember you," he said to Margaret, hastily, and turned again toward the tall windows. "Good-by."

"It is so dark," Margaret said, going beside him. "You will come back?"

"I will come back," he said sharply. "Good-by." He stepped across the sill of the window onto the marble stairway outside;

he was black for a moment against the white marble, and Margaret stood still at the window watching him go down the steps and away through the gardens. "Lost, lost," she heard faintly, and, from far away, "All is lost."

She turned back to the room, and, avoiding the worn spot in the carpet and moving widely around Mrs. Rhodes's embroidery frame, she went to the great doors and opened them. Outside, in the hall with the rose-and-white tiled floor, Mr. and Mrs. Rhodes and Carla were standing with the captain.

"Son," Mrs. Rhodes was saying, "when will you be back?"

"Don't *fuss* at me," the captain said. "I'll be back when I can."

Carla stood silently, a little away. "Please be careful," she said, and, "Here's Margaret, come to say good-by to you, Brother."

"Don't linger, m'boy," said Mr. Rhodes. "Hard on the women."

"There are so many things Margaret and I planned for you while you were here," Carla said to her brother. "The time has been so short."

Margaret, standing beside Mrs. Rhodes, turned to Carla's brother (*and Paul; who was Paul?*) and said, "Good-by." He bowed to her and moved to go to the door with his father.

"It is hard to see him go," Mrs. Rhodes said. "And we do not know when he will come back." She put her hand gently on Margaret's shoulder. "We must show you more of the house," she said. "I saw you one day try the door of the ruined tower; have you seen the hall of flowers? Or the fountain room?"

"When my brother comes again," Carla said, "we shall have a musical evening, and perhaps he will take us boating on the river."

"And my visit?" said Margaret smiling. "Surely there will be an end to my visit?"

Mrs. Rhodes, with one last look at the door from which Mr. Rhodes and the captain had gone, dropped her hand from Margaret's shoulder and said, "I must go to my embroidery. I have neglected it while my son was with us."

"You will not leave us before my brother comes again?" Carla asked Margaret.

"I have only to put the figures into the foreground," Mrs. Rhodes said, hesitating on her way to the drawing room. "I shall have you exactly if you sit on the lawn near the river."

"We shall be models of stillness," said Carla, laughing. "Margaret, will you come and sit beside me on the lawn?"

1952

This Is the Life

or, Journey with a Lady

"H<small>ONEY</small>," Mrs. Wilson said uneasily, "are you *sure* you'll be all *right?*"

"Sure," said Joseph. He backed away quickly as she bent to kiss him again. "Listen, *Mother*," he said. "Everybody's *looking.*"

"I'm still not sure but what someone ought to go with him," said his mother. "Are you *sure* he'll be all right?" she said to her husband.

"Who, Joe?" said Mr. Wilson. "He'll be fine, won't you, son?"

"Sure," said Joseph.

"A boy nine years old ought to be able to travel by himself," said Mr. Wilson in the patient tone of one who has been saying these same words over and over for several days to a nervous mother.

Mrs. Wilson looked up at the train as one who estimates the probable strength of an enemy. "But suppose something should *happen?*" she asked.

"Look, Helen," her husband said, "the train's going to leave in about four minutes. His bag is already on the train, Helen. It's on the seat where he's going to be sitting from now until he gets to Merrytown. I have spoken to the porter and I have given the porter a couple of dollars, and the porter has promised to keep an eye on him and see that he gets off the train with his bag when the train stops at Merrytown. He is nine years old, Helen, and he knows his name and where he's going and where he's supposed to get off, and Grandpop is going to meet him and will telephone you the minute they get to Grandpop's house, and the porter—"

"I know," said Mrs. Wilson, "but are you sure he'll be all *right?*"

Mr. Wilson and Joseph looked at one another briefly and then away.

Mrs. Wilson took advantage of Joseph's momentary lapse of

awareness to put her arm around his shoulders and kiss him again, although he managed to move almost in time and her kiss landed somewhere on the top of his head. "*Mother*," Joseph said ominously.

"Don't want anything to happen to my little boy," Mrs. Wilson said with a brave smile.

"Mother, for heaven's *sake*," said Joseph. "I better get on the train," he said to his father. "Good idea," said his father.

" 'Bye, Mother," Joseph said, backing toward the train door; he took a swift look up and down the platform, and then reached up to his mother and gave her a rapid kiss on the cheek. "Take care of yourself," he said.

"Don't forget to telephone the minute you get there," his mother said. "Write me every day, and tell Grandma you're supposed to brush your teeth every night and if the weather turns cool—"

"Sure," Joseph said. "Sure, Mother."

"So long, son," said his father.

"So long, Dad," Joseph said; solemnly they shook hands. "Take care of yourself," Joseph said.

"Have a good time," his father said.

As Joseph climbed up the steps to the train he could hear his mother saying, "And telephone us when you get there and be careful—"

"Goodbye, goodbye," he said, and went into the train. He had been located by his father in a double seat at the end of the car and, once settled, he turned as a matter of duty to the window. His father, with an unmanly look of concern, waved to him and nodded violently, as though to indicate that everything was going to be all right, that they had pulled it off beautifully, but his mother, twisting her fingers nervously, came close to the window of the train, and, fortunately unheard by the people within, but probably clearly audible to everyone for miles without, gave him at what appeared to be some length an account of how she had changed her mind and was probably going to come with him after all. Joseph nodded and smiled and waved and shrugged his shoulders to indicate that he could not hear, but his mother went on talking, now and then glancing nervously at the front of the train, as though afraid that the engine might start and take Joseph away before she had made herself absolutely sure that he was going to be all right. Joseph, who felt with some justice that in the past few days his mother had told him every conceivable pertinent fact about his traveling alone to his grandfather's, and her worries about same, was able to make out such statements as "Be careful," and "Telephone us the minute you get there," and "Don't forget to write." Then the train stirred, and hesitated, and moved slightly again, and Joseph backed away from the window, still waving and smiling. He was positive that what his mother was saying as the train pulled out was "Are you *sure* you'll be all right?" She blew a kiss to him as the train started, and he ducked.

Surveying his prospects as the train took him slowly away from his mother and father, he was pleased. The journey should take only a little over three hours, and he knew the name of the station and had his ticket safely in his jacket pocket; although he had been reluctant to yield in any fashion to his mother's misgivings, he had checked several times, secretly, to make sure the ticket was safe. He had half a dozen comic books—a luxury he was not ordinarily allowed—and a chocolate bar; he had his suitcase and his cap, and he had seen personally to the packing of his first baseman's mitt. He had a dollar bill in the pocket of his pants, because his mother thought he should have some money in case—possibilities which had concretely occurred to her—of a train wreck (although his father had pointed out that in the case of a major disaster the victims were not expected to pay their own expenses, at least not before their families had been notified) or perhaps in the case of some vital expense to which his grandfather's income would not be adequate. His father had thought that Joe ought to have a little money by him in case he wanted to buy anything, and because a man ought not to travel unless he had money in his pocket. "Might pick up a girl on the train and want to buy her lunch," his father had said jovially and his mother, regarding her husband thoughtfully, had remarked, "Let's hope *Joseph* doesn't do things like that," and Joe and his father had winked at one another. So, regarding his comic books and his suitcase and his ticket and his chocolate bar, and feeling the imperceptible but emphatic presence of the dollar bill in his pocket, Joe leaned back against the soft seat, looked briefly out the window at the houses now moving steadily past, and said to himself, "This is the life, boy."

Before indulging in the several glories of comic books and chocolate, he spent a moment or so watching the houses of his hometown disappear beyond the train; ahead of him, at his grandfather's farm, lay a summer of cows and horses and probable wrestling matches in the grass; behind him lay school and its infinite irritations, and his mother and father. He wondered briefly if his mother was still looking after the train and telling him to write, and then largely he forgot her. With a sigh of pure pleasure he leaned back and selected a comic book, one that dealt with the completely realistic adventures of a powerful magician among hostile African tribes. This *is* the life, boy, he told himself again, and glanced again out the window to see a boy about his own age sitting on a fence watching the train go by. For a minute Joseph thought of waving down to the boy, but decided that it was beneath his dignity as a traveler; moreover, the boy on the fence was wearing a dirty sweatshirt, which made Joe move uneasily under his stiff collar and suit jacket, and he thought longingly of the comfortable old shirt with the insignia "Brooklyn Dodgers" which was in his suitcase. Then, just as the traitorous idea of changing on the train occurred to him, and of arriving at his grandfather's not in his good suit became a possibility, all sensible thought was driven from his mind by a cruel and unnecessary blow. Someone sat down next to him, breathing heavily, and from the quick flash of perfume and the movement of cloth that could only be a dress rustling Joe realized with a strong sense of injustice that his paradise had been invaded by some woman.

"Is this seat taken?" she asked.

Joe refused to recognize her existence by turning his head to look at her, but told her sullenly, "No, it's not." Not taken, he was thinking, what did she think *I* was sitting here for? Aren't there enough old seats in the train she could go and sit in without taking mine?

He seemed to lose himself in contemplation of the scenery beyond the train window, but secretly he was wishing direly that the woman would suddenly discover she had forgotten her suitcase or find out she had no ticket or remember that she had left the bathtub running at home—anything, to get her off the train at the first station, and out of Joe's way.

"You going far?"

Talking, too, Joe thought, she has to take my seat and then she goes and talks my ear off, darn old pest. "Yeah," he said. "Merrytown."

"What's your name?"

Joe, from long experience, could have answered all her questions in one sentence, he was so familiar with the series— I'm nine years old, he could have told her, and I'm in the fifth grade, and, no, I don't like school, and if you want to know what I learn in school it's nothing because I don't like school and I do like movies, and I'm going to my grandfather's house, and more than anything else I hate women who come and sit beside me and ask me silly questions and if my mother didn't keep after me all the time about my manners I would probably gather my things together and move to another seat and if you don't stop asking me—

"What's your name, little boy?"

Little boy, Joe told himself bitterly, on top of everything else, little boy.

"Joe," he said.

"How old are you?"

He lifted his eyes wearily and regarded the conductor entering the car; it was surely too much to hope that this female plague had forgotten her ticket, but could it be remotely possible that she was on the wrong train?

"Got your ticket, Joe?" the woman asked.

"Sure," said Joe. "Have you?"

She laughed and said—apparently addressing the conductor, since her voice was not at this moment the voice women use in addressing a little boy, but the voice that goes with speaking to conductors and taxi drivers and salesclerks—"I'm afraid I haven't got a ticket. I had no time to get one."

"Where are you going?" said the conductor.

Would they put her off the train? For the first time, Joe turned and looked at her, eagerly and with hope. Would they possibly, hopefully, desperately, put her off the train? "I'm going to Merrytown," she said, and Joe's convictions about the generally weak-minded attitudes of the adult world were all confirmed; the conductor tore a slip from a pad he carried, punched a hole in it, and told the woman, "Two seventy-three." While she was searching her pocketbook for her money —if she knew she was going to have to buy a ticket, Joe thought disgustedly, whyn't she have her money ready?—the conductor took Joe's ticket and grinned at him. "Your boy got *his* ticket all right," he pointed out.

The woman smiled. "He got to the station ahead of me," she said.

The conductor gave her her change, and went on down the car. "That was funny, when he thought you were my little boy," the woman said.

"Yeah," said Joe.

"What're you reading?"

Wearily, Joe put his comic book down.

"Comic," he said.

"Interesting?"

"Yeah," said Joe.

"Say, look at the policeman," the woman said.

Joe looked where she was pointing and saw—he would not have believed this, since he knew perfectly well that most women cannot tell the difference between a policeman and a mailman—that it was undeniably a policeman, and that he was regarding the occupants of the car very much as though there might be a murderer or an international jewel thief riding calmly along on the train. Then, after surveying the car for a moment, he came a few steps forward to the last seat, where Joe and the woman were sitting.

"Name?" he said sternly to the woman.

"Mrs. John Aldridge, officer," said the woman promptly. "And this is my little boy, Joseph."

"Hi, Joe," said the policeman.

Joe, speechless, stared at the policeman and nodded dumbly.

"Where'd you get on?" the policeman asked the woman.

"Ashville," she said.

"See anything of a woman about your height and build, wearing a fur jacket, getting on the train at Ashville?"

"I don't think so," said the woman. "Why?"

"Wanted," said the policeman tersely.

"Keep your eyes open," he told Joe. "Might get a reward."

He passed on down the car, and stopped occasionally to speak to women who seemed to be alone. Then the door at the far end of the car closed behind him and Joe turned and took a deep look at the woman sitting beside him. "What'd you do?" he asked.

"Stole some money," said the woman, and grinned.

Joe grinned back. If he had been sorely pressed, he might in all his experience until now have been able to identify only his mother as a woman both pretty and lovable; in this case, however—and perhaps it was enhanced by a sort of outlaw glory—he found the woman sitting next to him much more attractive than he had before supposed. She looked nice, she had soft hair, she had a pleasant smile and not a lot of lipstick and stuff on, and her fur jacket was rich and soft against Joe's hand. Moreover, Joe knew absolutely when she grinned at him that there were not going to be any more questions about nonsense like people's ages and whether they liked school, and he found himself grinning back at her in quite a friendly manner.

"They gonna catch you?" he asked.

"Sure," said the woman. "Pretty soon now. But it was worth it."

"Why?" Joe asked; crime, he well knew, did not pay.

"See," said the woman, "I wanted to spend about two weeks having a good time there in Ashville. I wanted this coat, see? And I wanted just to buy a lot of clothes and things."

"So?" said Joe.

"So I took the money from the old tightwad I worked for and I went off to Ashville and bought some clothes and went to a lot of movies and things and had a fine time."

"Sort of a vacation," Joe said.

"Sure," the woman said. "Knew all the time they'd catch me, of course. For one thing, I always knew I had to come home again. But it was worth it!"

"How much?" said Joe.

"Two thousand dollars," said the woman.

"Boy!" said Joe.

They settled back comfortably. Joe, without more than a moment's pause to think, offered the woman his comic book about the African headhunters, and when the policeman came back through the car, eyeing them sharply, they were leaning back shoulder to shoulder, the woman apparently deep in African adventure, Joe engrossed in the adventures of a flying newspaper reporter who solved vicious gang murders.

"How is your book, Ma?" Joe said loudly as the policeman passed, and the woman laughed and said, "Fine, fine."

As the door closed behind the policeman the woman said softly, "You know, I like to see how long I can keep out of their way."

"Can't keep it up forever," Joe pointed out.

"No," said the woman, "but I'd like to go back by myself and just give them what's left of the money. I had my good time."

"Seems to me," Joe said, "that if it's the first time you did anything like this they probably wouldn't punish you so much."

"I'm not ever going to do it again," the woman said. "I mean, you sort of build up all your life for one real good time like this, and then you can take your punishment and not mind it so much."

"I don't know," Joe said reluctantly, various small sins of his own with regard to matches and his father's cigars and other people's lunch boxes crossing his mind; "seems to me that even if you do think *now* that you'll never do it again, sometimes— well, sometimes, you do it anyway." He thought. "I always *say* I'll never do it again, though."

"Well, if you do it again," the woman pointed out, "you get punished twice as bad the next time."

Joe grinned. "I took a dime out of my mother's pocketbook once," he said. "But I'll never do *that* again."

"Same thing I did," said the woman.

Joe shook his head. "If the policemen plan to spank you the way my father spanked me . . ." he said.

They were companionably silent for a while, and then the woman said, "Say, Joe, you hungry? Let's go into the dining car."

"I'm supposed to stay here," Joe said.

"But I can't go without you," the woman said. "They think I'm all right because the woman they want wouldn't be traveling with her little boy."

"Stop calling me your little boy," Joe said.

"Why?"

"Call me your son or something," Joe said. "No more little-boy stuff."

"Right," said the woman. "Anyway, I'm sure your mother wouldn't mind if you went into the dining car with *me*."

"I bet," Joe said, but he got up and followed the woman out of the car and down through the next car; people glanced up at them as they passed and then away again, and Joe thought triumphantly that they would sure stare harder if they knew that this innocent-looking woman and her son were outsmarting the cops every step they took.

They found a table in the dining car and sat down. The woman took up the menu and said, "What'll you have, Joe?"

Blissfully, Joe regarded the woman, the waiters moving quickly back and forth, the shining silverware, the white tablecloth and napkins. "Hard to say right off," he said.

"Hamburger?" said the woman. "Spaghetti? Or would you rather just have two or three desserts?"

Joe stared. "You mean, like, just blueberry pie with ice cream and a hot fudge sundae?" he asked. "Like that?"

"Sure," said the woman. "Might as well celebrate one last time."

"When I took that dime out of my mother's pocketbook," Joe told her, "I spent a nickel on gum and a nickel on candy."

"Tell me," said the woman, leaning forward earnestly, "the candy and gum—was it all right? I mean, the same as usual?"

Joe shook his head. "I was so afraid someone would see me," he said, "I ate all the candy in two mouthfuls standing on the street and I was scared to open the gum at all."

The woman nodded. "That's why I'm going back so soon, I guess," she said, and sighed.

"Well," said Joe practically, "might as well have blueberry pie first, anyway."

They ate their lunch peacefully, discussing baseball and television and what Joe wanted to be when he grew up; once the policeman passed through the car and nodded to them cheerfully, and the waiter opened his eyes wide and laughed when Joe decided to polish off his lunch with a piece of watermelon. When they had finished and the woman had paid the check, they found that they were due in Merrytown in fifteen minutes, and they hurried back to their seat to gather together Joe's comic books and suitcase.

"Thank you very much for the nice lunch," Joe said to the woman as they sat down again, and congratulated himself upon remembering to say it.

"Nothing at all," the woman said. "Aren't you my little boy?"

"Watch that little-boy stuff," Joe said warningly, and she said, "I mean, aren't you my son?"

The porter who had been delegated to keep an eye on Joe opened the car door and put his head in. He smiled reassuringly at Joe and said, "Five minutes to your station, boy."

"Thanks," said Joe. He turned to the woman. "Maybe," he said urgently, "if you tell them you're *really* sorry—"

"Wouldn't do at all," said the woman. "I really had a fine time."

"I guess so," Joe said. "But you won't do it again."

"Well, I knew when I started I'd be punished sooner or later," the woman said.

"Yeah," Joe said. "Can't get out of it now."

The train pulled slowly to a stop and Joe leaned toward the window to see if his grandfather was waiting.

"We better not get off together," the woman said; "might worry your grandpa to see you with a stranger."

"Guess so," said Joe. He stood up, and took hold of his suitcase. "Goodbye, then," he said reluctantly.

"Goodbye, Joe," said the woman. "Thanks."

"Right," said Joe, and as the train stopped he opened the door and went out onto the steps. The porter helped him to get down with his suitcase and Joe turned to see his grandfather coming down the platform.

"Hello, fellow," said his grandfather. "So you made it."

"Sure," said Joe. "No trick at all."

"Never thought you wouldn't," said his grandfather. "Your mother wants you to—"

"Telephone as soon as I get here," Joe said. "I know."

"Come along, then," his grandfather said. "Grandma's waiting at home."

He led Joe to the parking lot and helped him and his suit-case into the car. As his grandfather got into the front seat beside him, Joe turned and looked back at the train and saw the woman walking down the platform with the policeman holding her arm. Joe leaned out of the car and waved violently. "So long," he called.

"So long, Joe," the woman called back, waving.

"It's a shame the cops had to get her after all," Joe remarked to his grandfather.

His grandfather laughed. "You read too many comic books, fellow," he said. "Everyone with a policeman isn't being ar-rested—he's probably her brother or something."

"Yeah," said Joe.

"Have a good trip?" his grandfather asked. "Anything hap-pen?"

Joe thought. "Saw a boy sitting on a fence," he said. "I didn't wave to him, though."

1952

One Ordinary Day, with Peanuts

M R. JOHN PHILIP JOHNSON shut his front door behind him and went down his front steps into the bright morning with a feeling that all was well with the world on this best of all days, and wasn't the sun warm and good, and didn't his shoes feel comfortable after the resoling, and he knew that he had undoubtedly chosen the very precise tie that belonged with the day and the sun and his comfortable feet, and, after all, wasn't the world just a wonderful place? In spite of the fact that he was a small man, and though the tie was perhaps a shade vivid, Mr. Johnson radiated a feeling of well-being as he went down the steps and onto the dirty sidewalk, and he smiled at people who passed him, and some of them even smiled back. He stopped at the newsstand on the corner and bought his paper, saying "*Good* morning" with real conviction to the man who sold him the paper and the two or three other people who were lucky enough to be buying papers when Mr. Johnson skipped up. He remembered to fill his pockets with candy and peanuts, and then he set out to get himself uptown. He stopped in a flower shop and bought a carnation for his buttonhole, and stopped almost immediately afterward to give the carnation to a small child in a carriage, who looked at him dumbly, and then smiled, and Mr. Johnson smiled, and the child's mother looked at Mr. Johnson for a minute and then smiled too.

When he had gone several blocks uptown, Mr. Johnson cut across the avenue and went along a side street, chosen at random; he did not follow the same route every morning, but preferred to pursue his eventful way in wide detours, more like a puppy than a man intent upon business. It happened this morning that halfway down the block a moving van was parked, and the furniture from an upstairs apartment stood half on the sidewalk, half on the steps, while an amused group of people loitered, examining the scratches on the tables and the worn spots on the chairs, and a harassed woman, trying to watch a young child and the movers and the furniture all at the same time, gave the clear impression of endeavoring to shelter her private life from the people staring at her belongings. Mr. Johnson stopped, and for a moment joined the crowd, then he came forward and, touching his hat civilly, said, "Perhaps I can keep an eye on your little boy for you?"

The woman turned and glared at him distrustfully, and Mr. Johnson added hastily, "We'll sit right here on the steps." He beckoned to the little boy, who hesitated and then responded agreeably to Mr. Johnson's genial smile. Mr. Johnson took out a handful of peanuts from his pocket and sat on the steps with the boy, who at first refused the peanuts on the grounds that his mother did not allow him to accept food from strangers; Mr. Johnson said that probably his mother had not intended peanuts to be included, since elephants at the circus ate them, and the boy considered, and then agreed solemnly. They sat on the steps cracking peanuts in a comradely fashion, and Mr. Johnson said, "So you're moving?"

"Yep," said the boy.

"Where you going?"

"Vermont."

"Nice place. Plenty of snow there. Maple sugar, too; you like maple sugar?"

"Sure."

"Plenty of maple sugar in Vermont. You going to live on a farm?"

"Going to live with Grandpa."

"Grandpa like peanuts?"

"Sure."

"Ought to take him some," said Mr. Johnson, reaching into his pocket. "Just you and Mommy going?"

"Yep."

"Tell you what," Mr. Johnson said. "You take some peanuts to eat on the train."

The boy's mother, after glancing at them frequently, had seemingly decided that Mr. Johnson was trustworthy, because she had devoted herself wholeheartedly to seeing that the movers did not—what movers rarely do, but every housewife believes they will—crack a leg from her good table, or set a kitchen chair down on a lamp. Most of the furniture was loaded by now, and she was deep in that nervous stage when she knew there was something she had forgotten to pack—hidden away in the back of a closet somewhere, or left at a neighbor's and forgotten, or on the clothesline—and was trying to remember under stress what it was.

"This all, lady?" the chief mover said, completing her dismay. Uncertainly, she nodded.

"Want to go on the truck with the furniture, sonny?" the mover asked the boy, and laughed. The boy laughed, too, and said to Mr. Johnson, "I guess I'll have a good time at Vermont."

"Fine time," said Mr. Johnson, and stood up. "Have one more peanut before you go," he said to the boy.

The boy's mother said to Mr. Johnson, "Thank you so much; it was a great help to me."

"Nothing at all," said Mr. Johnson gallantly. "Where in Vermont are you going?

The mother looked at the little boy accusingly, as though he had given away a secret of some importance, and said unwillingly, "Greenwich."

"Lovely town," said Mr. Johnson. He took out a card, and wrote a name on the back. "Very good friend of mine lives in Greenwich," he said. "Call on him for anything you need. His wife makes the best doughnuts in town," he added soberly to the little boy.

"Swell," said the little boy.

"Goodbye," said Mr. Johnson.

He went on, stepping happily with his new-shod feet, feeling the warm sun on his back and on the top of his head. Halfway down the block he met a stray dog and fed him a peanut.

At the corner, where another wide avenue faced him, Mr. Johnson decided to go on uptown again. Moving with comparative laziness, he was passed on either side by people hurrying and frowning, and people brushed past him going the other way, clattering along to get somewhere quickly. Mr. Johnson stopped on every corner and waited patiently for the light to change, and he stepped out of the way of anyone who seemed to be in any particular hurry, but one young lady came too fast for him, and crashed wildly into him when he stooped to pat a kitten which had run out onto the sidewalk from an apartment house and was now unable to get back through the rushing feet.

"Excuse me," said the young lady, trying frantically to pick up Mr. Johnson and hurry on at the same time, "terribly sorry."

The kitten, regardless now of danger, raced back to its home. "Perfectly all right," said Mr. Johnson, adjusting himself carefully. "You seem to be in a hurry."

"Of course I'm in a hurry," said the young lady. "I'm late."

She was extremely cross, and the frown between her eyes seemed well on its way to becoming permanent. She had obviously awakened late, because she had not spent any extra time in making herself look pretty, and her dress was plain and unadorned with collar or brooch, and her lipstick was noticeably crooked. She tried to brush past Mr. Johnson, but, risking her suspicious displeasure, he took her arm and said, "Please wait."

"Look," she said ominously, "I ran into you, and your lawyer can see my lawyer and I will gladly pay all damages and all inconveniences suffered therefrom, but please this minute let me go because *I am late.*"

"Late for what?" said Mr. Johnson; he tried his winning smile on her but it did no more than keep her, he suspected, from knocking him down again.

"Late for work," she said, between her teeth. "Late for my employment. I have a job, and if I am late I lose exactly so much an hour and I cannot really afford what your pleasant conversation is costing me, be it *ever* so pleasant."

"I'll pay for it," said Mr. Johnson. Now, these were magic words, not necessarily because they were true, or because she seriously expected Mr. Johnson to pay for anything, but because Mr. Johnson's flat statement, obviously innocent of irony, could not be, coming from Mr. Johnson, anything but the statement of a responsible and truthful and respectable man.

"What *do* you mean?" she asked.

"I said that since I am obviously responsible for your being late, I shall certainly pay for it."

"Don't be silly," she said, and for the first time the frown disappeared. "*I* wouldn't expect you to pay for anything—

a few minutes ago I was offering to pay *you*. Anyway," she added, almost smiling, "it *was* my fault."

"What happens if you don't go to work?"

She stared. "I don't get paid."

"Precisely," said Mr. Johnson.

"What do you mean, precisely? If I don't show up at the office exactly twenty minutes ago I lose a dollar and twenty cents an hour, or two cents a minute or"—she thought—"almost a dime for the time I've spent talking to you."

Mr. Johnson laughed, and finally she laughed, too. "You're late already," he pointed out. "Will you give me another four cents' worth?"

"I don't understand why."

"You'll see," Mr. Johnson promised. He led her over to the side of the walk, next to the buildings, and said, "Stand here," and went out into the rush of people going both ways. Selecting and considering, as one who must make a choice involving perhaps whole years of lives, he estimated the people going by. Once he almost moved, and then at the last minute thought better of it and drew back. Finally, from half a block away, he saw what he wanted, and moved out into the center of the traffic to intercept a young man, who was hurrying, and dressed as though he had awakened late, and frowning.

"Oof," said the young man, because Mr. Johnson had thought of no better way to intercept anyone than the one the young woman had unwittingly used upon him. "Where do you think you're going?" the young man demanded from the sidewalk.

"I want to speak to you," said Mr. Johnson ominously.

The young man got up nervously, dusting himself and eyeing Mr. Johnson. "What for?" he said. "What'd *I* do?"

"That's what bothers me most about people nowadays," Mr. Johnson complained broadly to the people passing. "No matter whether they've done anything or not, they always figure someone's after them. About what you're going to do," he told the young man.

"Listen," said the young man, trying to brush past him, "I'm late, and I don't have any time to listen. Here's a dime, now get going."

"Thank you," said Mr. Johnson, pocketing the dime. "Look," he said, "what happens if you stop running?"

"I'm late," said the young man, still trying to get past Mr. Johnson, who was unexpectedly clinging.

"How much you make an hour?" Mr. Johnson demanded.

"A communist, are you?" said the young man. "Now will you please let me—"

"No," said Mr. Johnson insistently, "*how* much?"

"Dollar fifty," said the young man. "And *now* will you—"

"You like adventure?"

The young man stared, and, staring, found himself caught and held by Mr. Johnson's genial smile; he almost smiled back and then repressed it and made an effort to tear away. "I got to *hurry*," he said.

"Mystery? You like surprises? Unusual and exciting events?"

"You selling something?"

"Sure," said Mr. Johnson. "You want to take a chance?"

The young man hesitated, looking longingly up the avenue toward what might have been his destination and then, when Mr. Johnson said "I'll pay for it" with his own peculiar convincing emphasis, turned and said, "Well, okay. But I got to *see* it first, what I'm buying."

Mr. Johnson, breathing hard, led the young man over to the side, where the girl was standing; she had been watching with interest Mr. Johnson's capture of the young man and now, smiling timidly, she looked at Mr. Johnson as though prepared to be surprised at nothing.

Mr. Johnson reached into his pocket and took out his wallet. "Here," he said, and handed a bill to the girl. "This about equals your day's pay."

"But no," she said, surprised in spite of herself. "I mean, I *couldn't*."

"Please do not interrupt," Mr. Johnson told her. "And *here*," he said to the young man, "this will take care of *you*." The young man accepted the bill dazedly, but said "Probably counterfeit" to the young woman out of the side of his mouth. "Now," Mr. Johnson went on, disregarding the young man, "what is your name, miss?"

"Kent," she said helplessly. "Mildred Kent."

"Fine," said Mr. Johnson. "And you, sir?"

"Arthur Adams," said the young man stiffly.

"Splendid," said Mr. Johnson. "Now, Miss Kent, I would like you to meet Mr. Adams. Mr. Adams, Miss Kent."

Miss Kent stared, wet her lips nervously, made a gesture as though she might run, and said, "How do you do?"

Mr. Adams straightened his shoulders, scowled at Mr. Johnson, made a gesture as though *he* might run, and said, "How do you do?"

"Now, *this*," said Mr. Johnson, taking several bills from his wallet, "should be enough for the day for both of you. I would suggest, perhaps, Coney Island—although I personally am not fond of the place—or perhaps a nice lunch somewhere, and dancing, or a matinee, or even a movie, although take care to choose a really *good* one; there are *so* many bad movies these days. You might," he said, struck with an inspiration, "visit the Bronx Zoo, or the Planetarium. Anywhere, as a matter of fact," he concluded, "that you would like to go. Have a nice time."

As he started to move away, Arthur Adams, breaking from his dumbfounded stare, said, "But see here, mister, you *can't* do this. Why—how do you know—I mean, *we* don't even know—I mean, how do you know we won't just take the money and not do what you said?"

"You've taken the money," Mr. Johnson said. "You don't have to follow any of my suggestions. You may know something you prefer to do—perhaps a museum, or something."

"But suppose I just run away with it and leave her here?"

"I know you won't," said Mr. Johnson gently, "because you remembered to ask *me* that. Goodbye," he added, and went on.

As he stepped up the street, conscious of the sun on his head and his good shoes, he heard from somewhere behind him the young man saying, "Look, you know you don't *have* to if you don't want to," and the girl saying, "But unless *you* don't want to . . ." Mr. Johnson smiled to himself and then thought that he had better hurry along; when he wanted to he could move very quickly, and before the young woman had gotten around to saying, "Well, *I* will if *you* will," Mr. Johnson was several blocks away and had already stopped twice, once to help a lady lift several large packages into a taxi, and once to hand a peanut to a sea gull. By this time he was in an area of large stores and many more people, and he was buffeted constantly from either side by people hurrying and cross and late and sullen. Once he offered a peanut to a man who asked him for a dime, and once he offered a peanut to a bus driver who had stopped his bus at an intersection and had opened the window next to his seat and put out his head as though longing for fresh air and the comparative quiet of the traffic. The man wanting a dime took the peanut because Mr. Johnson had wrapped a dollar bill around it, but the bus driver took the peanut and asked ironically, "You want a transfer, Jack?"

On a busy corner Mr. Johnson encountered two young people—for one minute he thought they might be Mildred Kent and Arthur Adams—who were eagerly scanning a newspaper, their backs pressed against a storefront to avoid the people passing, their heads bent together. Mr. Johnson, whose curiosity was insatiable, leaned onto the storefront next to them and peeked over the man's shoulder; they were scanning the "Apartments Vacant" columns.

Mr. Johnson remembered the street where the woman and her little boy were going to Vermont and he tapped the man on the shoulder and said amiably, "Try down on West Seventeen. About the middle of the block, people moved out this morning."

"Say, what do you—" said the man, and then, seeing Mr. Johnson clearly, "Well, thanks. Where did you say?"

"West Seventeen," said Mr. Johnson. "About the middle of the block." He smiled again and said, "Good luck."

"Thanks," said the man.

"Thanks," said the girl as they moved off.

"Goodbye," said Mr. Johnson.

He lunched alone in a pleasant restaurant, where the food was rich, and only Mr. Johnson's excellent digestion could encompass two of their whipped-cream-and-chocolate-and-rum-cake pastries for dessert. He had three cups of coffee, tipped the waiter largely, and went out into the street again into the wonderful sunlight, his shoes still comfortable and fresh on his feet. Outside he found a beggar staring into the windows of the restaurant he had left and, carefully looking through the money in his pocket, Mr. Johnson approached the beggar and pressed some coins and a couple of bills into his hand. "It's the price of the veal cutlet lunch plus tip," said Mr. Johnson. "Goodbye."

After his lunch he rested; he walked into the nearest park and fed peanuts to the pigeons. It was late afternoon by the time he was ready to start back downtown, and he had refereed two checker games and watched a small boy and girl whose mother had fallen asleep and awakened with surprise and fear that turned to amusement when she saw Mr. Johnson. He had given away almost all of his candy, and had fed all the rest of his peanuts to the pigeons, and it was time to go home. Although the late afternoon sun was pleasant, and his shoes were still entirely comfortable, he decided to take a taxi downtown.

He had a difficult time catching a taxi, because he gave up the first three or four empty ones to people who seemed to need them more; finally, however, he stood alone on the corner and—almost like netting a frisky fish—he hailed desperately until he succeeded in catching a cab that had been proceeding with haste uptown, and seemed to draw in toward Mr. Johnson against its own will.

"Mister," the cabdriver said as Mr. Johnson climbed in, "I figured you was an omen, like. I wasn't going to pick you up at all."

"Kind of you," said Mr. Johnson ambiguously.

"If I'd of let you go it would of cost me ten bucks," said the driver.

"Really?" said Mr. Johnson.

"Yeah," said the driver. "Guy just got out of the cab, he turned around and give me ten bucks, said take this and bet it in a hurry on a horse named Vulcan, right away."

"Vulcan?" said Mr. Johnson, horrified. "A fire sign on a Wednesday?"

"What?" said the driver. "Anyway, I said to myself, if I got no fare between here and there I'd bet the ten, but if anyone looked like they needed a cab I'd take it as an omen and I'd take the ten home to the wife."

"You were very right," said Mr. Johnson heartily. "This is Wednesday, you would have lost your money. Monday, yes, or even Saturday. But never never never a fire sign on a Wednesday. Sunday would have been good, now."

"Vulcan don't run on Sunday," said the driver.

"You wait till another day," said Mr. Johnson. "Down this street, please, driver. I'll get off on the next corner."

"He *told* me Vulcan, though," said the driver.

"I'll tell you," said Mr. Johnson, hesitating with the door of the cab half open. "You take that ten dollars and I'll give you another ten dollars to go with it, and you go right ahead and bet that money on any Thursday on any horse that has a name indicating . . . let me see, Thursday . . . well, grain. Or any growing food."

"Grain?" said the driver. "You mean a horse named, like, Wheat or something?"

"Certainly," said Mr. Johnson. "Or, as a matter of fact, to make it even easier, any horse whose name includes the letters C, R, L. Perfectly simple."

"Tall Corn?" said the driver, a light in his eye. "You mean a horse named, like, Tall Corn?"

"Absolutely," said Mr. Johnson. "Here's your money."

"Tall Corn," said the driver. "Thank *you*, mister."

"Goodbye," said Mr. Johnson.

He was on his own corner, and went straight up to his apartment. He let himself in and called, "Hello?" and Mrs. Johnson answered from the kitchen, "Hello, dear, aren't you early?"

"Took a taxi home," Mr. Johnson said. "I remembered the cheesecake, too. What's for dinner?"

Mrs. Johnson came out of the kitchen and kissed him; she was a comfortable woman, and smiling as Mr. Johnson smiled. "Hard day?" she asked.

"Not very," said Mr. Johnson, hanging his coat in the closet. "How about you?"

"So-so," she said. She stood in the kitchen doorway while he settled into his easy chair and took off his good shoes and took out the paper he had bought that morning. "Here and there," she said.

"I didn't do so badly," Mr. Johnson said. "Couple young people."

"Fine," she said. "I had a little nap this afternoon, took it easy most of the day. Went into a department store this morning and accused the woman next to me of shoplifting, and had the store detective pick her up. Sent three dogs to the pound—*you* know, the usual thing. Oh, and listen," she added, remembering.

"What?" asked Mr. Johnson.

"Well," she said, "I got onto a bus and asked the driver for a transfer, and when he helped someone else first I said that he was impertinent, and quarreled with him. And then I said why wasn't he in the army, and I said it loud enough for everyone to hear, and I took his number and I turned in a complaint. Probably got him fired."

"Fine," said Mr. Johnson. "But you do look tired. Want to change over tomorrow?"

"I *would* like to," she said. "I could do with a change."

"Right," said Mr. Johnson. "What's for dinner?"

"Veal cutlet."

"Had it for lunch," said Mr. Johnson.

1955

Louisa, Please Come Home

"L OUISA," my mother's voice came over the radio; it frightened me badly for a minute. "Louisa," she said, "please come home. It's been three long long years since we saw you last; Louisa, I promise you that everything will be all right. We all miss you so. We want you back again. Louisa, please come home."

Once a year. On the anniversary of the day I ran away. Each time I heard it I was frightened again, because between one year and the next I would forget what my mother's voice sounded like, so soft and yet strange with that pleading note. I listened every year. I read the stories in the newspapers— "Louisa Tether vanished one year ago"—or two years ago, or three; I used to wait for the twentieth of June as though it were my birthday. I kept all the clippings at first, but secretly; with my picture on all the front pages I would have looked kind of strange if anyone had seen me cutting it out. Chandler, where I was hiding, was close enough to my old home so that the papers made a big fuss about all of it, but of course the reason I picked Chandler in the first place was because it was a big enough city for me to hide in.

I didn't just up and leave on the spur of the moment, you know. I always knew that I was going to run away sooner or later, and I had made plans ahead of time, for whenever I decided to go. Everything had to go right the first time, because they don't usually give you a second chance on that kind of thing and anyway if it had gone wrong I would have looked like an awful fool, and my sister Carol was never one for letting people forget it when they made fools of themselves. I admit I planned it for the day before Carol's wedding on purpose, and for a long time afterward I used to try and imagine Carol's face when she finally realized that my running away was going to leave her one bridesmaid short. The papers said that the wedding went ahead as scheduled, though, and Carol told one newspaper reporter that her sister Louisa would have wanted it that way; "She would never have meant to spoil my wedding," Carol said, knowing perfectly well that that would be exactly what I'd meant. I'm pretty sure that the first thing Carol did when they knew I was missing was go and count the wedding presents to see what I'd taken with me.

Anyway, Carol's wedding may have been fouled up, but *my* plans went fine—better, as a matter of fact, than I had ever expected. Everyone was hurrying around the house putting up flowers and asking each other if the wedding gown had been delivered, and opening up cases of champagne and wondering what they were going to do if it rained and they couldn't use the garden, and I just closed the front door behind me and started off. There was only one bad minute when Paul saw me; Paul has always lived next door and Carol hates him worse than she does me. My mother always used to say that every time I did something to make the family ashamed of me Paul was sure to be in it somewhere. For a long time they thought he had something to do with my running away, even though he told over and over again how hard I tried to duck away from him that afternoon when he met me going down the driveway. The papers kept calling him "a close friend of the family," which must have overjoyed my mother, and saying that he was being questioned about possible clues to my whereabouts. Of course he never even knew that I was running away; I told him just what I told my mother before I left—that I was going to get away from all the confusion and excitement for a while; I was going downtown and would probably have a sandwich somewhere for supper and go to a movie. He bothered me for a minute there, because of course he wanted to come too. I hadn't meant to take the bus right there on the corner but with Paul tagging after me and wanting me to wait while he got the car so we could drive out and have dinner at the Inn, I had to get away fast on the first thing that came along, so I just ran for the bus and left Paul standing there; that was the only part of my plan I had to change.

I took the bus all the way downtown, although my first plan had been to walk. It turned out much better, actually, since it didn't matter at all if anyone saw me on the bus going downtown in my own home town, and I managed to get an earlier train out. I bought a round-trip ticket; that was important, because it would make them think I was coming back; that was always the way they thought about things. If you did something you had to have a reason for it, because my mother and my father and Carol never did anything unless *they* had a reason for it, so if I bought a round-trip ticket the only possible reason would be that I was coming back. Besides, if they thought I was coming back they would not be frightened so quickly and I might have more time to hide before they came looking for me. As it happened, Carol found out I was gone that same night when she couldn't sleep and came into my room for some aspirin, so all the time I had less of a head start than I thought.

I knew that they would find out about my buying the ticket; I was not silly enough to suppose that I could steal off and not leave any traces. All my plans were based on the fact that the people who get caught are the ones who attract attention by doing something strange or noticeable, and what I intended all along was to fade into some background where they would never see me. I knew they would find out about the round-trip ticket, because it was an odd thing to do in a town where you've lived all your life, but it was the last unusual thing I did. I thought when I bought it that knowing about that round-trip ticket would be some consolation to my mother and father. They would know that no matter how long I stayed away at least I always had a ticket home. I did keep the return-trip ticket quite a while, as a matter of fact. I used to carry it in my wallet as a kind of lucky charm.

I followed everything in the papers. Mrs. Peacock and I used to read them at the breakfast table over our second cup of coffee before I went off to work.

"What do you think about this girl disappeared over in Rockville?" Mrs. Peacock would say to me, and I'd shake my head sorrowfully and say that a girl must be really crazy to leave a handsome, luxurious home like that, or that I had kind of a notion that maybe she didn't leave at all—maybe the family had her locked up somewhere because she was a homicidal maniac. Mrs. Peacock always loved anything about homicidal maniacs.

Once I picked up the paper and looked hard at the picture. "Do you think she looks something like me?" I asked Mrs. Peacock, and Mrs. Peacock leaned back and looked at me and then at the picture and then at me again and finally she shook her head and said, "No. If you wore your hair longer, and curlier, and your face was maybe a little fuller, there might be a little resemblance, but then if you looked like a homicidal maniac I wouldn't ever of let you in my house."

"I think she kind of looks like me," I said.

"You get along to work and stop being vain," Mrs. Peacock told me.

Of course when I got on the train with my round-trip ticket I had no idea how soon they'd be following me, and I suppose it was just as well, because it might have made me nervous and I might have done something wrong and spoiled everything. I knew that as soon as they gave up the notion that I was coming back to Rockville with my round-trip ticket they would think of Crain, which is the largest city that train went to, so I only stayed in Crain part of one day. I went to a big department store where they were having a store-wide sale; I figured that would land me in a crowd of shoppers and I was right; for a while there was a good chance that I'd never get any farther away from home than the ground floor of that department store in Crain. I had to fight my way through the crowd until I found the counter where they were having a sale of raincoats, and then I had to push and elbow down the counter and finally grab the raincoat I wanted right out of the hands of some old monster who couldn't have used it anyway because she was much too fat. You would have thought she had already paid for it, the way she howled. I was smart enough to have the exact change, all six dollars and eighty-nine cents, right in my hand, and I gave it to the salesgirl, grabbed the raincoat and the bag she wanted to put it in, and fought my way out again before I got crushed to death.

That raincoat was worth every cent of the six dollars and eighty-nine cents; I wore it right through until winter that year and not even a button ever came off it. I finally lost it the next spring when I left it somewhere and never got it back. It was tan, and the minute I put it on in the ladies' room of the store I began thinking of it as my "old" raincoat; that was good. I had never before owned a raincoat like that and my mother would have fainted dead away. One thing I did that I thought was kind of clever. I had left home wearing a light short coat; almost a jacket, and when I put on the raincoat of course I took off my light coat. Then all I had to do was empty the pockets of the light coat into the raincoat and carry the light coat casually over to a counter where they were having a sale of jackets and drop it on the counter as though I'd taken it off a little way to look at it and had decided against it. As far as I ever knew no one paid the slightest attention to me, and before I left the counter I saw a woman pick up my jacket and look it over; I could have told her she was getting a bargain for three ninety-eight.

It made me feel good to know that I had gotten rid of the light coat. My mother picked it out for me and even though I liked it and it was expensive it was also recognizable and I had to change it somehow. I was sure that if I put it in a bag and dropped it into a river or into a garbage truck or something like that sooner or later it would be found and even if no one saw me doing it, it would almost certainly be found, and then they would know I had changed my clothes in Crain.

That light coat never turned up. The last they ever found of me was someone in Rockville who caught a glimpse of me in the train station in Crain, and she recognized me by the light coat. They never found out where I went after that; it was partly luck and partly my clever planning. Two or three days later the papers were still reporting that I was in Crain; people thought they saw me on the streets and one girl who went into a store to buy a dress was picked up by the police and held until she could get someone to identify her. They were really looking, but they were looking for Louisa Tether, and I had stopped being Louisa Tether the minute I got rid of that light coat my mother bought me.

One thing I was relying on: there must be thousands of girls in the country on any given day who are nineteen years old, fair-haired, five feet four inches tall, and weighing one hundred and twenty-six pounds. And if there are thousands of girls like that, there must be, among those thousands, a good number who are wearing shapeless tan raincoats; I started counting tan raincoats in Crain after I left the department store and I passed four in one block, so I felt well hidden. After that I made myself even more invisible by doing just what I told my mother I was going to—I stopped in and had a sandwich in a little coffee shop, and then I went to a movie. I wasn't in any hurry at all, and rather than try to find a place to sleep that night I thought I would sleep on the train.

It's funny how no one pays any attention to you at all. There were hundreds of people who saw me that day, and even a sailor who tried to pick me up in the movie, and yet no one really *saw* me. If I had tried to check into a hotel the desk clerk might have noticed me, or if I had tried to get dinner in some fancy restaurant in that cheap raincoat I would have been conspicuous, but I was doing what any other girl looking like me and dressed like me might be doing that day. The only person who might be apt to remember me would be the man selling tickets in the railroad station, because girls looking like me in old raincoats didn't buy train tickets, usually, at eleven at night, but I had thought of that, too, of course; I bought a ticket to Amityville, sixty miles away, and what made Amityville a perfectly reasonable disguise is that at Amityville there is a college, not a little fancy place like the one I had left so recently with nobody's blessing, but a big sprawling friendly affair, where my raincoat would look perfectly at home. I told myself I was a student coming back to the college after a week end at home. We got to Amityville after midnight, but it still didn't look odd when I left the train and went into the station, because while I was in the station, having a cup of coffee and killing time, seven other girls—I counted—wearing raincoats like mine came in or went out, not seeming to think it the least bit odd to be getting on or off trains at that hour of the night. Some of them had suitcases, and I wished that I had had some way of getting a suitcase in Crain, but it would have made me noticeable in the movie, and college girls going home for week ends often don't bother; they have pajamas and an extra pair of stockings at home, and they drop a toothbrush into one of the pockets of those invaluable raincoats. So I didn't worry about the suitcase then, although I knew I would need one soon. While I was having my coffee I made my own mind change from the idea that I was a college girl coming back after a week end at home to the idea that I was a college girl who was on her way home for a few days; all the time I tried to think as much as possible like what I was pretending to be, and after all, I *had* been a college girl for a while. I was thinking that even now the letter was in the mail, traveling as fast as the U.S.

Government could make it go, right to my father to tell him why I wasn't a college student any more; I suppose that was what finally decided me to run away, the thought of what my father would think and say and do when he got that letter from the college.

That was in the paper, too. They decided that the college business was the reason for my running away, but if that had been all, I don't think I would have left. No, I had been wanting to leave for so long, ever since I can remember, making plans till I was sure they were foolproof, and that's the way they turned out to be.

Sitting there in the station at Amityville, I tried to think my self into a good reason why I was leaving college to go home on a Monday night late, when I would hardly be going home for the week end. As I say, I always tried to think as hard as I could the way that suited whatever I wanted to be, and I liked to have a good reason for what I was doing. Nobody ever asked me, but it was good to know that I could answer them if they did. I finally decided that my sister was getting married the next day and I was going home at the beginning of the week to be one of her bridesmaids. I thought that was funny. I didn't want to be going home for any sad or frightening reason, like my mother being sick, or my father being hurt in a car accident, because I would have to look sad, and that might attract attention. So I was going home for my sister's wedding. I wandered around the station as though I had nothing to do, and just happened to pass the door when another girl was going out; she had on a raincoat just like mine and anyone who happened to notice would have thought that it was me who went out. Before I bought my ticket I went into the ladies' room and got another twenty dollars out of my shoe. I had nearly three hundred dollars left of the money I had taken from my father's desk and I had most of it in my shoes because I honestly couldn't think of another safe place to carry it. All I kept in my pocketbook was just enough for whatever I had to spend next. It's uncomfortable walking around all day on a wad of bills in your shoe, but they were good solid shoes, the kind of comfortable old shoes you wear whenever you don't really care how you look, and I had put new shoelaces in them before I left home so I could tie them good and tight. You can see, I planned pretty carefully, and no little detail got left out. If they had let me plan my sister's wedding there would have been a lot less of that running around and screaming and hysterics.

I bought a ticket to Chandler, which is the biggest city in this part of the state, and the place I'd been heading for all along. It was a good place to hide because people from Rockville tended to bypass it unless they had some special reason for going there—if they couldn't find the doctors or orthodontists or psychoanalysts or dress material they wanted in Rockville or Crain, they went directly to one of the really big cities, like the state capital; Chandler was big enough to hide in, but not big enough to look like a metropolis to people from Rockville. The ticket seller in the Amityville station must have seen a good many college girls buying tickets for Chandler at all hours of the day or night because he took my money and shoved the ticket at me without even looking up.

Funny. They must have come looking for me in Chandler at some time or other, because it's not likely they would have neglected any possible place I might be, but maybe Rockville people never seriously believed that anyone would go to Chandler from choice, because I never felt for a minute that anyone was looking for me there. My picture was in the Chandler papers, of course, but as far as I ever knew no one ever looked at me twice, and I got up every morning and went to work and went shopping in the stores and went to movies with Mrs. Peacock and went out to the beach all that summer without ever being afraid of being recognized. I behaved just like everyone else, and dressed just like everyone else, and even *thought* just like everyone else, and the only person I ever saw from Rockville in three years was a friend of my mother's, and I knew *she* only came to Chandler to get her poodle bred at the kennels there. She didn't look as if she was in a state to recognize anybody but another poodle-fancier, anyway, and all I had to do was step into a doorway as she went by, and she never looked at me.

Two other college girls got on the train to Chandler when I did; maybe both of them were going home for their sisters' weddings. Neither of them was wearing a tan raincoat, but one of them had on an old blue jacket that gave the same general effect. I fell asleep as soon as the train started, and once I woke up and for a minute I wondered where I was and then I realized that I was doing it, I was actually carrying out my careful plan and had gotten better than halfway with it, and I almost laughed, there in the train with everyone asleep around me. Then I went back to sleep and didn't wake up until we got into Chandler about seven in the morning.

So there I was. I had left home just after lunch the day before, and now at seven in the morning of my sister's wedding day I was so far away, in every sense, that I *knew* they would never find me. I had all day to get myself settled in Chandler, so I started off by having breakfast in a restaurant near the station, and then went off to find a place to live, and a job. The first thing I did was buy a suitcase, and it's funny how people don't really notice you if you're buying a suitcase near a railroad station. Suitcases look *natural* near railroad stations, and I picked out one of those stores that sell a little bit of everything, and bought a cheap suitcase and a pair of stockings and some handkerchiefs and a little traveling clock, and I put everything into the suitcase and carried that. Nothing is hard to do unless you get upset or excited about it.

Later on, when Mrs. Peacock and I used to read in the papers about my disappearing, I asked her once if she thought that Louisa Tether had gotten as far as Chandler and she didn't.

"They're saying now she was kidnapped," Mrs. Peacock told me, "and that's what *I* think happened. Kidnapped, and murdered, and they do *terrible* things to young girls they kidnap."

"But the papers say there wasn't any ransom note."

"That's what they *say*." Mrs. Peacock shook her head at me. "How do we know what the family is keeping secret? Or if she was kidnapped by a homicidal maniac, why should *he* send a ransom note? Young girls like you don't know a lot of the things that go on, *I* can tell you."

"I feel kind of sorry for the girl," I said.

"You can't ever tell," Mrs. Peacock said. "Maybe she went with him willingly."

I didn't know, that first morning in Chandler, that Mrs. Peacock was going to turn up that first day, the luckiest thing that ever happened to me. I decided while I was having breakfast that I was going to be a nineteen-year-old girl from upstate with a nice family and a good background who had been saving money to come to Chandler and take a secretarial course in the business school there. I was going to have to find some kind of a job to keep on earning money while I went to school; courses at the business school wouldn't start until fall, so I would have the summer to work and save money and decide if I really wanted to take secretarial training. If I decided not to stay in Chandler I could easily go somewhere else after the fuss about my running away had died down. The raincoat looked wrong for the kind of conscientious young girl I was going to be, so I took it off and carried it over my arm. I think I did a pretty good job on my clothes, altogether. Before I left home I decided that I would have to wear a suit, as quiet and unobtrusive as I could find, and I picked out a gray suit, with a white blouse, so with just one or two small changes like a different blouse or some kind of a pin on the lapel, I could look like whoever I decided to be. Now the suit looked absolutely right for a young girl planning to take a secretarial course, and I looked like a thousand other people when I walked down the street carrying my suitcase and my raincoat over my arm; people get off trains every minute looking just like that. I bought a morning paper and stopped in a drugstore for a cup of coffee and a look to see the rooms for rent. It was all so usual—suitcase, coat, rooms for rent—that when I asked the soda clerk how to get to Primrose Street he never even looked at me. He certainly didn't care whether I ever got to Primrose Street or not, but he told me very politely where it was and what bus to take. I didn't really need to take the bus for economy, but it would have looked funny for a girl who was saving money to arrive in a taxi.

"I'll never forget how you looked that first morning," Mrs. Peacock told me once, much later. "I knew right away you were the kind of girl I like to rent rooms to—quiet, and well-mannered. But you looked almighty scared of the big city."

"I wasn't scared," I said. "I was worried about finding a nice room. My mother told me so many things to be careful about I was afraid I'd never find anything to suit her."

"*Any*body's mother could come into my house at any time

and know that her daughter was in good hands," Mrs. Peacock said, a little huffy.

But it was true. When I walked into Mrs. Peacock's rooming house on Primrose Street, and met Mrs. Peacock, I knew that I couldn't have done this part better if I'd been able to plan it. The house was old, and comfortable, and my room was nice, and Mrs. Peacock and I hit it off right away. She was very pleased with me when she heard that my mother had told me to be sure the room I found was clean and that the neighborhood was good, with no chance of rowdies following a girl if she came home after dark, and she was even more pleased when she heard that I wanted to save money and take a secretarial course so I could get a really good job and earn enough to be able to send a little home every week; Mrs. Peacock believed that children owed it to their parents to pay back some of what had been spent on them while they were growing up. By the time I had been in the house an hour Mrs. Peacock knew all about my imaginary family upstate: my mother, who was a widow, and my sister, who had just gotten married and still lived at my mother's home with her husband, and my young brother Paul, who worried my mother a good deal because he didn't seem to want to settle down. My name was Lois Taylor, I told her. By that time, I think I could have told her my real name and she would never have connected it with the girl in the paper, because by then she was feeling that she almost knew my family, and she wanted me to be sure and tell my mother when I wrote home that Mrs. Peacock would make herself personally responsible for me while I was in the city and take as good care of me as my own mother would. On top of everything else, she told me that a stationery store in the neighborhood was looking for a girl assistant, and there I was. Before I had been away from home for twenty-four hours I was an entirely new person. I was a girl named Lois Taylor who lived on Primrose Street and worked down at the stationery store.

I read in the papers one day about how a famous fortune-teller wrote to my father offering to find me and said that astral signs had convinced him that I would be found near flowers. That gave me a jolt, because of Primrose Street, but my father and Mrs. Peacock and the rest of the world thought that it meant that my body was buried somewhere. They dug up a vacant lot near the railroad station where I was last seen, and Mrs. Peacock was very disappointed when nothing turned up. Mrs. Peacock and I could not decide whether I had run away with a gangster to be a gun moll, or whether my body had been cut up and sent somewhere in a trunk. After a while they stopped looking for me, except for an occasional false clue that would turn up in a small story on the back pages of the paper, and Mrs. Peacock and I got interested in the stories about a daring daylight bank robbery in Chicago. When the anniversary of my running away came around, and I realized that I had really been gone for a year, I treated myself to a new hat and dinner downtown, and came home just in time for the evening news broadcast and my mother's voice over the radio.

"Louisa," she was saying, "please come home."

"That poor poor woman," Mrs. Peacock said. "Imagine how she must feel. They say she's never given up hope of finding her little girl alive someday."

"Do you like my new hat?" I asked her.

I had given up all idea of the secretarial course because the stationery store had decided to expand and include a lending library and a gift shop, and I was now the manager of the gift shop and if things kept on well would someday be running the whole thing; Mrs. Peacock and I talked it over, just as if she had been my mother, and we decided that I would be foolish to leave a good job to start over somewhere else. The money that I had been saving was in the bank, and Mrs. Peacock and I thought that one of these days we might pool our savings and buy a little car, or go on a trip somewhere, or even a cruise.

What I am saying is that I was free, and getting along fine, with never a thought that I knew about ever going back. It was just plain rotten bad luck that I had to meet Paul. I had gotten so I hardly ever thought about any of them any more, and never wondered what they were doing unless I happened to see some item in the papers, but there must have been something in the back of my mind remembering them all the time because I never even stopped to think; I just stood there on the street with my mouth open, and said "*Paul!*" He turned around and then of course I realized what I had done, but it was too late. He stared at me for a minute, and then frowned, and then looked puzzled; I could see him first trying to remember, and then trying to believe what he remembered; at last he said, "Is it possible?"

He said I had to go back. He said if I didn't go back he would tell them where to come and get me. He also patted me on the head and told me that there was still a reward waiting there in the bank for anyone who turned up with conclusive news of me, and he said that after he had collected the reward I was perfectly welcome to run away again, as far and as often as I liked.

Maybe I did want to go home. Maybe all that time I had been secretly waiting for a chance to get back; maybe that's why I recognized Paul on the street, in a coincidence that wouldn't have happened once in a million years—he had never even *been* to Chandler before, and was only there for a few minutes between trains; he had stepped out of the station for a minute, and found me. If I had not been passing at that minute, if he had stayed in the station where he belonged, I would never have gone back. I told Mrs. Peacock I was going home to visit my family upstate. I thought that was funny.

Paul sent a telegram to my mother and father, saying that he had found me, and we took a plane back; Paul said he was still afraid that I'd try to get away again and the safest place for me was high up in the air where he knew I couldn't get off and run.

I began to get nervous, looking out the taxi window on the way from the Rockville airport; I would have sworn that for three years I hadn't given a thought to that town, to those streets and stores and houses I used to know so well, but here I found that I remembered it all, as though I hadn't ever seen Chandler and *its* houses and streets; it was almost as though I had never been away at all. When the taxi finally turned the corner into my own street, and I saw the big old white house again, I almost cried.

"Of course I wanted to come back," I said, and Paul laughed. I thought of the return-trip ticket I had kept as a lucky charm for so long, and how I had thrown it away one day when I was emptying my pocketbook; I wondered when I threw it away whether I would ever want to go back and regret throwing away my ticket. "Everything looks just the same," I said. "I caught the bus right there on the corner; I came down the driveway that day and met you."

"If I had managed to stop you that day," Paul said, "you would probably never have tried again."

Then the taxi stopped in front of the house and my knees were shaking when I got out. I grabbed Paul's arm and said, "Paul . . . wait a minute," and he gave me a look I used to know very well, a look that said "If you back out on me now I'll I see that you never forget it," and put his arm around me because I was shivering and we went up the walk to the front door.

I wondered if they were watching us from the window. It was hard for me to imagine how my mother and father would behave in a situation like this, because they always made such a point of being quiet and dignified and proper; I thought that Mrs. Peacock would have been halfway down the walk to meet us, but here the front door ahead was still tight shut. I wondered if we would have to ring the doorbell; I had never had to ring this doorbell before. I was still wondering when Carol opened the door for us. "Carol!" I said. I was shocked because she looked so old, and then I thought that of course it had been three years since I had seen her and she probably thought that *I* looked older, too. "Carol," I said, "Oh, Carol!" I was honestly glad to see her.

She looked at me hard and then stepped back and my mother and father were standing there, waiting for me to come in. If I had not stopped to think I would have run to them, but I hesitated, not quite sure what to do, or whether they were angry with me, or hurt, or only just happy that I was back, and of course once I stopped to think about it all I could find to do was just stand there and say "Mother?" kind of uncertainly.

She came over to me and put her hands on my shoulders and looked into my face for a long time. There were tears running down her cheeks and I thought that before, when it didn't matter, I had been ready enough to cry, but now, when crying would make me look better, all I wanted to do was giggle. She looked old, and sad, and I felt simply foolish. Then she turned to Paul and said, "Oh, *Paul*—how can you do this to me again?"

Paul was frightened; I could see it. "Mrs. Tether—" he said.

"What is your name, dear?" my mother asked me.

"Louisa Tether," I said stupidly.

"No, dear," she said, very gently, "your *real* name?"

Now I could cry, but now I did not think it was going to help matters any. "Louisa Tether," I said. "That's my name."

"Why don't you people leave us alone?" Carol said; she was white, and shaking, and almost screaming because she was so angry. "We've spent years and years trying to find my lost sister and all people like you see in it is a chance to cheat us out of the reward—doesn't it mean *any*thing to you that *you* may think you have a chance for some easy money, but *we* just get hurt and heartbroken all over again? Why don't you leave us *alone*?"

"Carol," my father said, "you're frightening the poor child. Young lady," he said to me, "I honestly believe that you did not realize the cruelty of what you tried to do. You look like a nice girl; try to imagine your own mother—"

I tried to imagine my own mother; I looked straight at her.

"—if someone took advantage of her like this. I am sure you were not told that twice before, this young man—" I stopped looking at my mother and looked at Paul— "has brought us young girls who pretended to be our lost daughter; each time he protested that he had been genuinely deceived and had no thought of profit, and each time we hoped desperately that it would be the right girl. The first time we were taken in for several days. The girl *looked* like our Louisa, she *acted* like our Louisa, she knew all kinds of small family jokes and happenings it seemed impossible that anyone *but* Louisa could know, and yet she was an imposter. And the girl's mother—my wife—has suffered more each time her hopes have been raised." He put his arm around my mother—his wife—and with Carol they stood all together looking at me.

"Look," Paul said wildly, "give her a *chance*—she *knows* she's Louisa. At least give her a chance to *prove* it."

"How?" Carol asked. "I'm sure if I asked her something like—well—like what was the color of the dress she was supposed to wear at my wedding—"

"It was pink," I said. "I wanted blue but you said it had to be pink."

"I'm sure she'd know the answer," Carol went on as though I hadn't said anything. "The other girls you brought here, Paul—*they* both knew."

It wasn't going to be any good. I ought to have known it. Maybe they were so used to looking for me by now that they would rather keep on looking than have me home; maybe once my mother had looked in my face and seen there nothing of Louisa, but only the long careful concentration I had put into being Lois Taylor, there was never any chance of my looking like Louisa again.

I felt kind of sorry for Paul; he had never understood them as I well as I did and he clearly felt there was still some chance of talking them into opening their arms and crying out "Louisa! Our long-lost daughter!" and then turning around and handing him the reward; after that, we could all live happily ever after. While Paul was still trying to argue with my father I walked over a little way and looked into the living room again; I figured I wasn't going to have much time to look around and I wanted one last glimpse to take away with me; sister Carol kept a good eye on me all the time, too. I wondered what the two girls before me had tried to steal, and I wanted to tell her that if *I* ever planned to steal anything from that house I was three years too late; I could have taken whatever I wanted when I left the first time. There was nothing there I could take now, any more than there had been before. I realized that all I wanted was to stay—I wanted to stay so much that I felt like hanging onto the stair rail and screaming, but even though a temper tantrum might bring them some fleeting recollection of their dear lost Louisa I hardly thought it would persuade them to invite me to stay. I could just picture myself being dragged kicking and screaming out of my own house.

"Such a lovely old house," I said politely to my sister Carol, who was hovering around me.

"Our family has lived here for generations," she said, just as politely.

"Such beautiful furniture," I said.

"My mother is fond of antiques."

"Fingerprints," Paul was shouting. We were going to get a lawyer, I gathered, or at least Paul thought we were going to get a lawyer and I wondered how he was going to feel when he found out that we weren't. I couldn't imagine any lawyer in the world who could get my mother and my father and my sister Carol to take me back when they had made up their minds that I was not Louisa; could the law make my mother look into my face and recognize me?

I thought that there ought to be some way I could make Paul see that there was nothing we could do, and I came over and stood next to him. "Paul," I said, "can't you see that you're only making Mr. Tether angry?"

"Correct, young woman," my father said, and nodded at me to show that he thought I was being a sensible creature. "He's not doing himself any good by threatening me."

"Paul," I said, "these people don't want us here."

Paul started to say something and then for the first time in his life thought better of it and stamped off toward the door. When I turned to follow him—thinking that we'd never gotten past the front hall in my great homecoming—my father—excuse me, Mr. Tether—came up behind me and took my hand. "My daughter was younger than you are," he said to me very kindly. "but I'm sure you have a family somewhere who love you and want you to be happy. Go back to them, young lady. Let me advise you as though I were really your father—stay away from that fellow, he's wicked and he's worthless. Go back home where you belong."

"We know what it's like for a family to worry and wonder about a daughter," my mother said. "Go back to the people who love you."

That meant Mrs. Peacock, I guess.

"Just to make sure you get there," my father said, "let us help toward your fare." I tried to take my hand away, but he put a folded bill into it and I had to take it. "I hope someday," he said, "that someone will do as much for our Louisa."

"Good-by, my dear," my mother said, and she reached up and patted my cheek. "Very good luck to you."

"I hope your daughter comes back someday," I told them. "Good-by."

*

The bill was a twenty, and I gave it to Paul. It seemed little enough for all the trouble he had taken and, after all, I could go back to my job in the stationery store. My mother still talks to me on the radio, once a year, on the anniversary of the day I ran away.

"Louisa," she says, "please come home. We all want our dear girl back, and we need you and miss you so much. Your mother and father love you and will never forget you. Louisa, please come home."

1960

The Little House

I'LL have to get some decent lights, was her first thought, and her second: *and* a dog or something, or at least a bird, anything *alive*. She stood in the little hall beside her suitcase, in a little house that belonged to her, her first home. She held the front-door key in her hand, and she knew, remembering her aunt, that the back-door key hung, labeled, from a hook beside the back door, and the side-door key hung from a hook beside the side door, and the porch-door key hung from a hook beside the porch door, and the cellar-door key hung from a hook beside the cellar door, and perhaps when she slammed the front door behind her all the keys swung gently, once, back and forth. Anything that can move and make some kind of a friendly noise, she thought, maybe a monkey or a cat or anything not stuffed—as she realized that she was staring, hypnotized, at the moose head over the hall mirror.

Wanting to make some kind of a noise in the silence, she coughed, and the small sound moved dustily into the darkness of the house. Well, I'm here, she told herself, and it belongs to me and I can do anything I want here and no one can ever make me leave, because it's mine. She moved to touch the carved newel post at the foot of the narrow stairway—it was hers, it belonged to her—and felt a sudden joy at the tangible reality of the little house; this is really something to own, she thought, thank you, Aunt. And my goodness, she thought, brushing her hand, couldn't my very own house do with a little dusting; she smiled to herself at the prospect of the very pleasant work she would do tomorrow and the day after, and for all the days after that, living in her house and keeping it clean and fresh.

Wanting to whistle, to do something to bring noise and movement into the house, she turned and opened the door on her right and stepped into the dim crowded parlor. I wish I didn't have to see it first at dusk, she thought, Aunt certainly didn't believe in bright light; I wonder how she ever found her way around this room. A dim shape on a low table beside the door resolved itself into a squat lamp; when she pressed the switch a low radiance came into the room and she was able to leave the spot by the door and venture into what had clearly been her aunt's favorite room. The parlor had certainly not been touched, or even opened or lighted, since her aunt's death; a tea towel, half-hemmed, lay on the arm of a chair, and she felt a sudden tenderness and a half-shame at the thought of the numbers of tea towels, hemmed, which had come to her at birthdays and Christmases over the years and now lay still in their tissue paper, at the bottom of her trunk still at the railroad station. At least I'll use her towels now, in her own house, she thought, and then: but it's my house now. She would stack the tea towels neatly in the linen closet, she might even finish hemming this one, and she took it up and folded it neatly, leaving the needle still tucked in where her aunt had left it, to await the time when she should sit quietly in her chair, in her parlor in her house, and take up her sewing. Her aunt's glasses lay on the table; had her aunt put down her sewing and taken off her glasses at the very end? Prepared, neatly, to die?

Don't think about it, she told herself sternly, she's gone now, and soon the house will be busy again; I'll clear away tomorrow, when it's not so dark; how did she ever manage to sew in here with this light? She put the half-hemmed towel over the glasses to hide them, and took up a little picture in a silver frame; her aunt, she recognized, and some smiling woman friend, standing together under trees; this must have been important to Aunt, she thought, I'll put it away safely somewhere. The house was distantly familiar to her; she had come here sometimes as a child, but that was long ago, and the memories of the house and her aunt were overlaid with cynicism and melancholy and the wearying disappointments of many years; perhaps it was the longing to return to the laughter of childhood which had brought her here so eagerly to take up her inheritance. The music box was in the corner where it had always been and, touching it gently, she brought from it one remote, faintly sweet, jangle of a note. Tomorrow I'll play the music box, she promised herself, with the windows wide open and the good fresh air blowing through and all the bric-a-brac safely stowed away in the attic; this could be such a pretty room—and she turned, her head to one side, considering— once I take out the junk and the clutter. I can keep the old couch and maybe have it recovered in something colorful, and the big chair can stay, and perhaps one or two of these tiny tables; the mantel is fine, and I'll keep a bowl of flowers there, flowers from my own garden. I'll have a great fire in the fireplace and I'll sit here with my dog and my needlework—and two or three good floor lamps; I'll get those tomorrow—and never be unhappy again. Tomorrow, lamps, and air the room, and play the music box.

Leaving a dim trail of lighted lamps behind her, she went from the parlor through a little sunporch where a magazine lay open on the table; Aunt never finished the story she was reading, she thought, and closed the magazine quickly and set it in order on the pile on the table; I'll subscribe to magazines, she thought, and the local newspaper, and take books from the village library. From the sunporch she went into the kitchen and remembered to turn on the light by pulling the cord hanging from the middle of the ceiling; her aunt had left a tomato ripening on the window sill, and it scented the kitchen with a strong air of decay. She shivered, and realized that the back door was standing open, and remembered her aunt saying, as clearly as though she heard it now, "Darn that door, I wish I could remember to get that latch looked at."

And now I have to do it for her, she thought; I'll get a man in the morning. She found a paper bag in the pantry drawer where paper bags had always been kept, and scraped the rotten tomato from the window sill and carried the bag to the garbage pail by the back steps. When she came back she slammed the back door correctly and the latch caught; the key was hanging where she knew it had been, beside the door, and she took it down and locked the door; I'm alone in the house, after all, she thought with a little chill touching the back of her neck.

The cup from which her aunt had drunk her last cup of tea lay, washed and long since drained dry, beside the sink; perhaps she put her sewing down, she thought, and came to the kitchen to make a cup of tea before going to bed; I wonder where they found her; she always had a cup of tea at night, all alone; I wish I had come to see her at least once. The lovely old dishes are mine now, she thought, the family dishes and the cut glass and the silver tea service. Her aunt's sweater hung from the knob of the cellar door, as though she had only just this minute taken it off, and her apron hung from a hook beside the sink. Aunt always put things away, she thought, and she never came back for her sweater. She remembered dainty little hand-embroidered aprons in the hall chest, and thought of herself, aproned, serving a charming tea from the old tea service, using the thin painted cups, perhaps to neighbors who had come to see her delightful, open, light, little house; I must have a cocktail party too, she thought; I'll bet there's nothing in the house but dandelion wine.

It would seem strange at first, coming downstairs in the morning to make herself breakfast in her aunt's kitchen, and she suddenly remembered herself, very small, eating oatmeal at the kitchen table; it would seem strange to be using her aunt's dishes, and the big old coffeepot—although perhaps not the coffeepot, she thought; it had the look of something crotchety and temperamental, not willing to submit docilely to a strange hand; I'll have tea tomorrow morning, and get a new little coffeepot just for me. Lamps, coffeepot, man to fix the latch.

After a moment's thought she took her aunt's sweater and apron and bundled them together and carried them out to the garbage pail. It isn't as though they were any good to anyone, she told herself reassuringly; *all* her clothes will have to be thrown away, and she pictured herself standing in her bright parlor in her smart city clothes telling her laughing friends about the little house; "Well, you should have seen it when I came," she would tell them, "you should have seen the place the first night I walked in. Murky little lamps, and the place simply crawling with bric-a-brac, and a stuffed moose head—*really*, a stuffed moose head, I mean it—and Aunt's sewing on the table, and what was positively her last cup in the sink." Will I tell them, she wondered, about how Aunt set her sewing down when she was ready to die? And never finished her magazine, and hung up her sweater, and felt her heart go? "You should have seen it when I came," she would tell them, sipping from her glass, "dark, and dismal; I used to come here when I was a child, but I honestly never remembered it as such a mess. It couldn't have come as more of a surprise, her leaving me the house, I never dreamed of having it."

Suddenly guilty, she touched the cold coffeepot with a gentle finger. I'll clean you tomorrow, she thought; I'm sorry I never got to the funeral, I should have tried to come. Tomorrow I'll start cleaning. Then she whirled, startled, at the knock at the back door; I hadn't realized it was so quiet here, she thought, and breathed again and moved quickly to the door. "Who is it?" she said. "Just a minute." Her hands shaking, she unlocked and opened the door. "Who is it?" she said into the darkness, and then smiled timidly at the two old faces regarding her. "Oh," she said, "how do you do?"

"You'll be the niece? Miss Elizabeth?"

"Yes." Two old pussycats, she thought, wearing hats with flowers, couldn't wait to get a look at me. "Hello," she said, thinking, I'm the charming niece Elizabeth, and this is my house now.

"We are the Dolson sisters. I am Miss Amanda Dolson. This is my sister Miss Caroline Dolson."

"We're your nearest neighbors." Miss Caroline put a thin brown hand on Elizabeth's sleeve. "We live down the lane. We were your poor poor aunt's nearest neighbors. But we didn't hear anything."

Miss Amanda moved a little forward and Elizabeth stepped back. "Won't you come in?" Elizabeth asked, remembering her manners. "Come into the parlor. I was just looking at the house. I only just got here," she said, moving backward, "I was just turning on some lights."

"We saw the lights." Miss Amanda went unerringly toward the little parlor. "This is not our formal call, you understand; we pay our calls by day. But I confess we wondered at the lights."

"We thought *he* had come back." Miss Caroline's hand was on Elizabeth's sleeve again, as though she were leading Elizabeth to the parlor. "They say they do, you know."

Miss Amanda seated herself, as though by right of long acquaintance, on the soft chair by the low table, and Miss Caroline took the only other comfortable chair; my own house indeed, Elizabeth thought, and sat down uneasily on a stiff chair near the door; I must get lamps first thing tomorrow, she thought, the better to see people with.

"Have you lived here long?" she asked foolishly.

"I hope you don't plan to change things," Miss Amanda said. "Aunt loved her little house, you know."

"I haven't had much time to plan."

"You'll find everything just the way she left it. I myself took her pocketbook upstairs and put it into the drawer of the commode. Otherwise nothing has been touched. Except the body, of course."

Oh, that's not still here? she wanted to ask, but said instead, "I used to come here when I was a child."

"So he wasn't after her money," Miss Caroline said. "Sister took her pocketbook off the kitchen table; I saw her do it. She took it upstairs and nothing was missing."

Miss Amanda leaned a little forward. "You'll be bringing in television sets? From the city? Radios?"

"I hadn't thought much about it yet."

"We'll be able to hear your television set, no doubt. We are your closest neighbors and we see your lights; no doubt your television set will be very loud."

"We would have heard if she had screamed," Miss Caroline said, lifting her thin hand in emphasis. "They say she must have recognized him, and indeed it is my belief that Sheriff Knowlton has a very shrewd notion who he is. It is my belief that we all have our suspicions."

"Sister, this is gossip. Miss Elizabeth detests gossip."

"We were here the first thing in the morning, Miss Elizabeth, and I spoke to the Sheriff myself."

"Sister, Miss Elizabeth does not trouble her mind with wild stories. Let Miss Elizabeth remember Aunt as happy."

"I don't understand." Elizabeth looked from one of the tight old faces to the other; the two old bats, she thought, and said, "My aunt died of a heart attack, they said."

"It is *my* belief—"

"My sister is fond of gossip, Miss Elizabeth. I suppose you'll be packing away all of Aunt's pretty things?"

Elizabeth glanced at the table near her. A pink china box, a glass paperweight, a crocheted doily on which rested a set of blue porcelain kittens. "Some of them," she said.

"To make room for the television set. Poor Aunt; she thought a good deal of her small possessions." She frowned. "You won't find an ash tray in here."

Elizabeth put her cigarette down defiantly on the lid of the small pink box.

"Sister," Miss Amanda said, "bring Miss Elizabeth a saucer from the kitchen, from the daily china. Not the floral set."

Miss Caroline, looking shocked, hurried from the room, holding her heavy skirt away from the tables and Elizabeth's cigarette. Miss Amanda leaned forward again. "I do not permit my sister to gossip, Miss Elizabeth. You are wrong to encourage her."

"But what is she trying to say about my aunt?"

"Aunt has been dead and buried for two months. You were not, I think, at the funeral?"

"I couldn't get away."

"From the city. Exactly. I daresay you were delighted to have the house."

"Indeed I was."

"I suppose Aunt could hardly have done otherwise. Sister, give Miss Elizabeth the saucer. Quickly, before the room catches fire."

"Thank you." Elizabeth took the chipped saucer from Miss Caroline and put out her cigarette; ash trays, she thought, lamps, ash trays, coffeepot.

"Her apron is gone," Miss Caroline told her sister.

"Already?" Miss Amanda turned to look fully at Elizabeth. "I am afraid we will see many changes, Sister. And now Miss Elizabeth is waiting for us to leave. Miss Elizabeth is determined to begin her packing tonight."

"Really," Elizabeth said helplessly, gesturing, "really—"

"All of Aunt's pretty things. This is not our formal call, Miss Elizabeth." Miss Amanda rose grandly, and Miss Caroline followed. "You will see us within three days. Poor Aunt."

Elizabeth followed them back to the kitchen, "Really," she said again, and "Please don't leave," but Miss Amanda overrode her.

"This door does not latch properly," Miss Amanda said. "See that it is securely locked behind us."

"They say that's how he got in," Miss Caroline whispered. "Keep it locked *always*."

"Good night, Miss Elizabeth. I am happy to know that you plan to keep the house well lighted. We see your lights, you know, from our windows."

"Good night," Miss Caroline said, turning to put her hand once more on Elizabeth's arm. "Locked, *remember*."

"Good night," Elizabeth said, "good night." Old bats, she was thinking, old bats. Sooner or later I'm going to have words with them; they're probably the pests of the neighborhood. She watched as they went side by side down the path, their heads not yet turned to one another, their long skirts swinging. "Good night," she called once more, but neither of them turned. Old bats, she thought, and slammed the door correctly; the latch caught, and she took down the key and locked it. I'll give them the moose head, she thought, my aunt would have wanted them to have it. It's late, I've got to find myself a bed, I haven't even been upstairs yet. I'll give them each a piece of the junk; my very own, my pretty little house.

Humming happily, she turned back toward the parlor; I wonder where they found her? she thought suddenly; was it in the parlor? She stopped in the doorway, staring at the soft chair and wondering: did he come up behind her there? While she was sewing? And then pick up her glasses from the floor and set them on the table? Perhaps she was reading her magazine when he caught her, perhaps she had just washed her cup and saucer and was turning back to get her sweater; would it have been this quiet in the house? Is it always this quiet?

"No, no," she said aloud. "This is silly. Tomorrow I'll get a dog."

Pressing her lips together firmly, she walked across the room and turned off the light, then came back and turned off the lamp beside the door, and the soft darkness fell around her; did they find her here? she wondered as she went through the sunporch, and then said aloud "This is silly," and turned off the light. With the darkness following close behind her she came back to the kitchen and checked that the back door was securely locked. He won't get in *here* again, she thought, and shivered.

There was no light on the stairs. I can leave the kitchen light on all night, she thought, but no; they'll see it from their windows; did he wait for her on the stairs? Pressing against the wall, the kitchen light still burning dimly behind her, she went up the stairs, staring into the darkness, feeling her way with her feet. At the top was only darkness, and she put out her hands blindly; there was a wall, and then a door, and she ran her hand down the side of the door until she had the doorknob in her fingers.

What's waiting behind the door? she thought, and turned and fled wildly down the stairs and into the lighted kitchen with the locked back door. "Don't leave me here alone," she said, turning to look behind her, "please don't leave me here alone."

Miss Amanda and Miss Caroline cuddled on either side of their warm little stove. Miss Amanda had a piece of fruitcake and a cup of tea and Miss Caroline had a piece of marshmallow cake and a cup of tea. "Just the same," Miss Caroline was saying, "she should have served something."

"City ways."

"She could have offered some of the city cake she brought with her. The coffeepot was right there in the kitchen. It's not polite to wait until the company goes and then eat by yourself."

"It's city ways, Sister. I doubt she'll be a good neighbor for us."

"Her aunt would not have done it."

"When I think of her searching that little house for valuables I feel very sorry for Aunt."

Miss Caroline set down her plate, and nodded to herself. "She might not like it here," she said. "Perhaps she won't stay."

1964

The Bus

O<small>LD</small> Miss Harper was going home, although the night was wet and nasty. Miss Harper disliked traveling at any time, and she particularly disliked traveling on this dirty small bus which was her only way of getting home; she had frequently complained to the bus company about their service because it seemed that no matter where she wanted to go, they had no respectable bus to carry her. Getting away from home was bad enough—Miss Harper was fond of pointing out to the bus company—but getting home always seemed very close to impossible. Tonight Miss Harper had no choice: if she did not go home by this particular bus she could not go for another day. Annoyed, tired, depressed, she tapped irritably on the counter of the little tobacco store which served also as the bus station. Sir, she was thinking, beginning her letter of complaint, although I am an elderly lady of modest circumstances and must curtail my fondness for travel, let me point out that your bus service falls far below . . .

Outside, the bus stirred noisily, clearly not anxious to be moving; Miss Harper thought she could already hear the weary sound of its springs sinking out of shape. I just can't make this trip again, Miss Harper thought, even seeing Stephanie isn't worth it, they really go out of their way to make you uncomfortable. "Can I get my ticket, please?" she said sharply, and the old man at the other end of the counter put down his paper and gave her a look of hatred.

Miss Harper ordered her ticket, deploring her own cross voice, and the old man slapped it down on the counter in front of her and said, "You got three minutes before the bus leaves."

He'd love to tell me I missed it, Miss Harper thought, and made a point of counting her change.

The rain was beating down, and Miss Harper hurried the few exposed steps to the door of the bus. The driver was slow in opening the door and as Miss Harper climbed in she was thinking, Sir, I shall never travel with your company again.

Your ticket salesmen are ugly, your drivers are surly, your vehicles indescribably filthy . . .

There were already several people sitting in the bus, and Miss Harper wondered where they could possibly be going; were there really this many small towns served only by this bus? Were there really other people who would endure this kind of trip to get somewhere, even home? I'm very out of sorts, Miss Harper thought, very out of sorts; it's too strenuous a visit for a woman of my age; I need to get home. She thought of a hot bath and a cup of tea and her own bed, and sighed. No one offered to help her put her suitcase on the rack, and she glanced over her shoulder at the driver sitting with his back turned and thought, he'd probably rather put me off the bus than help me, and then, perceiving her own ill nature, smiled. The bus company might write a letter of complaint about *me*, she told herself and felt better. She had providentially taken a sleeping pill before leaving for the bus station, hoping to sleep through as much of the trip as possible, and at last, sitting near the back, she promised herself that it would not be unbearably long before she had a bath and a cup of tea, and tried to compose the bus company's letter of complaint. Madam, a lady of your experience and advanced age ought surely to be aware of the problems confronting a poor but honest little company which wants only . . .

She was aware that the bus had started, because she was rocked and bounced in her seat, and the feeling of rattling and throbbing beneath the soles of her shoes stayed with her even when she slept at last. She lay back uneasily, her head resting on the seat back, moving back and forth with the motion of the bus, and around her other people slept, or spoke softly, or stared blankly out the windows at the passing lights and the rain.

Sometime during her sleep Miss Harper was jostled by someone moving into the seat behind her, her head was pushed and her hat disarranged; for a minute, bewildered by sleep, Miss Harper clutched at her hat, and said vaguely, "Who?"

"Go back to sleep," a young voice said, and giggled. "I'm just running away from home, that's all."

Miss Harper was not awake, but she opened her eyes a little and looked up to the ceiling of the bus. "That's wrong," Miss Harper said as clearly as she could. "That's wrong. Go back."

There was another giggle. "Too late," the voice said. "Go back to sleep."

Miss Harper did. She slept uncomfortably and awkwardly, her mouth a little open. Sometime, perhaps an hour later, her head was jostled again and the voice said, "I think I'm going to get off here. 'By now."

"You'll be sorry," Miss Harper said, asleep. "Go back."

Then, still later, the bus driver was shaking her. "Look, lady," he was saying, "I'm not an alarm clock. Wake up and get off the bus."

"What?" Miss Harper stirred, opened her eyes, felt for her pocketbook.

"I'm not an alarm clock," the driver said. His voice was harsh and tired. "I'm not an alarm clock. Get off the bus."

"What?" said Miss Harper again.

"This is as far as you go. You got a ticket to here. You've arrived. And I am not an alarm clock waking up people to tell them when it's time to get off; you got here, lady, and it's not part of my job to carry you off the bus. I'm not—"

"I intend to report you," Miss Harper said, awake. She felt for her pocketbook and found it in her lap, moved her feet, straightened her hat. She was stiff and moving was difficult.

"Report me. But from somewhere else. I got a bus to run. Now will you please get off so I can go on my way?"

His voice was loud, and Miss Harper was sickeningly aware of faces turned toward her from along the bus, grins, amused comments. The driver turned and stamped off down the bus to his seat, saying, "She thinks I'm an alarm clock," and Miss Harper, without assistance and moving clumsily, took down her suitcase and struggled with it down the aisle. Her suitcase banged against seats, and she knew that people were staring at her; she was terribly afraid that she might stumble and fall.

"I'll certainly report you," she said to the driver, who shrugged.

"Come on, lady," he said. "It's the middle of the night and I got a bus to run."

"You ought to be *ashamed* of yourself," Miss Harper said wildly, wanting to cry.

"Lady," the driver said with elaborate patience, "please get off my bus."

The door was open, and Miss Harper eased herself and her suitcase onto the steep step. "She thinks everyone's an alarm clock, got to see she gets off the bus," the driver said behind her, and Miss Harper stepped onto the ground. Suitcase, pocketbook, gloves, hat; she had them all. She had barely taken stock when the bus started with a jerk, almost throwing her backward, and Miss Harper, for the first time in her life, wanted to run and shake her fist at someone. I'll report him, she thought, I'll see that he loses his job, and then she realized that she was in the wrong place.

Standing quite still in the rain and the darkness Miss Harper became aware that she was not at the bus corner of her town where the bus should have left her. She was on an empty crossroads in the rain. There were no stores, no lights, no taxis, no people. There was nothing, in fact, but a wet dirt road under her feet and a signpost where two roads came together. Don't panic, Miss Harper told herself, almost whispering, don't panic; it's all right, it's all right, you'll see that it's all right, don't be frightened.

She took a few steps in the direction the bus had gone, but it was out of sight and when Miss Harper called falteringly, "Come back," and, "Help," there was no answer to the shocking sound of her own voice out loud except the steady drive of the rain. I sound old, she thought, but I will not panic. She turned in a circle, her suitcase in her hand, and told herself, don't panic, it's all right.

There was no shelter in sight, but the signpost said RICKET'S LANDING; so that's where I am, Miss Harper thought, I've come to Ricket's Landing and I don't like it here. She set her suitcase down next to the signpost and tried to see down the road; perhaps there might be a house, or even some kind of a barn or shed where she could get out of the rain. She was crying a little, and lost and hopeless, saying Please, won't someone come? when she saw headlights far off down the road and realized that someone was really coming to help her. She ran to the middle of the road and stood waving, her gloves wet and her pocketbook draggled. "Here," she called, "here I am, please come and help me."

Through the sound of the rain she could hear the motor, and then the headlights caught her and, suddenly embarrassed, she put her pocketbook in front of her face while the lights were on her. The lights belonged to a small truck, and it came to an abrupt stop beside her and the window near her was rolled down and a man's voice said furiously, "You want to get killed? You trying to get killed or something? What you doing in the middle of the road, trying to get killed?" The young man turned and spoke to the driver. "It's some dame. Running out in the road like that."

"Please," Miss Harper said, as he seemed almost about to close the window again, "please help me. The bus put me off here when it wasn't my stop and I'm lost."

"Lost?" The young man laughed richly. "First I ever heard anyone getting lost in Ricket's Landing. Mostly they have trouble *finding* it." He laughed again, and the driver, leaning forward over the steering wheel to look curiously at Miss Harper, laughed too. Miss Harper put on a willing smile, and said, "Can you take me somewhere? Perhaps a bus station?"

"No bus station." The young man shook his head profoundly. "Bus comes through here every night, stops if he's got any passengers."

"Well," Miss Harper's voice rose in spite of herself; she was suddenly afraid of antagonizing these young men; perhaps they might even leave her here where they found her, in the wet and dark. "Please," she said, "can I get in with you, out of the rain?"

The two young men looked at each other. "Take her down to the old lady's," one of them said.

"She's pretty wet to get in the truck," the other one said.

"Please," Miss Harper said, "I'll be glad to pay you what I can."

"We'll take you to the old lady," the driver said. "Come on, move over," he said to the other young man.

"Wait, my suitcase." Miss Harper ran back to the signpost, no longer caring how she must look, stumbling about in the rain, and brought her suitcase over to the truck.

"That's awful wet," the young man said. He opened the door and took the suitcase from Miss Harper. "I'll just throw it in the back," he said, and turned and tossed the suitcase into the back of the truck; Miss Harper heard the sodden thud of its landing, and wondered what things would look like when she unpacked; my bottle of cologne, she thought despairingly. "Get *in*," the young man said, and, "My God, you're wet."

Miss Harper had never climbed up into a truck before, and her skirt was tight and her gloves slippery from the rain. Without help from the young man she put one knee on the high step and somehow hoisted herself in; this cannot be happening to me, she thought clearly. The young man pulled away fastidiously as Miss Harper slid onto the seat next to him.

"You are pretty wet," the driver said, leaning over the wheel to look around at Miss Harper. "Why were you out in the rain like that?"

"The bus driver." Miss Harper began to peel off her gloves; somehow she had to make an attempt to dry herself. "He told me it was my stop."

"That would be Johnny Talbot," the driver said to the other young man. "He drives that bus."

"Well, I'm going to report him," Miss Harper said. There was a little silence in the truck, and then the driver said, "Johnny's a good guy. He means all right."

"He's a bad bus driver," Miss Harper said sharply.

The truck did not move. "You don't want to report old Johnny," the driver said.

"I most certainly—" Miss Harper began, and then stopped. Where am I? she thought, what is happening to me? "No," she said at last, "I won't report old Johnny."

The driver started the truck, and they moved slowly down the road, through the mud and the rain. The windshield wipers swept back and forth hypnotically, there was a narrow line of light ahead from their headlights, and Miss Harper thought, what is happening to me? She stirred, and the young man next to her caught his breath irritably and drew back. "She's soaking wet," he said to the driver. "I'm wet already."

"We're going down to the old lady's," the driver said. "She'll know what to do."

"What old lady?" Miss Harper did not dare to move, even

turn her head. "Is there any kind of a bus station? Or even a taxi?"

"You could," the driver said consideringly, "you could wait and catch that same bus tomorrow night when it goes through. Johnny'll be driving her."

"I just want to get home as soon as possible," Miss Harper said. The truck seat was dreadfully uncomfortable, she felt steamy and sticky and chilled through, and home seemed so far away that perhaps it did not exist at all.

"Just down the road a mile or so," the driver said reassuringly.

"I've never heard of Ricket's Landing," Miss Harper said. "I can't imagine how he came to put me off there."

"Maybe somebody else was supposed to get off there and he thought it was you by mistake." This deduction seemed to tax the young man's mind to the utmost, because he said, "See, someone else might of been supposed to get off instead of you."

"Then *he's* still on the bus," said the driver, and they were both silent, appalled.

Ahead of them a light flickered, showing dimly through the rain, and the driver pointed and said, "There, that's where we're going." As they came closer Miss Harper was aware of a growing dismay. The light belonged to what seemed to be a roadhouse, and Miss Harper had never been inside a road-house in her life. The house itself was only a dim shape looming in the darkness, and the light, over the side door, illuminated only a sign, hanging crooked, which read BEER *Bar & Grill.*

"Is there anywhere else I could go?" Miss Harper asked timidly, clutching her pocketbook. "I'm not at all sure, you know, that I ought—"

"Not many people here tonight," the driver said, turning the truck into the driveway and pulling up in the parking lot which had once, Miss Harper was sad to see, been a garden. "Rain, probably."

Peering through the window and the rain, Miss Harper felt, suddenly, a warm stir of recognition, of welcome; it's the house, she thought, why, of course, the house is lovely. It had clearly been an old mansion once, solidly and handsomely built, with the balance and style that belonged to a good house of an older time. "Why?" Miss Harper asked, wanting to know why such a good house should have a light tacked on over the side door, and a sign hanging crooked but saying BEER *Bar & Grill*; "Why?" asked Miss Harper, but the driver said, "This is where you wanted to go. Get her suitcase," he told the other young man.

"In here?" asked Miss Harper, feeling a kind of indignation on behalf of the fine old house, "into this saloon?" Why, I used to live in a house like this, she thought, what are they doing to our old houses?

The driver laughed. "You'll be safe," he said.

Carrying her suitcase and her pocketbook Miss Harper followed the two young men to the lighted door and passed under the crooked sign. Shameful, she thought, they haven't even bothered to take care of the place; it needs paint and tightening all around and probably a new roof, and then the driver said, "Come on, come on," and pushed open the heavy door.

"I used to live in a house like this," Miss Harper said, and the young men laughed.

"I bet you did," one of them said, and Miss Harper stopped in the doorway, staring, and realized how strange she must have sounded. Where there had certainly once been comfortable rooms, high-ceilinged and square, with tall doors and polished floors, there was now one large dirty room, with a counter running along one side and half a dozen battered tables; there was a jukebox in a corner and torn linoleum on the floor. "Oh, no," Miss Harper said. The room smelled unpleasant, and the rain slapped against the bare windows.

Sitting around the tables and standing around the jukebox were perhaps a dozen young people, resembling the two who had brought Miss Harper here, all looking oddly alike, all talking and laughing flatly. Miss Harper leaned back against the door; for a minute she thought they were laughing about her. She was wet and disheartened and these noisy people did not belong at all in the old house. Then the driver turned and gestured to her. "Come and meet the old lady," he said, and then, to the room at large, "Look, we brought company."

"Please," Miss Harper said, but no one had given her more than a glance. With her suitcase and her pocketbook she followed the two young men across to the counter; her suitcase bumped against her legs and she thought, I must not fall down.

"Belle, Belle," the driver said, "look at the stray cat we found."

An enormous woman swung around in her seat at the end of the counter, and looked at Miss Harper; looking up and down, looking at the suitcase and Miss Harper's wet hat and wet shoes, looking at Miss Harper's pocketbook and gloves squeezed in her hand, the woman seemed hardly to move her eyes; it was almost as though she absorbed Miss Harper without any particular effort. "Hell you say," the woman said at last. Her voice was surprisingly soft. "Hell you say."

"She's wet," the second young man said; the two young men stood one on either side of Miss Harper, presenting her, and the enormous woman looked her up and down. "Please," Miss Harper said; here was a woman at least, someone who might understand and sympathize, "please, they put me off my bus at the wrong stop and I can't seem to find my way home. Please."

"Hell you say," the woman said, and laughed, a gentle laugh. "She sure is wet," she said.

"Please," Miss Harper said.

"You'll take care of her?" the driver asked. He turned and smiled down at Miss Harper, obviously waiting, and, remembering, Miss Harper fumbled in her pocketbook for her wallet. How much, she was wondering, not wanting to ask, it was such a short ride, but if they hadn't come I might have gotten pneumonia, and paid all those doctor's bills; I have caught cold, she thought with great clarity, and chose two five-dollar bills from her wallet. They can't argue over five dollars each, she thought, and sneezed. The two young men and the large woman were watching her with great interest, and all of them saw that after Miss Harper took out the two five-dollar bills there were a single and two tens left in the wallet. The money was not wet. I suppose I should be grateful for that, Miss Harper thought, moving slowly. She handed a five-dollar bill to each young man and felt that they glanced at one another over her head.

"Thanks," the driver said; I could have gotten away with a

dollar each, Miss Harper thought. "Thanks," the driver said
again, and the other young man said, "Say, thanks."

"Thank *you*," Miss Harper said formally.

"I'll put you up for the night," the woman said. "You can
sleep here. Go tomorrow." She looked Miss Harper up and
down again. "Dry off a little," she said.

"Is there anywhere else?" Then, afraid that this might seem
ungracious, Miss Harper said, "I mean, is there any way of
going on tonight? I don't want to impose."

"We got rooms for rent." The woman half turned back to
the counter. "Cost you ten for the night."

She's leaving me bus fare home, Miss Harper thought; I
suppose I should be grateful. "I'd better, I guess," she said,
taking out her wallet again. "I mean, thank you."

The woman accepted the bill and half turned back to the
counter. "Upstairs," she said. "Take your choice. No one's
around." She glanced sideways at Miss Harper. "I'll see you
get a cup of coffee in the morning. I wouldn't turn a dog out
without a cup of coffee."

"Thank you." Miss Harper knew where the staircase would
be, and she turned and, carrying her suitcase and her pocketbook, went to what had once been the front hall and there was
the staircase, so lovely in its still proportions that she caught
her breath. She turned back and saw the large woman staring
at her, and said, "I used to live in a house like this. Built about
the same time, I guess. One of those good old houses that
were made to stand forever, and where people—"

"Hell you say," the woman said, and turned back to the
counter.

The young people scattered around the big room were talking; in one corner a group surrounded the two who had
brought Miss Harper and now and then they laughed. Miss
Harper was touched with a little sadness now, looking at them,
so at home in the big ugly room which had once been so beautiful. It would be nice, she thought, to speak to these young
people, perhaps even become their friend, talk and laugh with
them; perhaps they might like to know that this spot where
they came together had been a lady's drawing room. Hesitating a little, Miss Harper wondered if she might call "Good

night," or "Thank you" again, or even "God bless you all."
Then, since no one looked at her, she started up the stairs.
Halfway there was a landing with a stained-glass window, and
Miss Harper stopped, holding her breath. When she had been
a child the stained-glass window on the stair landing in her
house had caught the sunlight, and scattered it on the stairs in
a hundred colors. Fairyland colors, Miss Harper thought, remembering; I wonder why we don't live in these houses now.
I'm lonely, Miss Harper thought, and then she thought, but I
must get out of these wet clothes; I really am catching cold.

Without thinking she turned at the top of the stairs and
went to the front room on the left; that had always been her
room. The door was open and she glanced in; this was clearly
a bedroom for rent, and it was ugly and drab and cheap. The
light turned on with a cord hanging beside the door, and Miss
Harper stood in the doorway, saddened by the peeling wallpaper and the sagging floor; what have they done to the house,
she thought; how can I sleep here tonight?

At last she moved to cross the room and set her suitcase on
the bed. I must get dry, she told herself, I must make the best
of things. The bed was correctly placed, between the two front
windows, but the mattress was stiff and lumpy, and Miss
Harper was frightened at the faint smell of dark couplings and
a remote echo in the springs; I will not think about such
things, Miss Harper thought, I will not let myself dwell on any
such thing; this might be the room where I slept as a girl. The
windows were almost right—two across the front, two at the
side—and the door was placed correctly; how they did build
these old places to a square-cut pattern, Miss Harper thought,
how they did put them together; there must be a thousand houses all over the country built exactly like this. The
closet, however, was on the wrong side. Some oddness of construction had set the closet to Miss Harper's right as she sat on
the bed, when it ought really to have been on her left; when
she was a girl the big closet had been her playhouse and her
hiding place, but it had been on the left.

The bathroom was wrong, too, but that was less important.
Miss Harper had thought wistfully of a hot tub before she
slept, but a glance at the bathtub discouraged her; she could
simply wait until she got home. She washed her face and

hands, and the warm water comforted her. She was further comforted to find that her bottle of cologne had not broken in her suitcase and that nothing inside had gotten wet. At least she could sleep in a dry nightgown, although in a cold bed.

She shivered once in the cold sheets, remembering a child's bed. She lay in the darkness with her eyes open, wondering at last where she was and how she had gotten here: first the bus and then the truck, and now she lay in the darkness and no one knew where she was or what was to become of her. She had only her suitcase and a little money in her pocketbook; she did not know where she was. She was very tired and she thought that perhaps the sleeping pill she had taken much earlier had still not quite worn off; perhaps the sleeping pill had been affecting all her actions, since she had been following docilely, bemused, wherever she was taken; in the morning, she told herself sleepily, I'll show them I can make decisions for myself.

The noise downstairs which had been a jukebox and adolescent laughter faded softly into a distant melody; my mother is singing in the drawing room, Miss Harper thought, and the company is sitting on the stiff little chairs listening; my father is playing the piano. She could not quite distinguish the song, but it was one she had heard her mother sing many times; I could creep out to the top of the stairs and listen, she thought, and then became aware that there was a rustling in the closet, but the closet was on the wrong side, on the right instead of the left. It is more a rattling than rustling, Miss Harper thought, wanting to listen to her mother singing, it is as though something wooden were being shaken around. Shall I get out of bed and quiet it so I can hear the singing? Am I too warm and comfortable, am I too sleepy?

The closet was on the wrong side, but the rattling continued, just loud enough to be irritating, and at last, knowing she would never sleep until it stopped, Miss Harper swung her legs over the side of the bed and, sleepily, padded barefoot over to the closet door, reminding herself to go to the right instead of the left.

"What are you doing in there?" she asked aloud, and opened the door. There was just enough light for her to see that it was a wooden snake, head lifted, stirring and rattling itself against the other toys. Miss Harper laughed. "It's my snake," she said aloud, "it's my old snake, and it's come alive." In the back of the closet she could see her old toy clown, bright and cheerful, and as she watched, enchanted, the toy clown flopped languidly forward and back, coming alive. At Miss Harper's feet the snake moved blindly, clattering against a doll house where the tiny people inside stirred, and against a set of blocks, which fell and crashed. Then Miss Harper saw the big beautiful doll sitting on a small chair, the doll with long golden curls and wide-lashed blue eyes and a stiff organdy party dress; as Miss Harper held out her hands in joy the doll opened her eyes and stood up.

"Rosabelle," Miss Harper cried out, "Rosabelle, it's me."

The doll turned, looking widely at her, smile painted on. The red lips opened and the doll quacked, outrageously, a flat slapping voice coming out of that fair mouth. "Go away, old lady," the doll said, "go away, old lady, go away."

Miss Harper backed away, staring. The clown tumbled and danced, mouthing at Miss Harper, the snake flung its eyeless head viciously at her ankles, and the doll turned, holding her skirts, and her mouth opened and shut. "Go away," she quacked, "go away, old lady, go away."

The inside of the closet was all alive; a small doll ran madly from side to side, the animals paraded solemnly down the gangplank of Noah's ark, a stuffed bear wheezed asthmatically. The noise was louder and louder, and then Miss Harper realized that they were all looking at her hatefully and moving toward her. The doll said "Old lady, old lady," and stepped forward; Miss Harper slammed the closet door and leaned against it. Behind her the snake crashed against the door and the doll's voice went on and on. Crying out, Miss Harper turned and fled, but the closet was on the wrong side and she turned the wrong way and found herself cowering against the far wall with the door impossibly far away while the closet door slowly opened and the doll's face, smiling, looked for her.

Miss Harper fled. Without stopping to look behind she flung herself across the room and through the door, down the hall and on down the wide lovely stairway. "Mommy," she screamed, "Mommy, Mommy."

Screaming, she fled out the door. "Mommy," she cried, and

fell, going down and down into darkness, turning, trying to catch onto something solid and real, crying.

"Look, lady," the bus driver said. "I'm not an alarm clock. Wake up and get off the bus."

"You'll be sorry," Miss Harper said distinctly.

"Wake up," he said, "wake up and get off the bus."

"I intend to report you," Miss Harper said. Pocketbook, gloves, hat, suitcase.

"I'll certainly report you," she said, almost crying.

"This is as far as you go," the driver said.

The bus lurched, moved, and Miss Harper almost stumbled in the driving rain, her suitcase at her feet, under the sign reading RICKET'S LANDING.

1965

The Possibility of Evil

MISS ADELA STRANGEWORTH came daintily along Main Street on her way to the grocery. The sun was shining, the air was fresh and clear after the night's heavy rain, and everything in Miss Strangeworth's little town looked washed and bright. Miss Strangeworth took deep breaths, and thought that there was nothing in the world like a fragrant summer day.

She knew everyone in town, of course; she was fond of telling strangers—tourists who sometimes passed through the town and stopped to admire Miss Strangeworth's roses—that she had never spent more than a day outside this town in all her long life. She was seventy-one, Miss Strangeworth told the tourists, with a pretty little dimple showing by her lip, and she sometimes found herself thinking that the town belonged to her. "My grandfather built the first house on Pleasant Street," she would say, opening her blue eyes wide with the wonder of it. "This house, right here. My family has lived here for better than a hundred years. My grandmother planted these roses, and my mother tended them, just as I do. I've watched my town grow; I can remember when Mr. Lewis, Senior, opened the grocery store, and the year the river flooded out the shanties on the low road, and the excitement when some young folks wanted to move the park over to the space in front of where the new post office is today. They wanted to put up a statue of Ethan Allen"—Miss Strangeworth would frown a little and sound stern—"but it should have been a statue of my grandfather. There wouldn't have been a town here at all if it hadn't been for my grandfather and the lumber mill."

Miss Strangeworth never gave away any of her roses, although the tourists often asked her. The roses belonged on Pleasant Street, and it bothered Miss Strangeworth to think of people wanting to carry them away, to take them into strange towns and down strange streets. When the new minister came, and the ladies were gathering flowers to decorate the church, Miss Strangeworth sent over a great basket of gladioli; when she picked the roses at all, she set them in bowls and vases around the inside of the house her grandfather had built.

Walking down Main Street on a summer morning, Miss Strangeworth had to stop every minute or so to say good morning to someone or to ask after someone's health. When she came into the grocery, half a dozen people turned away from the shelves and the counters to wave at her or call out good morning.

"And good morning to you, too, Mr. Lewis," Miss Strangeworth said at last. The Lewis family had been in the town almost as long as the Strangeworths; but the day young Lewis left high school and went to work in the grocery, Miss Strangeworth had stopped calling him Tommy and started calling him Mr. Lewis, and he had stopped calling her Addie and started calling her Miss Strangeworth. They had been in high school together, and had gone to picnics together, and to high-school dances and basketball games; but now Mr. Lewis was behind the counter in the grocery, and Miss Strangeworth was living alone in the Strangeworth house on Pleasant Street.

"Good morning," Mr. Lewis said, and added politely, "lovely day."

"It is a very nice day," Miss Strangeworth said as though she had only just decided that it would do after all. "I would like a chop, please, Mr. Lewis, a small, lean veal chop. Are those strawberries from Arthur Parker's garden? They're early this year."

"He brought them in this morning," Mr. Lewis said.

"I shall have a box," Miss Strangeworth said. Mr. Lewis looked worried, she thought, and for a minute she hesitated, but then she decided that he surely could not be worried over the strawberries. He looked very tired indeed. He was usually so chipper, Miss Strangeworth thought, and almost commented, but it was far too personal a subject to be introduced to Mr. Lewis, the grocer, so she only said, "And a can of cat food and, I think, a tomato."

Silently, Mr. Lewis assembled her order on the counter and waited. Miss Strangeworth looked at him curiously and then said, "It's Tuesday, Mr. Lewis. You forgot to remind me."

"Did I? Sorry."

"Imagine your forgetting that I always buy my tea on Tuesday," Miss Strangeworth said gently. "A quarter pound of tea, please, Mr. Lewis."

"Is that all, Miss Strangeworth?"

"Yes, thank you, Mr. Lewis. Such a lovely day, isn't it?"

"Lovely," Mr. Lewis said.

Miss Strangeworth moved slightly to make room for Mrs. Harper at the counter, "Morning, Adela," Mrs. Harper said, and Miss Strangeworth said, "Good morning, Martha."

"Lovely day," Mrs. Harper said, and Miss Strangeworth said, "Yes, lovely," and Mr. Lewis, under Mrs. Harper's glance, nodded.

"Ran out of sugar for my cake frosting," Mrs. Harper explained. Her hand shook slightly as she opened her pocketbook. Miss Strangeworth wondered, glancing at her quickly, if she had been taking proper care of herself. Martha Harper was not as young as she used to be, Miss Strangeworth thought. She probably could use a good, strong tonic.

"Martha," she said, "you don't look well."

"I'm perfectly all right," Mrs. Harper said shortly. She handed her money to Mr. Lewis, took her change and her sugar, and went out without speaking again. Looking after her, Miss Strangeworth shook her head slightly. Martha definitely did *not* look well.

Carrying her little bag of groceries, Miss Strangeworth came out of the store into the bright sunlight and stopped to smile down on the Crane baby. Don and Helen Crane were really the two most infatuated young parents she had ever known, she thought indulgently, looking at the delicately embroidered baby cap and the lace-edged carriage cover.

"That little girl is going to grow up expecting luxury all her life," she said to Helen Crane.

Helen laughed. "That's the way we want her to feel," she said. "Like a princess."

"A princess can be a lot of trouble sometimes," Miss Strangeworth said dryly. "How old is Her Highness now?"

"Six months next Tuesday," Helen Crane said, looking down with rapt wonder at her child. "I've been worrying, though, about her. Don't you think she ought to move around more? Try to sit up, for instance?"

"For plain and fancy worrying," Miss Strangeworth said, amused, "give me a new mother every time."

"She just seems—slow," Helen Crane said.

"Nonsense. All babies are different. Some of them develop much more quickly than others."

"That's what my mother says." Helen Crane laughed, looking a little bit ashamed.

"I suppose you've got young Don all upset about the fact that his daughter is already six months old and hasn't yet begun to learn to dance?"

"I haven't mentioned it to him. I suppose she's just so precious that I worry about her all the time."

"Well, apologize to her right now," Miss Strangeworth said. "*She* is probably worrying about why you keep jumping around all the time." Smiling to herself and shaking her old head, she went on down the sunny street, stopping once to ask little Billy Moore why he wasn't out riding in his daddy's shiny new car, and talking for a few minutes outside the library with Miss Chandler, the librarian, about the new novels to be ordered and paid for by the annual library appropriation. Miss Chandler seemed absentminded and very much as though she was thinking about something else. Miss Strangeworth noticed that Miss Chandler had not taken much trouble with her hair that morning, and sighed. Miss Strangeworth hated sloppiness.

Many people seemed disturbed recently, Miss Strangeworth thought. Only yesterday the Stewarts' fifteen-year-old Linda had run crying down her own front walk and all the way to school, not caring who saw her. People around town thought she might have had a fight with the Harris boy, but they showed up together at the soda shop after school as usual, both of them looking grim and bleak. Trouble at home, people concluded, and sighed over the problems of trying to raise kids right these days.

From halfway down the block Miss Strangeworth could catch the heavy scent of her roses, and she moved a little more quickly. The perfume of roses meant home, and home meant the Strangeworth House on Pleasant Street. Miss Strangeworth stopped at her own front gate, as she always did, and looked with deep pleasure at her house, with the red and pink and white roses massed along the narrow lawn, and the rambler going up along the porch; and the neat, the unbelievably trim lines of the house itself, with its slimness and its washed white look. Every window sparkled, every curtain hung stiff and straight, and even the stones of the front walk were swept and clear. People around town wondered how old Miss Strangeworth managed to keep the house looking the way it did, and there was a legend about a tourist once mistaking it for the local museum and going all through the place without finding out about his mistake. But the town was proud of Miss Strangeworth and her roses and her house. They had all grown together.

Miss Strangeworth went up her front steps, unlocked her front door with her key, and went into the kitchen to put away her groceries. She debated having a cup of tea and then decided that it was too close to midday dinnertime; she would not have the appetite for her little chop if she had tea now. Instead she went into the light, lovely sitting room, which still glowed from the hands of her mother and her grandmother, who had covered the chairs with bright chintz and hung the curtains. All the furniture was spare and shining, and the round hooked rugs on the floor had been the work of Miss Strangeworth's grandmother and her mother. Miss Strangeworth had put a bowl of her red roses on the low table before the window, and the room was full of their scent.

Miss Strangeworth went to the narrow desk in the corner, and unlocked it with her key. She never knew when she might feel like writing letters, so she kept her notepaper inside, and the desk locked. Miss Strangeworth's usual stationery was heavy and cream-colored, with "Strangeworth House" engraved across the top, but, when she felt like writing her other letters, Miss Strangeworth used a pad of various-colored paper, bought from the local newspaper shop. It was almost a town joke, that colored paper, layered in pink and green and blue and yellow; everyone in town bought it and used it for odd, informal notes and shopping lists. It was usual to remark, upon receiving a note written on a blue page, that so-and-so would be needing a new pad soon—here she was, down to the blue already. Everyone used the matching envelopes for tucking away recipes, or keeping odd little things in, or even to hold cookies in the school lunch boxes. Mr. Lewis sometimes gave them to the children for carrying home penny candy.

Although Miss Strangeworth's desk held a trimmed quill pen, which had belonged to her grandfather, and a gold-frost fountain pen, which had belonged to her father, Miss Strangeworth always used a dull stub of pencil when she wrote her letters, and she printed them in a childish block print. After thinking for a minute, although she had been phrasing the letter in the back of her mind all the way home, she wrote on a pink sheet: DIDN'T YOU EVER SEE AN IDIOT CHILD BEFORE? SOME PEOPLE JUST SHOULDN'T HAVE CHILDREN, SHOULD THEY?

She was pleased with the letter. She was fond of doing things exactly right. When she made a mistake, as she sometimes did, or when the letters were not spaced nicely on the page, she had to take the discarded page to the kitchen stove and burn it at once. Miss Strangeworth never delayed when things had to be done.

After thinking for a minute, she decided that she would like to write another letter, perhaps to go to Mrs. Harper, to follow up the ones she had already mailed. She selected a green sheet this time and wrote quickly: HAVE YOU FOUND OUT YET WHAT THEY WERE ALL LAUGHING ABOUT AFTER YOU LEFT THE BRIDGE CLUB ON THURSDAY? OR IS THE WIFE REALLY ALWAYS THE LAST ONE TO KNOW?

Miss Strangeworth never concerned herself with facts; her letters all dealt with the more negotiable stuff of suspicion. Mr. Lewis would never have imagined for a minute that his grandson might be lifting petty cash from the store register if he had not had one of Miss Strangeworth's letters. Miss Chandler, the librarian, and Linda Stewart's parents would have gone unsuspectingly ahead with their lives, never aware of possible evil lurking nearby, if Miss Strangeworth had not sent letters opening their eyes. Miss Strangeworth would have been genuinely shocked if there *had* been anything between Linda Stewart and the Harris boy, but, as long as evil existed unchecked in the world, it was Miss Strangeworth's duty to keep her town alert to it. It was far more sensible for Miss Chandler to wonder what Mr. Shelley's first wife had really died of than to take a chance on not knowing. There were so many wicked people in the world and only one Strangeworth left in town. Besides, Miss Strangeworth liked writing her letters.

She addressed an envelope to Don Crane after a moment's thought, wondering curiously if he would show the letter to his wife, and using a pink envelope to match the pink paper. Then she addressed a second envelope, green, to Mrs. Harper. Then an idea came to her and she selected a blue sheet and wrote: YOU NEVER KNOW ABOUT DOCTORS. REMEMBER THEY'RE ONLY HUMAN AND NEED MONEY LIKE THE REST OF US. SUPPOSE THE KNIFE SLIPPED ACCIDENTALLY. WOULD DOCTOR BURNS GET HIS FEE AND A LITTLE EXTRA FROM THAT NEPHEW OF YOURS?

She addressed the blue envelope to old Mrs. Foster, who was having an operation next month. She had thought of writing one more letter, to the head of the school board, asking how a chemistry teacher like Billy Moore's father could afford a new convertible, but all at once she was tired of writing letters. The three she had done would do for one day. She could write more tomorrow; it was not as though they all had to be done at once.

She had been writing her letters—sometimes two or three every day for a week, sometimes no more than one in a month —for the past year. She never got any answers, of course, because she never signed her name. If she had been asked, she would have said that her name, Adela Strangeworth, a name honored in the town for so many years, did not belong on such trash. The town where she lived had to be kept clean and sweet, but people everywhere were lustful and evil and degraded, and needed to be watched; the world was so large, and there was only one Strangeworth left in it. Miss Strangeworth sighed, locked her desk, and put the letters into her big, black leather pocketbook, to be mailed when she took her evening walk.

She broiled her little chop nicely, and had a sliced tomato and good cup of tea ready when she sat down to her midday dinner at the table in her dining room, which could be opened to seat twenty-two, with a second table, if necessary, in the hall. Sitting in the warm sunlight that came through the tall windows of the dining room, seeing her roses massed outside, handling the heavy, old silverware and the fine, translucent china, Miss Strangeworth was pleased; she would not have cared to be doing anything else. People must live graciously, after all, she thought, and sipped her tea. Afterward, when her plate and cup and saucer were washed and dried and put back onto the shelves where they belonged, and her silverware was back in the mahogany silver chest, Miss Strangeworth went up the graceful staircase and into her bedroom, which was the front room overlooking the roses, and had been her mother's and her grandmother's. Their Crown Derby dresser set and furs had been kept here, their fans and silver-backed brushes and their own bowls of roses; Miss Strangeworth kept a bowl of white roses on the bed table.

She drew the shades, took the rose-satin spread from the bed, slipped out of her dress and her shoes, and lay down tiredly. She knew that no doorbell or phone would ring; no one in town would dare to disturb Miss Strangeworth during her afternoon nap. She slept, deep in the rich smell of roses.

After her nap she worked in her garden for a little while, sparing herself because of the heat; then she went in to her supper. She ate asparagus from her own garden, with sweet-butter sauce, and a soft-boiled egg, and, while she had her supper, she listened to a late-evening news broadcast and then to a program of classical music on her small radio. After her dishes were done and her kitchen set in order, she took up her hat—Miss Strangeworth's hats were proverbial in the town; people believed that she had inherited them from her mother and her grandmother—and, locking the front door of her house behind her, set off on her evening walk, pocketbook under her arm. She nodded to Linda Stewart's father, who was washing his car in the pleasantly cool evening. She thought that he looked troubled.

There was only one place in town where she could mail her letters, and that was the new post office, shiny with red brick and silver letters. Although Miss Strangeworth had never given the matter any particular thought, she had always made a point of mailing her letters very secretly; it would, of course, not have been wise to let anyone see her mail them. Consequently, she timed her walk so she could reach the post office just as darkness was starting to dim the outlines of the trees and the shapes of people's faces, although no one could ever mistake Miss Strangeworth, with her dainty walk and her rustling skirts.

There was always a group of young people around the post office, the very youngest roller-skating upon its driveway, which went all the way around the building and was the only smooth road in town; and the slightly older ones already knowing how to gather in small groups and chatter and laugh and make great, excited plans for going across the street to the soda shop in a minute or two. Miss Strangeworth had never had any self-consciousness before the children. She did not feel that any of them were staring at her unduly or longing to laugh at her; it would have been most reprehensible for their parents to permit their children to mock Miss Strangeworth of Pleasant Street. Most of the children stood back respectfully as Miss Strangeworth passed, silenced briefly in her presence, and some of the older children greeted her, saying soberly, "Hello, Miss Strangeworth."

Miss Strangeworth smiled at them and quickly went on. It had been a long time since she had known the name of every child in town. The mail slot was in the door of the post office. The children stood away as Miss Strangeworth approached it, seemingly surprised that anyone should want to use the post office after it had been officially closed up for the night and turned over to the children. Miss Strangeworth stood by the door, opening her black pocketbook to take out the letters, and heard a voice which she knew at once to be Linda Stewart's. Poor little Linda was crying again, and Miss Strangeworth listened carefully. This was, after all, her town, and these were her people; if one of them was in trouble, she ought to know about it.

"I can't tell you, Dave," Linda was saying—so she *was* talking to the Harris boy, as Miss Strangeworth had supposed—"I just *can't*. It's just *nasty*."

"But why won't your father let me come around anymore? What on earth did I do?"

"I can't tell you. I just wouldn't tell you for *any*thing. You've got to have a dirty, dirty mind for things like that."

"But something's happened. You've been crying and crying, and your father is all upset. Why can't *I* know about it, too? Aren't I like one of the family?"

"Not anymore, Dave, not anymore. You're not to come near our house again; my father said so. He said he'd horsewhip you. That's all I can tell you: You're not to come near our house anymore."

"But I didn't *do* anything."

"Just the same, my father said . . ."

Miss Strangeworth sighed and turned away. There was so much evil in people. Even in a charming little town like this one, there was still so much evil in people.

She slipped her letters into the slot, and two of them fell inside. The third caught on the edge and fell outside, onto the ground at Miss Strangeworth's feet. She did not notice it because she was wondering whether a letter to the Harris boy's father might not be of some service in wiping out this potential badness. Wearily Miss Strangeworth turned to go home to her quiet bed in her lovely house, and never heard the Harris boy calling to her to say that she had dropped something.

"Old lady Strangeworth's getting deaf," he said, looking after her and holding in his hand the letter he had picked up.

"Well, who cares?" Linda said. "Who cares anymore, anyway?"

"It's for Don Crane," the Harris boy said, "this letter. She dropped a letter addressed to Don Crane. Might as well take it on over. We pass his house anyway." He laughed. "Maybe it's got a check or something in it and he'd be just as glad to get it tonight instead of tomorrow."

"Catch old lady Strangeworth sending anybody a check," Linda said. "Throw it in the post office. Why do anyone a favor?" She sniffed. "Doesn't seem to me anybody around here cares about us," she said. "Why should we care about them?"

"I'll take it over, anyway," the Harris boy said. "Maybe it's good news for them. Maybe they need something happy tonight, too. Like us."

Sadly, holding hands, they wandered off down the dark street, the Harris boy carrying Miss Strangeworth's pink envelope in his hand.

*

Miss Strangeworth awakened the next morning with a feeling of intense happiness and, for a minute, wondered why, and then remembered that this morning three people would open her letters. Harsh, perhaps, at first, but wickedness was never easily banished, and a clean heart was a scoured heart. She washed her soft, old face and brushed her teeth, still sound in spite of her seventy-one years, and dressed herself carefully in her sweet, soft clothes and buttoned shoes. Then, going downstairs, reflecting that perhaps a little waffle would be agreeable for breakfast in the sunny dining room, she found the mail on the hall floor, and bent to pick it up. A bill, the morning paper, a letter in a green envelope that looked oddly familiar. Miss Strangeworth stood perfectly still for a minute, looking down at the green envelope with the penciled printing, and thought: It looks like one of my letters. Was one of my letters sent back? No, because no one would know where to send it. How did this get here?

Miss Strangeworth was a Strangeworth of Pleasant Street. Her hand did not shake as she opened the envelope and unfolded the sheet of green paper inside. She began to cry silently for the wickedness of the world when she read the words: LOOK OUT AT WHAT USED TO BE YOUR ROSES.

1965

II

Unpublished

Portrait

THAT was the way she talked, and I used to listen, and watch her sitting with her legs swung over the arm of her chair, talking and smiling but not laughing. I don't think I ever saw her laugh.

> *Go walking through the valley,*
> *go walking through the valley,*
> *go walking through the valley,*
> *as we have done before.*

. . . There was a child dancing in the garden and I went out and spoke to it.

"Child," I said, "you are stepping on my flowers."

"Yes," said the child, "I know."

"Child," I said, "you are walking on my garden."

"Yes," said the child, "I know."

"Why?" I said.

"I am dancing," said the child; "can't you see?"

> *Go in and out the windows,*
> *go in and out the windows,*
> *go in and out the windows,*
> *as we have done before.*

. . . The little boy looked at me and he was crying.

"Look," he said, "my hands are dirty."

"Why are they dirty?" I asked him.

"I was digging to get my father," he said.

"Is your father dead?" I asked him.

"They hanged him," he said.

"Why did they hang him?" I asked him.

"Because he was alive," he said.

"Then why were you trying to dig him up?" I asked him.

"Because now he is dead," he said, "and they can't hang him again."

> *Go forth and face your lover,*
> *go forth and face your lover,*

go forth and face your lover,
as we have done before.

. . . Far off among the trees there was a little girl sitting, and when I came to her she looked at me and frowned.

"Leaves will fall on you," I said.

"I don't mind; I'm hiding," she explained.

"Why are you hiding here?" I said.

"It's darker than most places," she explained.

"Who are you hiding from?" I said.

"Everybody," she explained.

"Why?" I asked.

"They want me to comb my hair," she explained.

And now you two are parted,
and now you two are parted,
and now you two are parted,
as we have done before.

That was the way she talked, but I don't think I ever saw her laugh.

no date

The Mouse

THE new apartment into which Mrs. and Mr. Malkin moved on the first of October was large and comfortable. It had a woodburning fireplace, and a big kitchen, and was near Mr. Malkin's office; Mrs. Malkin had had the living room painted a soft rose, and the bedroom an equally soft blue, and the kitchen green, and then, in a sudden burst of what Mr. Malkin might have thought was wifely humor, she had taken the room Mr. Malkin had felt immediately was to be his study and had had it painted gray, a heavy slate gray. Mr. Malkin worked for an insurance company and had read somewhere that light, cheerful colors were best for work—Mr. Malkin's minor executive's office at the company had tan plaster walls and straight chairs—but Mrs. Malkin had been firm. "You're such a gloomy type anyway," she had said unkindly. She had relented to the extent of orange drapes and a bright rug, but Mr. Malkin never did like working in the room. Sundays, when Mrs. Malkin was moving cheerfully about in the kitchen, Mr. Malkin sat in his gray and orange room and pretended he was working, but at the end of the year, when he proposed repainting it, Mr. Malkin was to bring up as an unanswerable argument the fact that he felt he never had done any work in that room. And Mrs. Malkin was going to say that he never did any work anywhere anyway.

Mrs. Malkin had felt privately for a long time that it was her duty to see that her husband wasn't always as boyish as he intended to be; she had squashed with some enthusiasm his attempts to take up golf, had discouraged his friendship with an older member of the firm whom she thought patronizing, and had seen to it that at twenty-nine Mr. Malkin was always correctly dressed, good-mannered, childless, and taciturn.

Mr. Malkin liked his wife, or did until the terrible incident of the mouse.

The mice, both of them, had come with the apartment. The minute Mrs. Malkin had gone into the new kitchen and found the mousetrap the old tenant had left in the back of a cupboard, she had known she was going to have trouble. "They've been using this mousetrap right along," she told Mr. Malkin, "and you can see it hasn't done any good. Prints all over the kitchen."

"Trouble with this trap," said Mr. Malkin, getting down on his knees beside it, "they used the same trap over and over. Mice smell where traps have caught other mice, won't go near a trap that's been used."

Mrs. Malkin regarded her husband. "What makes you think you know anything about mice?" she asked.

"You get me a new trap," Mr. Malkin said, "and I'll have your mice caught for you."

Mrs. Malkin didn't remember to get a new trap until after the painters were finished and Mr. Malkin had put up the drapes and the pictures and she had had her new lampshades made and set them up. Then one night when she went out into her freshly painted kitchen to get a pack of cigarettes, Mrs. Malkin put her foot down on the mouse, which was racing for cover under the refrigerator. She screamed and ran into the living room, where Mr. Malkin was sitting and reading.

"I didn't know you were afraid of mice," Mr. Malkin said soothingly.

"I'm not," Mrs. Malkin said, "except I do hate to have one of them scare me like that."

"You get a trap in the morning," Mr. Malkin said, "and I'll have that mouse by night."

Mrs. Malkin got a trap the next morning, Mr. Malkin set it that night, and the mouse was caught, but just as Mr. Malkin was telling Mrs. Malkin, "You see, trouble with that old trap was that the mouse smelled where other mice had been caught," Mrs. Malkin heard a suspicious rustling in the newspapers behind the stove, and the next morning there were mouse tracks all over the sink.

"I'm going to have to get the exterminator," Mrs. Malkin said to Mr. Malkin over the breakfast table, "this cannot go on. I'm not afraid of mice—you know that—but they're making me so nervous."

"No one needs an exterminator for a couple of mice," Mr. Malkin said. "You just get me a trap today . . ."

Mrs. Malkin nodded, helped her husband with his overcoat, and kissed him goodbye. "You get that trap," Mr. Malkin said as he went down the stairs, "and I'll see that your mouse is caught by night."

Later that morning Mrs. Malkin called her husband at the office. "You get me a trap?" Mr. Malkin asked right away.

"A trap?" Mrs. Malkin repeated vaguely.

Mr. Malkin thought he detected a strangeness in his wife's voice. "Is there something wrong?" he asked.

There was a brief silence. Then: "What I called you about," Mrs. Malkin said, "I was glancing through your desk."

Mr. Malkin thought swiftly. He had obviously done something wrong; however, at the moment, he could remember nothing in his desk that would offend his wife. "I keep a lot of junk—" he began.

"I know," Mrs. Malkin said, "there's a little bankbook."

"A bankbook?" Mr. Malkin said.

"It's made out to the name of—let me see." There was a pause while Mrs. Malkin looked at the bankbook. "Donald Emmett Malkin," she said.

"Donald Emmett Malkin," Mr. Malkin said.

"There's a balance of twenty-nine dollars," Mrs. Malkin said, "a dollar a week for about six months."

"Twenty-nine dollars," Mr. Malkin said. "Well."

"You'd better see if you can get that money back," Mrs. Malkin said. "After all, it's almost thirty dollars."

"Yes," said Mr. Malkin. "I had forgotten about it. I'll get the money back."

"Who's Donald Emmett Malkin?" Mrs. Malkin said.

"Just a name," Mr. Malkin said vaguely. "A joke I had at the time."

"Donald for your father, Emmett for my father," Mrs. Malkin said. "You say you'll get that money back? Shall I leave the book out for you?"

"Yes," Mr. Malkin said. "It was probably just a joke."

"Probably," Mrs. Malkin said. "I saw the mouse, by the way."

"Frighten you?" Mr. Malkin said.

"I hate mice," Mrs. Malkin said, "it was all fat and funny. Well, I'll throw this little book out then, if you're sure you won't want it."

"Sure," Mr. Malkin said. He hung up with some relief.

When he got home that night, Mrs. Malkin met him at the door. She was wearing her wine-colored housecoat and had her hair sleek and straight down her back.

"I got the mouse," Mrs. Malkin said.

"In the trap?"

"No," Mrs. Malkin said gently, "just the mouse. I was too quick for her."

"For her?" Mr. Malkin was saying as he followed his wife into his study. The mouse lay in the center of the floor, on a piece of white typing paper. The mouse was, too, just the color of the walls. "For her?" Mr. Malkin said with more strength.

"I hit her with the frying pan," Mrs. Malkin said. She looked at her husband. "I was very brave," she said.

"You certainly were," Mr. Malkin said heartily.

"Then I put her on the piece of paper with the broom," Mrs. Malkin said, "and brought her in here. And I know why she was so fat."

Mr. Malkin bent over the mouse and saw why she was so fat, and then he looked up at his wife. From the look on her face, Mr. Malkin realized that she was the most terrible woman he had ever seen.

no date

I Know Who I Love

CATHARINE VINCENT began her life in a two-room apartment in New York; she was born in a minister's home in Buffalo; the shift from one to the other might be called her tragedy. When the devil prompted William Vincent to marry he did not prompt William further to inquire if his wife were to bear sons or daughters, or if the daughter were to be Catharine (named after William's mother, finally), thin and frightened, born with a scream and blue eyes.

When Catharine was twenty-three years old she found out that her father would have preferred a son, if he had to have any child at all. At that time she was still thin and noticeably frightened, with blue eyes and a faint talent for painting. She had eventually gone to New York alone; by the time she was self-supporting she had nearly forgotten her father, and her mother was dying.

William Vincent was a short heavy man, who affected a large mustache, which he thought made him look more the master of his house. He had become a minister shortly before his marriage because he had a vague feeling that in that way he was somehow certain of being right, and virtuous, and easily sure of his authority. He was not afraid of his wife, who was the only daughter of a grocer with no money, but he was afraid of the lady next door, and the brisk young man at the bank, and the butcher's delivery boy who made faces over unpaid bills, and asked insolent questions for which he could not be rebuked. William Vincent regarded his daughter as an unnecessary expense, as a trap, and as no true expression of God's will. He thought of his wife as an amiable woman whose place was in the home; practically the only person he felt really close to was God, in the heavy Bibles and the ponderous words, in the shabby church and the cheap hymns. Catharine early grew accustomed to hearing her father say across his small desk, or along the dull dinner table, "Do you think you are satisfactory, in God's sight or mine?"

After Catharine left home, while the train was pulling out of the station, she stopped thinking about her father and mother, except, later, for a weekly letter home. ("I am fine now, my cold is all gone at last. My job is fine, and they said it was all right about my being away three days. I guess I won't be able to leave work again for a while, so cannot expect to come home just yet.") Her father across the desk, her mother's small timid laugh, were emphatically and resolutely put out of her mind, until she was twenty-three and her mother died.

The doctor was there and Catharine waited outside in the apartment-house hall while the doctor and her mother spent the last few minutes together. "She never spoke at all," the doctor said. "She died very peacefully, Miss Vincent."

"Good," Catharine said. Her mother had waited until spring to die; next year she could have a fur coat. "What do I have to do about making arrangements?" she asked the doctor, waving her hand vaguely. "About burying her, and so on?"

The doctor looked at Catharine for a minute. "I'll help you with all that," he said.

Catharine spoke to strange people with soft voices, who told her she was brave, or patted her hand and told her her mother was happier now. "She's with your dear father," the maid in the apartment house said to Catharine, "They're together again at last."

With the funeral over and her mother gone, Catharine put the apartment back the way it had been before her mother came to live with her. The extra bed was moved out and the little table went back by the window. She spent five dollars on a new slip cover for the armchair, and she had the curtains cleaned. The only thing left of her mother was the old trunk full of her mother's memories and hopes. The little money from the sale of the furniture stored in Buffalo had paid for the funeral; Catharine had paid for the doctor and the medicine out of her salary and her fur-coat money. She asked the superintendent to put her mother's trunk in the basement storage room, and the evening before he took it down she opened it, to make sure everything was in moth balls and to take out anything she could use, and, finally, to set her mind dutifully to thinking of her parents.

For a minute or two her parents' memory would be centered in a flood of other memories, the thin teacher who snatched the drawing out of Catharine's hand and snarled, "I should have known better than to assign this to a stupid half-wit." Coming upon a boy named Freddie frantically rubbing out an inscription in chalk on a fence, and, when Freddie ran away, reading with hollow empty sympathy words he had been so anxiously erasing: "Catharine loves Freddie." And then her father: "Catharine, do the girls and boys in your school talk to each other about bad things?" The one or two parties, and the flowered chiffon dress her mother made. Her father sending her next door to get back a nickel she had lent to a school friend. And her mother: "I hardly think, dear, that your father would approve of that little girl. Jane. If I were to speak to her, very tactfully . . ."

And herself, coming back someday, a famous artist with a secretary and gardenias, stepping off the train where they were all waiting for autographs. And there was Freddie, pressing forward, and Catharine, turning slightly aside, said, "I'm afraid you must be mistaken. I never cared for anyone named Freddie." The tallest in the class, and thin, telling the other unpopular girls at recess: "My father doesn't like me to go out with boys. *You* know, the things they do." And finally, after school, staying by the pretty young teacher, saying, "Don't you like Mary Roberts Rinehart, Miss Henwood? I think she's a terribly good author."

The girls in school had called Catharine "Catty," the teachers and her mother and father had called her "Catharine," the girls in her office called her "Katy" or "Kitty," but Aaron had called her "Cara," "Strange Cara," the one note from him began. Catharine had held it in her hands, sitting by an open window at night and looking at the stars, in Buffalo, with her father moving around suspiciously downstairs; in New York, with her mother dead.

"Ratty Catty, sure is batty." Catharine remembered the jingle from the schoolyard and the notes passed from desk to desk, remembered it and turned it over in her mind while she leaned back with her feet on her dead mother's trunk and felt the soft upholstered chair against her shoulders, saw the traffic moving in the street below her apartment window, knew her job and her paycheck were waiting for her the next day. "Ratty Catty, sure is batty." Catharine smiled comfortably. There had been a kissing game at one of the few parties she went to, a

grammar-school graduation party, and Catharine, in the background, had unexpectedly had to come forward to kiss a boy
(what boy? she wondered now. Freddie again?). And the boy,
moving backward, saying, "Hey, listen," while Catharine
stood uncertainly. Then someone had shouted, "Catty's father
won't let her kiss a boy," and Catharine, trying to protect her
father, had begun a denial before she realized that it was infinitely worse to admit that the boy had turned away from her.
Then she told people, the other unpopular girls during recess,
"My father won't let me go to the parties where they play that
kind of game," or, "If my father ever caught me doing what
those other girls do!"

She went to business school, because her father needed
someone to help him with his numerous notes and the books
of sermons he might write someday, and held the idea of a secretary in his mind as a signal of success. At business school she
was no stranger; the pretty girls had all gone on to college, and
Catharine was with the other thin dull girls or fat girls who
were vivacious and had crushes on the men instructors. The
boys in the school were mostly earnest and hard-working, and
stopped in the halls to ask Catharine what she thought of the
typing test, and whether she had taken down today's assignment. Aaron came to the school in mid-semester, wearing a
yellow sweater suddenly into the typing class, standing thin
and small and graceful and smiling while the rows of students
sat mutely at their typewriters watching him.

"I fell in love with you right away," Catharine told him
afterward. "I never knew what hit me."

Once Catharine had asked her mother impulsively and inju-
diciously, "Mother, did you fall in love with my father?"

"Catharine," her mother said, letting her hands stand quiet
in the dishwater, "is there anything wrong, dear?"

High school had been worse for Catharine than any other
time in her life. When the other girls wore sweaters or beer
jackets and collected autographs, Catharine sat awkwardly
under a badly designed wool dress. Once, with money her
father borrowed from his brother, her mother bought Catharine a dark-green sweater and skirt, and when Catharine came
into school that morning, one girl said, "What'd you do, rob a

fire sale?" and another said, "Look at Catty, in the sweater she knit herself." Years later, Catharine told Aaron, leaning forward with her elbows on the table and her cigarette smoke blowing into her eyes, "I don't like clothes, at all. I think everyone makes too much fuss over them. I think the human body is too fine." When the girls with high-heeled shoes and curly hair went to sophomore proms and senior balls, Catharine and her three or four friends gave little hen parties where they served one another cocoa and cake, and said, "You'd be cute, honestly, Catty, if you had a permanent and wore some make-up." And Catharine, blushing, "My father would kill me." "You've got nice skin, though. Mine's always breaking out." "No, it isn't," Catharine said, or, "You're not fat, really. I only wish I looked like you, honestly."

A terrible thing happened to Catharine in her junior year in high school. One of her friends was to usher in a show put on by the local chapter of the American Legion. It was a performance of *The Mikado* and daughters of some of the members were going to usher, in evening gowns, with a chance to help with the make-up. Edna was the name of Catharine's friend, and the third and last night of the performance Edna managed to get Catharine invited to usher in place of another girl who was sick. At seven o'clock Catharine, in a blue crepe dress of her mother's which fitted badly and was cruelly improvised over the shoulders with a white organdy frill, met Edna in the lobby of the auditorium; Mrs. Vincent, who had come over on the streetcar with Catharine, said to Edna, "You'll be sure and see that Catharine gets home all right?"

"My mother and father are going to drive her home," Edna said. Mrs. Vincent kissed Catharine good-by, gave one sweeping suspicious glance over the auditorium, and went out to take the streetcar home. "How do I look?" Edna asked. "Look at me." She held out her skirt and Catharine, horrified, realized that Edna, with her bad complexion and straight hair, looked lovely. "I got a finger wave," Edna said, "and I'm wearing lipstick." Catharine realized even then that once or twice in any girl's life there will be an evening when she looks beautiful; she was not used enough to being ugly to be content to wait until an hour or two of beauty could do her real service.

"You look wonderful," Catharine said sickly, "how do I look?" She held her coat open and Edna said, "You look beautiful, listen, we're going to the party for the cast after."

Catharine stayed long enough after the performance to see Edna, with her finger wave uncurling damply and her wide skirts trailing after her, dancing dreamily in the arms of a stout middle-aged man who had been in the chorus; he giggled when he whispered in Edna's ear, and Edna rolled her eyes and slapped his face lightly, while her mother and father, tired and proud, sat at the side of the room and greeted casual acquaintances eagerly.

Catharine walked home, all the way, holding up the blue crepe skirt and not afraid that anyone would notice her. "It's the ugliest thing I ever saw," she was whispering to herself. "Daddy will be furious." Then, only a block from her home, she thought she was a beautiful glorious creature, walking in a garden, her long skirts moving softly over the ground, graceful, with people thronging around her for her autograph. "Please," she said softly, waving a fan, "please don't say I'm beautiful . . . I'm not really, you know," and a chorus of protests drowned out her voice, and she yielded, laughing softly.

Her father forbade her to speak to Edna again, and wrote Edna's father a sharp note, which was ignored. Her mother had to have the blue dress cleaned, because of the dirt on the hem.

"I don't think the ordinary run of person is able to recognize beauty when they see it," Catharine told Aaron later, years later. "I think that your common person tramples on beauty because it is so far above him."

"You always were an ungrateful, spoiled child," her mother said, moving uneasily on the bed.

"You're living off me, aren't you?" Catharine answered indifferently. "You eat, don't you? Doesn't the doctor come twice a week to see you?"

"You never had a spark of affection in you," her mother said.

"*Some*thing must make me take care of you and feed you," Catharine said.

Her mother pulled at the blankets, her hands thin and powerless. "I don't know what I did to deserve a daughter like you."

"You must have taken the Lord's name in vain," Catharine said. She was standing leaning against the doorway to the kitchenette, waiting for her mother's oatmeal to cook. She had had a long and dismal day at the office, it was getting on toward winter (the winter when she could have had a cheap fur coat if her mother had not come) and her mother showed no signs of getting better or worse. She was almost completely careless of everything except that she was twenty-three years old, and still tied down; the romance and glory of her life waiting still.

"If your poor father could hear that."

"My poor father can't hear anything," Catharine said, "and I'm happy about it."

Her mother tried to rise on the bed, tried to soften Catharine with tears in her eyes. "He was a good father to you, Catharine. You shouldn't say evil things like that."

Catharine laughed and went into the kitchenette.

When Catharine was twelve her mother tried to give her a party. She bought little invitation cards at the five and ten, and paper hats and small baskets to hold candies. She bought ice cream and made a cake, and bought a game of pin-the-tail-on-the donkey. "The whole thing didn't cost but about three dollars," she told Catharine's father. "I took most of the money out of my house money this week."

"There's no reason why Catharine should have expensive entertainments," her father said, frowning. "Her position as my daughter explains the absence of worldly frivolity in her life."

"The child has never had a party before," her mother said firmly.

"I don't want a party," Catharine told herself, alone upstairs in her room, lying on the bed. "I don't want any of the kids to come here." Her mother sent out the little invitations (Catharine Vincent, Thursday, August 24th, 2–5), and almost all of the twelve children invited had come.

The party was a miserable failure. Catharine, in an old dress with new collar and cuffs, and her mother in the dress she wore to church, greeted the guests at the door and sat them down in the living room where the little baskets of candy sat around on tables. The guests took the candy one piece at a time, played pin-the-tail-on-the-donkey as long as Mrs. Vincent wanted them to, and then sat quietly until one of them thought to say she ought to be getting home now. "But you haven't had your ice cream," Catharine's mother cried with bright gaiety, "you *can't* leave before the ice cream." Catharine's memories of that party were of her mother, working furiously, laughing and humming when she walked from place to place, her old dress showing constantly among the party dresses of the children; her mother saying "Well, don't you look pretty!" and "You must be the smartest little girl in Catharine's class."

Afterward, at the dinner table, her mother said encouragingly, "Did you enjoy your party, dear?"

"I told you they'd act like that," Catharine said without emotion. "They don't like me."

"Catharine has no business wanting parties if her friends don't know how to behave to her mother," Mr. Vincent said, devoting himself to a platter of liver and bacon. "You've worn yourself out and spent a lot of money to let the child have something she didn't need to have."

"Remember the party you gave for me?" Catharine said to her mother lying on the bed. "Remember that terrible party you insisted on having?"

"You are an ungrateful daughter," her mother said, moving under the blankets. "You always were a cold thoughtless child."

One day when Catharine was about fourteen her mother came into the bedroom where Catharine was cleaning her dresser drawers. Sitting on the bed, her mother said to Catharine's back, "Your father wants me to talk to you, Catharine."

Catharine, frozen, went on piling handkerchiefs and folding scarves. "What does he want you to talk to me about?"

"He thinks it's time I spoke to you," her mother said unhappily.

All the time her mother talked, apologizing and fumbling, Catharine sat on the floor folding and unfolding a scarf. "Have the girls at school been talking about things like this?" her mother asked once.

"All the time," Catharine said.

"You mustn't listen," her mother said earnestly. "Your

father and I are equipped to tell you the truth, the girls at school don't know anything. Catharine, I want you to promise me never to talk to anyone but your mother and father about these things."

"If I have any questions I'll ask Daddy," Catharine said.

"Don't laugh at your mother and father," her mother said.

Catharine turned around to look at her mother. "Are you all finished?" Her mother nodded. "Then please let's never talk about it again," Catharine said. "I don't want to talk about it again, ever."

"Neither do I," her mother said angrily. "It's hard enough to tell you anything at all, young lady, without having to talk about delicate subjects."

"You tell Daddy you told me," Catharine said as her mother went out the door.

"Did you love my father?" Catharine asked her mother lying on the bed, "did you ever love my father, Mother?"

"You never loved him," her mother said, moving against the pillow, "you were an ungrateful child."

"When you married him did you think you were going to be happy?"

"He was a good husband," her mother said, "he tried very hard to be a good father, but you only wanted to make trouble. All your life."

Catharine sat on the edge of the seat; she was nineteen and her hands were neatly on the booth table, her books beside her, her eyes on the door. If only someone comes in, just this once, she was thinking, if only one of the girls could see me, just this once.

"You look *très sérieuse*," Aaron said. "Coffee?"

"Yes, please," Catharine said.

"Now listen," Aaron said. "I ask you to come out for coffee with me because I think you're interesting to talk to. You can't just sit there and not say anything." Catharine looked up and saw he was smiling. "Say something witty," he said.

She got a minute to think when the waiter came over and Aaron ordered the coffee, but when the waiter was gone and Aaron turned politely to her, she could only shake her head and smile.

"Let me start a conversation, then," Aaron said. "What was the book you were carrying yesterday?"

"Did you see me?" Catharine asked before she thought.

"Certainly I saw you," Aaron said. "I see you every day. Sometimes you wear a green sweater."

Catharine felt that this had to be said quickly, urgently, before the moment got away from her. "I don't like clothes at all," she said. "I think everyone makes too much fuss over them. I think the human body is too fine."

Aaron stared. "Well!" he said.

Catharine thought back on what she had said and blushed. "I didn't mean to sound so vulgar," she said.

Another time, when Catharine knew how to answer more easily, Aaron asked her, "Why don't we go to the five and ten and buy you a lipstick?"

"My father would kill me," Catharine said.

"You could just wear it in school," Aaron said. "I want my girl to be pretty."

Catharine carried that "my girl" around with her in her mind ever afterward; she bought a lipstick and powder and rouge and nail polish, and put them on inexpertly in the girl's lavatory every morning before classes, and took them off each afternoon after leaving Aaron. Her father never knew; she kept them in a box in her pocketbook, and had a story prepared ("Gerry's family doesn't like her to wear make-up either, but she does anyway, and she asked me if I'd just keep these things—").

Aaron liked to sit with a cigarette hanging out of the corner of his mouth; he kept his eyes narrow when he talked, and the smoke from the cigarette went past his eyebrow. He smiled more than anyone Catharine had ever known, and she thought once that he looked satanic; she told him so and he smiled at her, smoke in his eyes.

"The devil is the only true god," he said.

Once her father frightened Catharine badly by saying to her abruptly at the dinner table "You're not running around with a young man, are you, Catharine?"

"*Catharine?*" her mother said.

"I was speaking to Mr. Blake this afternoon about a matter of business," her father said ponderously, "and he mentioned that he had seen Catharine walking out of her business school with a young man. No one he knew."

"It was probably one of the instructors," Catharine said in a clear voice. "I was probably asking about an assignment."

"I would not like to think that my daughter is associating with young men she is ashamed to introduce to her parents," her father said.

"Mother and Daddy have a great deal of faith in you," her mother said.

"It was probably Mr. Harley, our typing instructor," Catharine said. "I had to ask him about an assignment and we walked down the hall talking and out the door. I did the wrong assignment and had to find out what to make up."

"You should have told him to go to hell," Aaron said later when Catharine told him.

"Someday I will," Catharine said.

"Yes, Daddy dear," Aaron said in a high voice, "I am associating with a young man I am definitely ashamed to introduce to you, because he is a thief and a murderer. And he rapes young women. Even Mother wouldn't be safe with him."

Catharine shook her head helplessly. "He'd die," she said. "He'd just die."

When Aaron met Mr. and Mrs. Vincent he was very agreeable and Catharine was able to feel for a few minutes as though everything were going to pass off well. Aaron had escorted her home from school very properly and she had very properly invited him in. Her mother and father, sitting in the living room, watched Aaron and Catharine come in, and when Catharine said, "Mother and Daddy, this is Aaron, a friend of mine from school," her father came over and took Aaron's hand. "Pleased to meet you, my boy," he said.

"How do you do." Aaron stood next to Catharine, comfortable in his yellow sweater.

"Aaron is in school too," Catharine said to her mother.

"How do you like the school?" Catharine's mother said.

Conversation had continued without silences, they were sitting down, and Catharine met Aaron's eye and he smiled. She smiled back, and then realized that her mother and father were silently waiting. Aaron said smoothly, "Look at Cara's hands,

Mrs. Vincent. They're like white waves on a white shore. They touch her face like white moths."

Catharine met her father at the dinner table that night, with a sort of sick resignation that left her unsurprised when he said immediately, "I don't know about that young man." He thought heavily. "Your mother and I have been talking about him."

"It seems like your friends ought to be finer, somehow," her mother said earnestly. "With your background."

"He doesn't seem quite right, to me," her father said. "Not quite right."

"We'll find some money somehow," her mother said, "and see if we can get you another dress. Sensible, but pretty enough to wear to parties."

Sitting by the window with her mother's trunk open on the floor and her old report card ("English, B–, History, D, Geography, D") in her hand, Catharine, to spite her mother, thought about Aaron. Because the dull eyes of William Vincent and his wife were no longer on her, because she was loose, at least, from their questions ("Catharine, have you been seeing—") and their sudden quiet when she opened the front door, Catharine went to the little cedar box where she kept all her most secret treasures, and always had, and took out Aaron's only letter. In the box were a bright cotton handkerchief, and a tarnished silver charm bracelet. In her years in New York she had collected a match folder from a night club, and a printed note which read "We thank you for submitting the enclosed material and regret that we cannot make use of it." It had come attached to some watercolor impressions Catharine had sent to a magazine; she kept it because of the word "regret" and because it had been addressed to her name and addressed by someone there at the magazine, some bright golden creature who called writers by their first names and sat at chromium bars and walked different streets than Catharine did, from her apartment on West Twentieth Street to her typist's job on Wall Street. And at the chromium bars Aaron was sitting, and he walked quickly past the bright stores, and he might be in any taxi passing, smiling at someone with his quick sudden amusement saying, "Catharine? I once cared for a girl named Catharine . . ."

The Beautiful Stranger

WHAT might be called the first intimation of strangeness occurred at the railroad station. She had come with her children, Smalljohn and her baby girl, to meet her husband when he returned from a business trip to Boston. Because she had been oddly afraid of being late, and perhaps even seeming uneager to encounter her husband after a week's separation, she dressed the children and put them into the car at home a long half hour before the train was due. As a result, of course, they had to wait interminably at the station, and what was to have been a charmingly staged reunion, family embracing husband and father, became at last an ill-timed and awkward performance. Smalljohn's hair was mussed, and he was sticky. The baby was cross, pulling at her pink bonnet and her dainty lace-edged dress, whining. The final arrival of the train caught them in mid-movement, as it were; Margaret was tying the ribbons on the baby's bonnet, Smalljohn was half over the back of the car seat. They scrambled out of the car, cringing from the sound of the train, hopelessly out of sorts.

John Senior waved from the high steps of the train. Unlike his wife and children, he looked utterly prepared for his return, as though he had taken some pains to secure a meeting at least painless, and had, in fact, stood just so, waving cordially from the steps of the train, for perhaps as long as half an hour, en-suring that he should not be caught half-ready, his hand not lifted so far as to overemphasize the extent of his delight in seeing them again.

His wife had an odd sense of lost time. Standing now on the platform with the baby in her arms and Smalljohn beside her, she could not for a minute remember clearly whether he was coming home, or, whether they were yet standing here to say good-by to him. They had been quarreling when he left, and she had spent the week of his absence determining to forget that in his presence she had been frightened and hurt. This will be a good time to get things straight, she had been telling her-self; while John is gone I can try to get hold of myself again. Now, unsure at last whether this was an arrival or a departure, she felt afraid again, straining to meet an unendurable tension. This will not do, she thought, believing that she was being honest with herself, and as he came down the train steps and walked toward them she smiled, holding the baby tightly against her so that the touch of its small warmth might bring some genuine tenderness into her smile.

This will not do, she thought, and smiled more cordially and told him "hello" as he came to her. Wondering, she kissed him and then when he held his arm around her and the baby for a minute the baby pulled back and struggled, screaming. Everyone moved in anger, and the baby kicked and screamed, "No, no, no."

"What a way to say hello to Daddy," Margaret said, and she shook the baby, half-amused, and yet grateful for the baby's sympathetic support. John turned to Smalljohn and lifted him, Smalljohn kicking and laughing helplessly. "Daddy, Daddy," Smalljohn shouted, and the baby screamed, "No, no."

Helplessly, because no one could talk with the baby scream-ing so, they turned and went to the car. When the baby was back in her pink basket in the car, and Smalljohn was settled with another lollipop beside her, there was an appalling quiet which would have to be filled as quickly as possible with mean-ingful words. John had taken the driver's seat in the car while Margaret was quieting the baby, and when Margaret got in beside him she felt a little chill of animosity at the sight of his hands on the wheel; I can't bear to relinquish even this much, she thought; for a week no one has driven the car except me. Because she could see so clearly that this was unreasonable— John owned half the car, after all—she said to him with bright interest, "And how was your trip? The weather?"

"Wonderful," he said, and again she was angered at the warmth in his tone; if she was unreasonable about the car, he was surely unreasonable to have enjoyed himself quite so much. "Everything went very well. I'm pretty sure I got the contract, everyone was very pleasant about it, and I go back in two weeks to settle everything."

The stinger is in the tail, she thought. He wouldn't tell it all so hastily if he didn't want me to miss half of it; I am supposed to be pleased that he got the contract and that everyone was so pleasant, and the part about going back is supposed to slip past me painlessly.

"Maybe I can go with you, then," she said. "Your mother will take the children."

"Fine," he said, but it was much too late; he had hesitated noticeably before he spoke.

"I want to go too," said Smalljohn. "Can I go with Daddy?"

They came into their house, Margaret carrying the baby, and John carrying his suitcase and arguing delightedly with Smalljohn over which of them was carrying the heavier weight of it. The house was ready for them; Margaret had made sure that it was cleaned and emptied of the qualities which attached so surely to her position of wife alone with small children; the toys which Smalljohn had thrown around with unusual freedom were picked up, the baby's clothes (no one, after all, came to call when John was gone) were taken from the kitchen radiator where they had been drying. Aside from the fact that the house gave no impression of waiting for any particular people, but only for anyone well-bred and clean enough to fit within its small trim walls, it could have passed for a home, Margaret thought, even for a home where a happy family lived in domestic peace. She set the baby down in the playpen and turned with the baby's bonnet and jacket in her hand and saw her husband, head bent gravely as he listened to Smalljohn. Who? she wondered suddenly; is he taller? That is not my husband.

She laughed, and they turned to her, Smalljohn curious, and her husband with a quick bright recognition; she thought, why, it is *not* my husband, and he knows that I have seen it. There was no astonishment in her; she would have thought perhaps thirty seconds before that such a thing was impossible, but since it was now clearly possible, surprise would have been meaningless. Some other emotion was necessary, but she found at first only peripheral manifestations of one. Her heart was beating violently, her hands were shaking, and her fingers were cold. Her legs felt weak and she took hold of the back of a chair to steady herself. She found that she was still laughing, and then her emotion caught up with her and she knew what it was: it was relief.

"I'm glad you came," she said. She went over and put her head against his shoulder. "It was hard to say hello in the station," she said.

Smalljohn looked on for a minute and then wandered off to his toybox. Margaret was thinking, this is not the man who enjoyed seeing me cry; I need not be afraid. She caught her breath and was quiet; there was nothing that needed saying.

For the rest of the day she was happy. There was a constant delight in the relief from her weight of fear and unhappiness, it was pure joy to know that there was no longer any residue of suspicion and hatred; when she called him "John" she did so demurely, knowing that he participated in her secret amusement; when he answered her civilly there was, she thought, an edge of laughter behind his words. They seemed to have agreed soberly that mention of the subject would be in bad taste, might even, in fact, endanger their pleasure.

They were hilarious at dinner. John would not have made her a cocktail, but when she came downstairs from putting the children to bed the stranger met her at the foot of the stairs, smiling up at her, and took her arm to lead her into the living room where the cocktail shaker and glasses stood on the low table before the fire.

"How nice," she said, happy that she had taken a moment to brush her hair and put on fresh lipstick, happy that the coffee table which she had chosen with John and the fireplace which had seen many fires built by John and the low sofa where John had slept sometimes, had all seen fit to welcome the stranger with grace. She sat on the sofa and smiled at him when he handed her a glass; there was an odd illicit excitement in all of it; she was "entertaining" a man. The scene was a little marred by the fact that he had given her a martini with neither olive nor onion; it was the way she preferred her martini, and yet he should not have, strictly, known this, but she reassured herself with the thought that naturally he would have taken some pains to inform himself before coming.

He lifted his glass to her with a smile; he is here only because I am here, she thought.

"It's nice to be here," he said. He had, then, made one attempt to sound like John, in the car coming home. After he knew that she had recognized him for a stranger, he had never made any attempt to say words like "coming home" or "getting back," and of course she could not, not without pointing her lie. She put her hand in his and lay back against the sofa, looking into the fire.

"Being lonely is worse than anything in the world," she said.

"You're not lonely now?"

"Are you going away?"

"Not unless you come too." They laughed at his parody of John.

They sat next to each other at dinner; she and John had always sat at formal opposite ends of the table, asking one another politely to pass the salt and the butter.

"I'm going to put in a little set of shelves over there," he said, nodding toward the corner of the dining room. "It looks empty here, and it needs things. Symbols."

"Like?" She liked to look at him; his hair, she thought, was a little darker than John's, and his hands were stronger; this man would build whatever he decided he wanted built.

"We need things together. Things we like, both of us. Small delicate pretty things. Ivory."

With John she would have felt it necessary to remark at once that they could not afford such delicate pretty things, and put a cold finish to the idea, but with the stranger she said, "We'd have to look for them; not everything would be right."

"I saw a little creature once," he said. "Like a tiny little man, only colored all purple and blue and gold."

She remembered this conversation; it contained the truth like a jewel set in the evening. Much later, she was to tell herself that it was true; John could not have said these things.

She was happy, she was radiant, she had no conscience. He went obediently to his office the next morning, saying goodby at the door with a rueful smile that seemed to mock the present necessity for doing the things that John always did, and as she watched him go down the walk she reflected that this was surely not going to be permanent; she could not endure having him gone for so long every day, although she had felt little about parting from John; moreover, if he kept doing John's things he might grow imperceptibly more like John.

We will simply have to go away, she thought. She was pleased, seeing him get into the car; she would gladly share with him— indeed, give him outright—all that had been John's, so long as he stayed her stranger.

She laughed while she did her housework and dressed the baby. She took satisfaction in unpacking his suitcase, which he had abandoned and forgotten in a corner of the bedroom, as though prepared to take it up and leave again if she had not been as he thought her, had not wanted him to stay. She put away his clothes, so disarmingly like John's and wondered for a minute at the closet; would there be a kind of delicacy in him about John's things? Then she told herself no, not so long as he began with John's wife, and laughed again.

The baby was cross all day, but when Smalljohn came home from nursery school his first question was—looking up eagerly—"Where is Daddy?"

"Daddy has gone to the office," and again she laughed, at the moment's quick sly picture of the insult to John.

Half a dozen times during the day she went upstairs, to look at his suitcase and touch the leather softly. She glanced constantly as she passed through the dining room into the corner where the small shelves would be someday, and told herself that they would find a tiny little man, all purple and blue and gold, to stand on the shelves and guard them from intrusion.

When the children awakened from their naps she took them for a walk and then, away from the house and returned violently to her former lonely pattern (walk with the children, talk meaninglessly of Daddy, long for someone to talk to in the evening ahead, restrain herself from hurrying home: he might have telephoned), she began to feel frightened again; suppose she had been wrong? It could not be possible that she was mistaken; it would be unutterably cruel for John to come home tonight.

Then, she heard the car stop and when she opened the door and looked up she thought, no, it is not my husband, with a return of gladness. She was aware from his smile that he had perceived her doubts, and yet he was so clearly a stranger that, seeing him, she had no need of speaking.

She asked him, instead, almost meaningless questions during that evening, and his answers were important only because she was storing them away to reassure herself while he was away. She asked him what was the name of their Shakespeare professor in college, and who was that girl he liked so before he met Margaret. When he smiled and said that he had no idea, that he would not recognize the name if she told him, she was in delight. He had not bothered to master all of the past, then; he had learned enough (the names of the children, the location of the house, how she liked her cocktails) to get to her, and after that, it was not important, because either she would want him to stay, or she would, calling upon John, send him away again.

"What is your favorite food?" she asked him. "Are you fond of fishing? Did you ever have a dog?"

"Someone told me today," he said once, "that he had heard I was back from Boston, and I distinctly thought he said that he heard I was dead in Boston."

He was lonely, too, she thought with sadness, and that is why he came, bringing a destiny with him: now I will see him come every evening through the door and think, this is not my husband, and wait for him remembering that I am waiting for a stranger.

At any rate she said, "*you* were not dead in Boston, and nothing else matters."

She saw him leave in the morning with a warm pride, and she did her housework and dressed the baby; when Smalljohn came home from nursery school he did not ask, but looked with quick searching eyes and then sighed. While the children were taking their naps she thought that she might take them to the park this afternoon, and then the thought of another such afternoon, another long afternoon with no one but the children, another afternoon of widowhood, was more than she could submit to; I have done this too much, she thought, I must see something today beyond the faces of my children. No one should be so much alone.

Moving quickly, she dressed and set the house to rights. She called a high-school girl and asked if she would take the children to the park; without guilt, she neglected the thousand small orders regarding the proper jacket for the baby, whether Smalljohn might have popcorn, when to bring them home. She fled, thinking, I must be with people.

She took a taxi into town, because it seemed to her that the only possible thing to do was to seek out a gift for him, her first gift to him, and she thought she would find him, perhaps, a little creature all blue and purple and gold.

She wandered through the strange shops in the town, choosing small lovely things to stand on the new shelves, looking long and critically at ivories, at small statues, at brightly colored meaningless expensive toys, suitable for giving to a stranger.

It was almost dark when she started home, carrying her packages. She looked from the window of the taxi into the dark streets, and thought with pleasure that the stranger would be home before her, and look from the window to see her hurrying to him; he would think, this is a stranger, I am waiting for a stranger, as he saw her coming. "Here," she said, tapping on the glass, "right here, driver." She got out of the taxi and paid the driver, and smiled as he drove away. I must look well, she thought, the driver smiled back at me.

She turned and started for the house, and then hesitated; surely she had come too far? This is not possible, she thought, this cannot be; surely our house was white?

The evening was very dark, and she could see only the houses going in rows, with more rows beyond them and more rows beyond that, and somewhere a house which was hers, with the beautiful stranger inside, and she lost out here.

c. 1946

The Rock

B EING on the water was not precisely a unique, but rather an unusual, experience for Paula Ellison, and for the first few minutes that she sat on the small seat almost too close to the front of the boat, she was perfectly still, afraid not so much of upsetting the boat as of being unprepared when it surely did upset. She had gotten in first, and sat with her back to the island where they were going, watching the young man in the oilskin jacket as he helped first her sister-in-law Virginia, and then her brother Charles, into the more comfortable seats in the center of the boat. Charles, Paula thought, looked tired, and she thought further that she did not grudge him the better seat, or the reassurance of sitting next to Virginia, because Charles had certainly been so very ill, and was still not well, and looked tired after their journey.

"I'm so *excited*," Virginia said, and bounced in the boat almost like a child. Then she added, in the gentle voice both she and Paula were now using toward Charles, "How do you feel, darling?"

"Very well indeed," Charles said. "Very much better."

"It looks so *exciting*," Virginia said. "Look at it, all dark and rocky against the sky and that *perfect* sunset."

"What is that picture?" Charles asked. "*You* know the one."

"Like a pirate stronghold," Virginia continued ecstatically, "or a prison or some—"

Paula said with amusement, "Charles, do you think it entirely wise to bring Virginia to a place where she can indulge her romantic temperament so fully?"

Charles, without hearing her, said to Virginia, "Actually, I'm afraid it's only a rather ordinary summer resort." He smiled at his sister. "Do you think we might find one pirate for Virginia?"

Paula, without meaning to, looked over his head to the young man in the oilskin jacket who was running the boat, and found him at that moment looking at her, so that she turned quickly away and said, "It's cold."

"It *is* cold." Virginia pulled her coat closer around her.

"We're here so late in the year," Charles said.

Paula said immediately, "That's *much* better, you know; it means we'll be practically the only people and won't have to bother being sociable."

Virginia added, almost as quickly, "And I *always* think these early fall days are the best, after all. Relaxing," she added vaguely.

"Well, at least I didn't keep us from any vacation at all this year," Charles said.

"I never intended to take any vacation this year," Virginia said. "I *hate* going away in the summers, and the children are so much better off not going into public resorts."

"As you know," Paula said stiffly, "I rarely plan on a vacation at all. If it hadn't been for your insisting that you needed me—"

Charles laughed. "You worry too much," he said, turning from Virginia to Paula. "You don't have to fuss every time I mention being sick."

"You're not to think about it," Paula said.

"We all want to forget it," Virginia said.

"It's forgotten," Charles said. "How much longer will it take to reach the island?" From the inflection of his voice everyone immediately assumed that he was speaking to the young man in the oilskin jacket and did not know how otherwise to address him, whether as "driver" or "captain" or "ferryman" or perhaps "boy."

After a minute the young man said, "Nearly there."

"Does the island have a name?" Virginia asked.

"People round here call it mostly Rock Island," the young man said.

"Even *that* is exciting," Virginia said. She looked first at Charles and then at Paula. "Even that it should be named Rock Island. Like a stronghold, or a fort, or a—"

"Rock," Paula said.

"We land on the other side," the young man said, without being asked; it was as though every person whom he carried to the island asked the same series of questions, made the same comments, spoke of pirates and that picture, *you* know, and went on to ask how long now? and what was the name of the island, and as though the next question had to be "Where do we land?" or "Do we dock there?" or "How are you going to get the boat up onto those rocks?" and this time, for once, impatient and perhaps tired of ferrying, he answered the question before it could be asked. Paula, who thought that Virginia was again going to say "How exciting," said quickly, "Charles, are you tired?"

"No," he said, surprised. "Not tired at all; I'm feeling very well, really."

Although she had not intended to view this island, this site of her unexpected holiday, so soon, had meant ever since she stepped into the boat without being allowed a chance of turning around to keep her back steadfastly against the island and not turn, not turn, until she was close enough to touch it, Paula at last forgot her resolution and turned to look; she saw, looming impossibly large over her head and with the red sunset behind, a great black jagged rock, without signs of humanity or sympathy, with only dreadful reaching black rocks and sharp incredible outlines against the sunset and she said (thinking, I can always go back if it's *too* awful), "Charles, how do you feel?"

"I feel *fine*," he said sharply,

"It's just all *too* exciting," Virginia said.

As the boat came closer it appeared that the island was composed of a single rock instead of many; there were no pebbles or splinters of rock at the edges of the water in the little cove to which the young man guided the boat, and a series of steps leading up to the house above seemed to be carved out of the rock. The sun had gone by now and only a faint impression of the sunset lay in the sky; it had grown much colder and the coming darkness made the rock look blacker and the steps steep and wet.

"Can we get up there at all?" Paula said, leaning from the boat to look at the steps; realizing that she was expected to stand and move from the boat onto the steps she hesitated and then reflected that she could hardly stay on in the boat unless she chose to go back with the ferryman. I wish for once Virginia would move first, she thought, or Charles, and then rebuked herself with the recollection that after all Virginia could hardly climb over Paula in the end seat to get out, and Charles was ill. The young man stepped easily from the boat onto the rock and held out his hand to Paula, and she remembered that he had helped Virginia into the boat earlier, and took his hand and found herself with less grace than usual almost scrambling onto the rock steps. They were not wet, after all, or slippery, but seemed actually to press back against her feet as though holding firmly against her.

I like it here, she thought, surprising herself, and found the steps irresistible; before Virginia was even out of the boat Paula had turned and begun to climb. At first she only enjoyed the pressure of the steps under her feet, and then she raised her head and saw the house above her and she began to climb faster.

"Look at Paula, so far ahead," she heard Charles saying below her; he sounded cross, and she thought that perhaps he was annoyed with her for having spoken so much of his illness. Ahead of her the windows of the house showed light and then the door opened and someone came into the doorway, looking down and seeming to peer through the darkness.

"Who is it?" the woman in the doorway called.

Required to identify herself suddenly, Paula hesitated on the steps and then turned and looked behind her. Charles and Virginia were following her slowly, helping one another, and Paula felt first a small pang that she had not stayed with them, but had gone on so easily herself. Then, past the curve of the rock below her, she saw the boat going back, and was suddenly very frightened when she realized that the boat and the ferryman had never intended to stay with them; how will we ever get back? she wondered, and then smiled at herself, thinking that surely the ferryman must come back several times a day.

"Are you all right?" she called down to Charles and Virginia. "Shall I come back and help you?"

"We're all right," Virginia called up to her. "The steps are just a little steep for Charles."

Paula turned and climbed on up to the house while the woman in the doorway stood watching her. "So you've come," said the woman in the doorway when Paula was close enough for her to speak. "I'd almost given up expecting you."

Not a very gracious hostess, Paula thought. "We've been

late for everything all day," she explained. "Trains, busses, meals, everything."

"You'll have to take what you can get here tonight," the woman said. "Dinner's been done with for an hour, and the dishes washed and put away."

"I'm sure we won't want much," Paula said. She was displeased, and as she came up onto the last, wilder steps which led to the doorway she did not stop to look at the woman, but brushed past her and went inside. The room into which she came seemed to be made of the rock of the island, and for a minute she stood staring, forgetting the landlady behind her. A great fire burned on the far side of the huge room, and flickered against the walls in lines that might have been reflecting mica in rock, ran in light up and down the wide dark walls on which no pictures hung, and shattered itself oddly across and along the floor on which no rug lay. The furniture was huge and wooden, a great trestle table with benches on either side, and a long wooden bench with back and arms which brought the word "settle" to Paula's mind, and huge square wooden chairs, worn and smooth with use. There were no ornaments of any kind and no light except from the great fire.

Paula heard the landlady, still behind her in the doorway, calling down to Charles and Virginia that it was only a bit more to come, and then the landlady added very quietly, "You'll want to put in curtains and such, I daresay."

"Were you speaking to me?" Paula asked; there seemed no one else around.

"And flowers, I suppose."

Paula advanced to the fire and stood warming her hands. "It's a most unusual room," she said. She was trying to identify her own feelings; over and above everything else was a great despair and impulsive dislike of this house, this woman, this room; she tried to tell herself that it was the usual reaction to finishing a long journey and finding less comfort than she had been dreaming of since she left home. More than this, however, she was discouraged; this did not seem at all the sort of place in which to spend a belated vacation and she was anxious over how Charles and Virginia would feel about it. It'll be better in the morning when the sun is out, she told herself, and heard Charles and Virginia greeting the landlady.

"Did our suitcases come?" Charles was asking immediately; he had overseen their departure.

"This morning," said the landlady. "They're in your rooms."

"Splendid," said Charles. He came over to the fire and stood beside Paula. "Chill in the air," he said.

"It gets cold nights, this time of year," the landlady said.

"This is an extraordinary room," Virginia said. "It looks as though it's made out of rock."

"It *is* rock, as a matter of fact," said the landlady. "Most unusual. The greater part of the house is made of rock; I have a small booklet describing it for tourists, and I have put copies in your rooms. It is regarded as a most unusual house."

"It is *most* unusual," said Charles. "You are Mrs. Carter, of course?"

"Mrs. Carter," said the landlady, nodding. "Mr. and Mrs. Ellison."

"And Miss Ellison," said Charles, indicating Paula.

"Of course," said the landlady. "I have your rooms ready."

"Splendid," Charles said; he had taken command again now that there was no physical exertion required, and he looked patronizingly over Paula to say to the landlady, "Any chance of our having something to eat?"

The landlady waved her head back and forth sadly. "You came so late, you know," she said. "I can give you cheese, and beer; and perhaps, if you wanted to wait for a broiled chicken . . ."

"Just some tea for me, thanks," said Virginia.

"I should like some tea," Paula said.

"Whatever you can find, then, in a minute or so," Charles said. "Nothing that means any trouble."

The landlady nodded politely and went out of the room, and Charles, looking around with an odd smile, said "Well."

"Isn't it wonderful?" said Virginia. "That marvelous old woman, and this house . . ." she gestured at the walls and then, remembering, laughed and turned to Paula. "You know what she said to me, that funny old woman?" she demanded. "When I was just coming in the door, she whispered to me, was the tall woman with our party?" She laughed again. "Meaning *you*," she said to Paula.

"She didn't seem to like me," Paula said.

"These women are unaccountable," Charles said. "Remember she lives practically alone on this island."

"In this *wonderful* house," Virginia said.

It was substantially better in the daylight. They had slept in rooms adjoining one another, Charles and Virginia in a huge fourposter bed with curtains, and Paula in a small room with windows overlooking the water almost directly, and in the morning, lying awake in her bed, Paula was for a minute surprised at the moving reflections on the ceiling of her room before she realized that it was only the reflection of the sun on the water, reflected again through her windows. She rose from the bed and went to look out on the water and was shocked to see the steep and immediate fall of the island below her; this was the side of the island away from the steps they had come up the night before, and all this part of the house almost hung over the water. Looking down, Paula thought how in many ways this might be extraordinarily good for Charles after his illness, and good for Virginia and Paula too, since the whole aspect of the island lacked that cloying servitude which they all three hated by now, Charles from receiving it for so long, and she and Virginia from giving it; there was here no sense of heavy luxury and overrich surroundings, but only a very clear and distinct effect of an island out of sight of the mainland, sharp and strong alone on the water, and nothing below but solid rock and nothing more to do, perhaps, than endure the constant and incessant triumphs of water over rock, rock over water.

"I could spend all day," she thought, almost speaking aloud, "just standing somewhere watching the horizon, or sitting on a high rock, or walking down to the water and up again."

She put on a pair of heavy shoes, since if she were going to climb rocks she must be protected against their animosity, and went down the wide wooden stairs of the house into the stone room, where already this morning a fire was burning and the heavy furniture looked burnished in the sunlight through the windows. A clean napkin lay on the long wooden table and on it a heavy cup like the one she had had her tea from the night before, and a wooden trencher. Paula went to the door which she had learned led to the kitchen, opened it slightly, and called "Good morning."

"Well, there," said the landlady from somewhere within. "With us already?"

She swung the kitchen door wide and came into the stone room with an earthenware jug which she set down on the table. "Coffee," she said. "You'll have eggs, perhaps? And bacon? Fresh-made rolls?"

"Thank you," Paula said. Even the landlady seemed more cheerful this morning, and Paula thought that perhaps this was because she herself was not so sullen. "I'll have anything I may," she said, smiling. "I never dreamed I could be so hungry."

"It's being near the water," the landlady said profoundly. "You'll always have good appetite here. I've known them eat a whole chicken at a sitting."

"Tell me," Paula said, coming closer to look at the earthenware jug of coffee, "your dishes are so unusual, and so lovely. Where did you ever find them?"

"They came with the house," the landlady said. "I keep them because people seem to think they belong."

"They do, indeed," Paula said.

"Hard to wash clean," said the landlady, disappearing again into the kitchen.

This morning the moving lines of the firelight on the stone walls were caught and pursued by reflections of sunlight, and the broad windows overlooking the sea and the rock glittered until Paula wondered if the island could be seen from the mainland as a bright light on the horizon. She poured herself a cup of coffee from the earthenware jug, admiring its weight and solidity, and stood with her cup by the window, looking out. When the kitchen door opened she said without turning, "What is the rock the island is made of? I'd really swear it was black."

"Jet?" said the landlady's voice, musing, "malachite? I don't remember, but it's in the little book."

Paula came to the table and sat down, and served herself

with eggs and bacon onto the wooden trencher. The landlady stood by, silently, and when Paula began to eat she said, "You'll see my other guest this morning."

"Another guest?" said Paula.

"You'll be wanting to meet him as soon as possible," said the landlady.

"Who is he?" said Paula, but the landlady was going into the kitchen. She finished her breakfast and lighted a cigarette, and came back to the window with her cigarette and her coffee cup, and pulled one of the great wooden chairs around to sit in, so that she was almost hidden by the back of it and was surprised for a minute by the landlady's scolding voice until she realized it could not possibly be addressed to her.

"She's been and gone, of course," said the landlady. "You ought to have come an hour ago." There was the dull sound of the wooden trenchers being stacked together and the landlady's voice went on, "I can't after all keep coming to look for you when I want you; there are people here needing food and bedding and attention, and where you've gone I can never tell."

Since she was eavesdropping, Paula thought that the only thing to do was stand up immediately and go to the table for more coffee as though she had not been listening at all, which turned out to be more difficult than she thought, when she saw the landlady's surprised face.

"She's here again, then," the landlady said. "This will be the other guest, Miss."

I hope she doesn't fall to addressing all her guests so impertinently, Paula thought, and turned to smile at the other guest; she felt an immediate shock of recognition, as though this were someone she had known all her life, and then realized that she had never seen him before. "How do you do," she said, and then stopped because she did not know his name.

"How do you do, Miss Ellison," he said courteously but in such a low voice that she was not completely sure if he had called her by name. He seemed so frightened of her that she refrained from asking his name, but only smiled again and said, "I was admiring the view of the water from the window."

"That's why I like an island," he said. His tone and his manner were precisely those of someone excruciatingly shy, who cannot always stop to frame sensible remarks. He was very small, and held his hands in front of him in an attitude of cringing, and the only fact against his being so terribly shy was that he did not avoid looking at her, as a shy person would, but kept his eyes fixed upon her in a sort of hypnotized stare, and, staring back rudely, Paula thought that his eyes must be almost the color and texture of the rock itself.

"I was waiting for your sister-in-law, actually," he said.

"She'll be down in a while," said Paula, trying not to smile. Virginia was small and lovely, and shy little men like this always found her reassuring. "She was very tired after our trip yesterday, and I expect she'll sleep late."

"You'll *do*, of course," he said ineptly.

"Thank you," Paula said with gravity. "Have you been here long?"

"Quite a while," said the little man vaguely. "A very long time, in fact."

"I understand that this is quite a popular spot earlier in the year."

"Moderately so. Never more than a few people, that is." He looked at her earnestly. "Not many people feel at *home* on an island," he said.

"I suppose only a certain sort of person would find this stimulating," Paula said. She glanced out the window again and down to the sea below. "It's an excellent place for my brother to be, right now; he's been very ill, and needed precisely this kind of lonely, stimulating spot."

"It will probably do him a great deal of good," said the little man politely.

"I hope so," said Paula. She was thinking of how such a concrete, limited world as an island and the sea might be extraordinarily helpful to Charles, since he would be given no choice except rock or water, and could not waste his mind in a thousand distractions; he might come to see everything, as she sternly hoped, in terms of solidity and fluidity, and learn that the rock was, as a place to live, far preferable to the sea. Perhaps, even, confining Charles to an island for a while would result in his taking an island away with him and being thus enabled to preserve for himself this kind of firm rock to live on always . . . The little man disturbed her by saying, "You mustn't be *entirely* sure of the rock, you know."

"I beg your pardon?"

"Well, it's been here for a number of years, of course . . . and rock is a hard thing to get rid of . . ."

"I don't understand."

"It doesn't matter at all," he said nervously. "Your brother's illness—it's given you a good deal of worry?"

"Of course," she said; she had mentioned Charles's illness originally as a sort of warning; it would be wisest, she felt, to let the other guest know immediately that Charles had been very ill indeed and must not be disturbed, and must not, indeed, be allowed to disturb others with vagaries left over from his illness. She had not expected, however, that the conversation might allow this little man to feel that he had any right to ask more personal questions; a polite murmur of sympathy was the most she had felt was required of him.

"It's been very difficult for you," he said.

"Do you expect to be here long?" She hoped she did not sound too emphatic; these little men were sometimes hard to discourage and yet, on the other hand, they might be so easily affronted.

"Not much longer now." He smiled at her, and again she thought that his eyes in the timid face were much like the rock under her feet. "I intend to walk up to the high rock this morning," he said. "The highest point on the island. You can't miss it."

"It must be very interesting," she said flatly.

"I shall be there all morning," he said. "Just follow the path that begins under your windows. Good-by."

As she stood staring at the doorway out of which he had gone so suddenly she heard footsteps on the stairs, and a moment later her sister-in-law came into the room.

"Charles is feeling very tired and plans to stay in bed," she said. "Good morning, Paula dear."

"Good morning, Virginia. I'm so sorry about Charles."

"Is this coffee?"

The landlady came in, bustling and fussing at Virginia; Virginia would have fresh-baked rolls and bacon, and perhaps a gently boiled egg? Would Virginia have peaches brought from the mainland this morning? And the poor sick gentleman; would he have a tray?

Paula stood at the window and watched Virginia breakfast; already the sharp air of the sea outside had made her impatient with being indoors, and she found herself unwilling to move into the room when Virginia invited her to sit at the table and take more coffee; the window was at present as close as she might reasonably go to the outdoors, and she must remain within sight of the sea.

"*Wonderful* coffee," said Virginia. "I'm so hungry."

The landlady came over to the window and leaned out, standing near Paula.

"He'll be up on the high rock," she said softly.

"I know, he—"

"Mrs. Carter," said Virginia, "might I possibly have another of your incredible muffins?"

The landlady hurried off and into the kitchen, and Virginia said, without turning around, "Isn't she unbelievable?"

"Would you like to go for a walk this morning?" Paula asked. "If Charles is resting, you and I could go exploring."

"*Love* to," said Virginia. "All over the island—I can't wait."

The kitchen door swung open and the landlady returned, saying as she came, "The tray has gone up to the poor gentleman, and I hope he feels the better for it."

"Mrs. Carter," said Paula deliberately, "will you tell me the name of your other guest?"

"You ladies will be wanting fresh coffee," said the landlady, peering into the coffee jug; "shame on me for letting you waste yourselves on this."

"What other guest?" said Virginia as the landlady hurried off again.

"An odd little man," Paula said.

"And the view," said the landlady, returning, "you'll be wanting to see the view."

"My sister and I thought we might walk over the island this morning," Paula said.

"Indeed you will," said the landlady, "and if the poor gentleman upstairs calls, I'll be right here."

"Where would you suggest we start?" Paula asked.

"Well," said the landlady. She stopped, thinking, her hands on her broad hips, and frowning slightly. "Most people," she said, "prefer the steps down to the sea and then the path around the seashore. Or if you turn to the right as you leave the front door, you will find a path that takes you through our garden. If it were earlier in the year I might suggest bathing in the cove, but delicate young ladies do not care for bathing when the weather is chilled. Or perhaps—"

"What about the path that starts under my window?"

"That of course," said the landlady, "takes you just back down to the seashore again. Only if you go so far away and the poor gentleman upstairs should happen to call . . ."

"We'd better stay near the house," Virginia said.

"You were asking about my kitchens," said the landlady to Virginia. "If the other lady chooses to go walking and yet you want to stay within hearing of the poor gentleman upstairs, I would account it a pleasure to show you my kitchens."

"I should love to see them," Virginia said. "Paula?"

"The other young lady is aching to be outside," the land-lady said. "Some of us cannot resist the sea." She smiled po-litely at Paula and then turned again to Virginia. "If you are finished with your coffee," she said, "it might be as well to start before the day is much along." As Virginia rose, the land-lady said over her shoulder to Paula, "We'll see you back, then, by lunchtime. Mind the slippery rocks."

"Ah—Johnson," said the little man. "Yes, Johnson."

"I'm Paula Ellison, Mr. Johnson."

"Yes, of course. It was Virginia Ellison I was—yes, of course."

"Marvelous view up here."

"Isn't it? You'll be tired of the sound of your brother's voice, I expect?"

"Why, I don't know that I am, particularly. Of course, he's been so very ill."

"Yes."

"It's been quite a strain on both of us."

"Both of us? Oh, yes, Virginia, I see."

"We've had to take *very* careful charge of him."

"Of course. It must have been most upsetting."

"Well—tiring."

"Your own brother. Yes, I quite understand. And his wife such a—may I say?—such a *dependent* person."

"She did as much as she was able."

"Of course. As much as she was able, yes."

"She is not strong. And she had the children."

"Let me confess—I *do* dislike children. You do too, I take it?"

"Well . . . not of course my own nieces."

"Of course not. Your own brother's children. But with the responsibility so much on you, and your sister-in-law so dependent, and the children too—it is not surprising you have been allowed to exhaust yourself."

"It has been very tiring, yes."

"And then of course in addition there would be the realization that there is actually no tie like that of flesh and blood. No love like that between brother and sister."

"We have always been very close, Mr. Johnson."

"Of course. Unusually so, I daresay."

"Perhaps we have. Too close, perhaps."

"Neither of you could do very well without the other, I suppose. And it is so hard when one is ill."

"Very hard."

"I suppose you have never been so ill?"

"Never."

"But I daresay if you *were*, your brother would care for you as attentively as you care for him."

"If he could, yes."

"He has so much more to worry about. His children, his wife."

"He would hardly have much time for *me*."

"His wife would need him. She is so dependent, she could hardly spare him to care for his sister. Only his sister, when his wife and children need him at home."

"I am sure she would be most concerned if anything happened to me."

"Most concerned, yes. She is really very fond of you, I suppose."

"We are very fond of each other. Quite companionable."

"Perhaps your mutual concern over your brother brought you even closer together. You share one dear object, after all."

"Charles is very dear to both of us."

"Of course. His wife is probably with him now."

"I ought to go back."

"Not at all. If she is there, you can hardly be needed."

"Now then," said the landlady heartily, "here you are, back again much before you're wanted. My little joke," she added, looking at Paula's frown. "I am indeed a great joker. And you didn't stay long. Nothing to worry about with your sister, neither. She's up with the poor gentleman has been so ill, and I daresay gives him better medicine than any of us could, with the smile on her sweet face. And so you met Mr. Arnold?"

"Arnold? He said his name was Johnson."

"And so it is, if he says so. I'll be calling you Arnold or Heathen or something, give me my head; I never could remember a name and that's the truth. So you met him, whatever he chooses to call himself?"

"I ran into him by accident."

"So you did, dear, so you did. And you'll be wanting to know now where you can meet him next?"

"Nothing of the sort," said Paula stiffly. "I was about to go up—"

"To the high rock again? He won't be *there* by now. Tomorrow maybe. Try late tonight in front of the great fire, after the rest of us are abed. *There* you will find him."

"Certainly not," said Paula.

"Well, then it'll take you a while," said the landlady. "And the things he can tell you and all. Solid rock," she continued smoothly as Virginia came into the room, "and standing here since no one knows when."

"How is Charles?" Paula asked Virginia.

"Feeling much better, thank you," Virginia said.

"I'll just go up for a minute."

"Please don't," said Virginia hastily. "I mean, he said he was going to try to sleep and it would he better not to disturb him."

"And then of course there's Virginia, so weak, and so safe."

"She's not entirely safe—"

"Not entirely. But for all you or I could do . . ."

"She's very fond of me."

"And very fond of Charles. But so dependent. So pretty, too, and so weak, and so fragile. Such a pretty girl."

"I have been very necessary to her."

"Of course now that Charles is better you will not be quite so necessary. They will have each other again."

"That is as it should be."

"As you say. That is as it should be. And you?"

"I shall go home again, I suppose."

"Home?"

"I have a small apartment. I left there of course while Charles was so very ill. It was necessary for me to stay with Virginia."

"But now you will go back?"

"I have not been asked to stay with Virginia."

"They have each other again. And the children, and their home. I suppose they will feel sorry for you?"

"Sorry for me?"

"That you have gone, I mean. Sorry to be without you."

"I suppose so."

"See how the fire shines on the walls. It is perfectly safe here in this room, of course. This room is solid rock. It is only in the rest of the house that fire might be a danger. The rest of the house is of wood."

"Virginia, will you come exploring with me *today*?" Paula stood by the window; it was her daily habit now to take her breakfast there, sitting in the great wooden chair, where she could keep sight of the sea. During the day she found the sound and the smell and the sight of the sea almost a necessity for her, and at night she either sat late in the rock room with the great fire roaring before her and the sound of the sea all outside, or lay straight and silent on her narrow bed with the windows open onto the cliffs below and the sea almost in her room. "We've been here almost a week, and I don't believe you've so much as stepped outdoors."

"It makes me nervous," said Virginia. She smiled across the coffee jug at Paula. "I think I'm beginning to feel caught in by the island. Almost homesick for land on all sides instead of sea."

"Charles likes it."

"Sometimes," said Virginia. "Sometimes he's as much afraid as I am."

"Afraid, Virginia?"

"*You* know," Virginia said, gesturing vaguely. "You get to feeling so sort of cut off from everything. No way of escape. No way to get home again."

"I thought I'd run up and see Charles after breakfast," Paula said. "Is he sleeping?"

"Resting, anyway. Why don't you put it off until after lunch?"

"I will probably not be back. I intended to take a lunch with me and spend all day on the rocks."

"What can you find to *do* out there?"

"I find it stimulating, nothing but the sea and the rocks and nothing between them but me."

"And do you run across the other guest?" Virginia asked innocently.

"I sometimes gather shells, but there are no very interesting ones."

"You spoke once of another guest," Virginia said insistently. "Didn't you once mention an odd little man?"

"Suppose I just run up and say good morning to Charles, and spend just a minute trying to cheer him up?"

"He's cheerful enough. Why don't you wait till tonight?"

"I'd like to see him now, if you're sure you don't mind."

Silently, Virginia followed Paula upstairs and into the room Virginia and Charles shared. Paula had been here daily since they came, but Charles had not yet come downstairs, protesting that he was convalescing well enough in his bed, with the smell of the sea in his room and its sound in his ears always, and the landlady's good food brought to him regularly. He looked better, Paula thought; he had more color in his face—surprising, since he had not been outdoors or even had fresh air in the room—and he was astonishingly vigorous for someone who had been so very ill for such a long time.

"Good morning, Charles dear," she said as she entered. "And how well you look today!"

"I feel splendidly well," Charles said from the bed. He hoisted himself up slightly and turned his cheek for his sister's morning kiss. "*You* look well, Paula."

"I love it here. I'm afraid Virginia is bored, though."

"Is she?" Charles smiled over Paula's head at Virginia. "I don't think so," he said.

"You must try to get outdoors, Charles, and get nearer the sea. I can't tell you how invigorating I find it."

"Perhaps *you* do," Charles said. "Virginia and I prefer it indoors. We like our sea through windows."

"And *here*'s the poor gentleman's breakfast," said the landlady, bustling in with her tray. "Did he think I had forgotten him? When I was only waiting for hot corncakes from the oven? And see that you eat all of it, my poor Mr. Ellison, and we will have you well in no time at all."

"Will you have your breakfast, darling?" Virginia asked. She came closer to the bed. "Excuse me, Paula; let me come in here and see that his tray is right. Darling, are you hungry? I had such a wonderful breakfast downstairs."

"Good morning, Miss Ellison," said Mr. Johnson from the doorway. Paula looked up, over the heads of Charles and Virginia and the landlady and saw him, somehow taller, standing leaning against the doorway. "And how are *you* this morning?"

"I had eggs, and homemade sausage, just as you have, only I didn't have these wonderful corncakes. Just try one, darling. I believe Mrs. Carter made them especially for you."

"And how is your poor sick brother? *Is* he any better? And your sister-in-law, how is she?"

"Good morning, Mr. Johnson," Paula said.

"I beg your pardon, dear?" said Virginia, looking back at Paula over her shoulder. "Did you ask Charles something?"

"I doubt if she will bother with *me*, Miss Ellison. I doubt very much if she would ever be interested in me now."

Paula turned and stared, first at Charles and Virginia, who was bending over him laughing and feeding him, and then at the landlady, who was watching Paula silently and with an expression which might have been humorous.

"Mrs. Carter—" Paula said.

Mrs. Carter shrugged.

Mr. Johnson went on smoothly, "It had to be one or the other of you, you see; I told you I was waiting for your sister-in-law, but you *would* come first. It was your decision, you know; I would have been satisfied with either."

"Just don't try to answer him, dear," Mrs. Carter whispered. "There's no answer he'll take." She put a protective arm around Paula. "Try to hide behind me," she said very softly.

"No use, Mrs. Carter," he said, and, smiled sadly. "No use at all, you know." He nodded at Paula. "*She* knows," he said, and went swiftly and silently away.

c. 1951

The Honeymoon of Mrs. Smith

W HEN she came into the grocery she obviously interrupted a conversation about herself and her husband. The grocer leaning across the counter to speak confidentially to a customer straightened up abruptly and signaled at her with his eyes, so that the customer, in a fairly obvious attempt at dissimulation, looked stubbornly in the opposite direction for almost a minute before turning quickly to take one swift, eager look.

"Good morning," she said.

"What'll it be for you this morning?" he asked, his eyes moving to the right and left to insure that all present observed him speaking boldly to Mrs. Smith.

"I don't need very much," she said. "I may be going away over the weekend."

A long sigh swept through the store; she had a clear sense of people moving closer, as though the dozen other customers, the grocer, the butcher, the clerks, were pressing against her, listening avidly.

"A small loaf of bread," she said clearly. "A pint of milk. The smallest possible can of peas."

"Not laying in much for the weekend," the grocer said with satisfaction.

"I may be going away," she said, and again there was that long breath of satisfaction. She thought: how silly of all of us—I'm not sure any more than *they* are, we all of us only suspect, and of course there won't be any way of knowing for sure . . . but still it would be a shame to have all that food in the kitchen, and let it go to waste, just rotting there while . . .

"Coffee?" the grocer said. "Tea?"

"I'm going to get a pound of coffee," she said, smiling at him. "After all, I like coffee. I can probably drink up a pound before . . ."

The anticipatory pause made her say quickly, "And I'll want a quarter pound of butter, and I guess two lamb chops."

The butcher, although he had been trying to pretend indifference, turned immediately to get the lamb chops, and he came the width of the store and set the small package on the counter before the grocer had finished adding up her order.

One good thing, she was thinking about all this—I never have to *wait* anywhere. It's as though everyone knew I was in a hurry to get small things done. And I suppose no one really wants me around for very long, not after they've had their good look at me and gotten something to talk about.

When her groceries were all in a bag and the grocer was ready to hand it to her across the counter, he hesitated, as he had done several times before, as though he tried to gather courage to say something to her; she was aware of this, and knew fairly well what he wanted to say—listen, Mrs. Smith, it would start, we don't want to make any trouble or anything, and of course it isn't as though anyone around here was *sure*, but I guess you must know by now that it all looks mighty suspicious, and we just figured—with an inclusive glance around, for support from the butcher and the clerks—we all got talking, and we figured—well, we figured someone ought to say something to you about it. I guess people must have made this mistake before about you? Or your husband? Because of course no one likes to come right out and *say* a thing like that, when they could so easily be wrong. And of course the more everyone talks about this kind of thing, the harder it is to know whether you're right or not . . .

The man in the liquor store had said substantially that to her, fumbling and letting his voice die away under her cool, inquiring stare. The man in the drugstore had begun to say it, and then, blushing, had concluded, "Well, it's not *my* business, anyway." The woman in the lending library, the landlady, had given her the nervous, appraising look, wondering if she knew, if anyone had told her, wondering if they dared, and had ended by treating her with extreme gentleness and a sweet forbearance, as they would have treated some uncomplaining, incurable invalid. She was different in their eyes, she was marked; if the dreadful fact were not true (and they all hoped it was), she was in a position of such incredible, extreme embarrassment that their solicitude was even more deserved. If the dreadful fact *were* true (and they all hoped it was), they had none of them, the landlady, the grocer, the clerks, the druggist, lived in vain, gone through their days without the supreme excitement of being close to and yet secure from an unbearable situation. If the dreadful fact *were* true (and they all hoped it was), Mrs. Smith was, for them, a salvation and a heroine, a fragile, lovely creature whose preservation was in hands other than theirs.

Some of this Mrs. Smith realized dimly as she walked back to her apartment with the bag of groceries. She, at least, was almost not in doubt; she had known almost certainly that the dreadful fact was true for three weeks and six days, since she had met it face-to-face on a bench facing the ocean.

"I hope you won't think I'm rude," Mr. Smith had said at that moment, "if I open a conversation by saying that it's a lovely day."

She thought he was incredibly daring, she thought he was unbelievably vulgar, but she did not think he was rude; it was a word ridiculous when applied to him.

"No," she had said, recognizing him, "I don't think you're rude."

If she had ever tried to phrase it to herself—it would hardly be possible to describe it to anyone else—she might have said, in the faintly clerical idiom she had learned so thoroughly, that she had been chosen for this, or that it was like being carried unresisting on the surface of a river which took her on inevitably into the sea. Or she might have said that, just as in her whole life before she had not questioned the decisions of her father but had done quietly as she was told, so it was a relief to know that there was now someone again to decide for her, and that her life, inevitable as it had been before, was now clear as well. Or she might have said—with a blush for a possible double meaning, that they, like all other married couples, were two halves of what was essentially one natural act.

"A man gets very lonesome, I think," he had told her at dinner that night, in a restaurant near the sea, where even the napkins smelled of fish and the bare wood of the table had an indefinable salty grain, "a man alone needs to find himself some kind of company." And then, as though the words had perhaps not been complimentary enough, he added hastily, "Except not everyone is lucky enough to meet a charming young lady like yourself." She had smiled and simpered, by then fully aware of these preliminaries to her destiny.

Three weeks and six days later, turning to go in through the door of the shabby apartment house, she wondered briefly about the weekend ahead; she had been naturally reluctant to buy too much food, but then, if it turned out that she *should* be there, there would be no way to buy more food on Sunday; a restaurant, she thought, we will have to go to a restaurant— although they had not been together to a restaurant since that first dinner together since, even though they did not actually have to economize, they both felt soberly that the fairly large mutual bank account they now had ought not to be squandered unnecessarily, but should be kept as nearly intact as possible; they had not discussed this, but Mrs. Smith's instinctive tactful respect for her husband's methods led her to fall in with him silently in his routine of economy.

The three flights of stairs were narrow and high, and Mrs. Smith, with the immediate recognition of symbols she had inherited, had always had, potentially, and was now using almost exclusively, saw the eternal steps going up and up as an irrevocable design for her life; she had really no choice but to go up, wearily if she chose; if she turned and went down again, retracing laboriously the small progress she had made, she would merely have to go up another way, beginning, as she now almost realized, beginning again a search which could only, for her, have but one ending. "It happens to everybody," she told herself consolingly as she climbed.

Pride would not allow her to make any concessions to her position, so she did not try particularly to walk silently on the second floor landing; for a minute, going on up the next flight, she thought she had got safely past, but then, almost as she reached her own door, the door on the second landing opened and Mrs. Jones called, piercingly and as though she had run from some back recess of her apartment to the door when she heard footsteps.

"Mrs. Smith, is that you?"

"Hello," Mrs. Smith called back down the stairs.

"Wait a minute, I'm coming up." The lock on Mrs. Jones's door snapped, and the door closed. Mrs. Jones came hurriedly, still a little out of breath, down the landing and up the stairs to the third floor. "Thought I'd missed you," she said on the stairs, and, "Good heavens, you look tired."

It was part of the attitude that treated Mrs. Smith as a precious vessel. Her slightest deviation from the normal, in the course of more than a week, was noted and passed from gossip to gossip, a faint paling of her cheeks became the subject of nervous speculation, any change in her voice, a dullness of her eye, a disarrangement in her dress—these were what her neighbors lived on. Mrs. Smith had thought early in the week that a loud crash from her apartment would be the sweetest thing she could do for Mrs. Jones, but by now it no longer seemed important: Mrs. Jones could live as well on the most minute crumbs.

"Thought you'd never get home," Mrs. Jones said. She followed Mrs. Smith into the bare little room which, with a small bedroom, a dirty kitchen, and a bath, was the honeymoon home of Mr. and Mrs. Smith. Mrs. Jones took the package of groceries into the kitchen while Mrs. Smith hung up her coat in the closet; she had not bothered to unpack many things and the closet looked empty; there were two or three dresses and a light overcoat and extra suit of Mr. Smith's; this was so obviously only a temporary home for them both, a stopping-place. Mrs. Smith did not regard her three dresses with regret, nor did she particularly admire the suits of Mr. Smith, although they were still a little unfamiliar to her, hung up next to her own clothes (as was his underwear in the dresser, lying quietly beside her own); neither Mr. nor Mrs. Smith were of the abandoned sort who indulge recklessly in trousseaus or other loving detail for a preliminary purification.

"Well," said Mrs. Jones, coming out of the kitchen, "*you* certainly aren't planning to do much cooking this weekend."

Privacy was not one of the blessings of Mrs. Smith's position. "I thought I might be going away," she said.

Again there was that soft, anticipatory moment; Mrs. Jones looked quickly, and then away, and then, sitting herself down firmly upon the meager couch, obviously decided to come to the point.

"Now, look, Mrs. Smith," she began, and then interrupted herself. "Look, why this 'Mrs.' all the time? You call me Polly, and from now on I'll call you Helen. All right?" She smiled, and Mrs. Smith, smiling back, thought, how do they find out your first name? "Well, now, look here, Helen," Mrs. Jones went on, determined to establish her new familiarity immediately, "I think it's time someone sat down and talked sensibly to you. I mean, you must know by now pretty well what people are saying."

Here we are, Helen Smith was thinking, two women of the singular type woman, one standing uneasily and embarrassed in front of a window, wearing a brown dress and brown hair and brown shoes and differing in no essential respect from the other, sitting solidly and earnestly, wearing a green and pink flowered housedress and bedroom slippers—differing, actually in no essential, although we would both deny indignantly that we were the same person, seeking the same destiny. And we are about to enter into a conversation upon a fantastic subject.

"I've noticed," Mrs. Smith said carefully, "that there's a lot of unusual interest in us. I've never been on a honeymoon before, of course, so I can't really tell whether it's only that." She laughed weakly, but Mrs. Jones was not to be put off by sentiment.

"I think you must know better than that," she said. "You're not *that* wrapped up in your husband."

"Well . . . no," Mrs. Smith had to say.

"And furthermore," Mrs. Jones went on, looking cynically at Mrs. Smith, "you're not any blushing eighteen-year-old girl, you know, and Mr. Smith isn't any young man. You're both people of a reasonably mature age." Mrs. Jones seemed to feel that she had made a point here, and she said it again. "You are both people who have outlived their youth," she said, "and naturally no one expects that you're going to go around billing and cooing. And *furthermore* you yourself are old enough to show some intelligence about this terrible business."

"I don't know what kind of intelligence I ought to show," Mrs. Smith said meekly.

"Well, good heavens!" Mrs. Jones spread her hands helplessly. "Don't you realize your position? *Everyone* knows it. Look." She settled back, prepared to demonstrate reasonably. "You came here a week ago, newly married, and moved into this apartment with your husband. The very first day you were here, people thought there was something funny. In the first place, you two didn't act like you were the types for each other at all. You know what I mean—you so sort of refined and lady-like, and him . . ."

Rude, Mrs. Smith thought, wanting to laugh; he said he was rude.

Mrs. Jones shrugged. "In the second place," she said, "you didn't look like you belonged in this house, or in this neighborhood, because you always had plenty of money, which, believe me, the rest of us don't, and you always acted sort of as though you ought to be in a better kind of situation. And in the *third* place," Mrs. Jones said, hurrying on to her climax, "it wasn't two days before people began to think they recognized your husband from the pictures in the paper."

"I see what you mean," Mrs. Smith said. "But a picture in the paper—"

"That's just what started us really thinking," Mrs. Jones said. She enumerated on her fingers. "New bride. Cheap apartment. You made a will in his favor? Insurance?"

"Yes, but that is only natural—" said Mrs. Smith.

"Natural? And him looking just like the man in the paper who mur—" She stopped abruptly. "I don't want to frighten you," she said. "But you should know all about him."

"I appreciate your concern," Mrs. Smith said in her turn, coming away from the window, to stand in front of Mrs. Jones so that Mrs. Jones had to look up from her seat on the couch. "I know all these things. But how many newly married couples are there who make wills in each other's favor? Or take out insurance? And how many women over thirty get married to men over forty? And maybe sometimes the men look like pictures in the paper? And with all this talk and gossip about us all around the neighborhood, you notice no one's been even sure enough to say anything?"

"I wanted to call the police two, three days ago," Mrs. Jones said sullenly. "Ed wouldn't let me."

"He probably said," Mrs. Smith said, "that it was none of your business."

"But everybody's *wondering*," Mrs. Jones said. "And of course no one can know for sure."

"You won't know for sure until . . ." Mrs. Smith tried not to smile.

Mrs. Jones sighed. "I wish you wouldn't talk like that," she said.

"Well," said Mrs. Smith reasonably, "what exactly is it you want me to do?"

"You could get some kind of information," Mrs. Jones said. "Something that would let you know for sure."

"I keep telling you," Mrs. Smith said, "there's only one way I can ever know for sure."

"Don't *talk* like that," Mrs. Jones said.

"I could run away from my husband," Mrs. Smith said.

Mrs. Jones was surprised "You can't run away from your *husband*," she said. "Not if it isn't true, you couldn't do that."

"I have really no grounds for divorce," Mrs. Smith said. "It is a very difficult subject to mention to him."

"Naturally, you wouldn't have discussed it," Mrs. Jones said.

"Naturally," Mrs. Smith said. "I could hardly search his clothes—there is nothing, I happen to know, in the pockets of the suit hanging in the closet and searching his overcoat pockets and his dresser drawers would hardly turn up anything convincing."

"Why not?"

"Well, I mean," said Mrs. Smith in explanation, "even if I discovered, say, a knife—what difference would it make?"

"But he doesn't do it with—" Mrs. Jones began, and stopped abruptly again.

"I know," Mrs. Smith said. "As I recall the details—and I haven't read much about them, after all—he generally does it—"

"In the bathtub," Mrs. Jones said, and shivered. "I don't know but what a knife would be better," she said.

"It's not our choice," Mrs. Smith said wryly. "You see how silly we sound? Here we are, talking as though we were children telling ghost stories. We'll end up convincing each other of some horrible notion."

Mrs. Jones hesitated for a minute over her own reactions,

and finally decided to be mildly offended. "I really only came up," she explained with dignity, "to let you know what people were saying. If you stop to *think* about it for a minute, you ought to be able to understand why someone might want to help you. After all, it's not me."

"That's why I think you ought not to worry," Mrs. Smith said gently.

Mrs. Jones rose, but as she reached the door she was unable to keep herself from turning and saying urgently, "Look, I just want you to know that if you ever *ever* need any help—of *any* kind—just open your mouth and scream, see? Because my Ed will be up as fast as he can come. All you have to do is scream, or stamp on the floor, or, if you can, race downstairs to our place. We'll be waiting for you." She opened the door, said with a voice that she tried to make humorous, "Don't take any baths," and went out. Her voice trailed up from the stairs, "And remember—all you have to do is scream. We'll be waiting."

Mrs. Smith closed the door rather quickly and, before she started to think, went out to the kitchen to see to her groceries, but Mrs. Jones had put the things away. Mrs. Smith found the pound of coffee, and measured water into the coffeepot, thinking of her promise to the grocer that she would finish the pound of coffee herself. Mr. Smith drank coffee sparingly; it made him nervous.

Mrs. Smith, as she moved about the bleak little kitchen, thought, as she had often before, that she would not like to spend her whole life with things like this. It had not been so in her father's life, where a peaceful, well-ordered existence went placidly on among objects which, if not lovely, had at least the pleasures of familiarity, and the near-beauty of order, and Mrs. Smith, who had then been Helen Bertram, had been able to spend long days working in the garden, or mending her father's socks, or baking the nut cake she had learned from her mother, and pausing only occasionally to wonder what was going to happen to her in her life.

It had been clear to her after her father's death that this patterned existence was no longer meaningful, and had been a product of her father's life rather than hers. So that when Mr. Smith had said to her, "I don't suppose you'd ever consider marrying a fellow like me?" Helen Bertram had nodded, seeing then the repeated design which made the complete pattern.

She had worn her best dark blue dress to be married in, and Mr. Smith had worn a dark blue suit so that they looked unnervingly alike when they went down the street together. They had gone directly to the lawyer's, for the wills, and then to the insurance company. On the way, Mr. Smith had insisted on stopping and buying for the new Mrs. Smith a small felt dog which amused her; there had been a man selling these on the street corner, and all around his small stand were tiny wound-up dogs which ran in circles, squeaking in shrill imitation of a bark. Mrs. Smith brought the box with the dog in it into the insurance company and set it on the desk, and while they were waiting for the doctor she had opened the box and found that there was no key to wind the dog; Mr. Smith, saying irritably, "Those fellows always try to cheat you," had hurried back to the street corner and found the stand, the salesman, and the performing dogs gone.

"Nothing makes me more furious," he told Mrs. Smith, "than to be cheated by someone like that."

The small dog stood now on the shelf in the kitchen and Mrs. Smith, glancing at it, thought, I could not endure spending the rest of my life with that tawdry sort of thing. She sometimes thought poignantly of her father's house, realizing that such things were gone from her forever, but, as she told herself again now, "I had my eyes open." It will have to be soon, she thought immediately after, people are beginning to wonder too openly. Everyone is waiting; it will spoil everything if it is not soon. When her coffee was finished she took a cup into the living room and sat down on the couch where Mrs. Jones had been sitting, and thought, it will have to be soon; there's no food for the weekend, after all, and I would have to send my dress to the cleaners on Monday if I were here, and another week's rent due tomorrow. The pound of coffee would be the only detail unattended to.

She had finished her fourth cup of coffee—drinking by now hastily and even desperately—when she heard her husband's step on the stairs. They were still a little embarrassed with one another, so that she hesitated about going to meet him just long enough for him to open the door, and then she came over to him awkwardly and, not knowing still whether he wanted to kiss her when he came home, stood expectantly until he came politely over to her and kissed her cheek.

"Where have you been?" she asked, although it was not at all the sort of thing she wanted to say to him, and she knew as she spoke that he would not tell her.

"Shopping," he said. He had an armful of packages, one of which he selected and gave to her.

"Thank you," she said politely before she opened it, it was, she knew by the feel and the drugstore wrapping, a box of candy, and with a feeling which, when she felt it again later, she knew to be triumph, she thought, of course, it's supposed to be left over, it's to prove the new husband still brings presents to his bride. She opened the box, wanted to take a candy, thought: not before dinner, and then thought, it probably doesn't matter, tonight.

"Will you have one?" she said to him, and he took one.

His manner did not seem strange, or nervous, but when she said, "Mrs. Jones was up here this afternoon," he said quickly, "What did she want, the old busybody?"

"I think she was jealous," Mrs. Smith said. "It's been a long time since *her* husband has taken any interest in her."

"I can imagine," he said.

"Shall I start dinner?" Mrs. Smith asked. "Would you like to rest for a while first?"

"I'm not hungry," he said.

Now, for the first time, he seemed awkward, and Mrs. Smith thought quickly, I was right about the food for the weekend, I guessed right; he did not ask if she was hungry because—and each of them knew now that the other knew—it really did not matter.

Mrs. Smith told herself it would ruin everything to say anything now, and she sat down on the couch next to her husband and said, "I'm a little tired, I think."

"A week of marriage was too much for you," he said, and patted her hand. "We'll have to see that you get more rest."

Why does it take so long, why *does* it take so long? Mrs. Smith thought; she stood up again and walked across the room nervously to look out the window; Mr. Jones was just coming up the front steps and he looked up and saw her and waved. Why does it take so long? she thought again, and turned and said to her husband, "Well?"

"I suppose so," Mr. Smith said, and got up wearily from the couch.

no date

APPENDIX

Biography of a Story

O N the morning of June 28, 1948, I walked down to the post office in our little Vermont town to pick up the mail. I was quite casual about it, as I recall—I opened the box, took out a couple of bills and a letter or two, talked to the postmaster for a few minutes, and left, never supposing that it was the last time for months that I was to pick up the mail without an active feeling of panic. By the next week I had had to change my mailbox to the largest one in the post office, and casual conversation with the postmaster was out of the question, because he wasn't speaking to me. June 28, 1948, was the day *The New Yorker* came out with a story of mine in it. It was not my first published story, nor my last, but I have been assured over and over that if it had been the only story I ever wrote or published, there would be people who would not forget my name.

I had written the story three weeks before, on a bright June morning when summer seemed to have come at last, with blue skies and warm sun and no heavenly signs to warn me that my morning's work was anything but just another story. The idea had come to me while I was pushing my daughter up the hill in her stroller—it was, as I say, a warm morning, and the hill was steep, and beside my daughter the stroller held the day's groceries—and perhaps the effort of that last fifty yards up the hill put an edge to the story; at any rate, I had the idea fairly clearly in my mind when I put my daughter in her playpen and the frozen vegetables in the refrigerator, and, writing the story, I found that it went quickly and easily, moving from beginning to end without pause. As a matter of fact, when I read it over later I decided that except for one or two minor corrections, it needed no changes, and the story I finally typed up and sent off to my agent the next day was almost word for word the original draft. This, as any writer of stories can tell you, is not a usual thing. All I know is that when I came to read the story over I felt strongly that I didn't want to fuss with it. I didn't think it was perfect, but I didn't want to fuss with it. It was, I thought, a serious, straightforward story, and I was pleased and a little surprised at the ease with which it had been written; I was reasonably proud of it, and hoped that my agent would sell it to some magazine and I would have the gratification of seeing it in print.

My agent did not care for the story, but—as she said in her note at the time—her job was to sell it, not to like it. She sent it at once to *The New Yorker*, and about a week after the story had been written I received a telephone call from the fiction editor of *The New Yorker*; it was quite clear that he did not really care for the story, either, but *The New Yorker* was going to buy it. He asked for one change—that the date mentioned in the story be changed to coincide with the date of the issue of the magazine in which the story would appear, and I said of course. He then asked, hesitantly, if I had any particular interpretation of my own for the story; Mr. Harold Ross, then the editor of *The New Yorker*, was not altogether sure that he understood the story, and wondered if I cared to enlarge upon its meaning. I said no. Mr. Ross, he said, thought that the story might be puzzling to some people, and in case anyone telephoned the magazine, as sometimes happened, or wrote in asking about the story, was there anything in particular I wanted them to say? No, I said, nothing in particular; it was just a story I wrote.

I had no more preparation than that. I went on picking up the mail every morning, pushing my daughter up and down the hill in her stroller, anticipating pleasurably the check from *The New Yorker*, and shopping for groceries. The weather stayed nice and it looked as though it was going to be a good summer. Then, on June 28, *The New Yorker* came out with my story.

Things began mildly enough with a note from a friend at *The New Yorker*: "Your story has kicked up quite a fuss around the office," he wrote. I was flattered; it's nice to think that your friends notice what you write. Later that day there was a call from one of the magazine's editors; they had had a couple of people phone in about my story, he said, and was there anything I particularly wanted him to say if there were any more calls? No, I said, nothing particular; anything he chose to say was perfectly all right with me; it was just a story.

I was further puzzled by a cryptic note from another

friend: "Heard a man talking about a story of yours on the bus this morning," she wrote. "Very exciting. I wanted to tell him I knew the author, but after I heard what he was saying I decided I'd better not."

One of the most terrifying aspects of publishing stories and books is the realization that they are going to be read, and read by strangers. I had never fully realized this before, although I had of course in my imagination dwelt lovingly upon the thought of the millions and millions of people who were going to be uplifted and enriched and delighted by the stories I wrote. It had simply never occurred to me that these millions and millions of people might be so far from being uplifted that they would sit down and write me letters I was downright scared to open; of the three-hundred-odd letters that I received that summer I can count only thirteen that spoke kindly to me, and they were mostly from friends. Even my mother scolded me: "Dad and I did not care at all for your story in *The New Yorker*," she wrote sternly; "it does seem, dear, that this gloomy kind of story is what all you young people think about these days. Why don't you write something to cheer people up?"

By mid-July I had begun to perceive that I was very lucky indeed to be safely in Vermont, where no one in our small town had ever heard of *The New Yorker*, much less read my story. Millions of people, and my mother, had taken a pronounced dislike to me.

The magazine kept no track of telephone calls, but all letters addressed to me care of the magazine were forwarded directly to me for answering, and all letters addressed to the magazine —some of them addressed to Harold Ross personally; these were the most vehement—were answered at the magazine and then the letters were sent me in great batches, along with carbons of the answers written at the magazine. I have all the letters still, and if they could be considered to give any accurate cross section of the reading public, or the reading public of *The New Yorker*, or even the reading public of one issue of *The New Yorker*, I would stop writing now.

Judging from these letters, people who read stories are gullible, rude, frequently illiterate, and horribly afraid of being laughed at. Many of the writers were positive that *The New*

Yorker was going to ridicule them in print, and the most cautious letters were headed, in capital letters: NOT FOR PUBLICATION or PLEASE DO NOT PRINT THIS LETTER, or, at best, THIS LETTER MAY BE PUBLISHED AT YOUR USUAL RATES OF PAYMENT. Anonymous letters, of which there were a few, were destroyed. *The New Yorker* never published any comment of any kind about the story in the magazine, but did issue one publicity release saying that the story had received more mail than any piece of fiction they had ever published; this was after the newspapers had gotten into the act, in midsummer, with a front-page story in the San Francisco *Chronicle* begging to know what the story meant, and a series of columns in New York and Chicago papers pointing out that *New Yorker* subscriptions were being canceled right and left.

Curiously, there are three main themes which dominate the letters of that first summer—three themes which might be identified as bewilderment, speculation, and plain old-fashioned abuse. In the years since then, during which the story has been anthologized, dramatized, televised, and even—in one completely mystifying transformation—made into a ballet, the tenor of letters I receive has changed. I am addressed more politely, as a rule, and the letters largely confine themselves to questions like what does this story mean? The general tone of the early letters, however, was a kind of wide-eyed, shocked innocence. People at first were not so much concerned with what the story meant; what they wanted to know was where these lotteries were held, and whether they could go there and watch. Listen to these quotations:

> (Kansas)   Will you please tell me the locale and the year of the custom?
> (Oregon)   Where in heaven's name does there exist such barbarity as described in the story?
> (New York)   Do such tribunal rituals still exist and if so where?
> (New York)   To a reader who has only a fleeting knowledge of traditional rites in various parts of the country (I presume the plot was laid in the United States) I found the cruelty of the ceremony outrageous, if not unbeliev-

able. It may be just a custom or ritual which I am not familiar with.

(New York) Would you please explain whether such improbable rituals occur in our Middle Western states, and what their origin and purpose are?

(Nevada) Although we recognize the story to be fiction is it possible that it is based on fact?

(Maryland) Please let me know if the custom of which you wrote actually exists.

(New York) To satisfy my curiousity would you please tell me if such rites are still practiced and if so where?

(California) If it is based on fact would you please tell me the date and place of its origin?

(Texas) What I would like to know, if you don't mind enlightening me, is in what part of the United States this organized, apparently legal lynching is practiced? Could it be that in New England or in equally enlightened regions, mass sadism is still part and parcel of the ordinary citizen's life?

(Georgia) I'm hoping you'll find time to give me further details about the bizarre custom the story describes, where it occurs, who practices it, and why.

(Brooklyn, N.Y.) I am interested in learning if there is any particular source or group of sources of fact or legend on which and from which the story is based? This story has caused me to be particularly disturbed by my lack of knowledge of such rites or lotteries in the United States.

(California) If it actually occurred, it should be documented.

(New York) We have not read about it in *In Fact*.

(New York) Is it based on reality? Do these practices still continue in back-country England, the human sacrifice for the rich harvest? It's a frightening thought.

(Ohio) I think your story is based on fact. Am I right? As a psychiatrist I am fascinated by the psychodynamic possibilities suggested by this anachronistic ritual.

(Mississippi) You seem to describe a custom of which I am totally ignorant.

(California) It seems like I remember reading some-where a long time ago that that was the custom in a cer-tain part of France some time ago. However I have never heard of it being practiced here in the United States. However would you please inform me where you got your information and whether or not anything of this na-ture has been perpetrated in modern times?

(Pennsylvania) Are you describing a current custom?

(New York) Is there some timeless community existing in New England where human sacrifices are made for the fertility of the crops?

(Boston) Apparently this tale involves an English cus-tom or tradition of which we in this country know nothing.

(Canada) Can the lottery be some barbaric event, a hangover from the Middle Ages perhaps, which is still carried on in the States? In what part of the country does it take place?

(Los Angeles) I have read of some queer cults in my time, but this one bothers me.

(Texas) Was this group of people perhaps a settlement descended from early English colonists? And were they continuing a Druid rite to assure good crops?

(Quebec) Is this a custom which is carried on some-where in America?

(A London psychologist) I have received requests for elucidation from English friends and patients. They would like to know if the barbarity of stoning still exists in the U.S.A. and in general what the tale is all about and where does the action take place.

(Oregon) Is there a witchcraft hangover somewhere in these United States that we Far Westerners have missed?

(Madras, India) We have been wondering whether the story was based on fact and if so whether the custom de-scribed therein of selecting one family by lot jointly to be stoned by the remainder of the villagers still persists any-where in the United States. *The New Yorker* is read here in our United States information library and while we have had no inquiries about this particular article as yet, it is possible we shall have and I would be glad to be in a position to answer them.

(England) I am sorry that I cannot find out the state in which this piece of annual propitiatory sacrifice takes place. Now I just frankly don't believe that even in the United States such things happen—at least not without being sponsored by Lynching Inc. or the All-American Morticians Group or some such high-powered organization. I was once offered a baby by a primitive tribe in the center of Laos (Indochina) which my interpreter (Chinese) informed me I had to kill so that my blood lust was satiated and I would leave the rest of the tribe alone. But NOT in the United States, PLEASE.

(Connecticut) Other strange old things happen in the Appalachian mountain villages, I'm told.

As I say, if I thought this was a valid cross section of the reading public, I would give up writing. During this time, when I was carrying home some ten or twelve letters a day, and receiving a weekly package from *The New Yorker*, I got one letter which troubled me a good deal. It was from California, short, pleasant, and very informal. The man who wrote it clearly expected that I would recognize his name and his reputation, which I didn't. I puzzled over this letter for a day or two before I answered it, because of course it is always irritating to be on the edge of recognizing a name and have it escape you. I was pretty sure that it was someone who had written a book I had read or a book whose review I had read or a story in a recent magazine or possibly even—since I come originally from California—someone with whom I had gone to high school. Finally, since I had to answer the letter, I decided that something carefully complimentary and noncommittal would be best. One day, after I had mailed him my letter, some friends also from California stopped in and asked—as everyone was asking then—what new letters had come. I showed them the letter from my mysterious not-quite-remembered correspondent. Good heavens, they said, was this really a letter from *him*? Tell me who he is, I said desperately, just tell me who he is. Why, how could anyone forget? It had been all over the

California papers for weeks, and in the New York papers, too; he had just been barely acquitted of murdering his wife with an ax. With a kind of awful realization creeping over me I went and looked up the carbon of the letter I had written him, my noncommittal letter. "Thank you very much for your kind letter about my story," I had written. "I admire *your* work, too."

The second major theme which dominates the letters is what I call speculation. These letters were from the people who sat down and figured out a meaning for the story, or a reason for writing it, and wrote in proudly to explain, or else wrote in to explain why they could not possibly believe the story had any meaning at all.

(New Jersey) Surely it is only a bad dream the author had?

(New York) Was it meant to be taken seriously?

(New York) Was the sole purpose just to give the reader a nasty impact?

(California) The main idea which has been evolved is that the author has tried to challenge the logic of our society's releasing its aggressions through the channel of minority prejudice by presenting an equally logical (or possibility more logical) method of selecting a scapegoat. The complete horror of the cold-blooded method of choosing a victim parallels our own culture's devices for handling deep-seated hostilities.

(Virginia) I would list my questions about the story but it would be like trying to talk in an unknown language so far as I am concerned. The only thing that occurs to me is that perhaps the author meant we should not be too hard on our presidential nominees.

(Connecticut) Is *The New Yorker* only maintaining further its policy of intellectual leg-pulling?

(New York) Is it a publicity stunt?

(New Orleans) I wish Mrs. Hutchinson had been queen for a day or something nice like that before they stoned the poor frightened creature.

(New York) Anyone who seeks to communicate with the public should be at least lucid.

(New Jersey)   Please tell me if the feeling I have of having dreamed it once is just part of the hypnotic effect of the story.

(Massachusetts)   I earnestly grabbed my young nephew's encyclopedia and searched under "stoning" or "punishment" for some key to the mystery; to no avail.

(California)   Is it just a story? Why was it published? Is it a parable? Have you received other letters asking for some explanation?

(Illinois)   If it is simply a fictitious example of man's innate cruelty, it isn't a very good one. Man, stupid and cruel as he is, has always had sense enough to imagine or invent a charge against the objects of his persecution: the Christian martyrs, the New England witches, the Jews and Negroes. But nobody had anything against Mrs. Hutchinson, and they only wanted to get through quickly so they could go home for lunch.

(California)   Is it an allegory?

(California)   Please tell us it was all in fun.

(Los Angeles *Daily News*) Was Tessie a witch? No, witches weren't selected by lottery. Anyway, these are present-day people. Is it the post-atomic age, in which there is insufficient food to sustain the population and one person is eliminated each year? Hardly. Is it just an old custom, difficult to break? Probably. But there is also the uncomfortable feeling that maybe the story wasn't supposed to make sense. The magazines have been straining in this direction for some time and *The New Yorker*, which we like very much, seems to have made it.

(Missouri)   In this story you show the perversion of democracy.

(California)   It seems obscure.

(California)   I caught myself dreaming about what I would do if my wife and I were in such a predicament. I think I would back out.

(Illinois)   A symbol of how village gossip destroys a victim?

(Puerto Rico)   You people print any story you get, just throwing the last paragraph into the wastebasket before it appears in the magazine.

(New York) Were you saying that people will accept any evil as long as it doesn't touch them personally?

(Massachusetts) I am approaching middle age; has senility set in at this rather early age, or is it that I am not so acute mentally as I have had reason to assume?

(Canada) My only comment is what the hell?

(Maine) I suppose that about once every so often a magazine may decide to print something that hasn't any point just to get people talking.

(California) I don't know how there could be any confusion in anyone's mind as to what you were saying; nothing could possibly be clearer.

(Switzerland) What does it mean? Does it hide some subtle allegory?

(Indiana) What happened to the paragraph that tells what the devil is going on?

(California) I missed something here. Perhaps there was some facet of the victim's character which made her unpopular with the other villagers. I expected the people to evince a feeling of dread and terror, or else sadistic pleasure, but perhaps they were laconic, unemotional New Englanders.

(Ohio) A friend darkly suspects you people of having turned a bright editorial red, and that is how he construed the story. Please give me something to go on when I next try to placate my friend, who is now certain that you are tools of Stalin. If you *are* subversive, for goodness sake I don't blame you for not wanting to discuss the matter and of course you have every constitutional right in back of you. But at least please explain that damned story.

(Venezuela) I have read the story twice and from what I can gather all a man gets for his winnings are rocks in his head, which seems rather futile.

(Virginia) The printers left out three lines of type somewhere.

(Missouri) You printed it. Now give with the explanations.

(New York) To several of us there seemed to be a rather sinister symbolism in the cruelty of the people.

(Indiana) When I first read the story in my issue, I felt that there was no moral significance present, that the story was just terrifying, and that was all. However, there has to be a reason why it is so alarming to so many people. I feel that the only solution, the only reason it bothered so many people is that it shows the power of society over the individual. We saw the ease with which society can crush any single one of us. At the same time, we saw that society need have no rational reason for crushing the one, or the few, or sometimes the many.

(Connecticut) I thought that it might have been a small-scale representation of the sort of thing involved in the lottery which started the functioning of the selective-service system at the start of the last war.

Far and away the most emphatic letter writers were those who took this opportunity of indulging themselves in good old-fashioned name-calling. Since I am making no attempt whatsoever to interpret the motives of my correspondents, and would not if I could, I will not try now to say what I think of people who write nasty letters to other people who just write stories. I will only read some of their comments.

(Canada) Tell Miss Jackson to stay out of Canada.

(New York) I expect a personal apology from the author.

(Massachusetts) I think I had better switch to the *Saturday Evening Post*.

(Massachusetts) I will never buy *The New Yorker* again. I resent being tricked into reading perverted stories like "The Lottery."

(Connecticut) Who is Shirley Jackson? Cannot decide whether she is a genius or a female and more subtle version of Orson Welles.

(New York) We are fairly well educated and sophisticated people, but we feel that we have lost all faith in the truth of literature.

(Minnesota) Never in the world did I think I'd protest a story in *The New Yorker*, but really, gentlemen, "The Lottery" seems to me to be in incredibly bad taste. I read it while soaking in the tub and was tempted to put my head under water and end it all.

(California; this from a world-famous anthropologist) If the author's intent was to symbolize into complete mystification and at the same time be gratuitously disagreeable, she certainly succeeded.

(Georgia) Couldn't the story have been a trifle esoteric, even for *The New Yorker* circulation?

(California) "The Lottery" interested some of us and made the rest plain mad.

(Michigan) It certainly is modern.

(California) I am glad that your magazine does not have the popular and foreign-language circulation of the *Reader's Digest*. Such a story might make German, Russian, and Japanese realists feel lily-white in comparison with the American. The old saying about washing dirty linen in public has gone out of fashion with us. At any rate this story has reconciled me to not receiving your magazine next year.

(Illinois) Even to be polite I can't say that I liked "The Lottery."

(Missouri) When the author sent in this story, she undoubtedly included some explanation of place or some evidence that such a situation could exist. Then isn't the reader entitled to some such evidence? Otherwise the reader has a right to indict you as editor of willfully misrepresenting the human race. Perhaps you as editor are proud of publishing a story that reached a new low in human viciousness. The burden of proof is up to you when your own preoccupation with evil leads you into such evil ways. A few more such stories and you will alienate your most devoted readers, in which class I—until now—have been included.

(New Hampshire) It was with great disappointment that I read the story "The Lottery." Stories such as this belong to *Esquire*, etc., but most assuredly not to *The New Yorker*.

(Massachusetts) The ending of this story came as quite a jolt to my wife and, as a matter of fact, she was very upset by the whole thing for a day or two after.

(New York)   I read the story quite thoroughly and confess that I could make neither head nor tail out of it. The story was so horrible and gruesome in its effect that I could hardly see I the point of your publishing it.

Now, a complete letter, from Illinois.

EDITOR:

Never has it been my lot to read so cunningly vicious a story as that published in your last issue for June. I tremble to think of the fate of American letters if that piece indicated the taste of the editors of a magazine I had considered distinguished. It has made me wonder what you had in mind when accepting it for publication. Certainly not the entertainment of the reader and if not entertainment, what? The strokes of genius were of course apparent in the story mentioned, but of a perverted genius whose efforts achieved a terrible malformation. You have betrayed a trust with your readers by giving them such a bestial selection. Unaware, the reader was led into a casual tale of the village folk, becoming conscious only gradually of the rising tension, till the shock of the unwholesome conclusion, skillful though it was wrought, left him with total disgust for the story and with disillusionment in the magazine publishing it.

I speak of my own reaction. If that is not the reaction of the majority of your readers I miss my guess. Ethics and uplift are apparently not in your repertoire, nor are they expected, but as editors it is your responsibility to have a sounder and saner criterion for stories than the one which passed on "The Lottery."

Heretofore mine has been almost a stockholder's pride in *The New Yorker*. I shared my copy with my friends as I do the other possessions which I most enjoy. When your latest issue arrived, my new distaste kept me from removing the brown paper wrapping, and into the wastebasket it went. Since I can't conceive that I'll develop interest in it again, save the results of your efforts that indignity every week and cancel my subscription immediately.

Another letter, this one from Indiana.

SIR:

Thanks for letting us take a look at the nauseating and fiction-less bit of print which appeared in a recent issue. I gather that we read the literal translation.

The process of moving set us back a few weeks, but unfortunately your magazine and Miss Jackson's consistently correct spelling and punctuation caught up with us.

We are pleased to think that perhaps her story recalled happier days for you; days when you were able to hurl flat skipping stones at your aged grandmother. Not for any particular reason, of course, but because the village postmaster good-naturedly placed them in your hands, or because your chubby fingers felt good as they gripped the stone.

Our quarrel is not with Miss Jackson's amazingly clear style or reportorial observation. It is not with the strong motives exhibited by the native stone-throwers, or with the undertones and overtones which apparently we missed along the way.

It is simply that we read the piece before and not after supper. We are hammering together a few paragraphs on running the head of our kindly neighbor through the electric eggbeater, and will mail same when we have untangled her top-piece. This should give your many readers a low chuckle or at least provide the sophisticates with an inner glow. Also it might interest you to know that my wife and I are gathering up the smoothest, roundest stones in our yard and piling them up on the corner in small, neat pyramids. We're sentimentalists that way.

I have frequently wondered if this last letter is a practical joke; it is certainly not impossible, although I hope not, because it is quite my favorite letter of all "Lottery" correspondence. It was mailed to *The New Yorker*, from Los Angeles, of course, and written in pencil, on a sheet of lined paper torn from a pad; the spelling is atrocious.

DEAR SIR:

The June 26 copy of your magazine fell into my hands in the Los Angeles railroad station yesterday. Although I donnot read your magazine very often I took this copy home to my folks and they had to agree with me that you speak strait-forward to your readers.

My Aunt Ellise before she became priestess of the Exalted Rollers used to tell us a story just like "The Lottery" by Shirley Jackson. I don't know if Miss Jackson is a member of the Exhalted Rollers but with her round stones sure ought to be. There is a few points in her prophecy on which Aunt Ellise and me don't agree.

The Exalted Rollers donnot believe in the ballot box but believe that the true gospel of the redeeming light will become accepted by all when the prophecy comes true. It does seem likely to me that our sins will bring us punishment though a great scouraging war with the devil's toy (the atomic bomb). I don't think we will have to sacrifice humin beings fore atonement.

Our brothers feel that Miss Jackson is a true prophet and disciple of the true gospel of the redeeming light. When will the next revelations be published?

Yours in the spirit.

Of all the questions ever asked me about "Lottery," I feel that there is only one which I can answer fearlessly and honestly, and that is the question which closes this gentleman's letter. When will the next revelations be published, he wants to know, and I answer roundly, never. I am out of the lottery business for good.

1960

CHRONOLOGY

NOTE ON THE TEXTS

NOTES

Chronology

1916   Born Shirley Hardie Jackson on December 14 in San Francisco, California, first child of Leslie Hardie Jackson and Geraldine Maxwell Bugbee Jackson. (Leslie Jackson, born in England in 1891, came to San Francisco in 1905 with his mother and sisters to help support his financially struggling father, who had immigrated to America in the early 1890s. Outgoing and self-possessed even at age 14, he quickly found work as a printer's devil, and by the time he married, in March 1916, was a self-made man, a rising executive of the Traung Label & Lithograph Co. with a house in fashionable Ashbury Park. Geraldine, born 1895, was the socially ambitious daughter of Maxwell G. Bugbee, a prominent San Francisco architect. Family folklore has it that Shirley was conceived on her parents' wedding night, for she was born almost exactly nine months later.)

1918   Brother, Barry, born. (Throughout her life Geraldine Jackson will characterize Barry as her "obedient" child and Shirley as her "willful" one.)

1923   Family moves to Burlingame, an exclusive suburb 16 miles south of San Francisco, and lives for a year in rented rooms while their new house, designed by Grandfather Bugbee, is built. Jackson enters McKinley Grammar School.

1924   Household now includes maternal grandmother, Evangeline "Mimi" Bugbee, a devout Christian Scientist who takes Jackson to church and impresses upon her Mary Baker Eddy's belief that the material world is an illusion. Develops obsessive interest in mother's pastimes of Tarot cards, tea leaves, and Ouija boards, and, to the discomfort of the grownups, begins to spin fantasies—or describe visions—of an unseen world co-existent with our own. (Of her frequent childhood episodes of "clairvoyance" she would later say, "I could see what the cat saw.")

1928   At age 12 is an indifferent student who craves unsupervised hours spent alone reading at the public library or writing behind the locked door of her bedroom. Feels bitter mistrust of mother and Mimi after she discovers them reading her journals, poems, and other private papers.

Finds first close friend in Dorothy "Dot" Ayling, the unconventional, forthright daughter of a professional landscaper, who shares her interest in music, books, and crafts. Part of Dorothy's appeal is mother's dislike for her family's progressive politics and working-class background.

1930   In fall enters Burlingame High School as a freshman, where she excels in English but is otherwise a "C" student. Tutors Dorothy in English while Dorothy tutors her in math. Plays piano at home and violin in school orchestra, reads Lewis Carroll and Edgar Allan Poe, and continues secretly to write. Privately worries about her weight and popularity but openly defies mother's nagging efforts to "improve" her.

1933   In spring father is promoted to executive vice-president of Traung Label and in summer moves family to Rochester, New York, to oversee Traung's acquisition of the Stecher Lithography Co. Jackson enrolls as a senior at local Brighton High School, where she enjoys a reputation as an "eccentric" and "intellectual" but also feels fragile, uprooted, and friendless. Begins enduring correspondence with Dorothy Ayling.

1934   Graduates from high school and enrolls as freshman at the University of Rochester, where she lives on campus. Dislikes teachers and seldom attends classes. Grows intellectually curious about her "clairvoyant" mental states and, in the university library, begins lifelong self-education in abnormal psychology and the history and lore of witchcraft. Friendship with foreign-exchange student Jean-Marie "Jeanou" Bedel deepens into passionate attachment, and Jackson is briefly suicidal when, at end of school year, Jeanou returns to France.

1935   In the fall begins sophomore year at Rochester, but now lives at home with her family. Writes frequently to Jeanou, who will remain a correspondent for decades.

1936   In spring is expelled from Rochester due to poor grades and worse attendance, and suffers brief emotional breakdown. By fall resolves to write a thousand words a day and soon develops the disciplined work habits of a professional writer. Applies to Syracuse University, determined to earn a bachelor's degree in English or journalism.

1937   In fall enters Syracuse as a sophomore. Takes creative-writing class and joins a student writers' workshop.

1938   In March publishes short story, "Janice," in campus literary annual *The Threshold*; it attracts the attention of fellow sophomore Stanley Edgar Hyman (b. 1919), who says to friends, "Who is Shirley Jackson? I'm going to find her and marry her!" Hyman—a hyper-articulate English major from the Jewish tenements of Brooklyn, a professed atheist fascinated by Marx, Freud, folklore, and jazz—courts Jackson, helps her with classes, and recommends books to read. In spring, Jackson introduces Hyman to parents, who strongly disapprove of him; for his part, Hyman is too afraid of rejection to tell Orthodox Jewish father of the relationship. In fall Jackson begins junior year, during which she will publish five stories in *The Syracusan*, the monthly undergraduate magazine. Is introduced by Hyman to his mentor, Leonard Brown of the Syracuse English faculty, who will be her friend and literary champion until his death in 1960.

1939   Relationship with Hyman deepens, and couple agrees to marry upon graduation. In summer, while on family trip to California, parents urge Jackson to break off with Hyman; she suffers stress-induced allergies, and is briefly hospitalized in San Francisco. In fall Jackson and Hyman, with faculty sponsor Brown, plan a mimeographed "quarterly of the arts" called *Spectre*, which will run four issues in 1939–40. *Spectre*'s politics are progressive, its fiction and poetry experimental, and its satirical attacks on Syracuse faculty unsparing; Jackson focuses on writing for it at the expense of coursework. Through Brown, she and Hyman meet writer Malcolm Cowley, then assistant editor of *The New Republic*, and critic, poet, and fiction writer Kenneth Burke.

1940   In June, Hyman and Jackson graduate from Syracuse, he *magna cum laude*, she without academic distinction. Against protests of parents, couple moves to New York City and finds tiny apartment at 215 West 13th Street; they are married in a civil ceremony on August 13. (On her marriage license, Jackson gives birth year as 1919, shaving three years off her age and establishing a biographical falsehood she will maintain for the rest of her life.) Jackson's parents are dismayed by the marriage, and Hyman's father disowns and disinherits him. With help of Cowley, Hyman finds work as editorial assistant at *The New Republic*; Jackson takes many short-term jobs, including selling books at Macy's.

1941   Jackson works on short fiction and comic sketches; Hyman publishes book reviews in *The New Republic* and contributes regularly to *The New Yorker*'s "Talk of the Town" section. In fall, couple moves to cabin in Keene, New Hampshire, to concentrate on writing. War declared; Hyman is 4-F due to poor eyesight. On December 22, *The New Republic* publishes "My Life with R. H. Macy," Jackson's first story in a national magazine.

1942   Under Hyman's tutelage, reads 18th-century English novelists and discovers a touchstone in Samuel Richardson, in whom she finds "three attributes somehow lost today: peace, principle, kindness." In summer, couple returns to Manhattan when Hyman is offered job as staff writer at *The New Yorker*; after many short-term rentals, they settle into apartment on Grove Street, in Greenwich Village. Son, Laurence Jackson ("Laurie") Hyman, born October 3.

1943   Her "breakthrough year": publishes four short stories in *The New Yorker*, including "After You, My Dear Alphonse," "Afternoon in Linen," and "Come Dance with Me in Ireland." "Seven Types of Ambiguity" appears in *Story* Magazine.

1944   Publishes 11 more stories, six of them in *The New Yorker*. Writes opening chapters of "Elizabeth," a novel about a woman in league with the devil, but the work is soon abandoned. "Come Dance with Me in Ireland" reprinted in *Best American Short Stories 1944*.

1945   Publishes three more stories, and works on semi-autobiographical novel "I Know Who I Love." In spring, Hyman is invited to teach at Bennington College by faculty member Kenneth Burke; family relocates to North Bennington, Vermont, and rents a 14-room Victorian house on Prospect Street, about a mile from campus. Second child, Joanne Leslie ("Jannie") Hyman, born November 9.

1946   Household now includes Toby, a large dog of indeterminate breed, and, at Jackson's insistence, two cats, Ninki and Shax, whose offspring will be legion. Abandons "I Know Who I Love" for a satirical novel of suburban life based on childhood memories of Burlingame, California; writing quickly, completes first draft by Christmas. Hyman's father, resolving to be part of his grandchildren's lives, mends relationship with Hyman and Jackson.

1947   Through the agency of a Bennington acquaintance, literary scout Tom Foster, Jackson places Burlingame novel,

The Road Through the Wall, with newly founded publishers Farrar, Straus & Co. Resumes writing short stories, including "The Daemon Lover," and is eager to shape a collection for Farrar, Straus. Hyman's inner circle at Bennington includes Burke, fiction writer Ralph Ellison, poets Howard Nemerov and Ben Belitt, and college president Fred Burkhardt, all frequent visitors to the house.

1948   In February *The Road Through the Wall* published to few reviews and disappointing sales. Jackson engages Rea Everitt, of MCA Literary Management, to place her work in magazines. In late May writes "The Lottery," published in *The New Yorker* for June 26; the story is a *succès de scandale*, occasioning more letters from readers than any other work of fiction in the magazine's history. ("The Lottery" will be reprinted in *O. Henry Prize Stories 1949* and go on to become one of the most widely anthologized stories of the century.) In July publishes "Charles," the first of many family sketches, in *Mademoiselle*, launching secondary career as domestic humorist. Third child, Sarah Geraldine ("Sally") Hyman, born October 20.

1949   In April *The Lottery; or, The Adventures of James Harris*, a collection of 25 stories, published by Farrar, Straus to strong reviews and excellent sales. Publishes second family sketch, "The Third Baby's the Easiest," in *Harper's*, and signs contract with *Good Housekeeping* for eight similar pieces during the next twelve months. In summer Hyman, disenchanted with Bennington and weary of long weekly commutes to the *New Yorker* offices, resigns from the college and moves family to Westport, Connecticut.

1950   Chafing under arrangement with *Good Housekeeping*, which rejects several of her family sketches, and frustrated that, after the success of *The Lottery*, her more ambitious short stories are not commanding higher prices, engages new agent, Bernice Baumgartner of Brandt & Brandt. On June 14, television drama based on "The Lottery," written by Ellen M. Violett, broadcast live on NBC's *Cameo Theatre*. Jackson, drawing on memories of her unhappy years at the University of Rochester, begins new novel of a young woman's emotional breakdown; she calls it *Hangsaman*, after the "Hanged Man" of the Tarot deck, the card symbolizing the clairvoyant state.

1951   In April *Hangsaman* published by Farrar, Straus & Young to mixed reviews. "The Summer People," published in *Charm* the previous year, is chosen for *Best American*

Short Stories 1951. Fourth child, Barry Edgar Hyman, born November 21.

1952   In spring Hyman, invited by President Burkhardt to re-sume his old post at Bennington at a higher salary, moves the family back to Vermont; they rent a house on the college campus, and begin looking for a permanent residence in town. Jackson reworks family sketches, including "Charles," "The Third Baby's the Easiest," and the recently published "Night We All Had Grippe," into a book-length fictionalized memoir, *Life Among the Savages*. Begins research for new novel, *The Bird's Nest*, based on historical case study of a woman with multiple-personality disorder.

1953   The Hymans buy a 20-room house on upper Main Street, North Bennington, which, to the dismay of unwelcoming neighbors, becomes an intellectual salon, a poker den, and the site of noisy, crowded, hard-drinking weekend parties for the Bennington College English department. The furniture is sparse but the books number in the thousands, the jazz records in the hundreds, and the cats more than a dozen. Jackson, establishing a workspace in the front room, quickly and single-mindedly writes new novel. In June *Life Among the Savages* published by Farrar, Straus & Young to good reviews and very strong sales. In November Jackson is emotionally exhausted upon finishing her new book, *The Bird's Nest*.

1954   In winter and early spring suffers prolonged episode of depression, marked by unshakable drowsiness and inability to begin new work. In June *The Bird's Nest* published by Farrar, Straus & Young to enthusiastic reviews; Jackson is pleased, but refuses to grant interviews, sit for photographs, or make personal appearances on behalf of the book, a practice she will continue with all future publications. ("I just refer everyone to *Who's Who in America*, with great satisfaction," she writes in a letter to her parents.) Already a heavy smoker and coffee drinker, begins abusing amphetamines, which she has taken regularly for years to suppress appetite and boost energy.

1955   Sells movie rights to *The Bird's Nest* to Hollywood producer Ray Stark. Accepts commission from Random House to write a brief nonfiction account of the Salem witch trials for young-adult readers. Begins to shape second book of family sketches, which she will complete in spring of next year. Habitually counters effects of amphetamines with barbiturates and alcohol; the drugs aggravate her mood swings, food cravings, and emotional fragility.

1956   *The Witchcraft of Salem Village* published by Random House in the Landmark Books series. Reluctantly accepts invitation to participate in a one-week fiction workshop at the Suffield (Connecticut) Writers' Conference and is surprised by how much she enjoys the experience; she will return every summer for the next four years. "One Ordinary Day, with Peanuts," published in *The Magazine of Fantasy and Science Fiction* the previous year, is reprinted in *Best American Short Stories 1956*. Jackson, noting odd and fearful behavior in eight-year-old Sally, believes her daughter and classmates are being physically abused and ritually humiliated by their second-grade teacher. After she and a handful of anxious fellow-parents gather corroborating evidence from their children, Jackson spearheads movement to oust the teacher. Meets with principal and school board, who listen dispassionately but do not act, and is made a figure of fun and contempt by the teacher's many supporters and in local newspaper reports. Jackson's allegations are never proved, and they widen the rift between the Hymans and their North Bennington neighbors. In this and coming years, townsfolk will harass the Hymans with anonymous hate mail, soap their windows with swastikas, and repeatedly dump garbage into the bushes lining their front sidewalk. Feeling isolated, rejected, even hated by the community, Jackson becomes reluctant to leave the house, and everyday errands requiring social interaction—grocery shopping, trips to the post office—are increasingly fraught with anxiety.

1957   In winter and spring, quickly writes *The Sundial*, a darkly comic fantasy about a band of wealthy survivalists preparing for the end of the world. In January *Raising Demons*, a sequel to *Life Among the Savages*, published by Farrar, Straus & Cudahy to respectful reviews and good sales. In February, Hugo Haas's *Lizzie*, a film adaptation of *The Bird's Nest* starring Eleanor Parker, Richard Boone, and Joan Blondell, is released by M-G-M; movie suffers at box office from the simultaneous release of *The Three Faces of Eve*, a more memorable dramatization of multiple-personality disorder. In summer, with the children away at camp, the Hymans embark on a month of joint readings and talks at New England and Mid-Atlantic writers' conferences, including a week at Suffield and, by arrangement with Leonard Brown, a few days at Syracuse

University. At Sally and Joanne's instigation, writes one-act children's play, *The Bad Children*, a subversive retelling of the Hansel and Gretel story. Begins research for a haunted house novel.

1958   In February *The Sundial* published by Farrar, Straus & Cudahy to mixed reviews. In fall *The Bad Children* published in an acting edition by Dramatic Publishing Co., Chicago; it proves popular with school groups and amateur companies, and the royalties are split among the four Hyman children. Agent Bernice Baumgartner, after securing Jackson a lucrative three-book contract with Viking Press, retires from Brandt & Brandt; her successor is Carol Brandt, who will become a close friend. In December, delivers *The Haunting of Hill House* to her new editor, Pascal "Pat" Covici.

1959   Continually struggles with feelings of helplessness, fear, and inadequacy, and makes several false starts on a new novel. In October *The Haunting of Hill House* published by Viking to enthusiastic reviews and strong sales; agent sells film rights to producer-director Robert Wise and auctions paperback right for a then-unheard-of $67,000.

1960   In spring *Special Delivery: A Useful Book for Brand-New Mothers*, an anthology of humorous sketches and reassuring advice edited by Jackson, published by Little, Brown. Works with unaccustomed difficulty, but also with great satisfaction, on new novel. In fall, Laurie leaves for college, Hyman's father dies, and Jackson develops the chronic colitis that will trouble her the rest of her life. But, she reports to her parents, "I am making fine progress on my book; there's nothing like being too scared to go outside to keep you writing."

1961   Jackson is now essentially housebound, leaving home only to give the occasional public reading, usually in the company of Hyman. Joanne and Sally enroll at boarding school in Massachusetts, leaving nine-year-old Barry the only child still in Jackson's care. "Louisa, Please Come Home," published the previous year in *The Ladies' Home Journal*, receives Edgar Allan Poe Award for Best Short Story of 1961. At Christmas completes final draft of *We Have Always Lived in the Castle*, a novel three years in the making.

1962   In September *We Have Always Lived in the Castle* published by Viking to enthusiastic reviews and strong sales;

it appears on several bestseller lists, and is named one of *Time* Magazine's "Ten Best Novels of 1962."

1963   In August, Robert Wise's *The Haunting*, a film adaptation of *The Haunting of Hill House* starring Julie Harris and Claire Bloom, released by M-G-M; the movie delights Jackson and is well-received by critics. *Nine Magic Wishes*, a picture book commissioned by editor Louis Untermeyer and illustrated by Lorraine Fox, published by Collier-Crowell. Begins stint as occasional reviewer of children's books for Sunday *New York Herald Tribune*.

1964   "Birthday Party," a family sketch published in *Vogue* the previous year, is reprinted in *Best American Short Stories 1964*. Writes text for second picture book, *Famous Sally*, published posthumously, and begins a fantasy novel for children, never finished.

1965   Plans comic novel called *Come Along with Me* and writes six chapters, the first of which she reads at Syracuse University on April 26. In May is named recipient of the George Arents Pioneer Medal, the highest honor bestowed by Syracuse on its alumni, but because she is required to receive the award in person at her 25th class reunion, she declines ("I wouldn't attend that reunion for anything"). In early August, writes a curious letter to agent Carol Brandt, saying soon she will be leaving on a wonderful journey and must go alone. Days later, on August 8, Jackson dies of heart failure during an afternoon nap. In accordance with her wishes, there is no funeral or memorial service; her body is cremated, and the ashes are kept by the family. In December a final short story, "The Possibility of Evil," appears in *The Saturday Evening Post*, together with a memorial essay by Hyman. "I think that the future will find her powerful visions of suffering and inhumanity increasingly significant and meaningful," Hyman writes, "and that Shirley Jackson's work is among that small body of literature produced in our time that seems apt to survive."

Note on the Texts

This volume contains three books by Shirley Jackson—the collection of short fiction *The Lottery* (1949) and the novels *The Haunting of Hill House* (1959) and *We Have Always Lived in the Castle* (1962)—as well as a selection of 21 further stories and sketches, 15 of which Jackson published in magazines and anthologies but never collected, and six of which were published posthumously by her literary estate. It also contains, in an appendix, a posthumously published talk that Jackson frequently gave as a preface to public readings of her story "The Lottery."

The Lottery; or, The Adventures of James Harris was published by Farrar, Straus & Company, New York, in May 1949, when Jackson was 32 years old. It was her second book, following the novel *The Road Through the Wall* (1948), and comprised short fiction written between the summer of 1940, when she received her B.A. from Syracuse University, and the summer of 1948. Sixteen of the 25 stories and sketches collected in *The Lottery* first appeared, many in somewhat different form, in periodicals as follows:

"My Life with R. H. Macy," *The New Republic*, December 22, 1941
"After You, My Dear Alphonse," *The New Yorker*, January 16, 1943
"Come Dance with Me in Ireland," *The New Yorker*, May 15, 1943
"Seven Types of Ambiguity," *Story*, September–October 1943
"Afternoon in Linen," *The New Yorker*, September 4, 1943
"A Fine Old Firm," *The New Yorker*, March 4, 1944
"The Villager," *The American Mercury*, August 1944
"Colloquy," *The New Yorker*, August 5, 1944
"Trial by Combat," *The New Yorker*, December 16, 1944
"Men with Their Big Shoes," *The Yale Review*, March 1947
"The Tooth," *The Hudson Review*, Winter 1948
"The Lottery," *The New Yorker*, June 26, 1948
"Charles," *Mademoiselle*, July 1948
"Pillar of Salt," *Mademoiselle*, October 1948
"The Renegade," *Harper's Magazine*, November 1948
"The Daemon Lover" (as "The Phantom Lover"), *Woman's Home Companion*, February 1949

The nine remaining items ("The Intoxicated," "Like Mother Used to Make," "The Witch," "Flower Garden," "Dorothy and My Grandmother and the Sailors," "Elizabeth," "The Dummy," "Of Course," and "Got a Letter from Jimmy") appeared for the first time in *The*

Lottery. The autobiographical sketch "Charles" was later revised and incorporated into the text of Jackson's book-length fictional memoir *Life Among the Savages* (New York: Farrar, Straus & Young, 1953), pp. 23–30.

Jackson began writing short stories when she was in high school and contributed several to student publications when she was enrolled as an undergraduate at Syracuse University (1937–40). The humorous sketch "My Life with R. H. Macy," written in the winter or spring of 1941, was her first story to appear in a national magazine. By 1945 she had written some three dozen stories, more than half of which had appeared in *The New Yorker* and other periodicals, and had begun planning a collection with the working title "The Intoxicated." The table of contents for that collection was revised many times through late 1948, when a manuscript was submitted to Farrar, Straus under the title *The Lottery; or, The Adventures of James Harris*.

Among the previously unpublished items that Jackson included in *The Lottery*, "Elizabeth" was conceived, not as the long story printed here, but as the opening section of an unfinished novel that occupied her throughout 1944. In an outline for the novel, found among her papers in the Library of Congress and published by Joan Wylie Hall in her book *Shirley Jackson: A Study of the Short Fiction* (1993), Jackson describes her project as follows: "[This] novel is the story of one climactic day in the life of a woman who has figuratively leagued herself with the devil, and her figurative destruction. The story parallels in detail the discovery and condemnation of a witch, and the parallel will be stated in the title and chapter headings of texts from witchcraft cases at each stage." Indeed, the names of the principal characters of the story—Elizabeth Style (the witch), Shax (a petty demon), and Miss Hill (their victim)—are drawn from the pages of *Sadducismus Triumphatus* (1681), a collection of case histories in witchcraft compiled, with religious commentary, by the English cleric Joseph Glanvil. Although Jackson in the end abandoned her "Elizabeth" novel, she adapted her notion of using epigraphs from Glanvil for the four section-title pages of *The Lottery*.

The story "The Daemon Lover," one of the last written for *The Lottery*, was important to Jackson; through a subtitle incorporating the name of its title character, James Harris, it shared the bill as lead story in the collection. The title of the story, like the name "James Harris," were drawn from the old Scottish ballad "The Daemon Lover," seven stanzas of which serve as the collection's epilogue. To help give unity to the collection (and, like the epigraphs from Glanvil, to add a grace note of witchery), Jackson wove symbols and names from the story throughout much of the volume's other contents. For example, the name "Harris," variations on the name "James"

("Jim," "Jamie," "Jimmy"), and the imagery of the handsome man in the blue suit recur frequently and are usually attached to menacing or mysterious male figures on the periphery of the stories. Almost all the stories first published in periodicals were revised in small ways that—lightly, in passing—tie them into the "The Daemon Lover," the epilogue, or *Sadducismus Triumphatus*.

The first edition of *The Lottery* was scheduled to appear in February 1949, but due to errors in make-up—"they set it up in type all mixed up," Jackson complained to her parents in a letter dated December 18, 1948—printing was delayed by two months. Despite the best efforts of Farrar, Straus to correct the mistakes in composition, the epigraph to section one was accidentally deleted during the final stages of production, and the error was not corrected in subsequent printings. In 1950, *The Lottery* was published in London by Victor Gollancz Ltd. in a setting identical to the first U.S. edition except that the epigraph was restored. The present volume prints the text of the 1950 Gollancz edition.

In later American printings, *The Lottery; or, The Adventures of James Harris* went through many changes of subtitle. The first paperback edition (New York: Lion Books, 1949) was titled *The Lottery: Adventures of a Demon Lover*, and the second (New York: Avon, 1950), *The Lottery: Adventures of the Daemon Lover*. By 1965 Avon, which kept the book in print through the 1970s, dropped the subtitle altogether and sold it under the title *The Lottery*. When Farrar, Straus & Giroux republished the book in 1982 under its Noonday imprint, it was renamed *The Lottery and Other Stories*, the title by which it is best known today.

The Haunting of Hill House was published by The Viking Press, New York, in October 1959. An English edition, with pages photographically reproduced from the Viking edition, was published by Michael Joseph, London, in the following year. The novel, Jackson's fifth, was written in North Bennington, Vermont, between the fall of 1957 and December 1958. The present volume prints the text of the 1959 Viking edition.

We Have Always Lived in the Castle was published by The Viking Press, New York, in September 1962. An English edition, with pages photographically reproduced from the Viking edition, was published by Michael Joseph, London, in the following year. The novel, Jackson's sixth and last, was written in North Bennington, Vermont, between the spring of 1959 and December 1961. The present volume prints the text of the 1962 Viking edition.

The 21 items presented here as "Other Stories and Sketches" are gathered under two headings, "Uncollected" and "Unpublished." The 15 items under the "Uncollected" heading were published in magazines and anthologies between 1938 and 1965 but were never collected by Jackson. The six items under the "Unpublished" heading were found in typescript among Jackson's papers and were prepared for publication by her literary estate. Most of these stories and sketches have been previously printed in two posthumous collections of Jackson's writings, *Come Along with Me: Part of a Novel, Sixteen Stories, and Three Lectures*, edited by her husband, Stanley Edgar Hyman (New York: Viking, 1968), and *Just an Ordinary Day*, a selection of 55 stories, sketches, and prose fragments edited by two of her four children, Laurence Jackson Hyman and Sarah Hyman Stewart (New York: Bantam Books, 1997). Two of the "Uncollected" items, "The Third Baby's the Easiest" (1949) and "The Night We All Had Grippe" (1952), are autobiographical sketches that, after their initial periodical appearances, were revised by Jackson and incorporated into her book-length fictional memoir *Life Among the Savages* (New York: Farrar, Straus & Young, 1953). Two others, "Behold the Child Among His Newborn Blisses" (1944) and "It Isn't the Money I Mind" (1945), are collected here for the first time.

The items gathered under the "Uncollected" heading are arranged in the order of first print appearance. Their publication history is as follows:

> "Janice" was printed in *The Threshold*, the literary annual of Syracuse University, in March 1938. Stanley Edgar Hyman collected it in *Come Along with Me* (1968), the source of the text printed here.
>
> "A Cauliflower in Her Hair" was published in *Mademoiselle*, December 1944. Stanley Edgar Hyman collected it in *Come Along with Me* (1968), the source of the text printed here.
>
> "Behold the Child Among His Newborn Blisses" was published in *Cross Section 1944: A Collection of New American Writing*, a literary annual edited by Edwin Seaver (New York: L. B. Fischer, 1944). *Cross Section 1944* is the source of the text printed here.
>
> "It Isn't the Money I Mind" was published in *The New Yorker*, August 25, 1945, the source of the text printed here.
>
> "The Third Baby's the Easiest" was published in *Harper's Magazine*, May 1949, the source of the text printed here. Jackson revised and incorporated it into the text of *Life Among the Savages* (1953), pp. 55–79.
>
> "The Summer People" was published in *Charm*, September 1950. Stanley Edgar Hyman collected it in *Come Along with Me* (1968), the source of the text printed here.
>
> "Island" was published (as "The Island") in *The New Mexico*

Quarterly Review, Fall 1950. Stanley Edgar Hyman collected it, with Jackson's original title restored, in *Come Along with Me* (1968), the source of the text printed here.

"The Night We All Had Grippe" was published in *Harper's Magazine*, January 1952. Jackson revised and incorporated it into *Life Among the Savages* (1953), pp. 133–42. Stanley Edgar Hyman collected the *Harper's* version in *Come Along with Me* (1968), the source of the text printed here.

"The Visit" was published (as "The Lovely House") in *New World Writing* (No. 2), a paperback anthology of previously unpublished writing edited by Arabel J. Porter (New York: Mentor Books/New American Library, 1952). Stanley Edgar Hyman collected it, with Jackson's original title and dedication restored, in *Come Along with Me* (1968), the source of the text printed here.

"This Is the Life" was published (as "Journey with a Lady") in *Harper's Magazine*, July 1952, the source of the text printed here. It was reprinted under the revised title "This Is the Life" in *Ellery Queen's Mystery Magazine*, June 1958. Laurence J. Hyman and Sarah H. Stewart collected it (as "Journey with a Lady") in *Just an Ordinary Day* (1997).

"One Ordinary Day, with Peanuts" was published in *The Magazine of Fantasy and Science Fiction*, January 1955, the source of the text printed here. Laurence J. Hyman and Sarah H. Stewart collected it in *Just an Ordinary Day* (1997).

"Louisa, Please Come Home" was published (as "Louisa, Please . . ."), in *The Ladies' Home Journal*, May 1960. Stanley Edgar Hyman collected it, with Jackson's original title restored, in *Come Along with Me* (1968), the source of the text printed here.

"The Little House" was published in *The Ladies' Home Journal*, June 1964. Stanley Edgar Hyman collected it in *Come Along with Me* (1968), the source of the text printed here.

"The Bus" was published in *The Saturday Evening Post*, March 27, 1965. Stanley Edgar Hyman collected it in *Come Along with Me* (1968), the source of the text printed here.

"The Possibility of Evil" was published posthumously in *The Saturday Evening Post*, December 18, 1965, the source of the text printed here. Laurence J. Hyman and Sarah H. Stewart collected it in *Just an Ordinary Day* (1997).

The items gathered under the "Unpublished" heading were not dated by Jackson and are arranged in an order chosen by the editor of this volume. Their publication history is as follows:

"Portrait" was edited by Laurence J. Hyman and Sarah H. Stewart and published in *Just an Ordinary Day* (1997), the source of the text printed here.

"The Mouse" was edited by Laurence J. Hyman and Sarah H. Stewart and published in *Just an Ordinary Day* (1997), the source of the text printed here.

"I Know Who I Love" (1946), the opening section of an unfinished novel written in 1945–46, was edited and dated by Stanley Edgar Hyman and published in *Come Along with Me* (1968), the source of the text printed here.

"The Beautiful Stranger" (c. 1946) was edited and dated by Stanley Edgar Hyman and published in *Come Along with Me* (1968), the source of the text printed here.

"The Rock" (c. 1951) was edited, dated, and given its title by Stanley Edgar Hyman and published in *Come Along with Me* (1968), the source of the text printed here.

"The Honeymoon of Mrs. Smith" was edited by Laurence J. Hyman and Sarah H. Stewart and published (as "The Honeymoon of Mrs. Smith—Version II: The Mystery of the Murdered Bride") in *Just an Ordinary Day* (1997), the source of the text printed here.

The appendix to this volume presents "Biography of a Story" (1960), one of a handful of prepared talks that Jackson repeatedly gave at colleges and writers' conferences during the last decade of her life. A typescript of the talk was edited and dated by Stanley Edgar Hyman and published in *Come Along with Me* (1968), the source of the text printed here.

This volume presents the texts of the printings chosen as sources but does not attempt to reproduce features of their typographic design. The texts are printed without alteration except for the correction of typographical errors. Spelling, punctuation, and capitalization are often expressive features, and they are not altered, even when inconsistent or irregular. The following is a list of typographical errors corrected, listed by page and line number: 42.35, Coca Cola; 43.20, coke; 47.35, ref., and; 85.22, tieing; 110.28, star.); 136.18, suggestion,; 175.38, yoke; 204.35, maybe?") "I; 218.15, probably,; 280.12, gesture,; 321.28, kotting; 321.30, griping; 432.5 & 6, Donnell; 456.37, Clark; 502.37, sas; 511.28, sood; 589.4, Can; 589.26, shoulder said,; 589.33, said "After; 628.17, This; 634.29, attactive; 634.35, entrance,; 635.40, Mrs. Montague; 640.5, immediatey; 641.26, storm; 653.30, rather; 654.37, Heseemed; 776.27, as his; 787.11, 1948 was.

Notes

In the notes below, the reference numbers denote page and line of this volume (the line count includes headings). No note is made for material included in standard desk-reference books such as Webster's *Collegiate*, *Biographical*, and *Geographical* dictionaries. Quotations from the Bible are keyed to the King James Version. Quotations from Shakespeare are keyed to *The Riverside Shakespeare*, edited by G. Blakemore Evans (Boston: Houghton Mifflin, 1974). For further biographical background than is contained in the Chronology, see Lenemaja Friedman, *Shirley Jackson* (Boston: Twayne, 1975), and Judy Oppenheimer, *Private Demons: The Life of Shirley Jackson* (New York: Putnam, 1988). For a more detailed study of the text of *The Lottery* than is contained in the Note on the Texts, see Joan Wylie Hall, *Shirley Jackson: A Study of the Short Fiction* (New York: Twayne, 1993).

THE LOTTERY

3.8   Joseph Glanvil: *Sadducismus Triumphatus*] Glanvil (or Glanvill, 1636–1680), Oxford-educated clergyman, Fellow of the Royal Society, and Chaplain in Ordinary to Charles II, published his *Philosophical Considerations Touching Witches and Witchcraft* in 1666; a fifth and final edition, titled *Sadducismus Triumphatus; or, A full and plain Evidence, Concerning Witches and Apparitions*, appeared posthumously in 1681. In this book, a collection of case histories of hauntings, demonic possessions, and incidents of witchcraft in Europe, Glanvil called popular denial of the existence of witches "the triumph of Sadducism," alluding to the Sadducees, an ancient Jewish sect that rejected the teachings of Christ and denied the existence of angels, demons, and the afterlife. The documentary evidence of *Sadducismus Triumphatus*, and Glanvil's religious commentary linking skepticism about witchcraft to atheism, greatly influenced the thinking of Cotton Mather and the prosecutors of the Salem witch trials of 1692.

9.6   *Gallia est . . . partes tres*] Slight misquotation of the opening words of Caesar's *Commentari de Bello Gallico* ("The Gallic Wars," c. 50 BCE): "All Gaul is divided into three parts . . ."

35.1   *Trial by Combat*] In medieval Germanic law, a court-sanctioned physical contest between two persons to settle a dispute in the absence of witnesses or a confession.

41.4–5   Whelan's] American drugstore and soda-fountain chain of the early and mid-20th century.

41.5   *Villager*]   Weekly newspaper, founded 1933, serving the Lower Manhattan neighborhood of Greenwich Village.

51.9   Joseph Glanvil]   See note 3.8.

69.1   *After You, My Dear Alphonse*]   Catchphrase from the Sunday newspaper strip "Alphonse and Gaston" (1901–4) by Frederick Burr Opper (1857–1937). The strip featured two French tramps whose courtesy toward each other was sincere but comically excessive.

78.17–18   "Humoresque"]   *Humoresque* No. 7, in G-flat major; most popular of the eight brief piano pieces that Antonin Dvořák published under the collective title *Humoresky* (1894).

81.36   *The Home Book of Verse*]   Best-selling anthology of English and American verse (1912), edited by Burton Egbert Stevenson (1872–1962).

109.10–11   the Emporium]   From 1896 to 1995, San Francisco's chief department store, located at 835 Market Street.

109.24   Pig'n'Whistle]   Chain of soda-fountain restaurants that dotted the West Coast from the late 1920s through the early 1950s.

115.16   Joseph Glanvil]   See note 3.8.

166.7   Empson]   William Empson (1906–1984), English poet and literary critic. His *Seven Types of Ambiguity* (1930) is a critical study in the literary artist's use of ambiguity, which Empson defines as "any verbal nuance, however slight, which gives room for alternative reactions to"—and alternative readings of—"the same piece of language."

171.1   *Come Dance with Me in Ireland*]   See William Butler Yeats (1865–1939), "I Am of Ireland" (1932), refrain: "*I am of Ireland, / And the Holy Land of Ireland, / And time runs on,*" cried she. / "*Come out of charity, / Come dance with me in Ireland.*"

177.11   Joseph Glanvil]   See note 3.8.

184.1   *Pillar of Salt*]   See Genesis 19:23, the story of Lot's wife and the destruction of Sodom and Gomorrah.

184.8–9   Noel Coward people]   Witty, sophisticated, "high society" characters like those in the comedies of English playwright Noël Coward (1899–1973).

186.15   where that plane hit]   On Saturday, July 28, 1945, a U.S. Army B-25 bomber en route from New Bedford, Mass., to Newark, N.J., became lost in the fog above Manhattan and, at 9:50 A.M., crashed into the north side of the Empire State Building. Fourteen people died: the pilot, two crewmen, and 11 office workers on the 78th and 79th floors.

220.4   "God has given me blood to drink,"]   Cf. Revelation 16:6.

239.8   *drumlie*]   Scots: "perturbed," "gloomy."

239.30   Child Ballad No. 243]   The so-called Child Ballads comprise 305
narrative songs, many in several versions, collected by the American literary
scholar Francis James Child (1825–1896) and published in his *English and
Scottish Popular Ballads* (five volumes, 1882–98). From the eight versions of
"James Harris (The Daemon Lover)" collected by Child (Ballad No. 243),
Jackson here chooses, as an epilogue to *The Lottery*, the concluding eight
stanzas of Version "F," which, according to Child, was first recorded in Sir
Walter Scott's *Minstrelsy of the Scottish Border* (fifth edition, 1812). In all versions of the ballad, the young wife of a carpenter is reunited with her long-
lost lover, the seaman James Harris, to whom she had promised herself in
youth. Harris, now fabulously wealthy, persuades her to forsake her husband
and their young son and run away to sea with him on his splendid mystery-
ship. Not far from shore, the tempter reveals himself to be a demon, and, in
a "flash of fire" or by sheer brute strength, destroys the ship.

THE HAUNTING OF HILL HOUSE

241.1–2   THE HAUNTING OF HILL HOUSE]   In the text of an unpublished
talk (c. 1959) that she often gave as a preface to public readings of her work,
Jackson wrote the following as a demonstration of how her fiction "comes
directly from experience":

> I have recently finished a novel about a haunted house. I was [work-
> ing] on a novel about a haunted house because I happened, by chance,
> to read a book about a group of people, nineteenth-century psychic
> researchers, who rented a haunted house and recorded their impres-
> sions of the things they saw and heard and felt in order to contribute
> a learned paper to the Society for Psychic Research [London]. They
> thought that they were being terribly scientific and proving all kinds of
> things, and yet the story that kept coming through their dry reports
> was not at all the story of a haunted house, it was the story of several
> earnest, I believe misguided, certainly determined people, with their
> differing motivations and backgrounds. I found it so exciting that I
> wanted more than anything else to set up my own haunted house, and
> put my own people in it, and see what *I* could make happen.
>   As so often happens, the minute I started thinking about ghosts and
> haunted houses, all kinds of things turned up to enforce my inten-
> tions, or perhaps I was thinking so entirely about my new book that
> everything I saw turned to it; I can't say. [. . .] The first thing that
> happened was in New York City; we—my husband and I—were on
> the train which stops briefly at the 125th Street station, and just out-
> side the station, dim and horrible in the dusk, I saw a building so dis-
> agreeable that I could not stop looking at it; it was tall and black, and
> as I looked at it when the train began to move again it faded away and
> disappeared. That night in our hotel room I woke up with night-

mares, [which] had somehow settled around the building I had seen from the train. From that time on I completely ruined my whole vacation in New York City by dreading the moment when we would have to take the train back and pass that building again. [. . .] Anyway, my nervousness was so extreme, finally, that we changed our plans and took a night train home, so that I would not be able to see the building when we went past, but even after we were home it bothered me still, coloring all my recollections of a pleasant stay in the city, and at last I wrote to a friend at Columbia University and asked him to locate the building and find out, if he could, why it looked so terrifying. When we got his answer I had one important item for my book. He wrote that he had had trouble finding the building, since it only existed from that one particular point of the 125th Street station; from any other angle it was not recognizable as a building at all. Some seven months before it had been almost entirely burned in a disastrous fire which killed nine people. What was left of the building, from the other three sides, was a shell. The children in the neighborhood knew that it was haunted.

I do not think that the Society for Psychic Research would accept me as a qualified observer [. . .] but it seem[s] clear to me that what I had felt about that horrid building was an excellent beginning for learning how people feel when they encounter the supernatural. I have always been interested in witchcraft and superstition, but have never had much traffic with ghosts, so I began asking people everywhere what they thought about such things, and I began to find out that there was one common factor: most people have never seen a ghost, and never want or expect to, but almost everyone will admit [to] a sneaking suspicion that they just possibly *could* meet a ghost if they weren't careful—if they were to turn a corner too suddenly, perhaps, or open their eyes too soon when they wake up at night, or go into a dark room without hesitating first. . . .

Well, as I say, fiction comes from experience. I had not the remotest desire to see a ghost. I was absolutely willing to go on the rest of my life without ever seeing even the slightest supernatural manifestation. I wanted to write a book about ghosts, but I was perfectly prepared—I cannot emphasize this too strongly—I was perfectly prepared to keep those ghosts wholly imaginary. I was already doing a lot of splendid research reading all the books about ghosts I could get hold of [. . .] and at the same time I was collecting pictures of houses, particularly odd houses, to see what I could find to make into a suitable haunted house. I read books of architecture and clipped pictures out of magazines and newspapers and learned about cornices and secret stairways and valances and turrets [. . .] and then I came across a picture in a magazine which really looked right. It was the picture of a house which reminded me vividly of the hideous building in New York; it had the same air of disease and decay, and if ever a house looked like a candidate for a ghost, it was this one. All that I had to identify it was the name of a California town, so I wrote to my mother, who has lived in California all her life, and sent her the picture, asking if she had any idea where I could get information about this ugly house. She wrote back in some surprise. Yes, she knew about the house, although she had not supposed that there were any pictures of it still around. My great-grandfather [the architect John Stephenson Bugbee, 1841–c. 1891(?)] had built it. It had stood empty and deserted for some years before it finally caught fire, and it was generally believed that that was because the people of the town got together one night and burned it down.

By then it was abundantly clear to me that I had no choice; the ghosts were after me. In case I *had* any doubts, however, I came downstairs a few mornings later and found a sheet of copy paper moved to the center of my desk, set neatly away from the general clutter. On the sheet of paper was written DEAD DEAD in my own handwriting. I am accustomed to making notes for books, but not in my sleep; I decided that I had better write the book awake, which I got to work and did.

The complete text of this talk was edited and published by Stanley Edgar Hyman, under the title "Experience and Fiction," in *Come Along with Me* (1968), a posthumous miscellany of Shirley Jackson's writings.

242.1   *Leonard Brown*]   Leonard Stanley Brown (1904–1960), teacher of creative writing and pioneer of Marxist and Freudian literary criticism, was a member of the English faculty of Syracuse University for over 30 years. Upon his death, Jackson and Stanley Edgar Hyman published the following tribute in the Syracuse alumni magazine: "Leonard Brown was a fine teacher and a good friend. We will miss his understanding, his kindness, his gentleness. As two of his former pupils, who continued to value him as a personal friend long after we had left his classes, we want to express our sorrow at his loss. His was a stimulating and sympathetic mind; he enriched everyone who knew him well."

243.31–32   anonymous Lady . . . Ballechin House]   Ballechin House (1806–1963) was a Georgian estate house in Perthshire, Scotland, owned by the ancient Steuart family but unoccupied after the mid-1880s, when it was reputedly haunted by several spirits, including a ghostly nun. The house was made famous by Ada Goodrich-Freer (1857–1931), an English spiritualist who published papers on paranormal phenomena under the name "Miss X." Her book *The Alleged Haunting of B— House* (London: George Redway, 1899) describes her months-long tenancy of Ballechin in 1897 under the auspices of the Society for Psychical Research, during which she and fellow-researchers claim to have made frequent contact, via Ouija board, with "Ishbel," whom she surmised to be the ghost of Isabella Steuart (Sister Frances Helen), who died in 1880.

247.13   Alfred de Musset] French Romantic dramatist, poet, and novelist (1810–1857).

256.36–37   "In delay there lies no plenty,"] See Shakespeare, *Twelfth Night*, II.iii.47–52 (the Clown's song): "What is love? 'Tis not hereafter; / Present mirth hath present laughter; / What's to come is still unsure. / In delay there lies no plenty, / Then come kiss me sweet and twenty; / Youth's a stuff will not endure."

266.14–15   Journeys end in lovers meeting,] See Shakespeare, *Twelfth Night*, II.iii.39–44 (the Clown's song): "O mistress mine, where are you roaming? / O, stay and hear, your true-love's coming, / That can sing both high and low. / Trip no further, pretty sweeting; / Journeys end in lovers meeting, / Every wise man's son doth know."

268.1–2   sister Anne, sister Anne,] In the tale of Bluebeard ("La Barbe bleu" [1697], by French fabulist Charles Perrault), Fatima, Bluebeard's third wife, repeatedly cries for help from her sister Anne when Bluebeard threatens to hang her in the Blue Closet with the bodies of his previous wives.

280.13   "'These being dead . . . dead must I be.'] Cf. Dante Gabriel Rossetti, "To Death, of His Lady" (1870), a rendering of François Villon's "Le Testament" (1450): "Two we were, and the heart was one; / Which now being dead, dead I must be, / Or seem alive as lifelessly / As in the choir the painted stone, / Death!"

280.23   First and Second Murderers."] See Shakespeare, *Macbeth*, III.iii.

290.8   in Leviticus] See Leviticus 14:34–57.

290.9   *aidao domos*] See Homer, *Odyssey*, Book XI.

291.11   sowed with salt] Made barren. See Judges 9:45.

304.27   *Pamela*] *Pamela: or, Virtue Rewarded* (1740), epistolary novel by Samuel Richardson (1689–1761).

315.38   Winchester House] "Improvised" 160-room mansion of Sarah L. Winchester (1839–1922), heiress to the Winchester firearms fortune, in San Jose, California. Begun in 1888, it accreted room by room, at the owner's whim, into a random warren of lavishly appointed spaces.

318.40   what happened to Don Juan] In a scene from the Don Juan legend dramatized by Molière, Mozart, and Pushkin, the wicked Don mocks the statue of one of his innocent victims, a nobleman killed in a duel while defending his daughter's honor. The statue later appears at the Don's door, grabs him by the hand, and, when the Don refuses to repent his sins, drags him down to hell.

325.37   Borley Rectory] Anglican rectory (1863–1939) in Borley, near
Sudbury, Essex, built on the site of a former Benedictine monastery. Local
legend has it that, sometime in the late 14th century, a monk of that
monastery was put to death when his affair with a nun of a neighboring
convent was discovered; the nun, for her part, was sealed up alive inside the
convent walls. From the year of its construction, Borley Rectory was supposed to be haunted; a ghostly nun was observed on the grounds by residents and guests, and the house itself was troubled by violent poltergeist
activity.

331.15   *Clarissa Harlowe*] *Clarissa: or, The History of a Young Lady* (1748),
epistolary novel by Samuel Richardson.

339.18   Glamis Castle] The home of the Earl and Countess of Strath-
more and Kinghorne, in Angus, Scotland, and birthplace of Princess Margaret and Her Majesty Elizabeth, the Queen Mother. Built in the mid-14th
century, it has been the site of dozens of ghostly legends over six centuries.

341.15   Mrs. Foyster] The Rev. Lyonel Foyster and his young wife, Marianne (1899–1992), were residents of Borley Rectory (see note 325.37) in 1930–
35. During their tenancy the supernatural manifestations at Borley reached
their peak, as recorded by paranormal researcher Harry Price in his memoir
*The Most Haunted House in England: Ten Years' Investigation of Borley Rec-
tory* (London: Longmans, 1940). According to Price, Marianne Foyster was
continually harassed by spirits: she was struck by stones thrown by unseen
hands, was dashed to the floor by a bucking bed, and was sent "spirit messages," penciled on the walls in a strange, spidery hand, reading "Marianne,"
"Marianne help get," and "get light, mass, prayers here."

343.37–38   *filet de Luke . . . dieppoise,*] *Filet of Luke dredged in flour
and fried in butter,* or perhaps *poached in white wine with a shellfish reduction.*

347.24   *Sir Charles Grandison*] *The History of Sir Charles Grandison*
(1753), epistolary novel by Samuel Richardson.

362.16   from Foxe;] From *The Book of Martyrs* (1563), a monumental, lavishly illustrated history of Christian martyrdom, with special focus on English
Protestants from the 14th through mid-16th centuries, compiled by the Evan-
gelical scholar John Foxe (1517–1587).

363.11–12   "Was ever woman . . . wooed?"] Shakespeare, *Richard III*,
I.ii.227.

396.34   'The Grattan Murders,'] Cf. "The Rattin Family," Appalachian
murder ballad, collected in *Song Fest*, by Dick and Beth Best (1948, 1955, et
seq.), and other American song books. The murderer is Mr. Rattin, the head
of the family, come home after a night of heavy drinking.

402.12   Go walking through the valley] From the traditional English
children's song "Go In and Out the Window."

WE HAVE ALWAYS LIVED IN THE CASTLE

420.1 *Pascal Covici*] Pascal "Pat" Covici (1885–1964), Jackson's book editor after 1959, was an editor at Viking Press from 1938 until his death. Among his other celebrated authors were John Steinbeck, Saul Bellow, and Arthur Miller.

505.10 *Amanita pantherina*] Panther-cap mushroom, or False Blusher, an uncommon and deadly mushroom. Unlike the true Blusher, which it closely resembles, the flesh beneath its skin remains white upon cutting, whereas the Blusher's flesh turns pink.

505.10–11 *Amanita rubescens*] Common Blusher mushroom (see above).

505.13 *Apocynum cannabinum*] Dogbane.

OTHER STORIES AND SKETCHES

572.1 *Behold the Child . . .*] Cf. William Wordsworth, "Ode: Intimations of Immortality, from Recollections of Early Childhood" (1802–4), stanza 7: "Behold the Child among his new-born blisses, / A six years' Darling of a pigmy size!"

592.17–18 "She loved me . . . pity them."] Shakespeare, *Othello*, I.iii.167–68.

627.3 FOR DYLAN THOMAS] The Welsh poet and writer Dylan Thomas (1913–1953) was an admirer of *The Lottery*, and during his first U.S. tour, in the early spring of 1950, he asked his American host, the poet John Malcolm Brinnin, for an introduction to the author. Jackson and her husband, neighbors of Brinnin in Westport, Connecticut, hosted a Saturday-evening cocktail party in Thomas's honor, and, though she met him only on this occasion, Thomas made a lasting impression on her as both artist and personality.

727.6 *Go walking through the valley,*] See note 402.12.

735.22 Mary Roberts Rinehart] Prolific American writer of formula mystery fiction (1876–1958) about whose work was coined the phrase "The butler did it."

787.32 my agent] Rae Everitt (b. 1927), of MCA Literary Management, was Jackson's agent from 1948 to 1950.

788.8–9 fiction editor] Gustave "Gus" Lobrano (1903–1956) was Jackson's editor at *The New Yorker* from 1943 to 1953.

791.31 *In Fact*] Monthly newsletter devoted to media criticism and investigative reporting, published and edited throughout the 1940s by liberal journalist George Seldes (1890–1995). Seldes called his publication "An Antidote for Falsehood in the Daily Press."

THE LIBRARY OF AMERICA SERIES

The Library of America fosters appreciation and pride in America's literary heritage by publishing, and keeping permanently in print, authoritative editions of America's best and most significant writing. An independent nonprofit organization, it was founded in 1979 with seed money from the National Endowment for the Humanities and the Ford Foundation.

To subscribe to the series or to order individual copies,
please visit www.loa.org or call (800) 964.5778.

This book is set in 10 point Linotron Galliard,
a face designed for photocomposition by Matthew Carter
and based on the sixteenth-century face Granjon. The paper
is acid-free lightweight opaque and meets the requirements
for permanence of the American National Standards Institute.
The binding material is Brillianta, a woven rayon cloth made
by Van Heek-Scholco Textielfabrieken, Holland. Compo-
sition by Dedicated Business Services. Printing by
Malloy Incorporated. Binding by Dekker Book-
binding. Designed by Bruce Campbell.